The Rachel Prince Mystery Series: Books 1-3

DAWN BROOKES

The Rachel Prince Mystery Series Books 1-3

DAWN BROOKES

OAKWOOD PUBLISHING

This collection of novels is entirely a work of fiction. The names, characters and incidents portrayed are the work of the author's imagination. Any resemblance to actual persons, living or dead is entirely coincidental. Although real life places are depicted in settings, all situations and people related to those places are fictional.

www.dawnbrookespublishing.com
Paperback Edition 2019
Kindle Edition 2019
Paperback ISBN: 978-1-913065-03-4

A Cruise to Murder Book 1

DAWN BROOKES

A Cruise to Murder

A Rachel Prince Mystery

DAWN BROOKES

OAKWOOD PUBLISHING

www.dawnbrookespublishing.com
Paperback Edition 2018
Kindle Edition 2018
Paperback ISBN: 978-1-9998575-3-0

Chapter 1

"I can't do this anymore, Rachel. I've met someone else." The words pierced through her brain, like knives carving her in two.

Rachel awoke with a start, wondering where she was. The rhythmic chugging sound of a train on railway tracks reminded her immediately. Pushing the dream to the back of her mind, she looked around the busy train. The middle-aged woman with a teenage girl in tow, who had sat opposite Rachel at the start of her journey, had gone. She had been replaced by a younger woman with customary ear phones attached to her head and eyes glued to the mobile phone in her hand. A young man, presumably her boyfriend, was sitting next to her, reading a book and eating a sandwich.

Rachel noticed that the rather large man who had been sitting in the aisle seat next to her had also been replaced. An older man reading a newspaper was now beside her. Realising that she must have been in a very deep sleep, she automatically checked that her handbag was still in place. She had squashed it between herself and the side of the carriage when her eyes had begun to feel like lead and she realised that sleep was inevitable.

Reassured that it was still there, she took a quick look behind her to where the luggage compartment was and noticed her suitcase remained where she had left it. Vivid pink with white polka dots, it was hardly going to go unnoticed, even though it was now surrounded by other people's luggage. She had bought it to stand out and stand out it did.

Looking at her watch, she saw that it was now ten o'clock in the morning. She turned and looked out of the window, the sadness that had been wrenching her heart for weeks re-surfacing. Work had been busy, and she had pulled in extra hours to help dull the pain, but now she had stopped, it came crashing in on her again.

Blast Robert – get out of my head, she thought as tears stung the back of her eyes. Thankfully, phone-girl was too busy with her device to notice the tears.

The passengers around her were eating and drinking, so she assumed she must have missed the trolley service. Another hour and a half and the train would be arriving in Southampton. The smell of fresh coffee made her thirsty, and she needed to stretch her legs. Rachel decided to go for a walk and get some sustenance.

With an involuntary sigh that drew a sympathetic look from the man seated next to her, she excused herself and made her way through the train to the buffet car.

The train was now tearing through the countryside and felt like it was floating on air, except for the occasional shaking of the carriages from side to side. It was much busier than it had been at seven-thirty when she had first boarded in Leeds. The walk became an obstacle course as she fought her way past different-sized luggage overflowing into the aisles. She almost lost her balance as she moved through the carriages and felt the sway where they joined together.

Why did I agree to this holiday? She was pondering this thought when she finally arrived at the buffet car. Sarah had been so kind and sympathetic when Rachel had called her two months ago after Robert had decided to end their relationship and leave her broken-hearted and alone. Rachel had been engaged to Robert for a year, but she had noticed a change in him about six months prior to the breakup. At the time, distracted by assessments and not really able deal with it, she had put it down to the work strain they were both under and dismissed his moodiness.

Robert worked in Manchester as a police sergeant. They had met at a party and were immediately attracted to each other, discovering that they both went to church and were both in the police force. He had approached her while she was sitting with a group of friends.

"Would you like to dance?" It wasn't the best pickup line she had heard, but from the moment she looked into his dark-green eyes, she was smitten. It had seemed to be an ideal match, and it had been as far as Rachel was concerned.

Rachel had recently joined the force when they first met and was committed to staying in Leeds until her two years as a student officer were completed. Robert had been supportive initially, and when he asked her to marry him, she was over the moon. They agreed that she would look for work in Manchester once she qualified as constable.

That was before – this is now. Sorrow and pain coursed through her veins.

She bought herself a rather stale club sandwich and a cup of strong coffee and felt a bit better for having something to eat and drink. Grateful that she was not one of those people who starved themselves when they were unhappy, she was equally aware that she did not want to comfort eat and gain weight – especially being a fitness fanatic. Even she had stopped eating for a few days following the shock announcement from Robert eight weeks earlier though.

The memories once again invaded her senses.

She had gone to visit him in Manchester, and as usual arrived at his sister's house. Robert's sister, Louise, lived around the corner from his flat. She was a kind and patient woman with three children under the age of five and a husband who seemed to work all hours. Louise was committed to family life although Rachel couldn't help noticing that she looked exhausted most of the time. Rachel sometimes wondered if her husband deliberately missed getting home early in order to avoid having to spend time with the children or help with chores. She'd convinced herself that Robert would not be like that, and they would live as loving partners.

At least we would have done, if he'd got over his moodiness and more importantly, if he hadn't met someone else.

Rachel had arrived late on that Friday night and only seen him briefly.

"I'll collect you tomorrow morning at ten. We'll go out for lunch and spend the day together." He turned away before she could kiss him.

Her time was limited as she had to get back to Leeds on Saturday night to work on the Sunday. Looking back, she realised how foolish she had been, missing all the warning signs; but she had been studying frantically to finish her police assessments while planning for the future, and she was madly in love.

Louise had seemed quiet and distant over breakfast on the Saturday morning.

"Is everything alright?" Rachel wondered if she and her husband, George, had argued. George had left early in the morning and, unusually, had given Rachel a hug before he went.

"Yes, fine. I just need to get the children ready for their grandma." Louise had busied herself in the kitchen for the rest of the morning.

Robert arrived at around eleven o'clock, an hour later than they'd agreed. He didn't apologise for being late.

"I've only got time for lunch," he said brusquely.

"Oh, that's a shame. I was hoping we could go into town." She was disappointed, but tried to hide it, naively thinking he must have been called in to work – not unusual for police officers. Although a staunch believer in people's rights to protest, march, and all manner of other things, Rachel did sometimes wish they would spare a thought for the police. The police had to give up their days off and time with families to maintain public order. Even the most peaceful demonstrations could erupt into violence if rival factions got overheated.

Robert was quiet again.

"I've just got the one assessment left to do next week and then I'll be qualified. It won't be long before we can spend a lot more time together." Rachel tried to make the most of the time they had, overcompensating for his lack of speech by babbling on. They stopped outside her favourite café; the familiar smell of percolated coffee and baking filled her senses with a pleasing aroma. She entered the premises happily, looking forward to a romantic lunch, but Robert seemed to move away whenever she tried to hold his hand.

"I missed every signal. I was blind," she later told Sarah.

There was the usual queue of people waiting to be served, and they waited in line to order lunch and coffees. Rachel ordered her favourite home-made beef and potato pie and was about to tuck in when Robert grabbed her hand.

At last, some sign of affection. Then she looked into his eyes with a feeling of foreboding. He stared at her with a coldness she had not seen before; she was looking into someone else's eyes – these were not the happy eyes of her fiancé.

"I can't do this anymore, Rachel. I've met someone else. I love her and I want to marry her."

He threw himself back into the chair and took a deep breath. At this point, he looked away.

Rachel couldn't believe what she was hearing – her stomach was in knots and her heart was racing. Beginning to feel light-headed, she opened her mouth but realised she couldn't speak.

Taking advantage of the fact that she was unable to say anything, Robert continued. "I've tried, Rachel, really I have. I met Jessica through an inter-church thing – we started doing youth clubs together and things developed from there."

Rachel saw a look in his eyes that had once belonged to her as he began to speak about this woman whom he had dared to give a name. Somehow, thinking of this person as the other woman allowed Rachel to feel angry; but thinking of her as Jessica brought her to life as another person who had fallen in love with a man. Rachel's man.

Flabbergasted, Rachel shut down and went into autopilot. She could thank her police training for this skill because it helped her to survive the conversation – and it had become a matter of her survival. Her hand felt sore, and she realised that she had been twisting her engagement ring round and round while he was speaking.

"I need to go to the bathroom," she said, and then she got up and walked straight out of the café. At first, she didn't know where she was going, but after about an hour she realised she was heading for the train station. Her mobile phone had rung a few times with Robert's ringtone, but she declined the calls and turned it off. She knew she was not being very adult about this, but her heart had just been torn apart.

How else should I react? she asked herself, angrily. Tears fell down her face as she walked, and she had to use every ounce of strength to stop herself from sobbing in the street. A few people looked at her as she passed by with embarrassed fleeting glances, but no-one had asked if she was alright.

Sorrow had turned to anger by the time she reached the train station – anger with Robert for doing this to her, and anger at herself for missing all the warning signs. She saw that there was a train leaving for Leeds in ten minutes, so she sprinted to the platform.

Once on the train, Rachel had found a quiet compartment, unusual for a Saturday. She sat down and tried to take in all that had happened over the few hours that had been spent with Robert. Her happy, stable life had been thrown into turmoil, and she felt terrified of the fragility that overwhelmed her. The dark and devastating thoughts scrambling through her brain were totally new.

If only I had recognised the signs over the previous six months for what they were, the pain might have been a bit less and I might have been better prepared for what just occurred. She felt betrayed, angry, dreadfully sad; but most of all, she felt stupid. Her father had tried to warn her about long-distance relationships – not that Leeds and Manchester were that far apart.

"I am sure it will all work out for you," he had said after her engagement. "But just be aware that people can change, and you haven't known him that long."

Robert had asked her father's permission before proposing in the traditional way, and he had given it without hesitation. Rachel's dad, Brendan Prince, was a vicar in Hertfordshire where Rachel had been brought up. Robert had joked with her later, saying that her father had warned him: "Don't you hurt my daughter or you will have me to answer to." They had laughed about it then, but now Rachel wondered whether her wonderful dad had seen something in Robert that she couldn't or wouldn't see.

I don't suppose he asked my dad for permission to break off the engagement, she thought bitterly. How do I tell my parents?

When she got back to her flat, she realised she hadn't let Louise know that she wasn't going to collect her overnight bag. She turned her phone on and saw fourteen missed calls and numerous texts from Robert, all of which she deleted.

There was a text from Louise which read: "I am so sorry, Rachel, for what has happened. We only knew about it yesterday as Robert had kept it all to himself. Please let me know you are okay, I understand you will be angry and upset. The children send hugs and kisses."

Rachel replied: "Thanks, Louise, I have returned to Leeds. Sorry to leave without saying goodbye, but had to get away and take it all in. Love to the boys."

She received a sympathetic reply, but they had not communicated since, except when Louise had sent a parcel with her overnight bag and a *thinking of you* card. Robert had tried to call a few more times, but she had not replied. He did write one letter, which still lay unopened in her suitcase. She might open it with Sarah.

If only I hadn't joined the police force, I would never have met Robert. She knew it was silly to think that way, but her head was still reeling from the shock.

"You alright, love?" A voice behind her brought her back to the present. She had been staring out of the window opposite the buffet bar and hadn't realised there were tears streaming down her face. She gathered herself together, looking up at the buffet car attendant.

"Yes, I'm fine, thank you," she replied. *Pull yourself together*, she chastised herself, and then she made her way back through the train to her seat, after washing her face at the toilet sink.

Almost an hour had passed since she had left her seat. The train would soon be arriving at Southampton station. Thankful that her seat had not been taken and that her luggage was still in place, she sat down.

Get a grip, Prince!

Chapter 2

Sarah had at long last managed to get a good night's sleep aboard the *Coral Queen.* The ship docked at 5.30am, but she was woken by her alarm clock half an hour before.

Here goes. She heaved herself out of bed and groaned. Turnaround days were the busiest for crew members who had to make sure that all passengers disembarked, dealing with around 9,000 pieces of luggage, and then ready the ship for the new arrivals. The *Coral Queen* was one of the larger vessels on the oceans, carrying 3,500 passengers and 1,800 crew members, and she would be heading to the Mediterranean later that day.

The busiest crew members would be the stateroom stewards, of course, as they had to clean all of the passenger cabins thoroughly and have them ready for the new passengers in just a few hours. In addition to this, the whole ship had to be cleaned inside and out. Their work was checked by Heinz Linz, the Hotel Manager, who was meticulous with his inspections. The stateroom stewards knew that if he found one piece of dirt or debris, he would be down on them like a ton of bricks.

A knock at the door grabbed Sarah's attention. On opening it, she saw her friend and colleague, Brigitte.

"You look ready to roll." Sarah observed that Brigitte was dressed in shorts and t-shirt.

"I am. Can you believe it, I have never been to London?" Her French accent revealed her nationality.

"Well, enjoy yourself and I'll catch you later," said Sarah. "Make sure you do the London Eye."

"Top of my list," Brigitte called as she was already halfway down the corridor. "Missing you already."

"Yeah, really?" Sarah closed the door.

Turnaround was not such a bad day for the nurses, who had to restock the medical rooms and ensure that no drugs would go out of date during the next fourteen-night cruise, as well as collect health questionnaires in the passenger lounge. Janice had already placed the order for new supplies. Brigitte was taking the day off and heading to London for a few hours to see the sights on one of the tour buses. Passengers who were staying on board for back-to-back cruises were also given the option of a London tour.

Sarah and Bernard, a Philippine male nurse, were scheduled to be in the passenger lounge later, collecting questionnaires about recent vomiting or diarrhoea from the passengers. Sarah had discovered that seasoned cruisers did not admit to any such illness, knowing that they would be confined to their stateroom for a few days if they did. She hated telling new cruisers, who were just being honest, that their first few days would be limited to their rooms. It was a necessary precaution, however, because the Norovirus (Norwalk) could spread around a ship like a wildfire and ruin everyone's holiday. Medical and nursing staff would be called out *ad infinitum* to attend to every passenger or crew member who had picked it up.

Sarah had only encountered one episode of Norovirus early on in her cruising experience, and luckily the medics had managed to contain the outbreak in one small part of the ship. The *Coral Queen* boasted a high standard of hygiene, but buffets were lethal if this marauder invaded.

I would ban buffets altogether if it was left to me. Sarah knew that the restaurant and buffet staff did their best to ensure that passengers used hand gels on entering any dining area, but there were always a stubborn few who snubbed them.

The Canary Islands cruise they had just been on had turned out to be excessively busy. Lots of sea days always meant busy times in the medical centre. Sarah had been on call for the past seventy-two hours and had been up most nights, attending to minor ailments and injuries. Many of the ailments were due to excessive drinking by both passengers and crew. The crew tended to let their hair down during their time off in the bar below the waterline. Sarah had ventured into the crew bar on rare occasions, but it was not for the fainthearted.

"It's like a viper's nest down there," Janice, the senior nurse warned her when she first joined ship, but at least one visit to the bar was a necessary initiation for Sarah so that she knew what to expect during on-call hours.

Sarah had noticed that most nationalities tended to group together with their own countrymen. Seating was scarce in the crew bar whereas alcohol was abundantly available. During her very first cruise, she was having a drink with Bernard when a fight had broken out between a Romanian and a Russian, and it didn't end well.

Crowds gathered round as it turned nasty.

"So much for a quiet night," Bernard moaned, holding Sarah back. "Wait for security or you might end up hurt."

Security arrived and pulled the men apart. Sarah could see there was blood everywhere. She had spent the night helping the doctor to stitch the Romanian man's face. He'd ended up with stitches that ran from above his left eye down to his chin due to an injury sustained from a broken bottle.

Bernard had dealt with the Russian kitchen worker, who'd suffered a broken nose and had two front teeth knocked out.

"He was ugly before, now he's grotesque," Bernard whispered to her afterwards.

"You're incorrigible," Sarah replied.

"Serves him right for ruining my down-time."

"What happens to them now?" Sarah had asked Janice.

"Security are here to collect them. They will be locked up and thrown off ship at the next port without any fare home."

Discipline on board a ship had to be strict otherwise rival factions could create chaos. The crew knew the consequences of serious misdemeanours. Sarah understood the need, but couldn't help feeling sorry for the two men, knowing they would have very little money when they were escorted off the ship.

"There is a no tolerance policy towards this kind of violence," Janice explained.

Other drink-related mishaps commonly involved passengers with drinks packages and those who sneaked liquor on board. These passengers also accounted for many of the night-time call-outs. Occasionally there would be passengers or crew members who had taken drugs. Sarah had been surprised to discover that passengers could be locked up for drugs offences if security felt it necessary, but it was uncommon. Crew had to undergo regular drugs tests, and any who tested positive were also chucked off ship at the next port.

Sarah was thankful there had been no serious illnesses or injuries during the latest cruise. In general, both crew and passengers had been happy – barring a few disgruntled passengers who would never be satisfied. She smiled as she thought of how nice it would be not to have to see Mr Bragen ever again. Mr Bragen had been a passenger with a chronic leg ulcer who, in spite of having his own attending private nurse, insisted on turning up to one of the surgeries held twice daily to have his dressings checked. She would hear him before she saw him: a loud and uncouth man who always demanded to be seen straight away.

"No, I will not take a seat. Where's my nurse?"

Sarah would cringe before straightening up and heading out to the waiting area.

"Mr Bragen, please come through. What a pleasure it is to see you again."

"Like hell it is. Let's just get on with it and none of your British charm. I'm immune."

I couldn't agree more, and thankfully not all Americans are like you!

"As you wish." She would smile at Delia, his private nurse whom she had got to know quite well, as she wheeled him into the surgery.

"How do you put up with him?" she had asked privately. Delia had sniggered.

"I have very thick skin, and for the money he pays, I would do almost anything."

Delia helped Sarah to deal with this rude man, and she was right – he paid well and left generous tips. He even gave Sarah a gold brooch. She would have refused it, but he had sneaked it onto her desk while she wasn't looking, along with a *thank-you* card, on the last day. By then, she was too busy to track him down to return it.

Anyway, no more Mr Bragen. I can't wait to see Rachel today.

Sarah was three months into a nine-month contract with Queen Cruises, and she had finally got used to the shifts and facilities available aboard ship. It had taken a while to adjust from hospital life to that of a nurse on a cruise ship, but she enjoyed the work and managed to get some time off when the ship was in port. In many ways, working on a cruise ship beat hospitals on land. Time off was shared between herself, Bernard, Brigitte and Janice. The doctors also shared time off between themselves. As long as there was a doctor and two nurses on duty when the ship was in port, the others could go on land. Other than that, they were never really off duty because they had to respond to emergencies night and day.

Sarah had saved up quite a bit of time off so that she would be able to spend time with Rachel. Bernard and Brigitte had been happy to take extra trips on the Canaries cruise when she had explained Rachel would be travelling alone.

"Poor girl," said Brigitte. "Men are scum." She did a pretend spitting motion.

"Hey – am I invisible?" Bernard protested.

"You are not, but you should be." Sarah nudged him playfully. Bernard was in fact happily married with two children back home in Manila. 'Poor Rachel, she has had a horrid time. She was absolutely besotted with the man."

"As you can't bring yourself to say his name, I take it you didn't like him," Brigitte observed.

"To be honest, I never took to *Robert*." Sarah said the name pointedly. "Obviously, even if I had liked him, I wouldn't now, but he completely took over Rachel's life. Right from the start, he took her away from everything and everyone that she knew."

"Controlling then?" asked Bernard.

"Yes, it was subtle at first, but I recognised his controlling nature early on. The signs were there, but it was impossible to broach the subject with Rachel. Even when she phoned, he always seemed to be there. It was as if she wasn't allowed to speak without his permission. I was going to try to talk to Rachel about it, but I chickened out. She was so happy and I didn't want to make her sad."

"Perhaps as well, else she might not have been able to face you now when she needs you," said Brigitte.

"You're right, but I had already decided it was Rachel's choice, and I was going to try to like the man."

Sarah couldn't help thinking that Rachel was better off without him, but knew that it would take some time for her to recover from the breakup.

"As I said, men are scum." Brigitte folded her arms and glared at Bernard, who smirked.

"She's a fitness fanatic, so I'm just hoping that she enjoys the cruise and I have done the right thing persuading her to join me, especially as our time together will be limited. But it's got to be better than working all hours, which is the way that Rachel has been dealing with it."

"Don't worry, we will cover for you as much as possible. Anything to help a damsel in distress." Bernard turned to Brigitte. "As you see, not all men are scum."

That conversation had been a few days ago. Sarah was pleased that she worked with great people even though change was on the horizon.

Once Sarah was washed and dressed in her passenger deck officer uniform, she was ready for the day. She smiled to herself as she looked at the four different uniforms in her wardrobe.

"You have four uniforms to be worn on different occasions, and woe betide you if you get it wrong." Janice had given her a tour on her first day and then showed her to her living quarters. "There is a day uniform to be worn in passenger areas and a night uniform for the same areas. You can wear scrubs during surgery hours and when in the medical centre, and for formal nights you wear this baby." Janice held up yet another white starched uniform that was even more pristine than the others.

"I will do my best to comply," Sarah had answered, but what had seemed very confusing then was now second nature to her. As a nurse, she had officer status and proudly boasted two-and-a-half gold stripes on her epaulettes.

After putting on the day uniform, she made her way two doors down to see Janice. Janice had been senior nurse on the ship for a year, but she was moving to another ship after a short break to see her parents in Scotland. Sarah had been trained by Janice, and in spite of a fifteen-year age difference, they had become good friends.

Janice opened the door dressed casually in beige cotton trousers and the t-shirt Sarah had bought her as a leaving present. The bright yellow letters spoke volumes: 'LIFE IS FOR LIVING'.

"You'll never believe it, I slept in!" Janice exclaimed. "Thankfully, I packed last night so I'm ready to go."

"I'm going to miss you," said Sarah, to which Janice smiled.

"You'll be fine. You never know, you might get someone your own age to talk to."

"And I might get a dragon!" Sarah smiled wistfully, although she was not one to be negative. They hugged briefly, and then Janice turned to grab her hand luggage as her suitcase had been collected the night before and would be waiting for her in the baggage hall on the dockside.

"Good luck, Sarah, and enjoy yourself with your friend. I'd better get going before they keep me on board."

They walked together towards the lifts and hugged before Sarah took the stairs to the medical centre. Janice wasn't the only one leaving today. Marek, the junior doctor (or 'baby doc' as junior doctors are known on board a cruise ship), had completed his contract and decided that ship medicine wasn't for him. He missed his girlfriend, a ward sister at St Thomas's Hospital in London, so he had managed to get a job as a locum GP in Hackney. He was hoping to 'pop the question' as soon as he got to London.

Dr Graham Bentley would be staying, which was a good thing because he was so experienced in ship medicine and brilliant in an emergency. Dr Bentley was the chief medical officer and the first in command of the medical team.

It had taken Sarah a while to get used to the cruise-line hierarchy at first. The chief generally saw passengers and the baby doc was responsible for the health of the crew. The nurses saw both passengers and crew members, with the senior nurse ensuring everything ran smoothly and that passengers were billed appropriately.

Bernard and Brigitte were also staying, so at least Sarah could still have a laugh. They had similar senses of humour – humour that only nurses could share.

Among the many other staff moving on today, the one that was hardest for Sarah to take was Barry. The engineering officer was being moved to join the same ship as Janice. Sarah and Barry had got on from the first time they met and had become good friends. His impending move was one of the things that had stopped them becoming a couple; that and the small matter of his being engaged to the assistant cruise director on the ship he was soon to be joining. Sarah had fought off her feelings and Barry's advances, determined not to do to someone else what had been done to Rachel and having a stubborn belief in right and wrong. Her faith had taken a battering over the past five years, but although she no longer went to church, she still had a strong moral code that she couldn't quite shake off.

"It's perhaps as well he is leaving – it could only have ended badly." Bernard had comforted her the night before by helping her to avoid a long goodbye. Barry had made it obvious Bernard wasn't welcome, but at Sarah's request, he had stuck to her like glue, and Barry had finally given up.

Sarah knew that the long hours and the close proximity of other crew members resulted in multiple casual relationships on board. For some girls, it was their first time away from home, and they equated the freedom that came with it with being free to sleep around. It didn't always go to plan as the men often promised much and delivered little. Some of these relationships even ended up in crew presenting with venereal diseases. There was one crew member who attended surgery regularly for antibiotics, and no matter how much Sarah and the doctors tried to advise him to practise safe sex, he just didn't get it.

"Why should I? I can get treatment when I need it."

Marek had threatened not to treat him the next time, but they all knew that a doctor couldn't withhold the treatment, if only for the sakes of the girls that he slept with.

"One day you will have a resistant strain of the disease and then I won't be able to treat you. When that happens, you will be sacked to safeguard the rest of the crew."

Sarah took a deep breath as she unlocked the door and entered the medical centre.

Chapter 3

"It seems to be taking an inordinately long time to get there." Marjorie knew the journey from London to Southampton was only about seventy miles. She hadn't really been taking much notice of the road, but now she looked out of the window, she could see that the M3 was virtually at a standstill going north. Although she was travelling south, the car was going very slowly.

"What's happening, Johnson?" she asked the chauffer of the white Rolls Royce they were travelling in.

"We passed an accident a while back, ma'am, but we're almost at our turnoff. We have plenty of time."

Johnson hesitated as if he wanted to say something.

"Is there something else, Johnson?"

"You seem to be worried about something ma'am. Are you sure that you should take this trip alone? You have only just got over the accident and Lord Snellthorpe trusted me to look after you."

"You know that Ralph and I loved cruising and he would have wanted me to carry on." She wiped a tear away from her face. "I will be fine on board the *Coral Queen*. The staff will look after me and I have plenty of books to keep me occupied."

"Yes, I'm sure they will, madam."

Lady Snellthorpe was touched by Johnson's concern for her welfare. Her maid had told her that he had tried to get tickets for the cruise but found it was fully booked. The maid said Johnson had checked the day before, deciding to spend the money left to him by Lord Snellthorpe on the cruise, so that he'd keep an eye on her from a distance.

The nagging feeling returned.

Marjorie Snellthorpe was deep in thought. She hardly ever travelled in the Rolls, but the Bentley was in the garage having a re-spray following her minor bump the previous week. Her mind wandered back to that event. She had decided to go shopping on her own, much to the dismay of her housekeeper, Mrs Ratton. A car had crashed into the side of hers as she was turning a corner. The driver had seemingly come from nowhere, and when they collided, he stared at her menacingly. As he appeared to be getting out of the car, her first thought was that she was about to be a victim of road-rage, but a woman had come to her assistance. The driver had jumped back into his car and driven off at speed.

It had been traumatic, and when the police came, Marjorie had been unable to give them much information. She could remember the face of the driver, but nothing about the car, other than that is was possibly grey. The police had been sympathetic but unable to take it any further, and she had agreed that they were unlikely to be able to track the driver down.

She shuddered as she thought of the accident, still uncertain whether it had been deliberate. Marjorie had not thought so initially, but as she remembered how it had occurred and how intimidating the man had looked, a nagging feeling that it was not an accident wormed its way into her mind.

She had shared her concerns with her son, Jeremy, but he'd scoffed at her as he always did.

"Don't be ridiculous, Mother, you have been watching too much American television," he shouted. He always seemed to shout these days. "Why would anyone want to crash into you on purpose?"

"Why indeed? I'm sure you're right, Jeremy, perhaps I get a little over anxious since your father died. I miss him terribly."

Her son had changed the subject all too quickly and asked her for yet another injection of cash into the family business.

"Jeremy, you have had three large sums of money in the past twelve months. Why do you need more?"

She could see that her son was fighting to control his temper. He had always hated being challenged, but since taking over the management of the business, he had become overly quick to fly off the handle.

"Mother, you don't understand business. These are difficult times and we need to keep competitive."

"We're not in trouble, are we?" Marjorie was worried. Although she didn't understand the business, she did understand money management, and Ralph had always warned her about Jeremy's spending habits. She hoped rather than believed that the money was going into the business as she signed the cheque.

"Of course not. You just don't understand what it needs. Dad left it in a right mess."

Jeremy snatched the cheque. Marjorie didn't believe for a moment that this was true, but knew the pointlessness of trying to speak to her son when he was in that sort of mood.

"Oh well, Randolph and Philip are going to bring me in to explain the business and accounting side of things when I get back from my cruise, so I should understand it better then."

Randolph was the family lawyer and remained as loyal to Marjorie as he had been to her husband. He had called the previous week to say that he needed to speak with her and explain some things about the business, but that she should go and enjoy her holiday first. It could wait until she returned. Philip Mason was financial director of the company and a close friend of Ralph's. Randolph had explained he wanted Philip to be present at the meeting.

"I don't know why he feels the need to get you involved. I am managing things perfectly well. You have to trust me, Mother."

Before she had time to think about her reply, Jeremy had gone. The sadness of having a son who didn't seem to care about her returned, but it made her determined to do what Ralph would have wanted. Jeremy would just have to lump it. She feared it would not be good news awaiting her on her return, but she decided to try not to think about it too much until then.

The car stopped and she could see that they were at the cruise terminal. It looked busy, and for a brief moment, Marjorie wondered if Johnson might have been right about her travelling on her own.

It's too late now. She straightened up as Johnson opened the door to let her out.

Chapter 4

At long last, the train arrived in Southampton, and people were making a dash for the doors as if their lives depended on it. The elderly man who had been sitting next to Rachel had got off a stop earlier. Phone-girl and her boyfriend had gathered their things and gone to block the corridor, along with all the other people who hadn't yet wound down into holiday mode.

Rachel remained seated. It wasn't as if people needed to hurry as the train terminated here. She had plenty of time to get to the cruise terminal, and having attended far too many crowd-control events, she was happy to let the crowds disperse. She did keep one eye on her suitcase, though, just to be sure that it didn't leave without her.

After about five minutes, it was safe to get up and walk to her luggage without being crammed up against people. She noticed that a few other people had had the same idea and were casually gathering their things together, too.

She collected her suitcase and negotiated her way on to the platform, pausing to ensure that her hand luggage and handbag were securely in place before extending the suitcase handle and wheeling it along the platform towards the ticket barrier. She couldn't resist smiling as she noticed phone-girl and her partner, stuck in a queue at a different ticket barrier. Phone-girl was now chewing gum with mouth wide open and blowing bubbles.

Not a great look.

Once outside, Rachel joined the taxi queue. It appeared that the majority of people were heading to the cruise terminals with three sailings taking place today, so she heard a man in front say. After about twenty minutes of waiting, she got into a taxi and asked the driver to take her to the Mayflower Terminal where the *Coral Queen* would be berthed.

"You going on a cruise then?" he asked.

"Yes, I am."

"Where are you going?"

"Around the Med," Rachel replied. "I'm meeting a friend who works as a nurse on the ship."

"Oh, you'll get to see *Upstairs, Downstairs* then." The taxi driver laughed.

"Yes, I suppose I will. I hadn't thought of that." Rachel joined in and laughed for the first time that day, relaxing. She even started to feel a little bit excited.

"You'll see the ships any minute."

Just as he said that, she saw the enormous cruise ships in the distance. They became bigger and bigger as the taxi got closer.

"Wow! I don't think I imagined they would be that big. Which one is the *Coral Queen*?"

"That one on the right. We just have to do a bit of a circle and then we will be there."

Once at the gate, the taxi driver held out a pass that was checked by a security guard and then he was allowed through. As they pulled up at what appeared to be the terminal, there were more queues of people. The driver pulled in to the side, getting out to open her door.

On opening the boot, the driver stood aside as the ship crew came to collect her suitcase. After checking the label, they put it on a luggage crate and it was taken away. Rachel paid the taxi driver and walked towards the crowds that were heading inside the terminal.

"Bye, love, have a nice holiday," shouted the taxi driver and Rachel waved.

"Thanks, I think I will."

Once inside the terminal, she showed her ticket to a security guard at the bottom of an escalator.

"Go up to the next floor where you can check in and pass through customs."

The man stood aside. Once at the top, Rachel joined a long queue which was organised by makeshift barriers into the shape of a snake. She counted twelve desks at the end of the queue where people were checking in.

While standing in the queue, Rachel noticed people passing through on the right-hand side to two VIP desks where they were immediately checked in. She saw an elderly lady being pushed in a wheelchair by a uniformed chauffeur. The lady had beautiful white hair and was well-dressed in a fine silk dress with a white cotton jacket. Once at the desk, she was greeted warmly by the staff and taken through by one of the volunteers that Rachel had seen milling around. The chauffeur said goodbye and walked away, but then turned to watch. Rachel couldn't help but notice the look on his face as he watched the old lady go.

I wonder what he's worried about.

The queue started to move again, and she forgot about the old lady. Eventually, she arrived at one of the desks.

"Have you cruised before?" the lady at the desk asked.

"No I haven't," Rachel replied.

"Okay, I need to take a photo of you for your cruise card. The card will be your pass on and off the ship and also used for purchases while you're on board. I need to register a credit card to link it to."

Rachel handed over a credit card and signed a form permitting payment to be taken from her card at the end of the cruise.

"Look into the camera."

Rachel saw what looked like a web-cam. She was about to smile, but it flashed before she had the chance. She glanced at the photo on the screen that would be linked to the card. It made her look like one of her prisoners, but she wasn't that worried.

After all, who will see it?

She was then given a folded, cardboard map of the ship. Finally, she was handed a questionnaire to fill out in the departure lounge.

"Enjoy your cruise," said the lady. "Follow the crowds."

Next stop was security, and all her hand luggage was passed along a conveyor belt to be scanned. Rachel passed through a metal detector, and once given the all clear, she moved into an enormous room where people were being asked to wait until their key-card colour was called. She caught a glimpse of the elderly lady coming out of a lift at the top of the stairs and being wheeled towards the ship.

Rachel filled out the questionnaire relating to recent gastrointestinal upsets, of which she had had none. She looked around at her fellow passengers and was not surprised that there were lots of young people and families. Sarah had explained that cruises were likely to be taken by anyone now, and not just the elderly rich.

I guess we are all much better off than we used to be, thought Rachel. She had recently had a pay rise herself when she qualified as a police constable. *WPC Prince,* she thought proudly, finally allowing some self-satisfaction to surface. She had spent so much time being maudlin and was ready to allow a little bit of joy back into her life, deciding right then and there that she would be the old Rachel again: the girl who loved life and had a great sense of humour. It was time to put Robert in the past and get on with her life.

She felt better already, and her excitement mounted as she caught sight of Sarah collecting questionnaires. Sarah and Rachel had been friends since schooldays. They had lived two blocks away from each other, gone to the same church where Rachel's dad was the vicar, and ended up at the same university in Leeds. Sarah had studied for a nursing degree while Rachel studied history. They'd shared the flat where Rachel still lived from the second year of their student days, but Sarah had tired of hospital life and decided she wanted to travel.

Rachel had graduated with a first-class honours degree in history, but she hadn't known what she wanted to do for a career when she started the course. Initially, she thought about teaching, but one term in a secondary school convinced her it wasn't for her. In spite of her father's occupation, she had never considered pursuing theology, and her parents had always allowed her to choose what she wanted to do with her life. They had never pushed religion down her throat, either; she had realised for herself that she believed in God from an early age.

It was an incident that had occurred in her first year at university that sparked her interest in becoming a police officer, and her ultimate dream now was to become a detective and join the intelligence services. One day while studying in the shared sitting room at university, she'd heard a group of students come in. Some were speaking Arabic, and some were speaking in English. There had been recent terrorist attacks in France and Belgium, and she could hear that they were having a heated argument about them. They were not aware of her presence because she was sitting in a high-backed chair in a corner of the room – she had chosen the spot deliberately to do some studying.

While she couldn't understand a lot of the conversation because the students kept switching languages, she could hear that a couple of the boys and one girl were saying how awful the terrorist attacks were and that it went against Islam. However, a boy who sounded older than the others shouted them down, and whatever he said, they seemed afraid to challenge him. She heard words like 'holy war', 'infidels', and that the West was full of immoral people.

"LOOK AT HOW THE WOMEN DRESS!" he shouted. "They have no shame."

"It's a different culture," said another male voice. "We should not judge, Allah would not want us to judge."

"You are only saying that because you have been sucked in by their ways," one of the girls replied. "I have seen you hanging around with Bethany."

More Arabic shouting followed, and then Rachel heard some of them leave. Shocked by the parts of the conversation that she had understood, she took a peep around the chair to see if she recognised any of the remaining students. She was horrified to see that the man who had been doing all the shouting was Mohab from one of her history classes. She had spoken to him a few times during a study group and he'd seemed mild-mannered, even if he was a bit aloof.

One of the boys turned his head to check if anyone was in the room and she just managed to duck back behind the chair in time. She could feel her heart pounding; she felt frightened.

What will they do if they realise I am here?

She tried to convince herself that it was a free country and they were just having a political argument like many students do. Certainly, nothing she had heard gave any impression that they were plotting anything or that they would be likely to do so. Should she go to the police? What would she say if she did? That a group of students were discussing events that had occurred and were arguing about it – these sorts of arguments occurred in universities all of the time. In her history class, a few people stated they were republican and they would like to see the monarchy removed. It didn't mean that they intended to march on Buckingham Palace and kill the Queen! She reasoned that she needed to keep the conversation she had overheard in perspective; she didn't even know who the students were, apart from Mohab.

Later that night, Rachel had discussed it with Sarah, and although she'd agreed the conversation was disturbing, she'd also agreed that people were entitled to their views and no threats had been made.

"The only thing I can suggest is that you report Mohab to the anti-hate crime hotline to make them aware of his extremist views."

"Yes, good idea. I would never forgive myself if he turned out to be dangerous, and I hadn't done anything." Mohab's aggression and dominance had unnerved Rachel, even though some of the group had disagreed with him. She reported what she had heard, and as far as she was concerned, that was the end of the matter.

She had watched Mohab more carefully during the classes they shared, sitting a few rows back from him to see how he behaved. He behaved normally in classes and was respectful to the lecturers and other students, but occasionally she noticed a glimpse of anger in his eyes when certain girls entered the room, particularly Muslim girls who chose not to wear the hijab. Rachel knew some Christian men felt the same way about how girls from their churches dressed and behaved, so this alone was not a major cause for concern. Her own father had often had to calm down the more dogmatic members of his congregation.

About six weeks after the sitting room event, Rachel was returning to her halls of residence after a class when she noticed Mohab having a particularly heated argument with two boys. She saw two men approach him, show him a card, handcuff him and march him away. The boys he had been arguing with actually looked pleased and she wondered whether they too had reported him to the authorities.

It was at that moment she realised that she may have prevented a serious crime, and she knew what she wanted to do with her life. As soon as she finished her degree, she applied to the police force, and after passing the rigorous selection process, she was offered a trainee constable position.

Chapter 5

Sarah had agreed to meet Bernard in the medical centre before going off ship. The medical centre consisted of a passenger waiting area, two clinic rooms, a treatment room, an office and a clinical store. During a cruise, two surgeries were held for passengers and staff, one in the morning and one in the evening.

One member of the medical team held the emergency bleep at all times. When on call, they had to lug around a large suitcase on wheels which contained emergency equipment for any eventuality. Sarah had found this stressful initially, but once she had got used to the layout of the ship and discovered the quickest routes to any given area on board, it became easier. The most difficult places to access were those below the waterline as conditions were cramped. Engineering was the worst as the space was really tight.

"Hello, darling," Bernard greeted Sarah as she arrived. "We were just having coffee."

Sarah could see that Bernard was relaxing with Dr Graham Bentley while they had the opportunity. She poured herself a mug of filter coffee from the steel jug which had been sent up from the kitchens and joined them.

"I will be with the captain later so I will leave it to you two to welcome our new team members," Graham said. "The senior nurse is Australian and has worked on cruise ships for another cruise line, so you will need to brief her on how this girl runs. Her name is Gwen Sumner."

"Don't you worry, sir, we will sort her out," said Bernard with a mischievous glint in his eye.

"Mm, I will rely on you to be the sensible one, Sarah," continued Graham. "The new baby doc is called Alessandro Romano. He's Italian and has been working in refugee camps in the Middle East for a year. Before that, he worked in emergency care for a hospital in Rome so he should be able to cope. He may need guiding with medication names, but thankfully you two can prescribe and Brigitte is used to foreign sounding meds."

"It's as well he will be dealing with more crew than passengers. Some of our wealthier visitors might be too much of a culture shock after refugee camps," said Sarah sympathetically. "Come on, Bernard, time to go."

"Okay, you're in charge, Doctor," Bernard teased as they left the medical centre.

"I'll get you back for that one later," retorted Graham. He was happy to banter, but everyone knew who was in charge when leadership was required.

Sarah and Bernard left the ship, passing through security, and made their way down to the passenger waiting areas. The VIPs and people requiring assistance from volunteers were allowed to board immediately, and only if they had given a positive answer to the diarrhoea and vomiting question were they detained, so most of the action took place in the main waiting area.

Passengers were called through in order of the decks they were to be staying on. Sarah and Bernard collected the questionnaires as they queued to pass through security. It was a tedious job, but it had to be done in order to protect both passengers and crew from the unpleasant virus. As this was a summer cruise, the likelihood of norovirus was much lower than during the winter, but Graham would not be happy if they missed a potential outbreak.

"Oh, I can see Rachel," said Sarah.

"Where?" Bernard asked as he continued to keep one eye on the questionnaires being handed to him.

"Over there, in the pink t-shirt and jeans. There's a pink polka-dot suitcase next to her."

"You didn't tell me she was beautiful," said Bernard admiringly. "So sad she has a broken heart."

"She'll be alright." Sarah looked at her friend and saw that Bernard was quite right. Rachel was perfectly proportioned with long blonde hair, and she really was stunning.

"I hope so. She's far too beautiful to become a wallflower."

"Now the queue has died down, do you mind if I go and say hello?"

"Go ahead, I'll call you if anyone collapses," said Bernard, laughing.

Rachel had already spotted Sarah, and the women jumped up and down with excitement as they embraced.

"It's wonderful to see you, Rachel."

"You too, you look great. Obviously, life on the high seas is suiting you."

"You look good, too. I can't wait to show you around. I'll catch up with you after the safety drill tonight. What time are you eating?"

"I chose 6.30pm dining so that I could take in some shows and the gym afterwards," said Rachel.

"Trust you! What stateroom are you in?"

"I'm on deck nine – room 9003."

"Great, I'll catch you later. Your stateroom is on the starboard side at the front of the ship. I'd better get back to work."

Some of the other passengers smiled as Sarah left her friend.

A man sitting on the other side of the room had also been admiring Rachel's looks from afar.

Maybe when the job's done, I can have some leisure time with that one, he thought. He was a bit disappointed to see the woman in uniform arrive on the scene.

Perhaps as well I know she has a friend on the crew. I can't afford to draw attention to myself.

Chapter 6

Rachel headed towards the crowds as she heard her deck number called out and joined a line of people for a relatively long walk upwards via makeshift ramps. There had been a bottleneck at the beginning as people were being urged by the ship's photographers to have a pre-cruise photo taken, but Rachel had taken the opportunity to bypass it while a large family was being directed into position. After that, the walk was relatively simple. As she arrived at the entrance to the ship, her photo pass was scanned and she was on board the *Coral Queen*.

Waiters were handing out champagne or soft drinks to passengers on their arrival, and Rachel noted a few sales desks out to nab passengers as they boarded. Sarah had warned her about how expensive things could be on the ship. Rachel had been given a drinks package as part of her booking, meaning she would be able to choose from a limited range of wines or spirits and all soft drinks without extra cost.

She realised she was in the upper part of the ship's atrium and was struck by its opulence. The atrium spanned two decks and there were seats and pristine, shining tables scattered around. She could see a number of eating areas including a patisserie, a pizza lounge and a few coffee bars on the deck below.

She found herself a seat and noticed the old lady from the VIP entrance sitting with a glass of champagne, but not drinking it. The lady looked troubled. Rachel's instinct was telling her that something was not right, but her deliberating over whether to go and join her ended when a man and woman, who looked to be in their fifties, approached. The woman was incredibly well-dressed for a boarding day, wearing a blue silk dress with a laced V-neck.

"Are these seats taken?" the man asked in an American drawl.

"No, help yourself." Rachel smiled.

"Are you travelling alone, dear?" asked the woman.

Get right to it why don't you?

"Yes and no," Rachel replied. "I have a friend who works on board and she will be joining me for some of my trips. Where are you from?"

"We're from New York City, ma'am," said the man. "We take regular cruises and this is about our third around the Mediterranean. Rome is by far my favourite place. Isn't that right, Mildred? I'm Joe, this is Mildred. Do you have a name?"

"How do you do, Joe and Mildred. I am Rachel and my friend is called Sarah. She is one of the ship's nurses."

"Well hopefully we won't be meeting her in her professional capacity," said Mildred, laughing.

Joe chatted away, making easy conversation, and Rachel was happy to listen as she didn't want him to ask her what she did. She had debated whether she should tell a white lie while she was on board the *Coral Queen* and say she was a civil servant rather than a policewoman, mainly because she did not want to hear the inevitable "Evening all" jokes or stories about criminal relatives (or indeed anything work-related). She needn't have worried in this instance, though, as Joe and Mildred were happy to talk about themselves.

The announcement came over the ship's loudspeaker that passengers could go to their staterooms and Rachel excused herself. She noted she was currently on deck five and her cabin was on deck nine – *I must get used to calling it a stateroom*. When she had asked Joe and Mildred about cabins, they had been shocked.

"They're called staterooms, dear," Mildred had explained. "They are far grander than any cabins I have ever seen."

The lifts were packed with people, and even though there were six of them where she was standing, Rachel decided to run up the stairs. She had not done any exercise at all today, and she usually took in a morning run and an evening gym session. Having noticed a number of well-proportioned people milling around, she was determined not to gain weight over the next fortnight.

Cruise or no cruise, I will keep fit.

The stairs were wide with shiny banisters that had obviously been freshly polished. They rose in sections that enabled them to spiral up through the central area between the lifts. Rachel gulped in air when she arrived on deck nine, but felt stimulated by the exertion.

Large bronze plaques were on the wall with odd room numbers on one side and even on the other. Rachel hadn't yet worked out which side was starboard and which was port. She knew that starboard was right and port was left when facing the front, but she didn't know which way was the front.

Once she had worked out which side of the ship, the odd numbers were on and the direction her room was in, she stepped into the corridor.

Gosh, I knew it was big, but this corridor must be a mile long.

There were lots of people walking up and down a fairly narrow corridor and she had to step into indents where cabins – *whoops, staterooms* – were to let people pass who had a lot more hand luggage than she was carrying. She noticed that luggage was also starting to appear outside some of the staterooms and she passed a room with a 'do not disturb' sign on the outside.

Room 9003 was almost at the end of the corridor, a fair walk from where she had exited the stairs at midships. She noticed another lift area nearer to her stateroom and assumed there would be more towards the rear of the ship.

As she was making her way forward, she saw the old lady she had spotted earlier walking slowly along the corridor, dragging her hand luggage along behind her.

"Can I help you with that?" Rachel asked.

"No thank you, dear, I have already turned down one of the stewards, and he might be offended if he sees me accepting help from someone else. Although I'm beginning to wish I had taken him up on his offer."

The old lady smiled, and the worry appeared to leave her for the moment. Although she looked frail, her eyes were sharp, and Rachel suspected that she was a 'no-nonsense' type of woman.

"Where are you heading?" Rachel asked.

The lady looked confused for a moment, then checked her papers and answered, "I am in 9005."

"I think we will be neighbours then," said Rachel. "I was told midships was the more comfortable."

Tactless, she thought, slightly embarrassed. She had noticed the lady earlier passing through the VIP lounge and presumed she could afford the more expensive rooms.

"I thought I would try out a different part of the ship for a change," replied the old lady. Her eyes misted up momentarily before she blinked and came back to the present. "What about you? Is this your first cruise?"

"Yes." *Is cruise virgin stamped on my forehead?* "A friend invited me. She works on the ship as a nurse and decided I needed a holiday."

"How nice, I do hope you will enjoy yourself. Cruises can be great fun. I have done fifteen on this cruise line, which in my opinion is the best. This is my first one alone." Her eyes became sad again. "My name is Marjorie."

"I'm Rachel. My friend is called Sarah, but I'm not sure how much I will see of her. It depends how busy the medical centre is. I have brought plenty of books though."

They arrived at their staterooms and parted company. Rachel liked the old lady; she definitely had breeding, and Rachel didn't believe she normally roughed it – if having a balcony room at the front of a ship could be considered roughing it. Not the prying type, either, which Rachel liked - and needed.

Interested, but not nosey, she thought, wondering again whether something was troubling her new neighbour.

Chapter 7

Marjorie walked into her stateroom and saw that the double bed had been made up. Not for the first time, she wondered whether this whole cruise idea had been a mistake.

There's still time to leave the ship.

She had never felt so alone. For sixty years, she had been married to her beloved husband, and although she had good friends, she knew that she would have to face some tough decisions over the next few months that she couldn't discuss with them.

Her mind wandered to her only son who appeared so cold these days.

Where did we go wrong? She asked herself this question for the thousandth time, but knew that she and her husband had not made Jeremy who he was. She so wanted to be able to confide in him; she had wanted to cry on his shoulder following his father's death, but he had seemed detached both before and after the funeral. She only saw him when he needed money for the business that her husband had worked his fingers to the bone to build.

The rumblings from the directors had made their way to her ears, but Marjorie had remained loyal to her son for months, explaining that it was early days and he would become more like his father in time. In her heart of hearts, she knew that this was never likely to happen. Her husband had managed to rein him in, but now that he was gone, Jeremy was left to do things the way he wanted. He had always been a bit like a bull in a china shop, never having the sensitivities required for managing people in the way that his father had.

Perhaps we let him get away with too much when he was young.

Their only child had been born out of a difficult pregnancy and an even more difficult labour. Marjorie's blood-pressure had been raised during her pregnancy and she had been confined to her home for the majority of the time. Labour came one awful, stormy night – as if it had been a sign of things to come. She had awoken with terrible pain and was taken to hospital where she spent the next forty hours in labour. When the time for delivery came, it was long and protracted, and in the end the doctor was called in by the midwife to carry out a forceps delivery.

Marjorie could still remember the excruciating pain as the local anaesthetic hadn't worked. Eventually, their son had been pulled out, screaming at the top of his voice.

"You have a baby boy!" the doctor had announced, happily. She'd held out her arms to take her baby, but he'd been put into a cot by the midwife and wrapped in a shawl.

After this, Marjorie had bled, and she could see the concern on the doctor's face as he tried to stem the bleeding. She remembered staring at the ceiling, crying out for her husband, who wasn't allowed in the room, and she sobbed at the thought that she would be facing death alone. All the time, she could hear a screaming baby.

"Please let me hold my son."

She'd pleaded, but the midwife was too busy rushing around handing the doctor bits of equipment to try to stem the bleeding. A blood transfusion was put up. Eventually, Marjorie had been taken to theatre for an operation to stop the blood loss. She had woken in the early hours of the next morning and seen Ralph's head resting on her bed.

"Thank God!" he'd said as he woke up. "I thought I'd lost you." The tears, that he had obviously been holding back, filled his eyes. "You are never going through that again."

She'd found out later that during the night-time operation, her womb had been removed to stop her from bleeding to death. Going through 'that' again would never be an option.

Marjorie's thoughts were interrupted by a knock at the stateroom door, which she had left ajar.

"Hello, madam, my name is Josie and I will be your stateroom attendant for this cruise." The voice was loud and jolly and came from a pint-sized Philippine lady. "Is there anything I can do for you at the moment, madam?"

Marjorie was well aware of how busy the room stewards were at this time. She and her husband had usually had a suite with a butler in attendance when they'd travelled together. Although she could still afford this type of room, she had always thought it an unnecessary extravagance, but Ralph had loved to treat her.

Realising that Josie was waiting for an answer, she lifted her head. "Not presently, thank you, but if you could ensure that there is a regular supply of Earl Grey and camomile tea in the room, I would be grateful."

"Absolutely, madam."

Marjorie surmised that Josie knew she was a VIP passenger and likely to be wealthy, so the attendant would go the extra mile. Stateroom stewards provided a good service to all of the guests, but there were those who left generous tips, usually Americans. Marjorie was also aware that Josie was more likely to receive a generous tip from those with plenty of money, and would be hoping she would oblige.

"If there is anything you need, just call housekeeping, madam, and I will do my best. There is an emergency drill at 5pm. Let me know if you need any assistance, ma'am."

"Thank you, Josie, but I am quite agile for my age!" She couldn't help but smile as Josie slipped into 'ma'am' and 'madam' at random.

"Oh, your luggage has arrived, madam. Bring it in here," Josie instructed a man twice her size. He obediently brought in the luggage and placed it carefully on the plastic sheet that lay over the foot of the bed for this purpose. With that, they both left the room.

Marjorie remained where she was and could hear Josie knocking at the door of the nice young lady she had met in the corridor.

Rachel, I think her name was.

Chapter 8

Rachel checked out her room and appreciated its luxurious feel. She opened the balcony doors and stood on the balcony, enjoying the fresh air after travelling all day. She noticed the table and chairs that she could use for outdoor leisure and quiet times.

It was a pleasant day for England, but her room was facing the dockside so she couldn't watch any boats just yet. Instead, she watched men filling luggage trolleys and bringing them on board. She could also see what must be the bridge ahead of her as there were officers milling around in their white suits. It protruded out to the side as if floating in mid-air.

There was quite a bit of activity on the dockside as *Coral Queen* was due to sail at 4pm and it was now 3.30pm. She admired the well-oiled machine going on all around her and respected the efficiency.

Hearing a knock at the door, she went to answer it.

"Hello, madam. My name is Josie and I am your stateroom attendant for this cruise. Is everything to your satisfaction?" A very small woman with dark black hair was wearing a badge with her name on it over a maroon uniform.

"Everything's fine, thank you."

"Let me know if you need anything. Your luggage has arrived, madam. There will be an emergency drill at 5pm, madam."

"Please call me Rachel."

"Okay, madam Rachel," Josie replied, and off she bustled to the room next door.

Rachel chuckled as she brought in her suitcase and placed it on the bed so that she could unpack. This would all take some getting used to, but in the force, she called people sir and ma'am, so the situation was not entirely alien. She pulled in the suitcase and placed it on the bed so that she could unpack.

I think I might enjoy this holiday after all.

After unpacking, Rachel went upstairs to deck twelve. There a lively 'sailaway' party was rocking with music as people watched the ship manoeuvring through the Solent. A well-equipped deck confronted her with a large swimming pool, spa and children's pool along with a cocktail bar and a grill bar. Waiters strolled around offering cocktails to unsuspecting passengers, who were then asked to provide their stateroom card and sign a chit. All of these drinks would be added to the bill at the end of the cruise and could add up to a large sum over a two-week period.

"Don't take any cocktails off the waiters once you've had your free boarding champagne," Sarah had warned. "That's how the ship makes money when people first come on board – they think the drink is free, and once they realise it isn't, they are too embarrassed to refuse it. Stick to your drinks package allowance."

Rachel could see some people swimming already, and because of the hot summer afternoon, others had found sunbeds around the pool. A band played on a stage and the booming sound of the bass must have been audible from the dockside.

Rachel made her way to the side rails so that she could watch as the ship left Southampton. She couldn't believe how close some of the small sailing boats came, and every now and again, the ship would deliver a thunderous sound as the horn blasted to warn them to move away. A tiny dot of a motorboat with the word 'Pilot' on the side whose pilot had boarded to lead the ship safely out to sea before returning to port. Rachel looked forward to exploring the whole ship, but for now contented herself with watching people party and looking out to sea. The dock was becoming more and more distant as the ship moved away.

How on earth do you navigate a ship this size through this busy port? She admired the captain and the pilot immensely.

Rachel spotted a few passengers who she recognised from the departure lounge, including the man she had noticed watching her.

He also seemed to be travelling alone. He was good-looking in a dark sort of way, with black cropped hair and a physique that made him look ex-military. Something about him made her feel uncomfortable. Maybe it was his good looks, or maybe it was because she was wary of men at the minute. The last thing she wanted was a man in her life.

Rachel texted her parents to let them know that she was safely aboard and would be out of range for a few days until they made the first port of Lisbon.

Her father texted back. "Have a lovely holiday, we will miss you. Stay safe and give Sarah our love. Love you x"

She was aware her parents worried about her since her engagement had broken off, and they had tried to support her as best they could.

"Will do, Dad. Relaxing already, so looking forward to the cruise. Love to mum, see you when I get back xxx"

The hour after departure passed quickly and soon the passengers were summoned to muster stations. Rachel attended the compulsory safety drill, which consisted of a lesson on the different alarm sounds and how to put on a lifejacket. The latter had been fun as some people needed assistance adjusting lifejackets to fit around generous waists and chests. Each lifejacket had a torch, and a whistle attached to it so passengers could be seen and heard in the dark. Fire safety was also covered as a fire on board a ship could be fatal. Some passengers were taking the drill a lot more seriously than others, but the crew were all taking it very seriously.

Rachel knew how important it could be for people to pay attention to a drill which might seem meaningless at the time. She herself had attended terror-attack and chemical-attack drills and she knew that the majority of people would not know how to react in such circumstances. Rachel paid the utmost attention to the safety drill, and by the end she knew how to put on her life jacket and how to find her muster station in the dark without using the lifts. Sarah would laugh at her because her nickname at university had been SWOT as opposed to SWAT. The man-overboard drill had been a sobering moment as she had recently read about a man who had gone missing while on a cruise. *Missing Presumed Dead*, the headline had read.

After about thirty minutes, the passengers were dismissed, and the atmosphere returned to holiday mode. Rachel made her way back to her stateroom so that she could change out of her travelling clothes and have a shower before dinner. She took the stairs down to deck four and made her way towards the restaurant.

It was huge. She could see the sheer scale of the room from where she stood in a queue that had formed. A crew member had already sprayed Rachel's hands with hand disinfectant while the Maître D' was welcoming everybody as they arrived. When she got to the desk, she had to look up as the Maître D' towered above her at around six foot six.

"What is your room number, madam?"

"It's 9003."

"Ah, Miss Prince. Are you happy to sit with others?"

"Yes, that would be fine."

"This will be your table for the rest of the cruise, madam. Welcome aboard." He turned to a waiter standing by. "Table 305."

Rachel was led away and seated at a round table set for eight people. Another waiter pulled out the chair for her and smiled. Six people were already seated at the table and she felt a little bit like a fish out of water being on her own.

She needn't have worried.

"Hello, I'm David and this is my wife Florence," said a man sitting to her left. He was in his early sixties, Rachel thought, well-dressed, with greying hair, and his wife - who appeared to be some fifteen years younger than him, was glamorous.

"I'm Rachel," she responded and smiled at them both.

"We were just getting to know each other," said a lady opposite. She had bleached blonde hair and was around forty. "This is my husband Greg and I am Sue."

Rachel detected a Scottish accent. She nodded to Greg, who almost disappeared under the table, being quite short.

"I'm Jean and this is Brenda," said the lady next to the empty chair on Rachel's right. The two ladies were probably in their early fifties, and Rachel thought Brenda looked pale.

Animated conversation permeated the restaurant as people settled down for dinner. The place next to Rachel had been set, so the waiters were obviously going to give the eighth diner at table 305 a little more time to arrive before taking their orders.

"Is your partner running late?" asked Greg. A casually dressed man with a moustache, he seemed ill at ease. Rachel thought he must be mid-thirties.

"Sorry?" Then Rachel realised that he was referring to the empty seat. "Oh no. Erm, I'm travelling alone," she managed to say just as a man was seated next to her.

Blast, it's the man from the deck party.

"Sorry I'm late," he apologised. "My luggage took longer than expected." His accent was slightly foreign, but Rachel couldn't work out whether it was Italian or Spanish. "I am Carlos."

Carlos gave the impression of someone who was comfortable in his own skin. Rachel wished she could be like that. He managed to charm everyone into easy conversation, including her.

The waiter appeared.

"Good evening, ladies and gentlemen. Welcome to the *Coral Queen*. I am Stavros and this is Geraldine." A young waitress appeared at his side, smiling. "We will be waiting for you over the next few weeks and will do our best to satisfy your tastes."

Good English, but not perfect, Rachel noticed. They were given *à la carte* menus with a choice of up to five courses. Rachel's eyes nearly popped out.

The wine waiter, a Bulgarian man called Grigor, had already been to the table and introduced himself. The drinks were arriving during Stavros's introduction.

"Please to enjoy your drinks and we will be back momenta."

Stavros then moved on to the next table.

Rachel noticed Marjorie being seated at a table for two nearby.

"Are you sure you wouldn't like to sit with company?" she overheard Stavros ask.

"No, thank you, I shall be quite happy to eat alone." Marjorie looked overwhelmed and Rachel managed to catch her eye. She smiled, and Marjorie raised her glass of water in salutation.

As soon as Rachel saw Marjorie, she wished she had been seated next to her rather than the overly charming man to her right. She didn't want to be sucked in by anyone's charming ways and was annoyed that a single man had been seated next to her.

What are they up to? Are they matchmaking? She realised she was being silly. The Maître D' wouldn't know who she, or Carlos, was.

It was just a cruel twist of fate.

Carlos, on the other hand, seemed quite delighted that he had been seated next to her and made every effort to charm her. She decided to be polite, but aloof, and intentionally conversed more with the couple to her left rather than with him.

The dinner passed agreeably. Rachel liked David and Florence. Florence was a paediatrician, and she and David had met when his son had had an accident and had ended up being cared for by Florence. Recently widowed at the time, David had been desperately worried that he would lose his son, too. After the boy had been discharged from hospital, David had sent flowers to Florence and attached his phone number, but Florence had been aware of the ethics of having a relationship with a relative of a patient and had not called him.

"I could stand it no more," David said. "I know it might seem like stalking, but I had to know if she would consider going out with me and so I waited outside the hospital and followed her until she was off-site."

"I was thrilled to see him." Florence continued the story. "I had regretted throwing away his number so that I wouldn't be tempted to call him, and there he stood, in my local café. Of course, I didn't know then that he had followed me or I might have called the police." She nudged him gently at this point.

Rachel was delighted that after a rough time, David had found happiness with this charming woman.

"We waited for twelve months before announcing that we were going out together, which gave me enough time to explain to my son and daughter that I had met someone else. My son didn't mind at all as he already knew Florence, but my daughter, who was fourteen, made things difficult and left home at the earliest opportunity."

"That's the only sad bit," said Florence. "I tried everything to become friends with her, explaining that I didn't want to replace her mother, but she was anger personified. To this day, she hardly acknowledges me, even though she's now twenty-one."

Rachel couldn't imagine anyone disliking Florence, but then, she had not lost her mother at such a tender age so she couldn't judge.

There was only one tricky moment during dinner when conversation lulled and Jean had asked Rachel what she did. The table seemed to go quiet.

"I have just finished a training course and now I work in the public sector." This seemed to satisfy the other guests for now and no-one had asked for further details. Only Florence appeared to want to ask more, but Rachel sensed she understood her not wanting to elaborate.

With dinner over, coffees were served. Rachel had declined wine because she wanted to go to a show and thought she would have a drink in the theatre.

Carlos was hanging back after dinner, and he asked Rachel what she was doing next.

"I'm meeting a friend," she said, even though Sarah had said it would be late before she could join Rachel as she was having to show two new members of the medical team the ropes. Rachel excused herself, saying she had to dash.

In the ladies' room, Rachel came across Marjorie re-touching her lipstick.

"Hello," she said. "Did you enjoy dinner?"

"Yes."

Rachel thought she looked troubled.

"Are you going to the show?" she asked.

"Well, I was going back to my stateroom, but perhaps I will go to the show. I always find it difficult to sleep on the first night of a cruise."

"Perhaps we can go together?" Something about this woman made Rachel want to look after her, and she trusted her instincts.

"That would be nice," replied Marjorie. "Yes please."

Rachel took the old lady's arm, and they walked along from the stern to the bow where the theatre was situated. Rachel noticed Carlos in a crowd of people who were hanging around outside the rest room, and he looked none too pleased when she emerged with Marjorie. He turned his back and walked away.

Good riddance.

When she and Marjorie were walking back to their staterooms, Rachel had a feeling they were being watched. The feeling disturbed her, but she forgot all about it when she saw Sarah outside her room.

Sarah was in a different officers' uniform from the one she'd been wearing earlier. "About time too!" She laughed. "Living it up already?"

"For your information, we have just enjoyed a very pleasant show," answered Rachel. "This is my friend, Sarah. Sarah, this is Marjorie."

"Good evening, Lady Snellthorpe," replied Sarah. "The ship's chief medical officer, Dr Graham Bentley, knew your husband, I believe, and he asked me to send his regards and an invitation to join him for dinner tomorrow in the officers' dining room."

"Young Graham, of course! Please tell him I would be delighted," replied Marjorie. "Goodnight to you both, enjoy the rest of your evening. This old lady needs to go to her bed."

Rachel was curious, but not surprised by the conversation. She could tell a woman of breeding when she saw one.

"Goodnight, Marjorie."

Marjorie entered her stateroom feeling happy after spending a pleasurable few hours with the young woman called Rachel. She was delighted that Graham Bentley had remembered her and invited her to join him for dinner the next evening.

She reflected on the evening. The waiter at dinner had asked if she wanted to join other people or sit alone, and she had chosen the latter. In the past, she would have chosen to be sociable, but these days she felt a little edgy in new company and often experienced a need to withdraw herself. The whole cruise idea had become a bit overwhelming without Ralph by her side and she was now wishing she had brought a friend along for company. Johnson had offered to accompany her as had her maid, but she had been convinced she needed to do this by herself.

Blasted be your stubbornness, Snellthorpe, Marjorie chided herself. Oh well, it's too late now, and I will make the best of it.

On the whole, she viewed the cruise positively. It provided her with an opportunity to strive for independence and show Jeremy that weakness didn't mean walkover.

She had been enjoying people watching over dinner, and when she had seen Rachel seated at the large table, she'd almost asked the waiter to move her. Then she'd scolded herself. *A young woman doesn't want to have an old lady following her around.*

Something else was now troubling Marjorie. That young man at the table, I'm sure I've seen him somewhere before. Where was it? Oh, how I wish Ralph was here. My mind seems to be meandering these days.

Chapter 9

Rachel and Sarah nattered into the small hours.

"I've left my colleague, Bernard, showing the new team members round the ship," Sarah had explained when they'd met at Rachel's door. "And he's agreed to be on call. I have a great team to work with, but it's all change now as we've got a new senior nurse and a new baby doc."

"I'm sure it will be okay, I don't know anyone you can't get along with."

"It's so good to see you, Rachel, but you look like you've lost weight?"

"Only a few pounds, and I'm sure the ship's food will fatten me up. We had a three-course dinner tonight. It could have been five, but I abstained from two. I'm not used to that amount of food as you well know."

"I know. The food is wonderful, but you can't eat like that for too long. We get to eat in the officers' dining room, and sometimes at the infamous midnight buffet. A lot of staff aren't allowed in guest areas of the ship and rarely get above water level."

"That must be awful," sympathised Rachel. "It is rather upmarket, isn't it?"

"Yes. It's great fun as a nurse, although extremely tiring. Many of the crew work twelve to fourteen hours a day, and then they drink too much and romp too much in their time off."

"Really? Like being back at uni, then?"

"Worse because some of them don't have a clue about the meaning of safe sex and when they're drunk, they will go with anyone. We have a few who are renowned Casanovas and are always needing treatment for VD."

"Yuck, that doesn't sound so good. Don't tell me more or I won't be able to look the stateroom stewards in the eye."

"They're not all bad. Many of the Philippinos are married with families back home. They work to send money home so that their families can have a better life. Fidelity is not unheard of, but the bad are bad. Who is your steward?"

"Her name is Josie and I think she is from the Philippines."

"Yes, she is, and very hard working. You will be well catered for."

Rachel enjoyed hearing Sarah's stories while they shared a bottle of red wine, until eventually Sarah fell asleep. Rachel had pulled out the sofa bed in the room for Sarah so that they could chat until they were tired.

It took Rachel a little while to get used to the night time ship noises. She could hear the constant humming of air conditioning and engine noise, along with the rocking of the ship as it negotiated its way through waves. Eventually the rocking became soothing and lulled her into a slumber. She saw Carlos's face just before falling into a deep sleep.

By the time Rachel woke up, Sarah had left for work. She'd explained that she would need to return to her cabin to change her uniform before going to morning surgery. Rachel's room was really dark, but once she opened the heavy curtains, light flooded in. She could only see the sea as she was on the right-hand side of the ship, facing the Atlantic as the ship headed south. The sky was relatively clear, and it looked like it might be a sunny day.

Rachel decided to go and explore the gym, maybe go for a run before breakfast, so she pulled on a tracksuit and made her way to the upper decks. The gym was on deck sixteen, and she was pleased to see that there were only a few people using the facility. A small

Indian woman sat behind the desk and smiled at Rachel as she entered.

"Welcome, madam." She spoke perfect English. "Are you familiar with gym equipment?"

"Yes, I am."

"Okay, madam, help yourself. The female changing rooms are over there." She pointed to her left and then she handed Rachel a fresh white bath towel.

Rachel spent forty-five minutes working out on the treadmill, the bike and the rower, and felt a lot better for it. She then decided to go for a shower and postpone her run until the next day. All the while, Carlos's face kept popping into her mind. She became annoyed with herself for thinking about him although she was willing to admit to herself that he was attractive. Drop dead gorgeous, actually, but she didn't want to fall for his obvious charm, nor have a holiday romance that would go nowhere. Another part of her, though, was warming to the idea of a fling which showed that her heart was mending. It must be if she could be attracted to another man after what had seemed like a lifetime of pain. *You're getting ahead of yourself. All he has done is be polite over dinner.*

On the way back to her room, she saw Marjorie waiting for a lift. The old lady smiled.

"Good morning, my dear. It looks like you have been active already this morning."

"Good morning, Marjorie. Yes, I went to the gym, and now I'm just going to change for breakfast. Where are you heading?"

"I'm going to the main restaurant. What about you?"

"I think I'll head up to the buffet for breakfast – I saw it on my way down, then I'll take a tour of the ship."

"You have a good day, dear."

"Oh, I nearly forgot! Sarah invited me to dine in the officers' dining room tonight and she said she would pick us both up at around six. Is that alright with you?"

"That would be perfect. I'll see you then."

Rachel thought that Marjorie seemed a little more relaxed and wondered if she had been imagining the worry in her face. Sarah had explained that the chief medical officer had known Marjorie's husband well and that she and he had been very close, so understandably she must be missing him. *It's a shame she has to travel alone.*

Rachel got lost at least three times while she was strolling around the ship. She found it hard to familiarise herself with the huge floating five-star hotel, which seemed to offer every amenity going. The theatre she had attended the previous night at the front of the ship ran over two decks, providing a balcony and a stalls area. She found a cinema on deck fourteen, but noticed there was not a deck thirteen.

Her father had told her that sailors were very superstitious.

"If Apollo 13 had been a ship, it would never have been called that, and," he'd argued, irrationally, "it would never have got stuck in space."

"Really, Dad, the name caused the problem?" Rachel had given him her most derisive look.

"Mock me if you will, but sailors would never risk it."

"You're supposed to be a man of faith. How can you believe in such nonsense?"

"It's because I am a man of faith that I know there is more to the world than what we see."

Rachel had given up, exasperated.

Continuing her tour of the ship, she found a nightclub next to the cinema for those who wanted to stay up late. Bars were scattered throughout the ship and they all had different names that she didn't try to remember. The jogging area went the whole way around the ship on deck sixteen. On the upper decks, she discovered some false grass and a barbecue area, and there was a golf simulator somewhere, but she couldn't remember where she had seen it.

When she tired of trying to remember where everything was, she paused for a while and looked down from an inner rail to the pools where the party had been the night before. The grill bar was well and truly open and people were already lying on sunbeds with waiters walking around, serving drinks. Rachel saw that there were large racks containing blue-striped towels that could be used for the loungers and for drying after a swim. It had turned into a pleasant though not a hot day, but that did not deter people from wearing the flimsiest of bikinis and trunks.

Rachel also noted that there was a large outdoor cinema screen on the deck where she stood. In her room the previous night, she had found a *Coral News* magazine that listed all of the day's activities. She decided to go and get it from her room and find a quiet place to read.

She turned to leave.

"Rachel. What a nice surprise!"

Rachel felt slightly unnerved. "Carlos, hi. Have you been touring the ship?" she spluttered her words out.

"I have been wandering around for hours admiring the beauty of the ship, and now I see so much more beauty before my eyes."

She felt herself redden. Why did this man have such an effect on her? She decided to ignore the remark and was about to reply when she saw a furrow in his brow as he glanced away from her. Following his gaze, she studied the people below them but couldn't work out who, or what, had attracted his attention. She did spot Marjorie, though, making her way along the deck below.

Carlos quickly looked away, and Rachel surmised that he must just have been looking around.

"There is indeed much beauty to be seen on this ship."

He laughed as he looked towards the women bathing in the pool.

"Well, enjoy your day."

Annoyed and bemused, Rachel moved away.

Was I mistaken? If not, what had drawn his attention to the lower deck? There are so many people walking around, he must have noticed some bombshell to set his sights on. Rachel did not kid herself that she would be this man's only interest.

Rachel spent the rest of the day enjoyably reading a tense spy thriller, and the hours passed quickly. Against her better judgement, she had lunch at the grill bar and consumed more fat in that one meal than she normally ate in a week. After a whole day without thinking about Robert, which in itself was progress, she felt the tension of the past few months leaving, and admitted to herself that Sarah had been right to cajole her into taking this break.

The mysterious Carlos did keep cropping up in her thoughts though.

It's perhaps as well I'm eating elsewhere tonight.

Rachel dressed for dinner in a smart deep-blue cocktail dress which complemented her figure and clung to all the right curves. It was low cut, but not revealing. Her long blonde hair was brushed through and she had used curling tongs to add some waves. She applied her makeup in a simple way that highlighted her face. Looking in the mirror, she could see that she already had a healthy glow. Her eyes looked an even deeper blue than usual thanks to the reflection of the dress, and she looked happy.

Sarah was smug. "You look beautiful," she said. "But then you would look beautiful in a carrier bag! You are glowing."

"Thank you, and you look rather gorgeous yourself in that uniform. You know about men and their uniform fantasies."

They giggled. Their friendship had picked up where it had left off as all good friendships do.

Marjorie was ready and waiting for them when they knocked at her door.

"Hello, Lady Snellthorpe," said Sarah.

"Oh, do call me Marjorie." The old lady smiled.

"You look lovely," said Rachel, admiring Marjorie's dress sense. She had donned a Ralph Lauren evening dress of pale green and a chiffon scarf to match. Her shoes and handbag were a darker green, and they complemented her clothes. The ship was warm, but she wore a light jacket.

"And you look gorgeous," Marjorie said to Rachel.

"What did you do with yourself today?" asked Rachel.

"I spent most of the day in the ship's library, apart from one venture outside on the lido deck to get some fresh air. The day passed by nicely, and I read a travel adventure about a couple who trekked through Nepal, which provided some light entertainment." She winked at them. "It made me want to be twenty again."

Marjorie still looked spritely for her age – Sarah had told Rachel she would be eighty-five this year.

"You are looking well," Rachel said.

"Yes, I'm thankful that apart from a bit of high blood-pressure, I am in good health. I occasionally use a stick for support as my hips are not as strong as they used to be, but I can walk for miles on the flat. I may decide to go out on deck later. One of the things Ralph and I loved to do was to look at the stars at night."

Sarah linked arms with Marjorie and they started the long walk along the corridor to the lifts. As soon as they arrived in the officers' dining room, a dapper man in his late fifties came towards them. Rachel noticed he was in uniform with three gold stripes on his epaulettes. He was around six feet tall with a muscular physique, and the only sign of the good life was a slight belly paunch. His engaging smile reached his dark brown eyes, and his short fair hair only had a hint of grey to the sideburns.

"Lady Snellthorpe, how wonderful it is to see you again." He took her hand and lightly kissed it. Rachel felt she had been transported into a 1950s movie, but she warmed to his chivalry. "And you must be Rachel?"

"This is Rachel, my best friend, and this is Dr Graham Bentley, our chief medical officer," Sarah said, laughing.

"How do you do, Doctor."

"Tonight, you can call me Graham."

"Only if you call me Marjorie," interjected Marjorie.

"Come along then, Marjorie," he said and put her arm through his before leading them towards a table set for six.

"I hope you don't mind, but Lord and Lady Fanston will be joining us. I believe you know them, Marjorie."

Rachel noticed a slight reticence on Marjorie's part.

"A little. They are friends of my son Jeremy, really. I met them at a fundraising event that Ralph organised. They came along with Jeremy and his then wife, Flora."

"I didn't realise," said Graham, looking a bit embarrassed at inviting the couple. He didn't let it show for long though. Years of medical training had obviously given him the ability to hide his feelings. "They said they were friends, so I invited them along, hoping that they would look after Lady Snellthorpe during the cruise," Rachel heard him whisper to Sarah. Rachel saw for a brief moment that he was obviously annoyed.

As it turned out, a note was delivered to the table to say that Lady Fanston was suffering from seasickness and could Dr Bentley look in on her later? The evening passed in a pleasant, convivial manner and Rachel warmed to the charming but professional CMO. He made a fuss of Marjorie, who had visibly brightened when she heard the Fanstons wouldn't be joining them.

"I don't think she likes them," whispered Sarah to Rachel.

"No, I don't think so either. She is such a nice lady; it's so sad when people lose their soulmates, isn't it?"

"We're not going there tonight. Come on, get some champagne down you. To brighter days ahead."

Sarah clinked her glass against Rachel's in a toast.

"To brighter days ahead."

Chapter 10

Rachel walked Marjorie back to her room after the meal. Sarah was on-call and had been called away to an emergency after the main course. Apparently, a lady had fallen from a bar stool in one of the bars and the baby doc was already dealing with a crew member who was showing signs of appendicitis.

"It's interesting, getting the inside scoop into what goes on during a cruise," Marjorie said. "I had never given it much thought before, but I suppose, with thousands of passengers and crew on board, accidents and illnesses do occur."

"Yes, Sarah told me there is never a dull moment in the life of a ship's nurse. It's certainly not a revolving holiday for her, but she loves the work, and she does get to see parts of the world that she would never have seen otherwise. She has already been around the world once – not everyone can say that at twenty-five."

"Or eighty-five, dear. Ralph loved cruises in later life, but when we were younger, travel wasn't quite so easy and business kept him tied to England for most of his life. I'm pleased we got to travel over the past twenty years, and we had some marvellous holidays. There were some countries Ralph would never visit though. I would have loved to visit Asia and Africa but Ralph was never that adventurous. He loved Europe, and we often travelled to the USA, so I can't complain."

"You must miss him," Rachel replied with genuine compassion.

Marjorie sighed. "I do, but we had a wonderful marriage and not everyone can say that. You mustn't feel you have to look after me, you know. I am quite alright, and you are a young woman who needs to enjoy your cruise and spend time with young people, not an old codger like me."

"Oh, I am enjoying it so far, and you should understand that you are a delight to be with. I think you're as sharp as any of my friends. I like your company and I don't think you need looking after."

They said goodnight and Marjorie entered her stateroom. She had enjoyed another pleasant evening, apart from the near miss with the Fanston's. Marjorie hadn't elaborated over dinner, but she had not taken to the couple when she'd met them. They had spent the whole evening telling everyone how much they did for charity, but they didn't contribute to the fundraising at all. Ralph had been furious with Jeremy as they hadn't even paid for their tickets. Jeremy had given them tickets and seemed to want to impress them. The whole idea of the ticket price was that it paid for the dinner adding a little bit to the charity for those who didn't donate on the night. There had been a row between father and son, and Ralph had looked quite ill at the end of it.

Thank goodness for seasickness, she mused as she got ready for bed.

After walking Marjorie to her room, Rachel decided to go for a walk on the upper decks where she could get some fresh air. The champagne had made her head feel light for a while, but that was wearing off.

As she opened a door to go outside, a huge draught of air almost knocked her over and she noticed the ship lurching up and down a lot more than it had done during the day, even though she was in the midships area. They were travelling through the Bay of Biscay, and the captain had said in his announcement this evening that the sea would be slightly choppy overnight.

"Take that as captain-speak for nasty storm," Sarah had warned. "That means I am in for a very busy night – the Bay of Biscay can be a nightmare when it's rough, but don't worry, this baby is one of the best in the fleet and she will cope with the journey without too much discomfort. The stabilisers prevent her from rocking too much."

Rachel wasn't afraid of the sea. She liked the idea of seeing huge, undulating waves crashing against the ship, knowing that the liner could take it.

She didn't think she would be staying out on deck for long as the wind was picking up. Even on a ship this size, she was struggling to keep her feet on the ground. She noticed members of the crew tying things down to stop them from disappearing over the side. The man-overboard scenario at the emergency drill the previous night had made some passengers laugh at the time, but it was not funny to contemplate someone going overboard in seas like this, and she shuddered at the thought.

Passengers were now being encouraged to move inside, so Rachel went back in to the safety and the warmth of the internal areas. Once inside, she went and sat in one of the lounges where jazz music was playing. She liked jazz, but after rebuffing the interests of a few men who had been drinking heavily, she decided to retire to her room.

Why can't they just leave me alone?

She was still feeling like she was being watched, and no matter how much she told herself that she was being paranoid, she found the feeling difficult to shake off.

When she got back to her stateroom, she became more rational. She was not used to men approaching her all the time, but then, she had never been on a cruise by herself.

That must be what's unsettling me.

She stood out on the balcony for a while, watching the swell of gigantic waves. Huge breakers crashed into the side spraying the hull, but they were way below where she was standing. Because her room was in the bow of the ship, it was tossed up and down more than those in the middle.

The activities on *Coral Queen* produced a lot of light pollution, even in the vast darkness of the ocean. There were no other ships visible, and she couldn't see any stars through the overcast sky.

Rachel could just about make out the moon in the distance. The cacophony of sound produced by the waves rose above the noise of the musical activities on the lower decks.

Finally, at around 2am. Rachel went inside and climbed into bed.

An hour later, an unfamiliar noise woke her. The ship was still rocking up and down and side to side, but it now sounded like someone was trying to get into her room.

Maybe it's Sarah.

Bleary eyed and unsteady on her feet, she made her way to the door. Looking through the spy hole out into the corridor, she could only see the wall opposite. She unlocked the double lock and opened the door cautiously. Her heart raced as apprehension gripped her and she put her head outside to see where the noise was coming from. The corridor was clear.

At that moment, someone tapped her from behind. She almost leapt out of her skin, but managed to suppress a scream.

An American voice she recognised from the room next to hers broke the silence.

"Are you alright?"

"Yes, I thought I heard a noise, but it must have been the storm."

"Did it sound like someone trying to get in your room, ma'am?"

"Yes, it did."

"Don't worry, it was a drunk trying to get into the room next door to you. I saw him off. He was on the wrong deck."

"Oh, I see," said Rachel, suddenly becoming aware that she was wearing a flimsy cotton nightdress and was in the corridor in the middle of the night with a man. "Thank you, I think I'll go back to bed now." Then she turned to him again. "What did the man look like?"

"Let me see now – just over six foot, but he wore a hat and scarpered pretty quickly when he realised he was in the wrong corridor. It happens a lot on cruise ships, ma'am, don't be alarmed. The old lady didn't come out so I guess she didn't hear."

The man turned and went back to his room, and Rachel closed her door, but she couldn't get back to sleep. The ship was still being tossed about, but this wasn't what was keeping her awake. Was it a coincidence that someone was trying to get into Marjorie's room, or was there something sinister going on? Carlos's face came back into her head – had he been watching Marjorie when she had met him on the deck the previous day? What was going on?

She told herself that she needed to get some perspective. Her police training and experiences were starting to give her a warped view of the world. Sarah had said it was the same for nurses: they see so much illness that it is sometimes hard to believe that there are people in the world who are healthy.

Could that be what is happening to me? Rachel had spent so much time catching criminals that maybe she thought a criminal lurked around every corner. She pulled a pillow on top of her head. *Oh boy, I need this holiday.*

Chapter 11

After a very restless and disturbed night, Rachel awoke to a knock on the door. She staggered to answer in the dark and was greeted by the ever-cheerful Josie.

"Sorry, madam… Rachel, I was going to do your room. I didn't realise you were asleep. Shall I come back later?"

"Yes, please."

As Rachel closed the door, the first thing she noticed was that the ship was moving normally with just a slight rocking motion. She opened the curtains to a glorious, clear sky, and she couldn't believe it when she looked at her watch and realised it was 11am.

She picked up the phone and asked for coffee to be sent to her room and then went for a shower. When she got out of the shower, she heard a knock at the door and a kitchen waitress brought in a pot of coffee. Rachel gave her a tip and closed the door behind her. She had left the demons of the previous night in her bed and told herself to relax and enjoy her holiday.

Opening the doors on to the balcony, she sat outside with her coffee. It was warm, and although the sun was more or less above the ship, she could see the reflection shining on what was now a calm blue sea. It was as if last night had never happened and the morning had cleaned everything away – the angry sea had gone; the threatening dark and the tumultuous thoughts had all disappeared with it. She was on a cruise ship with a lovely old lady in the room next door and her friend close by. There was absolutely nothing disturbing going on, except in her head.

The phone in her room rang.

"Hello."

"Hi, Rachel. How was your night?" It was Sarah.

"Alright. considering the storm," Rachel replied, deciding to forget about the weird events. "Were you busy?"

"Afraid so. Anyway, I am calling to see if you want to meet up this afternoon for an hour. I am busy the rest of the day."

"Yes, that would be great." They arranged to meet later and Sarah hung up.

Having looked through the *Coral News* at the activities for the day, Rachel decided to have lunch and then go to an art auction. Not that she could afford to buy any art, but she liked looking at paintings by famous artists, and she enjoyed window shopping. In addition to that, there was the offer of free champagne. After the auction, she would meet Sarah for tea, and then take it from there. She had planned to discuss her concerns about the visitor in the night with Sarah. However, this morning she was able to shrug them off and decided that her friend had enough to think about without worrying that Rachel was losing her mind.

During the night, Rachel had decided to ask Marjorie if anything was bothering her, without telling her about the man at her door. She concluded that it would just put unconfirmed suspicions into an elderly lady's head and frighten her unnecessarily. In addition, Marjorie might think the girl she had befriended was a bit unhinged and start avoiding her. The morning light had brought back the rational Rachel, and it was that person who was going to enjoy her cruise.

The weather had turned much warmer as the ship headed south towards Lisbon. The capital of Portugal was to be the first land stop of the trip. Rachel dressed in a pair of smart-casual white cotton trousers and a short-sleeved pink cotton top, then donned a pair of pink sandals.

She went for a buffet lunch and found herself a salad to eat, amazed at how much food people managed to pile onto their plates all in one go. The buffet was noisy and busy, and she wondered whether others had also missed breakfast or whether they ate like this at every meal.

After eating, she made her way to deck fourteen, above the lido deck, and found a single sun lounger free. This part of the deck formed a circle similar to a balcony, and steps led from it down to the pool. Rachel sat on the sun lounger for a while, observing her surroundings. She could clearly see the swimming pool, spa and children's pool below. The pool was large enough for a swim, but only half the length of the pool she was used to, and far too busy to tempt her in.

A band set up on the stage as the smell of burgers and sausages wafted through the air from her left. The grill bar seemed to be permanently open and especially popular, and she noticed for the first time an ice cream bar next to the cocktail bar to her right.

The pools were at the back of the ship, away from the quieter areas. She watched as people left towels on the sun loungers when they went off for lunch in the buffet bar – something that was strictly forbidden. Other people were walking around, looking for loungers, and Rachel thought it was unfair that most of them had been reserved, but it was not her responsibility so she left it to the pool attendants to prevent this from happening.

Waiters made regular rounds, offering people drinks. Some people were sleeping in the sun, which Rachel knew they would regret later. Some people were applying sun cream frequently and reminding their children to do the same while others were not bothering.

Poor Sarah – it will be sunburn she will be treating later on.

Rachel realised she didn't have any sun cream with her so she sat in the partial shade. As she was one of the few people not wearing a bathing costume, she wasn't too worried.

After watching people for a while, she turned to face the sea and got her book out to read as she had half an hour before the art auction started. She heard a familiar voice to her left and was dismayed to see Carlos chatting to a young woman in his normal charming style. She tried not to look, but couldn't help herself.

He looked even more handsome today as the sun's rays were dancing in his hair. He had on a pair of khaki shorts that stopped just above the knees, and she could see his legs were as brown as his arms. His calves were strong and muscular as if he worked out, and he was wearing flip-flops. He was carrying his t-shirt in his left hand, and his torso was just as she'd expected: toned, but not overly worked-out.

Moving her gaze up to his head, she noticed how his jawline was perfectly set in his face. Not a feature was out of place, except, if she was being picky, his ears, which stuck out ever so slightly. He smiled at the woman he was talking to and his white teeth contrasted with his tanned face.

Rachel was just about to see who he was talking to when the woman moved and he caught her looking at him. She looked away quickly as he came towards her.

"There you are," he said. "I have been looking for you everywhere. I was most dismayed not to see you at dinner last night."

"I had dinner with my friend in the officers' dining room." For some reason, she didn't mention the presence of Marjorie. She wanted to ask him who he had been talking to, but thought that would give him too many signals that she was interested.

"I see, my loss was their gain. Did you enjoy hobnobbing with the officers?"

Rachel didn't like the insinuation, and before thinking, replied rather sharply, "I had a lovely dinner with my friend. Not that it's any of your business."

He looked a little bit taken aback, and then, with a pretence at hurt, he said, "I did not mean to offend you, but you must realise that any man who sees you would want to get to know you better."

His smile disarmed her, and she laughed.

"You say some crazy things." She saw he was about to sit on the side of her lounger and she got up quickly. "Would you like this lounger? I'm afraid I need to go."

"Mamma Mia! You can't leave so soon. Where are you going?"

"To the art auction on deck six."

"I was just on my way there myself, so in that case, I shall accompany you." Before she could protest, he had helped her to her feet and was marching her off towards the lifts.

They arrived at the auction in plenty of time and registered their presence. They were each given a bidding card in case they wanted to buy anything and were encouraged to browse the lots, which Rachel was keen to do.

The auction lots were originals and limited edition prints in various sizes and formats, all numbered. The large pieces with elaborate frames were standing on easels, and smaller pieces were hanging on makeshift walls.

Carlos made polite conversation, but he did stand back and allow her to browse, giving the appearance of browsing himself. He looked distracted, glancing around as if he was waiting for someone.

That girl he was speaking to upstairs, I suspect.

Then he moved away and left her browsing for a while.

She wasn't going to let his presence spoil her appreciation of all the art pieces and she paused to look at some prints by the Ukrainian artist Anatole Krasnyansky. She liked brightly coloured work, and his held a mixture of surrealism with a sense of structure and purpose. She was looking at a print of his *Russia Red Sunset* when she lost sight of Carlos.

She sighed and moved around the room, looking at the many varied prints. There was even a Picasso original for sale.

Other prints she browsed were by Salvador Dali and Thomas Kinkade. There were hundreds to look at, and after about an hour, she realised that the auction was about to start.

Carlos appeared by her side.

"Shall we find a seat?" he asked and handed her a glass of champagne.

"There are two over there." Rachel pointed out.

"Oh no, these will be better just there." He led her away to two seats that weren't very well positioned at all. As she sat down, she saw Marjorie three rows in front on the opposite side to where they were seated.

Carlos must have realised Rachel was looking at him, perplexed.

"I thought I saw a friend over there from Rome, but it is not him," he said quickly.

His explanation was perfectly plausible, and it was a packed auction room.

It's just a coincidence.

The auction began with a rather prolonged introduction and sales pitch, followed by a few giveaways. After this, the paintings were brought to the front one by one and auctioned off.

It was actually quite exciting. Rachel could have afforded some of the cheaper lots, but she didn't want to spend her spare cash at the moment. She noticed Marjorie bidding for a Dali. Rachel was not surprised that Marjorie would like art and having a spend might help ease some of the pain she must be going through. The bidding was in US dollars, and Rachel was trying to do the calculations in her head. Marjorie bought the painting for around £2,500 by her calculation.

After about an hour, Rachel looked at her watch and turned to Carlos.

"I need to go, I'm afraid. I am meeting my friend, Sarah, for tea before she goes into evening surgery."

"Will I see you at dinner?" he whispered.

"I will be there, so yes," she replied.

She waited for him to move, but realised that he was staying so she got up and left. The confused thoughts returned again as she made her way down to deck five where she would meet Sarah. She liked Carlos and was definitely attracted to him, and she sensed he was attracted to her, too, but there was something else going on that she couldn't put her finger on. It was like an itch that couldn't be scratched and it was disturbing.

She saw Sarah as she walked down the stairs into the main atrium, realising that she hadn't been inside any of the shops on board yet. The sea days were flying by. Sarah greeted her warmly, and they moved into the patisserie which was less busy than the other areas because passengers had to pay for cakes and drinks in there.

Sarah smiled at one of the waiters and he came over to serve them.

"I'll have a cappuccino and a slice of that delicious looking strawberry cake," said Sarah.

"A coffee for me and a slice of blackcurrant cheesecake, please," said Rachel, handing over her payment card.

"No payment, ma'am." He smiled at Sarah before walking away.

"Oh, he's sweet on you," said Rachel, laughing.

"He's nice, from the Czech Republic. We met in surgery two weeks ago. He's been following me around ever since, but in a nice rather than a weird way."

"I'm pleased you know the difference," said Rachel, thinking of a few of the stalkers she had had to deal with as a policewoman. No stalking was acceptable, but it was hard to differentiate between the annoying-but-harmless kind and the downright dangerous kind. The police took the problem much more seriously than they had in the past, and Rachel told Sarah how her sergeant was obsessive about it.

"He's probably been burned in the past. I bet someone ended up seriously harmed or even killed," said Sarah. "I have worked with doctors who have become so cautious that they end up wasting thousands of pounds ordering unnecessary tests. It's usually because they missed a cancer and a patient died as a result. Some doctors never forgive themselves while others accept their own fallibility."

"You're right. He let someone go that he should have charged, and they went on to kill. I have arrested some right scumbags, who are relatively harmless, and then I arrest someone who appears to be an outstanding citizen, but there is something in the eyes that makes me want to lock them away for the rest of their lives. Of course, it ends up being down to the courts and how much evidence we can gather. Then there are people who drop charges before it goes to court. It's a complicated world out there. Anyway, tell me more about the waiter. Do you like him?"

"If you mean *like*-like, then no. He's nice enough, but not my type. I'm a bit wary of cruise ship relationships because word gets around and life is just too hectic. I could do without the complications."

"What's your new baby doc like then?" asked Rachel.

"He's nice. His name is Alessandro Romano, but thankfully he prefers Alex. He's good under pressure, which is what we need because he has to do the bulk of the work while Graham goes off seeing passengers who don't really need him, but who demand to be seen. Alex has already had to deal with the broken wrist of an engineer and a miscarriage of a crew member."

"Oh dear, poor woman. I didn't think you could deal with all that sort of stuff on board."

"It's amazing, Rachel, what we can do. We have X-ray machines, scanners, and a blood lab. The only thing we can't do is operate, so sometimes we have to do an evacuation. The woman will need to go to hospital in Lisbon for a check-up. The other thing we have," Sarah whispered, "is a morgue."

Rachel had taken a few trips to morgues and seen a post-mortem as part of her training, but it was not something she wanted to think about.

"By the way," she said instead, "I think you are going to be seeing some lobsters tonight as there were loads of people out by the pool without sun cream."

"I suspected as much. People forget how damaging the sun can be out at sea because they feel a breeze."

They moved on from work talk and Rachel decided to tell Sarah about Carlos.

"I've been a bit silly. I have met this guy called Carlos who sits at my dinner table. I noticed him on the lido deck the first day of the cruise because he's really handsome and he seems interested, but what's the point? It's just a two-week holiday."

"A two-week holiday where you could have some fun. Just take it as it comes and try not to stress about it – if something comes of it, then great. If not, you will have had a nice holiday and some fun with a guy, no strings attached."

"You might be right, you know, but then you could let your hair down a bit and find some handsome officer to go out with."

"Maybe I will. Changing the subject, I have got shore leave tomorrow as Alex and Brigitte are staying on board. I think she's quite sweet on him, but the new senior, Gwen, will be staying behind too, so she won't get a look-in."

"Oh yes. You haven't told me about your new senior."

"Nothing to tell. Workaholic, but okay – you know the type."

After Sarah had left, Rachel changed for dinner and felt excited anticipation about seeing Carlos. She'd decided to take Sarah's advice and just enjoy his company without pinning any hopes on it becoming a romance.

Looking in the mirror, she was pleased with what she saw. She had chosen a maroon cocktail dress that her father had bought her when he took her shopping before the cruise. He had insisted on kitting her out with enough dresses, including evening dresses for the three formal nights when the captain and crew would be present, and champagne and canapés would be served before dinner. This dress was ideal for this evening. It accentuated her figure without being over-dressy – she didn't want to appear to be making too much of an effort. It was a hard balance, but she felt that she had achieved it.

A light smattering of makeup and her hair flowing freely, she put on a shawl to cover her shoulders during dinner: a rule for diners eating in the main restaurant. As she left her room, she was feeling slightly nervous.

So much for being relaxed about it, she admonished herself, but smiled happily nonetheless. She hadn't thought about Robert for two whole days, and that had to be good.

David and Florence were pleased to see her.

"We missed you last night," Florence said kindly.

"I have a friend who works on the ship so we met for dinner," answered Rachel.

"You look radiant," said Brenda, who was already seated with Jean.

Rachel blushed, and then as she heard the voice behind her, she blushed even more. Thankfully the lighting was dim and people were chatting so they didn't notice.

"Good evening." Carlos announced himself. "How beautiful the ladies look tonight." His eyes swept the table, but rested on Rachel. "How was tea with your friend?" he enquired.

"It was very nice, thank you. How was the end of the auction?"

"I didn't stay long," he answered. Rachel got the feeling he wasn't being entirely honest.

Perhaps he's a compulsive liar.

She smiled at him.

Chapter 12

On the third morning of the cruise, the ship was docked in Lisbon.

The day before, Marjorie had met another widow, Freda, while playing bridge in the card room on board ship. They'd got chatting and were both pleased to find someone to share time with. Freda, Marjorie had discovered, had been the wife of an ex-diplomat and had been based in various embassies around the world. They had moved back to Scotland when Freda's husband had retired and spent many happy years catching up with old friends and family.

"My husband died a year ago following a stroke," explained Freda. "He was out playing golf when he collapsed, and unfortunately he never regained consciousness. It's perhaps as well," she continued. "He would have hated being disabled and was a firm believer in euthanasia."

Marjorie could empathise with Freda with regard to the sudden loss of a spouse after decades of marriage. "It must have been hard," she said, remembering how hard it still was for her after Ralph's death.

"It was awful, to be honest. I just wanted to die myself. If it hadn't been for the children and grandchildren, I'm not sure what I would have done. I don't even like to think about it. I still find it difficult to go on sometimes, even with the support of family – the days and nights can be so long, can't they?"

"Yes, they can," Marjorie acknowledged. "Life is never the same, that's for sure."

Marjorie realised how cathartic it had been to talk to someone about her loss. *Another person who understands the deep sense of grief which nothing will alleviate.* When Marjorie had discovered Freda was going on the same trip in Lisbon the next day, she had been delighted.

Marjorie had been seated close to Rachel the previous evening and thought she had looked very happy. She still couldn't remember where she had seen the man who was with her before, though, in spite of racking her brains for two days.

Oh, old brain, I wish you could remember things.

She had gone to bed, deciding to think about it before she went to sleep. She had read somewhere that if you thought about something before going to bed that you would remember it during the night.

It didn't work.

Marjorie and Freda met up at breakfast, and afterwards went along to the theatre, where groups were gathering to join their various coach trips. Marjorie had booked the trip on the first day and was looking forward to visiting the Gulbenkian Museum, renowned for its private art collection. After that, they would be taken on a narrated tour through Lisbon, and she and Freda had decided they would stop off at the far end of the harbour and visit one of the larger hotels for afternoon tea.

The museum turned out to be everything Marjorie had expected, and more. It was huge and spacious inside as they entered through the main hallway. As they were on a tour, they had round stickers with numbers attached to their chests, and followed the tour guide who explained about the collections, but they only managed to see a fraction of the exhibits due to time constraints.

"You could spend a week in here and still not see everything," Marjorie remarked.

"Yes, I agree. I do love art, don't you? It's a shame we won't have time to see the Lalique collection as well."

Marjorie also liked Lalique and had a few pieces of the glassware herself. René Lalique was famous around the world for his unmistakable style of glass sculptural design. He produced anything from small sculpted animals to large bowls and vases and his work was sought after worldwide. Nevertheless, she was much more interested in paintings, and thrilled to see works by Rubens, Rembrandt and Turner. There were also pieces by Renoir, and she was in her element admiring the works of these great masters of art. Delighted with her Dali purchase the previous day, she was taking full advantage of the time they had, browsing the masterpieces.

Freda seemed to be enjoying the sculptures, particularly those that reminded her of her times overseas.

"We saw so many great works of art in many different parts of the world," she said.

Marjorie felt that although her own sense of loss was deep, Freda's seemed to eat her apart. *I wonder if any of us are ever happy again after the loss of our soulmate*s. She chastised herself for being maudlin and reminded herself how both she and Ralph had promised each other they would try to go on and enjoy life if the worst should happen to either of them.

After the museum tour, Marjorie and Freda had lunch in the café before rejoining the coach for the rest of the trip, chatting all the way. Because both of them had been to Lisbon many times before, they didn't feel the need to listen too carefully to the tour guide.

The coach driver dropped a number of passengers off at the far end of the harbour.

"You will need to make your own way back to the ship," the tour guide advised as they left the coach, and they agreed to be back at the *Coral Queen* by five.

Marjorie and Freda sat in the Botanical Gardens for a while, enjoying the scented perfume of the tropical flowers that were grown there. At three o'clock, they decided to find a grand hotel with excellent service and enjoy afternoon tea with cakes and scones.

"It has always surprised me how we British still long for the luxuries of home, even when abroad," said Marjorie. "It's no wonder that some foreigners find us annoying. Did you find this when you lived abroad?"

"Yes," replied Freda. "Seamus always insisted on haggis for Burn's Night, even when we were based in Morocco. It had to be shipped over in a diplomatic pouch." She chortled at the memory. Freda had a lovely laugh, and Marjorie was pleased that she appeared to be happier in herself. Thcy had spent much of the day sharing memories, and Marjorie noticed that Freda had difficulty staying in the present.

Marjorie also noticed that although they were of a similar height and build, the other woman did not appear to pay the same attention to her appearance. Her hair was a little dishevelled whereas Marjorie's was immaculately well styled and groomed. Freda's nails looked worn, and her face showed the marks and lines of someone who had smoked for many years, and who probably liked a drink too many. Marjorie had never smoked, but she did like the occasional brandy at bedtime and drank socially. Perhaps as a diplomat's wife, Freda had spent most of her life having to entertain guests and host parties, so this might have taken its toll on the woman.

Looking out of the window, Marjorie realised it was raining. She looked at Freda.

"Do you have a coat, dear?"

"No, I don't seem to have brought one," Freda replied.

"Never mind," said Marjorie. "I have an umbrella and a jacket. Why don't you wear my coat and hat? I'm always prepared for every eventuality."

"Oh, thank you, that is so kind. If I get wet, my rheumatism plays up awfully."

Freda took the coat and put on the hat as they left the hotel to find a taxi to take them back to the ship. They stood at the side of the road, waiting for a gap in the traffic so that they could cross to the other side. A large crowd gathered around them as everyone seemed to be waiting to cross at the same time.

Marjorie looked across the road and saw Rachel and her friend in the distance, heading their way.

Perhaps we could all share a taxi…

Her thoughts were shattered as she heard the loud beep of a vehicle horn, and she watched in horror as a lorry jackknifed right in front of her.

There was a huge commotion, and she looked around for Freda. Moments later, she saw her hat in the road. Her coat, along with Freda, was lying underneath the lorry.

Dropping her umbrella, Marjorie froze to the spot while the rain lashed down onto her head.

Chapter 13

Rachel had slept well, in spite of feeling some disappointment that Carlos hadn't offered her a kiss on the cheek, or even a clichéd compliment, when they had parted the previous night. In fact, their goodbye had been rather awkward. Putting her disappointment aside, Rachel got up early and worked out in the gym before having breakfast. Then she made her way to the main atrium to meet Sarah.

Sarah arrived around fifteen minutes late, looking tired. She had on a pair of cropped cotton trousers and a white printed cotton t-shirt. Her hair was down today, and the long naturally wavy light-brown locks reached the middle of her back. Rachel admired her friend appreciatively. Both women were used to wearing uniforms in their jobs and enduring the constraints this entailed, including tying back hair and wearing little or no jewellery, but they both liked bling when off duty.

"I'm sorry I'm late." Sarah was still breathless from rushing. "We were up most of the night dealing with burns. One woman had serious sunburn, and we had to arrange for her to go to the burns unit today at the local hospital."

"Will she be okay?"

"Yes, it's just precautionary really, and they can provide her with a supply of dressings to cover the worst of them. She was lucky. I think if she had been out in the sun for much longer, she would have been in trouble. Anyway, that's enough about me. Come on, let's hit Lisbon."

The two women walked off the ship arm in arm, chatting and laughing just like old times. Sarah wanted to go into town first to do some shopping and then they planned to walk the opposite way along the main promenade and see some of the sights that Lisbon Harbour had to offer. As they made their way to the shops, Sarah continued her stories of the previous night.

"Alex was called to see a drunken, abusive passenger in one of the bars who had hit his wife. Graham was seeing another passenger at the time who had not eaten enough following his insulin injection and suffered a hypoglycaemic episode."

Rachel knew that hypoglycaemia was when a diabetic's blood-sugar went too low and they needed immediate treatment before they went into a coma. She had been trained to spot the signs, which can mimic drunkenness, so that she could call the paramedics and initiate first aid where necessary.

"The drunk was too hot to handle for Alex, so security locked him up for the night, while Alex stitched his wife's eyebrow in the surgery."

"Domestic abuse doesn't confine itself to land then?" Rachel asked sadly.

"No, it doesn't, although they usually fight in their rooms. Not in one of the main bars."

"What happens next?"

"We asked the wife if she wanted to press charges and she said no, otherwise we could have had him arrested in Lisbon today. He will get a warning from the chief security officer and told that one more strike, and he's off ship. I expect security weren't too gentle with him, either, because he was fighting them, so he will have a few bruises himself today. The jury will be out as to whether this was a one-off, as his wife claims, or his usual behaviour."

They walked towards the town which was a couple of miles away from where the *Coral Queen* was docked. The temperature was a pleasant 28 degrees centigrade with clear blue skies, but Rachel had picked up from the captain's announcement before she'd left the ship that there was a chance of rain in the afternoon. Each morning and evening, the captain made an announcement over the ship's loudspeaker detailing where they were, at what speed they were travelling, and a weather update for the day or night. The cruise director followed on with announcements about activities available through the day or evening.

Rachel and Sarah arrived at the main square and entered the shopping areas through a large archway forming a gateway. The centre was pedestrianised, the streets cobbled and relatively narrow for a city. They enjoyed a pleasant couple of hours shopping and stopped off for lunch at one of the outside cafés.

Rachel found Sarah easy to talk to because she always listened and digested information before giving an opinion. Conversation flowed freely as they sat at a table, relaxed and replete after their lunch, drinking cappuccinos and watching tourists having their photos taken beside a man dressed as a clown. Rachel pondered whether to tell her friend about her concerns regarding Marjorie, but what was there to tell? A few feelings and a drunk trying to get into Marjorie's room were hardly conclusive proof of any sinister goings on.

"Come on," said Sarah after they'd finished their drinks. "I want to show you the prettier parts of Lisbon."

They got up and left the centre via the same archway through which they had entered and walked back towards the ship.

"We need to walk another couple of miles along the main road on the other side of the ship," Sarah explained.

They passed the *Coral Queen* on their journey, joining an avenue with a hospital on the right-hand side.

"That's a Hospital for Tropical Diseases," said Sarah. Rachel, exhilarated at being on land again, was enjoying the exercise, although the heat was becoming more and more humid.

"I think it's going to rain," she remarked, and Sarah agreed.

They continued their walk and took a right fork on to another avenue, which ran parallel to the one they had been walking along. The roads were busy and there was a lot of traffic noise. Rachel needed to raise her voice to be heard, but the views were lovely.

They came off the main road to visit the Botanical Gardens where they sat for a while and enjoyed ice cream until it started to rain. Neither of them had brought coats. Rachel looked at the skies where the clouds were now looking menacing. The rain was getting heavier, so they sheltered for a few minutes inside a café doorway.

"I think it's time to head back to the ship," said Sarah. "We can get a bus on the main road."

As they were walking towards the main road, Rachel caught a glimpse of Marjorie in the distance on the far side of the road. Crowds were building as people were trying to find shelter or make their way back to the ship. Suddenly there was the sound of a horn and she saw a lorry skidding in the road as the driver tried to slam on his brakes. His lorry jackknifed, blocking the boulevard.

Rachel and Sarah heard screams and immediately ran towards the commotion.

"Oh dear!" exclaimed Sarah. "Those are our passengers. I hope everyone is alright."

As they arrived at the scene, Rachel realised just how serious the situation was. An elderly woman was lying in the road, and Rachel knew she was dead before they got any closer.

"I'm the ship's nurse," called Sarah. "Please stand back and allow some room. Has anyone called for the emergency services?"

"I have," said a shocked-looking man in the crowd. Rachel lifted her head to look away from the body, finding herself relieved to see it wasn't Marjorie. She decided to do some crowd control, asking people to step back onto the pavement. As she did so, she thought she caught a glimpse of Carlos running in the opposite direction. It was only a passing glimpse before she became preoccupied with moving people away from the body.

"Please, everybody, stay around for a while as the police will want to ask if anyone saw what happened."

Rachel, now in full PC mode, noticed that Sarah had obviously decided there was nothing she could do for the woman in the road, and a man had covered the body with his coat. Rachel saw her friend helping the lorry driver, who had bashed his head on the windscreen, and admired the way in which her friend dealt with his injuries while calming him down.

"Is there anyone medical here?" shouted Sarah. Rachel could see she was trying to stem the bleeding from the man's head and keep him talking.

The emergency services arrived a few minutes later and took over from Sarah while the police were already taking notes and statements from people in the crowd. Rachel saw Marjorie standing at the side of the road, looking pale and shaken. She went towards the old lady and put her arm around her. Marjorie was soaking wet, and Rachel saw an open umbrella lying on the ground.

"Come on, Marjorie," she said, as she picked up the umbrella and covered both of their heads. "There's a bench over there. Let's sit you down, and then I will find a policeman to take a statement from you so I can get you back to the ship."

Marjorie tried to smile, but Rachel could see she was badly shaken.

Rachel found a policeman and sent him in Marjorie's direction. She then found Sarah speaking to another policeman and calling the ship. It was obvious that Sarah was going to be awhile as the policeman didn't speak much English and Sarah didn't speak Portuguese. They were trying to converse in Spanish.

"I need to get Marjorie back to the ship," she explained to Sarah.

"I didn't realise she was here. Yes, of course. I need to sort out some things here first. We'll meet up later, after dinner."

Rachel moved back towards Marjorie. The policeman shook his head and said he hadn't managed to get much out of her, but she could return to the ship.

"It appears to have been a tragic accident," he said in heavily accented English as he walked away.

Rachel helped Marjorie to her feet, and they crossed the road to flag down a taxi. Rachel held on to Marjorie's hand on the way back in the taxi. The old lady was shivering with cold and muttering words that were not making any sense.

"Please hurry," Rachel called out to the taxi driver. "This lady needs to see a doctor."

The taxi driver looked in the rear-view mirror and although Rachel was unsure whether he understood her words, she was certain he understood the situation and he put his foot down on the gas. Rachel was becoming increasingly worried as Marjorie became more incoherent and was only semi-conscious. She had found a blanket on the back seat of the taxi and wrapped this around the dear old lady, but this was now wet, too. Marjorie needed dry clothes, and she needed them soon.

"Stay with me, Marjorie," Rachel said, holding the old lady close and trying to warm her up with body heat. Rachel then called Sarah on her mobile phone and explained the situation.

"I'll call ahead and have a medical team waiting for your arrival, but they may turn her around to the hospital," Sarah explained.

"They can't do that!" cried Rachel, feeling hysterical. The taxi driver looked at her in the rear-view mirror again, concern in his eyes. "She would be all alone in a foreign country. They have to care for her."

After what seemed an age, the taxi arrived at the cruise terminal and was ushered straight through. Rachel was relieved to see Dr Bentley waiting on the dockside with a stretcher and a silver space blanket to treat hypothermia. There were two others with him. One was Bernard, and the other, Rachel presumed, was Alex. As soon as the taxi stopped, they opened the doors from the outside and went to work immediately. One of the crew members lifted Marjorie out of the car gently, and Dr Bentley wrapped her in the blanket while Bernard discreetly removed the wet clothing. They worked quickly, and all looked concerned.

"Please don't send her away," Rachel pleaded.

"She needs a hospital," said Dr Bentley.

"No," muttered Marjorie, and Rachel could see fear in her eyes. "No hospital," and then she became incoherent again.

Rachel looked at Dr Bentley, silently imploring him to do as Marjorie wished.

"Quick! Get her to the infirmary."

With that, Marjorie was strapped to the stretcher on wheels and moved swiftly away, with Bernard pulling and Alex pushing.

"Go and get dried off yourself," Bernard called back to Rachel. "Then come to the infirmary on deck two." Rachel was about to argue, but then realised that she was also soaking wet and feeling shivery herself. She started to follow the stretcher, but then she heard a call of dismay from behind her.

"Fare, ma'am. Please?" The taxi driver was following her.

"Oh, I'm so sorry. How much?" Before he had time to answer, Rachel shoved a twenty euro note in his hand, turned towards the ship and ran.

Chapter 14

She had to queue to get through security for what seemed like an age. There were crowds of passengers waiting for the lifts, carrying bags of shopping following their day out, so Rachel decided to take the stairs. She ran up six flights to her deck and walked briskly down the corridor. By the time she got to her room, she was feeling panicky, and very cold.

Please don't die, Marjorie. She kept saying the words to herself, over and over again.

Even in her state of panic, she realised that it would be quicker to take a hot shower to warm up before attempting to change into dry clothes. She put the shower on to the highest setting it would allow and stepped inside – removing her clothes once she was in the shower. She was shivering and her teeth were chattering, and in spite of the warm temperatures outside, she felt frozen. She realised this was partly due to the wet and partly the shock of the events that had just taken place.

Rachel spent a lot longer in the shower than she had intended because her legs had turned to jelly as the adrenaline kicked in as well as the after effects of running up the six flights of stairs on top of all the walking she and Sarah had done. She gave in to exhaustion and sat down in the shower for a while until she felt warmer and her muscles stopped trembling.

She managed to slow her breathing, taking deep breaths to bring her mind and body back under control. Her heart, which had been racing frantically, slowed down as she did this, and she gradually began to feel normal again.

It had taken Rachel almost an hour to compose herself. Now that she was in a condition where she could leave the room, she dressed in a pair of jeans and a light summer jumper over a t-shirt. She then headed down to deck two where she found the medical centre and was greeted by a small, brown-haired girl, she assumed was Brigitte.

"Is Lady Snellthorpe here?" Rachel asked, dreading the reply.

"Yes, she is. Are you Rachel?" The French accent was unmistakeable.

"Yes."

"Follow me. She is on the ward and sleeping. Dr Bentley has given her some sedation, and she is being warmed up as her temperature had dropped below thirty-six degrees centigrade, which is not good for anyone, let alone a woman her age. She's lucky she didn't have a heart attack."

"Will she be alright?" asked Rachel.

Brigitte didn't answer.

They walked into the ward and Rachel saw Marjorie lying on a bed, completely wrapped from head to toe in the silver space blanket. There was a heart monitor beside her, and Rachel could see that Marjorie's heart rate was just fifty beats per minute. She had a drip in her arm, and Bernard was sitting with her.

"I'll leave you with her for a while; I need to go get another IV bag," he said.

Rachel took a seat next to the bed and saw that Marjorie was asleep. The elderly lady looked deathly pale behind the oxygen mask that covered her face.

Bernard came back to the ward and smiled at Rachel.

"This one's a tough cookie," he said brightly. "My money is on her pulling through."

Rachel wasn't sure whether he believed this or whether he was trying to cheer her up, but it had the desired effect. She sighed a huge sigh of relief.

While sitting at Marjorie's side, she had a chance to look around the ship's infirmary and was impressed. It looked like a real hospital ward with four beds and all the modern equipment she was used to seeing when she was accompanying victims or criminals to a hospital on land.

She looked at her watch and realised it was six o'clock. They were due to sail.

"Sarah!" she exclaimed. "Where's Sarah?"

"She's aboard." Dr Bentley entered the ward. "She's had to go and get warmed up herself because she was soaking wet, too. That's the last time she gets shore leave." He was joking, but there was a look of concern in his eyes as he came closer. "She should really be in a hospital, you know, but I have called her son back in England and he has consented to us keeping her on board. He asked to be kept informed. The captain has agreed with my decision to abide by both of their wishes."

As if on cue, the ship's engines started up and Rachel felt slight movement as the *Coral Queen* set sail.

"Was her son alright? Is he flying out to join us at the next stop?" Rachel asked.

"I'm afraid not," whispered Dr Bentley. "In fact, he was rather abrupt."

Rachel was horrified. She would have been on the next plane if it had been her mother.

Dr Bentley checked that all was well with Marjorie and then went to help with evening surgery as it was busy in the waiting area outside. Bernard asked if Rachel was happy to stay with Marjorie while he helped with the surgery as Sarah was supposed to be on duty. Rachel agreed – glad to be alone with her thoughts for a while.

What was it Marjorie was mumbling about in the taxi? "My fault – my coat." None of it made sense. And did I really see Carlos? If so, why had he been running away rather than helping?

All of the sinister thoughts of the past three days jumbled themselves around in Rachel's tired mind.

A crew member entered the ward. "Senior asked me to bring you some food, ma'am," he said and laid a tray down on a table which he pulled towards her.

"I'm not sure I can eat anything."

"I'll leave it there, ma'am, just in case. Can I get you anything to drink?"

"A strong coffee, please." She smiled at him. A six-foot-tall Indian man, he had a solid build and was wearing black trousers with a white tunic over the top. His name badge said Raggie. "Is that your name?"

"No, ma'am, but no-one can pronounce my real name, so I decided on Raggie. People still call me Reggie rather than Raggie, though, so I can't win! I am the medical team steward and I make sure they are all looked after good."

Rachel looked at the food as Raggie left the ward. It was fresh salmon and spring vegetables with sautéed potatoes. In spite of saying she didn't feel hungry, she actually managed to eat almost all of it.

Stress reaction, she thought as she drank the contents of a whole thermos of coffee.

Every now and again, Bernard or Brigitte popped in to check on Marjorie and write down observations on her chart. Rachel was pleased to see that there was a slight pinkness returning to her face, and her temperature on the monitor was now thirty-six degrees while her heart rate had come up to sixty. Rachel laid her head on the bed, and with flashbacks of lorries, a dead body and crowds of people whirring round in her head, she fell asleep.

"Wake up, sleepy head."

Rachel opened her eyes. "Sarah! Thank goodness you're alright. I thought you'd missed the sailing, but Dr Bentley told me you hadn't."

"It was touch and go for a while because the ship can't wait too long for anyone. I made it in ten minutes before sailing. How are you?"

"What time is it?" asked Rachel, realising that there were no windows in the infirmary.

"Eleven o'clock. I decided to let you sleep."

Rachel looked at Marjorie. The oxygen mask had been removed, and she was still asleep, but her colour was back to normal.

"She'll pull through," Sarah said. "She's going to sleep all night, though, after the sedation, so you should go to bed. Brigitte is going to take care of her for the night."

"What happened to that poor woman?"

"No-one knows. Nobody seems to have seen anything. One minute she was standing waiting to cross the road, and the next minute she was in front of the lorry. The driver had no way of stopping in time in that rain."

"Is he okay?"

"Yes, he went to hospital for stitches and was in shock, but no serious injuries. The lady who was killed had been with Marjorie, according to one couple who were standing close by. The police have settled for tragic accident as far as I'm aware although it could have been suicide."

"Or..." Rachel finally let out what had been nagging her all day. "She could have been pushed."

Sarah looked shocked at the thought, "You're tired, Rachel. Passengers don't get pushed in front of lorries. By all accounts, she was travelling alone, was widowed and had a very close family."

"Is she in your morgue?"

"No, if passengers die ashore, then it is down to the local police to investigate and the coroner will decide on the cause of death. The family have been informed and are flying out to Lisbon. They will be able to repatriate the body once they have identified her."

"I thought Marjorie was going to die in the taxi." Rachel's bottom lip quivered. "She was losing consciousness before my eyes and I was completely helpless. It was horrible." The tears that had been close to the surface came out now that the horror of the day was gone.

"You did the right thing, Rachel. Graham said you saved her life by wrapping her up and using body warmth. He was impressed, and he also said that he wouldn't want to argue with you. What was that all about?"

"I wouldn't know!" Rachel managed a laugh as she remembered how she would have pushed the trolley on board ship herself, or at least been arrested trying, if he hadn't agreed to care for Marjorie.

"Come on, Rachel, it's time for bed. I for one am dead beat."

Rachel kissed Marjorie's forehead, and then Sarah took her arm and led her away. They parted at the lifts and agreed to meet up the next morning as Rachel would be down to check on Marjorie.

"Some holiday you're having so far!" Sarah looked uncertain. "I'm almost feeling guilty for persuading you to take this cruise, and I can assure you that nothing like this happened until you came on board."

Rachel returned to the comfort of her room, feeling stiff from falling asleep in an awkward position, and opened the balcony doors to listen to the sea. She loved the sound of the waves crashing against the ship. She looked up into the sky and could see that it was clear again and the night was warm.

As she lay on her bed, she started to rationalise the events of the day. Tragic accidents did happen, and the old lady could have just tripped into the road. Or maybe she had wanted to end it all and kill herself. It wouldn't be the first time Rachel had come across a widow who couldn't go on after the death of a partner.

Or she could have been pushed. The thought popped into her head as she drifted off.

Chapter 15

Rachel woke at six in the morning and decided to go for a run then to the gym. She pulled on her light cotton sports trousers and a t-shirt and headed up to deck sixteen. The ship was relatively quiet with just a few people milling around. Crew were already hard at work washing down decks and putting out fresh towels. Today was a sea day, and the ship was due to arrive in Barcelona the next day.

Rachel ran around the whole of deck sixteen three times, feeling the need to clear her head. She had put the thoughts of the awful accident in perspective, but she remained concerned for Marjorie. The old lady had looked so frail the day before.

"Good morning." She was dragged back to reality by the presence of another jogger at her side. He was a tall, thin man dressed in shorts and jogging vest with dreadlocks tied in a ponytail.

"Good morning." Rachel smiled back.

"It's a great morning for a run," he continued in his lovely Jamaican accent. "I like to get out before it gets too hot, and as you can see, I don't need a suntan."

Rachel laughed politely, but remained distracted. Any other time, she would have been happy to chat with this lively man, but she stopped running when they got near the gym.

"Enjoy your run," she said.

"Have a great day," he replied and continued jogging.

After a forty-five minute workout, Rachel headed back to her cabin where she showered and changed into a sleeveless cotton sundress before going to deck fourteen for a buffet breakfast. By this time, people were already claiming sun loungers with towels and books before going for breakfast themselves. Children were swimming and calling out gaily to one another. The reflection from the sun created dancing shimmers of light on the sea below, and the clear blue sky promised a beautiful day ahead – very different from the day before.

Rachel was wondering how hot it was going to be today when, as if on cue, the captain's voice came through over the loudspeaker. The sea would be calm and the temperature likely to reach 32 degrees this afternoon. There was a reminder about sun cream, then some other announcements that Rachel couldn't hear over the noise of conversations and the clattering of dishes in the main buffet area.

Rachel helped herself to fruit and muesli and found a table by a window. She could hear a Jamaican man singing as he brought around teas and coffees and recognised him as the happy jogger she had met earlier.

"Coffee, tea?" he would ask in between lines of a song she didn't recognise.

"We meet again, beautiful lady," he said as he poured her a coffee from the thermos on his trolley.

Rachel smiled at him. He was singing about sunshine as he moved away, and he certainly did bring sunshine into a room. All of the guests appeared to know him and he had short conversations with each one, complimenting the ladies and joking with the men. Rachel liked the buffet on deck fourteen because it lacked the formality of the reserved restaurants. She had not yet had breakfast in the restaurant for that reason. It was nice to start the day in an informal, albeit frantically busy part of the ship.

After breakfast, she returned to her cabin to collect her camera and a book before going down to deck two to see how Marjorie was. Rachel entered the ward and was relieved to see Marjorie sitting up in bed, wide awake and chatting to Dr Bentley.

"My dear," she smiled at Rachel, "I understand you saved my life yesterday."

"Hardly," replied Rachel. "It was Dr Bentley and his team who did that, but I am so pleased to see you looking better. How are you feeling?"

"A few creaking bones and a bruise on my arm, courtesy of the good doctor here." Marjorie laughed and looked very much like the proud and capable woman Rachel had come to know.

"I'll leave you two to it. I think the patient is back to her formidable self, and I am no match." Dr Bentley smiled. "You will be pleased to know that she has made a full recovery and insists on returning to her stateroom later today, as she says my fees are too high." He walked away laughing, obviously as pleased as Rachel was to see Marjorie well again.

Rachel sat down at the bedside and gave Marjorie a small bunch of dried flowers she had managed to pick up from one of the gift shops on deck five.

"Thank you, my dear," Marjorie said. Rachel noticed that in spite of her good humour, Marjorie was looking tired and drained, with a hint of sadness behind the smile.

"I'm so sorry about yesterday," said Rachel. "It must have been awful for you to witness the accident. I understand the lady was with you at the time?"

"Yes, she was. Her name was Freda McDonald. We had met the day before and were spending the day together. Two old widows – sharing stories of times past." Marjorie's voice faded away and her eyes became watery. "We were about to cross the road and get a taxi back to the ship, when suddenly, I heard the horn—"

Rachel didn't say anything; she was allowing Marjorie to relate the story in her own time and didn't want to interrupt.

"I must have dropped my umbrella. As I saw Freda lying in the road, I realised at once that she was dead. Death is expected at our age, but what a violent way to go—"

Again Marjorie's voice trailed off for a moment while she seemed to be recalling the event.

"She said she wanted to die, you know, to be with her husband."

"Do you think she did it on purpose?" asked Rachel, barely able to comprehend the thought.

"No, I don't. She said that she had contemplated suicide in the past, but that she would never do that to her children and grandchildren. Besides, we had had such a lovely day, and she was laughing and talking."

Rachel was relieved that it was unlikely to have been suicide. "An awful accident then," she concluded.

"It would appear that way," said Marjorie, but she seemed to Rachel to be holding something back.

"Was there anything else?" she probed.

"You'll think I'm a crazy old woman, but I can't seem to shake off the feeling that I am being watched. It started at the beginning of the cruise, and I kept telling myself that it was my imagination because I was travelling without Ralph for the first time. At times, I wondered if it was Ralph watching over me, but as well as not believing in that sort of thing, I feel it's menacing rather than reassuring."

Rachel could hardly breathe. "Go on," she encouraged. "I don't think you're crazy at all; tell me more."

"It sounds odd, I know, but I had the same feeling yesterday in Lisbon. Quite a few times I looked around to see if there was anyone watching me, but apart from lots of faces from the ship, I couldn't find any evidence. The awful thing was that as Freda lay there in the road, I kept thinking it was my fault and that it should have been me instead. And what was worse, I was relieved that it wasn't me – is that terrible? I was filled with terror and shock and couldn't move."

At this point, Marjorie broke down in tears and Rachel gave her a handkerchief.

"It's not terrible to think like that. I think it's quite normal, in fact, to feel a sense of relief mixed with guilt at surviving an incident like the one you experienced. One thing I am certain of though: it wasn't your fault."

"But it was my coat and hat." She almost whispered the words, and the significance of what she was saying finally dawned on Rachel. Remembering seeing Carlos running, she felt sick at the thought of him being involved in this.

Before she could think or say anything more, Sarah entered the ward, smiling.

"It's good to see you two looking well, especially you, Lady Snellthorpe."

It was a relief to change the subject for a while so that Rachel could compose her thoughts, and Marjorie seemed to welcome the break too as they laughed and shared good-humoured banter.

Finally, Sarah said, "Do you mind if I take Rachel away for a minute, Lady Snellthorpe?"

"Of course not," replied Marjorie. "You young things go and chat."

Rachel was reluctant to leave, but something in Sarah's eyes made her think it was important.

"We have had word from the Portuguese police and coroner's office." There was a look of concern on Sarah's face. "They are not certain about this by any means, but a young boy appears to have witnessed Mrs McDonald being pushed into the road by a man in the crowd."

"Could the boy identify the man?" asked Rachel.

"No, apparently not. He was standing close to the elderly ladies, but because of his height and the speed at which it all happened, he only saw the push."

"Is he sure she was pushed?"

"He swears by the story. His parents say he was fascinated by the raindrops rolling down the lady's waterproof coat when it happened. The police believe him, and the coroner says that there is a mark on her back that could have been caused by a push. Without the boy's testimony, he would have put it down to injury from the accident."

"This is terrible," said Rachel. "So it was deliberate?"

"There doesn't seem to be a motive, though. The police say she was unknown to anyone on the ship and are wondering if it was a random killing if it does turn out to be a killing at all. Security on the ship have been informed, but whether the pusher was a passenger or not is unclear."

"Oh, he is on this ship, of that I am certain. And I don't believe she was the intended victim, either."

"What do you mean?"

Rachel explained to Sarah the things that had been nagging her for days: the feeling that she or Marjorie was being watched; the man outside Marjorie's room in the middle of the night; and finally, what she had learned this morning: that Mrs McDonald had been wearing Marjorie's hat and coat.

"You see, they were a similar height and build, and from behind, Mrs McDonald would have looked like Marjorie. I believe she is in danger, but the killer may think that he has got away with murder."

"How so?"

"If he fled the scene, he will believe that Marjorie is dead, and hopefully she will be safe for now."

The only thing that Rachel didn't share was her concern that Carlos might be involved in some way, partly because she did not have a shred of evidence that he was, and partly because she didn't want to think about the possibility.

"We need to let security know. Do you think we should tell Marjorie?"

"It's hard to say, but I think she's been through enough. She already has some inkling that someone is after her, but thinking and knowing are two different things."

"And the reality is, we don't really know at all. It could all be coincidence and the Portuguese boy may just have an overactive imagination. The police aren't actively looking for anyone, but they have let all the ship's captains who were docked that day know that they may have a killer on board. If there is a killer, though, it is much more likely that he is on board this ship rather than any of the others." Sarah paused. "Security has carried out some routine checks and all passengers and crew are back on board, except for poor Mrs McDonald. The problem is, we don't really have a clue what the person might look like. The boy can't even confirm that it was a man who did the pushing!" Sarah looked concerned. "I have to go back to work now because I am on call, but I will catch you later. I will let Dr Bentley know your concerns so that he can alert the captain."

Rachel was left stunned, still finding it difficult to comprehend what might be happening. Now, in addition to her concerns about whether Carlos was involved (something she would investigate herself), she had to work out who might want Marjorie dead, and why.

She went back into the ward area and saw that Marjorie had fallen asleep again. *It must be the sedation*, she thought. *I wonder if I can persuade her to stay another night in the Infirmary.*

Meanwhile, she had work to do. But how do you go about investigating a murder on a cruise ship without any real suspects?

Chapter 16

Rachel put the telephone down in her room. Marjorie had insisted on being discharged from the ward and was on her way up in a wheelchair. Sarah had called to say that Brigitte was escorting her to her stateroom.

Rachel got up from her bed where she had fallen asleep and noticed that the worry lines were returning to her forehead when she looked in the mirror. *At least this time, it isn't anything to do with Robert.* She could take some comfort from that. She heard talking in the corridor and went out to greet Marjorie.

"They can't keep a good woman down, can they?" Rachel approached Marjorie and gave her a kiss on the cheek.

"I would rather be in my room," replied the old lady, looking tired. Her face was drawn, and although she appeared calm, Rachel noticed she was shaking slightly.

Marjorie got up from the wheelchair, and Brigitte said goodbye, mouthing "Look after her" to Rachel. Rachel nodded.

"Thank you, Nurse," said Marjorie.

"Can I help you into your room and get you something to drink?"

"That would be very kind, Rachel, thank you."

They entered the stateroom and found a huge bunch of flowers in a vase on the table, along with a bowl of fruit and a note. Marjorie picked up the note and smiled.

"They must be from Jeremy," she announced, but then Rachel noticed a flicker of disappointment as she read the note. "They are from the captain, how kind of him."

Marjorie handed the note to Rachel.

"Dear Lady Snellthorpe, wishing you a swift recovery, and may I offer my sincere apologies for your unpleasant experience yesterday. If there is anything I can do, please relay a message via Dr Bentley, who will be keeping an eye on you. Yours sincerely, Captain Peter Jenson."

Rachel thought it a lovely touch, but she could understand Marjorie's disappointment that her son had not sent her any messages. Not for the first time, Rachel felt a searing anger towards a man she had never met.

"Here you are." Rachel handed her a cup of Earl Grey tea.

"How did you know I like Earl Grey?"

"Observation," replied Rachel. "Is there anything else I can get for you?"

"No thank you, dear. I will eat in my room this evening as I am out on a trip tomorrow in Barcelona." Rachel admired her tenacity and determination to carry on and felt even more protective than ever. "You go out and enjoy yourself. I don't want these unfortunate events to ruin your holiday."

"I'll look in on you tonight if your light is on," said Rachel. "Otherwise I will see you tomorrow after your outing."

Rachel returned to her room and dressed for dinner. For the first formal night on the ship, women donned evening gowns and men wore tuxedos. The captain and all his officers would be present.

As soon as Rachel entered the dining room, she felt an arm rest on her shoulder. She turned to see Carlos beaming down at her and she felt familiar butterflies in her stomach. *Don't fall under his spell,* she warned herself, without much success.

"You look breathtakingly beautiful tonight," he said as he held her apart from him and gave her an appraising look up and down. She had on a red strapless evening gown with a matching bow above the left breast, and even with her wrap covering her shoulders, she was attracting appreciative glances from other men as they entered the dining room.

Her blue eyes shone as she smiled and relaxed for the first time that day. Carlos looked incredibly handsome in his tuxedo, and he was annoyingly confident and assured as he took her arm and led her to their table.

Dinner passed pleasantly. No-one at the table seemed to know about the events that had unfolded the day before, except perhaps Carlos. He kept giving Rachel looks as though he wanted to say something, but then changed his mind.

For her part, Rachel tried to probe him with questions about where he was from and what he did, but he was evasive. In between, he was charming, and his commanding presence meant that the others on the table wanted to speak with him just as much as she did.

So much for being skilled at information gathering. It was much easier when Rachel was questioning suspects or victims because she could be more frank.

After dinner, Carlos escorted her to the main atrium to meet with the captain and his officers. They were handed a glass of champagne, and Rachel was feeling a lot more at ease, partly because she had already had two glasses of wine with dinner, and now the champagne was filling her stomach with a warm, pleasant glow. She wasn't used to drinking in quantities and her head was swimming. Carlos was more attentive than he had been thus far in the cruise, and she was enjoying his closeness.

Then she abruptly remembered her suspicions.

"Did you enjoy yourself yesterday?" she asked.

"In Lisbon?" He didn't wait for her to acknowledge this. "It was alright. I went into town that was all. I have been to Lisbon many times before."

"Oh, I see. Did you not visit the western end of the harbour?"

"No, I returned to the ship from town." Rachel noticed a brief hesitation and a flicker of his eyes before he answered. Just enough to tell her he was lying.

Rachel stiffened slightly.

"I'm tired, I need to go to bed," she said, suddenly turning away. He grabbed her hand and pulled her towards him, and she felt breathless as he looked into her eyes.

"I will see you tomorrow," he whispered and kissed her lightly on the lips. Rachel summoned all of her willpower and strength in order to prevent this becoming a deeper kiss and broke away for the second time.

"Goodnight," she mumbled and left the atrium.

She didn't return to her room immediately. Deciding to get some fresh air first, she took a walk around one of the upper decks. She passed the outdoor movie screen and noticed that a film was showing, but she didn't stop to watch.

Her thoughts were confused. If it were not for the Marjorie thing, she would be enjoying her time with Carlos much more, but the nagging doubts in her head kept her from trusting him.

After about an hour of staring out to sea, Rachel returned to her stateroom. Marjorie's light was out, so she went straight to bed, and immediately her head hit the pillow, she was wrapped in dreams concerning romance and murder.

Rachel woke at seven the next morning after a restless night and saw that the ship was docked in Barcelona. Knowing that Sarah was working, Rachel had booked herself on to one of the coach tours to Montserrat for the morning, and afterwards she would meet Sarah to go to Las Ramblas for some shopping.

As she opened her door, she saw Josie in the corridor. "Good morning, ma'am Rachel," the Philippine woman said.

"Good morning, Josie. Have you seen Lady Snellthorpe this morning?"

"Yes, ma'am, she left early to go on her outing. Dr Bentley visited her and escorted her to her meeting area."

Rachel was relieved. "See you later."

"Have a nice day, ma'am Rachel," said Josie as she entered one of the staterooms armed with new bed linen and towels.

Rachel walked up the corridor towards the theatre where she would be meeting her tour guide. She was given a blue sticker with a number nine printed on it, indicating which tour group she would join, and then she sat and waited patiently until her number was called.

The group followed one of the crew members down to deck four where they passed through the usual security before leaving via a ramp down to the port side. The others in the group had obviously done this before, and Rachel followed them to a coach with a large number nine sign displayed in the window. The passengers were all greeted by a Spanish woman, who introduced herself as Maria, and the coach driver called Patrick.

Once on the coach, Rachel found a seat. It wasn't long before an Asian family sat around her, a teenager sitting next to Rachel.

"Hi, I'm Vindra," the girl said. "You're very pretty."

"I'm Rachel," she replied, laughing. "And so are you!"

Vindra was thirteen going on twenty, and turned out to be a chatty, outgoing young girl who entertained Rachel with stories of her school-life in Kent.

"If she annoys you, tell her to shut up," said the woman on the seats parallel to theirs. Rachel noticed she had much more of an accent than Vindra and wore a beautiful blue sari. *Silk*, Rachel thought. *She must be quite hot.* Sitting next to her was a man who appeared to be in his forties, wearing a smart short-sleeved white shirt and brown trousers.

"She is not annoying me," said Rachel, politely.

Vindra was dressed less formally than her parents, wearing pink shorts to mid-thigh and a vest with the word 'Lisbon' sprawled across the front. She smiled at Rachel, a beautiful smile that showed off her white teeth, and her deep brown eyes shone.

You are going to be a heartbreaker.

Rachel enjoyed the chatter and listened to the family as they laughed together. On the seat in front of Vindra's parents were two young boys who, Vindra told her, were six and eight. They were playing video games from what Rachel could make out.

"They would be searching for Pokémons if they had mobile phones, but Dad won't let them have one yet because they are too young," explained Vindra. "I do let them use mine, but Dad told me off in Lisbon because they kept getting in people's way while they were chasing after the Pokémons."

The guide drew the passengers' attention to the various landmarks on the drive up to Montserrat. The Benedictine Monastery was perched on the mountainside with spectacular views. Once the coach stopped, Rachel parted with the group and decided to go for a wander by herself.

The monastery was spectacular to look at, and she admired the basilica which the guide had said was Romanesque. In spite of the number of people there, Rachel thought how peaceful it appeared, and she admired those who lived, worked and prayed there.

She caught sight of some of the monks and followed them into the main building. Here she found beautiful architecture and evidence of a life that had not changed in centuries. She sat for a while and enjoyed the peace and tranquillity until a group of tourists arrived with a tour guide who had a rather loud voice. Rachel watched the group for a short time and realised the guide was speaking French. Rachel had studied the language at school to A level and was able to hold a relatively fluent conversation, but she was struggling to make out some of the guide's words. They were probably technical, relating to the architecture around her.

She left the monastery and headed in to the main plaza where the shops were situated. Ordering a cup of coffee from an outside café area, she watched as people crowded into the small souvenir shops. There were a number of tour groups visiting, some from her ship and some from another cruise ship she had seen in the port. The Mediterranean was busy at this time of year and tourism brought a welcome boost to the Spanish economy, which was not in the healthiest of conditions.

Rachel joined the rest of her group for lunch, provided as part of the tour package, and Vindra insisted she join her and her family to eat. Rachel liked this girl and was pleased that her parents allowed her to express herself so openly. She had met some Asian parents through her line of work who baulked at their children becoming a part of the western culture and still encouraged arranged marriages. Vindra had explained to Rachel on the coach that her father was a strict Hindu, but that he had agreed to allow his children to choose their own marriage partners.

"He would prefer them to be Asian," Vindra said, "but will accept them, whoever they are."

Rachel acknowledged the difficulties of integration into western culture for those who had not been brought up in the West, and understood the concerns of parents as her own parents found some aspects of western life difficult, too. Having a vicar as a father, she sometimes felt she was more aligned to the morals of other cultures than her own. Even though her brother had renounced Christianity and lived with his girlfriend, Amy, Rachel's parents still welcomed Amy and her daughter from a previous relationship into their home.

"Life's complicated," her father had said. "We are not here to judge people, but to live as honestly before God as we can."

Rachel agreed with this sentiment, and although she knew what she believed, she understood that for many, her way of life was archaic.

She was brought out of her reverie by Vindra.

"Rachel, come on! It's time to go back to the bus."

With that, Vindra took Rachel's hand as though leading a small child back to the coach.

Vindra continued her nattering all the way back to the cruise terminal, and Rachel half listened and half dozed through the journey.

Sarah was waiting for her as she got off the coach.

"Looks like you had fun," Sarah said, smiling.

"I did, actually. Vindra is entertaining and beautiful, inside and out. I hope she stays that way."

"Well, come on, you. It's time to go to Las Ramblas. Remember to hang on to your bag as there are a lot of thieves around, but it is quite spectacular. You will love the stalls and the cafés."

"You forget I am trained in self-defence and have a black belt in Karate."

"I did forget, sorry. I feel much safer now."

Sarah took Rachel's arm, and they began their walk.

The temperature was 30 degrees centigrade as they entered Las Ramblas, and Rachel loved it immediately. Stalls flanked both sides of the road, selling various wares. Cafés were also on both sides of the road, and outdoor seating areas were set up all along the centre so that people could stop at any time they wanted to for a drink or food.

"Look at him!" Rachel exclaimed as she saw a man dressed in a skin-tight suit, painted gold and balancing upside-down on one hand, staying absolutely still.

"Human statues," remarked Sarah. "People have their photos taken beside them and put money into the caps or containers. Look, there's someone doing just that."

Rachel watched a child standing next to the man while his mum took a photo on her mobile phone. The child then put some coins into the man's gold top hat.

"It makes a change from busking," said Sarah.

"Indeed it does. Oh, I do like it here, Sarah."

"I knew you would. Come on, let's keep walking."

The two young women spent a pleasant couple of hours wandering up and down Las Ramblas, and Rachel bought a Barcelona tea towel for her mum and a pair of brightly coloured socks for her dad with a picture of Barcelona's football stadium sewn into them. It was only when they sat down to have coffee and ice cream that they discussed the events of the past few days.

"Graham did decide to alert the captain to your suspicions, and the captain was aware of the report given by the Portuguese police, but there is not much else that can be done. The captain and

Graham agree with your view that the killer, if there is one, believes he has been successful and that Marjorie should be safe."

"I do hope so," replied Rachel. "But what if he sees her?"

And what if Carlos is involved? She kept that thought to herself.

"The Captain has alerted security but they have nothing to go on. No description and no real evidence that it was a murder at all when it comes down to it."

"You're right, it could all just be a nasty sequence of coincidences, I suppose." Rachel hoped rather than believed this to be true.

"He has also assigned a security officer to keep an eye out for Marjorie, but it will be difficult because they have so much to do with actual disturbances that go on throughout the ship. They had to arrest someone last night and found cocaine in his luggage. Thankfully only for personal use, but we do get drugs on board as we can't search all the passengers' luggage."

By the time Rachel returned to the ship, she felt quite calm. Sarah went back to work and Rachel went and sat on her balcony. The late afternoon sun glittered, and Rachel dreamily enjoyed the weather while watching the coaches returning way down below her.

It was getting close to sail away time when she saw what she assumed were the final two coaches arriving. She watched as passengers got off and became alert when she saw Marjorie being assisted from the penultimate coach. Rachel was pleased that Marjorie had made it out for the day and watched as she stood upright.

She was about to look away when, to her horror, she saw Carlos get off of the same coach about ten people behind Marjorie. Reaching for her binoculars, Rachel focussed the lenses on him. It was hard to see whether he was following Marjorie or whether this was yet another coincidence.

Rachel put the glasses down as her heart sank into the pit of her stomach and her head throbbed. Had she been right to be suspicious of Carlos?

Dear God, no! she pleaded.

Chapter 17

The man was livid when he got back to the ship. He had gone on land to check his bank account, but no money had been added. He had then spent most of the day trying to get his mobile phone to work. It was a burner phone he had picked up a day before the cruise so that it couldn't be traced, but the damn thing wasn't working.

I'll kill that stupid man when I get hold of him.

Then he caught sight of the woman and couldn't believe his eyes. He joined the coach trip she was on, bribing the driver, and confirmed it was her. How had she survived?

It gradually dawned on him that he had killed the wrong woman and he felt a knot in his stomach. He had relaxed for the past couple of days as the adrenaline had subsided and he had started to let his guard down again. He always liked to celebrate his kills with a woman and he had just the one in mind. He couldn't believe his bad luck.

When he got back to the ship, he was angry, but from his calm outward demeanour, nobody would have known it. Years of preparation and training as a hitman had given him the ability to hide his feelings beneath an outwardly charming facade. After his first kill at the age of seventeen, when he had been sick for two weeks, he had been determined that this would never happen again, and he had trained himself well. He kept to a rigid routine of exercise and mental discipline, teaching himself to behave perfectly normally, even moments after a kill.

He wasn't keen on killing a woman in her eighties, and now he had killed another one by accident. This had never happened before.

Doubts about this job plagued him again. It wasn't his normal hit, and he had been in two minds about taking it, but money was tight and he needed the work. A killer always needed to stay in practise; he'd heard of others who lost the edge when they had big gaps in-between jobs. He was stashing money away so that he could retire at forty because he didn't want to be in the killing game for ever. It wasn't something he took pleasure in, but he did take a certain pride in his work, and he had never failed an assignment before.

The mobile signal was working again; it had been off all day, in spite of his being on land. He looked at the screen: sixteen missed calls. Blast! Well, at least he knew what this was all about.

He was about to do a call back when the phone rang in his hand. Cursing to himself, he answered.

"You damn well missed her, you idiot. You said it was done! I've been trying to get you for two days."

"Calm down, will you. I saw her today, so I realised. What happened?"

"You tell me!" The shouting continued down the phone. "You killed the wrong woman. What kind of killer are you? You need to get this done, and it needs to look like an accident, which might prove difficult now. Do they suspect anything?"

"No, no. I heard the crew talking when I got back to the ship the other day and they said there had been an accident. It's fine, no-one suspects. I will do it, but I need to leave it a few days for the memory of the other one to die down, just in case. There's still plenty of time."

"Make sure you do and text me when it's done. No mistakes this time. Remember to use this number."

The man on the other end of the line hung up; he hadn't even sounded concerned that someone else had been killed.

Well, if he doesn't care, I certainly don't. I'm not in the business of caring, but I guess I am going to have to pull back a bit on the relationship that I've been developing. Just when things were starting to get interesting.

He made his way down to the bar and ordered a brandy before starting his planning.

This one would have to be different.

Chapter 18

Marjorie enjoyed a pleasant day out on the coach tour although she couldn't help thinking about Freda and how her family must be feeling. There was also the nagging doubt that perhaps Freda had been pushed, and if so – who would want to do such a thing? The concern about the fact that Freda had been wearing her hat and coat had subsided somewhat as Marjorie persuaded herself that there was no way she could have been the intended victim. She mulled over in her mind whether anyone would want her killed and the idea was preposterous. Although Jeremy stood to inherit everything when she died, the business had always been profitable, giving him a very generous salary and bonuses.

Marjorie had tried really hard to dispel all of these thoughts from her mind, and she felt the tears falling down her cheeks as she wished Ralph was still alive. He would have known exactly what was going on and would have reassured her that she had just witnessed a terrible accident and was in shock. This made her feel better as she felt the warmth of Ralph sitting next to her once again, whispering words of comfort. Sometimes the pain of losing him was too much to bear. Freda had understood that, and the only consolation that Marjorie could gain from the tragedy was that Freda was now with her beloved husband.

Not being one to dwell in self-pity, Marjorie resolved to pull herself together. Ralph had made her promise that she would make the best of life if he departed before her and said he would be keeping an eye on her from above to make sure she did, and she smiled at the thought. The coach tour guide was starting to explain exactly where they were on their journey and she put the headphones on to listen.

The tour took in the Olympic Ring on the outskirts of the city before heading on to Gaudí's unfinished masterpiece, the cathedral. Most of the tour involved sitting and listening, which was all Marjorie could manage today anyway because her bones still ached from the hypothermia she had experienced. Dr Bentley had not wanted her to go on a tour at all today, but she had persuaded him to let her in spite of his reservations.

Everyone had been so kind, and if it had not been for Rachel, she didn't know what would have become of her. Spending time with Rachel had renewed her faith in young people; she was such a kind and caring girl, and the sadness that had been in her eyes at the start of the cruise had started to dissipate. Marjorie was determined that Rachel should be allowed to enjoy her holiday and she didn't want her feeling that she needed to look after a silly old woman who had got herself into a fix.

The guide was talking about thousands of years of Barcelona history and famous sights such as monasteries and basilicas when Marjorie drifted off to sleep. She was brought to a sudden awakening when the coach stopped, and as she opened her eyes, she saw that they were back at the ship. The tour guide helped her to her feet as she had stiffened up a little and the driver lifted her down the steps onto the ground. Marjorie gave them both a gratuity and thanked them for the tour before one of the crew members arrived to escort her back on board the *Coral Queen*.

"Did you have a nice trip, ma'am?" he asked as he handed her an iced flannel to refresh herself with, followed by a cool drink of squash.

"Yes, thank you, it was interesting."

"I will accompany you on board, madam."

Marjorie looked at the smart man who offered her his arm, detecting an Australian accent.

"There's really no need," she replied. "I can manage."

"Doctor's orders, madam."

"Oh well, in that case." Marjorie gratefully took the young man's arm and was pleased of the support as she was starting to feel a little lightheaded. These dizzy spells had worsened since she'd been in the hospital ward, and she wasn't sure whether they were a normal reaction to what she had experienced or something else. She hadn't yet mentioned them to anyone, but thought she might need to if they continued.

Once she was safely back on board ship, she was escorted all the way to her stateroom where she ordered a pot of coffee as she was too tired to make tea. The stateroom had been cleaned and left looking immaculate by Josie, who had topped up the tea supplies. It had been another very hot day, and she was pleased to be in her air-conditioned room.

The telephone rang in her room.

"Hello, Mother." She heard Jeremy's voice at the other end. "I understand you have been unwell."

His tone was crisp and to the point. "Yes, it was an awful event. I met a friend on board and she fell into the road and was run over. I was in shock and they say I suffered hypothermia."

"Well I hope you will be more careful in the future, Mother. Are you well now?"

"Yes, I am much better, thank you. There was a lovely girl—"

"Sorry, Mother. I can't speak for long. I have to go into a meeting. Enjoy the rest of your cruise. Bye."

"Bye, I love you." She knew he had hung up before she finished.

Oh well, at least he called.

Chapter 19

It had been six days since Freda had died and Rachel was beginning to put it to the back of her mind, deciding it was just an unfortunate accident after all. The doctor and the captain had arrived at the same conclusion and everybody was more relaxed.

That afternoon, Sarah had explained to Rachel that the Portuguese police had allowed Freda's body to be released for repatriation to Scotland, also concluding that it had been an accidental death. They could not confirm the boy's story, and none of the other witnesses had seen anything sinister or suspicious.

"It looks like the boy had an overactive imagination after all."

"Yes, I'm sure you're right," agreed Rachel. "Marjorie seems much happier in herself, too. She says she has been feeling jittery since her husband died and the accident sent her into shock."

"Well, the captain has had her followed for the past five days since she left the infirmary and nothing suspicious has been spotted by the undercover crew members, so he has called them off."

"Did Marjorie know?"

"No, no-one knew, not even Graham. The captain kept it all very hush-hush until he was sure that she wasn't being followed. They checked off all the passengers on the same trips, and apart from a family from Ontario, there was no overlap. The poor family has been police checked and everything, and there are no links to the UK at all, let alone to Lady Snellthorpe or her family."

"That's wonderful news," Rachel said.

"Now you can concentrate on that dishy Italian, at last!" Sarah laughed. "I've got a date myself tonight with the deputy head of security. We got to know each other when I had to explain what had happened to Marjorie."

"You kept that under your belt." Rachel giggled.

"It only happened today. Hot off the press, and you are the first to know, of course."

Rachel had left Sarah to go and get ready for her evening and had stopped in on Marjorie before returning to her own room. They were ten days into the cruise and nothing further had caused any concerns. Marjorie's son had phoned her twice, and this seemed to please the old lady, although Rachel still got the impression they were not overly close.

Rachel beamed at the thought of seeing Carlos. As Marjorie seemed so much happier, she could now unwind and enjoy her time with Carlos without suspecting him of any wrong-doing. She had only managed to spend a little bit of time with him over the past few days as he had been distracted.

"Work stuff," he had explained when she'd asked. However, this evening, he was taking her to the theatre after dinner.

She was excited and nervous at the prospect of spending some time with Carlos after the evening meal. Choosing a casual cotton summer dress with short sleeves, she put on a pair of white sling-back sandals. Her skin was starting to look tanned, and it gave her a healthy glow. She spent time applying a thin layer of makeup that complemented her features, and she was pleased with the result.

Carlos was waiting for her outside the dining room and he escorted her to the now familiar table. Conversation flowed freely as each of the dinner companions had developed a familiar, relaxed camaraderie. Sue and Greg had been initially reserved, but even they engaged in quips and teases at the table.

Jean looked at Rachel. "Beautiful as ever," she remarked and Rachel blushed as she felt all eyes move towards her. She bore her beauty in a reserved way and didn't think about it until people brought it to her attention.

She changed the subject. "Have you been off ship today?" The ship had been docked at the island of Corsica, and was now on the way to the final stop before the return home, Gibraltar.

Jean and Brenda didn't usually venture too far from the ship as they liked to be close by. Brenda suffered from health anxiety, and although she was making progress, she still found new places difficult to explore in a totally relaxed way. Jean appeared to accept this and was supportive of her friend.

It was Brenda who replied. "Yes, we did today. We went on a tour to an aromatherapy craft factory and then went on to a vineyard for wine tasting and ate locally made nougat."

"Oh, I am envious," Florence chipped in. "We nearly went on that trip, but we went for a walk around the old town by ourselves today. David said he couldn't take another coach tour."

Florence gave David a pretend glare, and he squeezed her arm.

"Sorry, love, next time."

The dining room was busy this evening, and Stavros and Geraldine were rushed off their feet. Lobster was on the menu, and most of those at Table 305 chose that as the main course.

"I think we will all be needing to shape up when we get back home," said Greg as he watched his wife finish up her dessert. Sue had a healthy appetite, and Greg reminded her of it frequently, which Rachel had found embarrassing at times. Sue actually took no notice of him whatsoever in this regard and chomped her way through as much food as was laid on the table.

As dinner finished, each couple gradually dispersed, leaving Carlos and Rachel alone together, finishing an after-dinner cappuccino.

"It is nice to have you to myself for a while," said Carlos as he gazed into her eyes.

Rachel liked having his attention, and although she wanted the relationship to develop, she still had reservations about a holiday fling and where it would lead. There was also a much smaller, but still nagging doubt about who this man was. He gave nothing away, and even exercising all her womanly charm, she barely knew anything about him. He said he wanted to forget about life on shore and enjoy the moment. Above all else, Rachel feared he was married. She had almost cleared him of any involvement with Marjorie, but if he was married, that would explain his secrecy.

Rachel decided that although she wanted to enjoy this night, she had to find out more about this man if they were to become anything other than friends. She opened her mouth to ask him, but before she got the opportunity, he leaned in towards her and kissed her lightly on the lips. She pulled away slightly, aware of waiters and other diners still in the vicinity.

"What's the matter?" he asked.

"Please don't do that," she responded, knowing that she was sounding silly and her voice had taken on a slightly higher pitch. She turned, took her shawl from the back of the chair and walked away before he had the opportunity to move.

Once outside the restaurant, she picked up her pace until she found herself running towards the upper decks.

"Rachel, stop!" She heard his voice at a distance behind her. Once she arrived on deck twelve, she stopped and gazed out to sea, not knowing what on earth had got into her.

Well, that was mature! she scolded herself. I'm just not ready.

She finally acknowledged that her problem was still Robert and the unwelcome fact that he had shattered her trust in men. Facing up to this reality, she leaned over the ship's rail and cried a deep, sobbing cry that released some of the excruciating pain that she had been bottling up for months. A few people passed by and discreetly looked away, continuing on with their night-time strolls.

After crying for about an hour, she began to feel calm again. All these weeks, she had been throwing herself into her work, trying to avoid the inevitable chasm of emptiness and pain that was like a boil that had to be burst before it could heal. Meeting Carlos had been wonderful, she acknowledged, but it had also made her face up to the lack of trust she now had towards the opposite sex. Fearing he might be married added to the dilemma. She enjoyed his attention, and when he kissed her, it sent electric shocks through her body, but was it all a show?

Would he turn out to be another Robert?

She didn't even know what he believed. How would he feel about her religion? Would he understand? Did he believe in God? Most of all, though, it was the anger and misery that Robert had caused that tormented her.

"I hate you, Robert," she shouted. "I was ready to give my life to you, you're a contemptible rat. You behaved shamefully, and I hope you live in misery for the rest of your life."

Her words were lost in the night sky, and the noise of the waves drowned them out. Rachel stopped, shocked at the vehemence she'd felt in her heart – that gentle heart that had been so easily broken. These were not nice feelings. She was having visions of some of the people she had arrested who had shouted and cursed and sworn, giving off nothing but anger.

She settled herself.

I cannot go there, but I cannot give my heart away so easily again. I must protect it at all costs.

She stood upright, lifted her head and walked back towards her stateroom, determined to put Carlos out of her head before she made a huge mistake.

Deciding to walk to the bow of the ship, she went down the most forward steps to avoid the crowds who tended to use the centre stair and lift areas as they gave easier access to all of the entertainment areas. It was dark as she made her way down the outer steps first before going inside to descend to deck nine. As she walked along the corridor towards her stateroom, she had the feeling of being watched again, but there was no-one in sight. Josie's assistant came out of one of the staterooms and Rachel nodded to him, keeping her head down so that he couldn't see she had been crying.

When she entered her stateroom, she found the balcony doors open, which was unusual. *Josie must have left them open by mistake.* Walking out onto the balcony as it was a nice, warm evening, and the sky was clear, she could hear noises coming from Marjorie's room next door and called out. The balcony screens were such that she couldn't see into Marjorie's room unless she peered round from the front, which she only did when she knew Marjorie was on the balcony.

"Good evening, Marjorie," Rachel shouted, but there was no reply. Perhaps she was going to bed, and it was difficult to hear above the waves. Rachel decided to call it a night and went back into her stateroom.

An hour later, she awoke as she thought she heard Marjorie's door close and movement next door. Rachel got up and dressed quickly into a pair of slacks before knocking at her neighbour's door.

"Good evening, my dear." Marjorie was fully dressed and looking a little flushed.

"Good evening. Erm, I just thought I would check in on you. Have you been out?"

"Come in, dear. Yes, I went to the theatre with Mr and Mrs Hutchinson, a couple I met on one of my trips. They are really sweet – from Dallas, you know."

Rachel was feeling an uncomfortable adrenaline surge again as she entered the room. She noticed the balcony doors were closed, and the room looked untouched since it had been made up by the stewards earlier.

"Are you alright, Rachel?" Marjorie was staring at her.

"Yes, sorry. I was asleep, I think I must have heard you and wanted to say goodnight. I will leave you to it, then." Rachel turned to go, but then she noticed there were tablets on the table at the side of Marjorie's bed. "Are those your painkillers? I almost forgot, Sarah asked me to swap them for slightly weaker ones." Rachel had no idea why she was saying this, but she grabbed the pills before Marjorie could object. "I think I left them down in the medical centre, I'll go and get them for you."

With that, she turned and rushed down to deck two. There was no-one there, and the area was closed off, but Rachel could see a light coming from the infirmary so she knocked.

Bernard answered. "Hello, Rachel, Sarah's off tonight," he said in his Philippine accent. "Hot date!"

"Oh yes, sorry, I forgot. Do you have any paracetamol? I seem to have run out and I've got a splitting headache."

"Are you alright? You look like you've seen a ghost."

"I'm fine, just a bad head."

"I'll go and get you some tablets."

Bernard came back with a full packet of paracetamol tablets. "Do you want me to label them for you?"

"No, it's okay, I know what to do, thanks. Please bill them to my room."

Rachel went back to Marjorie's stateroom and gave her the paracetamol before leaving a rather confused looking lady staring after her. When she got back to her own room, she stared at the tablets she had taken from Marjorie, but they made no impression on her. One tablet looked like another, except illegal drugs, which she was pretty good at spotting.

She sat on her bed, thinking about what she should do now. There had definitely been someone in Marjorie's room earlier, and it hadn't been Marjorie. It wasn't the assistant steward either because she had seen him further down the corridor. The only other person with a legitimate reason to be there would have been Josie, and if it was not her, then who?

Rachel tucked the tablets into her bedside cupboard and decided that she would ask Josie in the morning if she had been making up Marjorie's room later than usual. As she drifted off to sleep, Rachel really did start to develop a headache and wished she had kept some of the paracetamol for herself. Thoughts whirred around in her head again, including visions of Robert and Carlos.

The next morning, Rachel woke early and decided to catch Josie before going for a run. She went into the corridor and saw a different steward, a stocky Asian man who smiled pleasantly.

"Good morning, ma'am."

"Good morning, I was looking for Josie."

"Sorry, ma'am, Josie burned hand last night. Gone help elsewhere. I help, ma'am?"

"No, thank you. It's alright, it wasn't important."

Her headache was returning. *Drat!*

She headed upstairs for her run, joining her singing Jamaican friend from the breakfast buffet as he ran at the same time most mornings. He usually made her smile, but today she was deep in thought, mulling over the events of the previous night. She wished she had her police uniform on so that she could ask questions formally, but that wasn't to be. The reassuring thought was that it was most likely to have been Josie in Marjorie's room rather than anyone else, and the worst that could happen would be that Rachel would look rather foolish having taken away the painkillers.

Daylight and running always help clear the head, she thought as she returned to her stateroom for a shower.

Chapter 20

Rachel took Marjorie's tablets to the medical centre shortly after breakfast and asked Dr Bentley to check them.

"There's nothing wrong with the tablets, these are the ones I prescribed." He looked perplexed. "What made you think there was a problem?"

Rachel explained about hearing noises in Marjorie's stateroom the night before and how she had initially thought it was the old lady herself. She explained about being woken up later when Marjorie had arrived back and how she had managed to remove the tablets with a cock and bull story about milder painkillers.

Dr Bentley frowned. "Look, you had a shock early on in the cruise and your mind is still coping with the fact that it was just a tragic accident. In the meantime, your policewoman mind-set is seeing villains behind every door where there are none. When I started medicine, I was the same – every pain was cancer. Every symptom more serious than it actually was, and I developed a warped view of the world where everyone was seriously ill. But this was *my* world, not the real one."

It made sense. Rachel knew that her senses were in overdrive, and the stress of the broken engagement had made her work and study even harder than ever, immersing herself in criminology books. The accident early on in the cruise had re-awoken her senses, and she was just beginning to relax when the issue with Carlos had triggered another stress reaction.

"How do I learn to deal with it?" she asked.

"It takes time." Dr Bentley got up to leave as Sarah entered the clinic room with a cup of coffee. "You were suddenly awoken last night and your mind was overactive after hearing the noises earlier. You reacted, end of story. If it had been a crime scene, you would have saved the old dear's life, but it wasn't. No harm done."

Dr Bentley left the room.

"Sometimes I think I'm going mad," Rachel confided in Sarah.

"There's no-one I know who is saner," said her friend. "Come on, drink up, there's no need to worry. Apart from last night, you have been more yourself. Just put it down to experience."

"You're right, I guess all I've hurt is my pride. Thank goodness your Dr Bentley is so understanding. He didn't even tell me off about switching the pills."

"Those painkillers would be too strong now, anyway. They probably made her sleepy, so it was a good switch."

Rachel felt pleased that everything had been put into perspective. She made a note to herself to fit in some relaxation classes when she got back to work.

Sarah stood up. "I'd better get back to work. Are we still on for Gibraltar tomorrow?"

"Yes, but I don't know how you persuaded me to join you on the Barbary ape trip. I hate monkeys, and I hear these ones can be quite aggressive."

"I know, but I'm fascinated by nature, you know that. See you tomorrow in the atrium."

As Sarah went back to the waiting room to call her next patient through, Rachel returned to her stateroom to change into shorts before going to the upper deck in search of light entertainment and food. Deck fourteen was packed as ever with people sunbathing and swimming, but she managed to find a sunbed and made herself comfortable, stripping down to her bikini. Her skin glistened in the sun as she applied sun cream and she was pleased to see that her usually pale skin had developed a nice bronzed glow. She was always careful in the sun as she was prone to burning, and a childhood experience of painful blistering had taught her a lifelong lesson. She was also well aware of the risks of skin cancer from the sun's harmful rays, and this was an added incentive to apply frequent dollops of sun cream.

Rachel looked around, and all she could see were people and sunbeds. Children were swimming, and some people had chosen beds in the shade. Looking out to sea, she could see that the Mediterranean was beautifully calm and blue. There was something therapeutic about the way the ship bobbed gently up and down as it made its way in a westerly direction towards Gibraltar.

She was looking forward to visiting this headland of which her grandfather had spoken. He had been stationed in Gibraltar during the war and spoke fondly of what he called Mediterranean England. The colony still belonged to the United Kingdom, a fact which was occasionally under dispute by the Spanish who wanted to reclaim it.

Rachel pulled a book out from her bag and decided to spend some time reading. This was a pleasure she had largely given up as the majority of her reading in recent years had been textbooks or policing manuals. It was nice to read something completely different. She was avoiding romantic novels, and had picked up a crime thriller by Dee Henderson, an author she had discovered on a recommendation from Louise, Robert's sister. Many of the people in her books were broken for one reason or another, but they managed to find happiness and purpose through their work and relationships. Maybe there was hope for Rachel yet.

In spite of the buzz of activity all around her, Rachel managed to get lost in a fictional world for a while, but now she was hungry. She decided to do what everybody else did and leave her towel while she went into the buffet dining room to collect some lunch. Craving healthy food, she opted for a large bowl of Mediterranean salad.

Having gathered her salad, she was just about to make her way back outside to her sunbed when she saw a familiar figure in the pizza queue. Carlos looked as handsome as ever, and Rachel debated whether to avoid him or apologise for the previous evening. The decision was made for her as Carlos turned his head and saw her standing there. He left the queue and joined her.

"What the heck happened last night?" He sounded confused rather than angry, so she tried to explain.

"I'm sorry, I am just not ready for a relationship at the moment, and I don't do one-night stands."

"Okay, I understand. I can't say they are my cup of tea either, but can we be friends and see where things lead?"

His brown eyes were piercing her with an intensity that she had not seen before and he seemed genuinely relieved when she answered positively.

"Right, don't go anywhere. I will get a pizza and we can relax together."

Rachel waited, not sure whether this was a good idea because she was struggling with her feelings for this man. There was something mysterious about him, the way he wouldn't talk about himself or what he did for a living, and yet he had just shown a vulnerability which she hadn't seen before. It was new, and attractive. He was drop-dead gorgeous, as her friends would say, yet he was also interesting and able to converse on many different levels. She was drawn to him, and this could prove dangerous if she dropped her guard but having decided that she was not ready for a relationship, she would summon all her self-control to make sure that she was not put in a position of compromise.

Carlos rejoined her and they walked out to where she had been lying on a sunbed. He perched himself on the side of the bed and they chatted as if nothing untoward had happened. Ordering cocktails from one of the waiters who was passing, Carlos handed her a sangria. The drink was loaded with ice, and she found it refreshing as she felt it on the back of her throat.

She loosened up as they continued to chat for a while. Rachel found it quite distracting when he took his shirt and shorts off and sat in his swimming trunks on the edge of her bed. Close up, he was a lot more muscular than she had previously thought, and his biceps were firm.

"Look, there's a free bed." She pointed it out as someone got up on her left-hand side. He smiled at her teasingly as he moved over to the bed next to her and appeared fully aware of the effect he was having on her. Rachel felt completely relaxed now. Was it the sangria or was it the Mediterranean sun that was helping her to laugh again?

Carlos looked at his watch. "I need to go now, but I will see you at dinner later. Yes?"

Rachel felt slightly disappointed, but nodded. She watched him go and then decided to movc herself as the afternoon was turning into evening.

She was collecting her things together when she saw Marjorie.

"Hello," she said.

"Oh hello, Rachel. It's very hot out here, isn't it? I was just going to head back to my room and dress for dinner."

"Me too." Rachel smiled and took the old lady's arm. "Let's go together."

Chapter 21

He was bitterly disappointed not to have finished the job completely so that he could relax and enjoy time with the girl he had met. Having made his way into the woman's stateroom, all he'd had to do was wait until she returned. He could have had her over the side in seconds.

It had been planned down to the last detail. He'd waited until the cabin stewards had gone into the rooms, then he had managed to sneak into the room next door while the steward was collecting supplies to replenish teas. Hiding behind the curtains that were already drawn, he had waited for the steward to close the door before opening the balcony doors.

He was about to close them when he heard someone coming into the room. He mustn't be seen. Quick to react, he climbed over the rail and onto the old woman's balcony. He had gone in earlier and unlocked the doors while the steward had been cleaning the bathroom, but the curtains were still open so he couldn't hide.

He tripped over a table on his way into the room, then heard a woman's voice call out, so he closed the balcony doors quickly. Annoyed that he had been heard, he decided it was too risky to make the murder look like an accidental fall overboard.

I'll have to come up with another plan now.

His employer was becoming impatient and had called again when the ship was docked in Corsica. He had explained it would all be done by the time the ship got to Gibraltar and he would call from there.

It has to be tonight, then. I have to finish the job tonight so that I can get paid and get this ridiculous man off my back.

He couldn't believe how difficult it was to kill off an old woman, who appeared to have more lives than a cat. Not for the first time, he considered reneging on the job, but this was not possible. His reputation would be tarnished and no-one would hire him again. These things had a way of getting around, and he didn't want rumours spreading that he couldn't finish off a woman in her eighties – he would be the laughing stock. Being a hired killer was all about reputation, and competence and efficiency were key to maintaining a reputation and guaranteeing future hires.

He had taken this job on the back of a kill in the Alps that he had made look like a skiing accident. Delighted with the result of that job, he smiled as he remembered it. It had been successfully completed on the second day of the trip, and he had enjoyed a holiday as soon as it was over.

Luck had been with him that day. He'd heard his target storming out of the hotel early in the morning after a violent row with his wife and had no qualms about killing the man. In fact, he was looking forward to it as he couldn't abide men who hit women. Anyway, killing them was different, killing was business, nothing personal, and he killed cleanly. He was not into torture or anything of that kind.

He'd followed the man, who had made his job even easier by going off-piste to ski. It had been a beautiful morning. Luckily no-one was around as they were obeying the danger signs that were posted along the run. He prided himself on being an excellent skier, so once his target took off from the top of the slope, he seized the opportunity and followed him.

He saw the edge of the ravine coming up, and before the man got the chance to turn, he nudged him, sending him flying over the edge. Stopping momentarily to check, he knew his target would not survive the fall.

He had enjoyed the rest of the holiday while being paid a handsome sum for the job.

If only similar luck were with him on this trip. He had hoped for a repeat and looked forward to enjoying the cruise, but it wasn't to be. Not every job was easy, but he had planned this one in great detail, and the woman should have died in Lisbon. Instead, she was very much alive and inadvertently dodging his every move.

He was determined not to fail this time.

Chapter 22

Rachel felt truly happy for the first time in weeks, pleased that she and Carlos could be friends without the pressure of anything more. She was sure that she could control her feelings for him with only three days and four nights of cruising left. Adding the finishing touches to her makeup, she made her way down to deck four for dinner.

Carlos was waiting for her outside the dining room and he flashed one of his most disarming smiles at her. She felt her heart miss a beat at the sight of him and took a deep breath before taking the arm he offered her.

Yep, really under control!

Dinner was enjoyable as always, and Rachel noticed that Marjorie was seated at her usual table with an elderly man. She seemed happy, and they were engrossed in conversation. Rachel smiled at her and Marjorie waved.

After dinner, Rachel and Carlos were the last to leave the table as usual. Marjorie was enjoying something that looked like a coffee liqueur, and Rachel was floating on air that all was well again with her world.

"Where to this evening, ma'am?" Carlos joked.

"Let's go and listen to the string quartet in the atrium, shall we?"

"Your wish is my command."

They left together, Rachel remembering that she had one more thing she needed to do before she completely forgot about the Marjorie thing.

She turned to Carlos. "Will you find us some seats? I just need to go and get a shawl from my room so that we can enjoy a walk outside later."

For once, Rachel took the lift up to deck nine and made her way along the corridor. Relieved to see that Josie was back on stateroom duties, she headed towards her.

"Good evening, ma'am Rachel," said Josie, smiling.

"Good evening, Josie. Is your hand alright? I understand you burnt it." Rachel looked at the neatly bandaged hand.

"Yes, ma'am. It's feeling much better. The Doctor fixed it up nicely for me and the nurses will be changing the dressings each day to stop it getting infected."

Rachel wasn't quite sure how to broach the subject. "Did you finish early last night?"

"No, ma'am, I always finish my work." She looked alarmed as if she might get into trouble.

"Of course you do. I wouldn't have thought otherwise. I saw Daniel last night, though, working along our corridor and leaving my room," she lied. "It is normally you I see, so I was a bit worried about whether you had been seriously hurt."

"No, ma'am Rachel, I got waylaid with one of the guests who was having trouble sleeping and I had to go to housekeeping to get new pillows for him, so Daniel finished the last few rooms down your end. Housekeeping don't like the assistants going down there for items."

"I see," said Rachel thoughtfully. "So you didn't do Lady Snellthorpe's room last night?"

"No, ma'am." Josie was looking more concerned. "There wasn't a problem with the room, was there, ma'am Rachel? No-one said."

"Oh no, Josie, nothing like that. I missed you that's all. I'm really pleased to see you back. Goodnight."

"Goodnight, ma'am Rachel."

Rachel went into her room and struggled to breathe. She hadn't been imagining things after all, and if Josie was to be believed, it had not been her in Marjorie's room. The cobwebs fell away from her brain and she sprang into police mode.

Marjorie is in danger. I need to find her.

She changed into comfortable shoes and then marched rapidly along the corridor, almost knocking a tray out of Daniel's hands.

"Sorry," she muttered, but didn't stop. She ran down the stairs towards the restaurant, forgetting all about Carlos, and walked straight through to Marjorie's table. Second sitting dining had begun and there was a young couple seated at the table.

Stavros turned towards her. "Did you forget something, ma'am?"

"No, Stavros, I wanted to ask Lady Snellthorpe something. Do you know where she went?"

"No, ma'am. Sorry."

"I heard her saying she was going for a breath of air." Geraldine had been taking orders nearby and obviously overheard the conversation.

"Thank you, Geraldine." Rachel turned so quickly she just missed Grigor, the wine waiter, who was bringing wine to the young couple at Marjorie's table. "I'm so sorry," she spluttered and marched out of the restaurant at break-neck speed. A sense of urgency was building up in her. Although she was aware of the looks she was getting as she half-barged past people in her hurry to get out, she didn't care.

She opted for the lift, deciding to start on deck fourteen and work her way up from there. There were queues of people waiting for the lifts and she could feel her heart pounding in her chest as the frustration built. In spite of there being six lifts, they were all full with people going out for evening entertainment. Finally one stopped that she could get into, but just as she was pressing the 'close doors' button, someone else pressed the 'open doors' one. She glared at the man who was holding the lift open, obviously waiting for someone.

The man's companion eventually arrived, but then the lift stopped at every floor on the way up to deck fourteen. Rachel was beginning to curse herself for not taking the stairs, but she had a full stomach and it would have been counter-productive.

At last, the lift stopped at the right deck. Rachel decided to take a clockwise walk from her starting point, searching around the deck. She walked more slowly now, not wanting to miss Marjorie, and she noticed that the deck was eerily quiet. Most people were eating or enjoying shows, and apart from the bow where the outdoor cinema screen was, there were not many people around.

Having circled the front of the ship, she was heading to the rear when she thought she heard footsteps behind her. Looking round anxiously, she saw a drunken man making his way towards one of the doors leading inside. Rachel continued walking, and now all she could hear was the sound of distant music and the ship forcing its way through the waves.

The tension was building in her head and in her temples, and she was beginning to feel the night-time chill as she hadn't put on a shawl or jacket. Goose bumps were building on her shoulders as she turned the corner at the back of the ship.

Suddenly, she heard a scream and turned to see a body hurtling down the stairs towards her. She managed to run up the stairs just in time to catch the woman in her arms, and they both fell backwards. Rachel felt a searing pain as her left foot caught underneath one of the steps as she fell.

It took a while for her to get her breath back, but she knew immediately it was Marjorie lying on top of her, moaning.

"Marjorie! Are you alright?" Rachel managed to move slightly and shift the weight.

"I think so." Rachel was so relieved to hear her voice. "Thanks to you."

At that moment, a couple arrived as a good-looking man came down the stairs in a black dinner suit. His manner was reassuring, and he sent the couple away to find a crew member.

"What happened? Are you both alright? Does anything hurt?" His deep Italian voice filled the evening air. As Rachel was starting to feel agonising pain in her left ankle, everything looked a little hazy, so she tried to focus on the man's eyes. He looked away and glanced around, as if unsure what to do next, but he didn't need to decide as an officer appeared on the scene.

"Medical team are on the way, don't move, ladies."

Rachel just managed to ask the officer to look after Marjorie, who was now shaking, before she passed out.

Chapter 23

Sarah was on call, catching up with paperwork in the medical centre, when the emergency bleep went off.

"Two passengers injured deck fourteen, stern."

She called Brigitte to join her with the stretcher.

"Can you track down Dr Bentley and ask him to join us?" she asked reception, putting the phone down. On her way out of the medical centre, she saw that Alex was still there.

"Accident, deck fourteen. We might need you," she said as she pulled the hefty emergency bag along behind her. He finished whatever he was drinking from a mug and followed her. Brigitte ran in, and seeing that Alex was already carrying the stretcher, she followed them.

The medical centre was midships on deck two, so it was a long way to race up to deck fourteen. They took the crew lift and then ran along the deck to where they had been told the incident had occurred.

Sarah was shocked and horrified to see Rachel and Lady Snellthorpe lying on the floor. A small crowd had gathered around. "Clear the scene, please," she instructed the officer. "But keep hold of witnesses. Rachel!" Sarah called her name. "Rachel!"

The officer explained that Rachel had fainted shortly after he'd arrived, then she had come to, only to pass out again.

Rachel opened her eyes and tried to smile. "Marjorie?"

"She's okay, Doctor Romano is seeing to her. What happened?"

"Not sure, Marjorie fell, caught, landed…"

She passed out again.

Graham arrived and took over the assessment of Rachel's injuries.

"Did anyone see what happened?" Sarah asked the officer.

"No, but this gentleman was on the scene when I arrived." He turned to his right, but there was a no-one there. "Sorry, looks like he's gone. He was dressed in a tux so may have been on his way out. He did tell me that he arrived after another couple and they didn't see what happened, either."

Graham carried out his examination.

"Left ankle is badly swollen, probably broken. Right arm is cut up – she'll need a bit of glue, but I think she managed to land without hitting her head. No lumps or contusions." He proceeded to feel each vertebra along Rachel's spine, assessing for pain and asking Rachel if it hurt. Rachel was mumbling negatives. "Let's get her to the infirmary and do a full head injury assessment there. Try to wake her up, Sarah, and keep her awake. Put her in a collar and use the spinal stretcher until I have assessed her properly. Right, team, let's get on with it."

Bernard arrived with a spinal stretcher, and after applying a neck collar for support, he and Sarah moved Rachel onto this. Sarah knew that Graham needed to rule out spinal fractures, but according to the officer who had attended the scene, Rachel had been moving all of her limbs around before passing out.

Alex and Brigitte had already left with Lady Snellthorpe on the first stretcher. Sarah was concerned for Rachel and held her hand, speaking to her all the way to the infirmary and exchanging worried glances with Graham. Sarah knew they were both thinking the same thing: it looked very much like Rachel had been right all along and that there really was a threat to Marjorie's life. It was hard to believe that anyone would want to harm this sweet old lady, but obviously, someone did.

Before he left, Graham asked the officers to get the names of everyone present and find out if anyone had seen anything.

"I want to see security later, but for now, I need to make sure these passengers are assessed properly."

Once they were in the infirmary, he made a full assessment of both patients. Lady Snellthorpe had a few bruises to her right arm and chest, but other than being severely shaken, she was not seriously hurt.

X-rays of Rachel's back, ankle and knee were taken, and it was established there were no spinal fractures. The X-ray confirmed her ankle was broken, but it was a simple fracture. Rachel had become more alert, but was clearly still in pain. Lady Snellthorpe was in the bed next to her, looking concerned.

"Are you alright, my dear? I was so worried about you."

Rachel tried to smile, but Bernard was shining a torch in her eyes and she flinched instead.

"Apart from feeling like I've been in a boxing ring, I feel fine."

"You've got a broken ankle," Sarah explained. "We can't give you any painkillers until we're sure you haven't got a head injury. Can you remember what happened?"

"I had found out that the person I heard in Marjorie's room last night wasn't Josie, and so I went in search of her, fearing the worst." Rachel looked apologetically at Lady Snellthorpe, but continued, "I went to the dining room and one of the waiters said that she had headed out for air, so I started my search on deck fourteen. I searched from midships port side and went in a clockwise direction. When I got to turn to the stairs on starboard, rear, I heard movement. That's when I saw Marjorie and I just reacted by running up a few steps and catching her as she fell. I think I caught my left foot under the step as I fell and I landed on my right side. I didn't bang my head, and most of the fall was broken by my right hand and elbow. I think catching my foot helped me to support Marjorie."

"Did you see anyone else?" asked Graham.

"I saw a shadow at the top of the steps, but it was too quick. After I fell, a couple arrived, and then a good-looking man in a tuxedo appeared and helped. He may have seen who it was at the top of the steps."

Rachel tried to get up.

"Stay still, Rachel," said Sarah. "You're not going anywhere."

"No, young lady. Bernard is going to put you into a back slab, and then you'll need to go the hospital in Gibraltar tomorrow to see the orthopaedic surgeon who will probably put you in a walking plaster as the break seems to be a simple one. Now we know you didn't bang your head, you are going to have a pain killing injection and get some sleep."

Rachel turned to Lady Snellthorpe. "What do you remember?"

"I remember walking along the outside of deck fifteen, enjoying the evening air. Ralph and I always took a walk after dinner, so it's force of habit. I was looking at the stars and I could hear the waves crashing against the ship's side, as if they were objecting to this monstrous beast daring to break their rhythm, when I felt there was someone there. I turned to see and felt a shove in my back, and the next thing, I felt myself falling. Then I saw you were there, Rachel, catching me. As I lay on top of you, I thought you were dead and I went into shock, but then you spoke to me. You saved my life, dear."

Graham explained that he had called security and would explain to them what had happened, but he didn't want either Lady Snellthorpe or Rachel to be interviewed until the morning.

"You both need a good night's sleep. Bernard, please give a sedative to Lady Snellthorpe and pethidine injection to Rachel. Sarah will stay with you and a member of security will be outside the door."

He smiled at them both.

Sarah was pleased to be left alone with Rachel and Lady Snellthorpe. Bernard had given Rachel an injection, and she was already looking quite woozy while he was putting on the back slab plaster.

"What is a back slab, anyway?" she asked.

"It's a slab of plaster, left open at the front, that will support the break while allowing the limb to swell up underneath. Once the swelling is down, a proper plaster can be applied."

"Sorry about the apes." Rachel turned to Sarah.

"You did warn me you didn't want to see them, but I didn't realise you would go to this much trouble to avoid them," Sarah replied. "I am just pleased that you and Lady Snellthorpe are not seriously injured."

Rachel smirked at her friend.

"I'd hate to know what you consider a serious injury."

Chapter 24

The next morning, Rachel woke up feeling like she had been mauled. It took her a while to register where she was, but soon the events of the previous evening came to mind.

She managed to sit herself up in the infirmary bed. Her left ankle felt sore but supported, and she noticed the cuts to her right arm had been dressed. Her ribs felt tender where Marjorie had landed on her right side. Sarah was asleep in a chair at the side of her bed and Marjorie was lying awake in the bed to her right, looking shaken.

"Good morning." Rachel smiled at the old lady.

"Good morning, my dear." Marjorie sounded as low as she looked. Rachel noticed a tear falling down her face. "I'm so sorry you have been injured because of me."

"It's not you who should be sorry," said Rachel. "It's the person who tried to—"

Rachel stopped, seeing that the realisation that someone was trying to kill her was sinking into Marjorie's mind.

"Why?" she asked. "I'm just a doddery old lady who will be dead in a few years anyway."

"Perhaps whoever is doing this can't wait a few years." Rachel spoke quietly. "Do you have any idea who that could be?"

"The idea doesn't bear thinking about. I just can't believe it."

Sarah woke up at that moment and heard the last part of the conversation. "I hope you two slept well," she said.

"Hi," said Rachel. "That knock-out injection definitely helped, but I feel pretty sore now."

"I'll get you some pain killers and anti-inflammatories. We are docked in Gibraltar so will need to head to the hospital soon. Dr Bentley has phoned ahead."

Sarah left the infirmary and returned with four tablets and fresh water. She also handed Marjorie some tablets to take. Marjorie looked unsure.

"A sedative, and your blood-pressure pills. Do you have any pain?"

"No, dear, only pain in the heart, and I don't think there are any tablets for that," she said, looking away.

Rachel understood how difficult this must be for Marjorie and she could see that Sarah sensed it too. There was not much they could say to help, but they tried to keep Marjorie in the present with light conversation.

Dr Bentley came into the room accompanied by a smartly dressed man with the customary three gold stripes on his epaulettes, signifying his status as a senior officer. The man had short greying hair and stood tall at around six feet, Rachel estimated, and his uniform was tight, implying some recent weight gain.

"Glad to see you two looking better than last night." Dr Bentley smiled. "This is Chief Security Officer Waverley and he would like to ask you some questions. I have filled him in on your previous concerns, Rachel, but he will want to know more about all of the events. Are you feeling up to it?"

Rachel nodded and Marjorie remained quiet but attentive. CSO Waverley took a seat in between the beds and started by turning towards Marjorie.

"Lady Snellthorpe, firstly may I say how sorry I and the captain are that you have been attacked on board the *Coral Queen*. We take this sort of thing very seriously, and I will do everything within my power to find out who is responsible for this. I'll be reporting directly to the captain on the matter." He paused for a moment as if to allow the enormity of his words to sink in. "Please start from the beginning. Have you noticed anything out of the ordinary since the start of your cruise?"

Marjorie sighed a deep sigh.

"If only Ralph were here, he would know what to do," she said quietly, but then she straightened up and continued. "The only things I have noticed have been feelings which seemed silly at the time, but may or may not be important."

"Go on," Waverley encouraged.

"Well, I kept feeling I was being watched, but it didn't make any sense. I put it down to travelling alone for the first time since Ralph's death." She paused for a moment and Rachel could see she was trying hard to remain in control. "There was a man I recognised, but I can't remember where from, and that has concerned me all through the cruise."

"Who is this man?" The CSO leaned forward, taking notes.

"It's a man who sits at Rachel's dinner table and he seems to have become a friend." Marjorie looked apologetically at Rachel. "It is probably nothing. We met so many people through Ralph's work and his charities."

Rachel felt herself redden and her heart was beating rapidly. All eyes had now turned towards her.

"Do you know who Lady Snellthorpe is referring to?" asked Waverley.

"I think she means Carlos," Rachel answered softly.

"Please can you tell us about Carlos?"

"To be honest, I don't know very much about him at all. We met through the dining arrangements and have become friends, but I don't even know his last name." Rachel was starting to feel like a complete idiot and looked to Sarah for support. Sarah nodded encouragement.

"What does he do? Where is he from?"

"I've just remembered, I was supposed to meet him in the atrium last night, but I returned to my room to ask Josie about the noise I heard in Marjorie's room the night before. When Josie said it wasn't her, I forgot all about him and went in search of Marjorie. He never told me what he did. I tried to ask, but he said that he wanted to forget about work for a few weeks. I was feeling the same way, so I understood where he was coming from in that respect. He lives in London that's all I know."

Rachel wanted to tell them about her suspicions regarding Carlos, but she couldn't bring herself to do so. Not until she had challenged him herself.

"What table number do you dine at?" Waverley asked.

"Table 305," Rachel replied sadly. She felt Sarah squeeze her hand as the CSO turned his attention back to Marjorie, but not before jotting the table number down in his notebook.

"Please continue, Lady Snellthorpe."

Lady Snellthorpe glanced at Rachel before going on. "The next thing was the accident in Lisbon."

Rachel noticed the CSO shuffle in his seat, looking a bit embarrassed as Marjorie related the events of the accident that had taken the life of Freda McDonald. "She was wearing my coat and hat, you see, and when I looked at her in the road afterwards, I was shocked by how much it looked like me lying there. I was shaken to the core, but as it seemed to be a tragic accident, I put it to the back of my mind. I was also very ill afterwards so wasn't quite myself."

The CSO turned to Dr Bentley at this stage in the story. "We were alerted by the Portuguese police that a boy may or may not have witnessed someone pushing the lady into the road."

Marjorie let out a gasp at this point, looking shocked.

"I'm sorry, Lady Snellthorpe," said Dr Bentley. "It was my decision not to alarm you with that information because the boy's story could not be verified, and the coroner delivered an accidental death verdict a few days later. Security were aware, though, and kept a close eye on you."

Marjorie looked angry, but said nothing.

Waverley continued. "We had plain clothes security officers following you for a few days until the Portuguese police closed the case."

"I see," said Marjorie, clearly exasperated. "Once I began to feel well again, I carried on with the cruise as Ralph would have wanted me to, and I didn't notice anything else – other than the feeling of being followed, which could have been your men." She looked scathingly at CSO Waverley at this point. "Until last night, when I was definitely pushed. Had it not been for Rachel, I would not have been here to tell the story, and it would have appeared to be another accidental death."

Waverley coughed and turned to Rachel. "What about you, Miss Prince? Or should I say WPC Prince? Where do you come in?"

Rachel noticed that Marjorie looked surprised again at the mention of her being a policewoman.

"This is going to sound like I read too many novels, but I first noticed Marjorie before we boarded. I was in the departure lounge and I saw her enter through the VIP entrance. I couldn't help noticing how concerned her chauffeur looked as he left her and I thought it was odd."

It was Rachel's turn to look apologetically at Marjorie.

"Chance put us into rooms next door to each other and we became friends. I, too, had the feeling of being watched, and I had a gut feeling that Marjorie was in danger, but I couldn't see any reason for this. I have been working flat out to get through my PC assessments and thrown myself into work for several months, so I put it all down to an overactive imagination and stress."

Choosing not to mention Robert, Rachel went on to explain about the night of the drunk in the corridor outside Marjorie's room and how he had been sent away by another guest. She reiterated the concerns she'd had after Freda's death in Lisbon, which to all intents and purposes had been put down to a tragic accident, and then she went on to explain about the night she had returned to her room and heard noises in the room next door. She missed out any suspicions she'd had regarding Carlos.

"You must have thought I was mad, snatching the tablets away from your bedside table."

"I did wonder what that was all about," agreed Marjorie.

"Anyway, the tablets were examined by Dr Bentley and they were the ones he had prescribed, so I assumed that it had been Josie, the stateroom attendant, who had been in your room."

Dr Bentley looked embarrassed as Rachel recalled their conversation and how he had reassured her that her suspicions were all in her mind.

"I couldn't put it to rest completely until I had spoken to Josie. Sorry, Doctor. I went back to my stateroom last night and asked her about it, and she confirmed that she had not been anywhere near your room that night, Marjorie, because she had to collect pillows for another guest and she got behind on her work. At that point, I was really worried and went searching for you. The rest is history."

"Thank heavens you did," said Marjorie, and the others nodded agreement.

"Do you remember anything else from last night? Did you see who pushed Lady Snellthorpe?" asked Waverley.

"No. I have racked my brains, and all I saw was a shadow. I reacted on impulse to catch Marjorie before she landed. There was a man who came downstairs and helped us though. He may have seen something."

Waverley coughed again. "We can't seem to find him. The officer attending had asked him to wait around, but in the melee he seems to have disappeared. We think he was probably on his way out, and once help was at hand, he left."

Rachel explained how he had seemed distracted. "I was ready to pass out, but I remember he was looking around as if weighing up what to do next when the officer appeared on the scene. I don't remember much after that."

"I guess he was looking for help," said Dr Bentley. "He was probably worried about you both."

"I realise you have to go to the hospital any minute," said the CSO, "but we would like to get a detailed description of this man from you later so that we can try and trace him."

He turned back to Marjorie.

"There is no easy way to ask this, Lady Snellthorpe, but do you know anyone who would want you dead?"

Lady Snellthorpe looked thoughtful. "In all honesty, Officer Waverley. No, but if you want to know who would benefit the most from my death, it would be my son, Jeremy."

"I think I have taken up enough of your time." CSO Waverley got up to leave. "I will see you again later, Miss Prince."

Rachel nodded, but she was more concerned about Marjorie. How would the old lady cope if her son were arrested for attempting to murder her?

Chapter 25

Sarah pushed Rachel's wheelchair through security and off the ship. A taxi was waiting to take them to the clinic, and Sarah held the X-rays taken the previous night. The clinic was just a few minutes' drive away, and they were seated in the waiting room within ten minutes of leaving the cruise terminal.

A doctor called them through into a clinic room, and after examining the X-rays and Rachel's ankle, he agreed it was a simple fracture of the fibula bone at the base of the ankle. He had introduced himself as Mr Ram, and after mumbling for a little while, he turned his attention to Rachel.

"We can get you put into a lightweight walking plaster, but you will not be able to walk on it until the plaster is dry. Your cast will be fibreglass and it usually hardens within an hour, but I would suggest you don't walk on it until tonight. You will still need to support yourself with crutches to prevent you putting too much weight onto the ankle. I will prescribe some painkillers and anti-inflammatory tablets to reduce the swelling. You should go to your local fracture clinic when you return home and show them the X-rays. Chances are you will be in the plaster boot for six weeks, and then it will be another six weeks of physiotherapy until you feel normal again. What do you do for a living?"

"I'm a policewoman," Rachel replied.

"Ah, you will be confined to desk duties until your ankle is healed, I suspect, but you can go to work. Nurse! Fibreglass plastic boot, please, and crutches."

"A man of few words," said Sarah as Rachel was wheeled into the plaster room.

A tall nurse with light brown hair tied up in a bun which reminded Rachel of missionary nurses, came into the plaster room, wearing blue scrubs similar to those which Sarah wore when she was in the medical centre.

"Miss Prince?"

"Yes," answered Rachel.

"Hi, I'm Chloe. I'm going to apply your new plaster. Have you had painkillers recently?"

Rachel nodded.

"All I need to know then is what colour plaster you would like." Chloe brought out a trolley with an array of different colour packages.

"I had no idea there were so many different colours," Rachel said. "I'm tempted by the pink, but it might clash with my red dress. I think I'll just go for the plain beige one, please. It will go better with my other leg."

Chloe was very efficient at removing the back slab and applying the new plaster, and the whole procedure was over in fifteen minutes. After this, Chloe gave Rachel an instruction sheet on how to look after the plaster and prevent a deep vein thrombosis from occurring.

"By the way," Chloe called out as Rachel was leaving, "don't be fooled by how light that plaster is. It sets like rock, so don't go kicking anybody."

"I'll bear that in mind," Rachel replied, cackling.

As they were leaving the hospital, Sarah asked. "How do you feel?"

"A lot better after taking more painkillers, thanks. If you don't mind wheeling me around, I'm happy to go somewhere."

"I'm game! Let's go into town. It's a fairly flat walk, and even with the heat, it will be nice." The temperature was climbing as it got closer to midday, but it was a pleasant, dry heat rather than a humid heat, so Rachel agreed.

Town was busy with cruise ship passengers, and it all seemed rather familiar. Gibraltar was British, and it showed. The signs were in English and Rachel could hear English being spoken all around her.

They passed through a large archway into a big courtyard area with lots of cafés and outdoor seating. Sarah chose a spot in the shade and sat down. Pulling a chair towards Rachel, she ordered her to elevate her leg while they rested.

A waiter was soon with them and they ordered ice cold colas. "Anything to eat?" the waiter asked.

"You know what?" said Rachel. "I'm starving; I haven't eaten since last night." She chose fish and chips from the menu, and Sarah opted for steak and chips.

"The one thing I miss more than anything else is British chips," Sarah remarked. "I love foreign food, but you can't beat good old traditional chips."

Rachel agreed and found herself looking forward to getting back to Leeds after the trip was over although she still had the matter of Carlos to resolve.

"Work is going to love me!" she laughed. "I go on a cruise and come home with a broken ankle. By the way that doctor didn't ask for my medical insurance documents."

"Don't worry about that. The cruise line is paying for all your treatment, and Marjorie's. I reckon you will also be in line for some compensation."

Rachel smiled. "Now that's the best thing I've heard all day, but I hadn't even thought about it."

"They can afford it. I have known them reach five or six figure payout agreements rather than having an insurance claim brought against them. The cruise lines take the safety of their passengers very seriously, and its reputation even more seriously. The last thing they want is a bad headline. They are none too happy that there is a murderer loose on their ship I can tell you."

"I don't doubt it, I can't say I'm very happy about it, either. I wonder if it is the son that is behind this. It seems a very callous thing to do."

"It is an awful thing to think, isn't it? Poor Marjorie, she must be at her wits' end."

"I just hope the stress doesn't finish her off. I have grown so fond of her and would hate anything to happen to her."

"I know what you mean; she is very likeable, and whoever is behind this is a heartless psychopath. Speaking of fondness – what about Carlos? Do you think he's involved?"

"I sincerely hope not, but I can't be sure. At times, he does behave suspiciously, and I've had my doubts since the accident in Lisbon. I thought I saw him running away from the scene there, but he said he was nowhere near that area."

Sarah looked shocked. "You never said!"

"Everything seemed to settle down afterwards, and I was never one hundred percent certain it was him. I would hate to accuse someone wrongly, but now that Marjorie says she recognises him from somewhere, I am left with huge doubts. The thing is, we have become close, and I was hoping something would develop."

Rachel could see the sympathy in Sarah's eyes as she took a long drink of cola. "Maybe he's not involved at all," Sarah said. "Remember there's that other man you saw last night, too. Perhaps he saw something, or perhaps he is involved."

Rachel knew that CSO Waverley would be checking Carlos out even while they were seated in the café. It wouldn't be too hard to track him down from the seating plans.

"We will know soon enough, I guess. Do you think I will ever find the right man? It seems I'm destined to pick the wrong ones. It's hard to believe that six months ago, my whole future was mapped out, and now I'm like a ship without a rudder – to use a nautical expression."

At that moment, their meals arrived and they tucked in hungrily. Sarah spoke first.

"I think you will definitely find a good man. You and I have both had our man troubles, but there's still plenty of time, and to use another nautical expression – there are plenty more fish in the sea."

Rachel enjoyed the time with Sarah and, as always, felt much more normal in the presence of her friend. She wished they still shared a flat together; life would be so much easier with Sarah around.

Perhaps I can buy my own flat if the compensation is as good as Sarah suggests it will be.

After lunch, Sarah pushed Rachel up the main High Street which was packed with people and shops. As a tax haven, with no VAT added to goods, Gibraltar proved to be very attractive to cruise tourists with lots of money to spend. Neither Rachel nor Sarah were in the mood for extravagant spending although Rachel did buy her mum a pair of gold earrings and her dad a new camera case. Sarah topped up on toiletries and then offered to take Rachel back to the ship.

"You should get that leg elevated now to keep the swelling down," she said, and Rachel laughed.

"Okay, Nurse Bradshaw!"

They caught one of the regular buses that ferried cruise passengers to and from the terminal. Sarah folded the lightweight wheelchair and placed it in the aisle while Rachel manoeuvred her way on with the aid of crutches. Rachel was happy to get back to the ship and asked Sarah to take her straight to her room so that she could get some rest before facing the CSO again. She was dreading going to dinner, and she was particularly dreading what news there might be on Carlos.

Once in her room, she climbed onto the bed, took some painkillers and went to sleep.

Chapter 26

Rachel awoke to banging on the stateroom door. It took a moment for her to realise where she was as she still felt groggy. As she went to move, she felt the plaster on her leg and pain in her ankle, which reminded her of what had happened.

She hobbled to the door as she hadn't quite mastered the walking plaster technique yet. Looking through the spy hole, she saw Sarah and opened the door.

Her friend came bustling in. "I was so worried about you. I phoned three times, and you didn't answer, and I've been banging on the door for ages. I was just about to call Josie to open up."

"Sorry, I was out for the count. I think these painkillers are taking their toll. What time is it?" Her room was dark because she had closed the curtains before climbing into bed.

"It's eight o'clock. We set sail an hour ago and I think you may have missed your dinner."

"That's perhaps as well, I don't want to run into Carlos. I'll get something at the buffet. Are you joining me?"

"Yes, I will. I'll just give Waverley a ring and tell him we'll be along in an hour. Is that alright with you?"

Rachel sighed. "Yes, I guess we have to get it over with. Sarah, I really need to wash. How am I supposed to shower with this plaster in place?"

"Da-daaa!" Sarah opened a package she had been holding and held up a long plastic boot with a rubber seal at the opening. "Meet your shower helper. I'll show you how to put it on, and then you can do it for yourself after today."

Sarah helped Rachel pull the boot over her plaster and showed her how it secured itself against her leg, allowing her to get into a shower or bath without wetting the plaster.

"You're the best!" exclaimed Rachel.

"More good news to come. The captain has secured two luxury suites for you and Lady Snellthorpe to stay in for the rest of the cruise. They have large bathrooms and are on deck fifteen. You will have a butler and can order anything you like, on the house. Josie will pack up your room, and your belongings will be moved for you." Sarah was oozing excitement now.

"Okay, so what's the bad news?"

"You will have a security guard stationed outside your rooms for the rest of the cruise, and Marjorie will be escorted everywhere. From a discreet distance, of course."

Rachel groaned and went for a shower. It was a lot more difficult than she'd thought it would be, showering with her leg in plaster. Even with the plastic boot, she felt clumsy and awkward. They were later than they thought they'd be going up to the buffet for dinner, so Sarah let CSO Waverley know that they had been held up.

Rachel was glad of the crutches as she still felt unsteady walking on the plaster cast, but she knew she would master it soon enough. *Three more nights to go.* She was pleased that she would soon be home, having called her parents from Gibraltar. They had agreed to collect her from Southampton so that she wouldn't have to negotiate luggage and train travel with a broken ankle. She hadn't been completely honest with them about how she sustained her injuries, deciding to fill them in on the real story when she got back. For now, they just knew she had fallen down some steps and broken her ankle.

Sarah insisted Rachel sit down when they got to the buffet, and then she went and got food for her, returning a second time for her own food. *It is good to have Sarah around*, thought Rachel. They enjoyed their food, and the waiters, who normally didn't serve from the buffet, kept coming over to offer them more food or drinks.

After she had eaten, Rachel felt a bit more like herself, albeit a slightly light-headed self.

"How's Marjorie?" she asked.

"Still a bit shaken, but she has already been moved to her suite and is being waited on hand and foot by the butler you will share. I think it will be difficult for her until she finds out what and who is behind all of this although I think we all know the *who*!"

"Does her son know he is under suspicion?"

"I'm not sure. Waverley is going to fill us in on the investigation once we see him, and he wants to talk to you some more, so I suppose we should get on with it." Sarah smiled sympathetically. They got up to leave, but as they did so, Rachel spotted someone out of the corner of her eye.

"That's him! That's the man from last night."

"Where?" By the time Sarah had turned to look, the man had gone, and Rachel was not capable of going after him. "Did he see you?"

"I don't think so, he was looking the opposite way. If only he had come forward so that we could eliminate him from our enquiries."

"Now you are sounding like a police constable," said Sarah, laughing. "Come on, PC Plod, let's plod along to your new suite. Waverley will meet us there."

Rachel picked up her crutches and walked slowly towards the lifts. On arrival at deck fifteen, Sarah led the way to the starboard side, but this time they were heading towards the stern of the ship. The suite was at the very back in the corner, and Sarah pointed to another one in the opposite corner on the port side.

"That's Marjorie's room."

Rachel was pleased to arrive, and on entering the room, she let out a whoop. It was about four times the size of her balcony suite, and there was a separate seating area and a huge bathroom with a tub as well as a shower. She walked through to the lounge area and saw a large flat screen TV hanging on the wall, a settee which was also a bed, a computer on a desk and a huge fridge.

"Was this not in use?" she asked Sarah.

"Apparently both suites were vacated in Gibraltar as the family were heading over to an apartment they own in Spain before flying home."

"It's wonderful," said Rachel as she opened the fridge and found it fully stocked. There were flowers on the table and a fruit bowl filled with exotic fruits.

There was a knock at the door and Sarah went to answer it. CSO Waverley entered, smiling. It was the first time Rachel had seen him smile. That morning he had been very serious and his whole demeanour had reflected the gravity of the situation, but now he appeared a little more relaxed.

Perhaps because no more murders have taken place.

"I trust your new accommodation suits?" he said.

"Yes, I think it will do, thank you." Rachel noticed a tall, skinny man standing alongside Waverley, who he now turned to.

"This is Security Officer Ravanos. He will be guarding you and Lady Snellthorpe for the rest of the journey. He will be relieved at night by Security Officer McColgan."

Rachel was about to ask whether this was all necessary, but decided against it as she didn't want to cause any problems. On reflection, she was pleased that Marjorie would be protected.

"How will he guard both of us?" she asked instead.

"Well, Lady Snellthorpe will be his priority because we don't really think that you are in any danger. It is unlikely the killer knows who you are, but if you could let your guard know where you are going at all times, that would be helpful."

"How is the investigation going?" asked Sarah.

CSO Waverley pointed to a seat. "Do you mind if I sit down?" Rachel nodded towards the chair and Waverley sat. "I'm afraid we don't have any leads on the potential killer yet, but head office is going through the passenger manifest with a fine toothcomb and anyone with a criminal record will be brought to my attention by the morning. The police in London have been informed and they will start investigating the Snellthorpe family and business connections to see what that brings up. I have asked them not to alert Jeremy

Snellthorpe, just in case he is involved, so their enquiries will be discreet. At present we have no real leads, and the man who assisted you last evening has not come forward. We did put out a request over the ship-wide speaker during the day and will do so again tomorrow morning, in case he was off ship. We could do with a description from you, though, if that is possible?"

He paused for a moment.

"We have managed to find out more about your—" He coughed. "Your *acquaintance*, Carlos."

Rachel stiffened and sat up; he had her full attention. She had been dreading whatever it was she was about to hear.

"It turns out his full name is Carlos Jacobi. He is a Private Detective who was hired to keep an eye on Lady Snellthorpe and make sure she was kept safe. He hasn't been very good at his job by all accounts, but we can confirm that he is who he says he is, and that he is not under suspicion."

Rachel had stopped breathing, but she now felt huge relief mixed with anger. Carlos was not a murderer, but she was angry with herself as much as with him because she had obviously distracted him from his job.

"Who hired him?"

"He won't say. Says his clients are confidential and he won't budge on it. I think he probably doesn't want us telling his employer what a mess he's made of his job, to be honest. We have checked his ID, though, and his firm has done work for the Snellthorpe family in the past – mainly for the former Lord Snellthorpe."

"That's why Marjorie thought she recognised him," said Rachel. "Has he discovered anything while on board?"

"He says he thought he saw someone running away from the scene in Lisbon and gave chase, but lost sight of the man as he was prevented from getting far by the crowds. He then returned to the scene and saw you getting into a taxi with Lady Snellthorpe, so he knew she was safe. He continued following her, but spotted our men following, too, so he assumed she would be under permanent surveillance and relaxed his guard. As did we, unfortunately."

"I see," said Rachel. She now knew that she had seen Carlos running away in Lisbon, but not for the reasons she had feared. CSO Waverley's words also clarified why Marjorie had felt she was being followed.

"All in all, it's a bit of a mess. Our security team made themselves too obvious." Waverley glared at SO Ravanos, who appeared to squirm a little, and then looked back to Rachel. "Mr Jacobi was unable to give a description of the man he chased, other than he was about six feet tall with dark hair, and that description fits about five hundred passengers. I don't think the killer will try again though. He may think he succeeded with his last attempt."

I doubt that, thought Rachel.

"Surely he would have stayed around to check – unless the other passengers scared him off." Sarah echoed the same concern. "Wouldn't he have kept watch to make sure she was dead?"

"Well, if he did, he will know he wasn't successful," answered Waverley, looking uncomfortable. "I still think he will give up. He has made two unsuccessful attempts on Lady Snellthorpe's life, possibly three if we count the probability of it being he who was in her stateroom the other night. He will know that we are onto him now so he would be mad to try again. Nevertheless, we are not taking any chances, and Lady Snellthorpe will be guarded at all times. However, I think this crime will now only be solved by the British police, unless our passenger checks come up with someone of interest."

"What about Marjorie's friend?" asked Rachel.

"The police in Scotland have been informed, and they have broken it to the family that the death is now being treated as suspicious and a case of mistaken identity. That's all we can say for now, unless we can find out more. Now, Miss Prince, perhaps you could give us a description of the man who assisted you last night."

Rachel gave as full a description as she could, explaining that she thought she had seen the man leaving the buffet this evening, and with that Waverley left. Ravanos was posted in the corridor with both staterooms in sight. Sarah stayed for a while and then hugged her friend goodnight after making sure Rachel was going to be alright.

"Goodnight, Rachel. Sleep tight."

"I think I will with all of these tablets." Rachel laughed as she locked her door and looked at the time – half past midnight. She took her pills and went to bed, admiring the opulence of the room she was now in.

Carlos's face appeared before her as she drifted off. At least she didn't have to worry about him being involved any more, but she couldn't help but wonder if she would ever see him again.

Chapter 27

Marjorie woke in the middle of the night. Something in her dream had disturbed her, and now she couldn't remember what it was.

Oh dear, it's so frustrating.

She got up and made herself a cup of camomile tea. Perhaps that would help clear her mind.

Marjorie recalled the events of the previous night. The night had been beautiful, and she had been remembering many of the happy strolls that she and Ralph had taken in the past. One particular night had come to her mind.

It had been their diamond wedding anniversary a week before their final cruise together, and they had kept it low profile, having just a few close friends round for dinner. Ralph had said he would take her out for a special dinner on their cruise and, true to his word, that night he had wined and dined her as if they were in their twenties. He had been working hard and business worries had been concerning him, but on that night, he seemed to have left all of those concerns behind him.

After dinner, they had walked out on deck and he produced a small box from his pocket as they stood admiring the stars.

"I love you." It was a simple statement but Marjorie could see tears in his eyes as he looked at her. "I'm sorry if I've been a bit distracted. There's something going on in the business. I can't say much about it, but it's been a bit of a worry. Money is going missing and I think I know who is taking it." He had looked so sad. Marjorie just wanted to hold him. "Anyway, let's forget about that for now. Open your present."

She had opened the Tiffany box to see the most beautiful black diamond encrusted eternity ring. The stunning cut of the five diamonds almost took her breath away. Neither Ralph nor Marjorie was prone to extravagance, in spite of their wealth, which made the gift all the more special. She had taken the 24 carat gold ring out of the box and looked on the inner side at Ralph's request to find the engraving: RS, MS, 60 years.

She looked at the ring now and remembered that wonderful evening. Two months after that, Ralph was dead.

Marjorie brought her thoughts back to the previous night again. After recalling that wonderful night and admiring the precious ring on her left ring finger, she had felt a sudden shiver. She wasn't sure whether it was the sadness of her loss or remembering Ralph's business concerns that had caused it, but she had decided to return to her room.

In her dream she had seen herself walking purposefully along the deck towards the steps. It was at that moment she had sensed she wasn't alone and turned to look behind her. She felt herself falling again, and then she saw Rachel reaching out for her. But now she remembered what had woken her. As she had turned her head, she had felt the push, and at the same time she saw the inside of a man's left wrist underneath a black jacket.

How odd, she had thought as she fell, *no watch*.

Now, as she remembered that small detail, she wondered whether it was important.

Perhaps it was, perhaps it wasn't.

Her mind now turned to what Ralph had said about money going missing from the company. He had never mentioned it again, and she had learned over their sixty years of happy marriage not to pry. He would tell her when he was ready, but that opportunity had not arisen. His health had deteriorated rapidly on his return to work, resulting in the fatal heart attack.

Who was taking money from the company? Is that what my Solicitor wants to talk to me about on my return? If it is Jeremy, it doesn't make sense that he keeps asking for more money to inject into the business. Is he just spending it on his extravagant lifestyle and his even more extravagant wife?

Marjorie got back into bed and decided to take one of the sleeping tablets Dr Bentley had prescribed. She was determined to take much more of an interest in the firm when she got back to London. She would find out who was taking money and then sell up if that's what was required; she didn't need the money. The one thing she wasn't going to allow was her husband's work to be wasted on spongers and thieves.

Chapter 28

This blasted job's becoming impossible! How could that woman keep surviving? If I believed in fate, I would think that it's just not meant to be. No. Don't be stupid, it has just been bad luck, and now it's going to be nigh on impossible to get near to the old girl.

Once again, he contemplated leaving the job undone and taking the risk on how it might affect his reputation. There was more to it than that though. There was his pride. He had *never* failed, and he couldn't accept failure of any kind now. His dad had been a complete failure – a weakling who allowed people to tread all over him. He had despised the way his dad was always polite to people, even when they scorned him, and was determined never to let people use him in the same way. Killing for a living empowered him. He was always in control, having the ability to take away life whenever he chose, and that's what motivated him above all else.

If he let this woman live, he could pretend it had been his own choice to his friends (not that he had that many), but deep down, he would always know that it had been his only failure. He would not be able to live with that, and even more importantly, it made him afraid of how it might affect him when it came to future jobs.

He had to finish the job, in spite of the risks. It just had to be done.

He had ignored the numerous calls he'd received yesterday in Gibraltar.

He will just have to wait. I will tell him when it's done. Now I have that young woman to contend with as well.

The tension was building in his temples. A job that had seemed like easy money was becoming the worst job of his life. It was bad enough that all his other hits seemed to be deserving of death whereas this one was not on that level and challenged what was left of his conscience. Now he would have to tread very carefully so that he wasn't recognised while finishing this elusive woman off.

She's a strong old bird, I'll give her that. She should have died of fright by now.

He had watched the stewards move the old lady's luggage from her room and seen where they had taken it, noticing the guard outside her new room.

Well, he looks dopey enough, I can deal with him and then push her overboard.

It was the only way he could see of getting the job done. He knew it would be risky, but he was starting to feel desperate. Anxiety was never a good sign for a hitman. The sooner he got this job done, the better.

Tonight, he thought as he tucked into a fried breakfast in the buffet.

Chapter 29

Rachel availed herself of the opportunity to eat breakfast on the balcony of her new suite. The balcony was at least three times the size of the one in the previous stateroom and faced the sea behind the ship. She could see the foam the *Coral Queen* left behind and the waves eventually re-forming after being broken by the onward journey. The weather was still hot as the ship had entered the Atlantic and was off the west coast of Spain and Portugal. They would begin crossing the Bay of Biscay this evening and would be in Southampton in two days, docking at five in the morning.

Rachel's butler had been attentive, obviously under strict instructions to make sure that she had everything she required. He had introduced himself as Jeeves and for a moment she'd thought he was being serious, but then he explained his name was Mario. He looked and sounded Spanish, but explained that he was actually from El Salvador.

"I have wife in San Salvador and send money each month for family food," he explained in broken English.

"You must miss them," said Rachel, who had then been shown a number of photographs of his wife and three little boys, all under six. *It's perhaps as well you work away*, Rachel thought, but not unkindly. "Is Lady Snellthorpe awake?"

"Yes, ma'am. I have just taken her tea, she asked how you are."

"Will you tell her I will visit soon?"

Rachel turned away, not wanting to appear rude, but she needed some time to herself. Mario cleared the breakfast tray and left her in peace.

She was pleased to have free Wi-Fi and had been able to email her boss the previous evening to let him know that she would not be on street patrol on Monday, explaining why. Now she logged into her email account and found a reply.

"Dear PC Prince,

That's the last time you are allowed to go away on holiday! I have made arrangements for you to work alongside the desk sergeant for next week and PC Gabriel will cover your shifts. I have attached your new rota.

See you Monday at eight o'clock sharp.

Regards

Sergeant Smythe."

Short and to the point, as ever, she thought as she read through the email. At least he attempted a joke.

Rachel was not keen on desk duty; she enjoyed being out on the beat, but being a policewoman involved everything from emergency call outs to routine to the downright boring. She was pleased to have the email to her boss out of the way, and now she only had to work out how she was going to get to and from work for the next six weeks until the plaster could come off.

Her mind came back into the present and she logged off the computer and hobbled to Marjorie's room. Ravanos was sitting in the corridor and stood to attention when she passed. She smiled at him as she knocked on Marjorie's door.

Marjorie welcomed her in with a brisk hug and a kiss on the cheek.

"Hello, my dear. How are you feeling?"

"A lot better for a good night's sleep," Rachel replied.

"Would you like a cup of tea? Mario has just brought in a fresh pot."

"Yes please."

Rachel followed her out onto the balcony and joined her at the table.

"How do you like your room?" The old lady asked. Rachel smiled. "Sheer luxury, I wish I could enjoy it for longer."

"I remembered something in the night – well two things, actually. One is about the other night and one is more personal."

"Oh?" said Rachel, and she waited for Marjorie to continue.

"The first is that I remembered seeing the man who pushed me's left wrist. It seemed odd that he wasn't wearing a watch with a dinner suit. At least, I think it was a dinner suit. I noticed a black jacket cuff."

Rachel pondered this information for a moment. "Well, it could be he doesn't wear a watch, or it could be he was left-handed."

"Exactly what I thought! I think he was reaching out to push me with his left hand, but when I turned, he used his other hand. It all happened in a split second, but at least it might help narrow the field a little."

Marjorie seemed to be enjoying playing detective, and it was nice to see her more like herself again.

"All we need to do now is find a left-handed man with murder on his mind." Rachel poured herself another cup of tea. "What about the other thing?" she asked gently.

"Not long before my husband died, he had mentioned he thought someone was taking money from the business and that he knew who it was. I haven't thought about it since because I was too busy trying to cope with his death and then I had a lot of other matters to attend to. I left the business side of things to my son, Jeremy." Marjorie paused before continuing. "It might be Jeremy who has been taking money out of the business. Ralph was furious that he was too extravagant, spending well beyond his means. I think, after my husband died, Jeremy thought he would be in full control of the company, but Ralph named me as controlling partner."

"How did he react to that?"

"How Jeremy reacts to most things, like a bull in a china shop. It took a while for him to accept it, but I thought he had come round. Now I have this awful feeling in the pit of my stomach that my son wants me dead, but I hardly dare imagine it." Marjorie's face set with a new determination. "But this old lady is not that easy to get rid of and I will fight any abuse of my husband's fortune until my dying breath."

Rachel reached for Marjorie's hand, unable to find words to respond. Everything in her wanted to protect this dear woman from whatever and whoever wanted to harm her. A deep anger that she had never felt before made her determined to get to the bottom of this before anything else happened. Unlike CSO Waverley, Rachel was certain the killer would try again. He had already killed an unsuspecting old lady, and she had no doubt that wasn't the end of it. Hitmen had to see their work through or they would not be hired again. Rachel knew how it worked.

"I will get a message to CSO Waverley about the possibility of our man being left-handed. Do you want me to mention your son?"

"No, dear. I think that is something I will need to investigate with Randolph, our Lawyer, when I return home."

After her tea with Marjorie, Rachel told Ravanos what Marjorie had told her and asked him to pass this information on to the CSO. She then decided to enjoy one of the many films that were available for free on her suite's TV, but halfway through *The Greatest Showman* she drifted off to sleep.

A distant ringing sound broke into her sleep and it took her a while to realise that it was the telephone in her room.

"Hello," she mumbled, fighting sleep.

"Rachel! Are you alright?" Sarah sounded stressed. "I just wanted to check in with you before I go back to work. It's been bedlam today with accidents and people running out of medication."

"Don't worry about me, I'm fine. I think I will ask Mario to find me some lunch and then sleep some more before trying to hunt down Carlos at dinner tonight. Hey, I didn't ask about your date the other night?"

"It was good, and I think there will be more dates on the next sailing as we are both with this ship for the foreseeable future. I wanted to let you know that Waverley has drawn a blank on suspects and your knight in shining armour still hasn't come forward."

"No-one with a criminal record?"

"Yes, there are several, but none of them fit the profile of a professional killer willing to do away with old ladies. We have a jewellery thief, a fraudster, a wife beater and a juvenile drug user. There are fifty-three that haven't come through yet. As you can imagine, trying to find the criminal records of three and a half thousand passengers and eighteen hundred crew is not easy."

"I didn't realise he would be looking at crew members."

"He's prioritised those who joined the ship in Southampton, but I think it is unlikely to be a crew member."

"I agree," said Rachel. "Marjorie saw a jacket cuff which suggests a passenger to me. Anyway, she is going to stay in her room tonight so she should be safe."

"That's good. I'll call you after I finish shift tonight. I hope it goes well with Carlos."

"Thanks, speak later."

Rachel hung up, smiling at the thought of seeing Carlos at dinner.

Chapter 30

Rachel dressed up as well as she could for a woman wearing a plaster cast on her leg. She smiled at how she looked in the mirror. The dress she had chosen was sky blue cotton with long chiffon sleeves that would help to hide her arm dressing and the underlying wounds. From the knees up, she looked like a glamorous young woman enjoying a cruise holiday, but the plaster cast on her left lower leg reminded her that this was no ordinary cruise.

She applied the finishing touches to her makeup and added a lip gloss rather than lipstick, which complemented her full red lips. Once satisfied, she called Marjorie to let her know that she might be late back tonight and agreed to see her for coffee in the morning. Feeling a flutter of excitement at the thought of seeing Carlos again, she picked up her handbag and left the room.

Ravanos was seated in the corridor and he smiled at her. "Enjoy your evening, ma'am."

"Thank you, I will." She thought how boring it must be for him being on guard duty the whole time, but she hoped that his watch would remain boring as any activity would mean another attempt on Marjorie's life. She shuddered at the thought, and for a brief moment, wondered whether she should stay behind.

Don't be silly that's his job.

There was a queue for the lifts as people were making their way down for dinner, but Rachel managed to squeeze into one after a group of three people almost carried her along in their haste to make sure they got in. The lifts at this time of the evening were claustrophobic as people insisted on filling every square inch, not wanting to wait the extra few minutes for the next one to arrive. The majority were heading for the deck four restaurant, as was Rachel, but she decided to exit on deck six so that she could make her way through midships and then down the stairs.

This was the first time she had walked slowly along deck six, passing through the casino. As soon as she entered, she saw a familiar figure at the blackjack table. He looked different because he was sporting a moustache so she thought she was mistaken initially, but as he lifted his head, she recognised the eyes immediately.

He seemed unsure whether to acknowledge her at all. *Perhaps he doesn't recognise me,* she thought. She walked towards him and he smiled.

"Good evening."

"Good evening. I'm sorry to interrupt, but are you the gentleman who helped me and my friend the other evening?"

"Your friend?" He seemed momentarily startled. "Yes, of course, now I remember. You had both fallen." Other players were starting to listen in on their conversation as he spoke. "Oh dear, I seem to have lost again. Perhaps you would like to join me for a drink?" He picked up his chips and put them into his pocket before taking her by the arm.

"I was just heading for dinner, but yes, perhaps a quick drink."

They walked in uncomfortable silence towards a quiet wine bar where he ordered himself a cognac and Rachel a martini and lemonade. He then steered her towards a quiet corner.

"Did you not hear the announcements requesting you go to reception with regard to the accident?" Rachel took a sip of the drink he had bought her.

"I have to admit, I did hear the announcements, but I have been busy enjoying ship life. I hardly ever get away, you see." He smiled, but the smile didn't reach his eyes. "I wouldn't be able to help anyway, I didn't see anything."

"I see. Well, I must go, I'm meeting someone for dinner."

"Please finish your drink, and I promise I will go to reception with you afterwards if it helps."

As Rachel took another few gulps of her drink, she noticed that he picked his drink up with his left hand, and there was no watch on his left wrist. Her heart beating faster within her chest, she rose to leave, but began to feel confused and woozy, not knowing where she was. Feeling herself becoming more and more drowsy, she tried to stand, but her legs wouldn't carry her.

When she approached him in the casino, he tried to ignore her, but when she said that the old lady was her friend, he improvised. This whole business had been one shambolic mess after another. Now as he looked at her legs giving way under her, he was in turmoil over what to do next. He could just leave her there and go and finish off the old lady, but that wouldn't work now. The croupier knew who he was and had seen him with this young woman. Questions would be asked and they would find him. No, he would have to kill her as well.

Collateral damage. He sighed. Such a shame, she is so beautiful.

He had to remain professional, but he could feel beads of sweat appearing on his forehead. This young woman hadn't been part of the plan.

He waited for most of the people to leave the bar as they headed off to their various dinner activities. Seizing his moment while the bartenders were clearing away a large number of wine bottles and glasses from tables at the far end of the bar, he lifted Rachel from her seat, putting his left arm around her waist and picking up her handbag with his right hand. He half carried her along the corridor, speaking to her as if she was drunk while doing his best not to draw any attention to himself. It wasn't too difficult; most people were wrapped up in their own little worlds, so the few people who were still around barely cast a second glance.

"Almost there, darling." He spoke to her as an elderly couple gave him a sympathetic glance. Managing to get her to the lifts at the bow of the ship, he decided to take her up to deck fourteen. They could walk along the deck and take the rear lift up to fifteen.

It is going well so far, he thought as he began to calm down. He took out a pair of false spectacles from his pocket and added a beard, using the mirror in the lift. He didn't want anyone to recognise him.

The woman let out a moan and tried to pull away, but she wasn't strong enough.

"I'm sorry you had to be involved in this, but it will soon be over," he said.

They arrived at deck fourteen and he took the port side first. The stewards were busy restocking rooms and turning down beds so he felt secure they hadn't been noticed. Once they got to midships, he moved over to the starboard side to walk the rest of the way to the rear. They met one young couple on the way, but they were too busy kissing and giggling to notice him. The girl gave Rachel a quick glance, but then looked away.

By the time they reached the rear lifts, he was feeling a little bit out of breath. He decided to rest for a moment and sat the young woman down on the floor while he composed himself for the next part of the plan. All he had to do now was deal with the security officer on the next floor and hope the butler wasn't around.

Having gathered himself together, he lifted the drugged woman from the floor and entered the lift. He could feel adrenaline pumping through his body as he moved in for the kill. The woman was murmuring again and starting to struggle a bit more. She hadn't drunk the full dose, but the effects of the drug should last for a bit longer.

"Not long now," he said as he pulled her tightly towards him.

The lift doors opened, and he carried her out. He decided to pick her up and approach the end of the corridor where the security guard was seated.

The guard look surprised.

"Drunk too much. Hold onto her for a minute, will you?"

With that, he handed her over to the surprised guard, who almost dropped her. As he bent to catch her, the man picked up the chair and hit him over the head with it.

He left the woman on the floor, opening her door with her key card and dragging the unconscious security officer inside. Tying him up, he left the guard there. He was happy with his disguise; the guard would not have seen him for long enough to provide a detailed description, and even if he did, the first thing he would have noticed was the beard.

Moving quickly to pick up the chair and put it back in place, he lifted Rachel up off the floor and headed towards the old woman's room. He knocked on the door and held Rachel up in front of the spy hole.

It worked. The old woman opened the door.

"One word and she's dead," he said.

Rachel could hear noises piercing her brain. She could feel herself being carried along, but couldn't make any sense of what was happening. There was pain in her foot and her head was throbbing. She was trying to count the number of throbs: one, two, three, four, ouch! The pain in her head again.

Blurred corridors passed through her subconscious, but everything seemed unreal, like a piece of abstract art. She could feel an arm around her waist and tried to call Carlos, but sensed it wasn't Carlos holding her.

She felt the pain in her ankle again and could just about work out that she was on the floor. A shadow was dragging another shadow away, and now she was being held up outside a door. Her vision was returning, but things still appeared blurred.

Marjorie?

She felt herself being thrown onto a bed and she could hear voices.

"What have you done to her?" Marjorie's voice sounded distant, but Rachel could make out the words.

"Just a little drug. It's best for her in the long run."

"You're the man from the car, aren't you? So you're the one who has been trying to kill me." Marjorie sounded calm.

"Yes, and it hasn't been easy."

"Who is paying you? I will pay you double to cancel the job."

"Sorry, lady. That's not how it works. A contract is a contract and I have a reputation to live up to."

"I would still like to know who is paying you."

"I won't say."

"What now?"

"You both go overboard."

Rachel's brain started to come back to reality. She opened her eyes and saw him reaching out to grab Marjorie. Reaching for the fruit bowl, she picked it up and threw it with all her might.

"Damn!" the man shouted, blood on his face. "Looks like she will have to go first."

Rachel saw him push Marjorie out towards the balcony, then he turned on her. She felt him dragging her along the floor. The noise of the sea sounded much louder in her head and the pain in her ankle was excruciating.

Marjorie had been pushed to the floor and was struggling to get up. Rachel felt herself being lifted up and carried towards the barrier. She fought, but her strength wasn't there. Her mind was still numb and her limbs were struggling to co-ordinate.

It's now or never, she thought as the man heaved her up.

Chapter 31

Sarah was finishing up her paperwork when Brigitte popped her head around the door.

"There's a Carlos Jacobi here to see you, Sarah."

She went into the waiting room and saw the handsome Carlos standing there.

"Hello. I'm Sarah."

"I'm sorry to bother you, but I was hoping to see Rachel this evening. I waited at dinner, but she didn't arrive. I thought you might know where she is."

"She said she was going to dinner as usual and she was hoping to see you, too."

Sarah was worried. She picked up the telephone and called Rachel's room, but there was no reply. She then tried Lady Snellthorpe.

"Hello."

"Hello, Lady Snellthorpe, it's Sarah. Have you seen Rachel?"

"No dear, she called me at six o'clock and said she would probably be late tonight. I think she was going to see that young man. Is everything alright?"

"Yes, all's good, I just wanted to catch her, that's all. Is everything quiet with you."

"Yes, everything's fine. There's someone at the door, so I'd better go, dear. It's probably the guard telling me he's changing shifts."

The phone went dead. Sarah looked at Carlos and shook her head.

"She was going to meet you. Come on, let's go and see if we can find her. Lady Snellthorpe is okay."

They went back to the restaurant, but people were now going in for the second sitting. Sarah asked the Maître D' to keep a lookout for Rachel and page her if she came in. Carlos looked worried sick, but he was holding it together for now.

"Let's just try the bars in case she's fallen asleep. The painkillers have been making her a bit tired. If no-one has seen her, I will contact security. They may want to put out a ship-wide alert."

They had been through every bar on deck's four and five when finally they entered the wine bar and gave a description of Rachel. The staff shook their heads until a Romanian bartender said he remembered a woman of that description coming into the bar with a man.

"They sat over there." He nodded his head in the direction of where Rachel had sat. "I thought it was odd because she only had one drink, but he was almost carrying her out. I only noticed them leave because I dropped a glass and saw out of the side of my eye. Is that how you say it?"

"Which way did they go?" Sarah was not inclined to give an English lesson at this moment.

"Towards elevators, bow."

"Thank you," said Sarah, and then she relented. "And it's out of the *corner* of my eye." The bartender smiled.

"Where would they go?" asked Carlos.

"I don't know. Come on, we'll go to her suite. I carry a ship-wide door pass." She turned back to the bartender. "Would you call security and tell them Rachel Prince has been abducted and we are heading to her room? Do you understand?"

The bartender picked up the phone as they left. Sarah could feel the adrenaline pumping through her body, and she could see that Carlos was also tense. They took the lifts to the fifteenth deck and Sarah opened Rachel's suite door. They immediately saw the security officer, Ravanos, tied up on the floor. He was just regaining consciousness, but they left him for now and ran towards Lady Snellthorpe's room.

Sarah unlocked the door and followed as Carlos rushed in. Rachel was being lifted up onto the balcony. Carlos ran towards her as the man turned, but Sarah could see that he wouldn't make it in time.

Just then, she saw Rachel's leg do a somersault, and the man went overboard. Carlos rushed over to Rachel and picked her up. Carrying her into the room, he laid her gently on the bed. Sarah was relieved to find Lady Snellthorpe sitting on the floor of the balcony, looking shaken but unharmed.

"Well, I have to say, I am pleased to see you." The old lady smiled at Sarah as the younger woman helped her to her feet.

"Are you hurt?" Sarah asked.

"No, dear, just shaken. He was going to kill us both, you know."

Sarah nodded and put her arm around Lady Snellthorpe, helping her through to the suite as six security guards came rushing into the room, CSO Waverley at the front. Rachel was sitting up on the bed.

"Man overboard," said Sarah quietly. The CSO got on his radio while the other officers checked the balcony. "And one of your officers is tied up in Rachel's room."

Chapter 32

As Rachel saw Carlos running towards her, she knew he wouldn't make it in time. Hanging over the edge of the balcony with the man leaning over her, she drew her plastered leg back and gave one almighty kick which thrust upwards, catching his leg. The man lost his balance and dropped her before tumbling over the edge and down into the dark, black sea.

Momentarily, Rachel saw Sarah picking Marjorie up after she was whisked into the arms of Carlos. He carried her over to the bed and laid her down gently.

Rachel explained what had happened, how she had recognised the man in the casino and how he had lured her for a drink. She said how she had noticed he was left-handed just before the drug took effect, and that she couldn't remember anything else until she reached Marjorie's suite.

The man-overboard siren had sounded, and the ship had stopped, but Sarah explained it would be unlikely the man would be found as they hadn't called it straight away. The majority of the security officers were using searchlights to see if they could spot any sign of the man, but it was a futile search and impossible to find him in the dark. Rachel almost felt sorry for him until she remembered that he had intended to kill both her and Marjorie.

Sarah had made coffee for everyone although she handed Marjorie a glass of brandy as well.

"Does this mean we won't find out who was behind this?" asked Marjorie, sipping her brandy.

"Not necessarily," said Carlos, producing a phone from his pocket. "He dropped this when he fell and I caught it automatically when I reached for Rachel. I think it's a burner phone, and if we can unlock it, I suspect it will lead us to another burner phone."

Marjorie and Sarah looked confused. "Criminals use burner phones for illegal activities," Rachel explained. "They are untraceable and discarded after a job is done."

Waverley took the phone. "I will get onto it at once." He started to leave the room with a bounce in his step before turning back. "Does anyone know who that man was?"

"No, sorry," said Rachel. "He was playing blackjack, though, so someone from the casino might know his name. He also paid for the drinks in the bar with his room card, a cognac and a martini and lemonade."

Waverley smiled. "I think I will be offering you a job soon, young lady."

As he left the room, Rachel looked around at the three people who were now as close to her as anyone could be.

"You were marvellously calm," she said to Marjorie. "Even through my disorientated and muddled state, I could hear the calmness in your voice. How did you do it?"

"Ralph always said it wasn't British to be over emotional, and I thought if this was going to be my last few minutes on earth, I wanted my husband to be proud of me."

"He would be very proud. I think your attitude unnerved the man, and it brought me to my senses out of the fogginess of the drug."

"I am so pleased that you are safe, though, Rachel. I wouldn't have been able to live with myself if he had managed to—" Marjorie took another drink. "Although I wouldn't have lived anyway, would I?"

They all laughed, and it relieved some of the tension in the room.

Rachel smiled at Sarah and Carlos. "How did you know to come here?"

"It's a long story," said Sarah. "We have Carlos to thank for that."

"And a Romanian bartender," said Carlos.

The captain's voice came over the loudspeaker. "We are starting up the engines again, ladies and gentleman. Do enjoy the rest of your evening on board the *Coral Queen*."

The room went silent as they realised what this meant. Rachel reflected soberly that she had killed a man, and it wasn't a pleasant thought.

"That nurse did warn me the plaster was hard and not to kick anybody," she said ruefully.

Both Sarah and Carlos squeezed her hands in acknowledgement.

"You couldn't have saved him." Carlos poured her a drink of brandy. "It was you or him."

Chapter 33

Carlos helped Rachel back to her room. Her ankle was throbbing after being dragged along corridors and from kicking her assailant. Sarah stayed with Marjorie while the butler cleared her suite and then joined Rachel.

"Is she okay?" asked Rachel.

"Yes. She has had three brandies so I think she will sleep very well. She will either feel better or worse once we know who is behind all this."

Sarah and Carlos left Rachel to get some sleep. In spite of all the excitement, she drifted off into a deep sleep, only slightly aware of the pain in her ankle after taking some pain killers. Sarah had told her Dr Bentley would probably want to do another X-ray in the morning to make sure it hadn't been damaged.

The next morning, Marjorie joined Rachel for breakfast, and Sarah arrived shortly afterwards with Carlos and CSO Waverley.

"We have cracked the phone code, and the captain is heading towards shore so that we can get a satellite signal to call the number. There is only one number on the phone and that will be the one."

"What's the plan?" asked Rachel.

"We are going to text the number to say that the job is done. We have read previous texts and have picked up the general tone of the way the man speaks. His name was Stefano Davidson, and he is officially missing, presumed dead. We have gone through his room, but there is not a lot to go on, except that we now have his bank details. He texted them to the person employing him. He probably has numerous accounts, but I'm sure this will be the one he is paid into."

Waverley paused for a moment.

"Is there something wrong?" asked Rachel.

He looked at Marjorie, who responded, "Out with it, man!"

"Because we don't know who is responsible, after we have sent the text," he coughed, "Dr Bentley will need to call your son and tell him you have met with a tragic accident. This will not be pleasant for him, unless—"

"Unless he is responsible." Looking pale, Marjorie finished the sentence for him.

"Yes, ma'am."

"I don't think we have any alternative, do we?"

Rachel took Marjorie's hand. "Coffee?" she asked.

"Make it strong," the old lady replied.

Beeping from all their phones broke the silence as a satellite signal brought them to life. "Okay, let's do this," said Waverley, tapping into the phone: "*Job done, transfer money.*"

Two minutes later, a reply came through.

"About time! Once confirmed will transfer payment. Remember to destroy phone."

Waverley typed again. "Will destroy once money transfer confirmed. You do the same."

"Do they think it's an accident?"

"Yes, no investigation."

"Will let you know when money transferred."

"Right, now it's Dr Bentley's turn," said Waverley. As he left the room, he turned and added, "I will let you know when there are any developments. The captain will stay within satellite range for as long as he can."

Sarah went back to work after Rachel agreed she would have an X-ray once things settled down, and Rachel, Marjorie and Carlos decided to play gin rummy. Marjorie had offered to return to her room, but as much as Rachel would have liked to have been alone with Carlos, she was not going to let Marjorie sit alone, waiting for news.

Carlos was the perfect gentleman, and he brightened them both up, reminding Marjorie of some of the jobs he had done for her husband in the past. She seemed to enjoy the reminiscences.

"I am so sorry that I didn't look after you properly on this trip. I was told it was a babysitting role really, and that you were unlikely to be in any real danger. I let my guard down when I saw the ship's security watching out for you."

"I have to ask," said Marjorie, "who did hire you?"

"I shouldn't really say, but I suppose there's no harm you knowing now. It was your Lawyer, Randolph, but he hired me on behalf of someone else."

"And who might that someone be?"

Carlos' phone rang. "It's Randolph, I guess the news is out. I think I'd better answer it to keep up the charade for now." He pressed answer. "Hello."

Carlos left the room for around fifteen minutes. When he returned, Rachel waited patiently for him to explain.

"The news is out. I'm in the doghouse for allowing you to be killed, Lady Snellthorpe. Randolph says that Jeremy took it badly. I felt guilty lying to him, to be honest, but we need everyone to think the killer was successful so that whoever is responsible can feel relaxed."

Rachel looked at Marjorie who was visibly shaking now.

"I don't think it was your son," said Carlos, taking her hand.

"Why not?" asked Rachel, horrified that he might be raising false hopes in this tender lady's heart.

"Because Randolph just told me, I would have to answer to Jeremy when I got back. That it was he who paid Randolph to hire me."

The relief on Marjorie's face was obvious, and she allowed the tears that she had been holding back to fall. Rachel hugged her.

At that moment the door opened and in came the captain, Waverley, Dr Bentley and Sarah. They were looking pleased.

"The plan worked," said Waverley. "The money was transferred half an hour ago, and we have traced it back to a Phillip Mason."

Marjorie gasped. "He is financial director of the company."

"And he is being arrested as we speak. I think that investigators will find that he has been siphoning money from the company for a while, and he was obviously getting desperate for more."

"He was Ralph's oldest friend and would become joint controlling partner in the event of my death to prevent my son overspending," Marjorie explained. "No wonder Ralph looked sad. I thought he suspected Jeremy, but this would have been worse for him. Randolph told me that Ralph had planned to change his will, but died before he could do it."

"That explains it, then," said the captain. "I am so sorry, Lady Snellthorpe, for all you have gone through, and to you, Miss Prince. The cruise line will try to make it up to you in some small way, I assure you."

"Thank you, Captain." Marjorie was ever the lady.

"I have just got off the phone to your son again, Lady Snellthorpe," said Dr Bentley. "Despite giving me a piece of his mind, he is relieved that you are alive and well. He apologises for having been so distant and cold recently, but he has been so worried about the company seemingly leaking money and hadn't wanted to worry you. He said to tell you he is looking forward to dinner on Tuesday?"

Marjorie smiled. "That is our weekly dinner date. I expect this one could be interesting."

After all the events of the day, Rachel was pleased to be left alone at last. She stood out on the balcony, peering into the night sky then she stared at the letter in her hand.

"Goodbye, Robert," she said as she let it drop unopened into the ocean.

With a sigh of relief, she returned to the stateroom and got into bed, reflecting on the day. Marjorie had given her an open invitation to stay with her at any time. The captain had told her the cruise line was offering her a free luxury-suite cruise to a destination of her choosing, and a cruise-line representative had offered her a healthy sum by way of compensation on condition she signed a gagging order. Marjorie had been offered free cruises for life and an undisclosed sum of money for the trauma she had suffered. In addition to this, CSO Waverley had offered Rachel a job as a security officer if she wanted to take him up on it.

Best of all, Rachel thought as she put her head to her pillow for the last time on board the *Coral Queen*, *Carlos has asked me out on a date.*

THE END

Deadly Cruise Book 2

DAWN BROOKES

Deadly Cruise

A Rachel Prince Mystery

DAWN BROOKES

OAKWOOD PUBLISHING

Paperback Edition 2018
Kindle Edition 2018
Paperback ISBN: 978-1-9998575-5-4

Chapter 1

At three o'clock on a damp, drizzly morning, a man's bulky body could be seen floating face-downward in the Moskva River, should anyone crossing the Krymsky Bridge in Moscow peer below. The killer had spent days meticulously surveying the area, choosing time and place carefully to prevent that from happening.

By the time the lifeless body was found it should have been carried further south of where the killer now stood admiring his callous handiwork. Satisfied he'd completed the grisly task, he walked a few miles back to the lively bar that would serve as his alibi should he need one. He'd already made certain of being seen by several different people before slipping away. On his return, he'd get himself noticed again to give the impression he'd never left.

After slipping in to the bar unnoticed, he ordered a double vodka and bought the barman a drink before settling in a corner booth. Another man joined him and he handed over a thick envelope containing one thousand US dollars. Payment for the intelligence he'd received. Good information as it turned out.

Later that morning he awoke with a hangover. After packing a suitcase, he travelled by taxi to Sheremetyevo airport, but not before scanning the local radio channels in his apartment. Reports of the body of a Moscow businessman found in the river at dawn sounded low key. Initial police statements suggested the authorities were treating the death as suicide.

Perfect, just what the heartless killer had hoped. Everything was going to plan. "One down, one to go," he muttered before getting into his taxi.

Being booked on an afternoon flight to London, he called his sister and arranged to meet at the Ritz for dinner, explaining he planned to leave for Southampton the next day.

Once on board the plane, he reclined his seat and took a nap, pleased to be in the quiet of business class. It had been a busy three days.

Chapter 2

"It's not a great idea, letting you loose on another cruise after last year. You know I'm worried, don't you?"

The handsome Carlos hauled Rachel's suitcase from the boot of his 1970s Ford Capri. Rachel gazed into his sensitive dark brown eyes and laughed, remembering her first cruise – complete with a murderer on board.

"This one will be indulgent luxury, I'm confident."

"Well in that case, my lady, here we are at your first port of call." Carlos had driven up from London to Leeds, where Rachel had worked the night before, and brought her down to her parents' home in Hertfordshire this afternoon.

"Hm, in spite of a minor hiccup."

Carlos kept the Capri in immaculate condition, it being his pride and joy, but it remained prone to minor mechanical problems and he'd had to change the fan belt before they'd left as it was slipping. Feigning hurt, he took her hand.

Rachel's parents stood on the doorstep, unable to contain their excitement. Rachel rushed forward to hug her mother while her father helped Carlos unpack the rest of the car and shook his hand.

"Good to meet you again, Carlos. Will you be staying for dinner?"

Carlos looked unsure, still a little intimidated by Rachel's father, the Reverend Brendan Prince.

"Oh, do stay," Rachel cajoled, knowing how he felt, but eager for him to get to know her parents, whom she loved dearly.

Carlos coughed, nervously. "How can I refuse such a kind invitation? Thank you, I will."

The men carried the suitcase and bags indoors while Rachel and her mum walked through to the kitchen.

"He's afraid dad can't talk about anything but religion." Rachel laughed. "I've tried to explain that he's most eloquent and can converse about many things, but Carlos can't seem to get past it."

"And your dad doesn't get past how Robert treated you, breaking your heart and calling off the engagement. It makes it tough for him to accept another man in your life just yet. When he's overprotective, it makes him less easy going than usual."

"Oh, Mum. What are we to do with them? Carlos is not at all like Robert and Dad needn't worry, I won't be rushing into a serious relationship for a long time."

Her mother looked concerned at this revelation, but didn't press.

"They'll become used to each other. Your father's a reasonable man, and when he relaxes, Carlos might find him more approachable. He'll talk all day about cars!" Mrs Prince turned towards a pot of freshly percolated coffee.

"It's wonderful to see you, Mum."

"It's great to see you too, Rachel, we miss you. Your father and I worry about you taking another cruise, though, after what happened last year."

"Now you're sounding like Carlos. I'm positive that was a one-off." Rachel laughed again. "Sarah will be there, and I need a break, Mum."

Rachel wondered what her mother would think if she knew all she'd been going through and how much she needed a respite from policing. While her mother busied herself making drinks and preparing dinner, Rachel excused herself and took her coffee outside to the garden. Carlos and her father had disappeared; she assumed this was a positive thing, but hoped Carlos wasn't being given a pep talk.

Rachel lingered outside, sitting on a swing seat on the large paved patio and surveying the grounds where she had grown up. The vicarage stood tall, an imposing Victorian building with eight bedrooms and ample space upstairs and down. Generous sized gardens displayed an ancient oak, large acacia trees, an apple orchard and a multitude of shrubs lining the borders that shielded the vicarage from the church, next door. Rachel inhaled the refreshing smell of recently mown grass. Her father found gardening a therapeutic hobby; his garden was his haven where he went to unwind.

He took his job seriously and spent a lot of time visiting parishioners; hence, his church bucked the national trend of diminishing numbers. It was a two-edged sword, though, because it led to her father being permanently on call. Rachel's mum also kept busy by proxy, entertaining or supporting various causes and village activities, although the Parish Council had recently agreed to employ a youth worker to take up the slack.

Rachel took a sip of coffee, recalling the events of the last six months. It had begun one Monday evening when she and her colleague, Tim Bryson, responded to an emergency call. The street they were directed to was on a housing estate renowned for violence. They heard a commotion as soon as Tim parked the squad car, getting as close as he could to the noise, but the sounds were coming from behind a building with narrow access.

They hurried towards the noise and Tim gave chase to someone. He hadn't seen the other person in Rachel's line of sight, visible in the shimmering moonlight, and she froze as the glistening metal of a knife caught her eye. Running towards the second man, she realised it was too late to save the teenager he'd stabbed straight through the heart in merciless fashion.

Shocked, she reached for her radio as the man lunged forwards, still wielding the bloodied knife. It caught her stab vest rather than her neck; she fell and her attacker raised his knife again.

Rachel had managed to loosen the telescopic truncheon she carried while going for her radio with the other hand, and she wielded it with enough power to knock the man off balance. As soon as he was down, she got to her feet and hit him anew as he sought to stab her from the ground. This time, he quietened down, so she could drag his hands behind his back and apply handcuffs.

She rushed over to the boy lying in a pool of blood and called for an ambulance and backup, but the boy was already dead. Rachel tried for what seemed like an eternity to resuscitate him before the ambulance arrived.

Tim came back. "Where the hell were you?" he shouted, but stopped as he registered the scene in front of him. Sirens and police appeared from everywhere. The ambulance arrived and paramedics took over from Rachel, confirming her fears that the boy was dead. The perpetrator was still on the ground, yelling abuse at anyone who would listen.

"Police brutality, that's what this is. That deranged woman hit me without provocation. I was just passing by, trying to help, when the *filth* came at me like a howling banshee."

There had to be an internal investigation, despite it being obvious the man was lying. Rachel's nerves were shot for several months as the court case seemed to drag on forever. After she had given evidence, alongside DNA found on the knife and in the boy's wounds, and separate evidence found at the scene, it was enough for a guilty verdict to be returned, convicting the man of murder. Rachel felt relieved the trial was over, even though the image of that young boy, attacked for his mobile phone, would stay with her forever.

Reaching for the lukewarm coffee, she realised Carlos was sitting next to her, sidling closer.

"How long have you been here?"

"Long enough – still getting flashbacks?"

"Yep, but less vivid than before. I'll be better once I've had a holiday. At least the court case is over and I can get on with my life. Did I tell you they've nominated me for a bravery award?"

Rachel didn't tell Carlos that the perpetrator, Steven Tansley, had vowed to get revenge. The police had never caught his accomplice, but she suspected Tansley was more mouth than action. Despite a history of violence dating back to his teenage years, he didn't appear to have the kind of influence that would put her in danger. Nevertheless, it would pay to remain alert.

"Yes, sweetheart, you did and you deserve it." Carlos held her hand for a while and they sat in comfortable silence. The silence was broken when they heard excited shrieking coming from the house. Rachel turned and saw Sarah, her best friend, running towards her.

"Rachel, I've missed you. I couldn't wait until tomorrow so your parents invited me over to dinner."

Rachel hugged her friend. "That's great! You look really well." Sarah had a healthy glow and exuded happiness. She worked as a nurse on the cruise ship Rachel would join the next day, and had shared in the adventures of the previous year when a hitman had been on board.

"Hello, Carlos, it's wonderful to see you too." Sarah gave him a warm embrace, and then turned back to Rachel. "I have enjoyed three months off after completing my first nine-month contract on Queen Cruises so I should look well."

"Dinner's ready." Rachel's mum appeared at the French doors leading out to the patio. The excited trio followed her back into the house and enjoyed a very pleasant home-cooked coq au vin. Rachel's mum, a superb hostess and accomplished cook, never failed to deliver.

Rachel and Sarah nattered away over dinner as if they had never been apart. The girls had been friends since school days and Sarah's parents were good friends with the Princes, attending the church where Rachel's father was vicar. There were a few nervous glances shared between Rachel's parents and Carlos over dinner, but while Rachel knew they worried about her going on a cruise, at least their joint concern brought the men closer together.

"Thank you for dinner, Mrs Prince, Mr Prince, but I must head back to London now," Carlos announced once they had enjoyed an after-dinner coffee. Rachel knew he was working on a difficult case, although he seemed unable to discuss too many details. As a private investigator, he worked on many mundane cases, but this latest one was more complex. Rachel was worried he might be in danger, but accepted the danger that came with both of their jobs and knew they would have to learn to live with it.

Rachel and Carlos had been attracted to each other almost immediately after meeting the year before and had been dating ever since. Neither of them was in any rush to settle down. Agreeing to allow the relationship to blossom into what was now a healthy romance, they had recently discussed the possibilities of Rachel moving jobs to London as they didn't see enough of each other, but Rachel was cautious following her broken engagement. She sometimes wondered whether she could ever give her heart to another man after the pain of Robert's betrayal. Carlos told her he would wait for as long as it took, confiding in her that he too was afraid of long-term commitment.

Rachel accompanied him to the car, and he held her tight.

"Be careful, my darling. Stay away from danger."

"The only danger on this cruise will be that I might gain weight." She kissed him on the lips.

"Call me tomorrow and when you are in New York."

"I will. Carlos, please be careful yourself, won't you?"

"Don't worry, I'll be fine. I'll collect you from the port in two weeks. Ciao."

Carlos climbed into his beloved car and drove away. Rachel remained outside, watching until his car disappeared from view in the evening sunset before returning to the house.

Day 0

Chapter 3

The next morning, Rachel woke before dawn but didn't move until bright sunlight penetrated the light curtains in her childhood bedroom. Looking out at the Hertfordshire countryside, Rachel brimmed with excitement. The sun was already burning away the remaining early morning mist.

Rachel was taking this break courtesy of Queen Cruises' generous offer of a free luxury cruise anywhere in the world. New York was a place she had always longed to visit – 'the city that never sleeps' had an exciting ring to it, and shopping was her top priority. The cruise had been booked months ago with Rachel hoping the court case would be over. Now, with Sarah's new contract starting, the timing couldn't have been better.

When Rachel arrived downstairs, her father was already up and dressed, and most of her luggage had miraculously loaded itself into the boot of his car. Rachel gave an exasperated sigh. He preferred to start early and had limited tolerance of tardiness. She should have known he'd be worried about traffic congestion and potential delays, so inevitably would want to leave extra time for the journey to Southampton.

"Dad, we don't need to leave for another hour," whined Rachel in a fruitless attempt to slow him down.

She texted Sarah to let her know they would be with her soon. The phone vibrated almost immediately; she looked at the screen.

"*I knew your dad would want to leave sharpish. I'm up and ready.*" Sarah's response was more patient than Rachel's. There was hardly any chance to say goodbye to her mother before she was bustled into the car.

"Enjoy yourself in New York, darling, and stay out of trouble." Her mother gave her a quick hug, rolling her eyes and turning to her husband. "Drive carefully, Brendan, there's plenty of time." She kissed him on the cheek.

Before long, they'd collected Sarah and nine-months' worth of baggage essentials for her second stint aboard the *Coral Queen*. They had sailed on the same ship the previous year. The drive to Southampton was uneventful; even the M25 motorway was relatively clear, a rarity. The girls discussed how they could meet up in between Sarah's shifts.

"I hope you'll manage with all the sea days on this cruise." Sarah had previously broached this with Rachel, but she was prepared, knowing there were six sea days each way with only two days in New York.

"Don't worry, I've brought a truckload of books and intend to chill and de-stress. I'll make full use of the luxurious suite your company has thrown in. I didn't get to experience the benefits first time round!"

Sarah smiled. "You've got that right. During the last trip I did to New York, though, we had rough weather mid-Atlantic. The medical team hardly came up for air."

"Is Dr Bentley on this cruise?" Rachel had become acquainted with members of the medical team last year and she liked the chief medical officer.

"Yes, Graham's still working on board, and Alex has stayed on as baby doc, so things are fairly stable now."

Rachel grinned at the term *baby doc*, a label used for junior doctors working on board cruise ships. She remembered Alex, an Italian doctor in his early thirties whose full name was Alessandro Romano. "Are the nurses the same ones? I hardly saw the senior nurse. Can't remember her name."

"Gwen Sumner, yes, she seems to have settled in for the long haul, and Bernard and Brigitte will also be there. I'm glad because we get on so well." At that moment, Sarah's phone rang. "Excuse me."

She pressed the call answer icon. "Hello? Oh hello, Bernard, we were just talking about you. What? Oh no! Will he be alright?

Okay. Yes, I can do that. I should be there soon – hang on a minute, Bernard—

How long before we arrive, Mr Prince?"

"We're approximately an hour away," answered Rachel's father.

"Should be there in about an hour." Sarah went back to the phone call. "Missed you too – will do. See you soon." Sarah frowned as she put her mobile away. "He sends his love."

"What's happened?"

"Brigitte's been called home to Dijon. Her father's been involved in a car accident and needs an operation, but he won't go for surgery until he's seen Brigitte."

"Will he be alright?"

"Bernard says they are not sure, and Brigitte left in a hurry early this morning, so I guess we won't know for a while."

"Oh dear, poor Brigitte. I was looking forward to meeting her properly on this cruise, but I hope he'll be alright. Does that mean you'll be short staffed?"

"Yes and no. There's a new nurse the cruise line has called out of induction so she'll get a baptism of fire. Sorry for the pun, Mr Prince. I'll need to help Bernard in the passenger lounge today, though, so won't be easing myself back into things."

"Oh well. At least they found a replacement in plenty of time," Rachel's father said.

"Yes, that's true, and you don't have to worry about me. I'll be happy in my lap of luxury," agreed Rachel.

"You mean in the gym!"

They all chuckled. Rachel felt inwardly disappointed as she had hoped to spend some quality time with Sarah, but understood that her friend had a job to do.

"That's all you need, first day back," she said light-heartedly.

"I guessed we might be busy, but wasn't expecting things to kick off quite so soon. At least Bernard will still be there."

"Is Bernard the nurse from the Philippines?" asked Rachel's father.

"Yes, he's from Manila. At least I've just enjoyed three months lounging around. I'm sorry I didn't see more of Rachel, but Mum misses me terribly when I'm away and she had sixteen trips planned for when I got home." Sarah rolled her eyes.

Rachel had also missed seeing Sarah and wanted to talk through what had happened with the stabbing and threats made by Tansley, but that would have to wait. They had spoken briefly when they'd snatched time together, but not since the threats.

The car arrived at Southampton docks and Rachel's dad drove towards the cruise terminals.

"You can take the lane on the right, Mr Prince. I'll show my crew pass to the security guards," directed Sarah.

They bypassed queues of traffic already building and pulled up outside the terminal where the magnificent *Coral Queen* was docked. Rachel got out of the car and showed her ticket to the port side crew. The crew quickly and efficiently removed the luggage from the car and stacked Rachel's on to mega-sized luggage trolleys.

Sarah showed her crew pass and grabbed her suitcase and bags before turning to Rachel. "I'll catch you later, Rachel. I need to walk along the port side to the crew entrance. Thank you for the lift, Mr Prince."

"You're welcome. Have a good journey – I'll tell your parents I delivered you safely."

Rachel hugged Sarah and then turned to her father. "Thanks, Dad. Here in plenty of time! Perhaps as well we left early." She kissed him on the cheek.

"Bye, Rachel. Stay safe, we'll see you soon."

Rachel watched her dad drive away before turning and entering the passenger terminal. This year she had a VIP passenger ticket and should be able to bypass the queues and go straight on board. She smiled, thinking of last year when she was a cruise virgin. She now felt like a seasoned cruiser and was looking forward to shopping in New York. Despite the slight setback with Sarah, she was determined to enjoy herself and take full advantage of the opportunity.

Bring it on.

Chapter 4

So much for boarding quickly, thought Rachel, finding herself jammed behind a sizeable fractious party checking in via the VIP entrance. Rachel watched the crowd advancing slowly ahead. They were speaking a foreign language that sounded Eastern European, but it wasn't clear where exactly until she made out a few words of Russian. A large Russian population had based itself in Leeds, and police personnel who wanted to go up through the ranks were encouraged to learn at least one other language, so Rachel had picked up a smattering of Russian. It helped if the suspects didn't realise they might be understood.

The group moved through security at a snail's pace with many demonstrating their displeasure. An English man, clearly the tour guide for the increasingly disgruntled group, worked his way through the crowd, explaining they would need to co-operate fully with security up ahead to speed up the process.

When he spotted Rachel, he asked, "Would you like to go ahead, Miss? We might be a while."

"If the party doesn't mind, then yes, please – otherwise I am happy to wait."

The guide spoke in fluent Russian to another man who appeared to be in charge to check whether it was okay to let her through first.

The man answered, "*Da*."

"My brilliant command of Russian tells me that was a yes," said Rachel.

The man acknowledged her with a smile. "Follow me, and I will take you to the front of the line." He had obviously picked up some

American colloquialisms as well as Russian. The British rarely use the term 'a line' for a queue.

Rachel followed him through the crowd. He looked aged late thirties. Short in stature, around five foot six, he was of slim build with thinning brown hair and slightly bulging dark-blue eyes. Wearing a grey suit with a white shirt and blue tie, he also wore a badge stating his first name, *Thomas,* and his company, *Ronson Tours.* As a policewoman, Rachel had processed this information automatically within seconds. It was all part of the rigorous training from probationer days.

Rachel felt eyes boring through the back of her head as the crowd parted to allow her through. The women looked around ten years younger than the majority of their male counterparts and were lavishly dressed in expensive-looking designer clothes. Most of them also wore high heels. Rachel guessed from previous experience that the long walk up through the tunnels and gangways to board the ship might cause some of the women to regret their choice of footwear.

"Here we are, Miss." Thomas stopped at the front of the queue.

"Thank you," said Rachel, smiling at him sympathetically, acknowledging he could be in for a long day. The group members were becoming increasingly boisterous the longer they had to wait.

"There is a problem with one of the scanners," Thomas explained.

Rachel was called forward by a security guard to pass through the entrance. Once through the scanners, she heard a huge roar of approval. The second scanner was now working and Thomas's group moved through.

Rachel walked uphill along the enclosed makeshift gangway, surrounded by members of the Russian tour group, barely understanding a word as they chattered away happily.

Not that good at Russian then.

They looked wealthy and walked with an air of self-indulgent superiority that suggested they were used to getting what they wanted. The mixture of strong but expensive perfume was at times overwhelming in the enclosed space – although a scent of Estée Lauder's *White Linen* felt more reassuring as it was her mum's favourite.

Once on board, Rachel was offered a glass of champagne. Taking a flute from the waiter, she ambled towards one of the food courts open to passengers, her stomach complaining over missed breakfast. There were a few others who had also boarded the ship early milling around – most people were not meant to arrive until after midday, although Sarah explained that the vast majority arrived earlier. As long as the disembarkation of passengers from the previous cruise had gone smoothly, people were allowed to board to wait in one of the many communal areas until their rooms were ready.

After eating a shrimp salad and finishing the champagne, Rachel moved into one of the lounges and sat people-watching for a short time. The Russian group gradually filed through, and Rachel spent some time counting them, getting to twenty before estimating it was a group of around thirty people in total, with stragglers still making their way on board. After becoming tired of watching them, she texted her father to let him know she was safe before calling Carlos.

"Hello, Rachel, I miss you already." Carlos answered the phone immediately.

"You don't see me that often and I only left you yesterday. You can't be missing me."

"Yes, I know, beautiful, but it's different because you're leaving the country."

"I'll be back before you realise I've gone." She smiled as his landline rang in the background.

"Sorry, darling, better answer this. I'm expecting a call – enjoy your trip and think of me. *Ciao.*"

"Bye, see you soon."

Rachel smiled again like a Cheshire cat after the call ended. They were not at the 'I love you' stage yet, but Carlos really had been a godsend over the past year. He was supportive without being suffocating and allowed her to be herself, something that her ex had never done. She hadn't grasped how stifling that relationship had been until she was able to look back objectively. Carlos was not at all stifling; rather, he was romantic while allowing her space. He had been her rock over the past six months and she wanted to reciprocate after this holiday.

Rachel spotted Sarah passing through the lounge, now dressed in an officer's uniform, heading towards the gangway leading to the passenger terminal. Sarah smiled and waved before making her way briskly towards the exit. Rachel stood up to stretch her legs and almost bumped into someone.

"Here you are again."

The voice came from behind and she turned to see Thomas standing there. She looked down because of their height difference.

"I'm not sure I introduced myself, my name's Thomas."

"Yes, I know, you're wearing a name badge. I'm Rachel," she replied.

Thomas looked down at his lapel sheepishly. "Whoops, I forget I'm wearing it most of the time. Are you travelling alone, Rachel?" His enquiry appeared sincere rather than a chat-up line, although it wasn't always easy to tell the difference.

"Not really. I have a friend who works on board and I've met a few of the crew before."

"If you would like to join any of our activities, please do. No offence, but a pretty face would brighten up my days. This could be a challenging cruise."

Coming from anyone else, this line would have annoyed Rachel, but Thomas appeared to be earnest in his request, although he might have worded it differently. She was used to men complimenting her beauty, but often wished they would just talk to her without bringing it up all the time.

"I'll bear that in mind, as long as you don't mention the pretty face bit again," she said firmly.

"Okay, it's a deal. Here's a list of our activities. Please join us for any of the ones that take your fancy."

Rachel took the piece of paper and looked at the long list, feeling rather sorry for Thomas. "Surely you're not expected to attend all these!"

"No," he chuckled, "just the ones with the initials *TG* next to them. Thomas Gabriel, at your service, ma'am. The cruise director has allocated members of the entertainment crew to run a lot of them. My job's just to keep the guests happy so they don't fall out or get bored." He leaned closer. "They are stinking rich – one of them is a Russian oligarch," he whispered. "There's also a diplomat among them, a group of businessmen, and lots of WAGs. I don't know who's who myself yet."

Rachel knew WAGs referred to *wives and girlfriends*. It would be intriguing to learn more about this interesting group; she was wavering, wondering what to ask Thomas. At that moment, one of the women called him away.

This cruise is going to be interesting besides relaxing, Rachel thought as the announcement for passengers to make their way to their staterooms whenever they were ready came over the ship's speakers. Opting to head up to her luxury suite on deck fifteen, she tucked the programme away in her handbag, deciding to look at it later.

I might well take Thomas up on his offer.

Chapter 5

Sarah and Bernard checked the passenger health questionnaires and were satisfied the results raised no concerns about a potential norovirus (Norwalk) outbreak. They returned to the ship through security, and on the way Bernard brought her up-to-speed with all the latest crew gossip.

"Guess what? I found out why Gwen asked for a transfer from the last ship," he boasted.

"Okay, I suppose you're going to tell me – so why?"

"She had a fliiiiing with the chief medical officer. Well, a bit more than a fling, actually, on Gwen's side. When she realised it was going nowhere and he wouldn't be leaving his wife, she worried about losing her job if news got out, so asked for a transfer."

"Wow! That I would never have imagined. Gwen seems so quiet and demure. Poor woman. And how – may I ask – did you manage to wheedle that information out of her?"

"Stingers!" Bernard looked overly pleased with himself. A stinger was his own special mix of spirits, a recipe he kept a closely guarded secret, refusing to tell anyone what went into the toxic cocktail. Sarah had sampled a glass once but, after the hideous burning sensations akin to swallowing acid had set her throat on fire, had vowed never to touch one again. The only recognisable spirit in the drink was vodka, but she had no idea what else it contained.

"I'm surprised she's still alive."

"Now, now – you know how everybody loves my special cocktail."

"Not exactly everyone," Sarah protested.

"Okay, not everyone," Bernard continued his bragging. "But ever since then, Gwen's been putty in my hands."

He rubbed his hands gleefully. Sarah looked sceptical – unable to imagine the Australian senior nurse being putty in anyone's hands.

"You wish!" She nudged Bernard good-naturedly.

They arrived at the medical centre in good humour. Gwen greeted Sarah, who found it difficult to conceal a smirk when looking at the boss.

"Welcome back, Sarah."

"Thank you, it's good to be back. I'm so sorry to hear about Brigitte's father."

"Yes, it's a sad situation, but let's hope for the best."

Sarah noted Gwen seemed happier and more settled than when they'd worked together previously. *Perhaps Bernard's stingers had a wider effect than expected.*

"Where's the new girl?" asked Bernard, mischievously. As he did so a tall, dour looking woman, skinny with cropped light-brown curly hair, dark green eyes and a wannabe attractive freckled face, entered the office. The woman's appearance was just how Sarah imagined the girl *George* from the *Famous Five* books would have looked, except more austere and a lot older – mid-to-late thirties, Sarah surmised.

"This is Lauren, our new nurse who has stepped in at short notice to help us out," announced Gwen. "Lauren's from Connecticut in the United States, but has been working in Africa for the past two years. Prior to that, she worked in emergency rooms – casualty to you Brits, Sarah. Lauren, meet Sarah and Bernard, your new colleagues."

Sarah smiled and attempted to shake hands. The other woman took the proffered hand, but dropped it again all too quickly.

"Hi, welcome aboard, good to have you with us. Bernard's a tease, so don't let him get to you," Sarah said.

"Hi," said Lauren, not offering any other words. Sarah looked at Bernard for help.

"Yes, I'm Bernard, at your service, ma'am. Anything you need to know – I'm your man." Lauren did smile at Bernard – almost flirtatiously, Sarah observed.

Strange girl, I do hope this won't be a difficult colleague. Ship life's too confined to work with troublesome personalities.

Gwen interrupted Sarah's train of thought. "Lauren's already met Graham and Alex, but will need a tour of the ship. I've explained the uniform policy and put her in Brigitte's room for now. The ship is full to the brim and we have six full days at sea, so I don't need to tell you how busy we'll be. Lauren is very experienced, so once she's familiar with the ship and its procedures, she won't need babysitting."

Thank goodness for that.

Bernard groaned in response to Gwen's announcement regarding the number of passengers on board. "It's been hard without you, Sarah. Now we have to do without Brigitte. Sorry, no offence." He looked at Lauren, who appeared to be somewhere else. Sarah wasn't even sure the woman had heard what Bernard said.

Gwen ended the meeting. "Meds are all stocked up – surgery starts straight after the emergency passenger drill. Bernard, can you show Lauren around the ship and explain where to go and what to do when on call? You're on call, Sarah. You've had quite enough holiday."

She laughed. This was the first time Sarah had seen Gwen laugh out loud, and it made her look much younger and more attractive. The senior nurse was older than the rest of them – early forties, Sarah thought – and had always played the congenial but aloof boss. She never joined in socially with the rest of the team, but considering the background Sarah had just discovered, it was not hard to understand why. Pleased that Gwen seemed relaxed, because it occurred to Sarah that Lauren might not know the meaning of the word, she felt at home already. She'd recently turned twenty-six, and her mother hoped she'd settle down once the travel bug was out of her system, but there was no hurry to comply.

Shortly after their gathering, once Bernard and Lauren had left, Graham came rushing through the entrance to the medical centre, beaming, and enveloped her in a bear hug.

"Sarah, it's good to have you back. We were almost the *A Team* again, weren't we, Sister?" He winked at Gwen.

"Almost." There was that laugh again.

Oh, this is going to be a great cruise. Perhaps Lauren will chill out once she gets used to us all and we can have some fun.

"What do you make of our new girl?"

"Only just met her, she seems fine," replied Sarah, tactfully.

"It might take a little while to adjust – the poor woman's been working in emergency hospitals in Mali where there's a humanitarian crisis. I expect Lauren's seen things hard to imagine, but by all accounts, she is a very capable nurse. I called the lead doctor from the aid organisation and he spoke highly of her capabilities."

Graham Bentley, the chief medical officer, always saw the best in people. An attractive man in his late fifties, he reminded Sarah of her own father. Standing at six foot tall, he kept himself fit, and the only signs of ageing were a few lines around his eyes and a slight paunch. Sarah immediately had guilt pangs about the negative opinion she'd already formed about her new colleague and determined to be a friend to Lauren.

"Well, catch you all later, I have an officers' drill to attend after the passenger drill. Alex is doing evening surgery with you. Call me if you need me." Graham left the office, chipper as ever, with a bounce in his step.

Sarah felt even happier to be back on board the *Coral Queen* after Graham's affectionate display, although it wouldn't be the same without Brigitte. It had been great to have a holiday, but there was nothing like nursing – she loved the job and preferred working on a cruise ship to anywhere else.

It was back to reality now, though. No sooner had Gwen handed over the emergency radio than a call came through to attend to a crew member in engineering who was reportedly light-headed. Sarah made her way down a deck to the mainly metallic area from where the main engines rumbled.

The man she had been called to attend to was Russian and didn't speak much English, but fortunately he had a friend to interpret. The other man, who introduced himself as Erik, shouted above the noise.

"He has light head for past few hours. He doesn't speak much English, but understands what you say." Sarah suspected Erik was Russian too. Knowing the patient's name already from the call out information, she was ready to carry out an assessment.

"Do you have any pain, Mr Popov?" Sarah also shouted.

Popov shook his head and said something to his friend.

"He says, please to call him Jefgeny."

"Okay, Jefgeny."

Jefgeny looked pale even though it was difficult to examine him properly with the dim lighting in this part of engineering. Sarah checked his vital signs and blood-pressure; all seemed normal.

"Do you have any chest pain?"

Jefgeny shook his head.

"Is the room spinning or do you just feel weak?"

The man spoke in Russian again and Erik replied, "No spinning, just light head and weakness."

"When did you last eat, Jefgeny?" she asked.

Jefgeny again spoke in Russian and Erik explained that he had not eaten since breakfast. "We have been fixing a problem with pumps," Erik said.

"Well, unless you want him to pass out, I suggest you send someone to get him some food and a hot drink with plenty of sugar." Sarah reached into the medical bag and handed Jefgeny some dextrose tablets. "These should help you feel better for now. I'm making you an appointment to attend surgery at 10am tomorrow for a blood test." She looked at Erik. "Does he understand?"

They both nodded. "*Da*," Jefgeny replied.

Sarah was satisfied it was nothing immediately serious – the engineering crew worked long hours in cramped conditions, and although it was difficult to be certain in the dim lights, she suspected Jefgeny might be anaemic, which would throw up other health concerns.

Dragging the emergency bag around obstacles, she felt every step, a stark reminder of how heavy it could be, but it had to accompany her when she was on call. She'd also forgotten how limited the space was in parts of engineering. This was the worst place on the ship when she was trying to treat people in a serious emergency because the corridors were so narrow, and parts were below the waterline, illuminated only by artificial light. Some areas could only be accessed via makeshift steps akin to loft ladders, and then through tight hatches, creating access difficulties at the best of times.

In this part of engineering, there were huge pipes and little space. It was similar to working on a submarine, she imagined, but a lot louder. Every sound was exaggerated, echoing backwards and forwards from the metal walls and floors.

Sarah decided to take the crew lift back up to deck two and the medical centre. Bernard and Lauren arrived back shortly afterwards, and she acknowledged them while continuing to restock her emergency bag.

Bernard spoke. "Busy already?"

"Yes, a Russian crewman in engineering, with low blood sugar. Should be okay, but I've asked him to come to clinic tomorrow morning for blood tests. He seemed pale – not that I could be certain in the dim lighting."

"I know what you mean. We've just come from engineering, met a few of the crew – everyone seemed alright, so you must have worked your magic."

"This is a huge ship, but I expect I'll soon find my way around." Lauren spoke for the first time, smiling at Bernard. Sarah watched the exchange with interest as Bernard seemed oblivious to the potential overtures of this rather strange new colleague.

"It takes a while. I kept getting lost during my first few weeks, particularly when on call, but we're here if you need help, and—"

"Can I see your notes?" asked Lauren, cutting Sarah off mid-sentence. Sarah handed her the written version of the records that would be typed on to the computerised medical system as soon as possible.

"Crew members receive free treatment courtesy of the cruise line, but you still have to account for every item used so that fresh supplies can be ordered when we're next in port."

Showing a sudden surge of interest, Lauren asked to see how the notes were added to the computer. Sarah brought up Jefgeny Popov's record and noted that he was listed as a US citizen, aged forty with no significant medical history. It seemed odd he didn't speak English, Sarah thought, but maybe he had only recently been granted citizenship.

"He may have succumbed to the scourge of cruise ship life, the habit of drinking too much alcohol – a trap many of the crew fall into," said Sarah while typing in the record. Lauren spent her time glancing at the record before her interest fell away as quickly as it had appeared.

The ship had set sail while Sarah was in engineering. They heard the announcement calling all passengers and crew to muster stations for the emergency drill.

"Here we go." Sarah smiled at the others as they made their way up to the passenger decks, dragging the emergency bag behind her, just in case.

Chapter 6

Rachel danced into the suite, twirling round and round. Her exuberance increased as she remembered the complimentary internet access, an obvious bonus because she could email Carlos while travelling. She grinned from ear to ear every time Carlos came to mind.

A knock at the door interrupted her blissful reverie. She opened it, delighted to discover the smart butler from the previous cruise would be attending to her. They had met after the captain had upgraded her for a few days towards the end of the cruise. Mario was from El Salvador and sounded Spanish.

Not surprising as Spanish is the national language of El Salvador.

"Hello, Miss Rachel." He entered, carrying her suitcase and other baggage. "It's good to meet you again. This year you will have relaxing cruise, yes?"

"That's the plan, Mario." The tall, thin butler was immaculately dressed with short, slick black hair that was well groomed, waves trained to be flat and shiny with the help of hair gel. After asking about his family, who lived in San Salvador, Rachel enquired, "Who is in the other suite?" There were two luxury suites, attended to by a single butler, at the rear of deck fifteen, one on port side and one on the starboard side. Rachel was occupying the starboard suite.

"That one is occupied by rich Russian and girlfriend. The whole corridor on port side to midships is occupied by Russian tour party," Mario said in broken English. "They wanted your suite too for diplomat but had to settle for superior balcony. They didn't want to be on different decks."

"Oh." Rachel pondered this information, not that keen about the possibility of bumping into Thomas regularly, but she was reassured he would at least use the opposite corridor. "Do you know which room their tour guide is in?"

"No, miss, but I can ask Grace, their stateroom attendant, when we meet later on, if you would like me to."

"Yes please, we met earlier – I would rather not bump into him too often on this deck, if it's possible to avoid it."

"Don't worry, Miss Rachel, I will find out. Is there anything you would like at the moment, Miss Rachel?"

"No, thank you. I'm sure you have plenty to do with your Russian guest."

Mario raised his eyebrows and shrugged his shoulders with a *c'est la vie* smile, leaving her to unpack.

The phone rang in the room. "Hello."

Sarah's voice could be heard among clanging in the background. "Hello, Rachel. Are you all settled in?"

"Yes, just unpacking. What about you?"

"Great to be back, but busy already. I can meet you after surgery this evening, if that suits?"

"Yes, that would be wonderful. Name the place and time and I'll be there."

"Jazz bar around eight o'clock?"

"Yep, see you then."

They said goodbye and hung up.

Rachel looked around, admiring the luxury suite. There was a huge bedroom with a queen-sized bed, a separate sitting room, a large bathroom with bathtub and shower. The rooms were elaborate, but tastefully decorated in pastels with exquisite artwork hanging on the walls. A large flat-screen TV was suspended above her bed, and another one hung on the wall of the sitting room. A welcome bottle of champagne sat on ice, but that could wait for another day.

After unpacking, Rachel walked out on to the balcony overlooking the dark-blue sea behind the ship to watch their departure, and she became lost, admiring the linear patterns made by the surf in the aftermath of the gigantic vessel cutting it apart. They stretched back for miles. The ship carried over three thousand passengers and two thousand eight hundred crew. Sarah called it a small city.

Rachel watched Southampton becoming a dot in the distance as they sailed away. The announcement came over the ship's loudspeakers, requesting passengers attend the compulsory emergency drill. Rachel left the room, but not before taking a quick glance into the rear corridor to check it was clear. She didn't mind coming across Thomas later, but would rather do it on her own terms until her suspicions that he was harmless were confirmed.

After dinner, Rachel sauntered along to the jazz bar where she and Sarah had arranged to meet up. The sound of a lively jazz band filled the air, and the room was already filling up with cheerful passengers. Her friend sat at a small round table by a window.

Sarah looked elegant, even in her officer's uniform. Rachel noticed she was armed with the large emergency bag and a glass of lemonade sat on the table.

"You're on call already then?"

Sarah stood and hugged her. "Yes, I drew the short straw, but can't complain because the others have been on call regularly over the past few months. Apologies in advance, I might get called away at any moment. We've already been busy." Sarah lowered her voice. "I've ordered you a glass of red, but as you can see, I'm on the soft stuff."

Rachel didn't ask any questions about her work as they were surrounded by other passengers. A waiter appeared, bringing Rachel's wine and setting it on the table with a small bowl of nibbles. Rachel thanked him.

"Thanks. I'll take any time I can get with you and be glad." She smiled at Sarah. "Have you eaten?"

"Yes, Raggie, the medical team steward, brought us food at the end of surgery. I think you met him last year. Did you have a luxurious dinner?"

"I did meet him, a lovely man from what I remember, and yes, my dinner was delicious. The chefs excelled themselves."

"What are your table companions like?"

"They seem pleasant enough, but won't be able to live up to last year's." Rachel grinned, remembering the lovely people she had met on the previous cruise. "There's a family of four who chatted amongst themselves, an older Canadian couple in their seventies, myself, and a quiet elderly man who's seated next to me."

Sarah laughed out loud. "I suspect Carlos phoned the maître d' to ensure that was the case!" Rachel joined in with her friend's laughter. "I'm on call until tomorrow night, so we won't be able to meet up tomorrow. Will you be alright?"

"Yes, don't worry about me. I'll go to the chapel service first thing, and afterwards will find some mischief to get up to. In fact, I met a tour guide leading a Russian group. He gave me their itinerary with an open invitation to join in with any of the activities."

"Oh, lucky you – how do you do it? Is this tour guide hoping for anything in return?" Sarah's brow furrowed.

"No, I don't believe he is – he seems harmless enough. He said he needs a distraction from the tour group. In fact, they're all on the same deck as me, but thankfully on the opposite side. A Russian oligarch's in the other luxury suite, with the rest of his party filling the rooms in that corridor."

"Sounds like you will have an interesting time. We're aware of that group because they've already insisted that Graham check up on one woman's blood pressure tonight. Three of them have also forgotten to bring prescribed medication with them, so he'll need to sort that out too. He might have his work cut out on this voyage."

"Poor Dr Bentley," said Rachel. "From what I witnessed as they were boarding, they could be quite a demanding group of people."

"Oh well, it makes for interesting cruising – never a dull moment," sighed Sarah. "Graham will have met worse and takes it all in his stride."

"Well, I will take the kind Thomas up on his offer, having taken a quick glance through their itinerary. They are doing a tour of engineering tomorrow. I'd love to explore life below the waterline, as you call it!"

"Small world, I've been down to engineering myself this afternoon." At that moment, Sarah's bleep went off, and she reached for her radio. "Sorry, Rachel, I have to go – speak tomorrow." She walked away, talking into the radio.

"Bye, hope it's not too busy," said Rachel, deciding to finish her glass of red wine before heading back upstairs to her stateroom.

Day 1

Chapter 7

"Jefgeny Popov!" Sarah called the name out in the medical centre waiting room. No-one came forward. "You can lead a horse to water, but you can't make it drink," she murmured to herself as she retired to the clinic room to look up the next patient on the list.

Surgery flew past as she saw a mixture of passengers and crew with various ailments and injuries. Sarah was dog-tired after being up most of the night on calls to passengers with minor scrapes, mostly due to too much alcohol. One lady called her out at 11pm having forgotten to bring her blood pressure tablets, so Sarah had supplied her with a pack from the treatment room. Typical first night calls, really. Medication given to passengers was recorded in a logbook, and then the cruise line charged passengers or their insurance companies for both the medicine and the consultation with a doctor or nurse on board.

With morning surgery finished, Sarah joined the other medical staff in Gwen's office for coffee.

"Well, that was a busy one." Graham joined them after seeing the final passenger attending surgery. "Is everyone okay?"

They all responded in the affirmative.

"Busy, but not complicated," said Bernard. "Lauren managed every condition without my help. I just sat back and admired her remarkable expertise." He smiled at the new girl.

"That's not quite true, I needed your help at least three times." She grinned back at him.

"Good to see you settling in," cut in Graham before the mutual admiration society had the chance to continue.

"Thank you, sir," Lauren responded.

"No need for the sir here. Call me Graham when we are staff only and Dr Bentley in front of passengers and other crew."

"Yes, sir – sorry, Graham."

Sarah was kicking herself for finding it so difficult to take to Lauren, so she made an attempt to get to know her. "Why don't you join us for lunch in the company dining room, Lauren?" she invited.

"Yes do," added Bernard. "Are you guys coming?" he asked the rest of the team.

"I'll be working on accounts – the bills are piling up already," answered Gwen.

"I've got to meet with the captain to give him an update," said Graham. "Alex, you need to deal with that problem downstairs."

"What problem?" enquired Sarah.

"A crewman was found dead in his cabin this morning. Poor fellow, looks like he had a heart attack in his sleep. Alex confirmed death first thing and called me. We left him there until we could bring him quietly to the morgue."

Sarah baulked at the reminder that they had a morgue on board the ship.

"Oh dear, that's sad. Who was it?"

"The man worked in engineering, according to the roommate. He hasn't needed a doctor since boarding ship. Medical application form unremarkable and pre-cruise check-ups were fine."

All crew members, including doctors and nurses, had to have a medical evaluation on land, which included lengthy form-filling, blood tests, X-rays and a physical examination, before stepping foot on a cruise ship. Medical evaluations cost a small fortune in some countries, but it was important from the cruise line's perspective to have healthy employees on board ship because Queen Cruises accepted responsibility for funding the medical care of the crew, and repatriation on account of illness or death, once they were aboard.

"What's his name?" enquired a concerned Sarah. "I met a man called Jefgeny Popov in engineering yesterday and made an appointment for him to come to clinic this morning, but he didn't show."

"The dead guy was called Erik Marinov," Alex answered, "but it was a roommate called Jefgeny who found him. They shared the room, but Jefgeny worked until 2am after swapping shifts with another crewman. When he got back, he assumed his friend was sleeping. On discovering him dead this morning, he called for a medic. After I confirmed Mr Marinov was dead, Jefgeny was in considerable distress, but I couldn't get much out of him. I'm just heading back down to deck C now."

"Erik interpreted for Jefgeny yesterday – he looked fit and healthy. Something worried me about Jefgeny's health, not Erik's. That explains why he didn't show up this morning. Can I join you, Alex? I'd like to find out how Jefgeny is."

"Yes sure. Come on, let's go. Do you want to come too, Lauren?"

"No thanks, I'll keep Bernard company."

Sarah raised her eyebrows, but Lauren didn't notice. Bernard shrugged his shoulders behind Lauren's back and grinned. Sarah put her tongue out at him and followed Alex down to the decks below the waterline where crew members had their cramped berths. The berths were still comparative luxury for some of the crew compared to what they left behind in their home countries. Sarah appreciated her good fortune, having a room above the waterline as an officer.

There were many decks below, and they walked down three sets of stairs before arriving at the right one. As always, Sarah noticed how the air got stuffier the further down they went. Stale cigarette smoke pervaded the air, making it even worse.

"Blooming cigarettes, I hate coming down here," muttered Alex in a voice barely audible. The bass beat of loud music emanated from some of the rooms where Sarah assumed crew, who worked nights or were on breaks, were enjoying down-time.

They walked single file as the corridors narrowed.

"I can never get used to the noise down here. How can anyone fall asleep?" asked Sarah.

"Sorry, can't hear."

Ignoring Alex's joke, Sarah continued her rant. "Music, if you can call it that, one might manage, but not the engine noises, all these vibrations and other creaks and groans." As if on cue, the rumbling sound of metal assaulted their ears, along with an irritating constant humming noise that Sarah certainly did not find soothing. The din reverberated off the surrounding metal, causing every sound to echo back at them.

"I do know what you mean, but I presume it's sheer exhaustion after twelve to fourteen hour shifts. It's probably no worse than living next to a busy motorway, I guess."

"If you say so." Sarah didn't sound convinced. She couldn't believe how negative she was feeling. "There's no way I would have renewed my contract if I'd had to live down here."

When they arrived at the cabin where the body of Erik had remained while morning surgery took place, she couldn't help thinking how tragic it would be to die in a small, airless cabin. With barely enough room for the two of them – made worse by the dismal darkness – Sarah held her breath as the pungent smells of body odour, dirty washing and stale cigarette smoke invaded her olfactory system. Added to this was the familiar, fetid smell of death all health professionals become accustomed to early in their training. Without a porthole, the cabin seemed unusually dark, despite the light having been left on. The light bulb barely broke through the shadows.

Alex took a quick look around. "We're safe to move him now. Most of the crew are at work – we'll put him on the stretcher and move him to the morgue. I'm glad he slept on the bottom bunk. Poor man looks heavy."

Sarah was hardly listening. She noticed Erik's bags had already been packed and placed in a corner. She looked at the bulky form of Erik, lying on the bottom bunk. Although his skin had taken on an ashen appearance, she recognised him as the man who, just yesterday, had appeared tough and robust when interpreting for his companion.

"He looked so healthy," she murmured.

Alex put a hand on Sarah's shoulder; she was welling up. *What on earth's the matter with me?*

"Graham and I did search for drugs earlier, but discovered nothing. There are no injuries or suicide note. Everything points to him dying in his sleep. Graham agreed that cause of death was probably a heart attack. The security team have been through the place while we've been in surgery, and they too detected nothing untoward."

"Have his family been informed?" Sarah asked.

"Not yet. We've checked his details, and he has a sister in Russia, but no relatives in the USA, despite being an American citizen. The details in his personnel file are sparse, according to the chief security officer. Someone in head office will inform the next of kin."

Sarah sighed. "How tragic, no-one to mourn his loss. Will there be a post-mortem?"

"Unlikely – too expensive. The death appears to be natural causes, and with no close relatives to demand answers, he'll probably be cremated in America."

With no sign of Jefgeny, and feeling like she needed to get a grip of herself, Sarah wanted to get away. "Do you need me to help you get him on to the trolley?"

They heard voices in the corridor and two security guards appeared.

"No thanks, these officers are just in time." Alex turned to them. "Come on, guys, let's move this poor man out of here."

Sarah left the crew quarters, a little overwhelmed. Only her second day back after a long break, and she was already tired from lack of sleep. She'd only met Erik briefly, but his death had come as a shock.

Sarah decided to return to surgery and catch up with paperwork from the morning; she had lost her appetite. Gwen was still in her office with the door open.

"What are you doing back here?" she called.

"I want to finish the paperwork and log items used this morning before taking a break. To be honest, I found it all a bit depressing downstairs."

"You'll get back into the swing of it. You've been thrown in at the deep end, haven't you?"

"I guess so. It was a busy shift so I must be feeling it more than I should."

"If it's any consolation, we all hate it when crew members die on board. We're like a family, even though we don't know everyone, so it's hard to take. But sudden deaths happen on ships as well as on land."

"I know, it's just that he doesn't seem to have anyone to grieve his loss, and his bags were all packed, ready to go to the purser's office, as if he never existed." Her eyes filled up again.

"Don't let it get to you. From what I can gather, he had half a dozen close friends who will miss him and grieve for him like family."

Gwen was right. Sarah thought about it and realised she was overreacting. Of course his friends would miss him.

"That reminds me, I must track down Jefgeny Popov. He still needs blood tests, and I think the loss of his roommate will have upset him."

Sarah walked into a clinic room and pulled up Jefgeny's records on her computer, glad of the distraction.

Chapter 8

The chapel was well attended, Rachel thought, considering it was nine o'clock in the morning and people were on holiday. It was to be an interdenominational service conducted by a visiting Baptist minister from a church in New York City.

A buxom bleach-blonde woman in her sixties sat next to Rachel. "I only came to meet the captain," she whispered.

"He's not here," replied Rachel.

"Just my luck," she grunted, but stayed anyway.

The pastor explained how he got to cruise regularly for free, in return for performing ministerial duties on board Queen Cruises. "Marriages," he explained, "are almost always performed by the captain or his deputy, though."

"Blast, looks like I'll have to find hubby number five." The woman next to Rachel nudged her.

"Number five?" Rachel mouthed.

"That's the way to do it, dear, hitch, fleece and run!"

Rachel liked this rather vociferous woman, but wasn't sure whether to believe her. If the diamonds adorning her hands and neck were anything to go by, she could well be telling the truth.

With her attention back on the service, Rachel found the bubbly minister made the whole thing fun and his jokes made her laugh. Not quite as much as those of the woman next to her, though. She didn't know all the hymns and choruses, but joined in as well as she could.

Feeling invigorated by the uplifting and entertaining hour, Rachel wandered over to the Voyager lounge where the Russian party would be meeting at 10am, prior to their tour of the engine room.

Recognising some of the men from embarkation, she was beginning to have second thoughts about gate-crashing, and was about to make a discreet exit when she was reassured by Thomas's entrance with a clipboard in hand. He waved enthusiastically, convincing her to join him and the gathering group.

Thomas spoke briefly in Russian to an unhappy looking man, who eventually moved away to join the others.

"Problems?" asked Rachel.

"Not really. A bit of jockeying for position among the ladies, apparently. Nothing too serious. One of the glamorous girlfriends is splitting the ladies off into a splinter group. There's quite a hierarchy among them, and the more senior ladies don't like it, so there might be a row brewing. I've told him, as long as there are no fisticuffs, there's nothing I can do about their internal squabbling, but I'll try to make sure they all enjoy themselves." Thomas grinned at Rachel. "Glad to see you took me up on my offer. It's good to have a pret… sorry, a friendly face."

"That's better, and thank you. I found it hard to resist a tour of the workings down below – it will be interesting to see how it all works."

"Personally, I'd rather be by the pool, but such is life." He sighed. "I need to check everyone is here and give them a tour badge to wear. Here's one for you." Thomas handed over a sticky blue badge with *Guest* printed on it and a pair of earmuffs, which she put around her neck. "We're just waiting for the chief engineer who will be taking us down. Come over, I'll introduce you – there are only ten of the group taking this tour."

Rachel followed Thomas over towards a group of six men who stopped talking as they arrived.

"This is Rachel, a fellow guest who will be joining us for the trip."

"Hello, we remember you from yesterday," said the tall man she had earmarked as the boss the day before. "Boris Stanislav – at your service, I look forward to getting to know you, Rachel."

A tall, well-built man with blond hair, Boris then turned to Thomas. "My father worked for government as naval submarine engineer, so I am very much looking forward to tour."

Rachel discerned an air of authority in Boris. Others in the group held back until they were invited to speak with him. She also noticed two burly men standing back, watching him continuously. One, short and bald with muscles the size of footballs protruding through a tailored black jacket, looked like a baddie straight out of a *Bond* movie. The other man was also powerfully built, but much taller with a head of thick dark-brown hair and a deep scar above his right eye, running the length of his face to his chin. They both looked menacing in a Mafioso way, but also slightly comical as they seemed to move in unison. However, Rachel thought they would make anyone think twice before approaching Boris without permission. She wondered if Boris would turn out to be the oligarch, deciding to ask Thomas when she had the chance.

"We are waiting for the chief engineering officer, Mr Stanislav, and then we'll get moving. There seems to be one missing from the tour group?"

"Who?" asked Boris.

"Mr Nikolai Stepanov."

"No problem, he is here now." They all turned and saw a man who appeared to be late-thirties, with jet black hair, moustache and bright, penetrating sky-blue eyes. He was strikingly handsome, in a dangerous-looking way.

The man nodded to Boris secretively. "Sorry I'm late, boss, I had to fill out some papers for the business we discussed last evening."

"Yes, yes. Never mind that now. This young lady is called Rachel, and she's joining us for the tour – a friend of Thomas."

The man took Rachel's hand in his and drew it up to his lips while holding her gaze. Rachel thought he had the most captivating smile ever, until she looked into frosty eyes and knew not to trust him.

"Charmed, I'm sure."

Rachel intuitively sensed the false charm; he made her skin crawl. She couldn't move her hand away quickly enough, subconsciously wiping it on the back of her trousers. Thomas came to her rescue by stepping between them and handing Nikolai a tour badge.

"Mr Stepanov, please wear this for our tour." He then took Rachel's arm and led her away. "Be careful of him," he whispered. "There's something about him that gives me the creeps."

"Me too. Thanks for the heads up, but I have no intention of letting Mr Stepanov anywhere near me."

"Good. Oh, at last!" Thomas turned in the direction of the door as two officers in bright, shiny whites entered the lounge. One of them, who Rachel assumed was the chief engineer, had four gold stripes on shoulder epaulettes.

"I'm not late, am I?" The officer looked at his watch.

"No, you're right on time," answered Thomas. "We are all present and correct with one extra." He gestured towards Rachel.

"Please could you let me have your name and stateroom number, madam?" Wearing a name badge with Steven Rafferty on it, the officer had a Scottish accent.

"It's Rachel Prince," she replied, surreptitiously showing him a card with her stateroom number on it while Thomas busied himself with Boris.

"Just a precaution, Miss Prince. Thank you." The officer moved away and spoke into his radio. Obviously receiving a satisfactory answer, he turned almost immediately and rejoined them.

"Good morning, everyone. Welcome aboard the *Coral Queen*. I am the chief engineering officer and this is one of my engineering officers, Ramjeet Singh. You will need to follow me at all times. Please be aware that conditions in some of the areas we will pass through are a bit cramped and you will need to walk in single file. Please do not leave the group at any time during this tour. I will lead the group and Officer Singh will bring up the rear. If you have any questions, I request that you ask them at the end of the tour and do not distract any of the workers from their jobs – if you want to get to New York on time." He laughed at his own joke and waited for the group to give a polite response. "Please wear the earmuffs you've been given when we enter engineering bays. Away we go then."

He headed towards the door with Boris hot on his heels and the group followed, along with the minders whom Rachel had subconsciously named Tweedledee and Tweedledum. Boris lost no time in picking the chief's brains.

Rachel walked with Thomas, but didn't want to ask too many questions while in such close proximity to the others. None of the Russian women had joined them.

"No women coming along?" she asked Thomas.

She recognised the voice of Nikolai, answering from behind. "Not a woman's tour, Miss Prince. Our women are attending beauty therapy this morning."

Rachel noted the veiled rebuke, but didn't take the bait.

"It's much noisier down here."

As they descended a number of different stairwells, so the sounds grew louder. Rachel slowed down in order to let Nikolai pass, but he stuck like glue. Unfortunately Thomas, distracted by others in the group, was unable to come to her aid again, being near the front and barely visible.

The corridors narrowed, and they moved along in single file so crew members could pass if they needed to. Tweedledee and Tweedledum remained close to Boris, who remained immediately behind the chief as far as Rachel managed to see, but an ever-increasing gap was emerging between the front and the rear of the group. Rachel sensed this was deliberate as the man immediately ahead of her was walking at a slower than natural pace.

The final member of the group ahead disappeared as he turned left. As Rachel's group turned the corner, she almost bumped into the man in front as he stopped abruptly. The straggler of the first group appeared to have been talking hurriedly to a crew member, but he stopped as soon as they arrived and continued on his way. The crew member, looking frightened, scurried past them as if he had seen a ghost.

"Hurry along, please," Officer Singh called from the rear, sounding frustrated. The man in front of her picked up his pace. Irritated by Nikolai getting ever closer behind her, she broke away.

They reached a pair of large metal doors, where Rachel finally made her escape from Nikolai, entering what appeared to be the main engine room. The noise sounded much louder as the engines thundered to new heights, making it difficult to hear anything. The humongous chains from the anchor that were wound around a huge metallic crank dominated the room and grabbed the group's attention. The deafening sound became worse, so the majority applied their ear protection.

The chief engineer tried saying something, and as the group gathered closer, he bellowed above the noise, but to no avail. Rachel gathered snippets about how the ship operated and how the anchor was winched up and down when needed – she didn't wish to imagine how loud that would be. Lots of crewmen in dark grey overalls continued their work around them. The room felt hot and airless while the dim lighting caused it to close in on the visitors, but Steven Rafferty seemed perfectly at home here. Apart from the fact he was raising his voice, you would not have known that he was standing in a partially lit tin can.

They moved through to a quieter room, larger and more spacious than the one they'd left. This room was filled with state-of-the-art computers and large glass dials. Officers sat or stood at various sub-stations around the room. The group could hear the Chief clearly now.

"This is the main engine room that makes the ship go and is the heart of the vessel." He spoke proudly. The room had a little natural light as a trickle of sunlight came through narrow windows near the ceiling. This area was above the waterline – just!

Before she'd learned very much at all, the tour ended hastily and the guests were escorted back to their original meeting place where the Chief answered various questions. Rachel excused herself, in need of fresh air. Having had her interest piqued, she mulled over what the connection might be between the frightened crew member and the man in the Russian party.

Chapter 9

After eating a hearty lunchtime salad from the buffet, Rachel took a stroll around deck fourteen above the lido deck where people splashed around in the many pools or sunbathed on loungers. The grill bar looked hectic and the smell of burgers and sausages made her hungry again. Rachel liked to keep herself in shape with regular gym workouts and jogging, so she walked past the enticing but deadly part of the deck.

Those things should come with health warnings.

Pausing at one of the side rails, she looked out at the deep blue Atlantic Ocean, appreciating that this would be her view for the next six days. She missed Carlos and decided to return to her room and email him.

"Rachel – where did you disappear to?" A voice arrested her in her tracks.

"Hello, Thomas. You were busy with your charges when I left, but I enjoyed the tour, thanks. I would have tracked you down later to extend my gratitude." Rachel felt embarrassed for not having remained behind to thank Thomas for his hospitality earlier. Her mind had been occupied by the puzzling encounter between the Russian and the crewman.

"Oh, that's no problem – my pleasure. The Chief made it informative, although a tad too cramped and noisy down there for my taste. Anyone who can work there for a full day with all that racket going on has my complete admiration and respect."

Rachel took the opportunity to quiz Thomas. "Yes, incredibly noisy. Did you see that crewman passing by? He might have known one of the men in your group."

"No, can't say I noticed anyone in particular. I suffer from claustrophobia, so was focussed on the person in front of me. Boris kept bombarding the Chief with questions after being specifically asked not to. I thought the Chief was very patient with him. No-one in this group would know a crewman, though, Rachel – they are poles apart. Every one of this party oozes success and wealth – even the bodyguards will be better off than we are."

He laughed. Rachel thought Thomas looked quite wealthy himself in his designer clothing alongside the Rolex on his left wrist, but didn't comment.

Thomas continued, "Maybe they heard someone speaking Russian, as I understood from the Chief there are quite a few Russians working in engineering."

Thomas didn't appear to be hiding anything, and what he said made sense. Why wouldn't they pass the time of day with one of their own countrymen?

"That's probably it," she answered. "A little mystery cleared up in my head."

"Where are you heading now, Rachel?"

"I'm going back to my room to email my boyfriend."

"A man should have known that one with such exceptional beauty would have a boyfriend somewhere."

"Thomas, stop saying things like that! If I suspect for one moment, you have ulterior motives for inviting me along to the tours—"

"Rachel, relax. I'm sorry, no offence intended. You don't need to worry about me." He looked around nervously, then whispered, "I'm gay – but would rather nobody in the tour party knew that. Russians can be very funny about these things, you know. They've not quite moved into the twenty-first century yet."

"Whoops – so sorry, Thomas, I didn't realise, and of course not. It's none of their business, or mine for that matter. I don't think you're being fair on Russians, though; I'm sure that many of them are very much in tune with the twenty-first century and would have no problem at all with your sexuality."

"Whatever." Thomas smiled cheekily and shrugged.

"Sorry again if I got the wrong end of the stick."

"No worries, I do a good cover-up act after years of practice." He sounded bitter. "I've only recently *come out* and am still getting used to saying it. It sounds ridiculous, but I come from a very macho background – my father was an RAF colonel, as was his father before him. Can you imagine they expected me to follow the family tradition and join up?" He cackled loudly.

"Does your father know?"

"OMG – No! He'd have apoplexy. As it is, he's disappointed that his only son hasn't followed in the family tradition. My mother knows – only told her six months ago when I started to get serious about someone. I dreaded the reaction, but there wasn't one – she said she'd always known. Mothers!" He shrugged his shoulders and continued. "Anyway, enough about me. Why don't you join us later? There's a Salsa lesson at five. I promise to protect you from any amorous Russians." He laughed, seeming more relaxed for having told her his secret.

"I've got your itinerary so will find you if I decide to take you up on your kind offer. Thanks again, Thomas."

"Don't worry about what anyone in the group thinks – Boris made it quite clear that you would be welcome to any of our activities. He believes I fancy you and I didn't put him right." Thomas winked and walked away, wiggling his hips playfully and looking triumphant.

Rachel grinned as she headed back to her room. Thomas was growing on her, and now she felt safe, she would be a lot happier joining in with him and his tour party. Still wary of Nikolai, she would play along with Thomas if required.

Sarah phoned while Rachel was emailing Carlos from her stateroom.

"Hi, Rachel – just checking in. Is everything alright?"

"Yes, everything's fine. I joined the engine room tour this morning – interesting, but I agree with you about the noise. How do people work down there?"

"With difficulty. I've spent more time down there since being back on the ship than I would care to. First seeing a Russian yesterday, and then today his roommate was found dead in the room they shared."

"Oh dear! How tragic. That's all you needed on your second day back. Are you okay?"

"Yes, fine now, but it's all a bit sad. The chap who died doesn't really have any family to speak of, and the only people who will be mourning his loss will be his roommate and his fellow crewmen. He worked in engineering and was one of the guys I met yesterday because he interpreted for his roommate, who didn't speak English."

"Are there any suspicious circumstances? Has security checked it out?" Being a police officer, Rachel had been called to sudden deaths occasionally, and always had to rule out anything suspicious before allowing a body to be moved. Such deaths had to be referred to the coroner and sometimes this resulted in a post-mortem, while others would be discussed with a GP to ask if they were happy to issue a death certificate for natural causes.

"Not this time, Rachel. We're not having any suspicious deaths on this cruise, so you just relax." Sarah sniggered. "Seriously, though, it looked like a heart attack in the night. There's no evidence of drugs or alcohol poisoning, which can occur, and no sign of violence or suicide, so I suspect we're looking at a natural death. Chief Security Officer Waverley, who you will remember from your last cruise, has cleared the room and not found anything suspicious. He will do some background checks on the man and his roommate, but I'm sure there will be nothing untoward."

"That's a relief – I really do want us to relax, and PC Prince would like to enjoy this holiday, but I'm so sorry you've been thrown back in at the deep end. Hopefully the rest of the cruise will be less eventful."

"Let's hope so, and at least you were nowhere near this one! I need to track down his roommate, though, because I'm concerned about him. I've just got back from engineering myself and he seems to be AWOL. He doesn't speak much English at all and he depended on the deceased, Erik, for translation. He's probably found a quiet corner to get drunk in."

"What makes you say that?"

"Well, when I saw him yesterday, even in the dim lighting down in engineering, he looked pale. He was supposed to come to surgery for an appointment this morning for blood tests, but he didn't show. Mostly when crewmen become anaemic, it's due to the excessive alcohol they consume on board, and they develop stomach ulcers or, worst-case scenario, liver cirrhosis. I still want to run those tests."

"Okay, now I get it. You'll be right, then, because the first thing a heavy drinker would do if upset would be to get drunk."

"Except that cruise ship procedure is so stringent. Most of the crew realise when to work and when to play. He'll be lucky if he keeps his job after going missing from shift, although I will ask Graham to fight his corner if he is passed out drunk somewhere."

"Is anyone looking for him?"

"Yes, actively at present – his friends are helping with the search. He went missing in the middle of his shift around midday but nobody reported it until I went looking for him an hour ago. His friends covered for him, hoping he'd come back. Security has been told to keep a lookout. I just hope he hasn't done anything silly."

"Like what?"

"Like throwing himself overboard." Sarah sounded worried.

"Wait – did you say he went missing at midday? That's when I was on the engineering tour. I saw a crewman looking scared, like he'd seen something frightening, and I'm sure he spoke to one of the members of the tour group, so he could have been Russian."

"Can you describe him?"

"Yes, about six-foot, skinny-looking with clothes hanging off him, and he had bright-red wavy hair and a moustache."

"Wow, Rachel – that's him. Do you know which way he went?"

"Not really, but he went in the opposite direction to the engine room because we were heading towards it. Sarah, he looked terrified. I've got a bad feeling about this."

"Me too – I'd better call Waverley. They'll need to do a ship-wide search. Are you sure he looked frightened rather than upset?"

"Hard to tell, but I would say he looked like he had just had a fright or a shock. His eyes were darting around and he rushed past rather than walked. The death of his friend could explain it, but I do hope it has nothing to do with the Russian he spoke to in the group."

"I'll call Waverley. My money's on him being in a drunken stupor somewhere below the waterline or in the crew bar, but if not, I'll keep you informed. Shall we meet up again tonight in the jazz bar? This time I'll be off duty."

"Yes, that would be great – see you around nine."

Rachel put the phone down with the distinct impression that yet again, this might be no ordinary cruise. She made up her mind to go to the salsa class and see if there was any more to that chance meeting between the Russian and the crewman in the corridor.

Chapter 10

Sarah put the phone down after speaking to Waverley for over half an hour. The turn of events had troubled him, it seemed, so he'd responded by being brusque and dismissive. He'd told Sarah in no uncertain terms that he would find Jefgeny Popov within the hour.

"The captain will need to know that things might be more complicated than we first thought, but I don't envision there being any relationship between a chance encounter with Russians in a corridor and Popov going missing," he snorted. "Let's hope your friend Rachel is wrong this time and the man is drunk in a corner somewhere."

"Yes, I'm certain he will be," Sarah replied, although she was anything other than certain.

"The team can make enquiries about this Russian group and carry out discreet background checks, although with diplomats in the party, we may run into problems. You realise that if it wasn't your friend suggesting the crewman looked frightened, I wouldn't be wasting any time on this."

"Yes, Chief, thank you. Perhaps it will be nothing. I'd better get back to work."

Sarah walked into one of the clinic rooms and sat down at a desk. Taking a deep breath, she hoped against hope all would be well with Jefgeny.

Shortly afterwards, the speakers in the medical centre burst into life as the captain made an unscheduled announcement.

"Good afternoon, ladies and gentleman, this is Captain Jenson speaking. The chief engineer has requested we stop the ship for a short while so he can deal with a minor problem in the engine room.

I would like to reassure passengers that the problem will not stop the ship from operating at its full capacity, but it is easier to fix with the engines switched off. We are currently in calm seas that will allow us to float without dropping anchor. Please accept my apologies for any inconvenience and rest assured you will be informed once we are due to be underway again. Please continue to take full advantage of all the wonderful facilities and entertainment, and enjoy your cruise aboard the *Coral Queen*. Thank you."

Sarah felt the ship's engines stop. In the silence that followed, it was easy to see they were at a standstill from the porthole in her clinic room.

"Minor problem in engineering indeed!" Graham blustered. Entering the room red-faced, he was followed by Alex, Gwen, Bernard and Lauren. "There'd better not be another dead body to deal with."

Sarah heard the strain in his voice and worried about his blood pressure with the stress he was exuding – not like him at all. The medical team was not used to crew deaths, although they were not unheard of. The occasional crew member fell or jumped overboard, but she had not come across this during her first year working for the cruise line. The occasional passenger death was far more likely, particularly on a world cruise due to the number of older people travelling with serious health problems. Despite an increase in younger people taking cruises these days, there remained a disproportionate number of elderly people on every sailing. She had only experienced one passenger death on board, plus the incident the previous year when a death had taken place in one port, but nothing like this.

"Don't worry, Graham, they'll find him off his head in some obscure part of the ship," said Gwen.

"Let's hope so. Anyway, the reason I'm here – Sarah, Gwen, we need to take another peek at the body – captain's orders. Tell me you didn't miss anything, Alex?" What Graham meant was that he hoped neither of them had missed anything.

Alex looked uncomfortable. "As far as I know, I didn't miss anything – there was nothing untoward," he replied, quietly. "Shall I do the passenger visits while you check?"

"Good idea, thanks." Graham calmed down a little.

Sarah saw Alex's head drop as he left and felt sorry for him.

Bernard and Lauren took over from Sarah, checking stocks and sorting out medicines. Sarah and Gwen followed Graham into the morgue. They stood back while Gwen pulled out one of the six shiny steel refrigerated drawers, available to store corpses when deaths occurred on board. This one contained the body of Erik Marinov.

Sarah gasped at the cold draught of air that enveloped them as the drawer opened. Erik was lying on his back, covered only by a plastic sheet that Gwen pulled back. A respectful silence descended, but it produced a macabre atmosphere.

"Dreadful business," muttered Graham. Sarah had never seen him so stressed, but understood his concern that Alex might have made a mistake. They exposed the naked body and Graham began his examination. He scrutinised every part of Erik from the top of his head to the bottom of his feet. "One bruise to his right arm. His roommate said he sustained it during an arm wrestling competition in the crew bar two nights ago."

"To think he was alive and arm wrestling recently, it's tragic," whispered Gwen to Sarah. Sarah nodded, but sensed Graham was not in the mood for chit-chat. He wanted to get his examination done as soon as possible.

He seemed satisfied he had examined the body thoroughly from the front. "Okay, Gwen, Sarah – pull him on to his side please." They did so and Graham repeated the same examination of the rear of Erik's body. "Okay, relax back, please."

They released Erik on to his back and Graham looked relieved. "Thankfully, I can find no evidence of foul play. We can't totally rule out suicide, but there was no evidence of drugs or medication in his room. We are back to probable cause of death as a heart attack."

It was as the condensation from the refrigerator cleared around the body that Sarah's attention was drawn to something else. She scrutinised a small birthmark on Erik's upper left arm that revealed a faint mark in the centre.

"What is it, Sarah?" Graham snapped.

"Erm, not sure. Would you take a look, please?"

Graham shot around to her side and examined the birthmark too. "I can't make it out. Gwen, can you get me a magnifying glass, please?" Gwen left the morgue and Graham stared at Sarah. "My God, I hope this isn't what I think it is."

They were silent as Gwen returned to the room and handed over the magnifying glass. Graham squinted with furrowed brow as he checked the mark, but they all realised what it was: a tiny speck from a needle carefully concealed within the darker part of the birthmark. The team was puzzled about what might have been injected into Erik's arm, but there was little doubt what it meant.

This was murder.

"Not a word to anyone outside the medical team – except to your friend, Sarah. This is not getting out, at least not until I've discussed it with the captain and the chief of security. We'll keep it from the new girl, too – we don't know yet whether she can be discreet enough to keep this under wraps. I would prefer to keep it as quiet as possible."

Graham marched out of the room with Gwen hot on his heels. Sarah stayed behind to close the drawer containing the late Erik.

"Sorry, Erik, we didn't realise, but we know what happened now. I'm positive security will find who did this to you."

Sarah had a sinking feeling that something awful had also happened to Jefgeny – unless, of course, he had committed the murder, which might also explain his disappearance. She couldn't believe he would have harmed his friend, though; they had seemed close.

Perhaps he suspects it was murder, or worse still, perhaps he knows who the murderer is. He's got to be hiding somewhere. Surely this is not going to be like Rachel's first cruise.

She determined to fill her friend in later this evening. Right now, she needed to do her job and perform the act of her life in front of Lauren.

Chapter 11

"Thank you for your patience, ladies and gentlemen, the problem is now resolved and we will start up the engines within the next ten minutes. Our course continues in a north-westerly direction towards New York and we will make up speed during the night. Please enjoy the rest of your day and take advantage of the exceptional facilities aboard the *Coral Queen*."

The captain's voice reverberated throughout the ship. Rachel wondered if this unscheduled stop had involved the search for the missing crewman.

As she entered the STARS Ballroom on deck five, she saw it was crowded with a lot more people than just the Russian party. Rachel spotted Thomas clutching his trusty clipboard, ticking off names, and his face lit up when he saw her.

"Rachel, I'm pleased you decided to come. One of the ladies has gone to bed with a headache and we have a male without a dance partner. Would you mind?"

"Not at all. I'd be happy to help, seeing as you've been so kind to me, as long as it's not Nikolai," she whispered.

"No problem. He's been ordered to stay behind and do some work for Boris."

A man walked over to them. Rachel recognised him as the person who had walked slowly in front of her on the tour earlier in the day.

"Rachel… sorry, I don't know your surname?"

"Prince," she replied. "Rachel Prince."

"Rachel Prince, allow me to introduce you to Mr Asimov. Mr Asimov, Rachel will be your dance partner."

"Charmed I'm sure," he sneered, holding out his hand.

Rachel disliked the abrupt man immediately, but smiled and offered her hand. She scowled back at Thomas, but he was already dealing with the next couple on his list. Mr Asimov didn't speak as they moved on to the dance floor and his penetrating gaze made her feel uncomfortable. He clearly wasn't happy about something and made no attempt to engage in conversation.

Asimov was smaller than her at around five feet eight inches. Middle-aged and grossly overweight for his height, he had wavy shoulder-length fair hair, was clean shaven, and wouldn't have been bad looking if he'd only lose the sullen look. He wore a loud Caribbean-type short-sleeved shirt with khaki knee-length shorts, the clothing completely out of synch with his dour demeanour. Through gold rimmed designer glasses, bloodshot grey eyes stared at her. *A drinker,* she mused.

"Are you enjoying your holiday so far, Mr Asimov?"

"It is satisfactory. I will be happier in New York," he replied in sharp, punctuated tones, raising his rather large nose at her, which made her want to burst out laughing.

Still no first name! This is going to be hard work.

Rachel had difficulty imagining dancing the salsa, a happy dance, with this miserable man. Thankfully, the Cruise Director arrived at that moment and took the microphone, introducing their dance instructors: a South American couple, dressed suitably for the part with bright, heavily sequined, happy clothing.

The class began with an introduction to a few basic steps where couples had to dance side by side while moving their hips rhythmically to the music. Rachel heard people laughing and having fun, but not Asimov. His moves weren't that bad, but the scowl never left his face.

"Do you like Latin dancing?" she asked.

"It's okay. I'm good, no?"

"You're good, yes," she said. "Did you enjoy the engine room tour this morning?"

"It was okay, I have background in engineering and have been on big ships in Russian navy, but I served in army."

Now we are getting somewhere. "Oh, how interesting. So how did the engine rooms compare?"

"All engine rooms alike on board ships. They may be different vessels, but they all work the same."

Pulling teeth came to mind. "Really? One thing I did notice was just how enclosed the corridors seemed, all a bit too cramped down there for me – that crew member struggled to get past us. Did you notice?"

"No, I didn't notice, I was concentrating on where we were going."

Rachel wasn't sure if he was lying, but she didn't get the chance to continue the conversation as the music stopped. The instructor paused to show them some new moves.

"Excuse me, I have to go and check how *my woman* is." Asimov spoke abruptly, turned and left.

Well I never! Rude man. Rachel moved away from the dance floor and went to join Thomas, who sat writing notes at a table to one side of the room.

"Did you realise he had the personality of a squid when you asked me to partner him? No wonder *his woman*, as he calls her, has a headache!"

Thomas laughed. "Sorry, Rachel, I didn't. I'm only just getting to grips with each of them myself. Don't you know who he is?"

"No – should I?"

"He's the oligarch. He's a billionaire and has a business empire spanning three continents, from what I can gather. I don't think any of the others like him very much – they seem frightened of him – but, according to Nikolai, he has a lot of influence in Russia."

"Blow me down with a feather! He didn't look like an oligarch – not that I have any idea what one should look like. But it doesn't excuse his blatantly rude behaviour. I never did get his first name."

"Let me see, it should be on my list – Vladimir, although he only likes to be addressed as Mr Asimov. It says here in my notes."

"There's a surprise – adds to his overinflated ego, I expect. There weren't any bodyguards with him – they seemed to be with Boris. Is he the diplomat?"

"Yes, and I find that strange, too. Those men follow Boris everywhere."

Rachel couldn't work out why this bothered her, but it did. There's something strange going on, but I'm at a loss to know what it is.

"Would you like to salsa with me?" asked Thomas. "I've finished for the next half an hour."

"Yes please. I must admit I enjoyed the dance, just not the partner."

"Come on then, let's hit the floor."

For the next thirty minutes, Rachel enjoyed herself. Thomas was fun to dance with, and his exaggerated salsa moves made her laugh – definitely an exhibitionist when he got going. It was not hard to imagine that with a less serious tour group, he would be a big hit. With his current group, she was sure he would have to curb his happy-go-lucky spirit somewhat.

A noticeable change of atmosphere had occurred as soon as Vladimir Asimov left, resulting in a considerably lighter mood. The Russians let their hair down, joining in with an American party who were happily shimmying to the music, in spite of some of the men grinding rather than rotating their hips. As soon as the class ended, Thomas was surrounded by people asking what activities they had booked for the remainder of the evening.

"It seems most of them have left their itineraries in their staterooms." Thomas rolled his eyes at Rachel once the final member had left. "Thankfully I carry spares."

"They seem to be relaxing a little, though, different from this morning. Did you notice how slow the tail end of the group walked on the engineering tour?" She decided she would quiz Thomas as he didn't seem to have anything to hide – apart from being gay.

"Yes, I did. Boris got really uptight about it, but the chief engineer wouldn't slow down."

"Oh, that's interesting."

"And I overheard one of the Russians talking about your crewman. Apparently, he almost spoke to Boris, but the minders shoved him away and he scuttled off."

"Did Boris know him after all?"

"Unlikely, otherwise his minders wouldn't have been so aggressive. What slowed your end down anyway?"

"Your Mr Asimov." Her eyebrows hit the ceiling as she continued. "He decided to walk at a snail's pace about ten minutes into the tour, but then picked up the pace after that crew member passed by, funnily enough."

"Do you think there's a link? Is there something going on?"

Rachel decided she had already said and learned enough, so ended the conversation.

"I doubt it. I can't imagine an oligarch or a diplomat having anything to do with a lowly engine room worker. Anyway, Thomas, thanks for the salsa class. I'll see you around. Can't believe we only boarded yesterday; it seems an age ago."

"It's going to seem like an eternity for me by the end of this one." He winked. "Still, I get well paid, and am hoping for a huge bonus if all goes well."

Rachel found the chief of security, Waverley, waiting outside her room when she got back.

"Chief, how nice to see you again. I do hope you haven't found any more murderers on board since the last time I cruised."

Ignoring her quip, Waverley tightened his lips. "Miss Prince, it's a pleasure. Do you mind if I ask you a few questions?" He lowered his voice. "It's regarding your tour this morning." He coughed. Rachel had noticed on the previous cruise he had a habit of coughing when he was nervous or had something sensitive to say.

Rachel opened the door to her suite. "Please call me Rachel and do come in. Would you like a tea or coffee?"

He coughed again. "No thank you, Rachel. Sorry to intrude, but Nurse Bradshaw, erm, Sarah said that you had seen a member of the crew during your engine room tour this morning who matches the description of a man who has gone missing."

"He's still missing then?"

"Afraid so – we did stop engines for a while to scour the sea, but to be honest, there was never any likelihood of spotting him if he did go overboard. He'd been missing for some time by then. We've alerted other ships in the area, but I fear his fate is sealed if he cannot be found on board."

"Let's hope that's not the case. The man I noticed appeared frightened so might be hiding somewhere."

"Would you care to expand?"

"Well, it was the way he scurried past with his head down. His eyes were bulging and darting here and there without looking at anyone. He spoke to one of the men in the tour party in Russian, but they could have been passing the time of day for all I know. I only caught a momentary glimpse when I turned the corner of one of the corridors down near the engine room. Their tour guide said the man tried to speak to the diplomat, Boris Stanislav, but was pushed back by his minders."

"This chance encounter can have little bearing on his going missing, but if he's on board, we'll find him. There has been another unfortunate development which Sarah will fill you in on later. I understand you are meeting her this evening."

"Yes, I am, but what is it?"

"Sarah will tell you, but it must be kept completely confidential, and if I were you, I would stay out of the matter. You're a passenger and a guest while on board this ship. Not an investigator." A twinkle in his eye could have been interpreted as meaning the opposite. "Unless you want to take me up on that job offer?" He didn't wait for a reply. "Have a pleasant evening, Rachel."

Rachel was left gawping.

Chapter 12

Eager to find out what Sarah had to tell her, Rachel found time dragging, so decided to take in a show. Waverley had well and truly sucked her in, giving her half a story.

I bet it was deliberate.

He still wanted her to join his security team after having offered her a job last year and been disappointed by her refusal. A frown attached itself to her forehead, annoyed at Waverley for playing her.

With the benefit of hindsight, she wondered if it might have been better to accept his offer. Following the stabbing in Leeds, and having suffered the fallout, she had regretted her decision to return to the police force, but reason told her it would have been career suicide to leave straight after qualifying. Every new police officer needed experience.

Well, I certainly got that!

She took a seat in the main theatre and ordered a cocktail, still frowning.

The lively show provided a welcome distraction from the thoughts whirring round in her head, both past and present. The main act, a comedian, had the audience in stitches, and it felt good to laugh. She guffawed along with everyone else and, not for the first time, admired the unbelievable talent that had chosen to work on board this exemplary floating hotel.

As the resident band and dance act finished the show, she saw Thomas sitting near the front of the stage along with around twenty of his party. Tweedledee was next to Thomas and Boris, with Tweedledum squeezed into a seat on the other side of Boris. Nikolai was there next to the man who had spoken to the crewman in the morning. Tall with silver-grey hair, a white beard and moustache, he wore silver-rimmed square glasses. Sitting to his right was the austere Vladimir Asimov. Next to Asimov was a woman with red hair tied up in a bun.

That must be 'his woman'. Rachel remembered how Asimov had referred to her. Deciding to move before they turned around and spotted her, Rachel headed out to make her way to the jazz bar to meet Sarah.

A crowd of people had the same idea and slowed her progress by milling around outside the entrance. Women were dressed up for the night, wearing evening gowns, and the men wore dinner suits. Trying to negotiate her way through another crowd waiting outside the public conveniences, she heard Russian voices behind her so picked up the pace. There was no point spending any more time with the arrogant Mr Asimov.

As she approached the jazz bar, she could hear ragtime music filtering out into the corridor, and when she entered, it was even more packed than it had been the previous night. Loud voices, raucous laughter along with saxophone music filled the air, and many of the passengers already looked worse for wear.

Rachel spotted Sarah at the table where they had met the night before, and Sarah waved her over. There was another woman with her who Rachel assumed must be the new nurse, Lauren, and Bernard, who she recognised from the last cruise, was there too. They were impossible to miss in their pristine white officers' uniforms, which Rachel knew was compulsory attire in public areas.

Bernard let out a wolf-whistle as Rachel approached and stood to hug her.

"Only you would do that in this day and age," scolded Sarah.

"What?" Bernard replied.

Rachel hugged him. "It's okay, Sarah, I'll let him off this once."

Bernard looked rebuked and feigned offence.

"It's a good job Brigitte isn't here otherwise he'd get one of her French lectures. I'm afraid feminism and political correctness haven't caught up with our Bernard yet."

"Well I think he's the perfect gentleman." The woman with them spoke up in a solemn tone, fracturing the light banter and mood of the moment.

"See?" said Bernard. "Someone appreciates me. This is Lauren, our new nurse. Lauren, this is Rachel, Sarah's friend."

Rachel put her hand out in greeting. "Hello, Lauren."

Lauren shook Rachel's hand, but quickly let go as if it was contaminated. *Odd girl.*

"What would you like to drink, Rachel?" asked Bernard. "I'm buying."

"Martini and lemonade – but I've got an all in drinks package so don't pay for it. Here, take my card."

Bernard walked through the crowd to the bar, and Rachel sat down. She found conversation with Lauren stilted and unnatural. The woman was at least ten years older than Sarah and Rachel, and clearly didn't want to be in their company, but she wouldn't go away. Sarah looked apologetically at Rachel, who was persevering in her attempt to make polite conversation with the American nurse.

"How are you finding life on board a cruise ship?"

"Alright."

"Have you nursed on a ship before?"

"No."

"Is it very different to working in hospitals?"

"No."

She's worse than Asimov!

Rachel gave up. Lauren's monosyllabic answers, along with the odd grunt, made her feel like she was interrogating a suspect who was taking the 'no comment' line. As soon as Bernard returned, however, Lauren's eyes lit up. Rachel couldn't help thinking this woman was immature at best, and odd at worst.

"You are more radiantly beautiful than ever, Rachel. How can that be?" Bernard continued in his usual teasing and flirtatious vein that Rachel laughed off, knowing he was happily married, but Lauren was giving her daggers.

"How's your wife?" deflected Rachel. This did the trick. Bernard was a devoted family man who loved his wife and children in Manila. He was a faithful husband who had not strayed during his three years intermittently working on cruise ships.

"She's doing very well. I have a four-month break after this cruise and fly home to Manila before rejoining the ship in Australia in the New Year. Milo is five years old, Janet is three and Mikey has just had his first birthday." Bernard took out his phone and waxed lyrical over the latest photos of his children sent by his wife. He had not seen his family in almost nine months, but sent most of his salary and tips home to support their keep. Nurse pay on board a cruise ship was good, Sarah said, and he earned far more than he could earn back home. This was one of the reasons that he, and many other members of crew from poorer countries, worked away from home.

"You must be looking forward to seeing them again," Rachel said.

He wiped a tear from his eye. "More than words can say."

Sarah took his hand and gave it a squeeze, while Rachel again noted a glare that would strike down dead coming from Lauren, only this time aimed at Sarah.

"Anyway, ladies, I'm on call from 6am tomorrow, so I'm going to call it a night."

Bernard got up to leave.

"I'll walk with you, I'm tired too," said Lauren.

Bernard glanced at Sarah, pleading for help, but got a shrug of the shoulders in return. "Goodnight, you two. See you tomorrow," she said.

Rachel watched them walk away and Sarah let out a deep sigh.

"He'd better be careful," said Rachel. "She looks smitten."

"She's misunderstood his friendly demeanour to mean he's interested, but I'm sure when push comes to shove, he'll put her straight. You'd think she'd take the hint when he spoke about his wife and kids, wouldn't you?" Her tone turned grave. "Shall we go up to your suite to talk – it seems to be getting louder in here?"

"That's just what I was thinking." Rachel finished her drink, and they headed back up to deck fifteen. As Rachel was swiping the door with her card key, Mario came out of Asimov's suite, looking frazzled.

"Good evening, Miss Rachel, good evening, Nurse Sarah. Can I get you anything?"

"No thanks," replied Rachel. "We're good – I take it you've been busy this evening?"

"It has been hectic for the past hour. Mr Asimov has several guests and they conduct some business in there. Every five minutes my buzzer goes off and they order something else. First it was vodka, then it was food, and just now, more vodka. I'm hoping they are happy now – but one man is not happy. They are arguing. By the way, Miss Rachel, the tour guide you asked about, Thomas, is staying two doors down from Mr Asimov in balcony stateroom number 1508."

"Thank you, Mario. You can forget about us for the evening, but can I request a pot of coffee around 7am please?" She looked at Sarah. "I want to hit the gym early before the other passengers get moving." Sarah nodded understanding.

"No problem, miss – goodnight to you both."

Rachel and Sarah entered Rachel's suite and switched on the lights.

"I forgot how nice these suites are," remarked Sarah.

The room was delightful, Rachel had to agree. "I am lucky, aren't I? All courtesy of Queen Cruises. You should have got a free cruise too for being traumatised last year. You know, I've not seen your room. Is it the same as the one you left?"

"Yes it is, and I'm lucky that officers have their own rooms. And I'm in a balcony suite, although it has a restricted view. I have to ask you – what did you make of Lauren?"

"Well I can't say she's the friendliest person I've ever met. She seems a bit strange, but maybe she's shy."

"Agreed – I keep trying to be friendly, but she rebuffs any attempt. The only person she appears to like is Bernard, but her behaviour towards him is just weird. Maybe she'll relax when she settles in. Thankfully Gwen's a lot happier, so I suppose I'll survive either way, and hopefully we'll get Brigitte back at the end of the cruise."

"Do you know how her father is?"

"No, not yet. I'm sure she'll be in touch tomorrow."

"Okay – I can't wait any longer. Waverley said you had something to tell me." Rachel cracked open the bottle of champagne that had been waiting since yesterday. Mario had refilled the ice bucket and left out two champagne flutes, which she now filled before taking a seat next to Sarah. "Cheers. Now spill the beans."

"Cheers – I'm still digesting it myself. After I spoke with you earlier, I told Graham and Waverley about your concerns over Jefgeny in the corridor, and Waverley informed the captain. The ship stop was to do a quick search of the surrounding sea, despite the impossibility of being able to find him at that late stage if he has gone overboard."

"Yes, Waverley told me about that, and that the man is still missing."

"Well what he didn't tell you was that the captain requested Graham take another look at the body of Erik Marinov, the man who died."

Rachel's ears pricked up as Sarah explained the events of the afternoon and about the suspicious needle mark hidden in the centre of a birthmark.

"If we hadn't taken a second look, we would never have noticed it. Alex took it badly at first, but Graham has reassured him on that score. But it appears Erik's death is suspicious. No-one can be certain because sometimes crew members get hold of drugs and inject themselves, but that would be into the brachial vein, not in the upper arm. We also checked he was right-handed. The needle mark, if it is that, was in the right upper arm, meaning it had been injected by his left hand if he'd done it himself."

"The prime suspect will be his roommate then. Do they suspect Jefgeny did it?"

"They've not ruled anything out, but yes, and it might be why he's hiding – if he's hiding."

"That seems the most likely scenario, but there's still an anomaly going on within the Russian group. I'm sure that Jefgeny was frightened of someone in that group. Thomas told me he tried to speak to Boris, the diplomat, but was pushed away by his minders."

"That's odd because engineering staff have no contact with passengers and it would be inappropriate to approach them in such a way – unless he heard them speaking Russian and just forgot himself."

"Mm, that thought has crossed my mind too, and that's what Thomas seemed to make of it. There was another man in the group who spoke to Jefgeny, too. If it weren't for Jefgeny's disappearance, and now the suspicious death, I would agree with Thomas, but it all seems too much of a coincidence. You know how I hate loose ends. I take it Waverley is doing background checks?"

"You'd better believe it – he doesn't want a repeat of last year, and he's not happy with the possibility of having another murderer on board. He'd be delighted if it were Jefgeny so he could close the case. All suspicion points to Jefgeny, or another crew member who knew Erik. Waverley's ordered a search of rooms on deck C to check for drugs and needles of any kind – the crew won't be happy, but Waverley's telling them it's a spot-check, which happens occasionally. The suspicious death part is being kept quiet – even Lauren hasn't been told."

"What about the Russian party?"

"Waverley's certain they're not involved, but after last year, he trusts your instincts. On the one hand, he's saying you should stay out of it; on the other, I think he'd like you to do some informal snooping. He won't ask you, though, because he would be in trouble with the captain then, and he doesn't want to put you in any danger."

"I've already started my sleuthing. I'll join the Russians for some of their planned activities tomorrow and see if I can find out anything else."

"What are you looking for?"

"To be honest, I have no idea, but I'm hoping to recognise it when I see it. The mysterious encounter this morning might have been innocent – all I've got is a tenuous link to the Russian party."

"Please be careful, Rachel."

"I will." She raised a glass to her friend. "Cheers! Here's to us and to cruise number two, whatever it may bring."

Chapter 13

"What the hell were you thinking of, trying to speak to that man this morning?" Vladimir Asimov shouted, beside himself with rage. He was not a patient man at the best of times, but Boris Stanislav was pushing him to the limit.

"How did you find out about that?" Boris shouted back, glaring at the minders.

"I'm informed of everything, you should understand that by now."

"The man tried to speak to me – I guess he was Russian. What would you have me do – appear rude? If anything brought attention to an innocent encounter, it was *your* minders throwing their weight around. I thought they would hit him – they scared him half to death."

Vladimir stomached people like Boris frequently: social climbers who crawled their way to the top of the pile, wanting to be seen with all the right people. But he didn't trust Boris one little bit, and for that reason, he'd assigned his own personal bodyguards to keep tabs on him.

"And I suppose you didn't know the man?" Vladimir noticed beads of sweat appearing on Boris's forehead and decided to let the matter go. He needed the diplomat's co-operation – especially his ability to carry items on board in his diplomatic bags. "Let's forget about it, shall we? But please try to be a little more circumspect in the future. I have a lot at stake, and neither of us can afford for anything to go wrong. We have to remember that someone must pay your boys' school fees, and you wouldn't want your wife to find out about your little indiscretions, would you?"

"I am not trying to harm the mission; it was an innocent misunderstanding. I promise to be more careful."

Vladimir dismissed the minders for the night. "Come, Boris, let us drink vodka and forget about this little incident."

Vladimir left the bedroom where he and Boris had held this private conversation and returned to the sitting room where the others were enjoying drinks. He caught Lucretia's eye and smiled, reassuring her all was well.

The party went smoothly and Boris appeared to have gotten over his telling off. *At least he doesn't sulk*, acknowledged Vladimir, *and while I have leverage, he will do as I tell him*. The effects of the neat vodka relaxed him as it reached the back of his throat before warming his insides. Tension in his muscles dissipated. Today had been challenging. First Nikolai had pleaded with him to slow the group down because he wanted to chat up some woman – the same woman Asimov had later been forced to dance with when Lucretia developed one of her headaches. Then his minders had informed him a crewman had tried to approach Boris this morning. That must have been the crewman that he'd seen passing them in the corridor – he thought he recognised the man, and wished he'd paid more attention to his face. But why did the woman, Rachel, want to know whether he'd seen the crewman?

Tension returning, his head throbbed and his neck tightened as thoughts jumbled around. Usually a calm man, he'd felt jumpy and suspicious since agreeing to do a favour for an old friend who had saved his life when they'd worked for the Russian army many years before.

Lucretia interrupted his chaotic ruminations, and he stared up into her beautiful round green eyes, her red hair now loosely wrapped around her shoulders. At thirty, in the prime of her life, she had the kind of dazzling beauty that took his breath away. Like a diamond.

"Come on, darling. You are being inhospitable. We are on holiday, let's dance."

If only you realised what was going on, he mused as he allowed her to pull him up from the sofa. Vladimir hated keeping secrets from her, but she would never allow him to do what he was going to do and would be safer if kept in the dark.

The rest of the party were enjoying themselves and classical music filled the air. He pulled her to him and they smooched before moving on to a waltz. Vladimir was a good dancer, but not as accomplished as Lucretia. He'd met her in St Petersburg when she'd played the part of Floria Tosca in the opera by Puccini and mesmerised him, both with her beauty and her voice. He'd only attended the opera reluctantly at the request of a friend who wanted to discuss a business proposition, and they'd occupied one of the best booths in the house. While his friend droned on about microchips and a new company he wanted to set up, seeking Vladimir's investment, Vladimir himself couldn't take his eyes off the woman on stage.

Later, he summoned one of his bodyguards and arranged for someone to deliver fifty red roses to the singer's room after the show, requesting an introduction. Having just come through a messy and expensive divorce, he wasn't looking for romance, but recognised from the moment he met this woman that she would hold him in the palm of her hand.

He could smell her perfume as they danced, drawing him into sublime tranquillity. When he held Lucretia in his arms, he forgot about everything except the two of them. He embraced her, comforted by the effect she had on him as it pulsated through his body.

He stopped dancing and looked into her eyes. "I love you."

The hour was late, and the others realised that their benefactor wished to be alone, so they left him with his woman.

Day 2

Chapter 14

Sarah tossed and turned all night with incessant worry about Rachel, Jefgeny and whether there was a murderer on board the *Coral Queen*. When she finally fell asleep, the sound of the telephone woke her again. On autopilot, she reached for the handset and flicked the light switch on the headboard, groggily answering, "Hello."

"Sarah, it's me." The crackly, hoarse voice was barely audible.

"Bernard?" She tried to shake herself awake, glancing at the time – 5am. "This had better be life or death. Do you realise what time it is?" she snapped.

"Sarah, it's really important. Can we meet by the pool?"

"Okay, give me fifteen minutes." She forced her weary body out of bed and took a quick shower. The nurses were woken at all hours when on call, so after her shower, she was not only awake, but alert and wondering what on earth was so important that Bernard had called her this early in the morning.

The crew pool was not visible from passenger areas, situated below and in front of the Bridge – where the captain and senior officers navigated night and day – that overhung the ship on both sides. Here, the crew got well-earned leisure time for themselves, and for many not allowed in passenger areas, it might be the only place they could breathe fresh air while at sea.

It was also where the crew let their hair down at occasional all-night parties. During these, they often called doctors and nurses to treat people who'd injured themselves falling over, or following alcohol-fuelled fighting. Senior officers turned a blind eye to most of the goings on as long as the behaviour didn't put other crew or passengers in danger. It was like any Saturday night in any big city, she had been warned when she first joined the ship.

At this time of day, all was deathly quiet, and a morning mist created an eerie backdrop to the pool. Sarah had grabbed a bacon sandwich and a flask of coffee from the crew buffet on the way. With no sign of Bernard, she sat on one of the second-hand loungers scattered around the pool. A 'Not in Use' sign explained why it was so quiet.

She finished her sandwich and was on her second cup of coffee when Bernard appeared. He looked dishevelled with dark bags under his watery eyes. Sarah had been about to scold him for being late, but seeing he was upset, she mellowed.

"What on earth's the matter?"

Tears poured down his cheeks. "I had too much to drink. Sarah, I didn't see it coming."

Sarah could imagine what he would say next even though he was struggling to speak.

"Okay, Bernard, just tell me what happened."

"On the way back to my room last night, I felt strange, unusually drunk. I'd only drunk three whiskeys – maybe I just hadn't eaten enough. I came over light-headed so Lauren offered to walk me back to my room."

His eyes filled with tears again.

"Go on."

"She invited herself in and said she would help me get undressed." At this point, he started sobbing. "You can guess the rest. I woke up this morning, and she was lying there, next to me. My head is throbbing. Sarah, I have never been unfaithful to my wife. How will I be able to face her or my children again?" Tears fell down his face.

Sarah sympathised, knowing despite his jokes and flirtations, he was a one woman man – until now, that was.

He has resisted offers from crew in the past. How did this strange woman worm her way into his bed, and how will he deal with it?

"Tell me you used something?"

"I don't think so. I can't even remember what happened – that's what's so strange. I can only assume we did it as she was lying there naked."

Sarah fought the urge to laugh at his innocent use of 'did it'. "Is she still there?"

"I guess so. I called you, dressed and ran. What am I going to do?" Tear stains marked his face.

"Look, Bernard, let's be rational – it's not the first time infidelity has occurred on a cruise ship and it won't be the last. You had too much to drink, end of story. Tell Lauren at the earliest opportunity it was a mistake and it will never happen again. Then you need to avoid spending any time alone with her for the rest of the cruise. It's not like she will be with us once Brigitte comes back."

And let's hope to God she's not pregnant! she thought.

Bernard stopped crying and Sarah gave him a hug. "Anyone who knows you knows how much you love your wife. I can't believe Lauren took advantage of your drunken state. You will get through this, and when the time is right, you can choose whether to tell your wife."

He grimaced at that part. "How did this happen? I always stay sober. I don't understand."

"I don't know how it happened, but it did. Now come on – time to get ready for work. Did you say you were on call today?"

"Yes."

"Well at least you'll be nowhere near her. I'll get her to work with me for the day, and from tomorrow, she's on her own. Are you okay going back? Do you need me to come with you?"

"I'll do it. I want to tell her as soon as possible," Bernard mumbled as he turned and headed back towards his deck, head-down, broken.

Sarah's heart went out to him – he and Brigitte had been her best friends since she'd joined Queen Cruises and she would not let this strange woman ruin his life.

I should have trusted my gut. There's something rotten about that girl – Africa or no Africa.

After getting back to her room, Sarah rang Rachel to arrange to meet up for tea this afternoon, deciding not to mention the Bernard thing at present. It wasn't her secret to tell.

On arrival at the medical centre, she spotted Lauren sitting with Graham and Gwen as bold as brass, chatting and drinking coffee.

"Sarah, good morning." Graham smiled. "I've let Alex go to get some sleep. He was up all night with a rowdy group of rugby players on holiday. They played rugby on the lido deck and one of them almost drowned! Idiots – three of them slipped and needed glueing, and one of them broke his arm rugby tackling a security officer sent to break up the party. Our security officer is no rugby player, but he's built like a battering ram."

"Oh poor boy, and poor Alex!"

"Indeed!" Gwen laughed. "Graham lets him loose on passengers rather than crew for a change, and this happens."

"Still, rather him than me! I'll do passenger surgery and you can cover crew, but call me if you need my help," said Graham, heading to the first clinic room.

"You're with me," Sarah snarled at Lauren.

"Oh, but I'm meant to be working with Bernard."

"Bernard's busy so I said I'd take you today, and tomorrow, you're working alone, with support."

Gwen looked at Sarah, shocked at her tone. Picking up something was amiss, she intervened.

"That's a superb idea, Lauren. You'll benefit from working with each member of the team so you get a feel for how we all operate. So that's settled, then."

Sarah smiled, gloating and fist-pumping in her head. *Gotcha!* Lauren glared at her, but had no choice but to follow Sarah into the clinic room.

The morning wasn't easy with a sulking assistant, but they were too busy for Lauren to give Sarah much trouble. The brooding Lauren could do her job like a sensible professional or be difficult. Sarah didn't care either way.

After surgery, Graham had passenger visits to attend to. Sarah would have liked to accompany him herself, but she didn't want to let Lauren get away. However, she needed to check how Bernard was because he was avoiding the medical centre.

"I'm sure Lauren would enjoy shadowing you with the passengers," Sarah suggested to Graham while they were having coffee.

"Excellent idea. Come on, Lauren. Time to work with the big chief." He was in surprisingly good humour, considering the events of the day before. Lauren followed him out, scowling and shooting daggers at Sarah.

As soon as they left, Gwen turned to Sarah.

"Are you going to tell me what that was all about?"

"Would you mind if I track Bernard down first?"

"No need, here he is."

Bernard rolled in, still looking tired, but at least he was forcing a smile.

"Well?" Gwen asked.

Looking at Bernard, Sarah spoke. "We need to tell Gwen, Bernard."

Bernard slumped into a chair. "You tell her please."

Sarah related the events of last night and this morning, and Gwen listened with the occasional nod of sympathy towards Bernard. Once Sarah had finished, Gwen turned to him.

"Did you tell her it was a one-off?"

He squirmed. "I couldn't, she'd left, and this was on my bed." He handed Gwen a note.

Gwen read it out loud, "*Thank you for an amazing night – can't wait for the next time*", Gwen peered at Bernard above her spectacles and guffawed, as did Sarah, despite herself.

"An amazing night, eh? Pity you can't remember it."

"It's not funny!" Bernard sounded like a petulant child before smiling sheepishly.

"Your private life is your concern, Bernard, but if this becomes a problem, I need to know. We're too small a team to have any friction; we have to pull together. Get this resolved quickly. I will not allow an unhealthy working atmosphere. Do you understand?"

He nodded.

"Let her down gently, and then behave as if nothing happened."

Sarah wondered if that might be easier said than done.

Chapter 15

Rachel had nothing planned for today other than meeting with Sarah at three o'clock at Creams for tea. Mario brought her coffee at 7am as requested, and she had already been for a run on deck sixteen followed by forty-five minutes in the gym.

"Would you like breakfast?" Mario asked.

"No thanks, Mario, I'll eat in the buffet."

Once in the buffet, she found an empty table tucked in a corner, away from the crowds, and took out the Russian tour party's itinerary, mulling things over again. She'd had little time to speak with Sarah, but her friend had told her Jefgeny Popov was still missing and there was a growing concern for his safety. He might have killed his roommate and then thrown himself overboard later that day. Rachel had to agree that seemed the most plausible of explanations. Nevertheless, it didn't sit well with her for reasons she couldn't explain.

While she was staring at Thomas's itinerary, a familiar Jamaican voice singing in the background drew her attention. She recognised the waiter from the previous cruise as they'd often met up during her morning runs. He hadn't been there this morning, so she'd assumed he'd moved ships, but here he was at her table, large as life, smiling with a gold tooth taking pride of place instead of an upper molar.

"Good morning, ma'am. Can I get you tea or coffee?" He didn't seem to recognise her at first, and then he said, "Didn't we meet last year – I never forget a beautiful face?"

"Yes we did, on my early morning runs. I didn't see you this morning, though."

"That's right – we did. I've got a calf injury so my running days are on hold. I do weights now so I might catch you in the gym."

"Yes, I'm sure you might."

"What can I get for you this fine morning?"

"Coffee please."

He poured her coffee and then continued to the next table, singing a few lines from *Summer Holiday* on his way. The waiter had extended his song repertoire since the last time they'd met, but he looked as skinny as ever, although more bulky around the arms and chest from his weight training. His dreadlocks had colourful braids running through them and were tied up in a ponytail.

This is what she loved about the buffet: the casual atmosphere was in stark contrast to the formality of the main restaurant where she ate her dinner each evening. Tonight was a designated formal evening where the captain and his officers met with passengers. Men would don tuxedos with a bow or black tie, while women would wear evening or cocktail dresses. Rachel appreciated the opportunity to glam up in a way she rarely experienced on land.

After a few sips of coffee, her attention returned to the itinerary in her hand. It listed many activities, including gaming lessons in the casino, sports trivia in one of the lounges, yoga, cha-cha lessons in the ballroom – which she decided to give a miss – and many others.

Rachel chose a wine tasting lesson at midday, thinking she might learn something. She had no clear plan, but the activities would help pass the time during sea days, and she liked Thomas. She hoped there wouldn't be anything to discover and the matter of Jefgeny and Erik would be a neat, albeit tragic, murder/suicide. This would be preferable to a murderer running loose on the ship – again.

Staff had cordoned a small area of the wine bar off for the wine tasting lesson. Thomas stood in the centre, armed with his usual clipboard, and beamed.

"Rachel, it's great you came. Please stay with me." He nodded her a warning towards Nikolai, knowing she wasn't keen.

Boris and his macho minders, Tweedledee and Tweedledum, sat at one of the tables, along with Nikolai and Vladimir Asimov, *his woman* hanging onto his arm. Rachel admired the woman's sultry beauty, hour-glass figure and gorgeous long red hair, which was flowing down her back while enhancing her porcelain-like facial features. The woman looked her way and smiled. Embarrassed at being caught staring, Rachel smiled back, and then turned her attention back to Thomas.

"I'm looking forward to this lesson, being a wine lover who doesn't understand what I'm supposed to be looking for when I'm poured a sample in a restaurant."

"I'm a scotch man myself, but I like a glass of wine too, and yes, this is one of the more useful sessions. Beats origami!"

Rachel chuckled and took a seat next to Thomas, then looked around, listening in to any conversations held in English. Nikolai looked agitated and stuck like glue to Boris today, whispering in his ear as soon as Asimov moved. They sat two tables ahead of her so she couldn't make out the words.

"Mr Asimov seems a lot happier today," Rachel whispered to Thomas.

"He seems much more relaxed when Lucretia is with him. He's the perfect gentleman then," Thomas acknowledged.

"Neither is wearing a wedding ring, so I assume they're not married?"

"No, I heard one of the others saying he had not long since come through a messy divorce that cost him a vast amount of his considerable wealth when they met. I don't think it will be long, though, he seems besotted."

"Well I grudgingly admit he seems to be a different person today."

"She is rather beautiful – a man could go straight looking at you two." Laughing out loud, causing a few heads to turn their way, Rachel thumped him on the arm. To anyone watching, it would appear they were striking up an early romance, and Rachel played along.

After the wine tasting session, she mingled. The ones she particularly wanted to get a handle on included Boris, Asimov, and the man who'd appeared to be speaking to Jefgeny the day before, but he wasn't there.

Rachel walked over to Boris, watched by the Tweedle twins. Grinning at her inner joke and ignoring them, she spoke to Boris.

"Thank you for allowing me to gatecrash some of your activities."

Boris looked a little bit uncomfortable, almost fearful as he looked at the short, stocky minder, Tweedledee. "It is no trouble at all. There is always one of the group who ends up not coming."

"Nevertheless, I'm grateful. May I buy you a glass of that exquisite wine we just sampled?" Rachel hoped he wouldn't get the wrong impression, but saw his wedding ring and assumed it would be okay. "Is your wife here? Perhaps I can buy her a drink too?"

"No, she is not here. They base us in America, but I am taking this cruise to conduct some business. When the ship returns to Southampton, we will continue on to the Baltic where the group will leave ship and I will fly back to New York from Russia." He still looked nervous and kept looking at his minders.

"In that case, it's just you and me, and as I owe Thomas a drink, I'm sure he'll join us." Then she looked at the Tweedle twins. "I'm sure these gentlemen can keep an eye on you from a distance."

The minders nodded and moved away, resulting in a more relaxed Boris. Rachel called Thomas over, and after buying drinks, found a booth away from prying ears.

"It must be so interesting being a diplomat. Do you like America?"

"It's alright. I haven't been stationed there long. Before I lived in Paris; I like France very much."

"Did you have to move?"

"Mother Russia decides where we should be." He spat out the words and she exchanged a cursory glance with Thomas, surprised at the venom in Boris's tone. As if sensing he had spoken out of turn and looking around, he continued. "Don't get me wrong, I love my country; it's just that my family had settled in France and my wife and I had to leave our two sons behind as they'd started university. My wife misses them and it makes life difficult."

"Paris is beautiful," said Thomas. "I've led many tours through the sights of that wonderful city. But I'm sure you and your wife will grow to love New York – there is so much to do there."

"How long have you known Mr Asimov?" Rachel wanted to move the conversation along, sensing Boris becoming morose.

Boris's face reddened. "Not long. We have business to conduct, that is all."

Now that reaction is interesting, thought Rachel, sensing the animosity and confirming her first impressions of Asimov.

Rachel saw Asimov speaking harshly to the Tweedle twins, who were now heading towards their table. Tweedledee spoke.

"Mr Asimov wants to continue with meeting now."

"Oh let the man finish his drink," said Thomas, but the minders were unmoved.

"I had better go. Thank you for the drink, Rachel. We will no doubt see you again at some of our other activities." He rose to leave, shaking Thomas's hand before the minders flanked him either side.

"That's an odd way to protect someone," said Thomas. "Normally the one being protected is in charge, but in that relationship, it seems to be the other way around."

"Yes, I had the same thought," remarked Rachel. She needed to find out more about that, but for now she felt hungry.

"You've hardly touched your wine, Rachel."

"I know, I don't drink that much. Not sure why I bought it. I think I'll get lunch now. Where are you heading next?"

"I'm lunching with ten of the group in the main restaurant. Tonight I'm accompanying Mr Asimov, Lucretia, Boris, Nikolai and three other ladies for dinner at the captain's table after the formal evening events are over."

"Impressive," she answered. "See you again soon."

Rachel rose from the booth seat, filing an idea that Waverley might want to get a seat at the captain's table. With luck, he might even wangle Rachel and Sarah in too.

She passed through the main atrium on her way to lunch and watched chefs creating the enormous ice sculptures they would display during the evening. There was a magnificent sculpture of the Empire State Building and an extensive array of other American themed creations, but the one that impressed her the most was the multi-coloured American flag with a ripple effect that made it appear to be blowing in the wind. Red, white and blue ice flowed through it to make it even more realistic, fifty stars representing the number of states in America. It was unsurpassed.

Rachel ate a light lunch in the buffet before heading down to the lido deck, and then walked around the ship for a while, thinking about what little she had discovered so far. A murder had been committed on board the ship and the chief suspect, Jefgeny Popov, was now missing, presumed dead. Some interaction had taken place between the missing man and at least two members of the Russian group. Did this have a bearing on his going missing soon afterwards? She thought it unlikely; he was probably on his way into hiding or suicide when she saw him in the corridor, otherwise he would have been at work in the engine room. That would rule out the Russians being part of a conspiracy.

What of Boris's reaction today? He obviously didn't like being part of this group and appeared to be guarded rather than minded. Why would that be? Her gut told her something was amiss, and after the events of the last cruise, she wouldn't be dissuaded from following the investigation through. She would try to get Waverley to agree to the next stage and see where it led.

She looked at her watch – time to meet up with Sarah.

Chapter 16

Sarah stayed with Bernard after morning surgery, in spite of being off duty. She wanted to make sure he was alright, so she attended a few on-board passenger injuries with him. He brightened up a little as the hours wore on and managed to banter with injured passengers in his usual way.

An elderly man had sprained his wrist while trying out the golf simulator. "I think I put a bit too much wrist into my swing," he explained.

"Perhaps you should save your strength for lifting cocktails," Bernard joked, and they immediately hit it off. As Bernard engaged with passengers and crew like his normal self, it seemed to be helping him forget the trauma of his shock awakening. Sarah would be glad once he'd managed to speak with Lauren and clear the air. Sadly, it wouldn't undo the faux pas of the previous night, and she worried about how he would live with that.

Gwen had called a team meeting for 1pm and Raggie, the medical team steward, would bring lunch up from the kitchen. Bernard and Sarah headed back down to the medical centre. The arrogant Lauren was already there, along with Graham and Alex. Gwen sat at her desk, while Raggie brought in extra chairs so that they could all sit down.

Gwen kicked the meeting off. "I thought it would be prudent to have a proper meeting as Sarah has now rejoined us and we've got a new team member, Lauren Blythe."

Bernard kept his head down, staring at the floor.

"We also have a number of passengers with long-term conditions, and as it's only our second sea day, Graham would like to update us on a few of these. I will let him go first, and then he and Alex can carry on with their work while we have a nurse meeting afterwards."

"Thank you, Gwen," Graham began. "There are five passengers I would like you to know about in case they call, and there are some I should warn you about, but I'm sure you will suss those out for yourselves!" He laughed. "Lauren, you're new to the ship so it's important that you learn and follow ship procedure at all times. If there is anything that you don't understand, I'm sure that Sister Sumner – Gwen – has already told you to ask. We are all very approachable, but there is a hierarchy on board a cruise ship that you may not be used to."

Sarah thought Graham sounded niggled about something and wondered if Gwen had filled him in on the Bernard situation, but doubted it. Nevertheless, something had rattled him. She felt curious as to whether she had missed something, but was pretty certain she had been listening. She paid double attention now.

"Of course," Lauren replied, sullenly.

Graham continued. "We have a seventy-year-old lady in 7160 with chronic obstructive pulmonary disease who carries portable oxygen when out and about on the ship. An oxygen concentrator was delivered to her room on embarkation day." He turned to Lauren again. "Are you familiar with concentrators?"

"They don't have them in the depths of Africa."

Missing or choosing to ignore the sarcasm, Graham explained. "Oxygen concentrators are big beasts, about the size of a large portable air conditioning unit – they convert room air to concentrated oxygen. She uses nasal specula rather than a mask so that she can carry on as normal without constantly removing the mask. You will only need to see her if she develops a chest infection while you are on call or if anything goes wrong with the equipment. Call me if in doubt – understood?"

"Understood," they replied in unison. The problems associated with a transatlantic crossing boiled down to the number of sea days if equipment broke down. They carried one concentrator and oxygen cylinders in the infirmary for emergencies.

"We also have a gentleman with lung cancer who's joined us for what he says will be his final cruise, having been given only a few months to live. Gwen and I have met with him and we will continue to take the lead in his care, so call us if needed. I just hope the poor man survives the journey – he's not in the best of health and I wonder if he fabricated the amount of time he has left when completing his medical questionnaire. However, it is what it is, and we will do our best.

"There's a teenager with a broken leg – broke it playing football a few days before the cruise. He's in plaster and may need one of you if the plaster needs replacing – he's a low risk for thrombosis, but be on the lookout, just in case. One of the Russians, a Mr Sergei Markov, is diabetic and hasn't brought enough insulin with him. He swears he did and it's gone missing, but he only has a third of a bottle with him, so will need fresh supplies – I'll leave that with you.

"Finally, another one of the Russians takes regular morphine tablets for chronic back pain. I've explained to him the importance of keeping supplies locked in his stateroom." Graham got up from his chair. "Well that's it from me. There are other passengers with medical conditions that are all on the computer if you get called out, but I thought I'd let you know about these five. I'll see you this evening, then."

Graham left the room.

"Do you have anything to report, Alex?" asked Gwen.

"No, most of the crew are in good health. Obviously they would be in better health if they didn't drink quite so much, but what can I say? Christine, the perfume shop manager, is five and a half months pregnant, but there are no complications at present. She will leave us on our return to England. There's the missing man who needs blood tests if he turns up, but that doesn't seem likely."

Alex got up and left the office. Neither of the medics had mentioned the late Erik Marinov.

Gwen continued the nurses' part of the meeting, explaining to Lauren what would be expected of her from tomorrow. Sarah was pleased Lauren would no longer be shadowing either her or Bernard, thinking it might be easier to work with her from a distance.

At the end of the meeting, Gwen turned to Bernard.

"Bernard, please show Lauren where the insulin is and how to sign it out so she can take a supply up to Mr Markov." She gave him a look of encouragement as he left with the enthusiastic Lauren trailing behind like a puppy dog.

"That should be that. He has the opportunity to bring an end to this awkward situation." Gwen exhaled a deep breath as if remembering something. Sarah felt guilty about knowing Gwen's secret. "I expect Bernard told you about an unfortunate relationship on my previous ship, and although different to this mishap – the eventual outcome amounted to the same thing. I just hope this girl takes no for an answer. Difficult relationships in the confined space where we all live and work together are not at all pleasant. I'm relying on you, Sarah, to do your best to get on with Lauren in spite of your friendship with Bernard. We can't have factions."

"I'll try, but she hasn't responded to 'friendly' yet."

Gwen groaned. "Well let's give it a go and see how it plays out. At least it's only for a fortnight. I've never seen Bernard drunk so don't understand how he managed to get into such a compromising state."

Sarah had to admit this had bothered her too. She'd worked with Bernard for nine months prior to her leave and he'd always remained in control of his faculties. For a start, medical staff could be called upon to assist even when not on call, so she didn't get it. Maybe he'd just let his guard down.

Gwen shuffled, waiting for a reply, staring at her, nonplussed.

"Sorry, I was miles away. I don't get it either, but I'm certain it will never happen again. I'd better go; I'm meeting Rachel for tea."

She omitted to say that Rachel was doing some sleuthing among the Russian contingent.

On her way out of the medical centre, Sarah almost crashed into Waverley. Then Lauren barged past her.

"See you later," Sarah called, but got no reply.

Waverley looked bemused. "Is something wrong?"

"No, I don't think so."

"Anyway, you're just the person. I wanted to have a word with you and your friend."

"I'm on my way to meet her for tea," Sarah replied.

"Could you both drop by my office afterwards? I'm sure she won't keep herself out of our little mystery so we may as well compare notes." He frowned, but couldn't hide a smirk. "Your friend does seem to have a dog with a bone attitude."

"Yes, it was the same at school. Rachel always uncovered wrong-doing. She put an end to a pocket money thieving racket by hiding out in the girls' loos and filming the gang bragging about it. They targeted weak kids and threatened them. She's always championed the underdog and detests bullies. I'm not surprised she's ended up in the police force."

"Well, well, well." Waverly stroked his chin.

"Anyway, we'll be there in an hour," said Sarah before dashing off to change from her blue scrubs into a white uniform for the passenger decks.

Bernard came out of the medicine room and saw that Sarah had already left. Gwen called him into her office, pleased to see him smiling.

"I take it your smile means it went well," she said.

"Not really, she's very angry and says it's all my fault that she has fallen for me – she says I led her on. I did try to explain that my flirting is just my way, and it means nothing."

"I expect that went down like a lead balloon!"

"How did you know? Yes, it seemed to make her angrier, and she gave me a ticking off."

"So why are you smiling?"

"Oh," he beamed, "that's because she says nothing happened. She said I passed out and that she got into bed with me, hoping that it would happen this morning, but when she woke up, I was gone."

Gwen sniggered, feeling pleased for Bernard. "At least there's no real harm done. Well, let that be a lesson to you – cut out the flirting."

"Don't worry, I've learned my lesson, and she's already told me I'm a huge disappointment to her, so thankfully she won't be renewing her affections. I can't wait to tell Sarah that I am still a faithful married man."

At that point, his on-call radio signalled he was needed elsewhere.

"Go on, off with you." Gwen couldn't help chuckling again, pleased that a potentially sticky situation had been averted with the minimum of fuss. She was finally starting to feel happy after the heartbreak of her own relationship.

If only nothing had happened there, she thought as she remembered the heart-wrenching pain she'd experienced when transferring away from the only man she'd ever loved. Exhaling loudly, she turned towards the computer to create invoices for medical treatments administered this morning.

Chapter 17

Rachel made her way down to Creams Patisserie and arrived at exactly the same time as Sarah.

"I can't get over how lovely you are in your shiny white uniform."

"You don't look so bad yourself," Sarah replied. They hugged and walked into the small café together. There was a surcharge on food and drinks in Creams so it was quieter than many of the public eating areas. They sat down and ordered tea while looking at the menu.

"Are you going to eat?" Rachel asked.

"I'll have something sweet. We had a working lunch during a team meeting."

The waiter came over to take their orders.

"I'll have a strawberry cheesecake, please, and tea," said Sarah.

"Chocolate cake for me and filter coffee, please," added Rachel.

As soon as the waiter had gone, the young women nattered about their day for a while and laughed a lot, something they always did when they were together. Once the food had arrived, and they were left to themselves, Rachel was keen to ask if there had been any developments in the case she was now informally investigating.

"Nothing further our end. Jefgeny is still missing. I bumped into Waverley on the way to meet you. He's acknowledged that you'll be looking into the Russians and wants us to stop by his office after tea for an information exchange."

"Oh, that sounds interesting. I wonder if he has anything meaty to share. I'm not getting very far with the Russians, but I'll share what I've discovered. Shall we do it all afterwards, then?"

"Yes, I'd far rather talk about trivia at the moment. It's been quite a day."

Rachel sensed Sarah had something on her mind, but knew that if her friend wanted to share it, she would. *It's probably something confidential to do with her work.*

"Okay, trivia it is. I went to a wine tasting lesson today and discovered many things I never knew before, ignoramus that I am!"

"Come on, then, spill the beans – I thought you looked blurry eyed."

Rachel laughed out loud. "The wine they got us to taste was pretty strong, and then I had a part-glass with Thomas and Boris afterwards – trying to get to know Boris, but our drink was short lived when the minders butted in. I'm not very good at lunchtime drinking."

"There's so much booze available on the ship, but officers have to watch the amount they drink, and our team has to be careful even when off duty as you never know when the next emergency might occur."

"This chocolate cake is scrummy," said Rachel as she took a big bite.

They spent the next hour discussing wine tasting and chocolate before Sarah looked at her watch.

"I guess we should go see Waverley. I need to get back to the medical centre for early evening surgery afterwards, and then change into yet another uniform for formal night."

The ship enforced an ultra-strict uniform policy for staff, and those allowed in the passenger areas wore different uniforms for different occasions. Sarah had told her previously that about a third of the crew never got to be in passenger areas at all. There were even different tiers of eating for those considered staff and those considered crew.

"Okay," Rachel replied. "And on the way, you can remind me about who eats where."

Before they left, Sarah signed the chit for payment. Rachel also signed as all her food and drink was free, courtesy of Queen Cruises.

They arrived at an office on deck three with a shiny bronze plaque on the door that read 'Security Office'. Sarah knocked and entered. Rachel followed and noted how pristine it was, like everything else on the *Coral Queen*. There was a monstrous oak desk with a veneer so shiny Rachel could see her reflection.

Chief Security Officer Waverly was seated on a large black leather office chair which swivelled away from them while he spoke on the telephone. He acknowledged them with his hand, without looking, motioning for them to take a seat. There was a small settee on one side of the room and two comfy chairs with a round glass table at the centre. There was also a fixed chair opposite the large desk.

Sarah opted for the settee and Rachel joined her, realising that in spite of her dealings with Waverley on the previous cruise, she had never been inside his office. Sarah smiled at her and they waited for the chief to finish his telephone conversation.

As soon as he put the telephone down, he swivelled his chair back towards them and rose.

"Sorry about that. Can I get either of you ladies a drink?" He moved towards them and took one of the seats.

"No thank you, we're good," Sarah answered for both of them.

Rachel felt like she was sitting in the headmaster's office at school waiting for Waverley to get to the point.

He looks tired, she thought, it can't be easy trying to investigate a murder on board a cruise ship while also being responsible for the safety of over six thousand people and answerable to the captain on all matters of security.

"I'll get straight to the point. First of all, Rachel – I realise you're not a member of the security team and you ought not to be involved in this investigation at all. The only reason you are here is because experience tells me you won't keep out of it."

He smiled grimly.

"I have been doing some background checks on our Russian crew members, Erik Marinov and Jefgeny Popov. First, Marinov had no criminal record. His background was clean, and he was a model employee for three years – no girlfriends; no fallouts with his friends who, incidentally, speak highly of him. We can find no motive for anyone to want to kill him, except perhaps his roommate."

He paused, allowing this information to sink in.

"Now to Mr Popov. He's also unmarried, brought up in the USA and a US citizen. He has a background in engineering and both parents are dead – other than that his background is a bit sketchy, but nothing pointing towards being a killer."

"If he was brought up in the USA, why couldn't he speak English?" asked Sarah. "When I saw him on embarkation day, he used Erik as an interpreter."

"That is odd. I don't know, but I'll certainly find out. Perhaps he was playing a joke on you."

"Is it possible the two men were in a relationship?" asked Rachel.

"I wondered that, but Mr Popov has a girlfriend on board. She is Slovenian and works in the casino. She is obviously distraught at his disappearance, but says she hasn't seen him since yesterday morning. I haven't told her his roommate may have been murdered; she insists they were good friends and confirms what others have said: that Erik took Jefgeny under his wing ever since he joined the ship two years ago. By all accounts, they got on well, and all eight Russians working in engineering corroborate this. All the others are clean. I had expected nothing else, to be honest – our pre-employment checks are rigorous."

Waverley didn't hide his defensiveness at this point. It was clear he had hoped the murder would have been a falling out between the two crew members that ended with the death of Erik Marinov.

"What about the girlfriend?" Rachel enquired.

"Eva Sipka – she has a clean record. No-one with a criminal record may work in the casino. She and Jefgeny have been seeing each other for the past six months and are in a steady relationship. It also turns out Miss Sipka might be pregnant; she's not yet had this confirmed by the medical team, but I have insisted she make an appointment to see Dr Romano for a pregnancy test and examination. As you can imagine, this has caused her even more distress."

"Oh my goodness!" gasped Sarah. "That's just what a girl needs – a partner who goes missing and a baby on the way."

"Welcome back to the *Coral Queen*." Waverley grimaced.

"Can I see a picture of the girlfriend?" Rachel asked.

Waverley walked over to his desk, fired up his computer and pulled up the record.

"Here you go, take a peek."

Rachel and Sarah both looked at the image of a woman in her twenties with dyed blonde hair. She had green eyes and her face was thin with pronounced cheek-bones.

"Thank you," Rachel said and returned to the settee.

"There is something else." Waverley's tone turned more serious.

"What?" asked Rachel, noticing that he appeared unsure of whether to give them any additional information.

"Someone ransacked Jefgeny's room last night. It's difficult to say whether the person or persons were looking for something or were opportunistic thieves. Both scenarios create problems for security. We have sealed off the room and changed the swipe code."

"Was anything taken?"

"They took a watch and a radio, but we don't know what else was there. We didn't find his passport when we searched the room yesterday and we have not touched the room since."

"What about CCTV?" asked Sarah.

"We don't monitor the crew passageways. The crew need to let their hair down sometimes."

He coughed and looked down at his shoes.

"Now we move on to the Russian party, although I can't see how they can be involved in this matter at all." He sounded frustrated. "But, I failed to follow your gut instinct last year, Rachel, and I do not want to make the same mistake. You understand I'm being over-cautious."

Rachel understood his frustration, certain that Asimov and Boris would have no qualms about making life difficult if they imagined for a moment they were under any kind of investigation.

Waverley continued. "There are thirty-two members in the group, twenty-one men and eleven women. Eight of the women are clean, with one of those being a renowned international opera singer, a Miss Lucretia Romanov. I saw her myself in Verdi's *La Traviata* a few years ago in St Petersburg." Waverley blushed at the reminiscence.

"That's Asimov's girlfriend," said Rachel.

Waverley coughed before continuing. "Anyway, two of the women have been fined for prostitution in the past, and one faced an assault charge after attacking her ex-husband's lover with a cricket bat."

"Nice," remarked Sarah.

"They released her after the victim dropped charges." Waverley coughed as per his habit, so Rachel guessed that something interesting was coming next. "Now for the men – it has not been easy to get much information about Vladimir Asimov, other than that he is a very rich man – self-made billionaire with a large empire. He is an ex-soldier who served in the Russian army during the cold war and had friends in the KGB. There have been rumours of links to industrial espionage, but nothing proven. There are also rumours his accusers tend to disappear, but as I say, these are rumours, and Russia sometimes thrives on disinformation and fake news.

"I have an old friend who is also ex-soviet army. He now works for the Russian police force. He will make some discreet enquiries for me, but has to be careful not to end up in trouble. Asimov is a powerful man in Russia. Anyway, I believe none of this has anything to do with our murder and is unlikely to be relevant.

"The other person of interest is Nikolai Stepanov."

At this point, Rachel sat up straight – he would definitely be on her list of suspects.

"Interesting," she said. "He appears to be a bit cloak and dagger."

"As well he might be," Waverley continued. "He's well educated – studied at Yale University where he did a degree in engineering."

"That gives us an engineering link," Rachel pointed out.

"Probably coincidence – anyway, he served in the Russian Navy as a chief engineer and is also rumoured to have links with organised crime. He works as personal assistant to Boris Stanislav, diplomat. We cannot find much background on Boris, other than that he's married, has two sons and works at the Russian embassy in New York. He has diplomatic immunity, but there are no rumours surrounding him. I've asked my Russian friend to dig up anything relevant in his background. The rest of the men have clean background checks and appear to be legitimate businessmen."

"What about the bodyguards?" Rachel asked.

"I have run their names and they are both ex-soldiers who boxed during their army days and provide personal security to Vladimir Asimov. What makes you think they are Boris's bodyguards?"

"Now that is interesting," said Rachel. "They are minding Boris, but I got the distinct impression he wasn't their boss and was happy to get away from them. I'm sure there's more to this setup, but whether it has anything to do with the crime on board this ship is another matter."

"Well, we don't want to get involved in any personal Russian business problems," said Waverley. A worried frown appeared on his face.

"All I've found out so far is that Boris does not seem happy. I suspect he's being guarded rather than protected, and you've just confirmed that." Rachel looked at Waverley and then continued. "I don't like Nikolai, but that doesn't mean he's up to no good. Asimov appears moody and must have assigned his own security to Boris for some reason. Mario said the Russians were arguing the other night, but I thought nothing of it at the time. There might be some unrelated shady business dealings. Nothing links any of them to the murdered crewman, or to the missing Jefgeny – so far." Exasperated, she added, "And who is the tall, thin man who said something to Jefgeny when we were on our tour of the engine room?"

Waverley got up again and moved across to his computer, pulling up images of all the Russian party for Rachel.

"That's him," she said as he scrolled through the photos.

"Let me see – he is Sergei Markov, also an engineer and also at Yale around the same time as Nikolai. He started a year earlier. He is fifty-three years old with a wife in Moscow, listed as next of kin – she does not appear to be on this cruise." Waverley ran his hands through his thinning hair. "We have to keep this in perspective – if we ran checks on all our tour groups and passengers, we would find something dodgy, so what we urgently need to do is find out what has happened to Jefgeny Popov."

"True enough," agreed Rachel.

"Sorry, but I need to get back to the medical centre," said Sarah.

"Yes, and I need to dress for the formal evening," said Rachel. "Is there anything else?" she asked Waverley.

"Yes, just stay out of trouble, and *do not* stir up a hornets' nest with the Russians unless there's anything relevant. My hunch is this is a murder/suicide for reasons we cannot yet explain."

"Guides' honour." Rachel smiled as she left Waverley's office, knowing exactly where she was going to sleuth next.

Chapter 18

Rachel studied her outfit in the mirror before leaving her suite. It had taken ages to decide what to wear to the formal evening. Most women would be wearing elegant full-length evening dresses with matching stole. That would have been her first choice, except she wanted to hide away in the Sports Bar next to the casino once the captain and his officers had finished their introductions.

Eventually, she opted for a royal-blue cocktail dress, appropriate for the evening, but not too dressy for the sports bar. The creative use of curling tongs produced soft waves through her hair. Satisfied with the result, she applied a light smattering of makeup and smiled at herself in the mirror, wishing Carlos was here to compliment her.

Rachel looked forward to seeing the men in their tuxedos, although none could look more striking than Carlos in a tux. A pang of guilt made her shudder, knowing he would be worried sick if there was any mention of the murder.

Mario passed her in the corridor. "Good evening, Miss Rachel, may I say you look radiant this evening?"

"Thank you, Mario. I see you're busy as usual." He had his hands full, carrying a tray towards Asimov's room.

"Yes, ma'am. Pre-dinner drinks for the men. They are having dinner with the captain so are not worried about attending the formalities until later."

"Oh yes, Thomas told me earlier."

Blast – she had forgotten to mention it to Waverley during their meeting. *Oh well, I don't expect it would have revealed much anyway,* she reassured herself.

"If you pick up any mention of a crewman from engineering, would you let me know?"

Mario looked concerned. "I hope you're steering clear of danger, Miss Rachel."

"Of course I am, Mario. They might know someone I met, that's all, and I don't want to appear nosey or I'd ask them myself."

The explanation didn't convince her, let alone Mario, but he nodded anyway.

"Goodnight, see you in the morning." Rachel walked towards the lifts and stairwell, deciding to take the stairs, even in high heels.

The main atrium was packed with dazzlingly dressed women. The men looked dapper in their smart well-pressed suits. A waiter offered her champagne, and she took a flute from his tray and helped herself to canapés. Thomas waved from across the room, gesturing he would come over to her. She laughed as he struggled through the crowds of people, who were excited to meet the captain for the first time. Formal evenings were a highlight of the cruise calendar for many passengers.

The captain stood, patiently shaking hands, having photos and selfies taken with as many people as he could before making his way towards the ice carvings where he would introduce the senior officers one by one. Rachel had met Captain Peter Jensen on the previous cruise and he spotted her as he passed by.

"Miss Prince, it's good to meet you again. I heard you were aboard." Being surrounded by passengers, he omitted to mention any trouble afoot. To look at him, you wouldn't imagine he had a care in the world.

Just what you need in a ship captain, she told herself.

"Good evening, Captain. It's a pleasure to be on the *Coral Queen* again."

"Captain, this way—" Voices called for his attention from every direction and he obliged the more excitable guests who wanted to shake his hand.

Thomas appeared. "This is like being at a pop concert," he said as he made his way over to her. "But no drugs! You look stunning this evening. You're always beautiful, but tonight you have excelled yourself."

"Hello, Thomas. You're rather dashing yourself. You do scrub up well – a tuxedo suits you. Is that Armani?"

"Yes – one of the perks of being single is I can splash out on expensive clothing. Isn't it exciting, seeing the captain?" Thomas glowed at the prospect of meeting Captain Jenson. Rachel smiled, not wanting to brag.

"Yes, it is one of the most surreal parts of cruising. Where are your charges?"

"Oh, most of them are around here somewhere." He waved his arms in the general direction of where he'd come from. "Mr Asimov and Boris are joining us soon, and then we'll meet the captain for dinner. I'm buzzing. I hope I'll be able to eat without dropping anything in my lap or spilling a drink."

"You'll be your normal, efficient self, I'm sure," she said, reassuringly. "Does that mean Boris gets rid of his minders for a few hours?"

"Yes, he does. In fact, he's told them to stay away from him. He and Mr Asimov had a heated debate about it. They forget sometimes I'm fluent in Russian."

Rachel's ears pricked up, and she grabbed two more glasses of champagne from a passing waiter's tray – handing one to Thomas.

"Tell me more," she whispered, conspiratorially.

"Well, I was waiting in Mr Asimov's suite for him to confirm arrangements for the evening when Boris barged in. He completely ignored me and marched towards Mr Asimov. 'Call them off, Vladimir, or the deal's off,' he shouted at him. 'I mean it – I'm fed up with them throwing their weight around. I can't breathe with them around all the time, so make it happen.' Mr Asimov shrugged his shoulders, saying he would deal with it. He then turned back to me, cool as you like, and told me in English to go through the evening's arrangements. It's because they speak such good English they forget about my Russian."

"I can't blame Boris for wanting space," said Rachel, thoughtfully. This confirmed what she had suspected: Asimov was having Boris watched, but what deal was Boris referring to, and did it have any relevance to the missing crewman?

The microphone burst into life, interrupting Rachel's thoughts, and the cruise director welcomed everyone before introducing the captain.

"Ladies and gentlemen, I give you – Captain Jensen." Loud applause followed the announcement, and the captain took over the microphone.

"Thank you all, and again, I welcome you aboard the magnificent *Coral Queen*. First, I would like to draw your attention to the wonderful ice carvings created by our own world-renowned chefs. They depict the state of New York and the American flag. We will dock in New York in five days' time, but in the meantime, there is plenty for you to enjoy aboard this magnificent vessel."

More applause followed, and Captain Jenson provided a brief history of his maritime experience before starting his introductions.

"Now I would like to introduce to you the finest senior officers I have had the pleasure to sail with." Further applause followed, and the captain introduced each of his senior officers, including the familiar CSO Waverley, the chief engineer, Steven Rafferty, and Dr Graham Bentley, CMO. There was a senior officer for everything, from housekeeping and hospitality services right up to the deputy captain.

Sarah wasn't there, and Rachel assumed she was busy in the medical centre. Alex stood with a group of other officers, and Lauren stood close to a few of the Russians Rachel recognised, including Sergei Markov, whom she had yet to speak to. She decided to ask Thomas to introduce her, but would need to invent an excuse for him to do so without arousing suspicion. It could wait because she had other plans for this evening.

As the captain finished, Rachel observed Dr Bentley being hurried away, followed by Boris, and then Thomas's radio came to life. He looked concerned as he listened to the message and paled before her.

"What is it?" she asked as he put the radio away.

"It's Nikolai. Someone has found him dead in his room. The doctor is on his way. I need to go – this is a terrible turn-up."

He turned away and headed towards the lift. Rachel followed.

"Wait, Thomas! I'm coming with you – you might need support."

He smiled appreciatively and slowed down. "I'd be grateful. Let's take the elevator – nothing like this has happened before. I'm not sure what I'm meant to do."

The lift was full of other passengers, so they spoke no more. Thomas was almost in tears – she wasn't sure what state he would be in when they arrived.

As soon as they got to deck fifteen, Rachel caught sight of Sarah, Graham, Alex and Bernard heading briskly towards them and the lifts with a stretcher. She assumed Nikolai's body was being transported down to the morgue.

"Make way, please," Dr Bentley called out to curious bystanders gathering in the corridor as the stretcher rushed past. Rachel recognised an IV bag being held in the air by Sarah as they raced towards the lift and realised what was happening.

"He's not dead." She gripped Thomas's arm, seeing he looked like he might pass out, and mouthed to Sarah that she would follow her down later. "Come on, Thomas. We need to find out what happened. Let the medical team do their job."

Rachel frog-marched Thomas towards a crowd of Russians gathered outside the stateroom she assumed belonged to Nikolai.

"Miss Prince, what brings you here?" Vladimir looked unhappy.

"I was with Thomas when he got the urgent call and came to ask if there is anything I can do."

"As you see, it seems to be under control. Mr Stepanov has taken ill, and the doctors have taken him to the infirmary."

A distraught voice sobbed out, "Taken ill? I thought he was dead."

Rachel noticed an elegantly dressed long-haired brunette sitting on a chair inside the stateroom, being comforted by two other women, one of whom was Asimov's *woman,* the famous opera singer.

Rachel took the opportunity to follow Thomas into the room. He walked towards the hysterical woman and took her hand, having regained control of himself, so Rachel could take in the scene before her.

The room was littered with miscellaneous empty wrappers tossed on the floor, left behind by the medical staff. Nikolai's suit hung over a chair where he had seemingly placed it neatly to dress for the evening. His shirt lay on the floor. She picked it up and noticed someone had cut it in half.

"The doctor cut it." The crying woman sounded more coherent. "They needed to put drip up. They got ready to do CPR."

Rachel nodded and put the shirt on the chair, noticing as she did so a pill bottle under the bed, which she picked up.

"I'll call down to the medical centre and ask how he is," she said.

"You can use phone in our room," Asimov's girlfriend said.

Rachel slipped the pill bottle into her clutch bag and followed the woman out of the room. "We haven't been introduced," said Rachel. "My name is Rachel; I'm sorry about your friend."

"I'm Lucretia. Thank you for being sorry, but Nikolai Stepanov is no friend of mine. He works for Boris." They entered her stateroom where Asimov sat on a sofa, wearing headphones. A vodka bottle alongside a half empty glass lay on the table. He smiled when Lucretia entered the room, but frowned on seeing Rachel.

"Rachel will call infirmary to find out how is Nikolai."

"Okay, the phone is there." In his usual abrupt manner, he nodded towards a phone on a desk.

As Rachel picked up the phone, the couple started a conversation in Russian and Asimov embraced Lucretia, speaking softly into her ear.

At least he can be nice, thought Rachel.

Gwen answered the phone and Rachel cautiously explained about the empty tablet bottle she'd found on the floor, checking Asimov wasn't listening. She needn't have worried – he and Lucretia had moved into the bedroom and were having a hushed conversation.

"What are the tablets called?" asked Gwen.

Rachel took the bottle out of her bag and was dismayed at being unable to make out the name due to the writing being in Russian.

Oh well, nothing else for it.

"Mr Asimov, would you mind telling me the name of these tablets, please? The label's in Russian."

Lucretia came into the room, followed by Asimov. "Where did you find this?" she asked.

"I found it on the floor in Nikolai's room. I wanted to tell the doctors in case he's overdosed by accident."

Lucretia took the bottle and her face blushed scarlet. "I'm not sure what you call them in English."

She handed the bottle to Asimov. With a big grin on his face, he looked at Rachel.

"I believe you call them *Viagra* in your country. They are for—"

"Thank you, I realise what they are for." Rachel spoke into the phone. "Apparently, they are *Viagra*."

Gwen chuckled at the other end. "I heard! I'll ask Dr Bentley to check – not your usual overdose tablets, but they can cause heart symptoms in large doses."

Rachel put the phone down and looked at Lucretia, avoiding any eye contact with Asimov, who was still chuntering in Russian, finding his own jokes very amusing.

"Thank you for allowing me to use the phone. Nikolai is unconscious, but stable. They're not sure what's wrong with him. If he doesn't improve, they will consider medical evacuation."

"Good riddance," muttered Asimov, drawing a glare from Lucretia.

"I'm sorry for Vladimir's ignorance. Nikolai is not well liked, but we hope he improves and we are relieved that the worst has not happened."

Rachel admired the way Lucretia held herself and wondered what on earth she saw in Vladimir Asimov – except, of course, his being a billionaire.

Each to their own, she thought as she left the stateroom, grimacing to herself at the idea of what an overdose of *Viagra* might do to a person.

Chapter 19

"CODE BLUE, 1512. Repeat, CODE BLUE, 1512."

Sarah was just changing into formal uniform after finishing a hectic surgery when the radio bellowed out the alert. Bernard was on call, but must need help. With a deep sigh and adrenaline pumping, she quickly changed back into her passenger deck uniform and raced upstairs to deck fifteen.

I hope it's not one of the Russians, but she knew intuitively that it would be.

By the time she arrived, Alex and Bernard were already there. A woman stood crying hysterically in the corner, and Sarah saw what looked like a body on the bed.

"I found him lying there," the woman screamed. "He's dead."

Alex quickly examined the body while Bernard prepared the defibrillator and resuscitation equipment. Bernard had already cut away the man's shirt for easy access to his chest. A couple rushed in, and the woman tried to console the weeping woman.

"Please, can you take the ladies elsewhere and make sure no-one else comes in?" Sarah instructed the man, who ushered the women out into the corridor.

"There's a pulse," said Alex, relieved. "It's weak, but there is a pulse. He's not breathing, though. Give him some breaths."

Bernard tipped the man's head back and attached a mask to his face, connected to an Ambu bag. He squeezed the bag to give some artificial breaths. Sarah attached oxygen tubing to the bottom of the bag and turned the portable cylinder on to give a high concentration of oxygen.

"If he doesn't breathe, we'll need to intubate," said Alex, sounding stressed. "Where's Dr Bentley?"

They all relaxed as the experienced Dr Bentley arrived and took charge. "What happened?"

"We got an emergency call," said Bernard. "Just as I was finishing a write-up, Alex got the call. We dashed up here together."

Alex took over the explanation. "A lady called saying she'd found a man dead. He appeared to be dead, but he has a weak pulse."

"Any signs of an overdose?" Graham asked.

"Not as far as we can see. According to the woman, he was getting ready to escort her to the captain's dinner this evening."

"Any injuries?"

"None. It looks like a heart attack – two young men on one cruise?" Alex sounded exhausted.

"Keep your voice down," hissed Graham.

"He's breathing now," interjected Bernard, "shallowly, but he's breathing on his own.

Sarah had a horrible feeling in the pit of her stomach and walked around the bed, but she couldn't see if there was an injection mark as Bernard had attached a blood pressure cuff to the upper arm.

"Okay, let's deal with what we have." Graham spoke calmly. "Sarah, get a drip in the arm, then we'll get him stretchered down to the infirmary and find out what's happened. For now we'll work on the premise he's had a cardiac event."

Sarah had difficulty putting the needle in the man's arm as the peripheral circulation rapidly shut down, but managed on the second attempt to find a vein. Bernard attached the drip to the cannula once it was in place while Alex and Graham got the stretcher ready.

"Call Gwen, ask her to have a bed ready and a CPAP machine available."

"What is CPAP?" A voice came from the doorway and Sarah noticed the man who had been there earlier.

"Ah, Mr Asimov," acknowledged Graham. "It's a machine that will assist with giving deeper breaths without the need for a ventilator – his breathing is shallow, but he's alive."

"Who is he?" asked Sarah.

"His name is Nikolai Stepanov," answered Bernard. "He is the personal assistant to Mr Boris Stanislav."

At that moment, Boris arrived looking almost as distressed as the woman. Frenzied activity came from the corridor as more and more Russians heard what was happening.

"I think it's time to go," instructed Graham as the crowd grew outside the room. "I'll call you later, Mr Asimov."

Bernard and Alex wheeled the stretcher while Sarah held on to the drip. Graham cleared the corridor ahead, reassuring passengers on the way that everything was under control. As they arrived at the lifts, Rachel came out of one with an anxious man looking like he might faint. Sarah assumed this to be Thomas. Rachel led the man away, giving her a knowing look and mouthing that she would call down to the medical centre later.

Once in the lift heading down to deck two, Graham became very serious, but gave Sarah a warning stare which she took to mean not to mention foul play. By the time they arrived at the infirmary, Gwen was prepared. They transferred Mr Stepanov on to a bed and attached the drip to a stand. His breathing remained shallow, but the bag of fluid had raised his blood pressure, bringing a little colour back to his face.

"What shall I put up next?" asked Sarah.

"Dextrose/saline," replied Graham. "Get a clot buster ready as well, just in case."

Gwen started up the CPAP which would cut in, giving Nikolai Stepanov deeper breaths if his own weren't enough. "Thank goodness for that," said Bernard. "My hand has cramped from squeezing the bag."

"Wuss!" Sarah laughed as the tension lifted because the situation had become less critical.

"Connect the heart monitor," instructed Graham, but Gwen was already on the case. "I'm going to need some blood. Let's do cardiac enzymes, but I want a complete blood screen. We need to know what's going on here."

"We're too far away for an evac aren't we?" asked Alex.

"Maybe, but he's stable now anyway, so let's give it until morning, if anything changes we'll need to consider speeding up or diverting." Medical evacuation was not an option from where they were in the Atlantic and wouldn't be ordered unless necessary and Graham was right: Nikolai Stepanov appeared stable.

"Telephone call for Sister." Raggie appeared in the doorway. Gwen left the room.

Bernard's radio sparked into life again, calling him to a crew member who had trodden on broken glass. "Drunk, I bet," he said. "Is it okay for me to go?"

Graham nodded assent and asked Alex to check the blood results. As soon as they were alone, Graham sprang into action.

"Right, Sarah. You know what we're looking for."

Sarah examined the upper right arm while Graham removed the blood pressure cuff from the left. He let out a deep breath.

"Thank God, nothing." He put the cuff back over Nikolai's arm and relaxed. "For a brief moment, I was terrified we might have a serial killer on board."

Sarah nodded, acknowledging she had been thinking exactly the same. Gwen came back, chuckling to herself.

"Well, I'm glad you've got something to laugh about," snapped Graham.

"I'm sorry. Rachel's just phoned – she found an empty tablet bottle in the man's room and she had to ask Mr Asimov the name of the tablets as the label was written in Russian." She giggled again.

"And?" Graham said impatiently.

"*Viagra*." She laughed out loud, almost losing control. "The label read *Viagra*."

Sarah thought Graham was about to lose it, but then he smirked.

"I see. My, my – do we know how many party pills he took?"

"No, but the bottle was empty. Rachel's going to make discreet enquiries and ask his female escort for this evening. He doesn't have a girlfriend – some of the ladies in the group are, erm, paid escorts. Rachel's not sure if that includes sex at present."

"The plot thickens! Next we'll have a brothel on board. The symptoms could be those of a *Viagra* overdose, but I don't think so. We'll bear it in mind. He could also have had illegal tablets concealed in the bottle, which seems more likely, his ECG is normal so are the cardiac enzymes. Is Rachel going to bring the bottle down?"

"Yes, later," replied Gwen.

"Where's Lauren?" asked Sarah.

"Where indeed?" growled Gwen. "She would have got the call at the same time as everyone else. I've just asked for her to be paged again."

Sarah detected Gwen struggling to contain her anger. All medical staff had a duty to respond to a *code blue*, without exception.

The door to the infirmary opened and Lauren breezed in wearing her formal evening uniform.

"There you are," grumbled Gwen, her tone sharp. "Where have you been?"

Graham excused himself while Sarah checked on Nikolai.

"To the captain's party – it was great—" She stopped and looked over at the bed, her face paling. "What happened?"

"What happened is that I called you to an emergency along with every other member of the medical team. As you can see, they are all here, while YOU have only just arrived."

"Who's that in the bed?" Lauren appeared oblivious to Gwen's frustration.

"For your information – his name is Nikolai Stepanov, and had you turned up earlier, you would have been fully aware of that and what has happened."

Sarah had never seen Gwen angry and busied herself with Nikolai's charts, pretending not to listen.

"Why did you not respond to your radio?" Gwen appeared to be softening slightly as Lauren looked like she might be ill.

"I muted it."

Whoops, wrong answer! Sarah cringed. She almost felt sorry for the idiotic woman, who hadn't appeared stupid before that moment.

Gwen's face reddened and her lips pursed tightly together as she shook her head in disbelief.

"You muted it?" she repeated through gritted teeth. "Perhaps we should continue this conversation in my office." Gwen turned on her heels. Lauren looked over at the man in the bed again, avoiding any eye contact with Sarah, before following Gwen.

"Is it safe?" Graham appeared from the lab area of the ward.

"Coward! Yes, they've gone into Gwen's office," Sarah replied. "I don't expect Lauren will miss a *code blue* again."

"Nor should she," Graham said. "I realise she's new and all, Gwen and I will make allowances for that, but between you and me, one more strike like this and she's out. She's already stepped outside of protocol once – now this."

Sarah wanted to ask what else Lauren had done, but Graham would not be likely to tell her, so she just nodded. Ship policies and procedures were paramount and had to be obeyed without exception. All staff had this drilled into them at induction, and many crew members learned the hard way with misdemeanours resulting in them being escorted off the ship at various ports around the world with no means of getting home. They all knew the rules.

Sarah felt exhausted. She'd only been back for two days, and there had been one suspicious death, one crew member missing, and now the near death of a passenger who was part of an important tour party. Graham looked worn out too – it must be hard for him. He carried the responsibility for the health and wellbeing of all passengers and crew, answerable only to the captain.

Gwen and Lauren came back to the ward.

"You can go now, Sarah," said Gwen. "Lauren will take the night shift and care for Mr Stepanov. Is the patient stable?" Gwen checked with Graham.

"Yes, his cardiac enzymes are normal, as is his heart rhythm, and he's breathing better – I have just stopped the CPAP. He's out of the woods. There doesn't seem to be anything remarkable with the blood results we have so far, either. It's a mystery. Alex will need to repeat the enzymes in a couple of hours."

"Okay, well I'll call it a night, too. Bernard is on call with Alex. Where is Alex?"

"He's gone to visit the passenger with chronic airways disease who might have a chest infection," replied Graham, turning to Lauren. "Any problems, call me, and as soon as he wakes up, I want to speak with him. I don't care what time that is – call me."

"Yes, sir," muttered Lauren, and this time Graham didn't correct her for calling him sir.

Sarah left Lauren after handing over and reminding her where everything in the treatment room was kept. "Give me a shout if you're unsure, I won't mind," she said, trying to be kind.

Lauren rolled her eyes. "I'm a very experienced nurse. I was qualified when you were still at school."

"Of course you are." Sarah walked away. *One who doesn't respond to emergency calls and tries to seduce my friend.* The sympathy train had well and truly left the station as far as Sarah was concerned.

On her way out, she caught sight of Rachel.

"I almost forgot you were coming. Let's go – my room, if you don't mind. I'm beat."

Chapter 20

Rachel went back to Nikolai's room after calling the medical centre and found Thomas and Natalia Fenenko, the woman who had found him. Natalia told them she worked as a paid escort. Boris joined them, jittery and agitated, pacing the room.

"How could this happen?" he repeated over and over.

"Did he have any illnesses?" Rachel asked.

"Not that I knew, he hasn't worked for me for too long."

"Is he likely to have taken an overdose?"

"I don't think so – but who knows what goes on inside another man's head?"

"He would not have taken an overdose," said Natalia, emphatically. "I saw him fifteen minutes before to confirm time to meet for dinner. He looked – how you say? – smug. He hummed well-known Russian song; he was happy."

"Perhaps he had a hidden illness," said Boris. "Anyway, I need to find papers Nikolai had, so please excuse me, ladies. See you later, Thomas." He took what appeared to be Nikolai's briefcase and left.

Thomas's colour had returned, but he still seemed incapable of doing anything, so Rachel took over.

"Can I get you a cup of tea?" she asked Natalia.

"I heard you British believe tea is answer to everything, but I would like vodka, please – there is some on his table there." She pointed towards the coffee table.

"Scotch," muttered Thomas, sitting himself down on Nikolai's sofa bed.

After pouring their drinks and opting for bottled mineral water, Rachel sat down next to Thomas and focussed on Natalia. "Thomas will need to write a report for his company. Do you mind telling us exactly what happened this evening? My name is Rachel, by the way."

Natalia explained how Boris had asked her earlier in the day to escort Nikolai to the captain's dinner. "I shouldn't say this, but Nikolai is not nice man, nobody likes him. He keeps requesting me, though, and the pay is good, so I do my job and give him good time."

Rachel assumed that the good time involved staying overnight. "Go on," she encouraged.

"I came to room at six-thirty prompt and knocked. He didn't answer, so I knocked again, loud. When he didn't come, I asked room steward from another room to unlock for me. She swiped door open, then I saw him lying on bed and told him to hurry. He wasn't moving. He looked white like sheet; I was sure he was dead. I screamed and pressed emergency button on telephone."

"Can you remember anything else? Did you notice this tablet bottle on the floor?" Rachel held up the empty bottle.

"No, I saw nothing except body on bed. I panicked and ran to door after calling for help, waiting for doctor. Male nurse and doctor arrived, then more people. Lucretia and Mr Asimov came to help me and other nurse arrived who asked him to clear room."

"Have you seen the tablet bottle before?" Rachel persisted.

Natalia looked embarrassed. "Yes, last night. He took pill out of drawer before going to bathroom to change."

"Did you see how many pills were in the bottle?"

"Yes, full bottle. I opened drawer to find out what he had taken. I suspected it might be drugs, but realised he needed pills to be man."

Ignoring the scorn, Rachel continued. "Can you think of anything else that appeared strange tonight? Did he seem unwell?"

"He looked well. He was gloating like he had won on horse or something – that is all."

Asimov turned up and suggested they leave Nikolai's room. He advised Natalia to join some of the others in the main restaurant for dinner.

"Thomas, we need to go for the captain's dinner."

Thomas followed him out of the room.

Rachel decided there was nothing more to discover and returned to her room, surreptitiously. She didn't want Asimov to know how close her room was to his.

The evening's events and wondering what had happened to Nikolai were giving her brain ache. What about the empty tablet bottle? An overdose seemed unlikely, considering Nikolai's mood, if Natalia was telling the truth. Unless the bottle contained illegal drugs, and he'd taken an accidental overdose of those.

Perhaps he had a heart attack – it happens.

Rachel headed down to the medical centre and bumped into Dr Bentley on his way out.

"Good evening, Rachel."

"Good evening, Doctor. How is he?"

"Recovering and stable. Sarah's in the infirmary if you're looking for her."

"Thank you. This is the empty pill bottle I found under Nikolai's bed. Natalia, the woman who found him, said it was full last night."

Dr Bentley took the bottle. "Curious! Thank you, Rachel. I don't think it's an overdose, and certainly not with these – the symptoms are all wrong, but I will ask Mr Stepanov about the empty bottle when he wakes." He slipped the bottle into his trouser pocket. Rachel noticed how fatigued he looked.

It can't be easy.

She proceeded through to the waiting room just as Sarah was leaving. They stopped by the buffet on the way to Sarah's room as neither of them had eaten anything substantial since lunchtime.

"I managed a few canapés before everything kicked off," remarked Rachel as she filled a plate with pizza and salad.

"You're lucky, I didn't even manage that. Surgery ran late, and I went to change into formals, but then had to change back when I got the emergency call. Seriously, what a day – again. First Bernard and Lauren, and then this. And Jefgeny is still AWOL – I guess he jumped after all." Sarah didn't pause for breath while filling a plate, choosing a high-fat, high-carbohydrate combo.

"What about Bernard and Lauren?" asked Rachel.

"It's a long story. Last night, Bernard got to his room and passed out, only to find Lauren in his bed this morning. He called me first-thing, beside himself."

"I can't believe it! He seems so happily married."

"Me neither, and what's more, I've never seen him drunk, let alone pass out. But as it turns out, once he explained to Lauren that there would be no repeat – of an event he couldn't remember, by the way – the wretched woman told him nothing had happened anyway because he'd flaked out. He's been floating on air since hearing that news. I still don't understand how he let himself get that drunk, though."

"Maybe he hadn't eaten enough," replied Rachel. "These cruises are becoming a bit too *Agatha Christie* for my liking."

"I know what you mean, but I'm hoping the only murder taking place will be that of Erik Marinov. Although that's one too many, it wouldn't be the first time a falling out among crew has ended up in a death. Rare, but not unheard of."

Rachel chewed over the events of the past two days, unable to take it all in. When they got to Sarah's room, they flopped into chairs and ate. Rachel hadn't realised just how hungry she was until that moment. Her friend looked shattered.

Sarah confirmed Nikolai had stabilised and what had happened with the rather eccentric Lauren.

"Serves her right she's been given the night shift."

"Ooh, that's not like you. She's really got under your skin, hasn't she?"

"I'm sorry, Rachel, but first, she would have taken advantage of Bernard when he's a married man, and then she swans into the medical centre after ignoring a *code blue* and enjoying an evening with the officers without a care in the world. Finally, when I did feel sorry for her and offered support following her rocketing from Gwen, what does she do? Bites my head off and tells me what an experienced nurse she is! I've a good mind to call the hospital where she trained and ask if she bought her qualification. I bet the Africans were glad to get rid of the weirdo."

Rachel laughed out loud following this rant. "I have to give it to her – I've never known anyone wind you up like this. Look, you're exhausted. You've only been back two days and have hardly slept. Get some sleep – we can catch up tomorrow."

"Actually, if you wouldn't mind, that would be great. I can't keep my eyes open much longer. Is there anything you need to tell me?"

"No, nothing that can't wait another day. It looks like the events of tonight are unrelated to your missing crewman." Rachel looked at her watch and realised it was after midnight. "I'll stop by the casino and catch a word with Jefgeny's girlfriend."

Sarah yawned. "Good idea."

Rachel got up to leave and Sarah dragged herself up and walked her to the door where they hugged.

"Catch you tomorrow, then," said Rachel.

After her meal, Rachel had got a second wind and made her way to the casino. She ordered a martini and lemonade, and asked the barman, "Can you tell me if Eva Sipka is working this evening?"

"Yes, she is on the roulette table."

Someone else ordered a drink, giving Rachel the opportunity to take a seat on a barstool with a good view of the roulette table. She took her phone out of her handbag and pretended to look at it. *Carlos would be proud of me,* but she knew he would more than likely be worried she was putting herself in danger. These thoughts did nothing for her concentration.

Arguing with herself that the facts pointed to a murder/suicide eased her conscience. It was time to focus on the woman at the roulette table.

Eva was tall, mid-twenties with long, shiny blonde hair. Although her face was pretty, her flint-like eyes showed a rugged determination. Rachel thought she looked prettier in real life than in the photo Waverley had shown her.

Rachel snapped a few photos with her mobile phone and studied them in close-up. This did not appear to be a woman grieving for the father of her child – if she was pregnant. In fact, Eva Sipka radiated happiness, joking with passengers gambling at her table, and with her colleagues. It could have been an act, but Rachel didn't detect any sign of loss.

That woman knows where Jefgeny is.

Chapter 21

"Did you do this?"

Boris looked visibly shaken as he followed Vladimir into his room after the captain's dinner, which had gone well considering the events prior to it. Now Vladimir had to deal with this irritating man instead of dancing with his beautiful Lucretia.

"Lulu, my darling, would you mind giving me a few minutes?" He scowled at Boris, took him by the arm and frog-marched him to his own room. "Please keep your voice down, you idiot. Lucretia knows nothing of our deal." He spat the words out while Boris fiddled with his swipe card.

"I will have nothing to do with murder."

"I have no idea what you're talking about," said Vladimir. "Why would I want to murder your PA? Anyway, he's not dead, is he?"

"Don't make out you don't understand why I'm asking. I told you he was blackmailing me. You were aware he wanted twenty thousand euros in return for silence."

"And I told you I would deal with him later," Vladimir barked.

"Exactly, but I didn't realise that meant attempted murder."

"I don't go around murdering people! I meant I would pay him and ensure he gets posted somewhere out of harm's way on our return to Russia. Siberia, perhaps." Vladimir chuckled.

"And that's it? I'm meant to accept you had nothing to do with this?"

Vladimir didn't like being challenged. Trying not to lose control and wishing he had not agreed to help his friend transport documents from the US, he glared at Boris. He had always known there would be risks with an unreliable pawn. Boris was likely to panic and give the game away at any moment, and his sudden belligerence annoyed Vladimir.

"You can believe what you like, but as far as I am aware, Nikolai is ill – unless, of course, *you* had anything to do with it. After all, it's you he is blackmailing."

"Don't be ridiculous!" Boris reddened again. Sweating, he loosened his tie and slumped down in a chair.

At least the idiot had quietened down. "Did you tell anyone else?"

"No, only you. Did you?"

"No, the only people who know about it are you, me and Sergei, who is trustworthy."

"What about your minders? They heard the conversation."

"My minders are well paid – they have no reason to tell anyone else. Look, this is an unfortunate illness. The doctor told me over dinner it was most likely drugs or a heart attack. It is convenient, yes?"

"It would have been more convenient if he'd died," blustered Boris, "but I still want nothing to do with that kind of thing. Just my luck he survived."

Boris put his head in his hands. He looked upset but appeared satisfied with Vladimir's answer.

"Everything will be alright."

"I guess so. I'm worried about breaking the law, that's all – this is a one-off job. You do get that, don't you?"

"Yes, yes," replied Vladimir. *At least, until the next time.*

He smiled to himself as he left the room.

Day 3

Chapter 22

The ship's soporific rocking motion soothed Sarah to sleep as soon as her head hit the pillow. She was in a deep slumber, dreaming of surfing off the coast of Hawaii. The waves enveloped her multi-coloured surfboard, along with that of a handsome black-haired hunk. The rise and fall of their surfboards made her feel alive. They were laughing as they approached a monster wave. As they were climbing it, finally nearing the top, her companion became separated from his board and disappeared under the water.

He cried out, "CODE BLUE, INFIRMARY!"

She woke up sweating in a panic before realising it was a dream.

"I REPEAT, CODE BLUE – INFIRMARY." The radio bellowing on her bedside table was not a dream.

Oh no!

She quickly climbed into her scrubs, taking a gulp of water before diving out of the room towards the infirmary. She rushed through the doors to see Bernard performing CPR while Alex stood at the head of the bed. Having intubated Nikolai Stepanov, he was delivering respirations in between Bernard's cardiac massage. Graham injected adrenaline directly into the patient's heart and other drugs through the IV tube. Gwen was drawing up and passing drugs as Graham barked out instructions.

This scene had played out a thousand times before in hospital casualty departments, but it was a first for Sarah on the *Coral Queen*. She took in the situation in a matter of seconds before leaping into action, adrenaline and muscle memory taking over.

Sarah ran towards the bed and took over from Bernard, who looked whacked. Cardiac massage was draining, and he looked like he'd been doing it for a while. Lauren was at the foot of the bed, writing down the drugs used on a chart.

"How long?" she asked Bernard.

"CLEAR!" Graham shouted. They all stepped back from the bed and Graham released a defibrillator shock. Nikolai's body jerked as the voltage shot through him, but it made no difference to the heart monitor that continued in a straight line.

"Forty-five minutes. Lauren put out the call; me and Alex were first on scene. Graham and Gwen have been here a while too. He's only had one shockable rhythm, and that was it, but—" Bernard spoke quietly as if Nikolai might hear, "he's not coming round."

Graham had obviously come to the same conclusion as he shook his head and stood back from the bed. "Stop what you're doing, folks." He looked at his watch. "Time of death 04.17. We'll need more blood, fluid and swabs for post-mortem and toxicology, Alex. They'll be tested when we hit New York."

Alex nodded and began the process of extracting blood from Nikolai's collapsed veins, along with fluid from the eyes. Lauren recorded time of death on the chart while Gwen removed the leads and tubes from the dead man. This was the first time someone had died in the infirmary and the team looked low, the atmosphere was gloomy. Quiet descended as each person processed the death and performed their various jobs like automatons.

"I'm going to order some coffee from the kitchen," said Gwen. After finishing their tasks and covering the body, they all followed after her, except for Bernard and Sarah.

"We'll move him," said Bernard.

Sarah and Bernard cleaned up the corpse of Nikolai Stepanov and wheeled him through to the morgue.

"I don't like this room," said Sarah. She looked at the six metal doors, each drawer comfortably capable of housing a body until they reached port. In spite of knowing that large cruise ships were required to have a morgue on board, she wasn't happy at the amount of use this one was getting.

"I would think it strange if you did," said Bernard, trying to cheer her up. As soon as they had put the body away in a refrigerated container, he winked at her. "I hope that's the last one – we only have four drawers left."

Sarah thumped his arm playfully, which made them both laugh. They made their way to the office to join the others for coffee.

"I'm really sorry, Gwen, I must have been in a deep sleep."

"Don't worry. We knew you'd been up all night on Saturday – I asked them not to call you at first, but I thought you'd want to know, so I put the call out."

Sarah smiled in appreciation, but noticed Lauren giving her a stony stare. "Thank you," she said to Gwen. Glaring back at Lauren, she added, "That was very thoughtful."

Now you're being childish, she rebuked herself.

"Okay, perhaps now the crisis is over, Lauren can tell us what happened," said Graham as he took a swig of coffee.

All eyes turned towards Lauren. "Everything was quiet, his obs were stable until he woke up and started thrashing about. I tried to calm him down and tell him what had happened, but then he fell back on the bed. I only just managed to stop him falling out. He'd pulled off the monitor leads, so I didn't see his vitals. I tried to rouse him, checked his pulse and airway. There was nothing, so I dialled the emergency through and started to resuscitate. Bernard arrived first, we tried to bring him round. Alex came next, then the rest of you, except for Sarah, who was asleep."

Sarah rolled her eyes at Bernard, who smirked.

"So we don't have a recording of his rhythm before he arrested?" asked Graham.

"No – sorry, sir, I didn't have time to put the leads back until Bernard arrived." Suddenly she started to cry. "We're all going to die! It's Novichok – I've been reading about it on the news. I'm certain this is it, and he coughed all over me before he died."

Graham gawped at her, astonished. "Of course it's not Novichok. The symptoms of a nerve agent death are completely different to what happened here. My dear girl, Russians don't carry nerve agents around like smarties."

"I think perhaps you should go to bed, Lauren," said Gwen, calmly. "You've had a difficult induction into cruise ship life. I can assure you this is far from normal. I concur with Dr Bentley. This. Is. Definitely. Not a nerve agent death, and I must insist that you do not repeat such thoughts to anyone on board ship. We do not want unsubstantiated rumours spreading like wildfire, causing alarm. Are we clear?"

Lauren nodded, wiping her eyes, whimpering.

Alex patted her on the shoulder. "Come on, I'll walk with you. It's most likely a tragic heart attack. You'll feel much better in the morning. It's been a stressful night for all of us."

Lauren heaved herself out of the chair slowly and walked off with Alex.

"Don't take her for a drink," Sarah muttered sarcastically under her breath, but the twinkle in Gwen's eye revealed she'd heard.

"How extraordinary!" Graham was still processing the outburst. "Perhaps working in Africa has warped her vision. I've never heard anything so absurd."

"We'd better keep a closer eye on her," said Gwen to Sarah and Bernard.

"Perhaps she's suffering from stress," said Bernard.

"I suppose it could be PTSD," said Graham. "No signs of it until now, though."

"Maybe she's got an over-active imagination," added Sarah. Unable to understand why she couldn't feel any sympathy towards Lauren, she didn't say any more.

"I'd better go and inform the captain we've had a second death. He's not going to be happy about it. I'll let Mr Stanislav and the tour guide know in the morning. Would you mind hunting out the next of kin, Gwen?"

"Already done, he has a brother in Moscow. I've emailed you the name and number."

"Thank you. Goodnight all. See you in a few hours."

After Graham had gone, Sarah poured another cup of coffee for herself, Gwen and Bernard. "I don't want to sound neurotic, but we are treating this as a natural death, aren't we?"

"I was wondering the same thing," said Gwen. "It's the Rachel influence."

"I refuse to work with a bunch of paranoid nurses." Bernard laughed. "One is quite enough."

"You're right. It was either a heart attack, or an overdose," said Gwen. "There're certainly no nerve agents on board this ship, and our Russian friends are enjoying a nice holiday the same as all the other passengers. Perhaps we're all jittery over the death of Erik Marinov. I don't imagine the two deaths are linked, but I can't help be sad about the tragic deaths of two young men on our watch."

Sarah looked at the time; it was 6am. She excused herself and decided to go and see Rachel for breakfast and fill her in on the night's activities.

Chapter 23

Getting out of the shower, Rachel heard knocking. She grabbed a towel robe and looked through the spyhole. Mario arrived with a pot of coffee just as she opened the door to let Sarah in.

"You're up early! I thought you'd sleep in this morning."

"Yes, I thought I'd keep up with the Princes and join you for breakfast. Is that okay, Mario?"

"Yes, ma'am. I will bring breakfast for two. Would you like cooked as well as cereal and toast?"

"Yes, I would please – I'm famished," replied Sarah.

"Me too, Mario, please," said Rachel.

Mario left and Rachel moved over to the settee and poured coffee for two. Sarah still looked weary.

"He died," Sarah whispered.

"I assume you mean Nikolai Stepanov?" answered Rachel, frowning. "What happened?"

"Suspected heart attack, but it could have been an overdose. Toxicology tests can't take place until we reach New York. Oh Rachel, it's so sad – he was only forty-eight."

"He looked even younger than that, I would have put him in his thirties," said Rachel. "I assume that this one is natural causes?"

"Everything points that way. Lauren says he woke and thrashed about before collapsing so it sounds like it. Afterwards the silly girl became hysterical, suggesting it was Novichok because she'd read about it in the news."

"A slight overreaction then?"

"Not half! As if we don't have enough to deal with without having a paranoid drama queen nobody likes. Rachel, that girl's unhinged."

"If it's any consolation, nobody seemed to like Nikolai either. I certainly didn't, but wouldn't wish him dead."

"Well, let's hope that's all the deaths on this particular sailing. Gwen's blaming you," Sarah said, laughing.

Rachel laughed too. "I was wondering that myself."

"I'm not superstitious, but I do hope there's not a third, although if Jefgeny is dead that would make it three, wouldn't it?"

"Maybe; I'm not sure Jefgeny is dead."

"What makes you say that?"

Mario knocked at the door and came in with a trolley laden with food. "You ladies looked hungry," he explained. "I've brought fresh coffee too."

"Thank you so much, Mario. We'll enjoy this. How is Mr Asimov? I met his girlfriend last night."

"She is nice lady," he replied. "They have early visitors this morning. Dr Bentley is in Mr Asimov's room along with Mr Stanislav and tour guide, Thomas. I am about to take coffee and tea there now. *Bon appétit*, ladies."

"Thank you," said Sarah and Rachel in unison.

Rachel poured milk on her cereal and topped up the coffee cups while Sarah tucked straight into her breakfast. "I never know when I might eat again, and getting up in the early hours always makes me hungry. There's nothing like the smell of fried breakfast and fresh percolated coffee. Anyway, tell me why you don't think Jefgeny is dead."

"I have no proof, but I studied Eva Sipka from a distance last night. The woman just didn't appear to be someone who'd lost the man she loved. Call it a woman's intuition, but I suspect she knows where he is."

"Did you talk to her?"

"No, I only watched. The roulette table was busy with passengers. I suspect the best time to catch her would be at one of the dinner or theatre times, but I will butt out and ask your Officer Waverley to speak with her."

"That's a good idea. The captain wouldn't want you getting involved again and Waverley could get into trouble. Are you still going to spend time with the Russians?"

"A little, but only because I like Thomas. He's fun, and he needs support. He'll take the death of one of his tour party personally."

Rachel and Sarah enjoyed the rest of their breakfast and sat on the balcony for a while, staring out to sea, drinking more coffee. Rachel felt happier when the colour came back to Sarah's face, but was tired herself. The Jefgeny case with its tenuous link to the Russians had been wearing. It was time to put it all behind her. It wasn't her case and there was nothing more to investigate.

Smokescreens weaving in and out of my head, that's all.

"Look at me, still in my bathrobe! I guess I won't be working out today, but I might go for a swim later. Not my favourite, but it could be fun competing for pool space."

"You do that. I'm pleased you're going to keep your head down, Rachel. I'm hoping the medical team gets a quiet spell too – we're bushed. I'll be happy to treat drunks and break up crew brawls rather than come across any more bodies."

"Sounds like a policewoman's lot!" said Rachel.

"Are you okay now? We haven't had a chance to discuss your court case, but can you forget about it?"

"Yes I can, it's over. In fact, Carlos has been nagging me about moving closer to him in London, and my parents would be happy for me to work somewhere in Hertfordshire, so I'll start looking for jobs when I get back. I've given Leeds constabulary four years of my life, so I'm not obligated to stay there any longer." Rachel didn't feel it was the right time to tell Sarah about the threats Tansley had made after the trial; she already had enough on her plate.

"And of course there is always cruise ship security. Waverley would love you on his team. Quite a few of the security team are leaving over the next two years – some are long past retirement age and the cruise line is pressuring Waverley to take on new blood."

"If it weren't for Carlos, I'd jump at the chance right now, but I wouldn't like to be away from him for nine months at a time."

"Sounds serious. I'm so pleased, Rachel. I like Carlos and he's good for you." Sarah didn't say how much she had disliked Rachel's ex-fiancé.

"He is lovely, but I'm still wary of commitment after Robert. I really believed I knew him; it shattered my confidence in my judgement."

"Rachel, you're a great judge of character, but we can all be blind when it comes to love. Trust me, Carlos is nothing like Robert, and from the way he looks at you, I can tell he adores you."

"He is wonderful and Marjorie loves him." Marjorie was a spirited elderly lady Rachel had met on her previous cruise, and they'd remained friends ever since. "Dad's as wary as I am, and he and Carlos prowl around each other like they're on eggshells. Mum says Dad's being overprotective and he'll come round. I do hope so because it's just not helping."

"I'm sure you're right. When the time is right, your dad will embrace Carlos for making you happy after the trauma you went through before. Anyway, I'm not sure where the time's gone, but I'd better sneak back to my room and get out of these scrubs before anyone sees me. Surgery starts in an hour."

"Are you on call?"

"No, Gwen's taking Lauren's on call as she's worried about her state of mind. Graham's on for the docs. Shall we meet for afternoon tea or in the jazz bar tonight?"

"Both, if you're free."

"Great – see you at three."

Sarah left and Rachel dressed, putting her bikini on under her clothes. It was time to pay Waverley a visit before getting back into holiday mode.

He was at his desk typing on his computer when he spotted her.

"Come in," he called. "Miss Prince," he coughed, "sorry, Rachel. Please don't tell me you're the bearer of bad news today."

"No, not exactly. I'm not sure I have any news, just a hunch."

Rachel didn't miss the caution on his face. "Take a seat and tell me about your *hunch*." He moved away from his desk and came round to the comfy chairs. Rachel joined him and told him about her observation of Jefgeny's girlfriend last night and her suspicion that Eva might know where Jefgeny was hiding.

"If he is hiding," she finished.

"I see – and you base all this on the premise that the woman looked happier than you would expect?"

Flushing, Rachel answered. "When you say it like that, it sounds odd, but yes, that's all I've got to offer."

"She has an appointment with Dr Romano this morning to determine whether she is pregnant. The best I can do for you is to ask him what he makes of her emotional state. We have already interviewed Miss Sipka, and she seems genuinely distraught – perhaps she's good at her job and manages to hide her grief. We are certain Jefgeny Popov is no longer on the ship. My team have even searched the lifeboats to make sure he's not hiding in any of these. He killed Erik Marinov after a row, and afterwards, filled with remorse, he threw himself overboard. That's my conclusion." Waverley emphasised his conviction by slamming a folder down on his desk.

Rachel understood his logic, but she still had her doubts about the facts. In spite of this, she determined not to get entangled in something that was not her concern. Waverley had become silent, making it clear her suspicions were something he didn't want to hear.

"Thank you for seeing me." Rachel left his office a fraction irritated by his attitude. "Well, CSO Waverley, I've done my civil duty. Now it's down to you," she mumbled to herself as she made her way towards the lido deck.

Chapter 24

A balmy day greeted Rachel out on deck, the ship rocking gently back and forth as soothing cross-waves passed underneath. Perching on a sun lounger overlooking the busy pools, she spent the morning sunbathing on the lido deck. The sun's rays reflected off two deep blue swimming pools, with crowds rushing in to take advantage of the opportunity to swim or bask in the sunshine. In the captain's morning bulletin, he'd said the temperature would be twenty-six degrees centigrade, providing plenty of heat even with the gentle sea breeze that swept across the deck every so often.

Waiters and pool attendants carried out their daily tasks efficiently and appeared whenever anyone was thirsty. Beefy aromas from the grill bar wafted down, reminding her she was hungry, but Rachel decided to make a move to the salad bar in the main buffet. The fried breakfast had provided more than enough fat for one day.

She pulled a summer dress over her bikini, picked up her book and vacated the sun lounger. On entering the buffet area, she had her hands squirted with hand disinfectant by a waitress – one of the many routines that took place on board a ship.

"Rachel!"

She turned around. Thomas was carrying a tray of what looked like Jamaican food.

"Hello, Thomas."

"Join me over there when you've got your food." He nodded towards a window table for four. Boris sat tucking into his lunch.

"Okay, see you in a minute."

There was a Jamaican theme today, and the staff were wearing brightly coloured clothing to match it. A diverse selection of

Jamaican delicacies was on display and she opted for a jerk chicken fillet to accompany her salad before negotiating her way to where Thomas and Boris were sitting.

"Did you hear about Nikolai?" Thomas asked.

Rachel wasn't sure whether she would be betraying Sarah's confidentiality if she replied honestly, so she carried on chewing, showing she couldn't speak.

"I'm afraid Nikolai passed away," Boris whispered.

"I'm so sorry," said Rachel. "That must be terribly upsetting for your party."

"Not really, people didn't like him and they didn't know him well. They are sad that someone has died, but not enough for it to be of any great concern."

Rachel stared in shock at his easy dismissal of the tragedy. Thomas explained.

"Russians aren't afraid to say what they think, Rachel. Unlike us, they are not constrained by politeness. That doesn't mean they're not concerned by the sudden death of one of their group, and Mr Stanislav has found the incident very distressing."

"Yes, it is most inconvenient. He has left me without a personal assistant for the rest of the cruise. It has been big upset for Natalia Fenenko, the poor girl who found him. She is very shaken."

"Have they said what caused his death?" Rachel asked.

"It was a heart attack or an overdose," answered Thomas. "They won't know for certain until he has a post-mortem. The family have requested repatriation to Russia for that, which the cruise line has agreed to. The insurance company will foot the bill and his brother is flying to New York to return home with the body."

"I see," said Rachel. "How is Natalia today?"

"She is okay; the ladies are taking her for pampering session in health spa," said Boris. "Russian ladies enjoy pampering. You are welcome to join them for some time, Miss Prince."

"Thank you, that's kind – I'll bear it in mind." Rachel detected a degree of agitation emanating from Boris and wondered what was on his mind.

They were distracted by sudden 'Oohs' and 'Ahs' as people gravitated towards the windows. Rachel followed their gaze and saw a large pod of dolphins swimming beside the ship.

"Aren't they gorgeous?" she exclaimed.

"Oh, they're awesome." Thomas beamed from ear to ear. Even Boris was smiling.

"Amazing creatures, and so intelligent," he said. "They are catching fish that ship is disturbing."

They remained transfixed by the spectacular display right before their eyes as the dolphins leapt through the air, diving in and out of the water.

The pod eventually disappeared from view.

"Now you wouldn't see that from an aeroplane," remarked a gleeful Thomas. He looked carefree again, and the sombre moments had passed. Boris still had a faraway look in his eyes as if something was weighing on his mind, but he returned to the present and smiled at Rachel and Thomas.

"If you will excuse me, I have some business to attend to."

"See you for the group massage, 4pm," Thomas called after him. Rachel gave him a look.

"Group massage?"

"Men only." He winked, then more seriously, he remarked, "To be honest, it will help them chill out. There's been too much tension in the air, particularly between Mr Asimov and Boris, and Sergei pops up from nowhere with alarming regularity. I swear that man never smiles – a more dour face, I've never encountered. Honestly, group dynamics, Rachel – be thankful you can hop in and out."

"I can't say I'd want to be around the sour-faced Asimov for very long, and Boris looks to be in a world of his own. Is Sergei the tall man with grey hair and beard?"

"Yes, that's him."

"I've noticed him from time to time. What does he do and where does he fit in?"

"As far as I'm aware, he's a businessman who part-owns some businesses with Mr Asimov. It's funny, I heard some of the others say he was at Yale at the same time as Nikolai, but they never spoke. That said, Sergei is older than him, so perhaps they never met."

"Still, you would expect old Yalies to have something to say to each other," remarked Rachel. "Maybe he imagined Nikolai was below him, being a PA."

"He seems to think everyone is below him. The party is generally more at ease when only one of the big three is present."

"Even happier when none are there, I suspect," said Rachel, laughing.

"Indeed. Anyway, I'm afraid I need to meet some of the ladies in the casino for a Blackjack lesson."

"Oh, can I come too?" The words were out of her mouth before she could stop them. *It can't do any harm, and perhaps Eva is off duty.*

"Please do. I hate gambling, but needs must." He held out his arm for Rachel to take.

On arrival at the casino, they saw a few men from Thomas's party and two women, none of whom Rachel had spoken to before. She recognised Eva Sipka coming towards them.

"Hello, I'm Thomas the tour guide, we're all here now."

"We will have the lesson on the other side of barrier."

Staff had put a makeshift security rope in place to cordon off an area of the casino, preventing other passengers entering. Thomas, Rachel and the rest of the group followed Eva. Rachel still didn't detect any sadness in the woman's demeanour or eyes.

The eyes are the window to the soul, her father had always told her, and she believed it. These eyes sparkled. *She is pregnant, then,* thought Rachel.

"Please, ladies and gentlemen, take seats around the table."

The table formed a large semi-circle in shiny mahogany with a golfing-green cloth cover. The group positioned the padded low-back stools around the semi-circular part. Rachel climbed up on to one next to Thomas. There were seven of them in all, and they stretched around the table while Eva moved to stand behind the flat edge.

It took the next thirty minutes to learn the rules of Blackjack and have a few practice games. Rachel found herself interested in the psychology of the game in spite of having a natural aversion to gambling. It was interesting to learn that despite them all playing against the dealer, the actions of one player could have a detrimental impact on other players, who might lose money when someone made the wrong call.

"You will find other players become impatient with you if you keep doing this," Eva explained.

Thomas nudged Rachel. "I might give it a go tonight, just to annoy people."

"You wouldn't!" The evil twinkle in his eye gave him away. It was such a pity he had to be with a serious group – he would be much better with party lovers. She felt sorry for him.

Some of the group lost interest towards the end of the game – in all likelihood, they knew how to play already. They dispersed, leaving Thomas, Rachel and one other man called Marat.

"Where you from?" Marat asked Eva.

"Slovenia, but I was born in Croatia. My parents moved to Slovenia when I was three."

"I have an uncle in Slovenia," Marat continued. "You are not wearing ring. No husband back home?"

Rachel noticed a brief flicker of unease.

"I hope to marry soon." Eva instinctively put her hand over her abdomen as if reassuring her unborn baby.

"Good luck with that. I had two wives – no more." He laughed.

"Until the next time, he means," joked Thomas.

Marat slapped Thomas on the back. "He's right – until the next time."

At this point, Marat got up and left the table, accepting defeat on the chat-up front. Thomas looked ready to leave too, but Rachel wanted to take advantage of the turn in the conversation.

"Does your boyfriend work on the ship?" she asked Eva, who looked around as if to check no-one was listening.

"He did, but no longer." Apprehension crossed the young woman's face.

"Will you return to Slovenia when you marry?"

"I hope to live in America. What about you? Do you have a boyfriend? You are very beautiful."

"How do you know I'm not her man?" asked Thomas.

Rachel suspected Eva had sussed Thomas out.

"My boyfriend is back in England, his name is Carlos," Rachel answered.

"She's breaking my heart," said Thomas, reaching for her hand.

"Eva – time for a break." A young woman with dark-brown hair tied in a ponytail approached the table.

"Thank you for the lesson." Thomas led Rachel away. "Sorry to desert you, but I'd better go for my man massage."

"Enjoy yourself," Rachel answered, but was miles away, mulling over the conversation with Eva, and more convinced than ever Jefgeny was still alive.

Waverley will have to believe me now.

Chapter 25

While she was on her way towards the main atrium, a man bumped into Rachel, causing her to drop her bag and spill its contents.

"I'm so sorry." The man stooped down to help her pick things up. "I can't have been looking where I was going."

"No harm done. Do I know you from somewhere?"

"I don't think so, unless you come from Nottingham?"

"No," she replied. "Anyway, thank you for helping. Goodbye." Tucking the clutch bag under her arm, she went in search of Sarah. She caught sight of her friend seated at a table for two by a window, staring out at the Atlantic.

"Penny for your thoughts," said Rachel as she leaned in to embrace her friend.

Sarah smiled up at her as she took the seat opposite. "Just daydreaming, wondering whether it was wise to take on another nine-month contract."

"But you love the work," Rachel said.

"I do usually, but these past few days have been extremely difficult. I don't feel like I've been off duty at all, I'm grumpy all the time, and on top of that, we now have an unreliable and peculiar colleague to cover for." Sarah lowered her voice to a whisper.

Noticing the strain telling on her friend's face, Rachel tried to encourage her. "Well tonight you're off and we'll enjoy a nice dinner – how would you like to go to the Steakhouse?" Sarah loved steak.

"Oh, I'd love that. Don't mind me, I'm just having a moment. How's your day been?"

"It's been good." Rachel decided not to mention the Jefgeny thing. "I lazed about sunbathing all morning, had lunch with

Thomas. He makes me laugh, so I'm behaving like quite the cruise passenger! We even spotted a pod of dolphins that put on a spectacular display for everyone in the buffet."

Sarah cheered up. "That's great, Rachel. Actually my day has been alright, apart from the lack of sleep. I saw children in morning surgery and made them laugh – they love getting good children stickers and cartoon plasters."

A waiter came along and took Rachel's order for tea, and she chose a chocolate cake from his trolley. Sarah opted for a waffle and strong coffee.

"It's amazing how much food is available. Where do they store it all?" asked Rachel.

"It's more difficult for six sea days as there aren't any stops to stock up, but there are huge storage facilities below decks with great big industrial freezers, fridges and racks of food. Every item of food is monitored, though, and they do run out sometimes when a particular meal is popular – then it's frantic for the kitchen staff."

"I don't know how the waiters manage those trays stacked high with dinners either."

"Trust me, they don't always. You'll hear the occasional clatter of metal when an accident occurs. I'm sure you'll witness one at some stage, but they are amazing and well trained by the hospitality officers."

As they finished their drinks and food, Sarah yawned. "I'm going to head back to my room to catch a nap before evening surgery. Shall we meet at eight?"

"That sounds perfect, I'll see you then – enjoy your sleep."

Rachel took a deep breath before heading downstairs to see if Waverley was in his office. He had a passenger with him, but motioned for her to wait outside, so she found a seat overlooking the sea.

Passengers milled along the corridors en route to destinations or activities. She watched a teenager whose parents were arguing about whether she could go off on her own to explore while they attended a quiz in the Sky View Lounge. People appeared happy. Rachel felt relaxed sitting there, but couldn't help being inquisitive regarding Jefgeny's whereabouts, and why he might be hiding. *Did he kill his friend?* Waverley seemed certain he had, but Sarah said they were close and she was worried about Jefgeny's health. Sometimes the most obvious explanation was the true one, but Rachel couldn't help wondering…

Waverley's door opened, and the passenger shook his hand, thanking him for his time. He gestured for her to come in.

"I suppose you want to ask where I've got to regarding Eva Sipka?" he said. Not waiting for a reply, he continued. "Miss Sipka is pregnant, Dr Romano says she's ecstatic. She told him she would like to vacate the ship in New York as she has relatives living in North Carolina. Dr Romano says she's twelve weeks pregnant, and he's advised her to get a scan at sixteen weeks. He asked who the father was, and she admitted it to be Jefgeny Popov. Dr Romano can find no evidence she believes Mr Popov is still alive. In fact, he says she broke down when he mentioned him."

An Oscar winning performance, no doubt!

Rachel paused before shattering Waverley's happy 'case solved,' dream. "I met Eva Sipka this afternoon when I joined a few of Thomas's tour party for a Blackjack lesson."

A frown appeared on Waverley's face. "Why do I feel this will ruin my day?" He gave a wry smile.

"Miss Sipka was unaware I knew anything about her situation, and as one of the men asked her a few innocent questions about boyfriends and so on, she opened up. She made it quite clear she expects to marry soon, and that she plans to live in the United States. There was no mention of the pregnancy, but she talks about a boyfriend in the present tense."

Waverley's face reddened, then he coughed. "She could have been spinning a yarn for the passenger's sake – she's hardly going to say her boyfriend is missing."

"You're right, but why say anything at all, and why flower the story with marriage and settling in America? You said yourself she asked to disembark in New York. Is that usual? If she's on her own with the father of her child presumed dead, surely she would want to work for as long as possible and return home to Slovenia to give birth? You also said Jefgeny's passport was missing."

Waverley put his head in his hands. "If what you are saying is true, we have a suspected murderer on board this ship and a crew member harbouring him." His voice raised a pitch.

"I'm afraid so," answered Rachel.

"Then I need to speak to the captain and bring her in for questioning."

"You could do that."

"I take it you don't agree?"

"Only that Eva's not the type of woman to give up the man she loves and the father of her child, and we can't prove she's hiding him. We only have a supposition. She's more likely to drop her guard when it appears no-one is looking for Jefgeny. At some point, Eva will tell a friend or lead you to him, if you're patient."

"I suspect you're right, but I will need to ask the captain's permission to follow her. Unfortunately she knows the security officers. I can't ask you to follow her because you're not allowed in the staff areas – we do have a new woman in training who Miss Sipka won't have met. This officer can keep watch, but if we have not found Popov by Friday, I will have to question her. Please keep out of this now, Miss Prince, and enjoy the rest of your cruise."

"That's fine by me, Officer Waverley."

Two can play formal.

Rachel dressed for dinner in a turquoise cocktail dress, this time using straighteners on her hair to rein in the waves appearing from too much sun. After applying a smattering of makeup, she was ready. The dark lines that had been under her eyes had all but disappeared and the sparkle had reappeared. The Tansley matter had passed from her mind, and a new job was the top priority after the holiday. She had already spent an hour looking at vacancies in the Metropolitan Police force, and also in Hatfield, not too far from London, and close, but not too close to her parents. It would be cheaper to live there than in London, too.

Entering the main atrium, she browsed around Customer Services before sitting for a while, admiring the shiny marble pillars circling the entertainment area where passengers congregated day and night while the ship sailed. She helped herself to an A4 sheet of daily news snippets from the UK. Deck four formed a part of the tiered atrium, also visible from deck five which encircled the area where Rachel now sat. It was accessible via a spiral staircase and a viewing lift that ran up through the centre of the ship for those who wished to admire each of the main passenger entertainment decks.

Rachel saw Sarah walking towards her and stood to greet her. The colour had returned to Sarah's cheeks. Her brown eyes shone against the backdrop of the white uniform and her brown hair was tied loosely back and perched on top of her head.

"You look much better, and beautiful." They hugged.

"You don't look so bad yourself. Come on, let's go eat. I'm ravenous again."

They walked up two flights of stairs to deck six and on to the steakhouse. As Rachel had pre-booked, the waiter led them to a table for two next to a window, away from the main eating area. Sarah had to be discreet in passenger areas and preferred not to draw attention to herself.

"This is perfect," said Sarah, choosing to sit behind a pillar with her back to the other tables.

"I thought you'd like it. I explained to the manager you would be joining me and we wanted a private area. He was very nice."

"That would be Martin Lonsdale, he's popular with passengers and staff."

"He called himself Marty," said Rachel.

"Yep, that's him. He worked in Vegas at some of the top steakhouses there."

"My mouth's watering already." Rachel concentrated on the menu.

A waiter appeared at the table. "Can I get you anything to drink, ladies?"

"Are you happy with Shiraz?" Rachel asked Sarah.

"Yes, that's fine, and a jug of water with ice, please."

The waiter left them to decide on their meals and returned with the water and the wine, asking Rachel to taste.

"Now I get to practise what I learned at the wine tasting session yesterday. Okay, I first have to check the wine's clear from above. Now I tilt the glass and scrutinise it against the white tablecloth." She was having fun with this, and the waiter was encouraging her.

"Next, ma'am, the smell."

"Yes, I smell it – this one smells spicy – and now my favourite part: the taste." Rachel took a small sip and swilled it around her palate before swallowing. "You know, that's not half bad!" she exclaimed.

"Thank goodness you didn't spit it out like they do when tasting more than one!"

Rachel nodded to the waiter, and he poured wine into both of their glasses before setting the bottle down on the table. He also poured them some water.

They ordered steak dinners, both opting for T-bone which included fillet and sirloin. Rachel asked for well-done and Sarah requested medium. The smell of steak filtering through the restaurant made Rachel feel hungry.

"I rarely eat steak, so this is a real treat for me, and I never eat T-bone, it's too expensive."

"Last time on board, I ate in here twice. Once with Daniel, the guy I dated for a while."

"Have you heard from him since he moved ships?"

"I get the occasional email, but he's not the one for me. That man's still out there, somewhere," answered Sarah, smiling.

"It's good to see you smile," said Rachel. "You've had a torrid return to cruise ship nursing."

"Yes, but today's been more normal. The sleep helped. The only irritation is that one of the Russians, Sergei Markov, has lost his insulin again. Lauren's taken him another vial from the ship's supply and Graham has given him a lecture on safeguarding medicines."

"Isn't that dangerous if a child should find it?"

"It's not ideal, but unless the child has a syringe and needle, they would be unlikely to come to any harm. Anyway, he thinks he threw it out in the trash with a tissue he'd used to wipe blood away. Probably drunk too much vodka."

"Yes, Mario says they like their vodka."

Rachel and Sarah enjoyed a succulent steak dinner and Rachel finally told Sarah about the threat Tansley had made after he'd been found guilty. Her friend looked alarmed.

"Is he dangerous?"

"He's small-time, I suspect, but there have been rumours of links to a drugs gang. I'm hoping he'll forget all about me, and anyway – I've made the humungous decision to find a job in the south."

"Oh, that's a relief. Does anyone else know about the threat?"

"No, I got an anonymous letter attached to the windscreen of my car. I can't even prove it came from him. I just know it was."

"You should tell Carlos and your senior officer, just in case."

"You're right. I didn't want anyone to think I was overreacting; I was so pleased the trial was done and dusted, I put it out of my mind. Carlos and my parents seemed worried enough about me coming on another cruise, I didn't want to make things any worse for them. Carlos has been under a lot of strain himself with a case he's working on."

"That's just like you, Rachel, always putting other people first."

"Pot and kettle comes to mind," said Rachel, laughing.

"Well I'm pleased you'll be leaving Leeds if it will be dangerous for you to stay there."

They finished their desserts and both had a Baileys.

"Drink up, Sarah. I've had an idea."

Chapter 26

"You can't be serious, Rachel!" Sarah's voice had taken on a screeching sound. "What if someone sees me? I could lose my job."

"The room's been untouched, waiting for forensics on land after the ransacking. There might be something in there that would give us a clue." Rachel didn't want to get Sarah into trouble, but was desperate to find out what had happened to Jefgeny.

"Rachel Prince, Waverley will not like this one little bit. Neither will Graham, for that matter."

"You want to find out what happened to Jefgeny? He might be lying ill somewhere." Rachel cringed at using emotional blackmail on her best friend. Sarah looked exasperated as she chewed her bottom lip, something she always did when pondering an issue. Rachel had first noticed it when they'd shared a flat together at university.

"Come on, then, let's go."

"Now?"

"You asked for it, and this is the best possible time, while most of the crew are still at work. Evenings and mornings are their busy times. Those not working will be in the crew bar or café. You'll need to change, otherwise you'll stick out like a sore thumb."

Rachel knew better than to argue the toss now, so meekly followed Sarah back to her room where her friend handed her a set of blue scrubs.

"You're kidding?"

Sarah shrugged, eyebrows hitting the ceiling. "Are you coming or not? Besides, you'll look good in scrubs."

Rachel gave her a look. "Don't push it!" She obediently donned the pale-blue trousers and short-sleeved top.

"Welcome to my world – here, put these trainers on. You can't wear those heels." Sarah was clearly enjoying this now. The trainers were a half-size too small for Rachel and pinched her toes, but they would have to do.

"Stay close and keep your head down if we pass anyone. You'd better tie your hair up. Use this."

Rachel tied her hair into a ponytail with the blue hair bobble. "At least it matches," she said, laughing.

"I always accessorise!"

"Yep, forgot that."

Sarah checked the coast was clear. Rachel followed her to the end of the corridor and through a door marked STAFF ONLY. Once through the door, Rachel resisted the temptation to take a peek in the crew bar.

They descended the same steps she had trodden during her engineering tour. At least she assumed they were, otherwise they were identical. When they reached a deck three floors below the waterline, Sarah slowed, motioning for her to stay still while checking the corridor. The noise level had risen, the grinding of metal extinguishing any sound from their rubber soles. Rachel stifled a cough as musty smoke residues irritated the back of her throat. Hoping it wouldn't make her gag, she regretted not having drunk more water during dinner.

About halfway along this narrow corridor, they came to a door screened off with yellow tape marked: SECURITY DO NOT ENTER. Rachel's heart beat faster as the realisation of what they were doing and the trouble they might get into sank in. She pictured her and Sarah being thrown off ship in New York and wondered whether to suggest they turn back, but Sarah had already opened the door. As a ship's nurse, Sarah carried a universal swipe key that would open any room on board in case of emergency.

Sarah held the door open. "Come on, quick," she hissed.

Rachel paused, but boots and voices entering the corridor further down removed any doubts and caused her to dive into the room and close the door. She stood with her back to it.

"Someone's coming."

Sarah's face looked deathly pale as they waited. The footsteps got louder and Rachel could almost hear her own heart thumping above the noise before the footsteps passed by the room and proceeded on their way.

"Must have been crew," said Sarah. "Right, let's get on with this. What are we looking for?"

"No idea, let's take a peek around. Good grief! It's so small in here, and dark. Where's the light?"

Sarah turned the light on, which cast shadows around the room, but didn't make it bright. "This is how it was when Erik was found. His was the lower bunk. Security packed his belongings, which are now in the purser's office." Sarah was staring sadly at the bed.

Rachel surveyed the room, taking in the scene. Cramped with single bunk beds against one wall, it had a small table with bottle stains and an ashtray still containing cigarette butts. Clothes were scattered on the floor from the ransacking on the day Jefgeny went missing.

That might have been Jefgeny throwing things together before going into hiding, thought Rachel.

"You search his pockets while I check the bathroom – you're the policewoman," said Sarah, handing Rachel a pair of surgical gloves while putting on a pair herself.

"Hm, nurses would make good criminals," Rachel teased, before turning out Jefgeny's pockets. Whoever had ransacked the room had emptied most of the contents onto the floor, so she found nothing.

She picked up a newspaper and checked for any writing or clues, but there were none. There wouldn't be any documents as Waverley would have those locked away.

"Found anything?" Sarah asked.

"No, nothing. You were right, there's nothing here." Rachel bent down to pick up a photograph frame from the floor and saw a photo of two men in high spirits, dressed as pirates in a port somewhere. "Is this Jefgeny and Erik?"

Sarah took the frame. "Yes, that's Jefgeny on the left and Erik on the right."

There was another small photo frame on the floor with a photo of Jefgeny and Eva.

"The ship photographers sometimes do snaps for the crew as keepsakes," explained Sarah.

"I don't think we're going to find anything here – unless all the films I've ever watched are true!" Rachel removed the photo of the two men from the frame, checking the back. Nothing. "Or not." She laughed, then she removed the back of the portrait of Jefgeny with Eva and saw something folded in half. "Jackpot!" she exclaimed.

Sarah came and sat beside her on the lower bunk bed. "What is it?"

Rachel opened the faded piece from a newspaper which contained another photo of two young men, standing either side of a pretty young woman with two small children. One of the men had long hair and a beard and moustache. The photo was in colour, although faded.

"The one on the right is Jefgeny. Do you agree?"

Sarah took the photo. "Yes, the red hair is a giveaway, and the woman has red hair too. I wonder who the others are."

Rachel looked at the picture again. "The other man looks familiar, but I can't place him. He's obviously the woman's husband or partner because they're holding hands."

"Perhaps they are Jefgeny's family or friends. The woman could easily be his sister," suggested Sarah.

"But why hide the photo?" Rachel was preoccupied, playing with the old piece of American newspaper in her hand when the headline jumped out at her.

PROMINENT BUSINESSMEN FOUND GUILTY. Two key witnesses go into witness protection after giving evidence in data theft trial.

Rachel skimmed the article, describing a trial involving a conspiracy to steal plans of a driverless car blueprint from Future

Motors, a major company in the USA. The article revealed that a man called Marian Krokowsky, an industrial engineer, and a Russian scientist named Jerzy Bobrinsky had entered witness protection. The US granted Krokowsky citizenship, and Bobrinsky defected. The prototype blueprint was worth an estimated one billion dollars, and Krokowsky and Bobrinsky had revealed the names of two prominent US senators, a US industrial espionage gang leader and his son, along with four Russian businessmen and politicians. The police had intercepted the handover, thanks to information provided by Krokowsky and Bobrinsky, resulting in four of the men being jailed for thirty years each. Two of the Russians working at the Russian embassy had had diplomatic immunity and were deported back to Russia. The rest were given jail terms of various lengths.

Sarah read the article over Rachel's shoulder. "Blimey! This is bigger than we imagined."

"Yes, I suspect that Krokowsky or Bobrinsky took on the new name of Jefgeny Popov, which is why you and Waverley had so little information about his past. Krokowsky, probably, as he was the industrial engineer. The man and woman in the picture must be related to Jefgeny, and it may be all he has left of his past. If Jefgeny is in witness protection, he would have had to sever all links with family. What a comedown, though, from industrial engineer to this."

Rachel looked around the room.

"Perhaps it's where he felt safe, and at least he was still using his engineering skills, getting three square meals plus full board and lodgings with a salary on top. If you think about it, a cruise ship is a great place to remain anonymous."

"Someone found out, though, and killed his friend."

"Do you suppose they were trying to frame him?"

"Or maybe Erik was killed by mistake."

"We have to tell Waverley, but I'm likely to lose my job for breaking ship's rules."

"I agree, we do need to tell Waverley. Can I sleep on it, Sarah? I want to think it through some more, and I'll work out a way of getting Waverley to show me this room without involving you. I want to try to keep you out of it." Rachel placed the photo back inside the paper and folded it up, after taking photos of all the evidence on her mobile phone. She placed the frames back on the floor where she had found them.

Sarah checked the corridor again, and they made their way swiftly back upstairs to her room. Rachel changed her clothes and hugged her friend.

"I'll work something out. It could still be a murder/suicide with no connection to Jefgeny's past." She sounded more reassuring than she felt.

"Thanks, Rachel, but if not, I'll just have to face the consequences. Waverley needs this information in case there is a connection." Sarah's eyes filled up and Rachel was ashamed at having dragged her into this.

"Yes, he does, but there will be a way of telling him without involving you, I'm sure."

Rachel left her friend, determined to protect her somehow.

What the heck is going on? Where are you, Jefgeny Popov?

Day 4

Chapter 27

At one stage during the night, Rachel could hear shouting in the corridor, but it settled down quickly. Restless at the startling discovery in Jefgeny's room, she pressed the button on her phone to check the time and groaned: 3am.

Turning over to get a drink of water, she heard someone trying the door of her room. Rachel leapt out of bed and raced to the door, peeping through the spyhole. The dark-brown hair of a man's head was just visible as he swiped the door and pressed the handle, but Rachel always double locked so no-one could get in. She frantically tried to control her breathing while watching the handle move again.

The man swiped repeatedly while she slowly took off the double lock and pulled the door open. Seeing the look of surprise on his face, she squared up to him.

"Who are you?" she demanded. He looked familiar, but appeared to be drunk.

"Sorry, I must have the wrong room," he slurred and staggered.

"Yes, you have," said Rachel, turning to shut him out. Before she had a chance to move away, the man put his foot in the door. Grabbing her, he spun her backwards, holding a knife to her throat. It all happened so quickly, she had no time to react.

He pinned her tight, walking her back through the room, holding the knife to the front of her neck.

"PC Prince, you have a debt to pay," he snarled in her ear.

Rachel's brain was doing somersaults, trying to work out why he looked familiar. Sucking in air, she croaked, "What are you talking about?" Her mouth was parched, but she figured the longer she kept him talking, the more chance she might have of disarming him. The blade was sharp against her neck, restricting her movement.

"My brother sends his regards."

"Tansley?"

"That's right. He would have come himself, but he's otherwise engaged. But you know all about that, don't you?"

The man walked her towards the balcony.

Not again! What is it with people trying to throw me overboard? She had found herself in the same predicament on her previous cruise. Seeing the irony of the situation, she burst into uncontrollable laughter.

Taken aback by her hysteria, the man loosened his grip. "Oh, you think it's funny, do you? Perhaps you'll be less amused when you take an early morning dip."

Rachel seized the opportunity as the man relaxed his grip to open the curtains. She quickly moved her left hand up against her chest, grabbing his right hand, and rotated his arm, keeping it close to her chest. She then bent forward and slipped behind him in rotation, still holding his right arm close to her, so that the knife was pointing upwards, away from her. As she twisted his arm, he dropped the knife, and she was able to deliver a swift blow to the back of his neck with both of her hands. He lost his balance for a moment and she kicked the knife away before picking up a chair and hitting him hard.

He still lunged at her, just like his brother had done. Managing to avoid the blow from his fist hitting her full in the face, she grabbed his hand and twisted his arm hard behind his back. Using all her strength, she carried on twisting until he cried out in pain.

"Better men than you have tried this before." She spoke through gritted teeth. Without releasing her grip, she pushed him towards the door. "Now open it."

He pulled the door open. Her lungs bursting from the effort of holding his arm in the same position, she pushed him along the back corridor to Asimov's room.

"Let go, pig!" he cursed.

"Knock on the door," she ordered. He knocked with his left hand, and Rachel was relieved when Tweedledum came out of another room. Tweedledee answered Asimov's door at the same time. An astonished silence ensued for a split second until Rachel broke it.

"Can one of you hold him while I call security?"

They grinned. "With pleasure." Tweedledee picked Tansley up and thrust him against a wall. "Would you like to fight me?" He pushed his face up against the man's nose. Tansley looked terrified now.

"No."

"Shame, I like to fight cowards who hit women." He punched the man hard in the stomach to show he meant business. Rachel grimaced as Tansley fell to the floor.

Asimov arrived at the door in his dressing gown and stared at Rachel, who had scratches to her arms and neck and a bruise to her face. Suddenly feeling exposed wearing her scanty nightclothes, but thankful for the two-piece shorts and shirt, Rachel started trembling.

Lucretia appeared. "What are you men doing? Bring her in here." She covered Rachel with a bathrobe. "Call security, Vlad."

Asimov did as he was told while the twins guarded the attacker who remained on the floor of the corridor. Two security guards arrived, and after taking a brief history from Rachel, took Tansley away. They told Rachel the CSO would come up to visit her within the hour.

Asimov looked confused, but Lucretia remained practical. She sat Rachel down, as Rachel was shaking uncontrollably, the adrenaline surging through her body in the aftermath of the attack. Lucretia handed Rachel a drink.

"Vodka, it will steady nerves," she said.

"Thank you." Rachel took the shot and swallowed it in one go. As the heat of the vodka reached the back of her throat, it made her cough, but it soothed her at the same time. "That hit the spot!"

"Another?" Lucretia asked.

Rachel nodded and did the same again. The trembling was settling and her emotions were back in check.

"Sorry for disturbing you, but I couldn't let him go to use the telephone," she explained.

"Did he try to rape?" Lucretia asked, putting her arm around Rachel. Rachel appreciated the woman's concern, but wasn't sure how much to say, not wanting them to know she was a police officer in case Asimov was involved in Jefgeny's disappearance.

"I'd rather not talk about it. Thank you so much for your help. I'd better get back to my room now until the chief of security comes."

"I understand." Lucretia spoke softly. "Vladimir will escort you safe to room." She nudged the confused looking Asimov.

"Yes, of course. Where is your room?"

Rachel smiled. "It's the suite opposite yours."

"Oh! Well come along then." He led her across the rear corridor, back to the safety of her room. She swiped the card in the door and he noticed the mess inside where the fight had taken place. "Looks like you need Mario. Shall I call for him?"

"No, thank you. I'll deal with it later."

"Where you learn to fight?" he asked with admiration in his voice.

"I'm a karate black belt." Rachel decided not to mention additional self-defence from the police academy. He seemed satisfied with the answer.

Seeing the weapon lying on the floor, he said, "If I were you, or if it had happened to Lucretia, I would have used knife." He pivoted and strode back to his room. Rachel saw Lucretia waiting in the doorway and waved before closing the door.

Rachel had showered, dressed and made a cup of coffee by the time Waverley knocked on her door. She presumed he would have a universal door swipe, so called out.

"Come in."

Her whole body was weak and jelly-like. She reasoned this was as a result of the adrenaline release, the fight and lack of sleep.

Waverley looked worried when he caught sight of her and squeezed her shoulder before sitting down opposite. "How are you?"

"I've been better." She forced a smile.

He was taking in the surroundings and looking at the knife on the floor.

"I haven't touched it. It's evidence. You'll need to fingerprint it, and won't find any of mine on it." Rachel's emotions had shut down; she was speaking on autopilot.

Waverley appeared relieved. "That's good. Please can you tell me what happened here?"

Rachel explained how she couldn't get to sleep and how, on hearing someone trying to get into her room, she'd surprised them.

"He seemed like a drunk, to be honest, but I was stupid because a drunk wouldn't have a key card to my room, and this man did."

"How did that happen?"

"I lost mine yesterday – I realise now it was him who bumped into me, knocking my bag out of my hands. The contents spilled out. He helped me pick them up, which must have been when he took the key. I assumed I'd lost it, and as they don't have room numbers or names on them, I thought it would be okay. I also double-lock at night, but I was tired and not thinking straight when I opened the door."

"Do you know this man?"

"No, I don't. He's the brother of someone I recently arrested for murder, so there was a resemblance. I received a threatening letter after the trial, but didn't take it too seriously. He said his brother sent his regards when he held the knife to my throat."

"What was the brother's name?" asked Waverley, taking notes.

"Tansley – Steven Tansley."

"That confirms it – the man's name is Ray Tansley. He'll be locked up now for the rest of the cruise and we'll hand him over to the police in New York. I need to bag up the knife. If you don't mind, I'll send someone to come and fingerprint the door and the key card he used to get in. Were you in one of the public areas when he bumped into you?"

"Yes, I was in the main atrium on my way to meet Sarah. It was just before three."

"We'll look at video footage from that time. We should have enough evidence, along with the knife and your testimony, to put him away for attempted murder, or at least aggravated assault. I need to ask you to drop in to see Dr Bentley later this morning. He'll write a full report of the injuries and take photos. I'll let him know to expect you. Is that alright? I can ask him to visit you here if you prefer."

"No, let your team come and gather any evidence they need. His fingerprints will be on the curtain and the balcony door. He was going to throw me overboard."

She grimaced. The irony was not lost on Waverley, who scowled.

"I'll let Dr Bentley know to expect you first thing. The perpetrator denies attacking you, says you invited him up to your room, but we have enough evidence to keep him locked up for the duration. With forensics as well, he won't get away with it. My team are searching his room as we speak and I suspect there will be more evidence to find there. He will not bother you again, Rachel." Waverley used her first name in a fatherly manner, which she appreciated.

"Thank you."

Rachel took a deep breath, relieved that she had escaped with her life again. Working as cruise ship security sounded pretty good to her right now.

Waverley got up. "Mario will ensure your room gets a thorough clean up once my team have finished. I suggest you stay away for a few hours this morning. I'll send them up around 8am, if that suits?"

Rachel looked at the time: 5am. "Yes, that will be fine."

Waverley left, and Rachel crashed out like a light in the chair where she sat.

Chapter 28

Chief of security, Jack Waverley, who stood at six foot four, prided himself on being physically fit for a fifty-six-year-old. He looked in the mirror back in his stateroom after taking a shave. Apart from carrying an extra stone, brought about by the attentions of Brenda, a senior cook in the bakery with whom he was having a relationship, he looked good.

He liked his work on the *Coral Queen.* It certainly beat the stress of working in the military police for the navy, where he had been a petty officer for twenty years. This cruise, though, was proving challenging, and he had a lot on his mind.

Before being called to Rachel Prince's room, he had been worrying she might be right about Jefgeny Popov hiding somewhere aboard ship. He still hoped his hypothesis about Popov killing his friend, Erik Marinov, would turn out to be true, but he had growing doubts having questioned the engineering crew further. They all confirmed Erik had protected Popov. On top of that, there was the quandary over where Jefgeny would get a syringe, needle and drugs that would kill the big man.

The more he thought about it, the more doubts he had, which left him with a thumping headache. Could one of the other crew members be responsible, and if so, who? As far as Waverley could work out, Erik had had no enemies. He'd worked hard and, unlike many of the crew, hadn't drunk very much, preferring to study engineering books in his spare time.

Jefgeny Popov was more of a mystery – kept himself to himself, spoke only in Russian (even though he must have spoken English, being a US citizen), but he also worked hard, and going AWOL was totally out of character according to Steve Rafferty, the engineering chief. Jefgeny's only weakness appeared to be the demon drink. His colleagues said he could hold his alcohol, and despite being able to drink more than most, he had never appeared drunk.

Waverley had been going through the case in his head, having informed Captain Jenson of Rachel's suspicions and got his agreement to have Jefgeny's girlfriend watched.

"Do what you have to do, but for pity's sake, don't let any harm come to the passengers," Captain Jensen had said. "Are we certain the Russian passenger died from natural causes?"

Waverley had answered cautiously. "As far as the medical team can tell, he died of a heart attack or an overdose. There is the empty pill box found in the room—"

"Found by Miss Prince, again. She seems to have a knack for being in the thick of things, and was one of the last people to see Popov before he went missing."

"You're not suggesting she had anything to do with it?"

"No – of course not! It's just a pity she's a passenger, rather than on your team – she seems such a bright young thing, and could be useful to you, but she *is* a passenger."

Waverley heard the veiled warning to curb her involvement. "Yes, sir. I don't see any need to involve her further, and Miss Prince has assured me that her only wish is to enjoy her cruise and go shopping in New York."

"Good – we can't have passengers put in danger – no matter how useful they might be."

The pressure had mounted – Waverley needed to solve the murder of Erik Marinov and find out what had happened to Jefgeny Popov, but his main priority was to protect the rest of the passengers and crew. He had been just about to fall asleep when his radio sparked into life, informing him of the attack on Rachel Prince. He couldn't believe it.

He returned to his room only too aware that this lovely young woman had almost been killed on his watch. Waverley was not a man prone to self-doubt, but even he wondered if he might be losing his edge. He looked again at his tired reflection in the mirror. This shouldn't be happening to him.

After shaving, he changed into his day uniform and marched into the main security station. As he entered, Ravanos and Brody stood to attention.

"It's okay, boys, be seated. Is our man securely locked away?"

"Yes, sir," answered Ravanos.

"Anything else to report overnight?"

"Not really," said Brody. "A rowdy group in the disco, but they didn't give us any trouble when we suggested they call it a night. One elderly man reported his watch stolen, but has just phoned to say he found it in his dress suit. We've got no further with the supposed jewellery theft."

Brody looked sceptical. Waverley knew about the case – a middle-aged passenger called Mrs Munro appeared to be the constant victim of jewellery thefts over several cruises.

"We'll leave that one to the insurance company, but keep up the pretence of looking for the missing jewellery."

"Sorry we had to wake you, sir," said Ravanos. "We knew you'd want to be informed of such a severe attack on Miss Prince."

"That's why I'm here. I need you to pull up security footage from the main atrium: timeline 2.30 to 3.30pm yesterday. Miss Prince says the man may have been someone who bumped into her deliberately and stole her room key card."

They carried out the laborious task of scrolling through video footage from different cameras, but it eventually yielded results.

"Stop there! That's Miss Prince. Scroll through slowly," Waverley instructed.

"There, sir." Brody pointed to a man bumping into her.

"Okay, scroll back and play it slowly. Yes, that looks deliberate. There, watch his left hand as he helps her pick up things with his right."

Sure enough, they saw him pick up the key card and slip it into his pocket before excusing himself and walking away.

"We only have a rear view – he's heading towards the shops. Pull the video from that area."

Eventually they found what they were looking for and identified Ray Tansley as the man who had bumped into Rachel.

"Gotcha," said Waverley happily. "Make copies of these so we can hand them over to the police in New York, and to the British police. The time has come for me to interview Mr Ray Tansley."

Waverley marched off with a spring in his step. Maybe his luck was changing.

Waverley arrived at the brig where the prisoner was being held and asked the officer on guard to bring the man to a small room nearby for questioning. Tansley came into the room wearing handcuffs and stared hard at Waverley. Thirty years old, the ship record had stated.

Waverley summed up the man in front of him. Six foot tall, rotund with cold eyes and tattoos lining muscular arms, he had a few bruises to his face and arms and a gash to the back of his head. Dr Romano had glued the gash together. A tough looking hooligan, Waverley concluded.

"What am I doing here? You've no right to lock me up. I'm the one that's been attacked by a loony woman. After inviting me up to her room, she turned demented."

"Really, and why would this woman attack you, Mr Tansley?"

"She obviously got cold feet. One minute, she gave me the come-on, the next minute she behaved like I was trying to rape her. You know what girls like that are like."

Tansley leered. Waverley gripped the pen in his hand, resisting the urge to punch the low-life in front of him. He had dealt with men like this all his life and found himself becoming less tolerant as he got older. He was pleased to see Rachel had inflicted some damage, and that alone consoled him. He marvelled at her resilience and the skill she must possess to disarm a man this size, punching well above her weight.

"I assume the knife in her room belonged to her, then?"

"Well, it's not mine, is it? What's more, I want to press charges against her."

"Please take a seat, Mr Tansley."

"My friends call me Ray." Tansley smirked.

I'd like to wipe that grin off your face. Waverley felt rage, but remained the picture of self-control as he spoke.

"Let me tell you where we're at, *Mr Tansley*. You are under arrest for the attack and attempted murder of a passenger on board this ship."

Tansley protested, but Waverley continued.

"We've recovered the knife as evidence, and as Miss Prince did not touch it, we are certain the only fingerprints to be found on it will be yours."

"So I carry a knife, but that's not enough to charge me. You can only charge me with carrying an offensive weapon."

"You appear to know the law, Mr Tansley. However, we also have CCTV footage of you deliberately bumping into Miss Prince yesterday and stealing her room key. With her testimony and your motive, I can assure you that you will be charged. We know you're the brother of someone she testified against and who later threatened her.

"Trust me, Mr Tansley, you will remain locked away in our padded cell for the next few days. After that, you will be handed over to the authorities in New York and will be locked away there. You are likely to be deported back to the United Kingdom for charges there. Either way, you will not be allowed any freedom on board this ship or on US soil. Personally, I hope they lock you up and throw away the key. Goodbye, *Mr Tansley*, I trust you will have a pleasant sailing aboard the *Coral Queen*."

Tansley shouted and cursed while being escorted back to the brig. Waverley walked away, punching the air, pleased with life.

Now, back to the Popov case.

Chapter 29

Hammering on the door roused Rachel from a deep sleep. After dragging herself up from the sofa and answering, she was greeted by two security guards.

"Sorry to disturb you, ma'am. We can come back later if you prefer?"

"No, now will be fine. Just give me five minutes and I'll leave you to it." Rachel rinsed the sleep out of her eyes and brushed her hair through before grabbing her handbag and leaving. She waved good morning to Mario, who was coming out of Asimov's room, drawing a concerned look as he shook his head in disbelief and blew her a kiss. She smiled weakly and headed upstairs.

The buffet was buzzing with people enjoying their holidays and filling up with as much food as they could eat before going about their recreational activities. Rachel felt envious, having had a stark reminder of the dangers of her day job.

Why, oh why did I get myself involved in another investigation? What's worse, I forgot about my night-time sortie in the depths of the ship when I spoke to Waverley this morning. Not that it would have been a good time to broach the subject. Now he won't let me have anything to do with the Jefgeny case, I've no idea how to keep Sarah out of it.

Her head hurt and her muscles ached.

After wandering around the buffet for about ten minutes, she finally filled a bowl with fresh fruit. The endless buffet options were too much for her today and the choice overwhelmed her.

She found a quiet place to sit. The welcome sound of her Jamaican friend singing as he pushed a trolley laden with hot drinks reminded her that all was normal.

"Good morning to my favourite lady. What can I get you this morning?"

"Strong coffee, please."

He poured the drink and moved along, not noticing, or choosing not to notice, the scratches to her neck. She had pulled on a polo shirt earlier and wore the collar up, but the marks had still been visible when she'd checked in the mirror. Her arms ached from the exertion of pinning Tansley's arm behind his back for so long – it had taken all her strength, powered by the will to live, to hold him in a vice-like grip, and her biceps were shouting about it.

Before she got up to leave, Thomas rushed over to her, his face filled with concern. He embraced her.

"I heard what happened last night. I'm so sorry – did he hurt you? Oh, your neck! Is that a bruise on your face?"

Rachel had to smile at how the words tumbled out of his mouth. He looked worried as he took a seat opposite.

"Thomas, calm down – I'm alright. Look, I'll tell you what's been going on, but you must promise not to tell anyone else – especially not any of the Russian tour party."

"I promise," he said, adding a cross my heart motion for good measure.

"Drinks?" Rachel's Jamaican friend returned with the trolley.

"More coffee for me, please," said Rachel.

"Tea with two sugars," said Thomas.

Once Rachel was satisfied that nobody else in the vicinity was in earshot or listening, she started.

"The man who attacked me last night is the brother of someone I got put away for murder. I work in Leeds as a policewoman and I witnessed a stabbing. After the trial, I received a threatening letter, and last night was an attempt at vengeance. The man would have thrown me overboard if I hadn't managed to turn things around. I didn't tell Asimov or Lucretia the full story because there's something else going on, and it might involve one of your tour party. I don't want them to know I'm a policewoman."

Thomas was a good listener and Rachel found it cathartic, talking to someone about the Tansley incident and his brother turning up last night.

"Well, you're a dark horse, I must say. I had you down as a model or a film star," he said, winking. "Are you going to tell me about the other thing then?"

"Perhaps later. I need to see the doctor so he can write a report of my injuries to go with the knife and other evidence from the attack last night."

Thomas's eyes widened. "Knife? OMG, Rachel!"

"I know, it was super scary, but at least he's locked up now."

"Good job – I'd like to get my hands on him even though I'm a pacifist. Where is he?"

"In the brig."

"Oh, I didn't think about that. I guess they must have a lock-up on board a ship this size."

"You'd be surprised what they've got on board this ship, Thomas," she teased as she got up. "I'll catch you later."

As soon as Rachel arrived at the medical centre, Sarah came rushing out.

"They told me what happened. Oh Rachel, I'm so relieved you're safe."

They hugged each other as Dr Bentley came out of his surgery.

"Why don't you both come in while I examine Rachel – if you don't mind, Rachel?"

"I'd love to have Sarah with me. Thank you."

They followed Dr Bentley into surgery, and after offering his condolences and support, he took a full history of the events of the night before. He examined Rachel, writing notes and using a tape measure to measure the size of the scratches and bruises. Dr Bentley then took several photos after asking Rachel's permission and uploaded them on to his computer.

He asked her if there had been any attempt at sexual assault. She assured him that her attacker had only had one goal, and that was to kill her in revenge for putting his brother behind bars.

"That's all I need from an evidence perspective. I'm sorry someone has attacked you on board a Queen Cruise again, though."

"This man would have attacked me wherever – he obviously supposed a cruise ship to be an ideal place for murder. I'm just pleased he didn't stab me first, but I guess it would have been too messy."

"Rachel, don't – it makes me shudder at the thought of how much danger you were in," pleaded Sarah.

"Sorry, but it's over and he's behind bars."

"Not quite bars on a ship, but we get the gist." Dr Bentley turned away from his computer and Rachel sensed he wanted to say something else. She looked at him. "While you're both here – I know it might not be a good time, Rachel, but I need to get something off my chest."

"What is it, Graham?" asked Sarah.

"It's this Marinov and Popov business – I'm sure you've not let it go, Rachel, which is why I want to go over some things that are bothering me."

Rachel looked sheepish. "What things?"

"The injection, for a start – we are so strict about drugs and crew members undergo regular screening. Neither had any history of drug abuse, so if Marinov's death involved Popov – where did he get a syringe, needle and the wherewithal to kill his friend? Killing in this way would be premeditated, which doesn't fit in with a heat of the moment kind of killing."

Dr Bentley seemed relieved to get his thoughts out in the open, and Rachel couldn't have agreed more. "We've both had doubts, and you have just confirmed what we've been thinking: that Jefgeny did not kill Erik Marinov. We also suspect he's hiding on board the ship and that his girlfriend, Eva Sipka, is helping him."

"What makes you think that, and if he is innocent, why doesn't he just come forward?"

Rachel didn't want to mention what they had discovered last night because she didn't want to get Sarah into trouble. She was not good at lying so she didn't speak for a while.

"Rachel spoke to his girlfriend, and she gave away little titbits of information that suggested Jefgeny is still alive," said Sarah.

"We need to tell Waverley."

"Already done," said Rachel. "He is having her watched and will pull her in before we get to New York if they don't find him by then."

"I still don't understand why he's hiding."

"Perhaps he doesn't trust the authorities, or maybe he has some other reason," offered Rachel. Keeping information from this kind and distinguished man didn't sit comfortably, but protecting Sarah's job came first. Sarah was also looking guilty, so Rachel took a different tack. "If you don't suspect Jefgeny – do you have another theory?"

"Not really – it would need to be someone who has access to syringes and needles and medication that can kill. There might be an illicit drugs racket on board, and if Erik found out about it, someone might have killed him to keep him quiet."

Rachel had to admit there was logic in the theory. "I hadn't thought of that, but that would explain the suddenness of the murder and the attempt at subterfuge. Perhaps Jefgeny knows about it too and that's why he's hiding. You said security carry regular tests out on crew?"

"They do, but if it's smuggling rather than drug taking, that's more complicated. We've got good security, but there are ways for the ultra-determined to get things on board a ship this size. I'll talk to Waverley and see if we can get some sniffer dogs on board when we call in at New York. In the meantime, I suggest you have a relaxing day at sea, Rachel."

"That's a great idea on both counts," said Sarah, pleased.

"Yes, agreed," said Rachel.

Dr Bentley was almost joyful having talked the matter through, as if someone had lifted a great weight from his shoulders.

Chapter 30

There was work to be done – first on her list was Thomas. Rachel pulled the dog-eared Russian itinerary from her handbag and studied it to determine the best place to track him down. After running a finger through the list of activities, she spotted a talk being hosted by one of the guest speakers entitled *Russian Art – influences past and present.* Thomas's initials were next to the session. The talk started at 11am so she had time to return to her room to see if there was an internet signal, her near-miss last night still preying on her mind.

Rachel felt much calmer having received an email from Carlos and was ready to continue her investigation. She hadn't mentioned the early morning encounter with Ray Tansley because she didn't want him stressing out about her. His email had been chipper and mentioned he'd resolved his recent issue and was now working a different case. She wished someone would solve her complex case – maybe it was a drug smuggling racket as Dr Bentley suggested. In that case, she would not need to tell Waverley about her excursion below the waterline last night.

Rachel arrived early at the Plato Lounge near to the Queen Art Gallery on deck six and took a seat. One of the crew was demonstrating the operation of a handheld remote to the guest speaker, who carried out a few sound and visual checks. She heard Asimov's voice as he entered the room with around twenty of the group. Lucretia was with him and she walked over to Rachel.

"How are you?"

"I'm much better now that man's locked away. Thank you for your help last night, I'm sorry I disturbed you."

"That was not a problem. I am light sleeper and Vladimir was happy to help damsel in distress. His bite is worse than his bark."

Rachel smiled at the misquote but appreciated the sentiment.

"Lulu," Asimov was calling for Lucretia to take her seat beside him.

"I'd better go. He doesn't like art, he is more technical man, but I love, so he comes with me."

Lucretia joined Asimov and he nodded to Rachel, not giving much away, but at least it was an acknowledgement. Rachel saw Boris in the group along with the tall grey-haired man called Sergei.

Thomas arrived armed with the clipboard and ticked off his list of attendees before spotting Rachel. As soon as he did, he joined her.

"My day has just got better." He flirted for effect in front of his Russian audience. Rachel smiled, and then he put on a brief act of seeing her scratches for the first time before whispering, "I'm free after this session if you want to talk."

"Yes, that would be fine. I have something to show you," she whispered back.

The speaker introduced himself as Mishka Orlov, a lecturer from the University of Pennsylvania, specialising in the history of art, and in particular, Russian artists. He was a natural orator who held the audience's attention for forty-five minutes; even Asimov looked as though he was enjoying himself, laughing at Mishka's jokes and listening intently. After a fifteen minute question time at the end of his talk, Mishka managed a quick plug of his latest book, with the same title as the talk, holding up a copy. He had several copies with him – books he offered to sign. Otherwise, the book was on sale in Coral Bookshop on deck five. Almost everyone attending bought a copy at $49.00 each, and a crew member was on site to swipe their onboard payment cards.

Rachel and Thomas left. "Where would you like to lunch?" Thomas asked.

"Are you happy with the grill? I feel like taking on some fat after my exertions last night."

"Suits me, let's go." Thomas took her arm, and they headed up to deck fourteen.

Once they'd stocked up with food, they found a table and chatted while they ate.

"He was a surprisingly good speaker – I thought the talk would be dry," remarked Thomas.

"I only attended to meet up with you, but I really enjoyed it," agreed Rachel. "If I imagined I might ever open a page of his book, he would have tempted me to buy one too."

"Yes, his talk did the selling for him, didn't it? I gather Lucretia loves that sort of thing. She drags Mr Asimov around all the art galleries. He's bought her a few special pieces too, apparently."

"Looks like a man in love, and she has a good influence on him," said Rachel. "It's a shame he can't lose that scowl."

"Men with money don't have to pretend, I guess," replied Thomas. "He doesn't seem to care whether people like him, and I hear he has a foul temper. It wouldn't surprise me if he was involved in some dirty dealings. Boris doesn't seem to like him at all, and the rest of the group are on the payroll in one way or another, from what I can gather."

"What about the women?"

"Wives, girlfriends or paid escorts – just having a good time at Asimov's expense. He has money to burn."

"Are you any wiser on where Sergei fits in?"

"Sergei Markov? I still can't work it out, other than his shared business interests with Mr Asimov – he isn't on the payroll and keeps himself to himself. It wouldn't surprise me if he was some sort of covert business manager or negotiator. He has some health problems too, from what I understand – he's diabetic. One of the nurse's has to keep supplying him with insulin, which is annoying the doctor."

"What makes you think he's a covert business manager?"

"No particular reason, except he and Mr Asimov have private meetings that not even Lucretia attends."

"How do you know?"

"Because they use my room when they want to talk in private."

"That is interesting," said Rachel.

They finished eating and Rachel studied Thomas. Deciding to trust him, she took her phone out of her handbag and scrolled through to the photos she had taken the night before.

"Thomas, do you read Russian as well as speak the language?"

"I'm familiar with the alphabet so can make out most words, why?"

"Take a look at the writing on this picture. Can you make out what it says?" Rachel handed him the phone.

Thomas used two fingers to enlarge the photo to help him focus and took reading glasses out of his shirt pocket. "Let me see, the first word is easy. It says *me.* Okay, the next word is *with*, then *Bianca.* I take it the writing is off the back of a photo?"

"Carry on," prompted Rachel.

Thomas looked at the photo again. "*And* is the next word, then a capital B, followed by o, r, i… OMG, it says *Boris*! Do you have the photo?"

Rachel, not sure how much she trusted Thomas, evaded the question. "What does the rest say?"

"Hm, it's a place name. Oh, that's easy, it says *St Petersburg 1999.*"

Rachel put her hand out for the phone and, scrolling to the photo, she zoomed in on the second man. Yes, it could be Boris Stanislav, but it was hard to be certain. Taking the plunge, she passed the phone back to Thomas.

"What do you think of this?" she said.

"The man on the right looks familiar. It might be Boris Stanislav, but it's quite faded, and the beard and moustache make it difficult to say. I'm not sure. Boris is a common name in Russia. Where did you get the photo and why is it important?" Thomas looked as if he was enjoying himself.

"I can't tell you that, Thomas." He looked deflated. "But you could do something for me, if you don't mind."

His eyes lit up. "Ooh, yes please. I love a bit of detective work."

"Can you get to speak with Boris? I'm sure he's hiding something, and the issue with the minders makes me suspect Asimov was having him watched. It might be nothing."

"I'll try. He likes cards, so I can take him to the casino tonight and see what I can find out. I'll ply him with drinks." Thomas rubbed his hands together, excited.

"Be careful, Thomas. I'm not sure what's going on, but it might be dangerous. Whatever you do, keep it natural. Also, try to get some information about his family. He has a wife and two sons, but does he have a sister or brother, and are they married?"

"You think that's Boris in the photo, don't you?"

"I'm not certain."

Thomas looked at his watch. "Time to go, I'm afraid. Golf simulation with some of the ladies!" He rolled his eyes.

Rachel smiled at him. "Make sure you flirt madly."

He laughed as he walked away.

Rachel hoped she had done the right thing involving him, but he was her closest link to the group, and the only one she could trust. Natalia was the other one who might help, but it was best to proceed cautiously. Another idea was developing in her head, but it would take some careful planning and she might need help.

Chapter 31

Guilt weighed heavily on Sarah's mind. She was not happy at concealing her foray into Jefgeny's room last night, and now Rachel had been assaulted. Worry for her friend whipped her head into a frenzy.

What if she puts herself in danger again?

There was only one thing for it and that was to see Waverley herself and confess. If it meant losing her job, so be it. At least Rachel would be safe.

The initial euphoria over Graham's theory had worn off. Although there might be some truth in it, for her it made no sense. It was ludicrous to envisage a drug smuggling cartel operating in secret below decks. Also, knowing Rachel would not stop and might end up dead worried her silly.

Two bodies are quite enough for one cruise.

Resigning herself to her fate, she finished morning surgery on autopilot.

Bernard popped his head through the door. "Hey, have you finished? We can get lunch if you're free?"

"That would be good. Will anyone else be coming? I can't face eating with Lauren today."

"Nope, just you and me. Lauren's gone with Graham to read the riot act to the Russian guy who keeps mislaying his insulin. Alex is finishing up, then going for a sleep after being up all night again, and Gwen is catching up with paperwork and billing."

"In that case, let's go." She powered down the computer.

"Can we eat in the officers' dining room? You never know when we'll get to eat a proper meal again. You're on call tonight." They usually ate in the buffet, but occasionally indulged in a bigger meal at lunchtime to stock up in case they missed an evening meal.

"That's fine. I just need to sign out the glue I used to fix a laceration before we go."

The storage room where they kept supplies and medicines locked away was neat as ever. Sarah filled in the logbook. "Looks like Lauren's been busy. She's signed out more meds than any of us."

"Might have been from the cardiac arrest – she did all the paperwork. And the poor girl has to keep supplying the Russian guy with insulin."

"Oh yes, I forgot about that. The cardiac arrest seems an age ago, but it was only yesterday, wasn't it?"

"I know what you mean. Come on, Sarah. I'm starving."

Sarah closed the book. "You're always starving. Be careful – your wife won't recognise you if the Michelin Man comes home."

"The Michelin Man?"

Sarah explained about an advert for tyres and the accompanying round Michelin Man, trademarked by the tyre company. "You need to spend time in the UK."

"And when might I do that? My whole life's spent on this ship, and in between I need to get home to see my family."

"I tell you what, let's see if we can swing it to take a day off when we dock in Southampton and do the London trip. I would love to show you round London."

"Wow, Nurse Bradshaw, you're on. It's a date."

"Better not mention it to Lauren, or I might find cyanide in my tea!"

Bernard nudged her as they made their way to the officers' dining room for lunch. "Hopefully she got the message loud and clear," he muttered.

Sarah enjoyed eating in the officers' dining room sometimes because it was waiter service with a full menu, not dissimilar to the one the passengers chose from. During her nursing training, she'd learned not to let stress affect her appetite or she would have starved long ago, stress being a nurse's lot.

One of the waiters, an Indian man called Rai, bantered with Bernard for a little while before taking their order. It always amazed her how many people Bernard knew on board; he had a gift for remembering names.

"I'll have pâté followed by a rack of lamb," said Bernard.

"And for you, miss?" asked Rai.

"Shrimp cocktail and chicken with basil, please."

Bernard poured them both some water. "What's on your mind, Sarah? I can tell you're worried about something."

"I'm concerned about Rachel more than anything. She seems to attract trouble these days."

"She sure does. Someone told me about the attack last night, but she's alright now, isn't she?"

"Hopefully," said Sarah. "It's been a depressing few days with the two deaths; I'll be glad to get to New York."

"Three deaths, more like, as your Mr Popov is probably shark bait somewhere."

"Bernard, that's horrible! Anyway, Rachel's not sure he is. She's convinced he's somewhere on board and hiding. Graham's now thinking along those lines too."

"So you're worried Rachel will get herself in some sticky situation again?"

Sarah nodded.

"She's a big girl, and from what I understand of last night, she can take care of herself. Don't worry, she'll probably get to the bottom of it like a young *Miss Marple* and then tell the chief of security whodunit."

Sarah laughed. "You've heard of *Miss Marple* then?"

"Oh yes, my wife loves those books, reads them all the time. We watched the series together on satellite television. We're not completely backward in the Philippines, you know."

"I never thought you were." She was about to apologise when she noticed the teasing glint in his eye. "How does your wife put up with you?"

"Why do you think she sends me away to work?"

They finished their meal and Bernard returned to the medical centre to collect the on-call bag for the afternoon. Sarah accompanied him, putting off her visit to Waverley's office for a while.

When they arrived back, Gwen was not in her office. There were sounds of a commotion coming from the infirmary. Walking in, they found Graham, Gwen and Lauren treating a young woman. Alex arrived almost immediately afterwards.

"What happened?" he asked, looking concerned.

"She collapsed in the casino," said Graham. "It doesn't appear to be anything serious, but she looks anaemic. Working too hard, I suspect."

"It's Eva Sipka, the girlfriend of the missing crewman. She's twelve weeks pregnant," said Alex.

"Oh," said Graham. "There's no blood loss and no abdominal pain, but perhaps we'll keep her in overnight just to be on the safe side."

Sarah groaned. "That's the end of my afternoon off."

"I'll look after her," Lauren piped up, looking gooey eyed at Alex.

Talk about Jekyll and Hyde!

"Thank you, Lauren. You get some rest, Sarah," said Alex kindly.

"Okay, I'm not complaining. I'll be back later to collect the on-call kit."

Sarah left the medical centre, pondering the weird girl that was Lauren. One minute she's Cruella Deville, the next minute, Florence blooming Nightingale. I really can't work her out. I expect there's some ulterior motive. She must fancy Alex now Bernard's out of bounds – astonishing.

Sarah approached Waverley's office, half hoping he wouldn't be there, but he was. She knocked on the door. He looked up from his desk and beckoned her in, looking weary.

"Nurse Bradshaw. What can I do for you – is Rachel alright?"

"I assume so, I haven't seen her since this morning. Has Dr Bentley been to see you?"

"Yes, he has." His tone sharpened. "He told me his ridiculous drug smuggling theory, and quite honestly, it's inconceivable we could have criminal activity of that level going on under our noses. Our security is rigorous, it's not possible. I'm sorry to disappoint, but I don't accept for one minute this is the case. I do wish people would stop playing amateur detective and leave me to get on with my work. I don't tell him how to do his job, do I?"

Sarah suspected this would not be a good time to confess her crime or she could end up sharing a cell with Ray Tansley.

"Oh well, if you're sure."

"Was that what you were here about?"

"Yes, sir. Sorry, I didn't mean to interrupt your work."

Sarah headed towards the door and Waverley followed her. "Look, Nurse Bradshaw – Sarah – I'm sorry for being short. It's been a long day and I still have a missing man who may or may not be on board. I'm going to speak to his girlfriend, despite what Rachel Prince might say. It's time to put this case to bed."

"I'm sorry, but Eva Sipka's taken ill. She passed out at work and is in the infirmary," said Sarah.

"GREAT! That's all I need. How long will she be there?"

"At least overnight," Sarah answered and walked away, sighing. She had a funny feeling Waverley's day was not going to get any better.

Oh well, at least I still have a job for now.

Chapter 32

On her way to Waverley's office, Rachel saw Sarah walking towards her.

"Hi, where are you heading?" asked Sarah.

"I'm going to see Waverley to discuss Jefgeny Popov."

"Not a good time – you're likely to get your head bitten off, even if you are a passenger. I've just been, but before I got the chance to confess about last night, he read me the riot act and told me in no uncertain terms to leave any investigating to him. He's annoyed about Graham getting involved."

"Blast, that's not what I wanted to hear."

"He's tired and stressed by all the trouble he's had to deal with. He'll calm down later. Why don't we get afternoon tea and then you can walk me back to the medical centre?"

"That sounds like a great idea." Rachel linked arms with Sarah and they made their way to their favourite haunt, Creams.

After ordering, Rachel explained what she'd found out from Thomas over lunch: how it seemed that Boris was related to or friends with Jefgeny.

"Do you think it's your Boris?"

"He's not *my* Boris, but I'm pretty sure it is. It would explain why Jefgeny tried to speak to him that first day when they met in the corridor. If it is, it also suggests that Jefgeny might be hiding from Boris or Sergei Markov, because he's the other one that spoke to Jefgeny."

"We don't seem to be getting very far, and the drug idea seems far-fetched. Despite what Graham believes – and Waverley didn't hold truck with Graham's theory, by the way – the most likely explanation is still that Jefgeny killed his friend and is hiding or dead."

"But how did he inject him, and what is the connection to the Russian group?" asked Rachel.

"I don't know. Perhaps the injection mark is not that at all, or maybe Erik took an overdose."

"Possible, but no suicide note? It doesn't make sense."

"None of it makes sense, Rachel. I just want it to end so I don't have to worry about you roaming around on your own, putting yourself in danger."

"It's okay, I'm not on my own. I've got a recruit."

"Who? Don't tell me – Thomas?"

Rachel smiled at the concerned look on Sarah's face. "I'll be fine, and Thomas is only going to do a bit of listening in for me – nothing dangerous."

"I hope you're right, because if Waverley gets wind of this, we'll both be in the doghouse. He's verging on apoplexy. The sooner we own up to what we did last night, the better."

"You said he's not in the mood for listening, so we'll just have to get on with it for now."

Sarah didn't look reassured, but at least she accepted things as they were.

They finished their tea, and Rachel walked Sarah back to the medical centre. When they got back, Bernard came rushing out to meet them.

"I'm glad you're here, Sarah. Lauren has gone missing and Graham's called me to help with a sick passenger on deck eleven. Alex is due any minute to check on Eva Sipka and Gwen's in her office, doing paperwork."

Sarah was livid. "I don't suppose you've told Gwen that Lauren is AWOL?"

He shook his head. "I daren't, she'll go mad." He turned and hurried away with the emergency case in tow.

Rachel looked concerned. "What's Eva Sipka doing here?"

"Sorry, I forgot to tell you, she fainted in the casino. She's fine – pregnant women can drop their blood pressure, and Alex suspects she's anaemic as well. She's in overnight. I wonder where that wretched woman is this time!"

Gwen came out of her office. "What wretched woman? Is everything alright?"

At that moment, Alex walked through the door and Sarah excused herself to accompany him for his examination of Eva. Rachel saw from Gwen's face that the situation was becoming clear.

She looked at Rachel.

"Where's Lauren?"

Rachel wasn't sure it was her place to say anything, so she shrugged her shoulders.

Sarah popped her head out of the infirmary. "Miss Sipka says Lauren's gone to her cabin to collect something for her."

"It's not good enough," muttered Gwen. "She can't just leave a patient unattended without telling me. That woman has no concept of ship hierarchy, thinks she can do as she pleases. Well I've had enough." Gwen wasn't as much speaking to Rachel as letting off steam. Sarah had gone back into the infirmary, and Rachel wasn't sure what to do.

"Can I get either of you some coffee?" Raggie appeared just in time.

"Yes please, Raggie. Rachel, do stay – I could do with a break. Come and join me."

Gwen motioned her to sit in one of three comfy chairs around a coffee table. There was also a two-seater settee, similar to the setup in Waverley's office. Rachel guessed senior officers had identical offices, and this one would be where Gwen's team held medical meetings.

"Sorry, Rachel, that was unprofessional of me. I trust you will use your discretion."

"My hearing's been playing up recently," Rachel replied, and they both laughed.

Gwen's computer pinged.

"Excuse me for one moment." Gwen moved over to the computer and tapped a few keys, her face paling.

"Are you okay?"

"Not really." She picked up the phone and spoke to whoever answered at the other end. "It's Sister Sumner, you need to come down here, now."

Rachel could tell this was something serious, but wasn't sure whether to go. "Should I leave you to it?" she asked, hoping Gwen would say no.

"You'd better, please, this is confidential. Have your coffee outside and see Sarah before you go, though."

Rachel was tempted to decline, but decided she might as well enjoy a percolated coffee.

She sat in the waiting room. Waverley burst through the doors, heading straight into Gwen's office, not noticing Rachel, whose radar was now on full alert.

What is Waverley doing here?

Raggie took coffee in to Gwen's office, but left the door ajar on his way out. He didn't spot Rachel either and left the centre, so she seized the opportunity and moved a chair closer to the office where she could listen in to what was being said.

"It sounded important, Sister. What is it?"

"Something's been bothering me about our new nurse. She seems to go missing far too often, and I noticed she's been signing out a lot of medication."

"Go on." Rachel detected from his tone that Waverley wanted the facts as quickly as possible.

"I pulled her CV and work history and realised she had worked at a hospital in Connecticut where I have a friend who is chief nurse. We go back a long way, but you don't want to know about that."

"Quite," said Waverley.

"Well, I decided to email her and ask if she knew anything about a Lauren Blythe who had worked there from 2006 to 2007. It was before her time, but she agreed to ask around. Emails have been a bit hit and miss over the past twenty-four hours, but I've just received one sent yesterday."

What does it say? Rachel had to stop herself saying it out loud.

"What does it say?" asked Waverley, sounding tense.

"It seems she left under a cloud. There were unsubstantiated rumours that drugs had been going missing from the ward."

"Are you telling me she might be a drug addict?"

"I wish it were that simple," Gwen answered. "The drug was insulin. Nothing was proven, but my friend has now interviewed all the nurses who worked there at that time, and they say in retrospect, there were a high number of patient deaths during her tenure."

Waverley gasped.

Gwen continued. "The thing is, none of them registered this in isolation, but now they all seem to say the same thing. My friend's predecessor encouraged Lauren Blythe to leave, feeling they didn't have enough evidence to call in the police. To cut a long story short, my friend has now involved the police who are looking into the deaths during that time period."

"Let me get this straight. You're telling me we might have a serial killer on board the *Coral*." Waverley's voice was shaking. "Are we sure it's the same nurse?"

"Certain. It prevented her from getting a job in a hospital again, according to my friend – mud sticks, but she got a job as an occupational health nurse at a company called Future Motors in Boston. She worked there until 2013, then moved to Africa."

Where have I heard that name before?

"NO!" Rachel couldn't stop herself shouting, which brought Waverley rushing out of Gwen's office.

"What the hell are you doing here?"

"Never mind that now. That company is where Jefgeny Popov worked until he reported some big players for industrial espionage. They tried to steal the prototype for a driverless car. Jefgeny ended up in witness protection. I suspect he saw her, and that's why he's in hiding. She knows who he is."

Sarah came out of the infirmary, picking up the last part of the sentence. "She was here after I'd seen him on the first day and took an interest in his record. I think she recognised him."

"You need to move quickly. She's gone down to Eva's room to get something. I'm sure that's where he's hiding," said Rachel.

"But even if you're right, why would she want to harm him?"

"I'm not sure yet, but she killed Erik Marinov with an insulin overdose, of that I'm certain."

"And Nikolai Stepanov," said Sarah as this new information dawned on her. "She was alone with him the night he died."

Waverley got on his radio. "Sarah, come with me. Sister, can you explain to Miss Sipka that her boyfriend might be in grave danger and ask her where he is hiding? Call me on the radio when you find out. Send Dr Bentley and Dr Romano after us – we may need them. I'll ask you how you knew about the witness protection thing later, Miss Prince."

Sarah grabbed an emergency bag and followed Waverley.

"I'm coming too, Sarah might need help," said Rachel.

Waverley shrugged his shoulders in resignation and Rachel brought up the rear.

Chapter 33

Rachel could feel adrenaline pumping and anxiety building as they made their way through the private staff area and down several flights of stairs. Eva's room was on Deck B, two decks below the waterline. Waverley took the steps two at a time and Sarah pursued hard on his heels. Rachel's stilettos kept catching in the metal grids of the steps until she risked going barefoot and took them off.

By the time they got to deck B, Waverley was panting and had to stop. Rachel sympathised, but didn't slow down. Sarah raced on ahead and arrived at the room first with Rachel right behind.

Sarah unlocked Eva's door. Lauren looked surprised when they burst in. They saw a man lying on the floor; Rachel assumed him to be Jefgeny.

"Thank God," said Lauren. "I was just going to call for help. He collapsed; I think he might be dead."

"Get out of my way!" Sarah pushed past her and checked Jefgeny's vital signs. Lauren turned to assist.

"Oh, no you don't!" said Rachel, pulling her back and pinning her arms behind her back. At the same time, she checked Lauren's pockets and pulled out two medicine bottles.

"Let go of me! What are you doing?" Lauren shouted, at which point Waverley arrived, followed soon after by two security guards. He took control of the situation.

"Get her out of here," he ordered the security guards, who applied handcuffs to Lauren's wrists and marched her away.

"Is he alive?" asked Rachel, handing the bottles to Sarah so she could identify what Lauren had given the man.

"Barely."

Waverley shouted into his radio. "CODE BLUE. Doctors to deck B, 1932, I repeat—"

He didn't need to repeat the call as Dr Bentley and Bernard came running through the door.

"Was that Lauren I just saw in handcuffs?"

"It's a long story," answered Sarah. "Insulin overdose."

"Clear the area," ordered Dr Bentley. "Get a line in." Bernard handed Sarah the equipment to work with. "Glucagon injection," Dr Bentley commanded.

Bernard drew up the solution using a syringe and needle, and Graham injected it into Jefgeny's leg. Rachel moved out of the already cramped room and joined Waverley in the corridor while the medical team worked hurriedly, but efficiently. She hoped they were not too late.

"He's coming round," said Dr Bentley. "Right, team, let's get him on a stretcher and up to the infirmary. He's out of the woods."

"Will he survive?" asked Waverley.

"Yes," answered Dr Bentley. "She's used long and short acting insulin, but it's easy to reverse when you know what you're treating. We'll monitor his blood sugars and treat him accordingly. He has a sugar solution going in through the IV line, so all will be well."

Sarah and Bernard wheeled Jefgeny away and Dr Bentley followed. Waverley looked exhausted as he picked up his radio.

"Send fingerprinting equipment down, and seal the room for forensics – we'll need evidence." He turned to Rachel. "Perhaps you would like to accompany me to my office and explain what you know. I will see to Nurse Death later." His smile was grim.

"You'd better tell me the full story," said Waverley when they arrived at his office. He poured them both a glass of mineral water from a bottle out of his fridge. "When did you work out it was the nurse?"

"Only when I overheard your conversation with Gwen. I realised then it involved her, and it makes sense now because she would have access to the crew quarters while the Russian guests wouldn't.

She also has access to medicines. Sarah said that one of the Russians kept losing his insulin – I suspect she was stealing it."

"What about the witness protection?"

"That's what Sarah and I wanted to confess today. We found out last night – don't blame Sarah, it was my fault." Rachel explained about their expedition downstairs the night before, and about finding the newspaper article and the photograph. "I'm still not sure of the relevance, although it seems that Jefgeny Popov and Boris Stanislav know each other. They may even be related. They must have recognised each other in the corridor when we took the tour of engineering."

"So has he been hiding from Mr Stanislav or Nurse Blythe?"

"The latter, I suspect, but he will answer that. She obviously recognised him from her time working at Future Motors. Perhaps she was involved in the initial conspiracy."

"That might be a leap too far, but it seems she's responsible for two deaths on board this ship, and one attempted murder. Case solved – looks like your Russians are innocent after all."

Rachel detected a hint of triumph in his voice and she couldn't blame him.

"I'm not sure all of them are innocent, but I grant you, they are not guilty of the murders."

"It's time for me to go to the medical centre to speak with Popov and his girlfriend. I suppose you want to tag along?"

"Yes please." She got up and followed before he could change his mind.

When they arrived at the medical centre, all appeared calm. Gwen escorted them through to the infirmary where Jefgeny was sitting up in the bed next to Eva. He looked tired and pale, but relieved.

"I need to ask you both some questions. Is that alright, Doctor Bentley?"

Doctor Bentley nodded tersely. "Don't be too long, we still need to run tests."

The pair looked frightened; both knew they would more than likely lose their jobs with the cruise line and not be able to work on board a ship again. Waverley pulled up two chairs and sat down, motioning for Rachel to do the same. He introduced Rachel, explaining that it was she they needed to thank that Jefgeny was alive. Realising the medical team were going nowhere, Waverley started his questioning.

"First, I need to ask you, Mr Popov, did you kill Erik Marinov?"

"No, sir, I did not."

"Do you know who did?"

"Not for sure, but I guess it was the nurse who tried to kill me."

"Why did you pretend that you couldn't speak English when I met you?" Sarah asked.

He looked at her. "I'm sorry, but since joining witness protection, I have trusted no-one."

"Who have you been hiding from?"

"I recognised man in Russian group. He was part of crime I reported before. They said they would never stop until they found us. My friend also went into protection. He is crazy – still visits Russia. I would never go again. I thought about coming to security, but these men have tentacles everywhere. When I decided to come to you later that day, I caught sight of the nurse in my room and thought I recognised her from the company, Fortune Motors. Terrified they had tracked me down and intended to kill me, I begged Eva to hide me – she no want to. She wanted me to come clean, but I was too afraid. It's not her fault."

"Never mind that now," said Waverley. "Where did you hide? We searched everywhere, including Miss Sipka's room."

"I hid in shaft above shower room. There is service hatch – engineers and electricians know these things. I hid there during day and with Eva at night."

"Does that mean your roommate knew of this, Miss Sipka?" Waverley asked.

"No, she works nights, so she did not know."

Rachel doubted that, but enough people would lose their jobs without adding to the tally.

"Is it Boris Stanislav you were hiding from?"

"No, he is my brother-in-law. We have not seen each other since I entered witness programme. He looked pleased and almost gave me away. Other man in the group may have recognised me, or maybe nurse was sent after me."

"Can you tell me the man's name?"

"No. I never met him, only saw from a distance. It's twenty years."

"It may have been a coincidence, Mr Popov. The woman seems to have been working alone; she even killed one of the Russians in the group. I'll show you photos of the men tomorrow to see if you can identify the man you recognised."

Jefgeny closed his eyes and Rachel noticed tears falling down his face. She couldn't be sure if they were tears of joy or sorrow.

"That's enough for now," Dr Bentley intervened. "Mr Popov needs time to recover. You can post a security guard down here if he's still in any danger."

"I don't think he is," answered Waverley. "But it can't do any harm. I'll send someone down. Perhaps you and I could get a drink later?" He looked at Dr Bentley.

"Yes, perhaps we will."

Sarah looked relieved that the spat between her two favourite men would be over soon.

"Good evening to you all. We will speak again tomorrow, Mr Popov. I will report to the captain. Murder case closed, Miss Prince. Russian business transactions are no concern of ours."

Rachel took that to mean *butt out.*

"Yes, chief," she answered.

Day 5

Chapter 34

The next morning, Rachel decided to speak with Thomas during the day, and then forget about the whole thing. The nagging doubt at the back of her mind would have to go away. She'd been convinced one of the Russians was involved in the two deaths on board, in particular Asimov or the mysterious Sergei. It didn't make sense, though, as neither had any link to Lauren. Waverley's Russian friend had come up with nothing, and Waverley had told him to forget about it.

Maybe Lauren had acted alone, a psychopathic serial killer who used her nursing skills to exercise her need for control by deciding who should live and who should die. Rachel shuddered. She remembered reading about a doctor and pathological liar, Harold Shipman, who'd murdered hundreds of patients over decades before he was eventually found out. She had studied the interviews at the police training centre. The detectives interviewing him had said he'd mocked them – always believing his intellect was superior and they wouldn't be able to catch him out, he'd then been haughty even in court. Lauren had displayed some of that contempt to both her and Sarah, and she disregarded authority, so she fitted the bill. Rachel found it hard to comprehend.

Another example she remembered of a serial killer in the medical profession was a nurse called Beverley Allitt. *Didn't she use insulin too?* She'd murdered four children and attempted to murder more while working on a children's ward.

Yep, thankfully they're rare, but perhaps Lauren was one of the few. I dread to think how many she murdered in Africa. Rachel shuddered again.

Mario brought her a pot of coffee and she took it out to the balcony, happy there had been no stormy days or nights with only two more sea days to go before they arrived in New York.

The telephone rang.

"Hello."

"Rachel, it's Thomas. I've found out something, can we meet up?"

"Yes, when?"

"Can you come to my room, 1508, this afternoon about three? I'm chock-a-block with activities until then. I have something you should listen to."

Rachel wrote the room number down on a pad next to the telephone. "Okay, see you then."

After putting the telephone down, she wondered what Thomas had discovered. *This could be the final piece in the puzzle.*

Rachel knocked on the door of 1508 and Thomas answered immediately, looking breathless with excitement. Sweating profusely, he walked over to his safe and took out a digital recorder.

"I carry this everywhere. I keep a digital diary in case I ever want to write my memoirs," he explained, laughing.

He sat down on the sofa and Rachel took a seat next to him, intrigued.

"They are speaking in Russian so I'll need to interpret for you." He pressed play. "*Tell me you had nothing to do with Nikolai Stepanov's death.*" Rachel recognised the voice of Asimov.

"*He was blackmailing Boris.*" She assumed this was Sergei speaking, and Thomas confirmed this by mouthing, "Sergei."

There was silence for a moment. "*I knew that, but it was in hand.*"

"It wasn't New York he found out about; it involved another matter. Not something that involves you."

"Astonishing! What other matter? I need to know about everything; I am taking big risk."

"It was nothing." Sergei sounded dismissive. "Boris had a brother-in-law who caused big trouble for us in the past. Nikolai discovered he was working on this ship. We planned to kill the man and didn't want Nikolai opening big mouth. We killed two birds with one stone."

"I don't believe what I'm hearing! You killed two men during this cruise? Unbelievable."

Thomas stopped the tape.

"They argue about it for a bit longer. Sergei explains that neither of the deaths could be linked to him; he has someone else on board who did the killings. I'll play and interpret the next bit, though, because it mentions that the wrong man was killed."

Thomas looked so pleased with himself, she didn't want to burst his bubble by telling him she already knew this.

Sergei spoke again and Thomas interpreted.

"We found out this man who took witness protection would be on this ship. We needed to get an accomplice on board to replace a crew member, so we arranged for a person's father to have an accident."

Rachel gasped – Brigitte's father had been an unwitting victim in this conspiracy.

"And this poor person's father – did you kill him too?"

"Of course not – he survived. He will recover. Anyway, we brought our accomplice on board and ran into some problems. They killed roommate by mistake after being caught in the man's room. Man we are looking for has killed himself – that's what accomplice says. Nikolai was greedy, and when he recognised Boris's brother-in-law, he threatened to expose him and get him killed – but I already knew about him."

Asimov took deep breaths before hissing, "Boris thinks I had something to do with Nikolai's death. Look, I signed up to do a favour for a friend, not to get involved with murder."

"*I always hunt traitors down. Russia does not tolerate betrayal.*" Rachel could hear the edge in Sergei's voice and she almost felt sorry for Asimov.

"Is there not an investigation?"

"No, they have assumed the first death to be murder/suicide, and the second heart attack or overdose. We drugged Nikolai to mimic a heart attack."

"I haven't asked what is in the documents I expect Boris to collect because I don't want to know. Now I do want to know."

"The information they contain is worth billions of dollars, and one of your companies will get the contract to manufacture a state-of-the-art stealth aircraft like the world has never seen. Russia will be grateful to you, my friend."

Thomas stopped the recording again. "That's it – Asimov leaves the room after that."

"We need to take this to the security chief right now." Rachel stood up to go, but noticed Thomas remained where he was with his head in his hands. "What's wrong?"

"Rachel, I'm not sure about this. I'm not a brave man, and this Sergei Markov goes around killing people – I don't want to die."

Rachel saw he was trembling, with tears in his eyes.

"Look, I realise it's difficult, Thomas, but we can't let them get away with murder. Not only that, they intend to steal some pretty high-level security information."

"I'm really scared, Rachel – you need to give me more time to think about this. My schedule's full for the rest of the evening. Give me to tomorrow morning."

"Alright, but then I will need to tell the chief whether you come with me or not." Rachel was frustrated, but understood why Thomas was scared, and he had good reason to be. She offered up a quick prayer for Thomas, but she remained determined to see Markov arrested for his part in two murders.

"I'll be in the Twilight Room at 10am tomorrow for a treasure hunt. Meet me there. I don't want anyone to see you coming in here in case suspicions are raised."

"Can I take the recorder?"

"No, there's a lot of personal stuff on there from the cruise. I will need to make a copy of that first. You can have it tomorrow, with or without me. One more thing, Rachel. Promise me you won't tell anyone about this until after we've met tomorrow."

Rachel knew not to push him at this point or she might lose him.

"Okay, I promise."

She hoped she wouldn't come to regret her promise as she watched him return the recorder to his safe.

Chapter 35

"I can't believe it," said Bernard, astonished to hear how close Jefgeny Popov had come to becoming the third victim of Nurse Psychopath. "You read about these things, but you never imagine they happen in real life."

A sombre mood clouded Gwen's office as the medical team tried to process the information they now had. Graham had insisted they discuss it and debrief after he had been to see the captain.

"She might have killed me," Bernard continued.

"She wouldn't have tried it on any of us," said Graham.

Gwen, Bernard and Sarah looked at each other, acknowledging how close Bernard had come to being a victim.

"Don't you realise, Bernard? You were her alibi while she snooped around Jefgeny's room. I think she drugged you that night." Sarah saw the confused looks on Alex and Graham's faces and explained about the second morning of the cruise when Bernard had woken up to find Lauren in his bed.

Graham put a hand on Bernard's shoulder. "I'm sorry about your experience and glad you were drugged rather than killed. Why do you think she went back to the room?"

"Who knows – maybe she'd left something behind that might incriminate her, or perhaps she wanted to find Jefgeny and kill him," said Sarah.

"How did she carry on nursing?" asked Alex.

"People like her are renowned for being manipulative, and according to my friend in Connecticut, she was. She'd also been clever, offering to rotate around the hospital so no-one got to know her well, and subsequently suspicions weren't raised. It was only after a keen-eyed ward nurse in charge of supplies noticed insulin stocks didn't tally with those being administered that she got caught."

"So why didn't they realise that she might be killing patients?" asked Graham.

"She came up with a convincing story about visiting a slum where diabetic patients couldn't afford meds. They checked her story and confirmed that she did a lot of good in the slums. The hospital hierarchy gave her the opportunity to jump or be pushed. She chose to jump."

"So they believed she was some sort of misguided *Robin Hood*?" said Sarah. "Did she kill patients at the hospital?"

"That investigation's only just started, but I suspect if she's killed on this ship with such audacity, she's killed before."

"Why would she kill people in hospital, but not in a slum or Africa?"

"That we may never know," said Graham. "Perhaps her warped mind enjoyed playing God, choosing who should live and who should die. We're not certain she has killed before, and she might well have killed people in the slums, and in Africa too. I've called the doctor there and told him the bad news."

"What about the other hospitals she worked at?" asked Sarah.

"Fiction," answered Gwen. "I've had emails from all the hospitals listed on her CV – none of them have heard of her. The only places we're sure she worked at are the hospital in Connecticut, Future Motors and Africa. The local police are interviewing staff at Future Motors. I'm not sure whether we'll get any more information about that for now. She'll be handed over to the authorities when we arrive in New York, along with the man who attacked Rachel."

"What interesting cruises we enjoy when you and your friend are together, Sarah," said Graham. "I hope if there are any more shared cruises, the most exciting thing we encounter is who pays for drinks in the officers' mess."

They were brought back to reality when Sarah's radio burst into life with a call to a child suffering from sunburn. Letting out an exaggerated sigh, she stood up and grabbed the emergency case.

"Only one more sea day left – hurray!"

Day 6

Chapter 36

Sarah woke following the best night's sleep she'd had in ages. Her evening had been light, and pleased not to have encountered any real emergencies, she'd prayed for the first time in ages before going to bed, thanking God that Bernard had not been one of the victims of Lauren's killing spree.

The happiness transferred over to the morning; it was the final sea day before they were due to arrive in New York, and Sarah was looking forward to shore leave and shopping with Rachel. She ordered a room service breakfast and changed into her scrubs as she was only working the two surgeries today. Gwen was taking the on calls for the day as she would also be on shore leave tomorrow. With New York being an overnight stop, they were alternating leave, with half the team having one day off and the other half the second. After six days at sea, it was important they all stepped on land again.

Sarah pulled the case into the medical centre and wheeled it into Gwen's office before starting surgery. She finally got to run the blood tests on Jefgeny, and they revealed he was anaemic with abnormal liver function, pointing to early liver damage from excessive alcohol intake. She and Alex were going over the results as Eva was also anaemic.

"Eva just needs a bit of iron and some folic acid to help her through the pregnancy," said Alex. "She'll be fine with that. It's sad she will lose her job – it won't help her with an application for American citizenship." He shook his head.

Sarah felt sorry for Eva, whose only crime had been protecting the life of the man she loved. Now it seemed that unless he stopped drinking, his life wouldn't be that long anyway. They walked through to the infirmary to deliver the news to both patients, starting with Jefgeny.

"Now, Mr Popov, I have to tell you you're severely anaemic, and more than likely you have a stomach ulcer caused by drinking. On top of that, your liver is struggling to cope with your alcohol intake and you have the beginnings of liver cirrhosis." Alex allowed this information to sink in.

"Can you cure me?" Jefgeny asked, head down.

"We can give you medicine to heal the ulcer and you will need to have a tube passed into your stomach in hospital on land to find out how bad the damage is. If you're fired from the company, the cruise line insurance will no longer cover you."

Sarah's heart broke as she looked at the terror on Jefgeny's face. He'd already been through so much.

Alex continued. "In terms of the liver, that's down to you. If you want to see your child grow up, you need to stop drinking."

It sounded harsh, but Sarah knew Alex was trying his best to provoke Jefgeny to help himself. She wasn't sure whether the man could stop drinking if he lost his job, his insurance, and his girlfriend got deported.

Eva looked at him, pleading with him. "Jefgeny, please, for me and for our baby."

Jefgeny looked down and nodded. "I try."

Alex seized his opportunity. "I'll start you on stomach medication straight away and give you an eight-week supply. Miss Sipka won't be able to drink during pregnancy so that should help you. Do you have anywhere to go when you get to America – any family?"

Sarah knew the answer to this, but said nothing. As part of a witness protection programme, Jefgeny would have had to sever all links to his past. She wondered how he'd ended up on the cruise ship rather than being given funding to start a good new life. She'd hoped to ask him, but for now she needed to start surgery.

After surgery, the team ate lunch in the medical centre, courtesy of Raggie who brought the food up from the kitchen. Once lunch was over, they all dispersed. They discharged Jefgeny and Eva, with Eva returning to work and Jefgeny being under house arrest, confined to his room until the next day. Waverley had assigned a security guard to him.

Gwen, Bernard and Sarah were finishing up the last of the coffee when Gwen's computer beeped to announce an incoming email. She sashayed to the screen.

"You guys need to see this." She turned the screen towards them. It displayed a photo of Lauren entwined in the arms of a man. Sarah recognised the man.

"I need to find Rachel," she said as she ran from the office with Bernard in hot pursuit.

Chapter 37

Rachel was late, but saw Thomas at the front of the room, giving the group some last-minute instructions regarding the treasure hunt.

"Divide into groups, a minimum of two and a maximum of four. The sheets on the chairs contain the clues for the treasure hunt. We will let groups depart at ten-minute intervals so we don't cause chaos around the ship. When the last group has gone, Rachel and I will follow to pick up any stragglers and help any of you who are struggling. Are we clear?"

"Clear," several people answered at once. Thomas beckoned to Rachel to take a seat, looking happier than he had the day before. Rachel watched the last group leave the room before speaking to him.

"Have you decided?" she asked.

"I have. I will go with you after this activity, on condition you join me on the treasure hunt," he teased.

"As you've already included me, I don't see how I can refuse. Anyway, it'll be fun. It's years since I did a treasure hunt. We need to speak with the security chief straight after, though."

"I know." He put his head down before marching off. "Come on, then, time to go." Rachel followed him – it was easy for them because Thomas had set up the hunt with the aid of the cruise director and knew where to find all the clues.

It wasn't long before they found a group of three people wandering around on deck four. Thomas looked at the last clue they had found on their sheet before pointing them towards the guest services area.

"Aren't you going to let me find any clues?" asked Rachel, disappointed.

"Sorry, we don't have time. The groups will become impatient if I'm not around to help them when they get lost."

Forty-five minutes later, after helping numerous groups with their clues, Thomas led the way to the rear of the ship. Rachel followed him up multiple flights of steps until they were in a private area with artificial grass.

"Where's this, then? I've never been up here."

"It's a private party area, not in use today. It's one of the areas we hired for the tour group. The next party's tonight."

"Ooh, it's luxurious. Is there a clue up here?" Rachel looked around some false cordylines for clues.

"No, Rachel, I'm afraid not."

Something in his tone made her turn around. She saw the gun in his hand before anything else.

"Thomas, why are you holding a gun?"

"You know why, Rachel."

"Are you saying it was you all along? How did you get that gun on the ship?"

"It's one of the many things I own. It's undetectable to scanners and comes apart to go through X-rays. A prototype, but trust me, it's deadly."

"So what happens now? You shoot me and throw me overboard?" Her voice sounded calmer than she felt, and she was speaking loudly.

"That's about the sum of it. I'm sorry, I had no idea you were a cop when I invited you to tag along. It was my mistake, but your snooping has brought about the inevitable outcome."

Rachel decided the only thing to do was to play for time. With a dry mouth, she spoke.

"Well you could at least tell me what this is all about. What about the conversation between Asimov and Sergei?"

He laughed. "I had you fooled there, didn't I? They were arguing about how to surprise Lucretia for her birthday on the return journey. Asimov is going to propose, but they had different ideas about the menu. They played into my hands – these Russians get so excited, it was easy to convince you they were arguing about murder."

"So they had no part in the deaths of Nikolai or the crewman?"

"None." He smirked. "My sister is a nurse on board the ship and she's been doing some final calls."

He laughed, obviously not realising that Lauren had been arrested. Rachel didn't want to spook him by telling him.

"The man – Popov, as he's now called – was responsible for putting my father and my brother in jail. He and another man caused my father to kill himself because my mother returned to England in shame. Lauren and I vowed to get revenge on them. My sister likes killing people – she confided in me she killed patients in a hospital where she worked. I got her a job at a company we were stealing plans from to keep her out of trouble, but on this trip, I've let her do what she likes to do."

Rachel couldn't help but be disgusted at how lightly he dismissed murder. Thomas was in full boastful mode, almost wanting to tell her everything it seemed.

"I killed one traitor in Russia the day before the cruise, and now I will kill Popov, but first, I'll kill his girlfriend in front of him."

The conversation was taking a sinister turn. Rachel hoped to keep him calm, because if he got angry, he might just pull the trigger.

"What about Boris and the industrial espionage? I don't understand."

"Ah yes, Boris. All he's doing is smuggling copies of plans for a state-of-the-art refrigeration system for a friend of Asimov. Minor stuff, but hard to get hold of in Russia. I'm the one who will collect the blueprints for the new stealth aircraft. Everything I told you is true, but I'm the mastermind. I took over the business of export from my father and got a job as a cruise tour guide because it's the perfect vehicle for meeting up with buyers and sellers. This one is personal, though – unfinished business. Anyway, Rachel, I need to get back to the group, so I'm afraid your time is up."

"Did you cause the accident that put my friend's colleague's father in hospital?"

"Your friend?"

"My friend's also a nurse on the ship."

He looked shaky now, but recovered quickly. "Yes, Rachel. You need to understand, this is not personal; it's business – a multi-million dollar business. I like you, I do, and had I known you were a policewoman, I wouldn't have invited you along for the ride, but it's been a pleasure."

He lifted the gun, but a pair of strong arms grabbed him from behind, causing it to fall to the floor. Waverley held him in a vice-like grip and called for assistance. His security guards had been waiting in the wings and they now approached and cuffed Thomas.

"You took your time!" shouted Rachel.

"Don't worry – you were never in any danger. Look behind you." She turned and saw an officer with a rifle waving at her. "He would have shot if things had got out of hand."

"Out of hand – what do you call out of hand?"

"Sorry, we needed the confession." Waverley shrugged.

Thomas looked confused and angry.

"Thomas, I couldn't sleep last night. So many things didn't ring true – least of all, your translation of the Russian conversation. I speak very little Russian, but I do understand a few words, and 'birthday' and 'party' kept coming up in the conversation you were translating. And they never mentioned Nikolai. There were other things too. I suspected you were American. Even though you have mastered the English accent, you make mistakes, such as 'line' for queue and 'elevator' for lift. On their own, they mean nothing, but last night, I put it all together and you became my prime suspect."

Thomas scowled. Waverley continued the story, looking chuffed.

"Miss Prince alerted me this morning, and we looked into you in great detail, Thomas Gabriel – or rather, Mr Timothy Blythe. We tracked down your mother, who hasn't heard from you in years. She says you are too much like your father."

"So what! You have no evidence I've done anything wrong. It's her word against mine. No court will convict me. I'll walk."

"Except that I'm wearing a wire – that's how they knew where we were." Rachel pulled up her outer blouse to reveal wires and a microphone. "Courtesy of the *Coral Queen*." She took the recording off and handed it to Waverley.

"I think you and your sister, who is already incarcerated in the ship's brig, will go away for a very long time, Mr Blythe. We will also hand over an important notebook I found in your safe to the FBI in the morning."

"How did you get in there?"

"Miss Prince has sharp eyes and watched you tap in the code and memorised it when she was with you yesterday. We copied it while you were busy with your guests. Mr Price will not be meeting up with you in New York as the police have already arrested him. There will not be much left of your little gang by the time Interpol has finished. You chose the wrong stooge, Mr Blythe.

"Rachel, Sarah's waiting for you in the main atrium – she almost gave the game away."

It was time to leave. "Goodbye, Thomas – or Timothy. I don't suppose we'll be meeting again. Nothing personal, of course!" She held her head up high and bounced down the steps, leaving Waverley and his officers to deal with Timothy Blythe.

Chapter 38

Sarah ran over as soon as Rachel arrived in the main atrium and hugged her tight.

"Oh, Rachel – I was so worried about you. Waverley assured me you had it all under control when I tried to put out a ship-wide alert for you."

"What made you do that?"

"Gwen got a picture through today. It was a newspaper cutting about an industrial espionage gang leader who killed himself. The photo showed Lauren and her brother, Timothy Blythe, at the man's funeral, embracing, and I recognised him as your tour guide friend."

"Yes, it seems Timothy Blythe became Thomas Gabriel courtesy of deed poll to hide his past, but continue with his father's business."

"I was going to warn you, but Waverley said you'd worked it all out and would get a confession out of him. It has worried me sick something would go wrong – there's no way I could have done it."

"And I couldn't do what you do, so we'll just have to keep doing our own jobs."

"Except Waverley will offer you a security officer's job again, I'm sure."

"He already did – last night."

"And?"

"I'd rather go shopping in New York tomorrow, if you're still up for it?" Rachel laughed.

"Absolutely," replied Sarah.

"One thing, though – the ship's brig will be overcrowded tonight!"

"That's Waverley's problem. Lunch?" asked Sarah.

"Definitely, I'm starving."

Rachel was called into a meeting in Waverley's office that afternoon. It surprised her to see Asimov and Boris sitting down when she arrived.

"Ah, Miss Prince has arrived so we can start." Waverley showed Rachel to a seat.

"I demand to know what this is all about," Asimov barked.

"Me too," echoed Boris.

Me three! thought Rachel, but kept her thoughts to herself.

"Of course, gentlemen. First, I regret to inform you your tour guide, Thomas Gabriel, has been arrested on suspicion of murder and conspiracy to commit industrial espionage."

Rachel couldn't help smiling at Asimov's open mouth as he stared in disbelief.

Waverley was in his element. "I have spoken with Ronson Tours and another guide named Jeremiah Radley will join the ship tomorrow and take over Mr Gabriel's appointments."

"Well that's settled, then," said Asimov, shifting in his seat as if to leave.

"Not quite, sir. I must insist that you indulge me in a theory before you leave."

The men looked impatient, but Rachel guessed what might be coming.

"If it were to come to my attention, that someone might commit a crime in New York involving the handover of certain sensitive information regarding refrigeration equipment, I would have to move swiftly and inform the authorities. These theoretical people have committed no such crime at present, but I would value your opinion, gentlemen, whether you think such a crime might occur."

Asimov reddened, but then smiled. "I believe no such crime will happen. What do you think, Boris?"

"I don't believe anyone will commit such a crime, Mr Asimov." Boris looked relieved, almost joyful.

"Excellent," replied Waverley. "As a precaution, I must insist that diplomatic bags remain on board the ship while we are in port. I apologise in advance for the inconvenience. However, following the murder of one of your group, we need to ensure your safety by making thorough searches of people who return from shore leave."

"Chief, I understand," said Asimov. Rachel admired the man's ability to admit and accept defeat. "I'm due to dress for dinner now, so if you will excuse me."

He rose from his chair and left the room. Boris also got up to leave.

"Just one moment, Mr Stanislav. I wanted to let you know your brother-in-law is safe aboard ship and willing to meet up with you in secret later this evening – here are the arrangements." Waverley handed Boris an envelope.

"I would be very pleased to accept, as long as it does not put him in danger. My wife, his sister, misses him terribly."

"I guarantee his safety," said Waverley.

Boris pocketed the envelope and left the office, smiling. Rachel couldn't help smiling too.

"Thank you for that – I was pleased to be here."

"We're not finished yet." He picked up the phone. "Send them in." Rachel looked towards the door and saw Jefgeny and Eva escorted into the office. "Please take a seat," instructed Waverley.

They sat down, holding hands, preparing for the worst.

"Mr Popov, Miss Sipka, the captain has asked me to convey his disappointment with some of your actions during this cruise."

"Sorry, sir," said Jefgeny.

"However, he has spoken with the cruise line and explained the circumstances of what has happened, and we have both spoken to your senior officers. They agree that you should both keep your jobs, if you would like them, on condition that no such thing happens again, and that you, Mr Popov, work with Dr Romano to overcome your health issues."

Jefgeny and Eva hugged each other. "Thank you so much, we will do everything you say."

"The United States of America owes you a debt of gratitude, Mr Popov. Dr Romano has arranged for you to have an endoscopy at 10am tomorrow at Queen Cruises' expense as you remain covered as an employee. Now I suggest that you both get back to work."

They beamed as they left. "Yes, sir."

Rachel was over the moon. "I can't wait to tell Sarah, she'll be ecstatic. She was so worried about Jefgeny."

"I love my job sometimes," said Waverley. "Enjoy the rest of the cruise, Rachel. I hope you will stay out of trouble for the remaining eight days, if that's at all possible."

"Oh, it's possible," Rachel said as she floated out the door.

THE END

Killer Cruise Book 3

Dawn Brookes

Killer Cruise

A Rachel Prince Mystery

This novel is entirely a work of fiction. The names, characters and incidents portrayed are the work of the author's imagination except for those in the public domain. Any resemblance to actual persons, living or dead, is entirely coincidental. Although real life places are depicted in settings, all situations and people related to those places are fictional.

Dawn Brookes
Oakwood Publishing

Paperback Edition 2019
Kindle Edition 2019
Paperback ISBN: 978-1-9998575-9-2

Chapter 1

As Rachel gazed up out of the rear window of the old Bentley, the glow from the sun appeared to be caressing the magnificent *Coral Queen*. The *Coral* had become a ship she was extremely fond of, in spite of a few minor hiccups from puzzling murder conundrums on the two cruise holidays she'd previously spent on board.

"Almost there, ladies." Marjorie's chauffeur broke the amicable silence in the rear of the car. Rachel was spending a fortnight accompanying her eighty-six-year-old friend, Lady Marjorie Snellthorpe, whom she'd met under stressful circumstances on her very first cruise. Afterwards they had become firm friends and Rachel had grown increasingly fond of the stoical older woman.

"Thank you, Johnson, my old bones were beginning to stiffen up. Are you alright, dear?" Marjorie smiled at Rachel.

"I'm great, thanks. I was just admiring the *Coral,* she's berthed over there."

"She is rather wonderful, isn't she?" replied Marjorie as they continued the drive towards the port's entrance. A few minutes later they were parked up at a drop-off area in front of the passenger terminal. Johnson leapt out of the car with surprising agility for someone much older than Rachel and opened the door for Lady Marjorie before moving round to let Rachel out.

He opened the boot, which had required packing with great precision due to its size, and the ship's crew were soon attending to their luggage. Johnson insisted on carrying the hand luggage for both of them, despite protests from Rachel, reminding her how she felt part of a bygone era whenever she was with Marjorie. Growing up in a vicarage, she was used to helping other people rather than being helped herself and being pampered didn't come naturally.

Her father, vicar of St Crispin's in the village of Brodthorpe, Hertfordshire, always set a perfect example of the 'give and you shall receive' philosophy. The only assistance the family had ever had came from a cook hired to help her mother during Rachel's early childhood. Rachel's mother was the perfect hostess and for the most part played the role of the vicar's wife well, with just the occasional rebellion. One such mutiny had occurred the previous week when Rachel was visiting for the weekend.

"I draw the line at overnighters with Girl Guides in the church, Brendan. It's just not going to happen."

"The overnighter or you being one of the responsible adults?" Her father had laughed.

"You know full well what I mean. I'm not cooking, baking, cosseting or babysitting a group of giggly girls. I'm very sorry Clara's ill, but my sympathy does not stretch to replacing all and sundry every time something goes wrong. I already have the village fête, the women's institute and your AGM to cater for this weekend, and now you're asking me to feed fifteen girls for two days and sleep – or not – in the church with them! No, Brendan. Enough is enough. Find someone else or cancel it, I don't care which."

Brendan Prince knew when he was beaten. He hugged his wife and conceded, looking pleadingly towards Rachel who'd agreed to step into the breach, and as it happened, had had enormous fun. Her mother had softened enough to supply meals while Rachel baked enough cakes to feed all of the Girl Guide troops for miles around.

Rachel stretched her legs after getting out of the car and ran up and down on the spot for a few minutes to shake away the effects of the relatively short car journey. She had already jogged around Hyde Park first thing, knowing that the day would be sedentary and not wanting to miss out on her daily exercise. No-one in the family understood where her fitness-fanatic behaviour came from except herself. The running bug she'd picked up at university when she'd found herself homesick and after feeling confined during the first year living in halls of residence. It became more of an obsession during her first year of police training when she'd failed to run down a youth who had knocked an elderly woman to the ground and snatched her handbag. Her colleague had stopped to give support to the woman and Rachel had given chase, but the youth had lost her after running up a hill with comparative ease and leaping over a wall. Disgusted with her apparent lack of fitness, she'd trained harder and harder and prided herself on never failing to run anyone down since.

Marjorie and Johnson waited patiently for her to finish jogging on the spot and retrieve her handbag from the car.

"Ready?" the old lady asked.

"Ready," replied Rachel, noticing the enthusiastic crowds building up both inside and outside the terminal.

As VIP passengers, courtesy of Marjorie's multiple cruises, which had more recently been extended to free cruises for life, they would not have to wait in the orderly snake-like queue forming in the terminal. Marjorie took Rachel's arm and they walked towards the entrance for platinum passengers. The staff welcomed them and asked if they needed assistance with their bags, which Rachel declined quickly, claiming them from Johnson before he could object.

"Goodbye, Johnson. Safe journey home, and enjoy your holiday," Marjorie intervened to prevent a scene.

"Thank you, My Lady, I will." He tipped his cap and waved until they'd passed through the passenger entrance towards security. Marjorie was offered wheelchair assistance for the long trek up to the ship's passenger entrance, which she graciously accepted. Rachel put one bag on her shoulder and extended the handle of Marjorie's hand luggage to drag it along behind her.

"Where's Johnson going for his holiday?"

"Where he goes every year – fishing in the Scottish Highlands. He loves it up there, walks for miles after spending hours on end ogling the water for signs of a catch."

"That explains why he's so agile," remarked Rachel.

"He's a keen fisherman," Marjorie continued. "I think that's the reason Ralph chose him as our chauffeur – it was something my late husband loved to do too. So the two of them would up-sticks and spend days sitting in front of some river, loch or anything else they could fish in."

"Sounds like it's not your thing."

"You're absolutely right, my dear. It's one pastime I've never been able to comprehend. Dreadfully dull, but each to their own, as they say. I never told Ralph, but I don't think it's fair to catch fish with a hook only to throw them back in the water again. Although to be fair, he did sometimes eat what he caught."

After slowly making their way up the makeshift ramp, not because the volunteer pushing Marjorie's wheelchair was slow, but because people joining the ship ahead of them were taking their time, they finally arrived on board where Marjorie insisted she could walk.

"I'll be alright now, thank you. I'm fine on the flat, really."

"Okay, Madam." The jolly volunteer made his way back with the empty wheelchair to assist with the next passenger needing help, but not before Marjorie had given him a generous tip for his kindness.

The initial impression on entering the grand atrium never failed to take Rachel's breath away. She couldn't help admiring the thick, shiny marble pillars, polished brass stair rails and the immaculate cleanliness.

Marjorie looked tired. "Shall we sit for a while?" asked Rachel, to which the old lady nodded. They found seats at a small table away from where the passengers were boarding. The surrounding tables were already filling up as some people had the same idea. Others were wandering around admiring the opulence of the atrium, which spanned two decks and formed the main hub of activity and the retail section of the vessel. A waiter who had been about to offer them champagne on boarding until he'd noticed Rachel's hands were full brought them complementary flutes to have while they sat.

"I do hope there's a crime on board so that we can do a bit of detecting," said Marjorie gleefully.

"And I do hope there isn't," replied Rachel, laughing.

Chapter 2

"Come on, Sarah, questionnaire time," called Brigitte.

Sarah looked up at her French colleague from where she'd been lounging after checking through new passenger records and pondering over who might need medical attention. Groaning, she hauled herself from the comfortable sofa in Senior Nurse Gwen Sumner's office. Gwen herself had taken the day off and joined back-to-back passengers on a coach tour to London.

"I love turnaround days and meeting new passengers, but honestly, Brigitte – if we have another cruise like the last, I'm out of here." Sarah had worked as a nurse for Queen Cruises for almost two years and considered herself fortunate that she'd only worked on the one ship so far.

A ship that also happens to be the largest in the fleet.

She smiled. The transatlantic crossing they had just returned from had resulted in the medical centre being inundated from day one. The return crossing was rough and passengers had struggled with the conditions, either falling down or throwing up all over the ship. In addition to that, the crew had been particularly accident prone, injuring themselves on a daily basis. Most of the injuries occurred when crew became unable to maintain their footing while rushing around attending to passengers.

"Be thankful it wasn't worse," said Brigitte.

"It was bad enough – I would say we're due a quiet spell, but Rachel and Marjorie are joining us today and you know what that means!"

"Noooo, it's not going to happen. Third time lucky – no murders this voyage, not even a hint of murder." Brigitte had missed the previous cruise Rachel had taken after her father had been involved in a car accident.

"Let's hope not. Anyway, I'm ready. Where's Bernard?"

"I don't know – he said he was going to enjoy his day off and sleep all day before surgery tonight."

Sarah sighed. The medical centre held two walk-in surgeries each day, and staff also attended emergencies night and day. The nurses and doctors took turns being on call, with the nurses usually triaging patients that might need to be seen by a doctor, treating many themselves. As a rule, Dr Graham Bentley, the chief medical officer, treated passengers while Alex Romano, the junior doctor or baby doc as he was affectionately referred to, managed the health of the crew.

"Did Alex do the London trip?"

"No, he said he was going to Portsmouth to visit the *Victory* or something. Whatever that is?"

"HMS *Victory*, it's an old gunship. I'm surprised you haven't heard of it as it played a major part in the Battle of Trafalgar during the Napoleonic Wars. I think we beat your lot, along with the Spanish."

"Pah, I never was interested in history, and least of all in war history. There's enough going on in the world today without harking back to the past."

"If only we would learn from history," Sarah muttered as they made their way off the ship to the passenger terminal.

"Those lads are going to be trouble," said Sarah as they made their way back on board after checking through passenger health questionnaires. A group of thirty young men aged between twenty-one and twenty-three were taking the cruise as a stag party. Sarah noticed the already boisterous and rowdy group causing consternation among some of the older passengers, while others looked less than patient, raising their eyebrows and rolling their eyes.

"I think you're right, they will be, but hopefully for security, not for us," answered Brigitte.

"Poor Waverley, he's already dreading this cruise with Rachel joining us. I do think his hands are going to be full keeping that lot under control."

"Not to mention them." Brigitte nodded towards an American all-girl group, similar ages to the boys.

"Mm, could be a satisfying blend or a toxic combination, a bit like Bernard's cocktails."

"Don't talk to me about Bernard or his cocktails."

Brigitte and Bernard had developed a good friendship, but it could be volatile at times due to their opposite personalities. Bernard, a nurse from the Philippines, could be a tease, while Brigitte was more serious and often spoke her mind before engaging her brain. It sometimes resulted in heated debate, but Sarah was thankful that underneath it all, they liked each other, and when push came to shove, they had each other's backs.

"He does like to experiment," Sarah laughed. "The only successful secret cocktail recipe he has produced is the Stinger – not that I like them. They are like Marmite: you love them or you hate them."

"They're alright I suppose, but I prefer wine, being French."

"Anyway, I'm going to track down Rachel and Lady Snellthorpe before dinner and evening surgery. See you later." Sarah tapped her friend and colleague on the shoulder and headed towards the main atrium.

She spotted Lady Marjorie's unmistakable head of bright white hair, immaculately permed, before seeing Rachel partially hidden by a pillar. She sneaked up behind her, holding her finger to her lips to alert Marjorie not to give the game away, and grabbed her shoulders from behind. Rachel calmly got up from her chair before hugging Sarah excitedly. They had been best friends since school.

"Why weren't you surprised?" Sarah felt disappointed.

"I saw you coming through the glass. If you want to surprise people, you're going to have to tell the staff not to do such a good job of the cleaning."

Rachel laughed as Sarah looked at the gleaming glass balustrade next to the table and realised what she meant – her reflection was clearly visible, not only in the glass, but also the table and the marble pillars.

"Hello, Lady Snellthorpe. It's lovely to see you again." Sarah hugged the old lady who had stood to greet her.

"Bah, you can do away with the Lady Snellthorpe business. Marjorie to you, and I'll brook no argument. You look lovely in that pristine white uniform, my dear, and it's a pleasure to see you again."

"Thank you," answered Sarah, standing back and studying the elderly lady. A spritely woman for her age, and immaculately dressed and manicured as usual. She recognised the sky-blue Ralph Lauren suit and the Armani blouse immediately. "You don't look so bad yourself. Are you keeping well, Marjorie?"

"Quite well, thank you."

Sarah joined them at the table and gratefully accepted a glass of orange juice from one of the waiters. Marjorie was unlikely to say even if she weren't well, a proud woman who believed in the stiff upper lip mentality that many people her age adhered to.

"How was the New York trip?" asked Rachel.

"New York was fine – no murder en route, unlike when you were with us, but the return sailing was rough the first few days. Lots of passengers were seasick. We haven't had much time to catch our breath, but this journey looks good. The forecast is favourable, and the multiple stops should keep people entertained, allowing the crew to get their land legs back again as we all get more shore leave."

An announcement came over the ship's loudspeakers informing them of a compulsory safety drill before dinner.

"I'd better go and drop this hand luggage off in our rooms," said Rachel. "I'll meet you at our Muster Station, Marjorie.

"Yes, I need to change uniforms quickly. One of the passengers spilt tea downstairs and my skirt was splashed."

"Barely noticeable," remarked Marjorie.

"I know, but better to give a good impression to passengers on their first day," answered Sarah, winking. She hugged Rachel and Marjorie again before leaving. "I can't wait to introduce you to Jason."

"We can't wait either, can we, Marjorie?"

"We are very much looking forward to it," answered Marjorie.

"I'll let you know when I can arrange it. Catch you later."

Sarah bounced away happily. She was indeed looking forward to introducing her new boyfriend Jason to Rachel. A best friend's appraisal was always welcome.

Chapter 3

The next evening, Rachel couldn't help but notice the brash Freddie Mercury lookalike making his way towards her. He'd been doing the rounds in the bar where she and Marjorie were having a quiet after-dinner cocktail.

"Oh dear. Here comes trouble," remarked Marjorie.

"Allo, darling." The stench of alcohol-fuelled breath almost knocked her out as the man sat on the bar stool next to Rachel. Around six-foot tall, with short dyed black hair, black moustache and large, prominent front teeth, he was already worse for wear. At eight o'clock in the evening, the night was yet young. He spoke with a cockney accent and his lecherous blood-shot green eyes told Rachel all she needed to know about him.

"How do you do?" Marjorie tried to intervene on her behalf. Rachel was used to unwanted attention, being tall with blonde hair, blue eyes, and told by so many how beautiful she looked. Being so attractive wasn't always a positive thing, but she could handle it. This man had already caused quite a commotion in the bar, a number of men standing up and threatening him, and the policewoman in Rachel had been inadvertently observing his behaviour since he came in. Almost as soon as he'd entered, he'd argued with a man in a suit. The man had grabbed his arm in an attempt to lead him out, but 'Freddie Mercury' had pushed him away, causing the man to shrug his shoulders and leave.

The man before her now was wearing a white Elvis Presley style jumpsuit decorated with ribbons and sequins. Not the normal white vest and trousers she remembered from seeing pictures of Freddie Mercury, if that was who he was imitating. He also wore smudged bright red lipstick, eyeliner and thick mascara – he had to be a member of the on-board entertainment. She got another whiff of alcohol mixed with cigarette smoke on his breath as he leaned closer, blocking Marjorie.

"I was talking to 'er, Grandma." His speech was slurred and he almost fell over as he grabbed Rachel's wrist. Rachel wanted to give him a swift karate chop for his rudeness to her elderly friend, but she made allowances for the fact he was in a drunken stupor.

"Sir, I respectfully suggest it might be better if you went elsewhere. I'm having a drink with my friend. Please take your hand off me." Rachel warned him, forcing herself to be as pleasant as she could muster.

"Oh, come on, give a geezer a break. You looking for a good time?" His grip grew tighter and he pulled her closer. Looking down at her wrist, Rachel noticed a red mark extending beyond where his hand was holding her tight. It was becoming painful.

"I am having a good time, thank you. Now, you're hurting me, so for the last time, please remove your hand."

"Or what?" he spluttered, spraying saliva over her dress. Rachel had had enough. Moving as quickly and stealthily as a panther, she grabbed his hand and twisted his arm behind his back in an instant, gritting her teeth.

"Or this—"

He cried out, drawing even more attention to the scene. Heads were turning all around.

"Alright, let go o' me."

Rachel noticed a large man getting up from another stool, looking angry. She released Freddie's arm as a security guard entered the bar and approached him.

"Mr Mercury, sir, I'm going to have to ask you to come with me."

Rachel gawped. "Really?"

The guard rolled his eyes and mouthed, "I know, it's what he likes to be called!"

The man tried to straighten himself and square up to the security guard, but his effort was a pathetic attempt, and he was no match for the strapping six-foot-three guard, whose name badge revealed him as Jason Goodridge. Rachel knew at once that he was a recent addition to the security team working on board the *Coral Queen*, and more importantly, he was Sarah's new boyfriend.

Mercury conceded defeat and allowed Jason to lead him out of the bar.

"Well, cruising has certainly been more interesting since I met you, Rachel Prince," chuckled Marjorie, eyes twinkling.

"It can be entertaining at times, although deadly and extremely annoying at others," Rachel retorted, mulling over her previous cruises tracking down murderers. It was fun travelling with Marjorie, who had asked Rachel to accompany her on this cruise around the Baltic Sea as she no longer enjoyed travelling alone and her son despised cruising. Rachel was only too pleased to oblige and they were happily ensconced in luxury suites at the back of deck fifteen with a butler shared between them. Marjorie insisted on paying for Rachel who had reluctantly accepted, knowing that once the old lady's mind was made up, there was no changing it.

"Do you suppose that was his real name?" asked Rachel.

"No, I don't think so. He looks like he might be one of the entertainers; I read in the *Coral News* there was a Queen tribute act on board. He may be a fanatic, or worse still, a member of the band, I suppose."

"Let's hope he's not one of the band or they will be one short – I can't see him sobering up anytime soon. Are they playing tonight?"

"I believe so, but I didn't notice where or when. Not my thing, I prefer heavy metal." Marjorie giggled again, causing Rachel to join in.

"Yeah, right!"

"You handled yourself well there, ma'am." A pleasant American voice interrupted their conversation. Rachel looked down from her bar stool to see a short, stocky man in his sixties with silver-grey hair and a snow-white moustache, similar to Marjorie's hair colour. He continued in his southern drawl, "He was getting on my last nerve." The man giggled at his own joke. "The wife told me to come to your aid, but you moved pretty quickly before I got the chance. I don't move as fast as I used to. May I buy you both a drink and would you like to join Mabel and me?" He pointed towards a table for four where an elegant bleached-blonde lady, wearing an emerald green dress, was waving. Rachel looked at Marjorie to check.

"Thank you. That would be most kind," the old lady answered. "I'll have another one of these splendid cocktails please."

Rachel smiled at the man and answered, "The same – if you're sure that's alright?"

"It would be my pleasure." He turned to a barman and ordered the drinks.

They made their way over to the table where Mabel was sitting.

"Howdy." The woman spoke in a high-pitched voice. "I haven't seen moves like that in a long time. Where d'you learn to do that?"

Rachel, always reluctant to divulge the fact she worked as a policewoman, answered honestly, "Karate black belt. I like to practise now and then."

"Well, he's lucky he didn't get the chop then, eh, Mabel?" The man laughed again as he arrived with two Blue Lagoons. "I'm Ron, by the way, and this is my wife, Mabel."

"I'm Rachel."

"And I'm Marjorie," said Marjorie with the twinkle that hadn't left her eye. It was obvious she was enjoying herself.

"That's a mighty fine upper-crust English accent you have there, Marjorie," said Ron, good-naturedly. "Are you two related?"

"No," answered Marjorie. "But I have come to view Rachel as a granddaughter over the past few years. She's become part of the family," she said affectionately.

Rachel smiled at the unexpected compliment and had to agree that she and Marjorie had become very close in recent months. Rachel had taken a job in the police force in north London, and knowing how expensive London was to live in, Marjorie had offered her a flat she owned in the West End at a much reduced rent. Rachel had been reluctant to accept the offer, but Marjorie had insisted.

"It's an apartment that was used by my husband for international visitors when he ran the business. Since Ralph died, it sits empty as Jeremy puts overseas people up at his home now. Gives him the opportunity to show off. I was mulling over the idea of selling the place so you would be doing me a huge favour occupying it. Save me the bother."

Rachel finally accepted, and despite a few guilt pangs, couldn't be happier with her new apartment just a short distance from Harrods in Knightsbridge.

Ron and Mabel turned out to be pleasant company. They explained they were from Texas with Ron owning a cattle ranch inherited from his grandparents.

"Daddy didn't want anything to do with it. Couldn't wait to escape, but I love it out there, solitary and wild. I would have given it all up for Mabel, though. She was born and bred in the city, but fell in love with me and the ranch in that order." He squeezed his wife's hand. "We're getting too old for all the work involved now; we haven't been blessed with children, so it looks like we might have to sell up the old place soon." He looked momentarily saddened by this proclamation, and Mabel squeezed his hand back. "But I have a great neighbour and his son who will buy us out whenever we're ready. We'll be able to live in the house for as long as we like, though."

"That guy who was bothering you ladies is lead singer in a Queen tribute band, you know. Only saw them perform last night and he was brilliant, although a bit too risqué for our liking," said Mabel.

"Oh really? They're supposed to be performing tonight, too," remarked Marjorie.

"Is that so?" Mabel pulled a copy of the *Coral News*, a daily brochure listing all activities and events available on board ship, from her bag. "Oh, so they are, eleven o'clock in the Culture Lounge. Let's hope there are two lead singers."

"Too late for me, I'm afraid," said Marjorie. "Otherwise I'd be tempted to see if he's sobered up by then. What about you, Rachel?"

"I just might go out of curiosity, if Sarah's up for it."

"Who's Sarah?" asked Mabel.

"She's my best friend who works on board as a ship's nurse. We're meeting up once she's finished work for the evening. Here she comes now."

Sarah walked in, looking dazzling as usual in her pristine white officer's uniform, compulsory attire in the passenger areas. She hugged Rachel and kissed Marjorie on the cheek.

"Hello, you two." She looked at Ron and Mabel. "Good evening, sir, madam."

Rachel introduced the couple and Sarah joined them. Ron enjoyed relating the story of Rachel's lightning moves fending off the troublesome entertainer, ending with the fact the man was supposed to be performing later in the evening.

"I can tell you want to go," said Sarah, laughing at Rachel's eager face. "I have heard about the band. They've joined us on a three month contract." Sarah sounded like they had already made an impression, but didn't elaborate.

Rachel nodded and the matter was settled.

"Can I get you a drink?" Ron offered.

"No, you cannot," interjected Marjorie. "It's my turn, but might I ask you to do the honours, Rachel? Here's my card."

After buying a round of drinks, Rachel sat down and told Sarah how they had inadvertently met Jason who had been the man of the moment, escorting Mr Freddie Mercury out of the bar following the unwelcome incident. Sarah blushed at the mention of Jason's name. Rachel was happy for her.

"We didn't get the opportunity to introduce ourselves, though."

"Freddie Mercury can't be his real name, can it?" asked Marjorie.

"No, it's not," Sarah replied. "His name is Dominic, Dominic Venables, but he will only answer to Dom – or Freddie. He is apparently going to change his name by deed poll soon, though, according to the drummer."

"My, my!" exclaimed Ron. "As long as we don't meet an Elvis Presley or Dolly Parton – not that I'd complain about the latter – on board ship, or I'll start thinking I'm ready for a rest home." They all laughed, good naturedly.

After finishing her drink, Marjorie stood up. "If you young things don't mind, it's time for me to retire."

"I'll walk you," Rachel offered.

"No need, dear. I'm going to take a stroll on the upper decks first."

Rachel knew that Marjorie and her late husband had always strolled around the open decks before going to bed, something Marjorie chose to do alone as she said it helped her feel close to him.

"Time for us to go too," declared Mabel. "I've got an appointment for a manicure early tomorrow morning."

Left alone, Rachel asked Sarah how her day had been.

"Relatively quiet – a healthy group of passengers so far. Day two and no murders – that's got to be a bonus."

"If you count boarding day as day one, then yes, so far, so good."

The cacophonous din of rock music blaring from the Culture Lounge greeted them.

"I've never been here before," said Rachel. "There's still so much to explore on board."

The band was warming up. The lounge was already full and the two friends struggled to find anywhere to sit. The cavernous room resembled a disco in many ways with a dance floor in front of the stage where the band was tuning instruments. The lighting was dim around the tables with kaleidoscopic rotating lamps flashing towards the dance floor and the stage.

"No sign of Freddie," said Rachel as they perched themselves on two bar stools on the edge of a large table.

"Gordon doesn't look happy," Sarah remarked.

"Who's Gordon?"

"Gordon Venables. He's the new cruise director, taken over from Matt who decided to join the Caribbean route."

Rachel saw a small, slim man with dark-brown hair, dressed in a navy-blue suit, frantically speaking into his radio just off the side of the stage. The other members of the band continued testing their instruments and microphones at mega-too-loud decibels. Rachel could barely hear Sarah, they were shouting above the thunderous sound of the bass.

"He does look stressed, poor man."

It was quarter past eleven and the crowd was becoming more boisterous and fractious by the minute. Gordon walked towards the main microphone.

"Apologies, ladies and gentlemen, there will be a short delay while we wait for our lead singer—"

"Boo, boo, boo!" the crowd yelled, drowning out the dulcet tones of the cruise director.

"Oh dear," said Sarah. "He's really not having a good day – one of the dancers in the early evening theatre show sprained her ankle and had to pull out of the second show, and now this."

"How do you know all this?"

"I was called over to the theatre to treat the sprain."

As if by magic, the lights dimmed, the band struck up a rousing intro and Freddie-cum-Dom paraded on stage, belting out a rendition of *Killer Queen*. It did the trick. His jumping and gyrating with the microphone attached to a mobile stand whipped the mainly middle-aged and largely inebriated crowd into a state of frenzy. A good performer, Rachel had to admit.

"The cynic in me says that was staged," she shouted above the noise.

Sarah was shaking her head, bemused and looking as confused as Rachel. The atmosphere was rocking with sound vibrations they could actually feel underneath their feet following the increase in volume. The sudden appearance of the elusive Freddie had caused the crowd to go into a feverish euphoria. Gordon ran off stage, wiping sweat from his forehead with a handkerchief.

Rachel watched the theatrical Freddie, mesmerised by his mannerisms. "I can imagine him practising in his bedroom, performing to old videos to be as good as this. Queen was before my time, but he seems about right. They certainly don't use mics like that anymore, as far as I'm aware."

"Thankfully. He's obviously an obsessed eccentric, but a brilliant performer," Sarah shouted back. "As long as he keeps the passengers happy, although I fear the band might end up being more trouble than it's worth."

An hour later, while the band left the stage for a break, Rachel and Sarah enjoyed the relative quiet.

"Do you mind if we call it a night? I'm on call in the morning," said Sarah.

"Yes, that's fine with me. They are a good group, I'll give them that – shame Mr Mercury doesn't behave a bit better when not on stage."

While waiting for Sarah to come out of the ladies, Rachel saw Dom-cum-Freddie standing in the corridor, yelling at another man. The lead guitarist she suspected, although she wasn't certain.

"If you think you're ever gonna be good enough to take over from me – forget it! Don't think I don't know what's going on behind my back. You're not good enough! You'll never be good enough."

Following this diatribe, Freddie barged past Rachel, knocking her left shoulder as he did so. The man who had been shouted at was too busy licking his wounds to see her either and he sulkily followed Freddie back towards the stage.

Sarah returned.

"He might be a good singer, but he's a real pain in the backside." Rachel glared after both men.

"What happened?"

"Mr blooming egocentric dinosaur barged into me after giving one of his band mates a tongue lashing. He really needs to learn some manners."

"Oh dear, I'm sorry. Don't worry, Rachel, I suspect he won't last long on board the *Coral Queen* if he starts annoying the passengers like that."

"I won't be complaining, but it will not be long before someone else does, I'm afraid. Anyway, no harm done, but someone might just lash out at him if he's not careful."

They parted company at the lifts and Rachel made her way up to deck fifteen and her luxury suite, *Killer Queen* still buzzing around in her head.

Chapter 4

The following morning, Rachel joined Marjorie for breakfast in her suite after going for a run around deck sixteen. Mario, their butler from El Salvador who she knew from previous voyages, brought in extra coffee on seeing Rachel.

"I knew you would want coffee, ma'am Rachel, so I took liberty of ordering extra."

"Thanks, Mario. I must be taking too many cruise holidays if you know me that well!"

"Not nearly enough, ma'am." He placed the tray on a table and left them to it.

They sat out on the large balcony facing the expansive sea behind the ship as their suites were situated, one either side, at the rear of deck fifteen. Today there was no sea view as they were docked in Copenhagen harbour. Rachel poured them both coffee and took in deep breaths of salt-filled air.

"Did you enjoy your evening last night?" asked Marjorie.

"It was incredibly noisy, but the tribute band was surprisingly good. My father was a fan of Queen in their early days so I'm familiar with some of their music. He keeps it secret from his parishioners, though."

"I don't see why. I am pleased I didn't come, though; I'm not a fan of loud pop music. Give me Brahms any day of the week. So the rather rude Dominic Venables managed to sober up in time, did he?"

"I couldn't swear to him being sober, but he did deign to turn up, fifteen minutes late, just as the crowd was getting agitated about the wait. It could have been a ploy for all I know, although the new cruise director looked stressed out of his head. Sarah said he'd had a bad first sea day. Anyway, that's enough about the obnoxious Dom if you don't mind? What would you like to do today, Marjorie?"

"Nothing too strenuous, if that's alright? Perhaps a look at the Little Mermaid as she's not long returned from touring the globe, I understand, and then changing of the guard at the palace. I'm happy to take a taxi if you want to do something more exciting, though."

"Nope, that sounds very good to me. I had quite a late night."

Rachel took a quick shower after breakfast and dressed in cropped denim jeans, a faded jade t-shirt and a pair of white Doc Martin sandals. Marjorie looked quintessentially British in a dark-blue summer skirt and jacket with a pair of fitted beige open-toed shoes and handbag to match. The cotton floral print blouse with colours that enhanced her outfit finished it off to a tee. Rachel admired her friend's dress sense. Marjorie always took time over her appearance and rarely had a hair out of place. Her white hair, recently permed, accentuated her almost regal demeanour. *She could have been a duchess as well as a lady.*

"I feel positively underdressed," she said forlornly.

"You look beautiful, my dear, as you always do."

"Not as glamorous as you, but it's too late for me to change now anyway."

Rachel took the old lady's arm and they headed towards the central lifts and down to deck three where they could leave the ship via security and makeshift steps. The ship's photographers were strategically positioned on the dockside, offering to take photos before passengers left for their outings. The happy duo obliged, before ambling along towards the building that formed the port's customs.

Just before they entered through a pair of open doors, the noise of someone gasping behind her caused Rachel to swing round. Following the gasping woman's gaze, she looked on in horror as a body hurtled downwards, towards the sea from somewhere near the top of the ship. A few other passengers had turned around too, and soon afterwards there was a loud splash.

Pandemonium followed and one of the passengers screamed. A life buoy was thrown into the water from one of the lower decks and the man overboard siren sounded. Two officers and a dock worker dived into the black water.

"Ladies and gentlemen, please move along." An officer quickly took charge and directed passengers away from the scene, while others screened off the area. Marjorie looked at Rachel.

"Was that who I think it was?"

"It certainly looked like it, but I didn't get a good enough look. It all happened so quickly. The jumpsuit looked about right, though."

They were hurriedly escorted towards the exit and, accepting there was nothing they could do, they complied, agreeing to continue with their day.

"It looks as though we'll have another 'accident' to look into after all. When we get back, that is."

There was a mischievous twinkle in Marjorie's eye. Rachel groaned aloud.

"This can't be happening."

Chapter 5

Rachel and Marjorie enjoyed their visits to the main tourist attractions in Copenhagen, and Marjorie was particularly pleased that the Little Mermaid statue had been returned to her rightful place.

"She certainly is well named," remarked Rachel, surprised at how small the statue actually was. "I don't understand why, but I imagined she'd be bigger somehow."

"I was surprised too, the first time I saw her, but I expect that's why she's called the *Little* Mermaid," Marjorie teased.

After taking some photos, they wandered around the harbour for a while, watching the changing of the guard at the Amalienborg Palace at midday before stopping for lunch.

"That was interesting, but I have to say the one at Buckingham Palace beats it by a country mile," commented Rachel.

"Ah yes, well that does take some beating. No-one does pomp and ceremony quite like the British – not that I'm biased. Here in Copenhagen, it is much more spectacular when the Danish queen is in residence, usually in the winter months."

The day glowed with brilliant sunlight and temperatures hovering around the twenty-two degree mark, making it pleasant but not too hot for Marjorie. Rachel recognised that her elderly friend looked tired after taking a walk around the Tivoli Gardens following lunch. Although still spritely for her eighty-six years and able to walk with the assistance of a stick for lengthy periods on the flat, she was slowing down.

"Would you like to return to the ship?"

"Not yet, dear. However, I am happy to rest a while. If we can find an English newspaper, you can park me at that hotel over there and then you can go exploring by yourself, if that's agreeable?"

They walked to the hotel near to the Tivoli Gardens and not too far from the river front. The concierge found a copy of the *Daily Telegraph* in English for Marjorie to read. After finding plush cushioned seats in the rather opulent lounge, Rachel ordered tea for the old lady.

"This reminds me of the ship's atrium," she remarked. "Are you certain you'll be alright?"

"Absolutely, I will catch up on the news from Blighty and enjoy a nice cup of tea. You go and enjoy yourself." Marjorie picked up the newspaper and soon became engrossed.

Rachel left the grand hotel and walked along the river front admiring the beautifully vibrant painted buildings that lined the area. She was considering returning to the hotel to join Marjorie when she heard English voices coming from a café to her right. There, seated at a table outside, she saw Brigitte and Gwen, Sarah's nurse colleagues, wearing mufti as they were obviously on shore leave for the day.

Gwen saw Rachel and stood up.

"Rachel, how nice to see you. Sarah told us you were on board with Lady Snellthorpe. Is she with you?" The Australian senior nurse gave Rachel a warm hug.

"We came out together, but I left her resting down the road at the Nimb Hotel while I did a bit more exploring."

Brigitte, the French nurse who Rachel had met on her first cruise, stood and gave her the traditional air kiss while touching each cheek, French style.

"Please join us, we were just about to order," Gwen invited.

Rachel sat down. "I will thank you."

Gwen handed her a menu. "What will you have? Our treat."

"Much appreciated. I guess as I'm in Denmark, I ought to have a Danish pastry."

"Ah, but which one?" Brigitte teased, going on to explain the many varieties of Danish pastry options while pointing out the more popular ones on the menu.

"Wow! I never knew that. I'm going to have the Snegl with cinnamon – that's the one I'm familiar with back home."

The waiter came to take their order.

"I'll have a croissant," Brigitte told him.

"And I'll have the Spandauer Danish, I love custard," Gwen explained. Rachel ordered her Snegl, and they all requested tea.

"How's your father?" Rachel asked Brigitte, aware he had been involved in a car accident the previous summer when the nurse had been called home at short notice.

"He is well now, thank you. Back to his normal bossy self so I'm glad to be back at sea."

"What about you, Rachel? How are you?" asked Gwen.

"I'm good, thanks. Started a new job in January – a new year, a fresh start. I'm working in north London, but living in a West End apartment thanks to Marjorie."

"That sounds expensive."

"It would be totally unaffordable, but Marjorie is glad to have someone living in it so she charges me a silly rent."

"I expect it's her way of paying you back for saving her life. How's the job in London, is it busy?"

"Incredibly, but I knew it would be when I took it. I'm working towards my sergeant's exams as well – glutton for punishment. The move to London means I'm closer to Carlos and following the near-miss and persistent threats from a man I helped put away for murder, it seemed like the right time to move." She had been a police constable for almost two years and still enjoyed her work, although it presented many challenges.

"I heard about that man. I do hope you don't have to use your sleuthing skills on this cruise." Brigitte laughed.

"We have been relatively quiet in terms of corpses," Gwen interjected light heartedly. "Since your last cruise, we haven't used the morgue next to the medical centre, but when Sarah said you were on board, Bernard warned us there was bound to be a body."

"Bernard has a wicked sense of humour." Rachel grimaced. "I guess you left the ship early this morning then?"

"You're not kidding! Yes, we like to take full advantage of shore leave when we get it," said Brigitte.

Gwen picked up on Rachel's serious expression and the guarded comment. "What do you mean by then? Has something happened?"

Rachel felt like a Grinch for upsetting the two nurses' day out, but explained what she and Marjorie had witnessed when standing at the dockside before leaving.

"Oh my goodness, Rachel! Did you find out what happened?" Brigitte exclaimed.

"No, we were ushered away pretty sharpish. A couple of officers dived into the water after the person – it appeared to be a man. In fact, I'm almost certain it was the lead singer of the Queen tribute band, Dom somebody or other, but that was only because of the white jumpsuit – it could have been anyone. I didn't notice which deck he fell from, but he wasn't flailing, which makes me wonder."

"I can't believe it," said Gwen, staring at Rachel closely as if to check whether she was winding them up.

Rachel shrugged her shoulders. "I seem to have that effect on the *Coral*."

"Do you think we should go back?" Brigitte asked Gwen.

"No, from what Rachel described, once he's dragged out of the water, he'll be transferred to hospital. If the worst has happened – well, we'll cross that bridge when we come to it."

Brigitte looked relieved. "In that case, I'm going to tuck in to my croissant," she said as the food arrived.

"What did you mean by that flailing remark, Rachel? Are you suggesting it wasn't an accident?" Gwen enquired.

"Not sure – it could have been. You know me, never satisfied unless there's a suspicious death to solve." Rachel could tell that Gwen wasn't convinced by the answer, but decided to stick with it as she didn't want to be responsible for ruining their day any more than she had already.

Rachel stayed with the two nurses for an hour, talking about other things, before deciding it was time to leave.

"I'd better go and find Marjorie in case she thinks I've got lost. It was lovely to meet you again – tell Sarah I'll meet her tonight."

"Will do. We're just going to visit an ice bar before returning to the ship."

"Oh, Sarah's hoping to take me to one of those when we get to Finland. Enjoy yourselves, I'm sure we'll catch up later."

Rachel left the two women and headed back to the Nimb Hotel. When she arrived, her friend was sitting comfortably, chatting to another elderly lady.

"There you are." Marjorie smiled. "I was wondering if I needed to send out a search party! Rachel, this is Gloria. Gloria's staying in Copenhagen for a week with her husband."

"How do you do?" Rachel greeted a short, casually dressed woman in her seventies. The woman had smiling blue eyes, dyed auburn hair and wore heavy makeup and lipstick.

"Hello there. Marjorie has been telling me all about you and your antics on board cruise ships." Gloria shook Rachel's hand, speaking with a pleasantly lilting Welsh accent. Embarrassed, Rachel blushed – she didn't want to discuss murderous cruises. Marjorie understood and piped up.

"Well, it's time we returned to our trusty steed, Rachel. We don't want to miss the boat, now, do we?" She couldn't resist turning back to Gloria and whispering, "Especially when there's been another murder."

"Get away with you," rebuked Gloria, not sure whether to take Marjorie seriously.

Marjorie winked at Rachel and then pulled herself up from the seat, straightening herself to get her balance before taking Rachel's arm.

"Did you hear my bones creak then?" Not waiting for an answer, she turned to her new friend. "It was good to meet you, Gloria.

Enjoy the rest of your stay. You chose the right hotel, I must say – the service has been excellent."

Gloria stood up and shook both women's hands. "It's been a pleasure, Marjorie, and don't forget, you'd be welcome in Carmarthen anytime."

"Thank you," answered Marjorie. Turning to Rachel as they left the hotel, she asked, "Did you have a nice time?"

"I did, I took a lovely walk along the river and bumped into Gwen and Brigitte. Do you remember them? They asked after you."

"I do remember them, very well. Brigitte is the French nurse who looked after me when I was in the infirmary and Gwen is the Sister. There's nothing wrong with these grey cells yet. Have they ascertained what happened to the person who fell overboard?"

"No, they didn't even know about it – they left early to ensure they got a full day out, but Gwen says that he would most likely be admitted to hospital in Copenhagen if he survived the fall, so nothing for them to worry about. If it was a fall."

"Oh no, Rachel, surely not? I was only joking when I said we would need to investigate, but I can see you've got that look in your eye." Marjorie smiled up at Rachel. "You don't think he fell at all, do you?"

Rachel was thoughtful. She had been pondering the man overboard scene they had witnessed and rewinding it over and over in her mind.

"I can't be certain, but no, he plummeted too quietly and too quickly. In fact, if it hadn't been for that woman gasping and our line of sight, no-one would have even noticed."

Marjorie sensed Rachel's need to mull things over in her mind and squeezed her arm before sighing.

"Let's get back, then, shall we?"

It was only after speaking about the falling man to Gwen and Brigitte, and now Marjorie that Rachel had come to the conclusion that he was probably unconscious when he went overboard. She would want to discuss it with the chief of security, Jack Waverley, whom she had met on the two previous cruises that turned out to be deadly. Waverley and Rachel had developed a mutual respect, although he wasn't always happy with her involvement in his investigations – the main reason being her passenger status. He'd offered her a job on his security team on both occasions, but she had declined. There were times when she would love to be working as a security officer on a cruise ship with the travel opportunities that it offered, but she had initially felt the need to consolidate her police training with practical work, and more recently she hated the thought of being away from Carlos for the amount of time that would be required if she took up this line of work. Carlos worked as a private investigator, and although this meant he travelled away at times, most cruise ship contracts were six to nine months.

On arriving back at the *Coral Queen*, Rachel and Marjorie discovered all was normal.

"You wouldn't imagine anything had happened this morning," remarked Marjorie.

Rachel could see exactly what she meant. Passengers were returning to the ship, and the crew welcomed them back with iced flannels and refreshments, just as they always did before the passengers climbed the steps to pass through security on rejoining the ship. It was surreal in many ways, considering what they had witnessed just six hours ago.

"If we hadn't seen it with our own eyes, we just wouldn't know," said Rachel, taking in a deep breath. Instead of heading for the gangway and steps, they walked to the front of the ship where they had seen the man fall. All was calm in the dark black water; Rachel spotted fish swimming near to the surface, but other than that, it was pretty murky.

Probably polluted from all the ships sailing in and out of the harbour.

Rachel looked upwards, re-enacting the scene in her mind's eye, but try as she might, she couldn't determine which deck he'd fallen from.

"Definitely higher than deck twelve," she said out loud. "The top of that crane was about level with him when I spotted him falling. He was also higher than that suspended platform there where the crewman is painting. Although he's moved around from where he was this morning, he's at the same level."

"Yes, I noticed him too," said Marjorie. "I remember thinking to myself that the crew always seems to be painting something or other outside when the ship is docked. I imagine cruise ships are painted more than any other vessel. Do you suppose it's necessary or to give them something to do?"

"You're right, now you mention it, there is always painting going on. I expect it's to stop corrosion from the salt water and other pollutants." Rachel's mind was elsewhere. She was only half concentrating on the topic of ship maintenance procedures as she was still picturing the falling body from this morning. "I wonder if that crewman noticed anything. He's quite high up so he might have."

"I doubt it, my dear, listen to all that racket going on from those cranes working over there, and the machinery was hard at it this morning. They began at eight o'clock when I sat on my balcony, and we're at the back of the ship where there isn't as much activity as there is here."

Rachel was disappointed, but agreed with Marjorie's logic. With all the banging and clanging around the dockside from cargo vessels being loaded and unloaded, it would be unlikely the crewman had noticed anything. Nevertheless, she zoomed in on him with the camera on her mobile phone and took a picture, just in case she needed to track him down later.

She showed the image of two men dressed in white overalls to Marjorie. "Technology these days is marvellous," declared the elderly lady. "I can't believe your phone can capture those dots of men with such clarity. They look like they are from the Philippines to me. Many cruise ship workers come from there."

"Agreed. I'll ask Chief Waverley if I need to, but I suspect you're right about them not hearing anything – when I zoom in, I can see they appear to be shouting to each other over the noise." She snapped a couple more photos of the front of the ship, and then noticed people staring down at her from their balconies. "Come on, Marjorie. Time to get back on board."

Passing through security, Rachel spotted Waverley speaking to two other guards. He saw her coming through.

"Miss Prince – I gathered you were on board. Lady Snellthorpe – what a pleasure it is to see you again."

Marjorie answered first. "Thank you, I feel much more secure now I've seen you." Rachel detected a hint of sarcasm in her voice.

Waverley coughed, as he seemed to do when nervous or distracted. "We do our best," he mumbled.

"What happened to that person we saw fall from the ship this morning?" Marjorie had him under the cosh and wasn't going to let up any time soon.

He coughed again, and this time his neck reddened. He looked towards Rachel for help. "Erm. I didn't realise you had witnessed that event. Perhaps we can talk about this later?"

Rachel noticed a large group of passengers were passing through security behind them. "Yes, we can do that. Come on, Marjorie, we'd better go and get ready for dinner."

Marjorie was chuckling like a naughty schoolgirl as they got into the lift. Rachel had to smile.

Once they'd got off on deck fifteen, Rachel spoke. "I suspected you had a darker side, Lady Marjorie Snellthorpe – the poor man didn't know where to put himself."

Marjorie was still chuckling. "Serves him right for bungling things up previously." She was referring to the cruise when they had originally met and Waverley had had Marjorie followed for a while.

"To be fair, it wasn't just Chief Waverley that messed up. Carlos wasn't great either, though I hate to admit it."

"Ah, but I can forgive him because he's a handsome young man, and he's made up for it since."

"I can see you're going to be incorrigible over the next few days," said Rachel, laughing.

Rachel walked Marjorie to her room and then crossed the rear corridor to her own suite. The luxury suites were magnificent. She appreciated the exquisite decor and the facilities were second to none. The suite had as much space as her apartment at home. The large sitting room overlooked one part of the balcony and the bedroom led out on to the other half, providing ample space for at least six people to sit outside in comfort. The suites were served by the butler, Mario, and he looked after them well.

She helped herself to a glass of mineral water from the well-stocked fridge and opened the doors to the balcony as her mobile phone rang with Carlos's designated ringtone.

"Carlos, hi." Her voice took on an endearing high-pitched note.

"Hello, darling. I knew you were on land today and wanted to hear the sound of your voice."

"It's wonderful you phoned. How are things?"

"Not too bad, I'm in Birmingham looking for a missing dog – stolen from a house in your neck of the woods, Knightsbridge. I've tracked the person who has it and I'm closing in. Lady's with me."

Lady was Carlos's two-year-old Springer Spaniel, a recent acquisition from a friend who'd emigrated, and she now accompanied him on his investigative tours. The two of them had become inseparable, and Rachel had grown almost as fond of the dog as Carlos was.

"Oh, I do hope you find the dog you're looking for. Why was it stolen?"

"Stolen to order. It's a golden retriever puppy from a champion breeder. The family is distraught, as you can imagine – the dog had become the children's pet, but I'm pretty confident I can get it back by tomorrow. Lady and I are going to pay a visit to the thief in an hour."

"Be careful, Carlos."

"Don't worry, darling. I've got a detective pal of mine meeting me at the house, ready to arrest the thief if he doesn't tell us where the dog is. Lady will sniff it out if it's in the house, but he'll have passed it on for sure. Anyway, that's enough about me. How's your cruise? Please tell me there are no dead bodies."

Rachel swallowed hard as she answered. She'd promised him after the last cruise that she would tell him everything in future because he hadn't known she'd been in danger. He'd been desperately unhappy she hadn't told him what was happening at the time.

"I don't think so—"

"*Mamma Mia!* Rachel – it can't happen three cruises in a row."

"As I say, I'm not certain, but Marjorie and I witnessed someone fall over the side when we were leaving the ship this morning, before we were ushered away. I don't know exactly what happened to the person. It was probably an accident anyway." *Surely one white lie couldn't hurt?*

It was quiet at the other end of the phone for a moment, but Carlos sounded more chipper when he spoke again.

"Well at least that won't involve you, whatever happened. Probably someone showing off to their mates."

"Could have been, and you're right, it doesn't involve me."

The line started to fade.

"The connection's bad now, Rachel, and I have to get ready to leave. Take care and enjoy yourself. Stay out of trouble."

"You too, and give Lady a treat from me. Bye."

Carlos hung up and Rachel kissed the phone automatically. Then her thoughts turned back to the body over the side situation.

Chapter 6

Following an exceptional five-course dining extravaganza in the *Coral* restaurant, Rachel and Marjorie met up with Sarah.

"Have you eaten?" Rachel asked.

"Yes, I grabbed a quick bite from the buffet. I suppose the pair of you dined well?"

"I must say, the lobster tasted exquisite," said Marjorie.

Sarah raised her eyebrows.

"Personally, I'm stuffed," said Rachel. "The chefs should be arrested for cooking up such irresistible cuisine."

"Since I became a cruise ship nurse, my culinary tastes have been extended beyond belief. Not always positively, but mostly so."

"Oh, do tell, what don't you like?" asked Marjorie.

"Well, durian certainly isn't my favourite."

Rachel looked confused.

"Oh, the fruit, you mean. It's popular in south-east Asia, isn't it?" said Marjorie.

"Yes, and you smell it before you see it. I could never enjoy it because it smells so foul. I did try a very small piece in Malaysia. The catering department doesn't bring it on board for obvious reasons."

The three women discussed food and drink as they made their way to an early evening show. The theatre at the front of the ship boasted luxurious tiered seating spanning two decks. They commandeered three seats at the rear so that Marjorie didn't need to negotiate too many steps. No-one mentioned the man overboard situation and Rachel could feel the elephant moving into the room.

"I met Gwen and Brigitte along the Nyhavn today," she prompted.

"Did you?" said Sarah. "I haven't seen them since they got back on board. I was on call, and they were in surgery when I handed the on-call bag over to Bernard for the night. That's why I only managed a rushed dinner."

That explains it. She obviously isn't aware we saw the man go overboard.

"I expect you were busy after the accident this morning," whispered Marjorie.

The troubled look on Sarah's face confirmed what Rachel had supposed. "How do you know about that?" she asked quietly.

"We witnessed it, didn't we, Rachel?"

"Yes, it happened just as we were leaving the ship." Rachel shot an apologetic glance at her friend.

"I'd hoped to keep you out of this one," groaned Sarah. "But I suppose you might have found out anyway."

Their conversation was interrupted as the cruise director Gordon appeared on stage and introduced the evening's main act, a singer who'd been on *America's got Talent.*

"Shall we talk about it afterwards?" whispered Rachel.

Sarah nodded.

Although the singing sounded respectable enough, Rachel found her mind drifting back to the morning and replaying various scenarios over in her head – drunken fall, bravado as Carlos thought, or push? It had looked like the Freddie Mercury lookalike, but it could have been another member of the band, or anyone else wearing a white jumpsuit for that matter.

Sarah ordered drinks, and when they arrived Rachel absentmindedly took hers from the waiter, before telling herself to switch off and enjoy the show – she would find out soon enough what had occurred.

The rest of the performance passed by in a blur until raucous applause brought Rachel back to the present. Sarah nudged her to move as they were blocking the aisle and people wanted to leave the auditorium. Marjorie looked happy.

"What a delightful evening. I've had a lovely day, but if you two young things don't mind, it's time for this old lady to retire. I expect you have things to talk about." Marjorie winked.

Rachel kissed Marjorie on the cheek after she and Sarah had escorted her to the lifts in the midships area.

"Goodnight, Marjorie. See you in the morning."

"Goodnight, Rachel. Goodnight, Sarah."

Sarah kissed her too, and then the two young women made their way to the Jazz Bar, one of the many bars aboard the *Coral Queen*, which also happened to be one of their favourite haunts, although the lively bar didn't provide a good opportunity to talk thanks to the volume of the music. Rachel suspected Sarah's desperation to keep her out of another investigation confirmed that the man overboard scenario was suspicious. If not, she would have said something.

They ordered drinks, Sarah asking for cola while Rachel had a martini and lemonade. Then Rachel gave Sarah a look.

"You're going to need to talk about it sometime."

Sarah led her towards the edge of the room where they claimed a booth from people just leaving.

"It was the lead singer from the tribute band."

"Was? That means he's dead then."

"Yes. They pulled him out barely alive, and after resuscitation and first aid, they took him to hospital, but he died shortly afterwards."

"Were you involved?" Rachel sympathised with Sarah, who looked shattered.

"We all were. We managed to get him round before the ambulance came, but he died of a brain haemorrhage."

"Is that unusual?"

"It could have been caused by his head hitting the water after falling from a great height, but witnesses believe he was unconscious when he fell."

"Yes, I thought the same. He just dropped like an inanimate object."

"It gets worse." Sarah looked around for a brief moment, checking no-one was listening. "He's the new cruise director's brother – that's how the band got the job, apparently. The entertainment officer, Rosa Doherty, is none too pleased as she didn't like Dom, or any of them, from the off. She wanted to sack them – she's had numerous complaints about them from female crew members, and some from passengers. What's more, Alex spent the night patching a few of them up following a brawl in their manager's room."

Alessandro Romano, better known as Alex, was the ship's junior doctor. Rachel had met him previously and liked him.

"I didn't realise they were brothers. When you told me their names before, it didn't register they had the same surname. So there could be motive among his band mates, if this is murder?"

"That's the only reason they haven't been sacked and escorted off the ship. Rosa wanted to give them the push this morning, but in view of events, Waverley says they must stay."

"Any idea what Waverley thinks?"

"No, he hasn't been near us today. From a distance, he looked stressed to say the least. He's been busy interviewing distressed passengers who witnessed the fall. The security team has also been stretched due to a rowdy stag party who have been causing trouble with a group of cheerleaders. Jason says the chief's at the end of his tether."

"Oh dear – and then Marjorie made things worse with a pointed jibe." Sarah looked confused. "She goaded him a bit over the incident, still miffed with him for having her followed on her last cruise."

"Poor Waverley." Sarah laughed. "He doesn't ever get an easy time of it, but it always seems much worse when you're on board. If you don't take him up on his job offer soon, he might ban you from travelling on the *Coral Queen* altogether."

Rachel feigned offence. "I can't be responsible for every crime committed on board this ship! Anyway, this one's nothing to do with me."

"You don't fool me, Rachel Prince – you can't resist a challenge. You will start sleuthing soon, if you haven't already." Sarah smiled grimly. "Just don't put yourself in danger, and remember you've got Marjorie to take care of. She's a frail old lady and the excitement won't be good for her."

"Bah! There's nothing frail about Marjorie – she's as tough as old boots, in the nicest possible sense. Anyway, she's already keen to get going on this – she's arranged for us to hold a war council in the morning so we can come up with an investigative action plan."

Sarah looked exasperated. "I don't know who's worse – you or her."

Rachel gave a mischievous smile and then said more seriously, "I will take care of her. I'm not looking for trouble, but we might do a bit of snooping. I feel sorry for Waverley and he might need my help."

"I don't think he'll see it that way, but I'll find out what I can from Jason, as long as you promise you won't do anything dangerous."

"Guides' honour," answered Rachel.

"Hey, you two." Bernard's cheerful voice cut them off.

"Bernard, great to meet you again." Bernard and Rachel hugged while Sarah moved along the bench seat to let him in.

"How can someone get more beautiful each time we meet?" Bernard said.

Sarah glared at him, knowing how fed up Rachel got with men constantly drawing attention to her looks, but Bernard remained oblivious. He was one of the few men who didn't attract a cutting remark in return.

"I thought you were on call tonight," Sarah said.

"I thought so too, but Gwen offered to do it because of the day we've had."

"That's nice of her," replied Sarah.

"Did you hear about our day, Rachel?" He leaned in. "I guess you heard the one about the singer in the drink?"

"Bernard, that's horrible!" Sarah admonished.

"Sarah's just been telling me about it – I understand the grapevine suggests it might not have been an accident."

Bernard giggled. "Well, it wouldn't be with you on board, would it?"

"I don't understand why everyone surmises it's anything to do with me!" She laughed. "It's your screening that's gone to pot – obviously you just let anyone on board cruise ships nowadays."

Following a period of banter, Bernard turned more serious. "The brawl last night sounds worse than we first believed."

"What do you mean?" asked Sarah.

"We imagined it to be a drunken argument that got out of hand, but according to my source, it was nastier than that. It turns out Dominic Venables had quite a few enemies, not least those in his own band. There were women involved too, with one of them swearing she'd kill him if he didn't get his act together."

"What women? They must have been crew if they were below the waterline."

"My source didn't see them, just heard the racket and told them to shut up or she'd report them. Poor girl works in housekeeping and was exhausted, says they were really loud."

Rachel listened intently. "That's a shame she doesn't know who they are. Do you know if any of the men were up top at the time of the incident this morning?"

"Graham says they all deny being up there and none of them have decent alibis."

"Oh, so Graham's getting the sleuthing bug now, is he?" said Sarah, clearly ruffled. "Really, I can't wait to hear what Waverley makes of that. What's the matter with you lot?"

Rachel laughed at her friend's angst and understood it to be concern over her getting involved following a few near misses in the past. A pacifist through and through, Sarah hated violence, although she'd witnessed her fair share as a nurse working in casualty on land and on a cruise ship. Nevertheless, she just wanted people to get along with each other and had always wanted to repair rather than destroy, a trait responsible for her becoming a nurse.

Bernard answered, "No worries there. Graham got the message last time, but he took Waverley for dinner tonight to try to help him relax after the day he's had. He also had to report all injuries sustained by passengers and crew over the past twenty-four hours in case they're related."

Rachel put her hand on her friend's arm. "Don't worry, Sarah, it'll be okay – sounds like some internal squabbling that's got out of hand, so at least there's not a killer running loose intent on inflicting random acts of violence or looking for more victims."

Sarah nodded. "I'm sorry, but I will never be able to understand the mindset of a killer – death is so final—" Her voice trailed off and alarm bells sounded for Rachel – there was something else on Sarah's mind she hadn't shared.

Now I'm worried.

They finished their drinks, said goodnight to Bernard, and took a stroll around the upper decks. Sarah explained that security had confirmed the man fell from the front of deck sixteen, so Rachel suggested they visit the would-be crime scene. No-one on the bridge had seen the incident because they were relaxing while the ship remained docked.

The deck appeared relatively quiet when they arrived as most of the action was occurring in the bars and lounges, although they encountered a few couples taking moonlight strolls. The sounds of distant music emanated from the ship's decks, but the most striking sound, the one that Rachel loved, came from waves sloshing against the side of the ship. As they were at sea again, the enormous vessel was tunnelling her way through the waves, her path resulting in the crashing noise as the waves objected. It was the most beautiful thing about night-time cruising and more pronounced at the bow of the ship.

"Oh, Sarah, look at the stars!" For a brief moment, they lost themselves in the beauty of the world around them. The water was pitch black and eerie beneath them, while the night sky above produced a glorious darkness, broken by the light from innumerable twinkling stars.

"I love nights like this," said Sarah. "They make me happy to be a cruise ship nurse. Sometimes I get to be wonderfully alone, in spite of the five thousand odd people on board. It makes me glad to be alive."

Another reference to life and death. Rachel felt anxiety about her friend. What could be making Sarah so morose? She needed to find out and help her.

"I know what you mean – it is rather special."

Their reverie was interrupted by the sounds of laughter as a group emerged from a door behind them and headed off towards the stern.

"I'd better show you where it all happened before you burst."

"Okay, thanks. Where do they say he fell from?"

"Port side, bow."

Sarah led the way and Rachel followed. Port referred to the left-hand side of the ship when facing forward as frequently it was this side of the ship that docked against a port's side. On this occasion, the ship had been docked starboard side in Copenhagen. No sign of what may have occurred just this morning jumped out at them. Rachel noticed a buoy tied to the rail and wondered if it had been thrown in the water after the man. A thought she dismissed as unlikely if they were looking at murder. *Besides*, she told herself, *it came from a lower deck.*

Sarah answered her unasked question.

"A buoy was thrown from deck twelve, not from here."

"It's looking more and more like murder," Rachel said thoughtfully.

They snooped around, but it was obvious they were not going to find any evidence. Waverley would have already done a sweep of the whole area and interviewed anyone in the vicinity at the time of the incident. No scuff marks were visible on the railings where Venables was reported to have gone over.

Rachel looked downwards and gasped, contemplating plunging into the depths from this height. She imagined that even if conscious, one might not survive such a fall. Looking at her watch, she realised it was after midnight and suddenly felt tired, but instead of saying goodnight, she turned to her friend and gently asked a question.

"Sarah, is something else bothering you?"

Sarah bit her lip, a sign of stress that Rachel recognised from their student days. She looked out to sea and Rachel watched the tears trickling down her cheeks.

"You'll think I'm silly," she said quietly.

Rachel joined her by the rail and put her arm around her. "Whatever is troubling you is not silly."

"Mum Skyped this morning to ask if they could have Pickles put down." Tears were now flowing freely down her face, causing tracks to form through her light foundation. "He's riddled with cancer and the vet said there's no more she can do. It seems trivial in the light of the death of a man on board, but I can't help it."

Rachel embraced her sobbing friend, who cried on her shoulder.

"I'm so sorry, Sarah, and it's not trivial. Pickles has been part of your family for eighteen years." Rachel remembered the little kitten being bought for her friend's eighth birthday and how he'd looked so much like a jar of pickle that Sarah had hugged him and named him Pickles. The Bradshaw family often joked about how he was more like a dog than a cat – he lacked the independence and aloofness of some cats and followed Sarah around whenever she visited home.

"They took him this afternoon," Sarah sobbed into Rachel's shoulder. There was little Rachel could say to console her friend. To Sarah, it was like losing a member of the family.

Sarah eventually stopped crying and wiped her eyes. "At least I got to see him one more time via Skype. Mum had him sitting on her knee. She'll be even more upset than I am, having looked after him since I've lived away for so long. Now I feel guilty for taking this job and not being there."

A chill developed in the night air as if it understood the significance of the moment. Sarah shivered.

"Come on, let's get you inside. I am truly sorry, Sarah. I'll pray for you and your family tonight."

"I'd appreciate that, Rachel. I'm going to call it a night. I'll catch you tomorrow."

Rachel watched her get into the lift at the front of the ship before walking towards the stern to make her way back to her own room.

Poor Sarah, what a day!

Chapter 7

Mario brought tea and coffee through to Marjorie's room where Rachel had joined the old lady on her extensive balcony. An early morning run around deck sixteen and forty-five minutes in the gym had left Rachel feeling invigorated. They had a sea day ahead so they could take their leisure.

Marjorie looked tired and a little pale. Rachel hoped she wasn't going down with anything.

"Are you alright?" she asked.

"Yes, dear, although I can't say I slept well last night. One of those disturbed nights, I'm afraid."

"I had a message from Chief Waverley. He would like to speak to us this morning. Would you like me to ask him to come up here or shall we venture down to his office?"

"Oh, make him come up here, it will give us home advantage."

"Okay, up here it is. Are you coming down for breakfast?"

"No, I think I'll eat out here on the balcony. You go off to the buffet, I know you prefer to eat there during the day."

"I'll just call Waverley before I leave."

Waverley agreed to meet them in Marjorie's room at 10am, giving Rachel time to shower, change out of her running gear and eat before he arrived. She made her way up to the buffet for breakfast before returning to Marjorie's room to wait with the old lady, who looked more like her normal self again, for the security chief.

At precisely 10am the expected knock came and Rachel opened the door. On close inspection, Waverley looked almost the same as he had done on her two previous cruises, tall with short greying hair, now thinning on top. A burly ex-navy officer, he had been chief of security for over a decade. But Rachel noticed some weight gain around the middle. His usually ruddy face appeared pallid beneath the tan, as if he hadn't been sleeping well, and there were dark lines under his penetrating deep-brown eyes.

"Chief Waverley, good to see you, please come in."

He followed Rachel outside to the balcony where Marjorie was enjoying the morning sun. Marjorie stood and invited him to sit down before doing so herself.

"Thank you for seeing me, ladies."

A second knock followed and Mario entered with a flask of fresh coffee and biscuits.

"I took the liberty of ordering coffee," explained Marjorie.

"Thank you." Waverley blushed and coughed, and Rachel wondered if he might still be smarting from Marjorie's barbs the day before.

"I'll try not to intrude on your day and won't keep you too long. I'm interviewing all passengers and crew who witnessed the tragic event that took place yesterday morning, and as Lady Snellthorpe indicated that you had both seen the man falling, I wanted to speak with you."

"What would you like to know?" asked Marjorie, clearly enjoying the chief's discomfort.

"Could you both describe what you remember about the incident?"

Rachel explained what they had witnessed and how the man appeared to plummet into the sea like a brick from on high. "I've gone over it a lot and it looked to me like he was unconscious before he went in. Of course, if it was suicide he may have chosen to dive in like that, but it certainly didn't strike me as a fall."

"Do you feel the same, Lady Snellthorpe?"

"Yes, I'm afraid I do. The poor man didn't cry out or anything, and I'm sure he would have done so if he'd fallen, unless of course he was so inebriated he didn't realise what was happening. Judging by the man's previous behaviour, intoxication wouldn't be completely out of the question."

"I understand you met him in the Rat Pack bar the night before he died."

"I would say encountered, rather than met. We certainly weren't introduced. The man was drunk and annoying Rachel, but she dealt with him quite admirably." Marjorie snickered.

"So I understand." Waverley looked at Rachel admiringly. "Did he have any bruises to his face when you, erm, encountered him?"

"No," answered Rachel, "although he had a lot of makeup on which might have masked bruising. He didn't appear to have any later either when Sarah and I watched the band play in the Culture Lounge. I did spot him arguing with the lead guitarist, though."

Waverley looked up from writing notes. "Do you have any idea what the argument was about? A few passengers mentioned seeing the two men argue but couldn't recall any details."

"Venables shouted at the lead guitarist – I think it was him – accusing him of trying to take over as lead singer, followed by a rant about the rest of the band back-biting about him. I put it down to rivalry and paranoia. I only overheard them because Sarah had nipped into the ladies and I was waiting nearby. He then barged right through me – I've still got the bruise on my shoulder to show for it."

"I didn't know that," said Marjorie, shocked. "Horrible man. He was a rather unpleasant fellow, Chief Waverley, but obviously I'm sorry that he is dead."

"You heard he's dead, then? Sarah, I suppose." He didn't wait for a reply. "Yes, he died in the ambulance before arriving at the hospital, a brain haemorrhage. There will be a post-mortem today, but initial examination does point to him being unconscious or semi-conscious when he entered the water."

"Do you know who wanted him dead?" asked Rachel.

"There's a queue of people. From what I can gather, the band often argued, but they've been together for eighteen years and the arguing happens to be part of who they are – totally harmless, according to Jimmy, their agent and manager who's also on board. Mr Venables managed to upset a few of the passengers, mainly due to drink and a bit of unwelcome fraternising, although I can't imagine a passenger killing him for that. To be honest, the entertainment manager was going to sack them yesterday morning, but then all this happened so she's had to keep them on at my insistence.

"My theory is a fight turned nasty, resulting in him ending up in the water. I haven't ruled out a drink-induced accident or suicide either. No-one in the band seems to have a clear alibi for the time of the incident so that hasn't helped narrow it down any." Waverley paused before giving Rachel a firm stare. "I would thank you to keep out of this one, Miss Prince. Leave it to the security team. We know what we're doing."

Marjorie made a choking sound and they both looked at her. Waverley looked concerned, but Rachel recognised from the twinkle in her eye that she was stifling a giggle.

"No problem, Chief, Rachel and I will forget all about the incident," she said sincerely.

"Thank you. I will not take up any more of your time. Have a pleasant day, ladies."

Rachel escorted him to the door. He looked at her again. "I mean it, Rachel. Stay out of it." He marched off down the corridor.

Rachel re-joined Marjorie who was now guffawing, which made Rachel laugh too. Once they'd stopped laughing like a pair of teenagers, Marjorie sat up straight.

"We need an action plan – first, let's write down our list of suspects."

"Maybe we should take his advice and stay out of it."

"We should," said Marjorie. "But we're not going to, are we, dear?" A disappointed frown appeared on her face.

"Well, I guess he might need our help, even if he doesn't realise it," sighed Rachel, cursing herself for ever having seen the man fall overboard in the first place. Carlos was not going to like it, but she couldn't resist doing a little bit of undercover investigating. She nodded to Marjorie, having made up her mind.

"Right then, who's our chief suspect?" asked Marjorie, taking out a pen and notebook from her handbag.

"The lead guitarist would have to be in the frame – he's the one who argued with Venables in the club, and it seems like a deep-seated rivalry or jealousy existed between them. Jealousy is always a good motive."

Marjorie wrote in her book, and then said, "Jealousy and money. There's also the agent."

"Or any of the other band members. We don't have enough information about them. We need to track them down and poke around a bit. I'll ask Sarah later for some more detail about the room brawl and who was involved in that. Bernard said a woman threatened him, but no-one knows who she is." Rachel paused. "It's interesting they still plan to perform, isn't it?"

"Typical of these entertainment types," said Marjorie. "*The Show Must Go On* – wasn't that a Queen song? Seems rather apt. It's in their genetics, unless, of course, they really don't care about the man's death. He certainly seems to have had more enemies than friends, and from what we experienced of him, it's not hard to imagine why."

"That might be right, but they're a heartless group of people if it's true. We'll need to find out when they next perform and where."

Marjorie picked up the day's copy of *Coral News* and scrolled through. "They're doing two evening shows in the Culture Lounge, one at eight and one at eleven. They're also doing a live show on the lido deck at two o'clock. Oh please, let's go to that one – the noise will be more tolerable in the open air."

Rachel nodded agreement. "That gives us a few hours this morning. What would you like to do?"

"There's a quiz at eleven in the Sky View Lounge, would you be happy to accompany an old lady to that?"

"Absolutely, let's go."

They made their way up to deck sixteen and entered the Sky View, situated at the bow of the ship. It spread across the whole deck with spectacular views of the sea from full height windows that enfolded the room in a semicircle. A glitzy circular bar dominated the centre of the room. Marble-topped tables were scattered throughout and avid quizzers arriving early settled in their teams. Gentle music played in the background.

Marjorie nudged Rachel. "Over there," she whispered.

Rachel looked over to the opposite side of the room from where they had entered and followed Marjorie's gaze to where the members of the tribute band and their entourage were having an animated conversation. The two women made their way across the room to where the band was seated on a horseshoe sofa with two round tables in front of them, laden with drinks. The rest of the party sat on stools around the tables. Marjorie walked towards a table in close proximity, facing the horseshoe.

"There's room for two here, Rachel."

One of the men in the band looked up, but then ignored them as they sat on cushioned armchairs. A waiter came along and took their drinks order, Rachel asking for lemonade and Marjorie ordering tea.

The three band members sat next to each other. Rachel recognised them from the show two nights ago. She pointed them out to Marjorie.

"The one on the left is the bass guitarist, alias John Deacon."

"He's rather dashing, isn't he?"

Rachel had to agree, the tall muscular man, who she guessed at being in his late thirties, was the best looking of the bunch. With long brown thinly permed afro hair, he wore a denim shirt with cropped jeans showing off his muscular calves. He stood out among the contingent for his good looks, and also appeared quieter than the rest.

"The one in the middle, doing most of the talking, is the lead guitarist, alias Brian May."

From what she could gather from the conversation, he was making frequent scathing and sarcastic remarks to the others. He was around six foot with long, wavy dark brown hair and bronzed skin, wearing jeans and ripped t-shirt exposing heavily tattooed arms and overly hairy chest.

"That tan looks like it came out of a bottle, and do you think he takes hormones? That hair!" whispered Marjorie. Rachel laughed, but had to agree. "He seems as nasty as the other one, suits the Neanderthal appearance," Marjorie continued as the man yelled at one of the waiters. "Uncouth, too – I haven't heard language like that since boarding school."

"The guy on the right is the drummer, alias Roger Taylor, and I assume the man in the suit is the agent." The drummer looked to be the oldest in the group, early fifties, Rachel thought. He had long crinkly greying hair, a grey moustache and wore horn-rimmed glasses. His shirt was open to the waist, displaying a smooth and shiny six pack.

"My goodness, whatever cream he's using on that chest, I want some." Marjorie was clearly enjoying playing amateur detective and made notes in her notebook. "He's the only one who doesn't take the lookalike aspect too seriously, methinks. My observations lead me to suspect it's either the uncouth one or the agent."

"If only it was as simple as identifying a murderer by their looks," said Rachel. "The agent looks shifty, though. What's he trying to do with that gum?"

They looked at a pot-bellied man in his mid-forties with ash brown crew-cut hair who, despite wearing a smart white suit, still looked bedraggled. He wore a gold stud earring, a bright yellow shirt, and was chewing gum aggressively, doing battle with the substance in his mouth.

An announcement came over the microphone to invite quizzers to collect quiz answer sheets from the assistant cruise director. The cruise director sat at the bar, so Rachel asked Marjorie to keep listening in to the band's conversation while she went over. After picking up one of the sheets and a pen from another crew member, Rachel made her way to the bar and ordered a drink she didn't need.

Gordon was slumped up against the bar on a bar stool, wearing a navy blue suit and a badge with his name and title displayed. His mouth smiled at her from beneath pained brown eyes, causing her heart to go out to him. The poor man had just lost his brother and had to continue performing his duty as director of entertainment for thousands of passengers seeking a good time. It was a big ask.

"Hello," she said. "We haven't met, but I'm Rachel, a friend of Sarah Bradshaw, one of the nurses."

"Gordon, I'm the new cruise director. Are you enjoying your cruise, Rachel?"

"So far, yes. Thank you." She thought about whether to broach the subject of his brother, but decided against it. She didn't want to upset him in a public lounge.

The assistant cruise director tapped him on the shoulder. "Sorry, Gordon, I need to get to the ballroom. Here's the list."

"Excuse me, Miss – hopefully we'll meet again."

Gordon took a deep breath and stoically made his way over to the microphone. Rachel went back to re-join Marjorie as the quiz was about to start.

They spent the next hour writing down answers to quiz questions, doing reasonably well, but not nearly as well as some of the teams who appeared to take the whole thing too seriously. The tribute band weren't taking part in the quiz, and at times became too raucous, causing passengers around them to hush them and attracting a scowl from Gordon. After being told off by an elderly gentleman nearby for the third time, the band and their hangers-on sauntered out of the lounge, still chatting loudly.

The winning team received prizes of a bottle of wine and a box of chocolates. Gordon acquitted himself well considering the pressure he must have been under, and came across as a natural entertainer. Following the conclusion of the quiz, pens were returned, and Gordon hastily marched out of the lounge.

"Did you glean anything from the brother?" Marjorie asked.

"No, I couldn't bring myself to broach the subject – not the right time or place. I did introduce myself as Sarah's friend. He looked pained, but something in his look bothered me. It was more angry pain than sad pain."

"There are many stages of grief and anger is one of them." Marjorie's voice trailed off and Rachel suspected she was referring to her own grief over the loss of her husband.

"You're right," Rachel said. "Did you pick up anything from the band's conversation?"

"Not really – they spoke a lot of drivel about girls, nightclubs and songs. Not a mention of the dead man. They don't appear or sound in the least bit sad. I don't suppose we'll be seeing any stages of grief among that lot. The only one that did seem out of sorts was the bass guitarist, who strikes me as a gentle giant – quietly spoken and not given to the verbal diarrhoea of the others."

"Perhaps he's the one we need to try to speak to," said Rachel.

"Agreed; he might even have a touch of sensitivity. Oh, the other thing I picked up is a new band member will be joining them tomorrow in Estonia. He's apparently not really new, more an old band member that had a fall out with someone – we can probably guess who – and is happy to help them out now."

"Good work, Marjorie. You have an eye for this sleuthing malarkey – now what say we go and get some lunch?"

"Yes please," Marjorie replied happily, seeming pleased with the compliment.

Chapter 8

The well-stocked buffet sported a dedicated theme each day as well as offering foods from around the world. Rachel and Marjorie filled their trays and ate outside. Afterwards, they made their way to the lido deck. They chose a table revealing a good view of the stage, but away from the giant overhead loudspeakers.

The deck was buzzing with activity along with happy splashes from the sparkling blue pools where children and adults vied for space. The Jacuzzi was being commandeered by a group of middle-aged women whose eyes fired daggers at a young couple daring to attempt entry. Meaty aromas from the grill bar on the next deck up wafted down to where they sat.

Rachel surveyed the rest of her surroundings. White peppery clouds formed overhead, but the sun was winning the battle thus far and the temperature had risen to a pleasant twenty-three degrees. The shouts and laughter from the pools and sun loungers surrounding them drowned out any sound of the sea waves that rocked the ship gently to and fro.

Shortly after they arrived, a game of water volleyball started up in the main pool. The teams consisted of officers versus crew with Gordon, the cruise director, providing a running commentary via a microphone. Among the officers playing was Alex, the junior doctor, and Rachel recognised Jason, Sarah's beau. The deputy captain and chief engineer also played in the officers' team. Gordon introduced the crew team that included two male dancers from the on-board dance troupe, an electrician and a maintenance engineer. Waverley was nowhere to be seen, but he didn't strike her as the pool game type.

"Here they come," said Marjorie, pointing towards the tribute band lugging heavy equipment up to the stage in preparation for their show. They seemed more subdued than usual, quietly going about their setup.

Perhaps they have been warned to behave.

After unpacking equipment and putting it in place, the men sat on the edge of the stage to watch the tail end of the volleyball game. The crew beat the officers by a considerable margin and Rachel wondered whether it could be a setup as a team building boost. The passengers applauded vigorously before filing back into the pool themselves and continuing with their own entertainment. Jason spoke to Gordon for a short time while the band tuned their instruments to suit the open air surroundings.

"I wonder what Jason's speaking to Gordon about?"

"By the way he's just patted him on the shoulder, I would say he's offering his condolences," said Marjorie. "Here's a waiter, Rachel, would you like a drink?"

They ordered mocktails and scrutinised the band closely. "This is frustrating," said Rachel. "We need to get to meet them somehow – it's alright watching, but we need to speak to them."

"Consider it done, my dear. They will be joining us after their show."

"What? Why – how?" Rachel stared open-mouthed.

"I spoke to their agent while you phoned Sarah after lunch and told him you were a huge Queen fan and that I am thinking of hiring them for your birthday later in the year. I told him I needed you to meet them to make sure they would be suitable and that we would be attending this performance to check them out. I used my title during the introduction, of course – it does come in handy occasionally!"

Rachel gawped, shaking her head admiringly. "Lady Marjorie Snellthorpe, you have to be the most sharp-witted and devious woman I've ever met. I would never have thought of that."

"Decades of experience as the wife of an international businessman do come with some knowledge of how things work.

Titles and money still go a long way, you know." Marjorie sniggered and the glint in her eye belied the piercingly sharp mind that accompanied it. A usually humble and unassuming woman, Marjorie rarely brought attention to her wealth or her title, but in this instance, Rachel was pleased she'd used both to full advantage.

"As long as they don't ask me too many questions about Queen or the game's up. Way before my time! My knowledge is limited to what I've read and what my father told me."

"I'm sure you'll ad lib marvellously. Anyway, they don't seem the enquiring type."

They laughed and enjoyed their drinks while waiting for the show to finish. Rachel felt glad when the band concluded as she reluctantly conceded they were not nearly as entertaining without the late Dominic Venables.

Jimmy, the manager, suddenly appeared at the side of the stage during the final song of the session. Mute applause followed from passengers who were not bathing or swimming in the pools as the lead guitarist and stand-in lead singer stormed off the stage and disappeared. Rachel observed Jimmy gather the rest of the band together after they had packed up their kit and escort them over to Rachel and Marjorie's table.

Marjorie stood, shook Jimmy's hand and introduced him to Rachel. Still battling with his gum from this morning, or perhaps having taken on a new piece, he shook Rachel's hand too.

"Ello, good to meet ya, Rachel. These are my boys, Dalton Delacruz aka John Deacon and Ray Lynch aka Roger Taylor. Nick's just gone to collect something from his room."

"No 'e's not," said Ray. "'E's got the 'ump cos no-one paid 'im much attention. I told 'im people just like a bit of background music, but you know 'ow 'e is. Mardy if 'e finks people ain't listening to 'im."

"I see, well, how do you do? I am Lady Marjorie Snellthorpe." Emphasis on *lady,* Rachel noticed. "And this is my granddaughter Rachel, who appreciated your performance."

The *boys*, as Jimmy had called them, grinned from ear to ear at this last part and nodded a greeting. They exchanged cursory looks as if not knowing what to do next.

"Please take a seat, gentlemen. Can I order you some drinks? You must be thirsty after that riveting performance."

Ray and Jimmy's enthusiasm went up a notch as Marjorie caught the attention of a waiter and ordered beers for the men and lemonade for herself and Rachel.

"I told the boys you might want us to do a gig for Rachel's birfday," said Jimmy. "You like Queen, then, do ya?" He glanced briefly at Rachel, but thankfully didn't wait for an answer, instead continuing to address Marjorie. "Can't say they were my cup o' tea, but the boys do a good job. As I said, Lady Snellforpe, they don't come cheap."

"Quite," said Marjorie. "Money isn't the issue here, but I would like to know more about who it is I'm hiring. I will need to meet, erm, Nick did you say? And the other band member – the one you mentioned the other night, Rachel. I think you said there were four?"

Rachel admired the way Marjorie had cut straight to the chase and dispensed with the blarney.

"Yes, a Freddie Mercury lookalike – a great singer," said Rachel on cue.

Nick arrived and caught the last part of the conversation. "Well, he won't be coming. Didn't you hear? He ended up in the drink. Singing with the angels now, or more than likely down there—" He pointed to the ground, smirking.

"Oh dear, how frightful! That must have been a terrible shock." Marjorie feigned horror.

"It must be hard for you to go on, I'm amazed you managed to sing so cheerfully," added Rachel beginning to enjoy the role play.

"To be honest, luv, he wasn't that good, and a right pain in the bum," said Nick dismissively, shrugging as he launched himself into a chair and lolled back casually.

"Creative temperament, you know the type," interjected Jimmy, chewing ever harder on his gum. His jaws tightened as they worked overtime, causing his saggy jowls to wobble in rhythm.

"I can't say that I do," said Marjorie. "What happened to the poor man?"

Cleverly, Rachel thought, Marjorie addressed her question to Dalton. Despite this, Nick answered while Dalton looked down at his shoes.

"No-one knows, he apparently fell overboard and hit his bonce. The doctors tried to save him, but he died in hospital in Copenhagen."

"That security geezer don't fink 'e fell. 'E finks 'e got pushed," said Ray, the drummer.

"Why would anyone want to push him overboard?" pressed Rachel before Jimmy could change the subject.

"Loads of reasons, luv," said Nick who looked her up and down appreciatively before continuing. "He always got someone's back up, argumentative plonker. If he wasn't arguing with someone, he would be seducing someone's bird."

"Now, now, Nick. Let's not speak ill of the dead," said Jimmy, chewing even more vigorously.

"But surely he wouldn't have had time to meet any women on board this ship to steal? We've only been at sea a few days."

"Don't you believe it," said Ray. "Dom worked fast and furious. As well as stealing birds, 'e always fell out with Nick 'ere. They 'ad a blazing row the night before 'e died."

"What are you implying?" Nick's face reddened and he looked ready to explode. "I didn't kill him. You had just as much reason to give him one after what he did to you and Jade."

Rachel inwardly smiled as this was all going to plan. The more they argued, the more they revealed and possible motives sprang to light.

"His brother had just as much reason to do him in." Dalton spoke so quietly the others didn't hear him as they continued to talk over each other, but Rachel heard.

"What makes you say that?" she prodded as he stared at his shoes again. He looked unsure, but she gave him one of her sweetest smiles, causing him to look up.

"Dom was knocking off his wife."

The men had quietened for a moment and caught Dalton's revelation.

"Whose wife?" asked Jimmy.

"Gordon's," answered Dalton.

Looks of genuine astonishment filled their faces. "You're kidding – no way," said Nick, open-mouthed. "That's the lowest of the low. How come you knew and we didn't? Are you making stuff up again?"

"Dalton's got a vivid imagination," interjected Jimmy. "Sometimes 'e's prone to embellishing the truf."

"No I'm not, I saw them. I took a walk in the early hours, the day he was killed. They were by the crew pool kissing in the shadows. I only noticed them cos a huge wave caused the ship to lurch. I caught them in a shaft of moonlight. I remember thinking the gleaming light could have been a spotlight on stage. They didn't notice me, though, too hard at it."

"Where was Gordon?" asked Ray.

"Working – I bumped into him soon after, heading out towards the pool, so I scarpered."

"Nice story, Dalton, but I saw Dom go to bed at one after I'd had my head glued. He was in no state to go prancing around the crew pool, I can tell you."

Dalton shook his head, tightened his lips and sulked, staring down at his shoes again.

Undeterred, Nick continued. "It could just as well have been Jimmy here. Hardly best buddies, were you?"

Jimmy looked decidedly uncomfortable about this revelation and the jaw burst into overdrive. If it had been a helicopter, he would have taken off. After chewing the gum into submission, he glared at Nick before looking at Marjorie pleadingly.

"Now, about this gig, ladies." He had clearly had enough of the direction the conversation had taken and was keen to get it back to its original purpose. "We will be back to being a band of four tomorrow, we've got an old band mate joining us in Tallinn, flown over specially."

"Yeah, and it's a good job he wasn't on board or he would have been the prime suspect," Nick threw in while facing off with Jimmy, clearly annoyed at being cut off in his prime.

Marjorie didn't pursue the subject and managed to defer her decision, dissipating the testosterone build up.

"We will need to meet again when your new man has settled in. We will attend a performance or two, and if Rachel likes what she sees, we will speak further. If I do hire you, it will be worth your while." The hint of generous remuneration caused Jimmy's eyes to light up. "There will be many wealthy guests at Rachel's party who could well follow up with invitations of their own. We are always looking for good acts for our circle of friends in London, not to mention the wealthy businessmen we entertain from all over the world."

Rachel knew she was being honest about everything, except a desire to hire this unruly bunch.

The men pushed their chairs back and rose to leave. Jimmy shook Marjorie's hand, obviously thinking they had the deal in the bag.

While Jimmy ingratiated himself sickeningly with Marjorie, Rachel spotted Waverley on the far side of the pool, scowling at them.

Whoops.

The group left and Marjorie looked triumphant.

"Wasn't that enlightening?"

"Yes, but look who's heading our way," said Rachel, inclining her head. Waverley was now marching towards them, having waited for the band to leave, and his face said it all. Clearly exasperated, he was struggling to keep his body language relaxed, but the red neck gave him away, as did the cough.

"Good afternoon, ladies. May I join you?" he said, smiling at a few passengers as they passed by.

"Chief Waverley, what a pleasant surprise," said Marjorie.

"We are just about to meet Sarah for afternoon tea in Creams," said Rachel. "Why don't you join us there?" She gave him enough eye contact to tell him they had information to share, but in a more private setting.

He got it immediately. Coughing, he replied, "I'll meet you there in twenty minutes."

Chapter 9

"If I see one more guy from that stag do, I'm going to jump overboard." Bernard flopped down on a chair in Gwen's office and let out a deep sigh. "Why couldn't they settle for a night out in Cardiff? No, obviously not good enough, so they decide to terrorise medical staff on a cruise ship. Well, I've had enough of them."

"It's not only us they're bothering," said Graham. "Those poor cheerleaders are sick of them too, not to mention the security team."

"Come on, you two bah humbugs. We were all young once," said Gwen.

"I was never that young," laughed Graham. "And I wouldn't have been able to afford a cruise for a stag do either."

"I can't afford a cruise now. If I didn't work on this ship, I wouldn't know they existed," moaned Bernard.

"Then be thankful and stop complaining," said Gwen.

Undeterred, Bernard looked at Sarah. "What do you think about them, Sarah?"

Sarah, still suffering from the loss of her childhood pet, answered absentmindedly. "They are boisterous, but they seem pretty harmless on the whole, I guess." Gwen looked sympathetic as Sarah had told her about Pickles when she'd asked her if anything was wrong this morning, noticing her eyes were swollen.

"Harmless?" chirped Brigitte. "I would like to give them all a good bit of French discipline."

"Not Madame Guillotine, I hope." Graham laughed. Brigitte scowled at him.

"Don't joke about such things. I am not proud of parts of French history, but you British have no room to talk."

"Sorry, no offence, and I agree those boys need a firm hand. Waverley will clamp down on them soon, I'm sure, and then they'll realise what discipline is."

They all laughed at this point. The medical team enjoyed their camaraderie and generally hit it off together. Bernard was the funny guy and usually made people happy, Brigitte could be blunt but was a pussycat underneath, Gwen, their team leader, reined them in when necessary and Sarah often provided the balance. Graham was the senior medical officer and liked to banter, but was well respected both in and out of the medical centre for his expertise and his poise in times of crisis.

Sarah looked around and noticed that the junior doctor was missing.

"Where's Alex?"

"He said he was going to check on the excursion staff to make sure they were all up-to-date with their medicals," said Graham. "I can't see why he didn't just check on the computer, but maybe he needed to stretch his legs."

The rest of the team shared some eyebrow raising and a joint smirk. "Yes, it's very important to stretch one's legs," laughed Bernard.

"What have I missed this time?" groaned Graham while draining his coffee cup.

"You'd better ask Alex. That's none of our concern," said Gwen, giving Bernard a warning look. "Haven't you got somewhere to be, Bernard?"

"Yes ma'am." He saluted and skulked out of the office.

"I'm going for lunch before taking a nap. I was up all night last night. Are you coming for lunch, Sarah?" asked Brigitte.

"Yes, anyone else?"

"I'll take a rain check on that one, I need to write some reports," answered Gwen.

"Me too. I'm meeting with Richard to discuss budgets – believe me, I'd much rather be with you."

Graham met regularly with the ship's administrator to justify current spending and put in bids for new equipment when they needed it. Sarah smiled sympathetically and followed Brigitte out of the medical centre.

Brigitte headed back to her room after lunch and Sarah wandered around the ship's library, choosing a light-hearted chick-lit book. Afterwards she made her way to the crew pool, armed with her reading material. The pool area was relatively quiet as most of the crew were at work or catching up on sleep. There was a group of Romanian barmen she recognised throwing a floating disc to each other in the pool, splashing about happily. They waved to acknowledge her and then carried on with their game.

Sarah walked over to a quieter side of the crew area where she found Gordon standing in the shadows of an alcove, staring at the wall.

"Hello, Gordon."

He almost leapt out of his skin before recovering himself. "Hello," he answered glumly.

"I'm so sorry about your brother."

"Not half as sorry as I am about my brother." His eyes flamed as he spat the words out with such venom, Sarah automatically took a step back.

"Perhaps you'd rather be alone," she said, hoping he would say yes. There was way too much testosterone floating round this ship for her liking.

"No, it's okay. It might be nice to have someone to talk to. Shall we sit over there?" He pointed to a table overlooking the sea. Sarah sighed, but reluctantly followed. They sat in silence while Sarah struggled, not knowing what to say.

"Have security said any more about how he died?"

In for a penny.

"They're not saying too much, but they reckon someone hit him over the head and threw him overboard. At first they said he might have fallen after drinking too much, but now they're saying it's suspicious. My parents are distraught – he's always been the bee's knees." The bitterness in his tone was clearly historical. "Anyway, they've flown over to Copenhagen with my sister to wait for the coroner to release him."

"I'm sure you could ask for compassionate leave, you know."

"To do what?" he snapped. "Join my parents crooning over their beloved favourite son? No thanks, I'd rather work." His eyes filled with tears, but the hatred emanating from them unnerved her.

"At least you've got Shirley on board. I'm sure she'll help you get through this."

He raised his voice several decibels. "OH YES, AT LEAST I'VE GOT HER!" He glared out to sea.

One of the Romanian barmen left the pool and came over. "Nurse, you alright?"

"Yes, I'm okay, thank you."

The man didn't leave. He stared at Gordon. "Come join us in the pool, man."

"No, I need to get back to work." Gordon pushed the chair back with such ferocity it fell over and stormed off.

"Sorry for interrupting, Nurse, but I didn't want to leave you with him. He behaving weird. And between you and me, he hated brother."

"Really? Why?"

"Not sure, but one of barmen heard them arguing. Not normal argue. He threaten to kill brother, and now look."

"Have you spoken to the security team about this?"

"No, they never speak to us. We not important, but you always kind to us so I not leaving you with him."

"Well, thank you, and I'll tell the security chief what you've said. It might be important."

"Okay, they know where we are if they need speak with us."

Sarah nodded, thanking him again for coming to her rescue before she made her way to Creams to meet Rachel and Marjorie for tea.

Chapter 10

Waverley arrived at the same time as Sarah, much to Rachel's disappointment. She had wanted to check her friend was alright after the previous night as they had not had time to talk properly when Rachel called to arrange the meet up.

"He doesn't look too happy," Marjorie chuckled.

"I suppose he imagines we've been snooping," giggled Rachel.

"What's so funny?" asked Sarah, who hadn't noticed Waverley coming up behind her. She joined them at the corner table they had deliberately chosen for its privacy.

"Marjorie was just telling me something funny." Rachel nodded, moving her eyes towards Waverley, telepathically signalling to Sarah not to ask any further questions.

Waverley hovered over the table, looking decidedly uncomfortable with a frown plastered on his face.

"Oh, do sit down, man," ordered Marjorie, to which he obediently responded, taking the fourth chair at the table.

"Well, as long as you don't mind me intruding on your tea. I do need to speak to you all if it's convenient."

Sarah appeared confused. Marjorie was in her element.

"You can speak to us all you like once we've ordered tea."

Waverley coughed. "Yes, of course."

The waiter saved him further embarrassment by appearing at the table, notebook in hand. They ordered tea and pastries. Waverley, more reluctantly than the rest of them, finally placed an order for coffee and a cookie under the watchful gaze of Marjorie.

"How was your morning?" Rachel asked Sarah.

"Busy as ever. The stag party continues to cause havoc, much to Bernard's disgust. He's getting tired of them."

"What have they done now?" asked Waverley.

"Nothing major – they're just injury prone, that's all. You know how young people are – they never look where they're going."

"You're not so old yourself, dear," said Marjorie kindly. She had heard about Sarah's cat and sympathised when Rachel told her, being an animal lover herself.

"I feel much older when up against them. It must be nursing – we grow up fast, and there is a four year age difference, which seemingly accounts for a lot in your twenties."

"Oh listen to Old Mother Time!" Rachel teased.

Sarah laughed. "I'm a bit of a grouch when it comes to boys behaving badly."

"I expect they would have fewer accidents if they drank less," remarked Waverley. "I envisage a couple of them being under house arrest before long. It doesn't help that the cheerleaders continue to mix with them, in spite of complaining about their behaviour. What are we supposed to do? My team is stretched to the limit trying to keep them in check, and at the same time, investigate an apparent murder."

All eyes turned to Waverley as the drinks and food were delivered to their table. Once the waiter had gone, Marjorie said what everyone was thinking.

"You've confirmed it was murder then?"

"Yes, either that or manslaughter. The coroner suggests from the evidence that the man was unconscious when he hit the water. The scans show no fluid in the nasal cavities, which is apparently significant. That and the witness statements we sent through to her confirm he didn't struggle for breath. She says that the bruise to Mr Venables's head was caused by trauma from a blunt instrument and there was a cut from whatever was used to hit him. The blow to the head caused a catastrophic haemorrhage to the brain fairly soon afterwards."

"But you brought him round, didn't you, Sarah?" said Rachel.

"Not me alone, the team did, but the bleed may have been a slow-burner followed by a rupture. It's not uncommon if the blow was particularly hard or if the person had an undiagnosed aneurysm."

"That's what the coroner says," said Waverley, admiring Sarah's explanation.

"So someone did hit him. I don't suppose it could have been a bang to the head following a fall?" asked Rachel.

"Not according to the coroner."

"Any idea who might have hit him?"

"Any number of people are in the frame for that." Waverley shrugged his shoulders and his drooping head and furrowed brow betrayed his worry and exasperation. "I can't get much information out of anyone. None of the band seems to have sensible alibis for the time of death, but they insist they all got on and were good friends."

Marjorie guffawed and Rachel laughed out loud, partly at Marjorie and partly because of the astonishment on Waverley's face at her outburst.

"Come on, you two. You've obviously discovered something, so out with it," said Sarah, looking sympathetically at Waverley.

Rachel explained about Marjorie's subterfuge and how the ruse had caused the men to join them after their performance on the lido deck.

"Very noisy it was too," interjected Marjorie. "Rachel says they weren't nearly as good without their lead singer."

Waverley stifled a tut as his impatience became visible at the interruption, but controlled himself and encouraged Rachel to continue with the story.

Once Rachel had explained how none of the band or even the manager seemed to have liked Dominic Venables and how they were all overly eager to point the finger at each other, Waverley sat back in his chair, confused.

"It doesn't change anything, I'm no nearer to knowing who hit him," he said.

"One of them could be lying, or maybe all of them. They seem to be doing a reverse alibi thing to make you work harder, and they probably find it amusing. I wouldn't trust them with a dime, as my husband used to say." Marjorie had a point. The tribute band members were the least likeable group of people Rachel had met in a long time. "And I wouldn't rule that shifty manager out, either," Marjorie added.

"I agree," said Rachel. "The way he chews that gum strikes me as overly aggressive. I have a gut feeling about him."

"Oh no, not your gut feelings!" Waverley almost smiled as he groaned. Rachel had got to the bottom of two cases of murder on her previous cruises on board the *Coral Queen* aided by her gut.

"There is something else," added Rachel. "One of the group, the one called Dalton, said that Dominic Venables was having an affair with his brother Gordon's wife. Gordon's the new cruise director."

"I'm well aware who Gordon is," snapped Waverley, immediately apologising for his outburst.

"The others didn't seem to know about the affair and scoffed at him – apparently Dalton is known for making things up or embellishing the truth, but he was pretty adamant that he saw them kissing at the side of the crew pool in the early hours before Venables was killed. He also says he bumped into Gordon heading that way afterwards."

"Do you believe him?" asked Waverley.

"He seemed sincere. He's much quieter than the others. He may have exaggerated the story, but I can't see why he'd make it up. Apparently Dom was a renowned philanderer—"

"That would explain Gordon's anger, if he did catch them out," Sarah interrupted.

"What do you mean, Sarah?" asked Waverley, gulping back his coffee and almost choking.

"Just before I came here, I found him in the crew area by the pool. He looked distraught, so I tried to comfort him, but he soon became vehemently angry. I would say the hatred in his eyes was caused by something other than his brother's death. It also sounded like their parents favoured Dom, and Gordon's very bitter about that too, so it may have been a mixture of grief and anger. I'm not saying he murdered his brother, which would be awful, but he didn't like him, and he did become enraged when I mentioned his wife."

"I noticed that anger in his eyes when Marjorie and I saw him in the Sky View Lounge. People do react differently to the death of a loved one, though, and we can't be certain the wife was having an affair. It might be sibling rivalry and now Gordon feels guilty because he hated his brother. But didn't you say Gordon got the band the job in the first place?"

"That's what I heard from Rosa Doherty. We got talking when I went to treat one of the dancers who had an ankle injury. Two of the band passed by and she muttered under her breath. I later asked her what that was all about and she told me she had made a mistake hiring them and shouldn't have allowed Gordon to persuade her to."

"So now we have at least five suspects, but do any of them fit the profile of a killer?" said Waverley. "Gordon has to be my chief suspect for now, judging by what you've just told me."

"If he deliberately got his brother on board, it could be premeditated murder," said Rachel thoughtfully.

"I realise you will find it difficult to stay out of this, Rachel, Lady Snellthorpe, but I would very much prefer it if you did—"

"Bah!" exclaimed Marjorie, interrupting Waverley. "Not going to happen, Chief, so we either club together, or Rachel and I find the killer for ourselves. We've found out a good deal of information for you so far."

Waverley answered tight lipped. "You stay with the band, I will speak to Gordon. Sarah, I shouldn't ask, but would you have a word with Shirley Venables? She might be more likely to open up to you as a nurse."

Sarah nodded. "I'll try. I can arrange a health promotion session for the dancers and quiz her. She's also due to see me about something else – confidential, so I can't go into it, but that might provide an opportunity. I'm sure I'll be able to wangle it somehow, but I'm not going to ask her if she was having an affair with her brother-in-law."

"I have no idea what my team are going to do with themselves while all these amateurs conduct enquiries," conceded Waverley.

"I do," said Sarah, nodding towards the public area outside the patisserie where a crowd of twenty youths were congregating.

"Ah, yes." Waverley smiled for the first time that afternoon. "Our delightful stag party."

"And the cheerleaders, of course," said Marjorie, laughing. "Whatever they are."

Rachel looked at her to see if she was teasing or whether she seriously had no knowledge of cheerleading. Marjorie was giving nothing away, but she winked as she sipped her tea. Admiring her elderly friend's elegance and poise, Rachel smiled affectionately.

Chapter 11

Jack Waverley came away from the meeting with Rachel, Lady Snellthorpe and Sarah grinning smugly. Let them chase the band around as much as they liked, that should keep them out of mischief, or more importantly to him, danger. He had grown fond of Rachel and Lady Snellthorpe and didn't want either of them putting themselves at risk on board his ship. Security was his concern and Rachel had been lucky to escape with her life on two previous cruises. He didn't believe in tempting providence too often.

He felt certain the tribute act would turn out to have cast iron alibis and agreed with Rachel: they were giving him the run-around in that respect. Despite knowing that the band argued a lot, he felt sure that underneath it all, they tolerated each other for their mutual love of music, such as it was. According to a member of the crew working in the casino, they stuck up for each other when push came to shove. They had rooms on her deck and she heard them laughing a lot in between incessant arguments. She told him these creative types often behaved like that: volatile one minute, effusive and lovey dovey the next.

He would focus on Gordon for now, although he remained to be convinced about the affair. The couple seemed happy enough, and he liked Gordon, preferring him to Matt. The previous cruise director had been an arrogant, pig-headed man who tended to upset the crew. Word got back to Waverley about these things from Brenda, his girlfriend who worked in the bakery. She didn't miss a thing, and keeping up with the gossip helped him to keep the passengers and crew safe.

Maybe the time had come to tie the knot again. He'd been thinking about it for months now, but hadn't quite plucked up the courage to ask Brenda, ten years his junior – a matter which bothered him. His daughter, Charlotte, liked her and had thus far been encouraging about his new relationship. This pleased him because Charlotte remained especially close to her mother who'd left him for one of his closest friends.

Waverley knew all about betrayal, and if Gordon was suffering, he understood exactly what he might be going through. He had never known anger like it when he'd found out he had been betrayed by two of the people he loved the most, but even in his darkest days he had never contemplated murder. Nowadays he tolerated the couple for his daughter's sake, but they would never be friends again as long as he had breath.

Waverley made his way towards guest services to check the cruise director's itinerary. He could have phoned down, but needed the exercise, concerned about his recent weight gain. He tapped his abdomen subconsciously as he arrived at the desk and asked for the document he needed.

A constant queue of people was present at the guest services desk during sea days with multiple requests and complaints, from lights not working to rooms being too hot or too cold and everything in between. The guest services staff performed their duty in the well-briefed fashion that had been drummed into them to assist with every eventuality, and they did so admirably.

Waverley stood by one of the marble posts on deck four, observing the crowds for a few minutes while scanning the document in his hands. He had fifteen minutes before Gordon would finish hosting a couples' quiz in the Plato Lounge. That was only one floor up so he took the stairs and stood at the rear of the lounge until proceedings concluded.

Gordon was nowhere in sight. Geraldine, the assistant cruise director, seemed to be in full control of the event and looked as though she relished being the centre of attention, but not as much as Gordon appeared to enjoy it. Waverley would hate it. Being reserved and preferring privacy, he kept himself to himself wherever possible. It must run in the family for Gordon, he mused as he watched Geraldine finish off the session with a joke, resulting in raucous laughter from the assembled crowd of couples.

Before he got the opportunity to ask her where he could find Gordon, his radio burst into life.

"Yes, what is it?" Irritation came through in his voice after being halted in his tracks.

"Sorry, sir, a fight's broken out on the lido deck." Ravanos sounded breathless.

"On my way." Frustrated, he heaved his shoulders up, sighed heavily and walked briskly towards the lifts.

Chapter 12

After the meeting with Waverley, Marjorie went back to her room for a shower and to change for dinner. Rachel took the opportunity to spend some time with Sarah. They walked along the upper decks, enjoying the fresh air.

"How are you? You said you were okay, but how are you, really?"

"Actually, I am alright. I cried myself to sleep last night, but today, work has taken my mind off things. This morning, Gwen asked what was wrong because she could see I'd been crying. She has been kind and supportive. I suppose being away from home helps – I don't have the daily reminder of the empty cat bed or anything like that. I expect Mum will feel it more than I will for now."

They walked side by side, Sarah dressed in uniform with two-and-a-half gold stripes on her epaulettes signifying her officer status, and Rachel casually dressed in lime-green crop trousers and a white vest top. They stopped at the inner rail on deck fourteen, overlooking the pools on the lido deck and enjoyed a casual conversation. Out of the corner of her eye, Rachel noticed Dalton speaking quietly to a woman at the side of the stage. He stroked her arm before she headed away. Rachel felt pleased for him that he had found someone else on board other than his negative band mates.

Sarah was looking in the opposite direction, watching children splashing in the pools when a scream drew both of them out of their reverie. Rachel spun her head away from the stage to the side of the main pool where two men were fighting, one grasping the other in a headlock. A young woman, probably early twenties, was screaming and crying for them to stop. Crowds of onlookers gathered quickly, but no sign of security.

Rachel and Sarah raced down the stairs and pushed their way through the crowd with Sarah commanding people to stand back while radioing down for security.

"Make way, please."

The onlookers at the front of the crowd reluctantly stepped aside. By now, one man was on the floor, bleeding badly from his head, while the other one continued to pummel him. Rachel thought if she didn't act quickly, the aggressor might kill him, so she grabbed the man on the top from behind.

"Please, sir, leave him. He's had enough."

Rage spilled from the man, who she was shocked to see was Gordon. With uncontrolled anger, he struggled from Rachel's grip, pushing her backwards, and jumped on the man again, leaving Rachel no choice. This time she was firm, arm locking him in a vice-like grip.

A few minutes later, Waverley and two other security guards, including Jason, arrived, taking over.

Sarah attended to the man on the ground. Calling for the on-call medic, she shouted to the waiters in the crowd.

"Someone get me the first aid kit and water. I need clean cloths too."

Rachel released Gordon so that Jason could handcuff him before leading him away.

"Get rid of these crowds," Waverley snarled at Ravanos, the other officer, who began gently ushering people back.

"Show's over, folks. Those who witnessed the incident from the beginning please take a seat and we will interview you shortly." He pointed to chairs under a canopy. "Otherwise, please clear the area. It will be open again as soon as the scene is cleared."

The inquisitive crowd moved slowly away, some muttering while others took seats as instructed. Many of the passengers, including those with children, had already left when the fight started.

"How is he?" Rachel handed Sarah water, a first aid kit and towels that had been brought by pool attendants.

"Pretty beaten up, but it looks worse than it is – faces always bleed badly. I'm not sure he would have been alright for much longer if you hadn't intervened, though."

"Who is he?"

"I'm not sure. I think he's one of the boys from the stag party."

"He is." A girl's blubbering came from nearby. "His name's Dave, he'll be the best man when Aled gets married."

Graham and Bernard arrived with the medical kit and helped Sarah stem the bleeding from Dave's face; he was now sitting up and mumbling to Sarah. Rachel recognised the situation was under control, so she led the girl away to one side and urged her to sit down.

"I'm Rachel, what's your name?"

"Tonya, I'm with a group of cheerleaders from Massachusetts. It was awful, I thought that crazy man was going to kill him. Doesn't he work on board?"

Ignoring the question, Rachel asked, "Why don't you start at the beginning and tell me what happened?"

They heard the sound of Waverley's cough before he appeared and introduced himself. Joining Rachel and Tonya, he handed them both a cup of tea.

"We were sitting by the pool having a laugh, that's all," said Tonya. "Dave was telling me how he'd caught one of the dancers snogging an older guy from a band on board ship. We were laughing about it when this guy, I'm sure he works on the ship, pulled him out of his seat and started yelling at him. Dave swore, told him to get a life, and the man punched him full in the face. I screamed, Dave fell over, just missing the pool, and the man leapt on him like a madman. He kept punching him. I shouted and cried, asking people to help – some ran away and others just watched. I even saw a couple of guys filming it on their mobile phones – how sick is that?"

Rachel put a hand on Tonya's arm as she continued to sob. By now the cheerleader was shaking.

"Did you recognise the men filming? Are they still here?" asked Waverley, handing her his lily-white handkerchief.

Tonya wiped her eyes and blew her nose, sniffing as she looked around. "That fat guy over there was one and the other one was older. He's not here now. He had long greying hair. He might have been in the band that played earlier."

Waverley looked confused and Rachel digested this information. Why would Ray Lynch be filming the fight?

The medical team were wheeling the shocked Dave away from the area.

"Can I go with him?" Tonya asked.

"Yes, of course, Miss," said Waverley. "Would you just give me your full name for my records in case I need to speak with you again?"

"Tonya Carson," the girl shouted as she ran after the medical team.

"Sounds like wrong place, wrong time to me," said Waverley.

"Obviously Gordon did know about the affair then if it was his wife they were referring to."

"Possibly, but it could have been any of the dancers – there are eighteen in the troupe and multitudes of older men on the ship. Gordon may have got the wrong end of the stick completely, idiot." Waverley shook his head in disbelief. "Now he's ruined his career, such as it was."

"What will happen to him?"

"He'll be put in the brig to cool off and then placed under house arrest. I'll have to interview him. If he wasn't a suspect in a murder investigation, I'd put him off in Tallinn in the morning, but as it is, I'm going to have to hang on to him as well as that rabble of a band. One of my officers will now be tied up babysitting outside his room until I get to the bottom of the murder of Dominic Venables. Gordon has just become my prime suspect, certainly has a temper from what that young lady told us. We'll need to see if the injured guy wants to press charges as well. Either way, Gordon's in big trouble – the cruise line will pay to compensate the young man for his silence if he agrees, and they'll want rid of Venables. They can't have employees attacking passengers – this is a nightmare.

"Perhaps Gordon Venables is just as bad as his brother – I don't know how he came to us with glowing references. I'll be going through his security file with a fine toothcomb. The captain will speak to the powers that be and see what they are prepared to offer the boy for his silence. It's a complete and utter mess, and for what? All because he overheard a stupid conversation between a couple of kids."

Rachel felt sorry for the chief of security. "I'm not sure he murdered his brother."

"Dare I ask why?"

"Think about it: if you had just murdered someone, wouldn't you want to keep your head down rather than get embroiled in a fight with one of the passengers? I accept he's livid about his wife possibly having an affair with his brother, but the rest doesn't add up."

"Killing isn't logical, Rachel. These things do happen – perhaps he can't rationalise at the moment. I don't know, maybe he's looking for someone else to kill."

He and Rachel looked at each other, suddenly concerned for Gordon's wife's welfare. Waverley picked up his radio.

"Get me Rosa, pronto!" he yelled.

They held their breath and waited. Waverley's radio lit up and he answered.

"Rosa, I need to know if Shirley Venables is with you." His shoulders relaxed. "Thank you. No, nothing at present, I'll talk to you later." He turned to Rachel. "She's in a dress rehearsal, been there most of the afternoon."

"Thank goodness for that," replied Rachel.

He stood up. "Thanks for what you did, you prevented a nasty situation becoming much more serious." He coughed, embarrassed. "Anyway, I need to go and interview the 'would be' filmmaker before the footage makes its way on to YouTube or CNN. I suppose you're coming?"

Sarah had left with the medical team so Rachel gladly followed Waverley over to where a bariatric young man was seated, looking at the mobile held in chubby, short-fingered hands.

"Good afternoon, sir," said Waverley. "I'm Chief Security Officer Waverley. This is Rachel Prince who broke up the fight I believe you witnessed. I understand you have mobile phone footage of the incident?"

"I sure do, Officer Waverley." The man had an American drawl. "Nasty incident it was too. Your security needs tightening up if you ask me."

Waverley's neck reddened. "May I see the footage?"

The man looked unsure, holding his phone tightly in his hand. "Well, I don't know about that. This is my personal property. I could sell this film to a news station, show them what goes on aboard your cruise ship."

Waverley's neck became a deeper red and his temple veins pulsated as he tensed. "Sir, maritime law applies to what happens on board a ship, and you are in possession of evidence I need. I either confiscate the phone or you show me the footage."

The man sighed deeply, his bulging grey eyes darting around. Rachel noticed he had no eyebrows and looked fearful of something. He reluctantly handed the phone over to Waverley.

"Just that video, mind," he said as Waverley prised the phone from his tightened hand.

Waverley looked at the screen, raised his eyebrows, scrunching up his face as he scrolled back to the beginning of the video. He held the phone so Rachel was able see. The film footage revealed why the young man was so possessive of his phone. It started with close ups of various women in bikinis before zooming in on buttocks and cleavages. Rachel frowned while Waverley looked at the man in disgust. The film swung round as a commotion occurred and showed the young guy Dave falling to the ground and Gordon going for him like a man possessed.

When they'd finished watching the film, the man held his hand out. Waverley leaned forward.

"Sir, I will be confiscating this phone as evidence and need your permission to copy the relevant footage."

"You can't do that! I refuse, and I need that phone."

"In that case, I'll show this and any other videos found on the device to the authorities when we arrive in Tallinn – where they have different laws to us – if that's what you prefer?"

"No, no – you can hang on to it and delete the video off the phone when you're done, as long as that's the last I hear of it. I haven't broken the law." The man was red and sweating.

"Name?"

"Arnold Blake."

"Room number?"

"9065, sir."

Waverley wrote the details down. "You can come to my office on disembarkation day and collect your phone, Mr Blake. My security officers will be following you closely. I suggest you make sure the only films recorded on any device from here on in consist of scenery. If I find anything illegal on this or any other device, I will report it to the relevant authorities. Do we understand each other?"

"Yes, sir. There's nothing illegal. I just like to admire – you know." His head dropped.

"You may go."

Arnold Blake heaved his enormous frame from the chair with some difficulty, but Waverley offered no assistance. Once he'd gone, Waverley let rip.

"Pervert! I'd like to put him in the brig if I thought he'd fit."

"Nasty piece of work, but I guess he doesn't have much luck with women. He might have health issues and his weight has nothing to do with his behaviour."

"I disagree, Rachel – it has everything to do with his weight. If he wasn't built like that, he wouldn't need to film women, would he?"

"Don't be ridiculous, you're showing your prejudice. I arrest perverts at least once a month and they come in all shapes and sizes. If it were that simple, I should arrest everyone over a certain weight, according to you."

Waverley looked suitably rebuked. "I don't like this sort of thing, that's all – if he'd been skinny, I'd have probably been personal about that, too. Sorry." He thrust the phone in his pocket. "I'd better help Ravanos interview the rest of this crowd. I'll talk to you and Sarah later."

He got up and headed towards half a dozen passengers still waiting to be interviewed. Rachel returned to her room to change for dinner.

Chapter 13

At breakfast the next morning, Rachel noticed Marjorie seemed off colour.

"Are you alright? You don't seem yourself."

"To be honest, I don't feel well. I have a migraine coming on. Do you mind if I stay on board today? Perhaps all the excitement has been a bit too much."

Rachel felt guilty for having allowed them to become embroiled in an investigation which strictly speaking had nothing to do with them.

"I don't mind at all. I'll stay with you."

"No, dear, there's really no need. I have Migraleve tablets with me, I'll take some and go back to bed. Once they kick in, I'll be better – it will be gone by this evening. Anyway, you're meeting Sarah. That girl doesn't get much time off – you must go."

Rachel considered it for a moment. Not wanting to disappoint Sarah but not wanting to leave Marjorie by herself if she was unwell, she was torn. However, seeing the determination in the old lady's eyes and knowing how independent and stubborn Marjorie could be, she opted not to argue.

"As long as I can escort you back to your room and ask Mario to check in on you while I'm out."

"That would be acceptable," Marjorie conceded.

Once she had settled Marjorie into bed, clucking like a mother hen, as her dear old friend chided, Rachel went downstairs to meet Sarah in the main atrium. While sitting at a table waiting, she watched people coming and going, preparing for their various outings. One of the luxuries of cruising was the excitement of waking up every morning in a different place or country and leaving the ship to go exploring.

She heard arguing coming from a nearby table and noticed the tribute band members once again having a heated discussion. A few women were with them, being just as loud as the men. Rachel sighed, thinking how tiresome they were.

They fell silent when Waverley approached. He said a few words then sat down. The conversation was now too quiet for Rachel to hear, but Waverley looked outwardly calm at least.

I wonder if he's quizzing Ray about filming the fight.

A couple approached the band's table from behind Waverley, but when they saw him, they turned and walked away. Rachel watched them meander round the customer services area looking at papers, but now and then they would surreptitiously glance over to the table where Waverley was seated.

Curious, she thought. She took out her phone and pretended to read from the screen while snapping a photo of the couple, whom she hadn't seen before, and then a short video of their behaviour. They whispered to each other before rushing off downstairs, presumably to vacate the ship.

Sarah finally arrived, wearing mufti for the land outing. Her eyes were still slightly swollen, suggesting she had likely cried again last night over Pickles. Rachel stood and hugged her, squeezing her arm at the same time.

"Where's Marjorie?"

"She's got a migraine, so she's gone back to bed."

"Oh dear, does she need any tablets?"

"No, she's brought her own along with her and has taken two. I did offer to stay, but she said she'd rather sleep it off. Mario's going to check in on her at lunchtime." Rachel noticed out of the corner of her eye the band heading downstairs. "How are you?"

"Better, thanks. Still sad, but I don't get that much time to think. It is for the best – I wouldn't want him to suffer, and he had a long life."

"Miss Prince, Nurse Bradshaw." Waverley spotted them and Rachel detected a note of irritation in his formal address.

"What have we done this time?" she whispered to Sarah.

"Pardon?" said Waverly.

"I said, 'Is that the time?' We're taking a trip today."

"Hmm." He knew she'd said something completely different, but didn't pursue it. "I've just been speaking to members of that tribute band. Funny how you're always around when I'm carrying out my enquiries."

"Sarcasm doesn't become you, and for your information, I was waiting for Sarah, who has just arrived. Yesterday, you gave me and Marjorie permission to speak to the men in the band – not that we've had any more opportunities with all the other goings on."

"In that case, I apologise. Have a good day, ladies." He marched off towards the rear stairs.

"He's insufferable sometimes. Yesterday we were included and today he's giving nothing away."

"Perhaps as well, Rachel. He can see your cogs turning as well as I can. He knows you won't let it go, but what say we go and join our tour before we miss the bus?"

Sarah laughed. She did seem brighter.

Not totally put off, Rachel continued while they walked down a deck to the exit.

"Waverley was talking to the band and some women with them in hushed tones. I expect he was asking about Ray filming the fight yesterday. In spite of what he says, they have to be high on his list of suspects, along with Gordon. I also spotted a couple I've not seen before behaving suspiciously when Waverley was with the group."

"Oh no," Sarah groaned. "You're not going to stop until you've got to the bottom of this, are you?"

Rachel grinned, and then turned serious. "To be honest, I am having second thoughts. I don't want all the excitement to make Marjorie ill – I forget sometimes just how old she is."

"I'm above telling you I told you so, but I did."

Rachel took her friend's arm. "I know. On a different subject, how's that young man, Dave?"

"He was kept in the infirmary overnight as a precaution. Graham needed to ensure there were no complications from the battering to his head. I suspect he also wanted to make sure news of the attack didn't spread like wildfire. His name's Dave Hughes and he's going to be the best man at the forthcoming wedding. He organised the stag do, I discovered. He needed some glue to his forehead and I'm sure he'll have a black eye this morning, but other than that, he'll recover. He even joked later on that he'd had worse on the rugby pitch."

"That explains his nose shape," said Rachel. "I thought it looked like it had been broken."

"Yes it has, but not yesterday, thankfully. That young cheerleader stayed with him for a few hours before rejoining her friends."

"Tonya," said Rachel, absentmindedly. "Do you imagine he'll sue?"

"I doubt it. The cruise line offers generous compensation for injuries aboard and they'll want to settle out of court if it comes to it."

They passed through security and found the group they would be with for their tour milling around at the side of the dock.

"That's Gordon's wife," said Sarah, "with the group over there."

Rachel recognised some of the dancers from the performance she had watched with Marjorie last night. Sarah had worked the previous evening, so Rachel and Marjorie had met up with Ron and Mabel, the elderly couple from Texas, and gone to the theatre together.

"Which one is she?"

"The one with the black bob."

Rachel saw a pretty woman, about the same height as her, wearing yellow cotton trousers and a tight fitting patterned vest with yellow speckles. She stood tall and straight and was wearing sunglasses that disguised her eyes.

"She doesn't seem the type to be snogging her brother-in-law."

"Pray tell me, what does the type look like?"

"Good point." Rachel chuckled. "Not like her, though. I wonder if Dalton is making it up."

"If that's the case, why would Gordon have attacked Dave yesterday?"

"I'm keeping an open mind. We need to talk to her."

Sarah put her arm through Rachel's and led her towards the coach that was now boarding.

"So much for my nice day out," she sighed.

They found two seats, Rachel keeping one eye on the dancers, paying particular attention to Shirley Venables. Sarah nudged her, giving her a disparaging glare.

The tour leader introduced herself before describing the highlights of the tour as the coach made its way out of the port and off to its destination. Rachel sat back.

"Sorry. You're right. Let's just have a nice outing."

Sarah smiled back, but her eyes said she wasn't convinced for one moment, and Rachel knew her friend was right.

They meandered along cobbled streets, taking in the sights and sounds of a new country. Sarah had an SLR camera with her, being an amateur photographer, and stopped whenever the opportunity to exercise her creative skills presented itself. Rachel didn't mind; she was pleased to see her friend happy and was well aware of how hard Sarah worked as a cruise ship nurse. It was important for her to have some down time as a tourist herself.

The streets were idyllic, or would have been if they weren't packed with cruise passengers. The locals were friendly and welcoming – the tour guide had explained that tourism was an important source of their income.

"Rachel, sit on that wall," Sarah directed, having spotted an attractive fountain with a church entrance in the field of vision behind. The sun was sending speckles of light through the leaves of a large willow tree to their left, and even Rachel recognised the ideal photo opportunity. She finally settled into the right position after numerous attempts that weren't quite right for her friend's eagle eye.

"I'm beginning to realise how a bride must feel on their wedding day!" Rachel rolled her eyes as she had to make yet another adjustment – her bag wasn't in the right place for Sarah, aka David Bailey.

"You still owe me for making me break every rule in the book on the last cruise, so don't you dare moan!"

"Now you're lowering yourself to emotional blackmail." Rachel laughed.

"Like you didn't use that as well!"

"Okay, you win. I know when to quit, just get it over with so we can have some lunch. I'm starving."

Sarah was right: Rachel had led her friend astray during her last cruise and put Sarah at risk of losing her job, something she had regretted immediately afterwards.

They bantered some more while Sarah took a range of casual photos. Just as she was about to put the camera away, the dancing group walked up the hill behind her.

"Would you mind taking a photo of the two of us?" called Rachel, making eye contact with the woman Sarah had identified earlier as Shirley Venables. Sarah shot her a warning glance. "What? It will be nice to have a photo together."

Sarah's eyebrows headed towards the sky as Shirley stepped away from the crowd.

"Sure, I'd be happy to," she said.

Funny, Rachel had presumed she was English, but the accent was German. Rather than trying to teach Shirley how to use the SLR, Sarah handed her a mobile phone to take the picture with, and then joined Rachel on the wall. The others in the crowd stopped and waited.

"Don't worry," said Shirley. "I'll catch up with you." They gladly walked on, laughing and joking after nodding or saying hello to Sarah.

After taking a couple of photos and showing the results to Sarah for approval, Shirley handed over her own mobile phone so Rachel could take a photo of her by the fountain. Rachel couldn't resist the temptation to take a quick scroll through Shirley's other photos once she had snapped a couple, while Sarah chatted amicably with the woman. After the photo shoot, they all headed in the direction the other dancers had taken.

The dance troupe had stopped at an outside café. Shirley rejoined her group.

Rachel nudged Sarah and mouthed, "Appointment!"

Sarah shook her head before leading Rachel away.

"Come on, Sherlock, let's get some food inside you."

"Did she say anything important?" Rachel asked.

"Yes, she told me her life story, and then confessed to having an affair and to her husband killing his brother – case solved, all in the three seconds we had!"

"You know, sarcasm doesn't suit you – you've been spending too much time with Brigitte," Rachel giggled.

They walked arm in arm down the cobbled road, laughing and joking until they found another café where they sat at an outside table and studied the menu.

"Right, seeing as you've dragged me away from our investigation, what do you recommend that's traditionally Estonian?"

Sarah gawped. "Our investigation? There's no 'our' about it." Her eyes caught Rachel's teasing smirk and she burst out laughing.

"I'll tell you what I found on the mobile phone after lunch."

"Rachel Prince – you didn't? Well don't tell me anything at the moment, I'm too hungry. We must have walked for miles. My feet are killing me."

"Well you will wear DCs when walking through cobbled streets."

Sarah looked down at her feet. Although her shoes were lovely, the soles were not suitable for the type of walking they had been doing.

"Okay, Miss Practicality, I wondered why you were wearing sturdy shoes on such a hot day. How was I to know you were going to drag me round every street in Tallinn? We are supposed to be on a bus tour."

"Yep, a bus tour marked as including moderate exercise, the brochure said."

Sarah picked up the menu and chewed her bottom lip as she did when she was concentrating. Rachel was delighted her friend was back to her normal bubbly self.

"So what do you recommend?"

"The last time I was here, I had a traditional dish with anchovies."

"Okay, anchovies with what?"

"On your menu, third down, Kiluvõileib – that's what I had. It's like an open sandwich made with whole anchovies, eggs and homemade rye bread."

"That sounds good, I'll try it."

The waiter appeared and they both ordered the traditional Estonian dish along with lemonade.

"I confess, I do cut the heads off the anchovies," whispered Sarah.

"You won't be alone there," replied Rachel.

Chapter 14

Marjorie awoke to a darkened room. Wondering where she was, she lifted a heavy head from the pillow before realising she was on a cruise with Rachel. Her hand automatically went to her head on remembering she had taken tablets to relieve a migraine. The pain had eased, but had left her feeling groggy.

She reached for the glass of water on the bedside table and reluctantly switched on the overhead light. After blinking a few times, she felt relieved to find the light didn't irritate her head. Mario had instructed her to call him on waking, so she did so.

The eager butler arrived within seconds as if he'd been hovering outside her room.

"Lady Snellthorpe, I worry about you." He smiled sincerely. "Would you like me to open the curtains?"

"Perhaps just a little, please. The room is very dark with them closed, but that's what helped me to sleep."

He walked to the far end of her bedroom and pulled the cord. The heavy full-length drapes opened a couple of feet, allowing light into the room.

"How are you?"

"Much better, thank you. The codeine in those pills made me a little woozy, but it will pass. I'll take the next dose shortly."

"Can I get you anything to eat, ma'am? It's past midday."

"No thank you, just coffee for now. I'm afraid these migraines make me feel sickly. I've got a few biscuits to munch with my pills."

After drinking coffee and taking a second dose of tablets, Marjorie felt well enough to get up. Donning a pair of light sunglasses, she left the room to go for a stroll. Mario had insisted on fussing and she'd had quite enough of his attention.

I expect Rachel put him up to it.

Marjorie looked at her watch: two o'clock. The ship was much quieter than usual, it being a port day, as the majority of passengers and some crew were enjoying the day on land. Others took advantage of the opportunity to stay on board and sit in peace on sun beds, often oversubscribed during sea days.

After breathing in the fresh air, she headed up to the Sky View Lounge where she anticipated it would be relatively quiet. The noise of children screeching as they played in the pool grated, despite being a sound she usually enjoyed. This seemed to be the only hangover from the migraine, reminding her it had not quite gone completely.

The enclosed Sky View was predictably peaceful with just a few dozen people scattered throughout its considerable expanse. She found a settee to park herself on and watched another cruise ship leave the port. People stood on the decks, waving to anyone who would wave back while their ship departed. Marjorie briefly wondered whether their ship was heading to St Petersburg as the *Coral Queen* would be doing later that evening.

A waiter brought her a pot of tea. Another reason Marjorie liked the Sky View Lounge and the atrium café was that they served tea in a pot rather than a mug. There were many things she had learned to tolerate in the modern world, even possessing a mobile phone, but a teabag in a mug was not one of them. Tea has to brew in a teapot and be poured at the right moment into a matching cup and saucer, preferably china rather than the white pottery that had been placed in front of her, but at least it was not a mug.

She smiled at herself.

Marjorie Snellthorpe, you're being a snob.

And on this point, I am happy to be so, replied her alter ego.

Sipping her tea, she heard familiar argumentative voices shattering the peace. Tutting at having her tranquil surroundings invaded, she sat forward to put herself in a position where it would be easier to rise from her seat.

"Lady Snellforpe, you're not leaving, are you?"

Timmy, was it?

Jimmy sat himself on the chair to the side of the settee, blocking her escape route.

"I was just wondering if you'd given any more fought to booking us. The lads are getting snapped up quick wiv bookings." He pulled a diary out of his pocket, reinforcing his point. "Now what date – October, weren't it?"

"Rachel's birthday is in October, but Mr Walker, I'm afraid I cannot commit to a booking until I've met the new lead singer and Rachel has heard him sing."

Not to be put off, Jimmy continued, "Mere formality, Lady Snellforpe – she'll love the new lad wiv the band."

"She may well," Marjorie spoke firmly, "but until she has seen and heard them together, I will not be making a booking."

Noticing the band manager's balloon deflating, Marjorie patted him on the arm.

"Would you like some tea?"

"Nah, don't drink the stuff, mineral water's fine for me."

Please would be nice.

Marjorie caught a waiter's attention and ordered more tea for herself and the water for the disappointed manager.

"Do you have any further information about the unfortunate death of your other lead singer, Mr Walker?"

"Not really. They still don't know whodunit, but I fink they might have arrested his bruvver, Gordon. That's what I 'eard from 'is wife anyway."

"Oh dear. Do you think it was him?"

"I don't fink Gordon could punch 'is way out of a paper bag, Lady Snellforpe, let alone kill 'is bruvver."

That's not what I heard, she thought, but continued, "Why have they arrested him then?"

"Not sure, I fink he got into a fight wiv some young geezer, so Ray says. I fink Dalton's made it worse telling everyone Dom was 'aving an affair wiv Gordon's wife."

"And you don't believe that's likely?"

"Who knows? Dom certainly put it about a bit – tried it on wiv every bird 'e met. Even tried it on wiv my wife."

"Really? How upsetting."

"Yeah, she told 'im where to go then told me straight away. I was angry, I can tell you that for a fact. He's lucky I didn't kill 'im myself. Trouble is, you'd be spoilt for choice wiv the number of people who would have liked to see 'im dead."

"Does that include you, Mr Walker?"

Jimmy scratched his balding head for a moment, rubbed his nose and bit down hard on his chewing gum – a nasty habit Rachel had remarked upon.

"I would 'ave that day, but I was away. By the time I met up wiv Dom, we had a blazing row, 'e promised me 'e would never do it again – even apologised, somefing 'e never did, so I forgave im and we agreed we wouldn't talk about it again. We never did." He sighed wistfully.

"You're lucky your wife didn't fall for his charms, I suppose."

"Yeah, Bee's a smasher to look at – could've 'ad anyone. I don't know what she sees in me, but we really are 'appy, always 'ave been. There's no way I would 'ave let Dom ruin that – no way." He raised his voice.

"Well thankfully, it wasn't ruined. So what makes you think he wasn't having an affair with Gordon's wife?"

"I don't know for sure, but it wasn't 'is style to be shy about it. He would always brag about 'is conquests to the boys. It doesn't fit his MO, if you know what I mean?"

"I see, so you really do believe Dalton is mistaken?"

"Look, Lady Snellforpe, Dalton's a nice lad – but not a lot between the ears. I expect 'e saw Dom wiv some bird and either fought it was Shirley or made the whole thing up. Unless, of course—"

"What?"

"Unless for the first time in 'is life, Dom was keeping 'is big gob shut. Anyway, I'd better go. Shall we meet up tonight after the band's played?"

"Is there another daytime show? I'm not quite the night owl."

"Yeah, tomorrow afternoon on the lido again. We'll meet you after that, then."

"That might not be convenient, Mr Walker, Rachel and I will be ashore for the day. However, we will come to one of the shows as soon as we are able."

Jimmy dropped his head and left Marjorie pondering over what he had told her and trying to remember it all so that she could tell Rachel when she saw her later. The only problem was, her head still felt muzzy from all the tablets she had taken, so she hoped she wouldn't forget everything. Time to return to her room – perhaps she could write it all down once she got there.

Chapter 15

"Did you enjoy your day out, dear?" Marjorie let Rachel into her room. Rachel was pleased to see her friend looking much improved from the morning. The colour had returned to her cheeks and the tension in her brow had almost disappeared.

"It was lovely, thank you, although we missed you. We did the historical tour as planned and visited the Old Town where we had a couple of hours' free time. We also bumped into Shirley Venables—"

"The wife of the angry cruise director." Marjorie finished the sentence for her.

"She happened to be on the same tour bus. We did manage to chat to her, but not for long as Sarah wasn't keen to intrude on her outing."

"Or her own, no doubt – and I can't say I blame her. She doesn't get much time off, does she? Anyway, what did you find out?"

"That she takes a good photo with a mobile phone and that she's a quiet sort of girl. That's about it. She doesn't seem the type to be snogging the likes of Dominic Venables in a public place – I wonder if Dalton's got it wrong. I took a quick peek at the photos on her mobile phone, but there wasn't anything obviously incriminating."

"Maybe Dalton does play economically with the truth as his friends intimated."

"But why lie about something like that? It doesn't make any sense."

"Perhaps he can't help himself. Some people are like that. I knew a girl many years ago who used to invent all sorts of things, so much so that in the end she convinced herself the stories she made up were true. Such keen and elaborate stories she told, could have made it as a successful author, but alas, lies were the undoing of her."

"How so?"

"Not satisfied with telling stories about herself and her own imaginary exploits, she started making up stories about other people – harmless stories at first, but when she got the attention she craved, the stories took on a dark and sinister turn. Any friends she had managed to hang on to soon gave her the cold shoulder."

"Did she tell any stories about you?"

"Oh yes – I had been a scullery maid in a Lord Grayson's household and learned how to pretend to be a lady. After that, I moved to London, pretended to be titled and sucked Ralph in by doing all sorts of creative things! To be honest, I found it amusing, but Ralph flatly refused to allow her in the house afterwards."

"What happened to her?"

"Emigrated, although that might be fiction too. We lost touch. Now, getting back to Dalton, the point is that there isn't always a reason people invent things – perhaps he's insecure. He's certainly not brash like the rest of the people he hangs around with, so it could be his way of drawing attention to himself. Or – he could be telling the truth, of course. Not all women are what they seem, and Shirley Venables may well have been kissing – I can't bring myself to say the other word – on the crew deck. And she could have been the same woman the young man saw in one of the passenger areas."

"Mm, I'll keep an open mind, but I'm more inclined to believe that Dalton made it up or was mistaken about the identity of the woman Dominic Venables was… ah hm… 'kissing'."

"I did discover more information about Mr Dominic Venables." Marjorie rubbed her hands gleefully with a glint in her eye. "Let's have tea before I reveal all. Mario will be arriving shortly with a fresh pot and a selection of pastries. I'm a bit peckish."

If it wasn't absurd, Rachel would have imagined that Marjorie's suite had been bugged as Mario arrived immediately her sentence was finished, carrying a tray laden with food. Rachel stared in disbelief at the pile.

"We'll be having dinner in a couple of hours!"

"I'm sorry, ma'am Rachel, but Lady Snellthorpe has hardly eaten all day, and if you don't mind me saying so, you have room to grow."

Rachel did keep herself in shape with hardly an ounce of fat, so she understood what he meant.

"You can't talk!"

Mario was tall and lean himself with slick black overly creamed hair, and now she looked at him more closely, she wondered if he had actually lost weight since she'd last seen him. After he'd left them, Rachel commented on it to Marjorie.

"Do you suppose he's ill?"

"I can't say I noticed. Remember, I only met him once before and it was under rather traumatic circumstances. Perhaps you should ask Sarah to give him a once-over."

Rachel decided to do just that. Not that Sarah would be able to tell her anything confidential, but she could at least draw her attention to it if he'd not been seen by the medical team recently.

"Okay, back to your Intel. What did you discover?"

Marjorie explained that she'd slept all morning and then got washed and dressed.

"Mario was clucking over me like I was a child," she huffed. Rachel laughed, knowing she had been responsible for that by making him promise to enquire after the old lady while she was out.

"I ended up stretching my legs on deck sixteen and wandered into the Sky View Lounge to sit for a while. I must have been feeling better because it's rather bright in there and I can't abide light during a migraine, but I chose it because it's also quiet and I was worried the noise from children playing might make the headache return." Marjorie went on to describe the goings on of various groups of people who passed through the lounge and watching another cruise ship sail away. "I was about to return to my room when who should turn up at my table but the band manager, Timmy Walker."

"Jimmy."

"That's right, Jimmy – he looks so much more like a Timmy, don't you think? But yes, him – seeing me, he came over to join me, mainly to ask when I might decide to book the band as they get snapped up and such like. I won't bore you with the details. After giving me his sales patter, he finally got on to talking about Dom, as he calls him. For all his car salesmen-type veneer, he did seem genuinely upset about the death."

Rachel thought it was probably more the money he used to make from the singer he was upset about, but didn't want to burst Marjorie's bubble.

"What did he say?"

Marjorie poured another cup of tea and finished off a breaded chicken finger fillet before answering. Rachel saw a glint in her eye as she sipped her tea.

"It seems that this Dominic Venables was a regular Casanova, usually with other people's wives."

"So I gather, but was there any new revelation? Did he say anything about Gordon's wife, Shirley?"

"No, he doesn't hold much truck by anything Dalton says, but he did mention his own wife had a near miss when Mr Venables tried to pull a fast one while Jimmy was out of town. Sounds like she was one of the few who managed to resist the deceased man's charm."

Rachel was thoughtful. She'd imagined Jimmy's wife to be an older woman, but that wouldn't necessarily put the lead singer off, she supposed.

"I know what you're thinking. I thought the same. Turns out his wife has kept herself in shape and is very attractive. He showed me a photograph and she is rather stunning – I told him she looked like an ex model. Jimmy – are you sure it's not Timmy? – laughed and explained he never knew what she saw in him, but they are very much in love."

"So she didn't succumb?"

"Apparently not. She showed Venables the door and informed him she would be telling her husband about his behaviour, and she did."

"That can't have done their working relationship any good."

"That's just it. Jimmy says they had a huge row, Venables assured Jimmy he wouldn't go near his wife again. He says they agreed never to talk of it and carried on as normal."

"How forgiving! Do you believe him?"

"He seemed sincere enough, but he also said that our Mr Venables would make a play for every woman he met."

"That puts me in my place as one of the many then," said Rachel, remembering how he'd made a beeline for her in the bar the night before he'd died.

"You have a far better fish to fry. That other fellow, Ray, said Walker and Venables argued all the time, didn't he?"

"It seems like they all argued, and still do. What a dysfunctional group of people. I'm amazed they didn't come to blows before." Then Rachel remembered that they had done just that a few nights ago.

They finished their tea and decided to get ready for dinner. Rachel returned to her room no nearer to knowing who might be responsible for the death of Dominic Venables, but mentally moving Jimmy higher up the list of suspects. The list that seemed to grow ever longer.

Waverley stood to attention, hovering outside the door to Rachel's suite.

"Mario told me you were with Lady Snellthorpe so I decided to wait," he said gruffly.

Rachel raised her eyebrows quizzically. *You mean you didn't want another ear bashing.* She smiled to herself.

"Will this take long? I'm about to change for dinner. Marjorie and I are meeting an elderly couple we have got to know during the cruise."

Two can play gruff.

"I don't mean to intrude, but I need a statement from you regarding the scuffle yesterday."

"Scuffle? A scuffle is when two people play at it. This seemed more like an unevenly matched boxing contest where one party continues to rain down blows while the other's out cold, but you know that already." She remembered the strength it had taken to pull Gordon off the prone Dave and the fear in the young man's eyes. "I don't want to appear rude, but I really don't have much time." She mellowed. "Perhaps I can come and see you later this evening or tomorrow morning?"

"I'm busy tonight, captain's dinner with some paying guests, but tomorrow morning will be fine. Would nine o'clock suit?"

"That will be fine, see you then."

Waverley turned on his heels and marched along the corridor. Rachel was exasperated, not able to work him out. One minute he was encouraging her to help and the next he was positively standoffish.

Perhaps the captain's told him to keep me out of it again.

Rachel quickly showered and changed into a jade green cocktail dress ready for dinner, choosing white open-toed shoes with a small heel and a deeper toned green stole to cover her shoulders. The mirror revealed a healthy glow developing as a result of spending time in the open air and she opted to apply only a light smattering of makeup without foundation. Then it was time to collect Marjorie, who had arranged for them to meet up with Ron and Mabel for pre-dinner drinks.

Marjorie was ready and waiting, dressed in a black evening dress with matching shoes and a red snug. Her bright-blue eyes twinkled under the light of the corridor.

"You look gorgeous," Rachel told her admiringly.

"And so do you, dear, but then you look divine whatever you wear. It's time young Carlos got his priorities straight."

Rachel's boyfriend, Carlos, had been exceptionally busy with his private detective agency and had been taking jobs that required him travelling both nationally and internationally. A recent case had taken him back to Italy to recover some stolen jewels taken from an estate in Norfolk. Carlos didn't mind travelling to Italy as he still had distant relatives there and it allowed him to catch up with their news. Lady, the Springer Spaniel, had travelled with him on his last trip and helped sniff out the hidden gems.

"If you mean what I think you mean, I'm not ready," said Rachel as she took the old lady's arm and led her down the corridor towards the lifts. Changing the subject, she remarked, "You appear to be a lot better than you did this morning. Has the head cleared?"

"Mostly, just a bit fuzzy, but at my age, fuzziness is not unusual." She laughed. "I'll stay on the wagon tonight, though."

"Good idea," agreed Rachel.

Chapter 16

Sarah hurried into the waiting room towards the end of a hectic surgery and noticed Shirley Venables sitting alone in a corner. She smiled and called her through to the clinic room.

"We meet again."

"Sorry I didn't say anything earlier. I forgot I needed an appointment until my phone beeped a reminder."

"No problem."

Sarah pulled up the woman's medical record on the computer and a reminder flashed as to why she was there, but she asked anyway.

"What can I do for you?"

"My pill implant needs changing."

"Okay. Have you had any problems with it?"

"None, just some spotting which can be annoying at times."

Sarah looked at the screen. Shirley Venables, thirty years old, married with no children. After checking her weight and blood pressure, Sarah asked, "Are you happy to have this implant removed and a replacement in the other arm?"

"Very happy, we're not ready for children." Sarah noticed the other woman's eyes filling up. "I don't want children with my husband."

"I see."

Shirley and Gordon had only recently joined the *Coral Queen* and Sarah hadn't got to know them very well. Obviously the events of the past few days had taken their toll.

"I'm sorry about Gordon being arrested."

"I'm not," said Shirley, starting to cry. Sarah handed her a box of tissues from the desk.

"Would you like to talk about it?" she asked softly. Shirley looked unsure, but Sarah smiled gently, encouraging her to take her time. "Let me get you some water."

After leaving the room to get glasses of water for them both and explaining to Gwen that she might be a while, Sarah returned to find Shirley sitting up straight. She handed over the water and wondered for a minute if the woman would cut and run, but she remained in her chair. Sarah shuffled her own chair round to face Shirley and prodded gently.

"Sometimes it helps to talk."

Shirley looked Sarah in the eye. She had big brown eyes underneath the false lashes that glistened with tears. Beneath the heavy makeup, she would be beautiful.

"Things are not good between us, they haven't been for a long time. I'm grateful for the break."

Sarah was beginning to believe the affair with Dom might have some truth in it. "Go on," she said encouragingly.

"We met on our first cruise contract. He's not good looking, but it didn't matter. We hit if off straight away. He seemed so funny and attentive, he made me feel like a beauty queen.

"After a whirlwind romance, we got married as soon as our contracts finished and we moved to Wales where Gordon originates from. I was happy there for the first six months, but we never went out. He didn't seem to have many friends, but then I realised he just kept me away from them.

"I began to get restless and feel like a prisoner in our home. I complained I was lonely – my family are in Munich. Neither of us could find work locally so we decided to apply to work on cruise ships again as a couple."

"Did you meet his family while you lived in Wales?"

"Only at the wedding. Gordon raged about his parents, he said they preferred his brother who had always been more outgoing. I didn't witness that at the wedding – they seemed a nice couple. They tried to talk to Gordon, but the relationship was strained. Gordon appeared standoffish and waspy whenever they spoke to him. They phoned a few times a week, but Gordon would always end the conversation on a negative note. I started to notice how insecure he could be and blamed his parents, but—"

Her voice cracked and Sarah waited patiently for her to continue. She placed a hand on the other woman's, encouraging her.

"It's not them, it's him. As soon as we started working on the *Jade Queen*, the ship before this one, he became obsessively jealous. Every time I spoke to another man, he would accuse me of having an affair. When I wasn't working, it became easier to be in our room rather than have to explain where I'd been and who I'd seen. I distanced myself from my fellow dancers and they thought I was snubbing them because I thought I was better than them."

Shirley paused again.

"Is he violent?"

"He's never hit me, if that's what you mean, but he's poisonous. He's aggressive without being physical. It started with accusations followed by an apology, but now it's much worse. I'm terrified of him because he shouts all the time – it's exhausting. I've stopped trying to reassure him because he never believes me."

She started to sob.

"But that's not right either. Whatever I do, nothing can convince him that I'm not seeing other men. Chance would be a fine thing – I have to account for my every movement.

"There was a man on the *Jade* – my dance partner, Miquel – he could see I wasn't happy. One day I broke down in training, upset because Gordon had called me a whore. Miquel asked me what was wrong and I told him. He put his arms around me and I cried on his shoulder, but Gordon burst into the room and saw. I became terrified when I saw the hatred in his eyes."

Sarah had seen that look by the crew pool and could understand her fear.

"He pushed Miquel away roughly. Miquel threatened him, but I pleaded with him to go. After that things got worse because he believed he had evidence of my infidelity. I withdrew into a shell and toed the line, hardly daring to speak to anyone – he even kept me away from any female friends. I felt more alone than I had ever been in my life.

"One night, after a blazing row, I told him I couldn't stand it any longer. That if he didn't stop, I would see my senior officer and ask for separation. He seemed shocked and calmed down, and then he applied for this cruise director's job and got it. Now I see he was just plotting to have yet more control. As cruise director, he has a full itinerary of all the activities. Before I could at least get fifteen minutes' peace, but since we've been on board this ship, he's followed me everywhere. He always knows where I am and turns up unannounced. I don't understand how he gets away from his job so often, but he seems to be able to delegate."

Sarah's heart burst with compassion for this woman.

"Was it worse when his brother came on board?"

"Much worse. I only met Dom once before when he sang at our wedding. Gordon warned me he was a womaniser back then. I wondered if it might help Gordon to have family on board, but he was more jealous of him than anyone. I would go so far as to say he hated him."

"Why did he help him to get the job in the first place?" asked Sarah.

"I really don't know – maybe he did kill him."

"Would he be capable of killing his own brother?"

"I've asked myself that question a thousand times and I'm still not sure. I didn't even know he could be physically violent until I heard what he did to that poor passenger on the lido deck. He hated Dom enough to kill him, particularly when he became convinced I was having an affair with him."

"What made him suspect that?" asked Sarah.

"Because it would appear that Dom stole every girlfriend Gordon ever had."

"Did Gordon tell you that?"

"No, Dom did when he made a play for me. He had drunk too much and started bragging about it, told me that since he'd been with every girl his brother had had, a wife would be no different. He grabbed me and kissed me in a public corridor of all places. I was shocked and pushed him away, but not before we had been seen by a young man."

Sarah remembered Dave's story and wondered if this had been the incident.

Shirley's eyes became fiery as she continued. "I told him if he ever touched me again, I would tell Gordon."

"What did he say to that?"

"He laughed in my face and patted me on the head. I hated him for what he'd done to Gordon, and in turn for what he'd done to me. I realised he had caused Gordon's behaviour.

"That night, Gordon accused me of having an affair with his brother. He said someone had told him, and not to deny it. I cried and asked him to go for counselling. I explained we couldn't go on like this, but that riled him even more. For the first time, he terrified me – I really thought he might hit me, but he stormed out and slammed the door. He didn't come back that night. The next day, I heard Dom had been killed and I went numb."

"Did you think Gordon had done it?"

"I wondered, but I can't believe it. I still don't. Yesterday, though, I did speak to my manager, Ms Doherty, about my situation and explained I was finding it difficult to work with Gordon becoming more and more volatile. She said she would try to get me moved, but I feared that would make him worse so I refused. Later, I heard what he'd done to that young man and that he was under house arrest. A few of the girls have been kind to me, so I bunked down on their floor last night. Today when I met you and your friend, it was the first time I've been free in a long time. I realise how unhappy I am and now I just want to get away from him."

Sarah hesitated for a moment. "Stay there, I'll be back in a minute." She asked Raggie, the medical team steward, to take coffee through to Shirley and explained briefly to Gwen what Shirley had told her. Gwen picked up the telephone.

"Leave it with me. Tell her that by the end of her show tonight, she will have new living quarters."

Sarah told Shirley what Gwen had said. The other woman's eyes lit up.

"Really? Is that possible?"

"Yes, it is. Not only that, but now your husband's under house arrest, he will not be able to follow you around."

Shirley looked at the clock. "I need to get back to work for the second performance. Can we do the implant tomorrow?"

"Yes, of course. Come to morning surgery and I'll do it then."

"Thank you so much." Shirley stood and embraced Sarah then bounced out of the door, emancipated. What an awful situation to find oneself in. Sarah shook her head in disbelief.

"The more time I spend on board this cruise ship, the more I feel like I'm living in some sort of soap opera," said Brigitte, stuffing goulash into her mouth in the officers' restaurant. Brigitte and Bernard had waited for Sarah to finish surgery following her delay. "I told you before, men are scum."

Bernard put his hand on his heart in feigned pain. "I admit some men are, but some women can be unpleasant too, especially ones from France." He sat back in his chair, puffing out his chest in mock victory.

"Stop it, you two, this is serious. That poor woman has been a prisoner in her own marriage."

"You're right. He deserves everything he gets from the sound of it." Bernard was a sensitive man who loved his family dearly and Sarah knew he was just as horrified as she was by the unfolding events. She patted his hand.

"So what happens now?" asked Brigitte.

"As luck would have it, one of the dancers finished her contract this morning and left the ship to stay with her family in Estonia. Gwen spoke with Waverley and Rosa and they have arranged for Shirley to move in with her old roommate, another dancer from the troupe, who is also one of the girls she was out with this morning. Waverley is going to tell the guard outside the room she was sharing with Gordon to bring him to his office for questioning while Shirley goes to pack her things to prevent a scene. He will then be told what has happened. She'll be safe while he remains under house arrest."

"There is one good thing that's come out of this," said Bernard with a smirk on his face.

"That is?" asked Brigitte.

"Murder solved without the need for Rachel." He smiled triumphantly.

"Yes, I suppose he is the most likely candidate, and he certainly had the motive. What a horrible brother, though. No doubt Waverley will be in his element if he can wrap the case up."

"As will the rest of us," said Brigitte. "I really don't like the idea of murderers roaming around the ship."

"Me neither," said Sarah, quietly. "I just hope we're not barking up the wrong tree."

They looked at each other before Bernard raised a glass. "A toast. To no more murders."

"To no more murders." They clinked glasses in celebration.

Chapter 17

Rachel walked Marjorie back to her suite after dinner, insisting the old lady have an early night to allow full recovery from the migraine that had plagued her on and off all day. Marjorie didn't argue, which Rachel took to mean she was still suffering.

"Sleep well, Marjorie. I'll see you in the morning." Rachel kissed her on the cheek.

"Goodnight, Rachel. Enjoy the rest of your evening." Marjorie winked.

After grabbing a summer cardigan from her own suite, Rachel headed off to the Jazz Bar to meet Sarah. Crowds were building up in the entertainment areas as the second run of the theatre show had finished, so Rachel had to negotiate her way through excited cruisers.

She heard the familiar sound of smooth jazz emanating from the bar before she entered. The bar was packed with people enjoying an evening out. Rachel squeezed past a group of elderly men who, on noticing her, parted politely to let her through.

Chivalry isn't dead after all.

Sarah, Brigitte, Bernard and Graham were easy to spot in their officer whites, and Rachel was pleased Gwen was with them as this was more of a rarity. Graham rose from his seat and shook her hand.

"How nice to meet you again, Rachel. I heard you were on board."

"Good to see you too, Dr Bentley, and the rest of you." She smiled. "I take it no emergencies are allowed this evening?"

They laughed, but Rachel spotted the emergency medical bag next to Sarah.

"Alex is dealing with a few minor injuries as we speak and Sarah is on call for us nurses," Gwen explained.

"What can I get you to drink?" asked Graham. "I'm treating the team tonight as a thank you for all their hard work."

"Yes, take advantage, it doesn't happen very often," Bernard teased.

"If you're sure – I'll have a martini and lemonade, please."

Graham made off towards the bar while Bernard and Sarah shuffled along their bench to allow Rachel to join them in their booth. Gwen and Brigitte sat opposite. Rachel looked admiringly around at the medical team, knowing from previous experience that the passengers and crew couldn't be in safer hands if the worst were to happen. They were a happy team who had recovered from the trauma of having a difficult and devious colleague joining them on her previous cruise.

"You're glowing even more than when we met the other night, Rachel," said Bernard. "Blooming, I would say. Love must be suiting you."

Rachel blushed while grinning at the small man who always had a happy demeanour, even under pressure. He had come through a difficult challenge on the previous cruise unscathed, despite finding himself in a vulnerable situation which, in retrospect, could have been extremely dangerous.

"I feel well. Sarah and I had a good day out today, Tallinn is a beautiful city." She chose to ignore his reference to her and Carlos.

"It is indeed. I have been ashore quite a few times there," said Gwen. "Where's Lady Snellthorpe?"

"I sent her to bed – she had a migraine today and couldn't join us on shore, so I wanted her to get some rest. If it was left to her, she would have battled on and joined us here."

"Good for you, that lady needs to take more care of herself." Graham had arrived back with a waiter in tow carrying a tray of drinks. "She's a rare breed these days, a real stalwart."

"I forgot you are acquainted with her." Rachel smiled.

"I knew her husband too, he was just the same. Pride of Britain, people like those two. Take note, Bernard."

"I will, sir." Bernard laughed. "By the way, Rachel, were you told the murder case has been solved without you?" He lowered his voice. "Chief Waverley is certain that the man in the drink was pushed by his brother."

Rachel raised her eyebrows. "Really? Marjorie will be disappointed, she's enjoying playing murder mystery sleuth."

"And you're not?" asked Sarah sceptically.

"Not at all, I'm wounded you should think so. I'm only too pleased if the case is solved. I don't want the reputation of being a bad omen on board this ship. I am well aware how superstitious you sailors are."

"Er, hum, I've never considered myself a sailor," answered Graham.

"Me neither," said Brigitte. "I am a nurse who happens to work on a cruise ship."

"No offence, but you know what I mean." Rachel enjoyed the banter.

"I'm afraid it will take more than a solved case to wipe your reputation clean," Gwen chimed in. "There was still a murder on board, something that only happens when you're cruising."

"Oh dear. In that case, guilty as charged, but hopefully no more. Why has Waverley decided it was Gordon after all? Not that I don't believe it, but there are still plenty of others with a motive."

Brigitte's radio went off, calling her away. "Catch you all tomorrow, I'm meeting up with some friends." She dashed off.

"Goodnight, don't get drunk," shouted Graham.

Sarah lowered her voice and explained what had happened during evening surgery and how Shirley had opened up about her marriage and the longstanding jealousy and control.

"Poor woman," said Rachel. "I actually feel quite sorry for Gordon too, though. Not that it excuses his behaviour towards his wife, but how awful to have a brother like that."

"It takes all sorts," muttered Graham. "I'm not happy this sort of behaviour was going on under our noses. I've checked through the man's medical records and he gets a clean bill of health from the doctors on his previous ship, both mentally and physically. Either he's a good liar, or the assessments weren't thorough enough – the man's clearly unhinged. I'm going to be meeting up with the administrators while we're in Russia and requesting we delve a bit deeper into the mental health of the crew on board our ships. We have to do better."

"Great idea," said Gwen. "Let's not blame ourselves, though. We learn from these incidents and do our best to improve things. However, some will slip through the net, regardless."

"None can be worse than Lauren," said Bernard, bitterly. "She was right under our noses."

"If you lot are going to be doleful, I'm going to bed," said Sarah, which brought the team back into the present. One thing about medics, Rachel had learned, is that they are quick to take advantage of the good times. Before long they were laughing and joking, with Bernard playing the jester that he was.

As the laughter subsided, Graham looked at his watch.

"It's after midnight, I'm going to turn into a frog if I don't get to bed soon." He stood up to leave. "Goodnight, team, we must do this more often."

"Only if he's paying," Bernard joked after the doctor had left.

"Behave yourself, Bernard," scolded Gwen before she turned to Rachel. "Are you coming to the wedding on Sunday?"

"What wedding?" Rachel looked at Sarah, shocked.

"Not me, silly. I haven't given her the invitation yet, Gwen," Sarah replied, leaning down towards her handbag and taking out two envelopes which she handed to Rachel. One was addressed to Lady Snellthorpe and the other was to Rachel herself. Puzzled, she tore open the envelope to find a *Coral Queen* headed wedding invitation:

PLEASE JOIN US FOR THE WEDDING OF

Eva Sipka & Darren Higgs

SUNDAY AT 2PM

THE CORAL CHAPEL

CORAL QUEEN

DINNER AFTERWARDS IN THE CREW CAFÉ FOLLOWED BY DANCING BY THE CREW POOL

"Now I'm even more confused. I know who Eva is, but who's Darren Higgs?"

Sarah lowered her voice. "Jefgeny Popov that was – he changed his name just to be on the safe side."

Rachel beamed. "Oh that's amazing – they're getting married, that's wonderful. How are they? Has Eva had the baby?" Her words tumbled out in her excitement. The couple had been on the previous cruise where Rachel had helped solve a crime.

"Slow down, Rachel. I've been so busy telling you about Jason and me, I forgot to fill you in on all that's happened to them. Eva had the baby last month, a boy named Erik after Jefgeny's – or rather, Darren's friend, who you will remember. Eva is now taking a further six month break to care for the baby and has returned to Slovenia. Darren is still working on board and sending money to support Eva. They have special permission to marry on board this weekend and Captain Jenson will conduct the service. They insisted on waiting until you were taking a cruise before they married because they desperately wanted you to be here for the occasion. As soon as they discovered you were travelling with someone else, they added an invitation for her. They are really looking forward to seeing you."

Rachel grinned from ear to ear. "And I them. I'm so happy. I can't wait to tell Marjorie, she'll be thrilled because I told her all about our adventures last summer."

Rachel bounced back to her stateroom at the end of the evening, but not before putting the invitation under Marjorie's door. She would explain in the morning. What a wonderful evening – no more worries regarding the murder, and a wedding to go to.

Chapter 18

Rachel awoke early. It was dark. She looked at her watch: 5am. Refreshed in spite of having only had a few hours' sleep, she got up and pulled on jogging trousers and sweatshirt, deciding to take advantage of the quiet and go for an early morning run.

A mist hung in the air, hovering over the ship and giving it an eerie feel. The sea looked black beneath the greyness; the sun should have been rising, but Rachel couldn't see it through the grey, despite the ship travelling due east.

After performing some routine stretches by the side rails, she took off at a steady pace along the outside of the deck. Normally she ran on the running track on deck sixteen, but today she wanted a change of scenery so she chose deck fourteen. The deck was silent except for muffled shouting in the distance. She plugged earphones into her ears and switched to music on her phone as she started to jog.

After she'd run twice round the whole deck, the mist began to lift just as she passed the rails overlooking the lido deck.

"What the heck?" She stopped suddenly and stared down at the main pool. "Hey you, stop!"

Rachel raced down the steps to find a man floating face-down in the pool. But before she had the chance to call for help, she felt a blow to the back of her head and everything turned black.

Seeing stars, Rachel found herself struggling for breath, submerged in the pool. Lifting her befuddled and drenched head to the surface, she managed to tread water towards the body and grab the man's jacket, pulling him to the side before clambering out.

An elderly couple were taking a morning stroll on the deck above.

"I need help," Rachel shouted. "Call security and medics."

The couple looked shocked, but did as they were instructed while Rachel tried to haul the wet body out of the water. The elderly man came to her assistance and they managed to pull him out. Dizzy and light-headed, Rachel was relieved to see Brigitte and Graham arriving.

"Help him." Rachel pushed Brigitte away.

More white uniforms were arriving, so Rachel allowed herself to be examined by Alex and put on a stretcher.

"How did he get there?" she heard Waverley shout. "Call Ravanos, now!"

Rachel turned round and recognised the man from the pool was Gordon Venables, coughing and spluttering as he was brought round following resuscitation. Waverley looked down at Rachel, concerned.

"Are you alright?"

After touching the back of her head and feeling the sticky viscosity of blood, Rachel grimaced.

"I'll be fine," she answered, looking at the blood on her hand. "I'm not sure my phone will be, though." Her heart sank as she saw her brand new iPhone floating in the pool. Waverley reached in to pull it out and handed it to her – the screen was blank.

"I want to get her to the infirmary for checks," said Alex. "You guys, take this stretcher." Two pool attendants appeared along with security officers and medics. Then Sarah arrived and took Rachel's hand.

"Come on, let's go."

Pleased to be moving as she was starting to shiver through the wet clothes, Rachel looked up at her friend.

"Is he going to be okay?"

"Yes, thanks to you. We'll talk more when you're out of these soaking clothes. They're bringing him down too. I'm getting flashbacks to your first cruise, Rachel Prince."

"Trying not to think about it," said Rachel. "So much for case solved."

The infirmary buzzed with hurried but controlled activity once they arrived. Rachel felt sleepy and kept being told to stay awake. Sarah helped her out of the sodden clothes and she was glad to be dry, although the white hospital gown was less welcome.

"Great, now I look like something out of *ER*."

The curtains were pulled around her and monitor leads attached to her chest and arm, a clip to her finger. Sarah checked the monitors and wrote notes while Bernard shaved a bit of hair at the nape of Rachel's neck away in order to apply glue to the gash at the back of her head.

"Looks to me like your shoulder took the brunt of whatever hit you, the bruising's already coming out," he said.

The activity outside the curtains sounded distant; Rachel couldn't focus enough to hear what was happening. Then the curtain opened and a worried looking Marjorie appeared.

"My darling girl." The old lady took Rachel's free hand and sat in a chair offered by Sarah. Rachel managed a smile.

"Sorry."

"Don't be. At least you're going to be alright. Don't talk yet. He's hovering outside, itching to come in, but Dr Bentley won't let him just yet."

Rachel knew she meant Waverley and was pleased for now not to see him; she didn't imagine she would make much sense.

Dr Bentley raised his voice. "Look, this is not a circus. Everybody out except the medical team. Sorry, Jack, that includes you. I'll call you when the patients are stable enough to be spoken to, but for now my team need to get on with their jobs without interruption."

Marjorie chuckled which made Rachel smile.

"My spinning head is a bit better now," she said. "Can I have a drink, Sarah, and is the drip necessary?"

"Yes, you can have a drink, and yes, it is necessary. Don't be difficult, you lost a lot of blood."

"Okay, in that case, no problem."

"What would you like to drink, dear?" asked Marjorie. "I'll find that nice medical attendant, Raggie, to get you something."

"Black coffee, please."

"Coming right up." Marjorie left to find Raggie.

"How are you feeling?" asked Sarah.

"Like I've been hit over the head."

"Can you remember what happened?"

"Vaguely. I'm wracking my brains at the minute, but I need to close my eyes."

"Try not to go to sleep, we need to make sure you remain conscious."

"I'll try. Coffee might help. I'm tired from last night, I only had a couple of hours' sleep."

"It did surprise me you were out so early. I was just finishing up treating a passenger when the code blue came through and couldn't have been more astonished to find you lying on a stretcher again. Really, Rachel, what is it about you that attracts violence?" Sarah frowned, her unusually dull hazel eyes close to tears.

"I don't know, but I'm here to tell the story. Come on, Sarah, cheer up. It could have been a lot worse."

"That's what bothers me, Rachel. I don't know what I'd do without you. You're my best friend."

Rachel squeezed her hand as Marjorie came back.

"Raggie is bringing coffee for you too, Sarah. You've had a shock," she said kindly.

Sarah smiled at last. "You're right. I'm overreacting again. I'm not rational at the minute."

Rachel sat up and Sarah fluffed up the pillows behind her before checking her monitors and writing notes on her chart at the end of the bed.

Pleased to see her friend appeared to be back in control, Rachel asked, "Can I get rid of these monitors? I feel like a high-tech robot with all these tubes and wires."

Dr Bentley appeared and said good morning tersely while checking the charts, and then he smiled at Rachel.

"It seems you have escaped yet another attack aboard our ship, young lady. You're out of the woods, but someone will need to be with you for the rest of the day, I'm afraid. We can remove the tubes and wires, though."

"Thank you."

"I can be with her," said Marjorie.

"Me too, in between surgeries," said Sarah.

"In that case, you can be discharged. I won't be able to keep Chief Waverley away from you any longer, though. Are you happy to see him before you leave, or would you prefer him to come to your room?"

"Before I leave, but can I have some breakfast first? I'm starving."

"You can indeed, Miss Rachel." Raggie appeared with a pot of coffee. "Trays are on the way from the kitchen. What can I get for you? There's food for everyone."

Jack Waverley was beside himself with worry and could sense his blood pressure rising as the realisation of what had occurred on board his precious ship sank in. He had just started to relax again after concluding that Gordon Venables murdered his brother in a fit of jealous rage. He hadn't been concerned about Gordon's denials – the evidence against him was mounting and Waverley felt sure that once all the facts were gathered, his man would crack. Now, that same man – supposedly under house arrest – had turned up almost dead in the main swimming pool.

After being turfed out of the infirmary, Waverley assigned a security guard to make sure Venables didn't move.

"Where's Ravanos?" he bellowed into his radio as he stormed out of the medical centre.

"He's outside your office, sir," came the reply.

Waverley marched towards his office in a rage, seeing the guard sitting outside.

"Wait there," he snarled.

After unlocking his office and going inside, he called down to the kitchen for coffee and toast, acknowledging the need to calm himself down before interviewing his inept security officer. He kept the blinds closed and put on a relaxation tape before sitting at his desk and practising the deep breathing exercises Graham Bentley had recommended.

The door opened and in came the ever ebullient Brenda with his breakfast. If anyone could help him to relax, it was she.

"I'm so sorry, darling." She placed the tray down and kissed him on the head, then his cheeks, then his lips. He found himself softening in her embrace and kissed her deeply, wishing he didn't have to work.

The lingering kiss came to an end. "You sure know how to make a man feel better."

"I do hope so." She smiled seductively. "Now, eat." She poured him some coffee. "I have to get back to work, but remember, I'm on a promise tonight."

As he watched her leave, he made up his mind – time to remarry. She understood him and was the best thing that had happened to him since his unnecessarily toxic divorce.

He opened the white vertical blinds shielding his office from the corridor and called Ravanos in. The man looked nervous.

"Sit," Waverley commanded.

Ravanos took the seat in front of his desk while he sat behind it and fired up his computer. He looked up at his officer, finding that his anger had dissipated and confusion had replaced it.

"How did Venables end up in the lido swimming pool?"

"I don't know, sir. I thought he was in his room until I got the call."

"Well, Houdini he is not, so admit it, man: did you fall asleep?"

"No, sir, I was awake all night. The only interruption came around 04.30 when one of the crew called me to sort out a disturbance in the corridor. I was only gone a couple of minutes. Just an argument between two of the entertainment team. They calmed down and went to bed."

"Do you think it was a ruse?"

"Looking back, it must have been, sir. Venables must have been ready to slip away; there's no way he would have had time to wake up, get dressed and leave otherwise."

Waverley was thoughtful. "Why would he want to do a disappearing act at that time in the morning? There's nowhere for him to escape to. What was he up to?"

"I'm really sorry, sir."

"Don't worry about it, sounds like we've both been played. I need you to find the crew who distracted you and interview them formally. They will be lucky if I don't get them fired. I'm going back to the medical centre to interview Venables, if Dr Bentley will let me in. At least he's agreed to let me speak to Miss Prince now that she's well enough to be discharged."

Ravanos heaved a sigh of relief and scurried out of the office before Waverley could change his mind.

Waverley pulled up the security record of Gordon Venables again and scanned through to check he hadn't missed anything. Next of kin, Shirley Venables, wife of twelve months. Enhanced DBS check clear, no name changes, worked for the cruise line for three years, one report of threatening behaviour towards a crewman Miquel Josephs, but complaint dropped by Josephs, and Venables promoted and moved to *Coral Queen* within six weeks.

Why was the charge dropped? There's always a reason – something isn't sitting right.

He picked up the phone.

"Call head office and get me the file on a Miquel Josephs working on the *Jade Queen* – urgently."

Next he pulled up the file on Shirley Venables. Dancer, good at her job, worked for the company for six years then had a break when she married Gordon Venables. Appraisals noted she had not mixed well with the dance troupe, which fitted in with her story. One warning for not turning up to do a show, said she had slept through – not unusual as they all worked long shifts on a cruise ship.

His eyes stopped reading and he studied the incident again, finding it linked to a private doctor's report that he couldn't access. He emailed the chief medical officer on the *Jade Queen* and requested information about the incident, explaining the situation and telling him that he needed to know if Venables was ever violent to his wife. He was beginning to sense he might be getting somewhere.

Still believing Venables to be guilty of murder, he shut down the computer and marched towards the infirmary.

Chapter 19

Marjorie brought some dry clothes from Rachel's room which the younger woman gratefully accepted, and she dressed ready to leave. On opening the curtains, Rachel saw Gordon lying in the bed opposite, looking bemused and terrified. He lifted up his head and stared at Rachel glumly.

"I understand you saved my life, thanks." His lips trembled as he mumbled the words.

"Anyone would have done the same thing," she answered, forcing a smile in spite of the pain in her neck and shoulder. He didn't seem to remember her from either of their previous meetings. "Did you know your attacker?"

"No, he grabbed me from behind and forced me into the pool. The last thing I remember is having my head dunked underwater and struggling to get away with all my might. I panicked because I can't swim, choked as I inhaled water, then everything went black. The next thing I remember is waking up here."

Rachel crossed over to his bedside and looked down on the puny man, remembering how just a couple of days ago he'd been beating the brains out of a young Welshman. Did he realise it was she who had pulled him away? If so, he was giving nothing away.

"I'm Rachel, this is Marjorie."

He looked up, not paying much attention to them, but nodded to Marjorie nonetheless.

"Gordon," he answered quietly. "I'm the cruise director, or should I say, was the cruise director?" His tone turned bitter.

"Was?" questioned Marjorie, obviously ready to continue the subterfuge.

Bernard sat at a desk in the background. Seemingly happy to let the conversation continue, he winked at Rachel.

"They suspect I killed my brother. He went overboard in Copenhagen."

"We are aware of that tragedy," continued Marjorie. "Didn't he fall?"

"They say someone pushed him over. It wouldn't surprise me either way – he drank heavily so could have fallen, and he had enough enemies to warrant murder. But he wasn't pushed by me. Now my wife's left me and I'm under house arrest, plus someone wants to kill me." He looked down at the bed and tears dropped like rain, causing a wet patch to form on the hospital sheet. His bottom lip trembled and his shoulders shook as the emotions were released.

Knowing his wife had taken advantage of the situation to escape from this hideous man didn't bring out too much sympathy from Rachel, but she tried to sound kinder than she felt.

"Do you have any idea who would want to kill you?"

"Not a clue. I don't know that many people on board this ship, apart from the entertainment staff. I guess someone in my brother's band might have it in for me if they think I did him in, but then again, they didn't like him that much either. The only other person who might want to harm me is—"

Waverley entered the infirmary alongside Dr Bentley, interrupting his flow.

"You were saying?" prodded Rachel. Gordon shook his head and looked down at the sheet.

Great timing, Chief.

"Glad to find you looking better, Miss Prince," said Waverley. "May I have a few words?"

"You can use Gwen's office, and then you're free to leave, Miss Prince." Neither the chief of security nor the doctor gave away that they knew Rachel, which she was grateful for. It would help if she managed to speak to Gordon again.

"I'll be back to speak to you soon, Mr Venables," said Waverley tersely.

Gordon nodded acknowledgement before looking down at the sheets again. Rachel and Marjorie followed Waverley to Gwen's office.

"Good to see you looking better, Rachel," said Gwen. "I'll leave you to it. Raggie will bring in a tray of tea and coffee."

"Thank you," said Rachel, grimacing as a pain shot through her neck. "I think I'll sit down, if you don't mind?" She sat down gingerly on the settee in the centre of the office. A large coffee table and two comfortable chairs surrounded it. Gwen's desk was at the rear with a formal office chair behind, similar to the setup in Waverley's office. A Gauguin print decorated the wall and some personal knick-knacks sat on the desk. A few medical journals lay on the large glass coffee table and marble coasters were stacked neatly in a classy looking coaster rack.

Marjorie joined Rachel on the sofa while Waverley placed his muscular frame in one of the chairs. He looked compassionately towards Rachel and warily at Marjorie.

Raggie brought in the tray of drinks and placed them on the table before leaving and closing the door. In spite of his obvious concern, Waverley looked rather chipper, like he had something to celebrate.

Maybe he's cracked the case.

"I can't believe this has happened to you again, Rachel. I can't apologise enough."

Rachel shrugged. "It wasn't your fault."

"Not directly, but the security team let you down nonetheless, and I take full responsibility for that. It appears a diversion occurred – manufactured, we believe – and Gordon Venables slipped out of his room without his guard noticing. The security officer didn't realise he was missing until we called down to find out how he'd escaped."

"I did wonder how he escaped house arrest. What was he up to?"

"We don't know. The team is going through security footage, but the cameras around the lido have been tampered with so I don't hold much hope."

"Do your men not watch the screens like I've seen on television?" asked Marjorie.

"I'm afraid not. Cameras are scattered throughout the ship, but they are not permanently monitored. They record information and we pull them out if an incident occurs. We saved footage of the fight Gordon Venables started the other day, but there's nothing from early this morning on the lido deck."

"I've never noticed those cameras. I did suspect there would be cameras hidden around the ship, though," said Rachel.

"Most of them are around the shops, bars and in the casino. We also scan the periphery of the ship in case anyone goes overboard. The ones on the lido deck aren't that well-hidden, to be honest, so anyone actively looking for them would be able to spot them. We've had more installed since the erm—" he coughed as per his habit "—events of your first cruise when Lady Snellthorpe was attacked. The cruise line is pretty anti surveillance on the whole, but we've had to move with the times – it was only a matter of time. We tread a fine line in relation to security versus privacy, but I can assure you there are no cameras in any private areas."

"I'm pleased about that," said Marjorie. "I do sometimes look at those smoke alarms in the suite and wonder."

"Staterooms, suites and private balconies are completely off limits, I can assure you. We also tend to keep our cameras hidden so as not to alarm passengers. Anyway, I digress. Can I ask what you heard and anything you remember from this morning, Rachel?"

"I didn't hear anything other than Ed Sheeran and Sam Smith."

Waverley looked perplexed.

"Oh, do come on, Chief, get with the times," said Marjorie. "They are two superb young English singer/songwriters and have huge followings."

Waverley coughed again. "I'm a classical fan myself, they must have passed me by."

Marjorie softened. "Me too, actually, but Rachel has introduced me to some of the more recent talents, many of whom I can't tolerate. But even this old girl can listen to the two Rachel mentioned."

"I expect my daughter knows who they are, she's about Rachel's age."

"Hello, you two – I am still here!" Rachel laughed.

"Oh yes, sorry – do continue," said Waverley.

"As I said, I had earphones in, so… hang on a minute, I did hear something just before I put my earphones in. I thought it was a muffled cry, but couldn't be certain so I dismissed it. In retrospect, it could have been Gordon."

"What time was that?"

"I guess it would have been around five-thirty. I'd done about fifteen minutes of stretching and gazing out to sea. After that, I ran a couple of times around deck fourteen, and on my third round the sun broke through the mist and I caught sight of two men in the pool, one being held under. I yelled something and ran down the steps.

"By the time I got to the pool, I saw a man I now know was Gordon Venables face down. The next thing, someone walloped me from behind and I found myself underwater. When I realised what had happened, I was more concerned about Gordon and just about managed to drag him towards the side of the pool and call some passers-by to help."

Waverley took notes. "It was definitely a man?"

"Ninety per cent certain, but I did only get a fleeting glance and they were both in the water. I didn't see him get out of the pool because there's a blind spot when you reach the top of the steps."

"I suppose it's too much to hope that you could give a description?"

"Sorry, it was misty, and the person wore a black hoody and a balaclava like a cat burglar. When I yelled, he turned to look at me, but the sun had disappeared and I only saw a profile. All I can tell you is it looked like a male, six foot tall, average build, wearing black. I didn't even recognise Gordon until I pulled him out of the water."

"I don't understand why he would be out there," said Marjorie. "Surely he wasn't going to swim for it."

Waverley put his notebook in his uniform pocket. "That's what I'm going to find out," he said. "By the way, what were you talking about when I came into the infirmary?"

"He was thanking Rachel for saving his life," said Marjorie.

"Mm." Waverley looked sceptical. "Well if you remember anything else, you know where to find me. I realise I was going to take a statement from you today with regards to the fight you broke up, Rachel, but under the circumstances that won't be necessary. I suspect the cruise line will be contacting you concerning compensation again."

Marjorie, giggling, nudged her. "At this rate, you'll be able to buy your own flat in London."

Waverley trudged off, muttering to himself.

"You are awful to him," Rachel scolded.

"Oh, really? I do quite like the man, and he did seem remarkably happy today, did you notice?"

"Yes, I did think that. I wondered if he had someone in custody for the murder, but obviously not."

"He looks like a man in love to me."

"I hadn't thought of that." Rachel hoped so – she had grown fond of the security chief, in spite of his mood swings. She knew he wanted her on his security team, and once again she pondered whether that might actually be a safer way to cruise.

"At least I'd get my own taser." She uttered her thoughts out loud, much to Marjorie's amusement.

"Come on, young lady. I imagine that blow to the head has addled your brain if you're considering joining cruise ship security."

They walked arm in arm towards the rear of the ship, taking the lift up to their suites.

Chapter 20

Sarah took over from Bernard in the infirmary so that he could help with morning surgery. Gordon had fallen asleep, so she took the opportunity to chat to Jason who was on guard outside to ensure he didn't slip away again. They hadn't been able to meet up for the past few nights due to opposing shifts.

Jason stood as she opened the door and smiled at her affectionately. They knew better than to embrace while on duty, so she settled for the sparkle in his eye.

"I'm glad it's you."

"I volunteered," he answered smugly. "How's our man?"

"Sleeping. What happened? How did he get away?"

"He gave Ravanos the slip, that's all I know. The chief's interviewing your friend, Rachel, to find out if she saw anything. She's brave, that girl, I'll give her that."

Sarah frowned. "Too brave sometimes. I worry about her, but it's in her nature to investigate. I just wish she didn't feel the need to do it on board this ship. It's fine when she's in uniform and armed with radio, whistle, stab vest, truncheon and the like, but here, she's completely unarmed and vulnerable."

He laughed. "The police don't carry whistles anymore, Sarah."

She poked him in the ribs. "You know what I mean."

"The chief still suspects we've got our murderer in there." He nodded towards the infirmary, behind the door.

"Is he right?"

"I guess so. It's not my investigation – he's put me in charge of the stag group and cheerleaders. What a handful they are."

"Lucky you… what do you mean, the cheerleaders?" A stab of jealousy momentarily caused Sarah alarm, but Jason seemed oblivious.

"I'm tasked with making sure the guys in the stag party don't cause them any bother. It's hard when they all seem to be pairing up – I can't tell them not to flirt with each other, much to the chief's disgust."

"How do you find Dave Hughes?"

"Haven't seen a great deal of him. He's quite brawny underneath that weak facade – I did notice him boxing a punch bag in the gym. I don't know how he let Gordon Venables get the better of him – seems like a complete mismatch to me."

"Perhaps he's trying to build up some muscle."

"Maybe, but he's got quite a six pack already."

"Kettle and pot!"

"Yeah, but I spent years in the army having mine drilled into me." He smirked flirtatiously.

Sarah recognised the footsteps coming towards them as Waverley headed their way.

"He looks happy," she whispered.

Jason stood to attention.

"Anything to report?"

"No, sir, he's sleeping. Nurse Bradshaw was just asking about the Welshman, Dave Hughes."

"Hm, I'm sure." Waverley's knowing smile told her their relationship had been rumbled, but then it was his job to be aware of what went on aboard the vessel. "I take it I'm allowed to wake him now?" he asked Sarah.

"Yes, come on through."

Waverley nodded to Jason to follow them and they walked towards the bed where Gordon Venables was out for the count.

Sarah approached him and gently touched his shoulder. "Mr Venables? Gordon?"

He woke, startled momentarily with the appearance of a rabbit in headlights, but calmed when he saw Sarah smiling at him. He looked behind her towards Waverley and Jason and resignation filled his eyes. He sat up slowly.

"Could I have a drink, please?"

"Yes, of course." Sarah handed him a glass of water. "Would you like a hot drink?"

"Tea, please."

"Gentlemen?"

"Tea as well," said Waverley.

"Coffee for me, please." Jason winked at her.

Sarah picked up a phone on the wall and dialled through to Raggie with drinks requests.

"Glad to find you looking better," said Waverley, taking a seat by Gordon's bed and removing a notepad from his pocket. Jason remained standing.

"I suppose you want to know how I got away."

"I know the how, but I don't understand the why."

"I received a phone call from someone saying they needed to meet me urgently about Shirley. They said she was in danger. You wouldn't have listened to me," he said bitterly, "so I called a couple of guys and asked them to distract the security guard from outside my room."

"Very enterprising," answered Waverley caustically.

"Anyway, the guy on the phone told me to meet him on the lido deck by the main pool. He must have been waiting for me in the shadows. As soon as I arrived, he jumped me and pushed me in the pool. I panicked – I can't swim."

Waverley rolled his eyes, disdain evident. "The pool isn't that deep."

"And I'm not that tall," Gordon snapped back. "I was scared; the man had me in the pool before I realised what was happening and he pushed my head underwater. I'm terrified of drowning. I don't remember any more."

"Who was he? Did you see his face?"

"No, it was dull and misty. I heard him say something – it sounded like 'That's for Mam', but it didn't make any sense."

Waverley sighed, frustrated. "Did you recognise the voice? Did he give a name? Anything?"

"I thought I recognised the voice on the phone, but I can't remember where from. He didn't give a name. He wore a balaclava and he was strong, that's all I remember. I didn't get a chance to see anything else. He didn't attack me to converse."

Ignoring the sarcasm, Waverley persevered. "Do you have any idea who it was?"

"No, unless it was one of Dom's mates."

"On that note, are you ready to confess to the murder of your brother?"

Sarah noticed panic fill Gordon's eyes.

They were interrupted by the arrival of drinks and Jason poured them and passed them around, winking at Sarah again.

"I didn't kill my brother. You can't still think I did! Surely, whoever tried to kill me also killed my brother."

"Unless they tried to kill you *because* you killed your brother," retorted Waverley.

Gordon took a deep breath and the panic in his eyes turned to anger – the anger Sarah had witnessed by the crew pool when he'd spoken about his brother.

"You have no evidence I killed him and yet you insist on locking me up. You've no right, and now you've caused my wife to leave me. Where is she?"

"Oh no, Mr Venables, you managed to cause your wife to leave you all by yourself. Fits of jealously, rage, controlling and abusive behaviour. You're a disgrace to our sex." Waverley's face had reddened, a witness to the strain he was under, but he quickly regained control. "Your wife is quite safe now."

"Well I want to see her." Gordon looked desperately to Sarah for help, but she had no inclination to assist in this matter. She shrugged her shoulders.

"That is quite out of the question. Your wife does not wish to be near you. Your employment has been discontinued as of yesterday – the sooner you confess to killing your brother, the sooner I can hand you over to the authorities. We're in Russia presently – I'm sure they will know how to deal with you. Your wife, of course, will remain an employee on board ship."

Gordon's fists clenched. He threw his tea at Waverley, who ducked and the tea hit Jason, soaking his pristine white uniform.

"Really, Chief? Is this necessary?" Sarah snapped as Waverley quickly cuffed Gordon to the bed rail.

"Sorry. Perhaps you'd better go and change," he said to Jason. "I'll take up your post until you get back."

Sarah accompanied Jason outside, handing him a roll of paper towelling used for covering the examination beds, and he thankfully wiped himself down.

"What's got into Waverley?"

Jason laughed. "At least it was only lukewarm tea."

Sarah loved Jason's ability to look on the funny side of life, one of the reasons they got on so well. She also recognised the fierce loyalty to his boss – something he'd learned in the army.

"You have to trust the man next to you has got your back," he'd told her when recounting some of his experiences. Some traumas he wouldn't share and she knew better than to ask – those conversations he reserved for his ex-army friends. Perhaps one day he would tell her.

Sarah returned to the infirmary, finding Waverley and Gordon chatting away like old friends. Bad cop had disappeared for now and good cop was in full flow. As she got closer, she heard them talking about football of all things.

Men! She would never understand them.

While Sarah and Jason were outside the infirmary, Waverley had recognised the funny side of what had happened and, thankful for his own lucky escape, had burst out laughing. Surprisingly, the petulant Gordon had joined in, and before long they were belly laughing at the ridiculousness of the situation.

"I don't mean to hit where it hurts, but you are going to have to come to terms with the fact that your wife wants a break from you," Waverley said as the laughter subsided.

Gordon looked down at his bed sheet. "I've made a right mess of things, haven't I?" Waverley didn't answer, but the look on his face showed concurrence. "How much trouble am I really in?"

"It's not looking good, and now someone wants you dead too."

"I really didn't kill my brother. You've got to believe me. I hated him, yes, and I feared he had got to Shirley. He's always hated me having anything he couldn't take away. Dalton told me they were having an affair. Yes, I could have killed him. I tracked him down that night and told him I'd found out about the affair. He laughed at me and said, 'Not yet'!"

"Did you believe him?"

"I wanted to, and now I do because he would have bragged about it as another conquest. Ironic, isn't it? For once, he'd failed, but I'd already had a go at Shirley."

"So believing your wife was having an affair, you killed him," Waverley persisted.

"No. I felt like it, but I didn't. I decided to tell Rosa he was upsetting passengers – which was true – and get him the sack. I found out after his death she already planned to sack them all."

"Didn't you get him the job in the first place? Why would you want him fired?"

"I thought it would be fun – we could leave the past behind us. He'd called me, begging me to get him a contract, told me he needed the work, convinced me he'd changed and we could make up, have a fresh start. Stupidly, I agreed. Secretly, I was always his biggest fan, lived in his shadow. Pathetic, isn't it? I just wanted us to be friends, but he had played me like he always did.

"As soon as I saw his smug face coming on board, I realised he hadn't changed one iota. I wanted to punch him in the mouth, but he's always been stronger than me. I'd gone down to greet him, but I turned around and went the other way. He was a bully and a misogynist, but I didn't kill him."

Waverley frowned. Either this man was a brilliant liar, or he was telling the truth, but that would cause huge problems.

Now what?

Gordon continued talking, looking a lot more relaxed. "He was the world's worst brother. He even supported an English football team, for goodness' sake."

"What's wrong with English football teams? I'm a lifelong Chelsea supporter."

"I'm a Cardiff City fan through and through. We didn't do so well in our last match with you guys, though."

Sarah entered the infirmary and raised her eyebrows at Waverley, who smiled back at her.

"No real harm done. It was only tea," he said sheepishly.

Sarah scowled at him, but didn't say anything.

Waverley rose from his chair and unlocked the handcuffs. "I don't think we'll be needing these."

"Thanks." Gordon brightened.

Waverley marched through the doors and took a seat outside, waiting for Jason Goodridge to return.

Chapter 21

Rachel and Marjorie were sitting on the balcony, enjoying watching the activity dockside in the port of St Petersburg, Russia.

"I'm so sorry to have ruined your day out." Rachel apologised for the fourth time.

"You really don't have to be. I've visited the city quite a few times, and at least it's an overnight stopover so perhaps Dr Bentley will clear you for going out tomorrow."

"Oh, no! That's not happening. We're not cancelling the ballet tonight. I know how much you are looking forward to it, and so am I. Sarah and Jason are coming too so we finally get to meet him properly. We're going and that's that."

"I'm not sure, dear. You should rest."

"I've rested since six o'clock this morning. If I have any more rest, I'll go spare." She looked at Marjorie. "If the shoe was on the other foot, you would go."

Marjorie caved. "You're right. I would, but should we ask Dr Bentley?"

"Certainly not, he'll err on the side of caution because he won't want to be liable. We'll just go. We'd better not say anything to Sarah until we get there either or she might dob us in."

"Dob us in? Whatever does that mean?"

"Sorry, I've picked up a few colloquialisms. It means tell on us – snitch and the like."

Marjorie laughed. "Are you ready for some lunch?"

Before Rachel had the chance to answer there was banging at the door. Marjorie let Sarah in.

"Hey, you two. How's the invalid?"

"Feisty," answered Marjorie.

Sarah laughed. "I take it she's being a difficult patient? I'm happy to take over now if you want to go ashore, Marjorie."

"I am here, you know. What is it when someone has been injured? I still have all my faculties despite receiving a blow to the head. Anyway, it's more my shoulder that hurts."

"And your pride by the sounds of it." Sarah joined them on the balcony.

"We were just talking lunch actually," said Marjorie.

"Yes, and I insist we go to the buffet because I'm not sitting still for much longer," said Rachel firmly.

Mario knocked and entered as if on cue. "Lunch, ladies?"

Rachel glared at Sarah. "I suppose this is your doing?"

Sarah shrugged. "Just for today – tomorrow you can be out and about again."

Rachel shot a warning glance to Marjorie, who looked uncomfortable but didn't say anything. They ordered food from the room service menu and hot drinks to go with it.

After Mario left, Rachel looked at Sarah. "Before I forget – have you noticed how thin Mario looks? I'm sure he's losing weight he can't afford to lose."

"I didn't, to be honest – I was focussing on the menu."

"Well take a peek when he returns. There's something not right. He looks gaunt and his eyes look too big for his head. I'm sure they didn't look like that before when we met."

Sarah looked thoughtful. "Does his hair look thinner?"

"I haven't noticed, sorry."

"Okay, but now, back to the patient in hand."

Rachel sighed. "Well at least tell me if they've managed to find out who attacked me this morning."

"No, Waverley interviewed Gordon who said he'd had a call from someone telling him Shirley was in trouble. He admitted to arranging the diversion and went to meet the person who'd allegedly phoned on the lido deck."

"I don't suppose he knows who that was."

"You're right – he doesn't. He said he recognised the voice from somewhere but couldn't place it and that the person said something like 'That's for Mam' when he pushed him under."

"How strange," said Marjorie. "This Gordon doesn't strike me as the most imaginative of men so I assume you and Waverley believe him."

"Yes, we do. I also believe him when he says he didn't kill his brother and I think Waverley has come round to that way of thinking now too."

"So we're back to square one," answered Rachel.

"*We're* not back anywhere. You're not to do any further investigating, Rachel Prince. Let Waverley get on with it."

Marjorie was about to object, but Rachel shook her head in warning. Sarah had gone into protective mode so it was best not to stress her out just yet.

Mario arrived with the lunch, and while he was placing the trays down and serving them, Sarah, true to her word, watched his every move carefully without him being aware.

"Bon appétit, ladies."

Sarah followed him to the door and had a quiet word before returning to the balcony.

"Well?" asked Rachel.

"None of your business," answered her friend.

"That's not fair."

"Okay, I've asked him to come to surgery to see Alex or myself and have some blood tests."

"Is it serious? It's not cancer, is it?" asked Marjorie, looking concerned.

"I don't think so. From my brief observation and his symptoms, it looks like he's got an overactive thyroid, but we'll need to take a history from him and do the blood tests and examine his neck. If it is what I think it is, he should respond well to tablets."

"Why hasn't he sought advice, do you think?" asked Marjorie.

"I don't know. It could be a fear that he'll lose his job if it's something serious."

"Yes, he supports his family in San Salvador, he told me that when I first met him," said Rachel.

Rachel decided not to ask any further questions about Gordon or Mario, and not to give Sarah any clue that she would still be going to the ballet this evening. Marjorie said she would stay on board today to build up her energy for the outing arranged for the next day and Sarah seemed satisfied with that.

They spent the afternoon playing scrabble in the ship's library after Rachel managed to persuade Sarah to allow her out for a little while. Eventually Marjorie was able to reassure Sarah that she would keep an eye on Rachel and that she should go and get ready for her date with Jason. Sarah reluctantly left them to it, but the light in her eyes suggested she would quickly get over any feelings of guilt.

"Thank goodness," Rachel said after she'd left. "I love Sarah to bits, but not when she's playing mother hen."

"You can't blame her for that. She's worried about you, and for that matter, I am too. Are you sure we shouldn't just stay here this evening?"

"Oh please, Marjorie. I'm like a caged tiger. It's fine being on the ship when we're at sea, but I can't bear the thought of not getting on land when I can see it through every window."

"Okay, dear, but I can tell you now: on this occasion, your friend is not going to be happy to see you."

"She will be eventually when she sees I'm alright." Rachel answered more positively than she felt and wondered if she was being foolish. Her head ached, but she wasn't sure if it was psychological, knowing she would be going against medical advice and common sense. But she had committed herself now and wasn't going to back down.

Entry into Russia had been by far the most difficult Rachel had yet encountered during her cruising experiences, but not as onerous as some had suggested it might be. Once they were through Russian security, the tour guide had gathered them together, and while they were on the bus, had advised them to stay in groups and keep their valuables closely guarded.

"Unfortunately, tourists are often targeted by thieves and criminal gangs, but stay together and you will be fine."

The guide was about Rachel's age, her hair dyed ash-blonde and shoulder-length with coppery roots. She had large green eyes and wore dark eyeliner underneath and on the lids, causing them to stand out even more. This was Rachel's first visit to Russia and she was overly excited at finally being off the ship. From the bus, she observed a vibrant city of people going about their lives. They passed a few landmarks, but Rachel missed the names because of a chattery group in front of her yelling at each other to be heard above the microphone.

"Some people are just plain rude," whispered Marjorie. "They'll be the first to complain if they miss out on directions, mark my words."

Rachel took the old lady's hand. "Never mind, we're going to have a lovely evening. I'm so pleased you agreed to accompany me in my folly. Thank you."

Marjorie raised her eyebrows. "As if I had a choice in the matter."

When they arrived at the theatre, they were surrounded by traders as soon as they got off the bus. Rachel took Marjorie's arm to protect her, but did manage to buy a Russian Fez.

"Dad's always wanted one of these. I promised I'd get him one."

She bartered the price down with the assistance of the tour guide, who was also keeping a watchful eye on Marjorie to make sure she didn't come to any harm.

They made their way inside the theatre and were led to a four-seater booth where an astonished and miffed Sarah was wide eyed.

Rachel hugged her. "Sorry, but I knew you wouldn't let me come if I'd told you."

"You should know better," Sarah said to Marjorie, who looked suitably admonished.

"Don't blame Marjorie, I insisted. I've been looking forward to this for months, so has Marjorie. Her husband had promised to take her the next time they visited St Petersburg, but he died before he could make good on his promise."

Sarah softened immediately. "I didn't know or we would have brought her with us."

"She wouldn't have wanted to cramp your style." Rachel smiled as she nodded towards Jason, who was entering the booth armed with drinks.

After Sarah got over her initial gobsmacked shock, she excitedly introduced Jason and relaxed just as Rachel had hoped she would. Sarah rarely stayed annoyed for long. Jason was the perfect gentleman, attentive to Sarah, but making sure that Rachel and Marjorie were well looked after. Rachel liked Sarah's new beau and hoped the relationship would flourish. For drinks, she stuck to mineral water at Sarah's insistence, although she wouldn't have wanted to drink alcohol anyway with the sore head she'd neglected to mention.

The Russians appeared to take their ballet very seriously, shushing and tutting at over-enthusiastic tourists who dared to whisper during the performance. The cast performed *Swan Lake*, something Rachel thought should have been familiar because she had heard it mentioned so many times, but she soon realised was not at all so. Watching a ballet in Russia struck her as the most wonderful way to spend an evening and her only regret was that Carlos wasn't there to witness it. He would have looked gorgeous in his tuxedo.

How was she going to tell Carlos she had become embroiled in yet another murder investigation? Come to think of it, why hadn't he phoned today? The IT wizard on board ship had managed to dry her phone out and get it working again and there had been no messages. Her muddled head wouldn't allow her to think for too long, though.

She noticed Marjorie wiping away tears from her eyes and realised that she too was thinking of the man she loved: her late husband.

Rachel hoped she had done the right thing by bringing Marjorie and that it wasn't proving too painful. She squeezed the old lady's arm.

During the break, Rachel looked around to see if she recognised anyone from the ship. There had been a couple of tour buses bringing people to the theatre and she hadn't recognised anyone on their bus. It was odd hearing Russian spoken all around her and she wondered how Lucretia Romanov, an opera singer she'd met during the previous cruise, and her oligarch boyfriend Vladimir were. He had been planning to propose on the return journey from New York.

I wonder if they're married.

Her reverie was interrupted by Jason bringing her a fresh glass of mineral water. He was hiding behind a pillar.

"What's the matter?" Sarah asked.

He groaned. "The stags, I just don't want to see them tonight."

"Where are they?" Rachel asked.

"Two o'clock."

The large group of young men, with young women interspersed among them, was sitting on the opposite side of the auditorium.

"I wouldn't have had them down as ballet fans," said Rachel.

"No, but the cheerleaders might be, and bees around the honey pot," said Sarah.

"Or pigs in muck," remarked Marjorie.

Rachel had taken out her binoculars and was observing the group to check they weren't annoying anyone. They seemed remarkably well behaved, considering their history.

"It's alright, they're not up to anything," she reassured Jason. "I can see Dave sporting a large black eye and Tonya hanging on his arm. Exemplary behaviour all round, as far as I can tell. They could have dressed a bit smarter, but other than that you can forget about them."

"They've probably been warned about any run-ins with the Russian police. They wouldn't stand for any nonsense," said Marjorie.

"Looking at him close-up, I think Dave looks familiar, but I don't know why," mumbled Rachel as she put the binoculars down and concentrated on the stage.

The second half was about to begin.

Chapter 22

Rachel slept fitfully as her shoulder continued to cause discomfort, but when morning came, she was in a sound sleep. The ringing of the telephone roused her.

"Hello?"

"Oh Rachel, I'm sorry, I've obviously woken you – would you like to go back to sleep?"

"No, I'm alright. What time is it?"

"Nine o'clock. I waited for as long as I dare, but I know you wanted to join the tour and we need to be dockside by ten."

"I didn't realise it was so late. I'll be with you in twenty minutes. Would you order coffee and croissants to your room?"

"Of course, see you shortly."

Rachel dived out of bed and into the shower, dressed quickly and was ready in fifteen. The only reminder of the previous day's injury appeared to be a bruise to the back of her neck extending over the left shoulder, along with the accompanying pain.

Marjorie was waiting cheerfully and looked pleased when Rachel arrived. "How's the wounded soldier?" she asked, giving Rachel a peck on the cheek.

"Much better, thank you, just a bit of a sore shoulder. I bet you've been awake for hours. Have I missed anything?"

"Not really. Sarah called to check up on you but I dissuaded her from phoning your room, explaining you probably needed a lie in. I promised to let her know if you didn't answer at nine, and she was going to race up here and let herself in. I've called to reassure her that you are quite well."

Rachel headed over to the table and poured herself some coffee while grabbing the croissants and lathering them with butter and jam.

"You know, I don't think I ate much yesterday. I'm starving."

Marjorie gave her *that* frown, telling Rachel without words that she had no idea what it was like to be starving, but refraining from regaling her with a lecture about the starving in Africa as she had on a prior occasion.

Marjorie's suite looked neat and tidy as always with the large flat screen television displaying CNN with the sound muted. The subtitles didn't reveal any good news so Rachel chose not to watch. The old lady had dressed smartly in a warm summer dress with a light cardigan over the top. Although this was a spring cruise, the weather had been exceptionally warm.

"You also missed His Lordship this morning. I wouldn't let him disturb you."

Rachel realised after a moment's confusion she meant Waverley.

"Did he say what he wanted?"

"Him, tell a batty old woman like me? No, he said it wasn't important and that he'd catch you later. I explained we would be out for the whole day. He asked if we could pop to his office after dinner this evening."

"We?" Rachel grinned.

"I'm sure that's what I heard, my hearing isn't so good these days."

"Your hearing is perfect, but I wouldn't go without you anyway."

Marjorie smiled with pleasure at the revelation. She picked up a jacket from the built-in wardrobe and took hold of her handbag.

"It's time we got a move on."

Rachel slurped down the rest of her coffee and, with a mouthful of croissant, ran to her room to clean her teeth and grab a jumper and handbag while Marjorie waited anxiously. By the time they'd picked up Sarah from reception and arrived dockside, their tour crowd had already gathered. The guide ticked them off in more ways than one and they boarded the bus taking them into St Petersburg for a shopping trip and some sightseeing. They were not allowed off ship in Russia except on supervised tours due to visa restrictions.

"Look who's here." Marjorie nudged Rachel and pointed to Ray, Dalton, Nick and another man occupying the long back seat of the bus, too busy talking to notice them.

"That must be the new lead singer," said Rachel.

"Not quite new – remember Nick told us he left previously following a fight with Dominic Venables over a woman. According to Nick, he had more reason to kill Dominic than anyone and had threatened to do so."

"With the best will in the world, we can't place him at the crime scene, more's the pity. I don't want to know, anyway. Let Waverley get on with it."

Rachel thought she recognised the new man but couldn't place him. Marjorie raised her eyebrows and threw Rachel a sceptical look, but didn't go there.

Instead, she said, "Look who else has joined the tour."

Rachel took the aisle seat next to Marjorie while Sarah sat across from them. Shirley Venables climbed on to the bus with the same group of women as she'd been with in Tallinn. She looked happy and attractive.

"And just to complete the party—" It was Rachel's turn to nudge Marjorie, who stood up to find out who she meant. "It's the stag party and the cheerleaders."

"Oh dear, I do hope this doesn't turn out to be a carbon copy of *Murder on the Orient Express*."

"More like *Seven Brides for Seven Brothers* the way they're carrying on. Anyway, there's nowhere to hide a body."

"Behave, you two," Sarah scolded.

The bus passed some of the more popular tourist attractions before stopping at a bazaar where they could use their luncheon vouchers. The tour guide explained they could then spend an hour shopping in the marketplace, but suggested they didn't go off alone and to stick to the Government approved souvenir shops.

"That charge treble the price," remarked Marjorie cynically.

"Don't worry," said Sarah. "We'll wander around the traders' stalls."

After the bus dropped them off, they sauntered into the busy bistro to have lunch. On finding a table, they sat down and perused the menu. Rachel saw Shirley heading towards their table.

"I wanted to thank you for everything you did for me the other day."

Sarah blushed, never comfortable being the centre of attention. "I didn't do anything really, but I'm pleased things are working out for you. It can't be easy."

An embarrassing silence hung in the air until Marjorie broke it.

"Hello, dear. My name is Marjorie – why don't you join us for lunch?"

"Oh, I wouldn't want to impose," said Shirley.

"You wouldn't be imposing, please do join us," Sarah encouraged. "I should have invited you myself. This is Lady Snellthorpe, a friend of mine and Rachel's. Rachel you've already met."

Rachel smiled and pulled out a chair next to her, which Shirley gratefully accepted.

"Thank you and I'm pleased to meet you, Lady Snellthorpe."

Marjorie scowled. "Less of the Lady here, please call me Marjorie."

Rachel studied Shirley while she spoke to Sarah and Marjorie, pleased with how relaxed she seemed. The worry lines that had been so evident on her forehead had disappeared and her demeanour looked generally at ease, with just the occasional frown. Her bright green eyes reflected in the light of the café window.

Marjorie nudged Rachel's foot under the table. "Have you decided what to eat?"

"Sorry, I was miles away." She concentrated on the menu, relieved by the English translation next to the Russian. "I'll settle for a beef sandwich and tea, I'm not feeling very adventurous today."

The waiter took their lunch vouchers and brought their food. Sarah and Shirley chatted away like old friends.

Marjorie looked pleased with herself. "Now about our shopping. I want to buy Russian stacking dolls – Matryoshka, I believe they are called – for my housekeeper, Mrs Ratton, and for my maid, and a fez for Johnson. Jeremy will be content with a bottle of vodka, and for that matter, so will I. How about you?"

"A Fabergé egg and a tea towel for my mum – she collects tea towels. Matryoshka dolls for my niece, and I'm not sure what to get for Carlos. My brother will settle for vodka I'm sure and his partner will be happy with duty-free perfume."

"We'll find something for Carlos, but I fear if we don't get going, we might run out of time."

They said goodbye to Shirley who rejoined her group to go window shopping.

"Let's hit the stalls, then," said Marjorie, taking charge. "Will you be looking for anything, Sarah?"

"Nothing in particular, but if I spot anything, I'll stop."

After they'd walked around the packed marketplace and made their purchases, time was running out for meeting back at the bus. Marjorie turned out to be a proficient haggler and managed to get everything she needed while helping Rachel with the necessary bartering. Rachel just enjoyed the vibrancy of the market. She took note of the fully armed unsmiling police, who reminded her of how lucky she was not to be armed as a policewoman in the UK. The day would likely come when police had to carry guns – there were already more armed officers than ever before as a result of acts of terrorism, but the temptation to shoot first and ask questions later bothered her a great deal. She often debated it with her colleagues, some of whom were all too eager to carry guns. She hadn't even got to the stage of carrying a taser yet, but would be undertaking training in the near future.

All the security guards on board the *Coral Queen* carried tasers and had access to arms if required, Waverley had told her during one of their many conversations. She wondered how the investigation was progressing.

I expect the killer is one of the people on our bus, she mused uncomfortably. A member of the tribute band would be a likely suspect if suspicion moved away from Gordon.

"Come on, Rachel, you're dawdling." Sarah grabbed her arm. "You need to find something for Carlos. How is he, by the way?"

"I'm not sure. I tried ringing him last night and today, but his phone went straight over to voicemail. The last time I spoke to him, he was in Birmingham, about to break up a dog snatching racket. I'm beginning to worry. I've been so distracted by matters aboard the ship that I hadn't given much thought to it, but now I've tried to contact him without success, it's concerning."

"He's probably in a poor signal area."

"Maybe, but he usually tries to contact me when he knows I'm on land with a signal. We've been two days here and not a word. I'll try his office when we get back to ship."

"Did you hear from him in Tallinn?"

"Just a text saying the Birmingham thing was a bit complicated and not to ring him as he was doing some undercover work in between stakeouts. I thought he was referring to that day, but perhaps he has his phone off if he's still undercover."

"You know what you're both like when you've got something to investigate. I'm sure he'll be in touch today."

Marjorie, aware of Rachel's worry, squeezed her arm. "All will be well. He's sensible and will contact you as soon as he can. Now come on, dear. Let's find him a present. That will cheer you up."

Rachel, trying to extinguish the myriad of scenarios playing out in her head and assuage the feelings of guilt over being too wrapped up in her own problems, followed her friends.

Chapter 23

Shirley Venables entered the room where Sarah had just finished evening surgery. The fearful eyes and pallid face told Sarah something was seriously wrong.

Shirley handed her an envelope.

"What is it?"

The other woman remained mute, but nodded to Sarah to open it. Sarah noticed Shirley trembling as she took out a folded piece of *Coral Queen* headed stationery.

DON'T THINK YOU'VE GOT AWAY WITH IT. THERE'S NO ESCAPE. WATCH YOUR BACK.

The letters had been cobbled together using words from magazines, something like one would see in a television drama.

"I found it under the door of my room when I got back."

Sarah turned over the envelope and saw it was addressed to Shirley using similar cut-out words.

Placing it down on her desk, she said, "We need to show this to security, but I don't want to put any further fingerprints on it." Sarah took a pair of surgical gloves off a shelf and put them on, then slipped the paper back inside the envelope.

She picked up the telephone and called Waverley. There was no reply from his office so she had him radioed to meet them there urgently.

"What does it mean? Got away with what?"

Shirley was too distraught to answer for a few moments.

"I don't know what it means," she said eventually. "The tone is Gordon's, but how could it be? He's in the infirmary, isn't he?"

Sarah took her hand. "No, he was discharged this morning, but he's still under house arrest. Let's go find the security chief and show him the letter."

Sarah quickly explained the situation and where she was going to Gwen.

"I can take the on-call bag with me."

"No you won't. I'll cover until you get back. Brigitte and Bernard are having the evening off."

"Thank you." Sarah was pleased Gwen had come up trumps because she couldn't be sure how long the matter would take. "I'll be back as soon as I can. I'll call you on the radio."

Waverley's office was in darkness when they arrived, so they took a seat outside and waited. Sarah found distracting Shirley difficult and inwardly cursed Waverley for being so slow.

She tried a topic that might help the woman relax. "How did you get into dancing?"

Shirley stopped hand wringing for a moment, but continued to look down at them. Sarah noticed the wedding ring had been removed.

"My mum loved ballet but had to give up due to health problems, so she was determined to encourage me. I took ballet lessons from the age of three, but when I went to my first musical I fell in love with show dancing. I became enthralled by the dancers' creativity that resulted in the show saying so much more than it would have done otherwise. I now know all about choreography, of course, but back then I was mesmerised.

"I turned to my mum at the end of the show and told her that was the kind of dancer I wanted to be. She tried to push me to continue ballet for a while afterwards, but accepted that my heart wasn't in it, so she supported me in taking up dance classes in a local community centre. We didn't have a lot of money, but eventually I got a scholarship to go to a dance school in Berlin. The hardest thing was leaving my mum behind, but she wouldn't have it any other way. She wanted me to fulfil my dreams and I did, until I met Gordon. Now everything's ruined."

"It doesn't need to be," said Sarah gently. "It's tough right now, but it won't be like this forever. You have years of dancing ahead of you and you're really good. Who's saying you won't end up in a West End show some day?"

"Do you think so?"

Wondering if she might have been a little over optimistic, Sarah was relieved to see the looming figure of Waverley heading towards them. He could clearly tell by the look on Shirley's face something was seriously wrong so nodded curtly to Sarah before unlocking his door.

"Come inside, ladies. Please take a seat. Can I get you something to drink?"

"Mineral water for me, please, I'm on call," said Sarah.

"I'll take water too, please. I have a show at nine."

Sarah doubted Shirley would be able to perform, but didn't say anything.

After getting drinks and placing glasses on the coffee table, Waverley sat in a comfy chair opposite the sofa they occupied.

"Would you mind telling me what this is all about?"

Sarah handed him a pair of men's surgical gloves followed by the envelope.

"It's about this."

Waverley dutifully donned the gloves before taking the envelope. Sarah removed hers and stood up to wash the powder off her hands in the small WC at the back of Waverley's office. When she returned, she could see he was studying the contents of the letter.

"I don't understand," he said finally. "Why would someone threaten you? Gordon wouldn't dare."

"Don't you mean he wouldn't be able to?" asked Sarah.

Waverley looked uncomfortable and coughed. "Strictly speaking, he could, but he wouldn't, I'm certain of it."

Both women looked confused, and then Shirley looked angry.

"You let him go! How could you? You told me I would be safe." Her voice rose to screech proportions.

"He gave me his word he would not approach you in any way. Dave Hughes, the man he assaulted, said he didn't want to press charges, said it was a misunderstanding, and I don't have enough evidence to prove Gordon killed his brother. He's no longer under house arrest, but he has to report to my officer, Ravanos, and tell him exactly where he's going whenever he goes out."

Shirley looked terrified and Sarah was incredulous at Waverley's stupidity in letting this potentially dangerous man go. She would speak with Waverley in private about her feelings. She took Shirley's hand to prevent her from saying anything she might regret.

"I assume, then, you will have him re-arrested. The letter can only be from him."

Waverley loosened his collar and placed the letter and envelope carefully in an evidence bag before picking up the telephone.

"Send Ravanos to my office, pronto," he barked.

Poor Ravanos, he was not having an easy time of it. *He might be losing his job at this rate*, thought Sarah.

Ravanos arrived after about five minutes and looked warily at Shirley.

"You wanted to see me, sir?"

"Where's Venables?"

"He's in the crew bar with a few of the entertainment team."

"I need his movements since his release."

Ravanos took a notepad from his pocket. "He was released from house arrest at thirteen hundred. Stayed in his room until fifteen hundred when he reported he was going to the crew dining room for a snack as he hadn't had lunch."

Waverley coughed impatiently at the additional details, but he had asked so he would just have to listen to a blow-by-blow account.

Ravanos continued, "Returned to his room at seventeen hundred, went for dinner in the staff dining room at nineteen-thirty then to the crew bar where he's been ever since."

"Your job now, Ravanos, is to verify those details step by step. I need times and people who can confirm seeing him. Don't leave anything out. I don't suppose he's been in any of the passenger areas?"

"No, sir. You gave strict orders that he was to remain in crew only parts of the ship, sir."

"Quite. Off you go then."

Ravanos got to the door, but Waverley called him back.

"Ravanos, stop. First, I need you to go and find Venables and escort him here. I need to speak to him."

"Yes, sir."

Waverley looked sympathetically towards Shirley. "Mrs Venables, even if your husband did send this letter, it's pure posturing on his part. He wouldn't dare touch you."

"And that's meant to reassure me?" Shirley stared at the chief in disgust.

"Sarah?"

If he hoped for support from Sarah, he wasn't going to get any.

"Come on, Shirley. We will let the chief get on with his job. I expect he will keep a closer eye on your husband from now on," she said caustically. Sarah knew she was sailing close to the wind being subordinate to a senior officer, but she really did wonder if Waverley wasn't getting too long in the tooth for his job. If so, it didn't bode well for finding the killer roaming around the ship.

"I'll do whatever I need to do to keep both passengers and crew safe," he retorted. She felt his eyes boring into the back of her head as she closed the door of his office.

"Don't worry. He might be embarrassed, but he'll do the right thing. He always does," she told Shirley.

"Thank you. Do you mind walking with me to the theatre? I need to get ready for my show, and even though he's not supposed to be in the passenger areas, he'll know exactly where I will be and when. He will have studied my work schedule down to the last detail. I expect he's still been allowed to keep a copy in the room."

Sarah was only too pleased to be of help and walked with Shirley, handing her over to her friends when they arrived at the entertainers' dressing room. She squeezed Shirley's arm and kissed her on the cheek.

"Everything will be fine. You're safe."

After depositing Shirley, Sarah returned to the medical centre to find Gwen in her office.

"Quiet as a mouse for a change," Gwen informed her.

Sarah explained what had gone on and Gwen too looked surprised that Gordon Venables had been allowed to roam free, albeit in the crew areas of the ship.

"Poor Waverley," she said. "I think he's under pressure with the murder investigation and the constant fracas caused by our young stags. He will feel the error of his ways deeply, I fear. Thankfully, no real harm has been done."

"Apart from scaring the poor woman out of her wits," said Sarah. "I don't think Gordon Venables will be allowed out of sight of security again, though."

Chapter 24

Rachel caught sight of Sarah walking hastily away from Waverley's office as she and Marjorie turned a corner to meet with the security chief as arranged. He sat at his desk, staring into space, but when he saw them, he suddenly stood up and walked towards the door. Flustered, he coughed.

"Oh, Rachel, Lady Snellthorpe, do come in."

"You were expecting us?" Rachel had a sneaking suspicion he'd forgotten all about their appointment.

"Yes, of course. Please sit down, can I get you a drink?"

"If you're offering, I'll have a small scotch," said Marjorie.

"Just water for me. I had wine with dinner and I'm meeting Sarah in the Jazz Bar later if she isn't called out."

Waverley handed Marjorie a scotch and pulled a bottle of mineral water from the fridge. Rachel remained impressed with the facilities senior officers had in their offices, but they clearly weren't enough to console the security chief when he had so many conundrums to solve. She wondered if whatever was on his mind had anything to do with Sarah.

"I thought I saw Sarah in the corridor just now."

"Who?"

"Sarah, with Shirley Venables."

Waverley coughed again, indicating to Rachel that it had been her friend's visit that had brought about his ruffled appearance.

"Yes, I'm sure Sarah will tell you about it later anyway as there doesn't seem to be any confidentiality on this ship, so I might as well fill you in. Mrs Venables received a poison-pen letter – well more of a poison-print letter, actually." His attempt at humour couldn't conceal the concern in his voice. "The words were put together from printed matter, probably magazines. Here, take a peek, but don't touch it."

He laid the letter out on the coffee table, contained in a plastic evidence bag. Rachel and Marjorie stared in horror.

"Who would send such a thing?" asked Marjorie. "Don't tell me her husband gave you the slip again." As Marjorie laughed, Rachel noticed the redness rising from Waverley's neck to his face. She shot Marjorie a warning glance to go easy.

"As a matter of fact, I ordered his release this lunchtime on condition he kept us informed of his whereabouts, and I don't know why people all jump to the same conclusion. Why would he send it?" Waverley's defensiveness betrayed his guilt, and even Marjorie gave him a brief look of sympathy.

"You no longer suspect he killed his brother then?" Rachel changed tack.

"No, I don't." Waverley took a drink of water and continued, "Obviously, I can't rule him out completely, which is why I've kept him aboard ship, but it seems unlikely from what he's told me. He's very honest about his rage at his brother, but I think he looked up to him in a way, just couldn't stand up to him. Then that young man said he didn't want to pursue him for assault. He even encouraged me to 'let the poor man go', as he put it – quite benevolent of him, I thought."

"Thankfully not all people are consumed by malice," said Marjorie.

"I may be putting Gordon Venables back under house arrest, though. I can't take the risk of him harming his wife, but if he sent that letter, he's a bigger fool than I gave him credit for. I'll be speaking to him after you ladies have left. I can see he's just arrived."

Waverley walked to the door and spoke to the security guard, Ravanos, as he and Gordon Venables took a seat outside.

"I can see you're busy, so please don't feel the need to delay. Marjorie said you wanted to see me."

"Yes." He glanced towards Marjorie, unsure whether to continue, but decided to do so. "I wanted to ask if you have discovered anything new about the tribute band members. If Venables is innocent, it has to be one of them."

Marjorie gasped and Rachel, flabbergasted, eyed him with suspicion. "Why are you asking me? I thought you wanted us to stay out of your investigation."

Looking flustered, he answered, "I'll explain. One of our security officers, erm, fell down some steps last night and had to be admitted to hospital in St Petersburg." He coughed again and looked at them both, trying to gauge their reaction. Seemingly encouraged, he persevered. "To make matters worse, since early this morning, another guard has gone down with chicken pox, and Dr Bentley says he can't work until all the spots stop blistering. Normally, we would manage, even with two down, but there is so much going on with the stag party, the murder investigation and a spate of robberies. My team is struggling to deal with it all." He rubbed the top of his head where the hairline was visibly receding and sighed. "That's why I took the risk of letting Venables go on condition he remained in the 'crew only' part of the ship, didn't go near his wife and informed Ravanos of his every movement. We can't pick up a replacement for the injured officer until we return to Southampton. Rachel, I can even offer you a temporary contract with excellent remuneration."

His pleading eyes made Rachel laugh. She looked at Marjorie, who was stifling a giggle.

"I don't think so, thank you, but we might do some informal snooping if it doesn't ruin Marjorie's holiday. I haven't spoken to anyone from the band since the gig on the lido deck. They were on our tour bus today but didn't notice us."

"You don't need to worry about me," Marjorie said keenly. "I've been to the ballet in St Petersburg and that was the most important thing for me. Ron and Mabel are sharing the next two trips with us and I'm sure they won't mind looking after this old girl if Rachel needs to be elsewhere. Are you sure you wouldn't like the temporary contract, Rachel? It would give you a trial run to see if you might like to be a security officer in the future."

"How much is a generous remuneration?" Rachel grinned at Waverley.

Waverley relaxed back in his seat and smiled for the first time since they'd entered the office. "It would be more than a month's salary for a few days work. You're also due compensation for the incident yesterday – our insurance negotiator will be in touch about that."

"Thanks again for the offer, but I still don't want to take the contract. I will agree to do some informal investigating. Marjorie and I will see what we can find out, if anything. The murderer obviously believes they've got away with it if Gordon is innocent, but I'm sure you haven't ruled him out entirely?"

"Not at all. I'll take you up on that offer as long as you're both discreet. I can't have you putting yourselves in danger if you're not in our employ. I can't seem to get anything out of that lot anyway. I've done background checks into all three, along with their manager – two of them have been arrested in the past for drugs offences – both cited as personal use. The manager also has a previous conviction for fraud, but over twenty years ago, and nothing since."

"I can guess which two have the drugs offences," said Marjorie.

"Me too, Nick and Ray?"

"For once, Miss Prince, and with respect, Lady Snellthorpe, you're wrong," said Waverley gleefully. "It was the manager Jimmy Walker again, but his crime goes back donkeys' years, and Dalton Delacruz."

"Now that does surprise me, but as you say, it was for personal use and not unheard of in their line of work."

"Did you find out why Ray videoed the fight between Gordon and Dave Hughes?"

"I did enquire, he said it was instinct – apparently gets out his phone whenever he spots an incident – says it might make him rich one day. He surrendered the footage, and to be honest, it was poor quality, jumping all over the place. He was probably drunk when he took the video."

"He won't be giving up the day job, or in his case, the night job, anytime soon, then?" Rachel got up to leave. Marjorie looked at Waverley with a twinkle in her eye.

"You are having a difficult time of it, aren't you?"

"You'd better believe it." He chuckled. "It used to be such a cushy number working on a cruise ship. Things are looking up for me, though." Rachel noticed him fiddling with the box he had shoved in his pocket on their arrival.

Once out of earshot of Waverley's office, Marjorie took Rachel's arm. "Come along, Rachel Prince, this calls for a celebration. We are now semi-official sleuths."

Rachel wasn't convinced about involving Marjorie as she rubbed her left shoulder, still smarting from the pain of her near miss. The last thing she wanted was for Marjorie to be in any danger. She looked at the white-haired old lady fondly and determined she would protect her at all costs.

"What do you suppose he hid in his pocket when we arrived?"

"An engagement ring, of course. He's positively glowing. If that's not a man in love, then I'm in my dotage."

"You're a savvy one, that's for sure, and certainly not in your dotage. I take it you're joining us in the Jazz Bar this evening?"

"If you don't mind? I'm far too excited to sleep. Perhaps we can go to the Culture Lounge or whatever they call it afterwards – might as well get started."

They could feel the beat from the bass throbbing through the floor and drowning out any chance of speaking. Sarah was in uniform and dragging her on-call bag behind her. Marjorie put her fingers in her ears as they squeezed through hordes of middle-aged people enjoying the songs of their youth. Rachel hung on to Marjorie to make sure the frail old lady didn't get pushed over by exuberant patrons.

They managed to snag a recently vacated table in one of the recesses of the nightclub. Rachel caught the eye of a waiter and ordered drinks.

"I'm not sure this is such a good idea. What are we hoping to find out? And I'm decidedly conspicuous in uniform," Sarah complained, not at all happy that Waverley had recruited Rachel and, by implication, Marjorie into his investigation.

Rachel thought her friend could be right: the chances of them discovering anything during a performance were negligible, but Marjorie had seemed so keen, and she didn't want to disappoint her.

"Now we're here, let's just have a drink. We don't have to stay for long."

The three women sat in silence, watching the band perform. The replacement lead singer delivered as loud and competent a rendition as his predecessor, but lacked the charisma of the late Dom Venables. The band played *The Show Must Go On*, which seemed nostalgic and appropriate in view of what had happened.

"We're not going to find out anything. This is silly, and Waverley should not have asked you to get involved at all. I don't know what's got into him." Sarah had continually stated this throughout the evening, and Rachel had done her best to reassure her friend they would be careful. She sighed, knowing that Sarah had a point, especially as she had already been attacked once. Now the killer probably knew who she was. Could one of the band have hit her over the head? It was a disturbing proposition.

Looking at the lead singer, Rachel suddenly realised where she'd seen him before.

"That man, the new lead. He was the guy hanging around the atrium that day Waverley spoke to the rest of the band!" She took out her phone and scrolled past pictures of St Petersburg and Tallinn to the photo of the couple she'd snapped on the day Marjorie had had a migraine. "Look, it's him!"

Sarah and Marjorie studied the photo. "You're right, but what's the significance?" asked Sarah.

"It means they were on board the ship when we arrived in Tallinn. We'd docked and people were leaving the ship, but they didn't have any hand luggage, and Jimmy said the new singer would be joining the cruise that day. I wonder if he's been on board all along, with the woman in the photo. Apparently, he has as much reason as any of them to kill Dom Venables, and now look. He's stepped into his predecessor's shoes very comfortably, don't you think?"

"If you're right, he has to go to the top of the suspect list," said Sarah.

Marjorie looked pleased. "Put us in charge and case solved almost immediately. We do need to check whether he was already on board when we got to Tallinn, though. He might have arrived early and joined the ship that day. It's not impossible."

Marjorie was right. They needed to find out the man's identity and when he joined the vessel, but they seemed to be getting somewhere at last.

"On that note, shall we call it a night?" Rachel asked. The others agreed, and as if on cue, Sarah's radio beeped, calling her to a medical incident.

Chapter 25

The *Coral Queen* docked in Helsinki, Finland on Sunday morning, where Rachel and Marjorie took a private tour to the Nuuksio Reindeer Park. Marjorie had expressed an interest in visiting the park when they were making plans the day before, but time was limited due to the need to be back for the wedding of Eva and Darren (formerly Jefgeny). Ron and Mabel chipped in with the hiring of a private car, giving them the opportunity to do both.

Rachel would have liked to have seen more of Helsinki, but didn't want to miss the wedding, and as Sarah had been asked to work, she had decided to shelve the ice bar experience for a future cruise. Marjorie narrowed the options down to either seeing reindeers close up or heading to town for shopping. Rachel thought this was a no brainer.

"I'll take the reindeers."

The delight on Marjorie's face confirmed she had made the right choice. They were duly rewarded with a pleasant and comfortable car journey, plus the enchanting experience of being able to feed the reindeers by hand.

"Such gentle and placid creatures," remarked Marjorie.

Rachel agreed: they oozed calm, and for an hour, any concern over the investigation into her own attack and the murder of Dominic Venables was dissipated by the serenity of the magical experience among the beautiful reindeers.

"It's like all my childhood dreams come true. The idea of walking among the reindeers and meeting Rudolph was always far more exciting to me than receiving presents."

"What an extraordinary child you must have been," said Marjorie wistfully.

"Don't get me wrong, I still liked the presents," Rachel added, "but I love animals. Sarah would have enjoyed this, I'm sure. If she hadn't been a nurse, she would have been a vet."

"Where is she?" asked Mabel.

"She's on duty, doing morning surgery, and then she's helping decorate the crew area ready for the wedding later."

One of the reindeers interrupted the conversation, giving Rachel a gentle nudge, requesting more food. She giggled.

"Alright, you, here, take some." The plucky animal took the food from Rachel's hand.

After taking photos, feeding the animals and wandering around the park for an hour, they retired to a tepee where a log fire burned brightly in a central fire pit. Marjorie had been as excitable as Rachel all morning and was now in her element.

"How delightful," she said. "I love the smell of forest and burning wood."

"Well I'm loving the aroma of that coffee," said Mabel. "Let's find a seat."

They sat on fur-covered benches close to the log fire. The older people had chilled off, having spent so much time outside – it was a clear day, but with a brisk wind blowing, the temperature had dipped into the late teens. They soon warmed up when served traditional coffee and freshly made cinnamon cake.

The outing ended too soon for Rachel, who would have loved to have gone for a long walk through the national park. She determined to come back one day and do just that. The private car driver returned them safely to the ship and received a generous tip from Ron for his trouble.

On exiting the taxi, they heard the loud voices of Nick, Ray and the new lead singer, providing Rachel with a stark reminder of her promise to Waverley the day before. She groaned, attracting inquisitive looks from Ron and Mabel who knew all about the death of the obnoxious singer, but not about the attack on Rachel, or her and Marjorie's part in the investigation.

"Is something the matter?" asked Mabel.

"I enjoyed being out in the countryside for a while, that's all. Now I have to decide what to wear to a wedding!"

"What exciting lives you two lead. We need to get out more, Mabel." Ron put his arm affectionately around his wife's shoulder.

The company parted ways as Ron and Mabel were taking a shuttle bus into the city centre. Marjorie paused to purchase some souvenirs before going through port security.

Rachel watched the rowdy group of musicians who appeared to be leaving to go out for the afternoon. Dalton and Jimmy weren't with them, but a woman appeared from one of the souvenir shops and joined them. It was the woman Rachel had seen with the replacement lead singer a few days before, for certain.

I must remember to ask Waverley who they are and when they first boarded the ship. If they were on board prior to the murder, it added to the likelihood that one or both of them could have been involved in Dom's death.

Did the other members of the band realise they were on board?

Another disturbing thought entered Rachel's head: the whole band might be implicated, making Marjorie's flippant remark about *Murder on the Orient Express* a chilling possibility.

Surely not?

The entourage passed within inches of Rachel, but were too wrapped up in conversation to notice her. It was the first time she had seen them laughing and joking with no arguments. Rachel's gaze followed them until they boarded the next shuttle bus heading into town.

It took ages to decide what to wear to the wedding, the dilemma being that Rachel had only brought a mixture of casual clothes and evening dresses, but nothing in-between. Finally, she settled on an aquamarine cocktail dress, white stiletto shoes, a white jacket and handbag to match.

Having spent so much time choosing a dress, she had little time to do anything with her hair, so the long blonde mane was quickly brushed through and tonged into loosely flowing waves. Marjorie was already walking along the back corridor towards her room as Rachel dashed out.

"I see you didn't have any problem choosing what to wear, elegant as always." Rachel loved Marjorie's outfit: a lush pink suit with matching fascinator. It was the perfect choice for a wedding.

"Coming from someone who would look beautiful in a bin bag, that's rich."

Rachel took her friend's arm and they made their way upstairs to the chapel, arriving suitably early. Rachel spotted Jefgeny, now Darren, standing nervously at the front, talking to friends. The chapel was already two-thirds full with crew from all over the ship. Sarah called them over to where the medical team was seated in a row.

"We saved you seats."

The medical officers stood out from the other guests because of their whites and gold striped epaulettes. Rachel greeted them with a cheery hello as Marjorie sat next to Sarah and Rachel sat next to her.

"I do hope nobody gets ill." Marjorie leaned over to address Dr Graham Bentley, whom she and her husband had known for years. "Otherwise, young Graham, you will have to leave discreetly."

Rachel never asked why Marjorie called the senior medical officer, who had to be in his fifties, 'young Graham'. It was obviously a private joke shared between them.

"Don't you worry, Lady Snellthorpe, our French angel can deal with most things."

Brigitte was the only absentee from the medical team. She had been at home in France when the rest of them had got to know Eva and Jefgeny.

Rachel recognised a few of the crew from the casino where Eva worked and could hear a group of men speaking Russian.

"I assume they're from engineering?" she questioned.

"Yes, the groom's friends. The best man is one of them. It's such a shame his sister can't be here, but it would be too dangerous for him," Sarah answered.

Jefgeny had been required to sever all ties with family when he bravely reported a conspiracy at a company he worked for in a prior life, hence his new name.

"I can't get used to thinking of him as Darren. Is Eva's family here?"

"Her mother's over there." Sarah pointed to a lady in her fifties with tightly pursed thin lips, wearing a floral dress. She looked austere, in spite of the brightly coloured attire.

"She doesn't look very happy considering it's her daughter's wedding," Rachel whispered.

"Rumour has it she doesn't approve of her daughter marrying a Russian. That's Eva's sister and brother-in-law next to her. Apparently the mother doesn't approve of the brother-in-law either, so at least Darren will be in good company."

"Is that little Erik?" Rachel saw a baby wrapped in a lime-green shawl being held by Eva's sister.

"Yes, he's gorgeous. I've already had a cuddle."

Jefgeny/Darren spotted Rachel and made a beeline for her. Before she could stand up, he'd smothered her in a warm embrace.

"We were so pleased you accepted our invitation. I can't thank you enough for everything you did. You, Sarah and Dr Romano."

Alex Romano and Sarah still worked closely with the Russian engineer to deal with his alcohol addiction and the beginnings of liver cirrhosis. Rachel was thrilled to see him looking so happy. There was still a slight discolouration to his skin, but his emerald eyes shone brightly now that he was overcoming his problems.

"It's wonderful to see you too, I was delighted to be invited. This is my friend, Marjorie."

Darren bowed the top half of his body to Marjorie. "I am honoured you are attending our wedding, Lady Snellthorpe."

Ship's etiquette even applied to weddings, it seemed.

Darren seemed uncomfortable momentarily. Marjorie sensed his unease and dispensed with any class barriers immediately.

"Do call me Marjorie. All my friends do, and any friend of Rachel's is a friend of mine." She took his hand. "Is that your son over there?"

The Russian's chest almost burst out of his ill-fitting suit as he proudly collected the baby and brought him over to them.

"This is Erik Higgs, we gave him my new surname."

Marjorie cooed over the baby and soon found herself holding the young Erik as the groom was retrieved by the best man. Captain Jensen arrived along with Waverley and they shook hands with Darren before checking on last-minute details with the pianist.

The chapel went silent as Eva arrived, wearing a traditional white wedding dress and veil. The dress was simple in design with a round neck and the minimum of fuss. Eva was walked down the chapel aisle by a man in his fifties.

"Her father," Sarah mouthed.

"Thank heavens he looks happier than her mother," Marjorie whispered.

The ceremony was simple and traditional, verging on Catholic as both bride and groom came from Catholic backgrounds. Captain Jensen officiated with an ease that demonstrated his experience. As soon as the ceremony was over, he congratulated the couple and departed at a polite juncture, understanding that his presence would suffocate the crew's joy and prevent them from being themselves.

Marjorie had held Erik throughout the service and he'd drifted off to sleep in the comfort of her arms.

"He reminds me of Jeremy when he was a boy. I do miss not having grandchildren, but Jeremy's never shown any interest in having children and his second wife is a socialite. I can't ever imagine her having children, even though she's twenty years younger than my son."

Rachel squeezed her arm.

The wedding attendees gathered round in groups and began to vacate the chapel after being advised food and soft drinks would be served in the crew café and alcohol in the bar. Rachel and Marjorie decided to leave after the service as they didn't want to intrude or make anyone uneasy. Darren and Eva came to collect Erik, and Darren hugged Rachel again while Eva thanked them for attending.

"It was a lovely service," said Rachel.

"Thank you. I am the happiest man in the world," Darren announced.

As the new Mr and Mrs Higgs left, Rachel thought he certainly looked it.

Chapter 26

Rachel and Marjorie opted for a table on deck fourteen overlooking the lido deck where a live band was playing in honour of the sailaway party.

"Time's rapidly passing and we are no nearer to finding out whodunit!" said Marjorie petulantly.

"Waverley told me after the wedding he's now going back to the theory of it being an accident. He's even considering allowing Gordon Venables loose again and back to work!"

"That would be a mistake, I fear, if only for the sake of his downtrodden wife. It's traumatic enough for a woman to try and escape the clutches of a dangerous and controlling man without being confined on board a cruise ship with him."

"In Waverley's defence, he did emphasise that Gordon would be sacked if he made any attempt to contact his wife during the sailing. He must be under pressure from above with Gordon's deputy having to stand in for him and others covering her work. If he is allowed back, Gordon will be transferred to another ship as soon as possible."

"Be it on their head if the cruise line is happy to employ a man who presents a real danger to his wife and violently attacks a passenger."

"Ah, there is also news on that front. Waverley found out quite by chance during his routine background checks that Dominic Venables had a son. Guess what the son's name is?"

"Is it Dave Hughes, by any chance?"

"You guessed it! His mother never married, but his father on the birth certificate is registered as Dominic Venables. The information only came to light after Waverley pulled up a historic assault charge citing Venables as the victim. The attacker, a teenager, went for him during a gig in Cardiff. The teenager was named as Dave Hughes, but he got off with a caution after police put it down to a 'domestic'. Apparently, the boy's mother explained her son was angry about being abandoned as a baby and Venables didn't press charges. Waverley interviewed Hughes again today and it turns out he and his estranged father had been communicating via Facebook, and when he heard his dad's band would be playing on board the *Coral Queen*, Dave persuaded his best friend to hold his stag do on board – sort of a final effort. It seems he imagined a great reconciliation."

"Well, that adds a new flavour to the pot, doesn't it? It seems our list of suspects is increasing."

Rachel acknowledged the fact. "Waverley thinks Hughes caused that fight deliberately because of the friction between his father and Gordon, who has no idea that the young man is his nephew."

"I suppose that's possible, but it seems a bit extreme. How would he know how his uncle would react?"

"I wonder if his estranged father had told him about Gordon's weak spot. Dom probably bragged about how he would get Shirley Venables to sleep with him – he was certainly arrogant enough to say something like that."

"It might have been better for Dave Hughes not to have become acquainted with his father, if that's the case. If he did provoke the fight, it explains why he dropped the charges and encouraged the chief to release Gordon Venables. Perhaps, unlike his father, he has a conscience."

"We only have his word he patched things up with his father, though," said Rachel as she stared into her empty glass.

"You're right. He does need adding to the suspect list. Did you find anything on the replacement lead singer?"

"No, Waverley hasn't looked into him, but promised he'll check and come back to me."

"We really are no closer to the truth. Do you imagine it could have been an accident?"

"Not in a million years. I suspect someone wanted it to look like that, and if Gordon is innocent, the murderer framed him deliberately on realising murder was suspected."

"Or found it convenient."

"Yes. We still can't rule Gordon out, but he goes to the bottom of the list for now. Trouble is with so many candidates, I'm no longer sure who should be at the top. We will keep our new lead singer up there as a question mark until we find out when he boarded."

"Agreed. I would also put Nick Garrett up there. He's a nasty piece of work and there was obviously a lot of friction between him and his so-called friend."

Rachel wrote the two names down along with possible motives. "I think we need to put Dave Hughes up top now too. Family feuds run deep, and if he has an abandonment grudge, he may well have argued with his father. He had obviously been violent towards him previously."

"Then there's Timmy Walker."

"Jimmy," Rachel corrected automatically.

"Yes, Jimmy Walker – I still think he looks like a Timmy – a man who had a lot to lose if the band walked away from him. We also only have his word that he forgave Venables for trying to seduce his wife."

Rachel added the two names. "That leaves Ray Lynch and Dalton Delacruz."

"There doesn't seem to be much of a motive for either of them to kill the man. Lynch seems happy enough with his role as the drummer and all we have on Dalton is that he is economical with the truth."

"Unless his leaning towards fantasies extended to arguing with Venables, who found out Dalton had told his brother about his attempted seduction of Shirley. That doesn't make sense, though, because Dom didn't seem to mind who found out. In fact, he would probably have revelled in it. Those two join Gordon at the bottom of the list for now."

"And there is one more," Marjorie said thoughtfully.

"Who?"

"Shirley Venables. She had every reason to want Dominic Venables dead – already suffering a life of torment with an over-controlling husband, frightened at what her husband might do if he became convinced she was having an affair with his brother, and knowing that either way, her husband wouldn't believe her."

"I must admit, I hadn't put Shirley in the frame, but I suppose she and Dom might have argued, and the argument could have gotten out of hand. Knowing what we do of the Venables ego, we can assume he wouldn't have backed down, and a woman desperate for respite from the false accusations of her husband may understandably have turned to violence, however unlikely. Perhaps he attacked her and she defended herself. The only problem with that is I'm sure it was a man in the pool trying to kill Gordon."

"Do you know that for certain?"

"Almost, but I didn't get a clear look at him because of the mist, and until I shouted, he had his back to me. But the shape looked like that of a man, and I'm pretty sure my recollection doesn't fit Shirley's frame. Gordon also said it was a man."

"What if he's lying? If he did suspect his wife, it would explain the accusation in that letter she received, wouldn't it?"

Rachel mulled it over for a moment and accepted the possibility. "We'll add her to the bottom of the list, but I just don't have Shirley Venables down as a cold-blooded killer."

"No," said Marjorie. "But as you suggested, if the first incident turns out not to have been an accident, even if it was self-defence, and she had reason to believe her husband suspected her, he would have had permanent leverage over her. She's desperate enough to be free of him."

"The hole in this theory is that a man called Gordon on the telephone to say his wife could be in danger. Shirley wouldn't be strong enough to push him in the water, and by all accounts, he was already under suspicion for the murder and locked up. I can't see her putting herself at risk in that way." Rachel caught the eye of a waiter. "I need a martini – our list has just grown!"

After dinner, Rachel walked Marjorie back to her suite. It had been a busy day and she wanted her friend to get some rest. On arrival back in her own suite, she decided to email Carlos again. There had been no reply from his office phone or his mobile the day before, and worry had been building up in her throughout today when she didn't hear from him again.

After emailing, she opened the doors on to the balcony and found herself imagining different scenarios about where Carlos was, none of them pleasant. When he didn't contact her after they'd docked in Russia, initially she'd felt relieved, not wanting to tell him about the attack, but now concern had set in. It was nearly four days since receiving the last text, and the tension was now setting her nerves on edge. Marjorie had been doing her best to keep her mind occupied, and discussing the list of suspects had helped.

She pulled the suspect list out of her handbag and placed it on the table. The only sounds she could hear came from the breaking of the Baltic waves against the side of the ship to her left. The scene was eerily black.

During their briefing – Marjorie had taken to calling the meetings 'briefings' or 'war councils' – they'd decided to follow the stag party on their tour the following day. A quick call to Waverley and a bit of checking on his part had revealed the boys were booked on a Stockholm sightseeing excursion, and Sarah had reluctantly agreed to join Rachel and Marjorie for the same excursion. The excursions desk was closed, but Waverley had called one of the team in to provide tickets for three.

When Waverley called her suite to confirm that the excursion was booked, Rachel went through the suspect list briefly over the telephone and he agreed they should continue to investigate, but was still hoping to close the case as an accident/unexplained death. He reasoned the attack on her and Gordon could have come from one of the band, convinced Gordon had murdered their friend. The coroner in Copenhagen didn't have enough evidence to conclude that it was murder, particularly as she had since discovered evidence of high levels of drugs and alcohol in the victim's system. As the drug found in his system turned out to be LSD, the coroner explained an alternative scenario to Waverley, suggesting the man may have thought he could fly, apparently a common hallucination linked to LSD use. Waverley appeared to be coming to the same conclusion.

Much to Rachel's disgust, Gordon Venables had been reinstated as cruise director on condition he stayed away from his wife.

"I told him, if he's seen within one hundred yards of her, he will be in the brig," Waverley assured Rachel.

Dr Bentley was none too happy about the situation either, Sarah told her when she phoned after surgery.

"He's worried. He says an obsessive man like that is unlikely to leave her alone. I'm frightened for her, Rachel."

Rachel had to agree. Waverley was taking a huge risk with this one and she couldn't work out why. From what she had known of him in their previous dealings, he made mistakes, but he didn't strike her as a risk taker. What he was doing now seemed out of character.

He can't have told the cruise line about the attack on the passenger.

Rachel found herself equally surprised Captain Jensen had agreed to the man's reinstatement. This reckless behaviour didn't make sense, unless there was something Waverley wasn't telling her.

The sound of her mobile telephone ringing made her jump from her reverie. Leaping up from the table, she almost slipped, realising she hadn't even kicked off her stilettos from the wedding.

Where was her phone? She clambered over the chair that had fallen to the floor and, dashing into the sitting room of her suite, saw the phone on the sofa. She looked at the screen and pressed the answer button.

"Carlos, where have you been? I've been so worried about you."

"Sorry, it's not Carlos."

"Is that you, Greg?" asked Rachel, recognising the voice of Carlos's assistant.

"Yes, he asked me to call you yesterday, but I was following a bloke around all day and I forgot."

"So where is he and why have you got his phone?"

"I don't have all the facts because he's gone off grid on this one. It turns out the case he's working on is much bigger than one missing dog. He said there could be a trace on his phone so he gave it to me to put them off the scent, asking me to let you know. He picked up a pay-as-you-go and was heading up to the Scottish Highlands. That was on Friday. He texted my number on Saturday to tell me he was following up another lead and had boarded a ferry to Dublin."

"I see," said Rachel, trying to control the palpitations pounding through her chest. She didn't know whether to laugh or cry. "Is he in any danger?"

"Nothing he can't handle, Rachel. Don't worry, he can take care of himself."

"Is Lady with him?"

"Yeah, it's thanks to her that he's got this far, he says. She sniffed out a secret room when he went to collect the missing dog. Turned out they found cages full of designer puppies, stolen to order. He was livid – him and his detective friend cajoled the guy into helping them with their enquiries on condition he gets some leniency."

"Okay, thanks for telling me. Oh, and Greg?"

"What?"

"Next time he asks you to contact me, make sure you do it the same day."

He sounded suitably rebuked. "Sorry, promise," he said, ending the call.

Rachel felt most of the tension dissipating. As she sighed deeply and looked heavenwards, she prayed, "Thank you, Lord. Why on earth didn't I just trust you in the first place?"

Her father had always told her it was much harder to have faith when trials came and things didn't go to plan, and she had to admit that on this occasion, her father was right.

Chapter 27

It had been a frustrating day. Rachel had found it difficult to concentrate on the beautiful city of Stockholm because she had been champing at the bit to find out why Dave Hughes wasn't with his friends on the tour and still fretting over the whereabouts of Carlos. Marjorie and Sarah made the best of the trip, annoyingly determined to look on the bright side of everything while Rachel took a rare journey into the doldrums. The other two women allowed her space, sensing her mood, but even that made her miserable.

When they got back to the ship, Sarah put her arm around her friend.

"Oh Sarah, Marjorie, I'm sorry. I've been a right pain in the butt today; I don't understand what came over me."

"Well you did get a blow to the head." Sarah laughed, clearly detecting it was alright to joke again.

"You do have a lot on your mind," said Marjorie kindly.

"That's no excuse. Only last night, I was relieved to find out Carlos was safe and thanking God, and today I behave like a petulant schoolgirl."

"It's the adrenaline drop," explained Sarah. "You've been on tenterhooks for days with adrenaline and cortisone coursing through the veins, and those hormones have plummeted today, leaving you feeling drained. From one adrenaline junkie to another, trust me, it's quite normal."

Rachel slapped her head. "You're right – you know what else? I haven't been running or gone to the gym since Friday – no wonder I'm so grouchy." The realisation that there was a cause for her mood immediately made her feel better. "How strange, I'm fine now."

Sarah mock wiped her brow. "Thank goodness for that."

As they passed through security, they saw Waverley hanging around in the background. He nodded curtly, indicating not to speak, so they passed on by.

"I wonder what he's up to," said Marjorie when they alighted the lift on deck four and headed to Creams Patisserie, one of their favourite haunts.

"Not sure," said Rachel. "It wouldn't surprise me if it's to do with Gordon Venables. I was thinking about the whole situation with him last night and something doesn't sit right."

"I thought the same," said Sarah. "Either Waverley's lost his marbles or he's up to something."

"Oh, you mean he might be using him as a kind of bait," said Marjorie.

"Something like that, because even if Dom Venables did imagine he was a bird and try to fly off the balcony, the attack on Gordon was very real. I can assure you of that from the residual pain in my shoulder. There's still the evidence that Dom was unconscious on hitting the water, which they all seem to be conveniently forgetting."

"I think you're right," said Marjorie. "Of course, he's putting Gordon out there to see if there's another attack on his life. But Waverley told us he was short-staffed – surely he doesn't have spare security guards who can follow him?"

"They have caught the thief stealing jewellery from passenger rooms, which has helped," Sarah explained. "Sadly it was a cabin steward whose contract hadn't been renewed. We all hate it when any of the crew commits crimes like that – it looks bad on us all."

"A bit like corruption in the police force," said Rachel grimly. "And there seems to be far too much of that if you ask me."

"So the stateroom steward was taking an unofficial bonus." Marjorie cackled.

"It's not funny," scolded Sarah.

"It's not the end of the world either, dear. Expensive jewellery should be locked in the safe or in the purser's office, so a few knick-knacks are hardly going to break the bank for the majority of passengers."

"It's not that, it's the breach of trust," argued Sarah.

"Sarah's right," said Rachel. "You need to be able to trust the crew."

"I've lived long enough to accept that isn't always possible, and when you remember the poverty many stewards leave behind in their homelands, it might be the temptation is too great. After all, cruise ships are the epitome of luxurious extravagance, aren't they?"

Rachel caught the naughty twinkle in Marjorie's eye, but could sense indignation building in Sarah so she felt it a good time to change the subject.

"Where do you suppose Dave Hughes was today?"

"I overheard one of the guys saying when they got back to the ship that he had a hangover and stayed behind, although the groom-to-be joked about it being funny that Tonya was also ill today."

"Ah," said Marjorie. "A secret liaison."

"Not that secret by the sounds of it," added Rachel.

They finished their pastries and teas before heading back to their respective rooms to change for dinner.

"I'm on call tonight, so I'll catch you tomorrow," said Sarah. "Let me know if you get anywhere with the Gordon thing, though."

"Will do," agreed Rachel as she kissed her friend on the cheek. "Where's Jason, by the way?"

"I'm not sure, working somewhere. He caught the jewellery thief," Sarah answered proudly.

Before Marjorie could say anything, Rachel took her arm and led her towards the lifts where they turned to wave to Sarah.

"I wasn't going to tease her any further, you know," Marjorie declared.

"Of course not." Rachel winked.

The next morning, Rachel and Marjorie split up to follow their respective action plans. Rachel stopped by Waverley's office after breakfast. The security chief looked chipper, radiating a newfound confidence.

"Good morning, Rachel. I just wanted to tell you we have dropped the investigation into Dominic Venables's death."

Open mouthed, Rachel found herself speechless.

"In the light of the drugs business and his general state, the company has, erm, advised me to rule out foul play from our end."

Rachel recognised what was happening. "How convenient," she said.

A momentary frown crossed the chief's face and Rachel suspected he was not altogether happy with this outcome either, but would have to toe the party line.

"As for the attack on Gordon Venables and yourself," he coughed, "that investigation continues. Our main line of inquiry is that it was one of the band, suspecting Gordon had killed their friend."

"What about Dave Hughes?"

"Unlikely. He would have been recovering from the assault on himself, so I don't think he would have gone near his uncle so soon afterwards."

"Does Gordon realise yet he has a nephew?"

"No, Mr Hughes doesn't want Gordon Venables told. He wants to put the whole thing behind him and get on with his life."

"Also convenient," Rachel murmured.

"Pardon?"

"Nothing. Did you find out when the new lead singer boarded?"

Waverley reached for a piece of paper on his desk. "A red herring, I'm afraid. Mr and Mrs Travers boarded on the afternoon of our arrival in Tallinn and moved to the crew quarters on deck A."

"The afternoon, you say? That can't be right. I saw them in the morning."

"You are mistaken, Rachel, they boarded at 3.30pm."

Rachel took out her mobile phone and pulled up the photo, placing the phone down deliberately on Waverley's desk.

"Is that a mistake, then?"

The furrowed brow showed confusion penetrating the previously happy face of the chief of security.

"When was this taken?"

"You can see from the time and date stamp, I snapped it on the morning in question, while you were speaking to the band members and before you spoke to me and Sarah."

He picked up her phone and enlarged the image with his fingers on the screen. He tapped names into his computer and pulled up the photos of the new lead singer and his wife. They both compared the images.

"Unless they are twin brothers married to twin sisters, I would say they are the same couple," said Rachel triumphantly.

Waverley slumped back in his chair. "I don't understand this at all. I will look into the matter, but it still has no bearing on the death of Dominic Venables. *Accidental* death."

"You can't believe that?" Rachel was astonished.

"I can and I do. Leave it with me – if I find out anything, I'll come back to you. It's probably a computer error on the boarding time, we do get the odd glitches in the system."

Rachel left, frustrated and angry.

"Insufferable arrogance of the man! Sheer blind stupidity."

This type of frustration was becoming a regular visitor to her life. Conversations with Carlos leapt into her mind about incidents at work where closing cases sometimes got in the way of finding the truth. Compromises she was uncomfortable with sprang up like a geyser ready to explode.

She found herself walking briskly towards her next destination, the determined look in her eyes a warning to anyone not to test her resolve. She would get to the bottom of the death of Dominic Venables, which was no more an accident than her being hit over the head and pushed into the pool. He may not have been a likeable character, and was apparently a junkie to boot, but that didn't mean his murderer shouldn't be brought to justice.

Rachel marched into the Sky View Lounge. The stag group happened to be participating in a marshmallow eating competition. Her indignation rose as she saw Gordon officiating.

This fiasco is getting worse.

Slamming herself down in a seat close to the front, she drew a nervous stare from a nearby couple. After taking a few deep calming breaths, she regained her composure and requested mineral water from a waiter, smiling reassuringly at the couple who tentatively looked away.

Her focus turned to the spectacle in front of her. The participants had to place as many marshmallows in their mouths as they could without chewing or swallowing, and the one who could hold the most at once was the winner. A few of them gave up fairly quickly and graciously accepted defeat, but the more competitive continued with the sickening display. Gordon and his assistant watched for any attempts at swallowing and Rachel noticed buckets nearby in case any of them threw up.

Gross!

Rachel could have gagged a few times herself in spite of having a fairly healthy stomach. The couple nearby retreated after the woman began to look a little green.

Gordon looked smug at being reinstated as cruise director and he gave Rachel a huge smile and a wave. Her smile hid the contempt she felt over his behaviour towards his wife – he had no idea she was aware – and her disgust that he had been allowed to go back to work as if nothing had happened after attacking one of the men now participating in the competition. Her smile was more at the irony of the situation.

It seemed Dave Hughes and the groom-to-be, Aled Lewis, were the most competitive because both looked about ready to regurgitate the contents of their mouths, and in all likelihood anything left in their stomachs, but neither would concede. Dave's face still had the bruises left from his previous meeting with Gordon and the latter was clearly enjoying adding to the young man's pain by encouraging him to take one more marshmallow. Just when it looked like both men would indeed vomit, Gordon's assistant hissed something in his ear and he brought proceedings to a close.

"Ladies and gentleman, in the name of decency, I declare it a draw."

Hugely relieved, the men turned away and spat the contents of their mouths into the waiting buckets, to the sound of cheers and jeers from their friends and amused passengers who had gathered to watch. Gordon awarded both men a lanyard with Queen Cruises Champion engraved on a plastic medallion and shook hands with them as if they were long-lost friends. Dave's eyes betrayed a steely cold gaze that sent chills down Rachel's spine; she was sure she had her man.

Gordon quickly departed and left the gang of young men to their back-slapping and congratulatory teasing, each jostling to be heard above the other. Dave Hughes looked pale as he approached Rachel.

"Hi," he said warily. "The security bloke said you wanted to have a word with me. He told me you saved my bacon the other day by the side of the pool."

Rachel slapped her most disarming smile on to her face as she encouraged him to take a seat.

"Catch you later, boys," he shouted to his mates.

"Lucky blighter," one of them remarked. "What do they see in him?"

"I'm Rachel." She had rehearsed the next part of her speech with Marjorie until it sounded convincing. "I witnessed the assault on you the other day, and wanted to tell you that I am happy to make a formal complaint about the whole thing to the security team to ensure that man never works again."

He looked nervous. "No!" He raised his voice and Rachel feigned alarm, moving away from him.

"Sorry, I didn't mean to shout. It's just the whole thing has been traumatic for me. I want to forget about it. In fact, I've already told the chief to drop it."

"Really? I'm surprised, are you sure that's wise? That man shouldn't be allowed to get away with what he did to you. He's even back at work – rubbing your face in it, that's what I'd call it."

The hatred in Dave's eyes gave him away again, but he quickly regained control.

"It was nothing. In fact, it was a family spat. Don't tell anyone, but he's my uncle, and I deserved it. Don't worry, I'll get him back." The malice became evident in his voice during the latter part of the statement. Rachel wanted to rattle his cage a little bit more.

"That's very forgiving of you, but it was still assault, uncle or not. I'll tell the chief I want to make a formal statement."

Rachel moved as if to leave. He gripped her arm aggressively, his eyes pleading.

"No, please, don't – you'll ruin everything."

"But he has to be dealt with," she said sympathetically. "People like him should be punished. In fact, I'd like to do it myself."

"What do you mean?" he asked.

"Well if it was left to me, I'd throw him overboard."

The young man's eyes welled up. "My dad was thrown overboard."

"I'm so sorry, I didn't realise. Was your dad that superb singer in the Queen tribute band?"

"Yes." He looked down at his clenched fists. "And I intend to get the killer."

"OMG! You think it was your uncle?"

"I know it was, so you have to understand, he will be punished, but the security chief's told me they don't suspect him of murder, so if he gets arrested he'll only get done for assault. Don't you see? He'll get away with murder."

"What are you going to do?"

"I can't tell you. I nearly got to him the other day, but he survived." He looked determined. "Next time I'll make sure."

Rachel was puzzled he hadn't recognised her as the person who shouted at him to leave the man alone, but relieved to see Jason come into the lounge. Her plan had worked – she'd got the confession.

"I'm sorry, Mr Hughes, I can't let you do that." Dave's eyes darted from Rachel to Jason, who was approaching them. "There's nowhere to run."

Rachel took the phone out of her pocket and handed it to Jason. "Everything's on there, but please let me have it back ASAP. I'm expecting a call."

Before Jason led Dave Hughes away, Rachel spoke to the young man.

"Believe me," she said, "attempted murder is better than committing the real thing. You're too young to go away for life, and if it helps, I'm almost certain it wasn't your uncle that killed your dad."

Dave looked back at her. "So you think it was drugs that killed him?"

"Perhaps, but if there is a killer, I don't believe it's Gordon Venables. He doesn't have it in him."

"Who are you?"

"Just someone trying to enjoy a holiday." She shrugged as Jason took the young man away. "And oh how I wish I could do that."

Chapter 28

Marjorie arrived in the main atrium in plenty of time for her meeting with Jimmy Walker. She ordered tea and sat gazing out to sea through the large windows that allowed torrents of light into the area. The marble floors shone with polish, as did the spiral staircases leading to the upper part of the atrium. The brass banisters were so shiny they could be used as mirrors.

If one sat here all day long, she mused, one would see the invisible crew who keep the public areas immaculately clean and tidy.

The public toilets were a perfect example. She had never known a time when soap or towels were lacking. Spillages were magically cleaned up immediately by a member of the crew who no-one noticed or acknowledged. The daily routine continued like the well-oiled machine it was. Rigorous training kept the crew on their toes, Sarah had assured her and Rachel, with work regularly inspected by senior officers throughout every department.

The atrium was busy, being a sea day. The cruisers had had four straight days of land stops and now they were enjoying the hospitality the ship had to offer before the next stop. Marjorie had finished her first cup of tea before the band manager arrived. He came alone at first as per her request, with the rest of the band due half an hour later.

The loud voice shattered her musings. "Allo, Lady Snellforpe, good to see ya again."

I do wish he would learn some diction. He can say 'the', so why can't he say 'thorpe'?

"Good morning, Mr Walker. I trust you enjoyed some relaxation over the past few days. Tea?"

"I'll 'ave coffee, ta."

Marjorie requested coffee from the waiter, who had seen Jimmy arrive, and another pot of tea for herself.

"The lads went ashore while I worked. Never a minute's rest, managing a band, what wiv bookings and rooms and making sure they've got everyfing they need."

"Yes, I'm sure it's a full-time job. You do seem to manage them well, though. My granddaughter liked the new singer, but not as much as the previous one, she told me."

Jimmy's jaw dropped.

"However, she's willing to have another listen when they play this afternoon, and afterwards I will make my final decision. It is such a shame about Mr Venables."

"Well, as I said, 'e could be difficult at times wiv 'is temperament an' all, plus the fact men couldn't let their wives out of their sight. Like I told ya, 'e even 'ad a go at mine."

"Quite. I still can't get over how forgiving you were over that incident; it must have riled you. My late husband would not have shown so much grace."

Marjorie noticed Jimmy fiddling with his collar as the memories came back. "Yeah, well, as I said, I was angry and could 'ave done for 'im the day I found out, but we made up. In business, you 'ave to let things go. We needed each other and 'e promised it wouldn't 'appen again, like."

"Artistic people do sometimes push all social boundaries, don't they?"

"Yeah, they can do, I suppose." He took a slurp of coffee from the mug that had arrived while they chatted. Marjorie thanked the waiter, but Jimmy didn't seem to notice him at all.

And he'd be the first to call me a snob.

For a moment, she was distracted by the loud slurping noises he made as his jaw performed somersaults to keep the gum in place while drinking.

"Do they know yet who done for him, as you put it?"

"They don't fink anyone did now. Last I 'eard they put it down to an accident. Now saying 'e was drunk and off 'is 'ead on drugs." He snorted in disbelief.

"You don't think it an accident, I take it?"

"Dom was a lot of fings, but a junkie ain't one of 'em. 'E never touched the 'ard stuff; a bit of pot now and again, but not what they say 'e took."

"What do they say he took?"

"LSD! Lady Snellforpe, the lads are clean, they don't do drugs, and Dom always warned them off such stuff. Said if they needed those kinds of drugs to be creative, they weren't good enough to work wiv." Jimmy's voice rose a few decibels and people stared at him, although he remained oblivious. He waved his hands in the air and chewed harder on his gum as if to prove the point. "My lads are clean."

Deciding to bring him back down from the ceiling, Marjorie suggested ordering drinks for the imminent arrival of 'his lads'. He recovered himself and she imagined how exhausting it must be to have a volatile temperament – up one minute, down the next. She couldn't see the point. People might criticise the stoical British temperament, but she would take that any day rather than the constant roller coaster ride many seemed to live by these days.

Maybe I am too old, she pondered while Jimmy rattled on about contracts and costs and bookings. Her attention returned when he stopped speaking and looked at her, obviously waiting for an answer to a question she hadn't caught.

Seeing the open diary in his hand, she guessed.

"We'll need to wait until this afternoon for that."

He slammed the diary shut, disappointed. Relieved at having guessed the right answer, Marjorie realised she was tired and wished Rachel had accompanied her. This investigating business might be all well and good, but she was not used to dealing with people like Walker.

Chastising herself for her weakness, she concentrated on the job in hand as the rest of the band made their entrance heard and approached the table.

"I was just telling Lady Snellforpe 'ow you don't do drugs, boys."

"Too right we don't," said Nick. "And I don't believe Dom did either."

Marjorie would have counted 'pot', as Walker called it, as a drug, but didn't want to split hairs. They obviously believed there was a distinction between what they did and drugs.

"You can't argue with what they found at autopsy," said Ray.

"I'm sure he did all sorts of things we didn't have a clue about," said Dalton.

"Oh, don't start again, Dalton. Come out of cuckoo land for a bit, won't you?" Nick hissed.

Dalton blushed and stared down at his shoes. Marjorie sympathised with him; he seemed a sensitive sort and the constant bickering must wear him down.

No wonder he seeks attention through fantasy.

Jimmy turned to the new lead singer who had a woman hanging on to his arm. He had short ginger hair and a moustache, presumably to resemble Freddie Mercury. His hair was unmistakable from the photo Rachel had shown her and Sarah a few days earlier.

"This is Fred and Millie."

"Fred as in Freddie Mercury?" Marjorie enquired.

"Ironic, isn't it?" Fred didn't have the cockney accent most of the band shared. "It is my real name. Inevitable I would play him, I was named after him. My parents' fault, huge fans."

"Oh, did you play Freddie Mercury before with the band?"

His jawline became jagged as he answered. "No, I should have been lead singer, but the venerable Dom Venables took over not long after we started out." He glared at the rest of the band. "And what a mistake that turned out to be," he added.

With so much testosterone flying about, it's a wonder they ever got anything done.

"But he's our leading man now, eh?" Jimmy interjected, trying to divert the conversation.

"Dom got his comeuppance." Fred was not to be dissuaded that easily.

"Now, now, Fred – let's not talk ill of the dead."

"I don't see why not," Nick argued. "No point pretending he was anything but bad news – we could have been famous now if it weren't for him holding us back."

"Come on, Nick, that was never gonna happen," said Ray, who seemed to be the only person satisfied with his lot.

"We don't know that – we should have made our own music, not lost our identity being a stupid tribute act."

"I agree," said Fred. "We used to make our own music until the esteemed Dom joined and convinced these losers to be a tribute. He actually thought he might be Freddie Mercury reincarnated – it's laughable. For a start, they happened to be alive at the same time – Mercury died in 1991 and Dom was born in 1969. Do the maths!"

"I never thought of that," said Dalton.

The rest stared at him in disbelief.

Not the shiniest tool in the box. Marjorie chuckled inwardly, but at least it brought about a change of subject as the rest of the group teased Dalton mercilessly over his faux pas.

Rachel and Marjorie met up and compared notes before arranging to see Waverley in his office prior to lunch. They found him whistling a tune as they arrived. His door was wide open.

Marjorie nudged Rachel. "I told you he's in love," she whispered.

Waverley turned just in time to catch the two women sniggering. He looked confused, but didn't comment.

"Come in, ladies, take a seat."

They sat on the sofa and he took one of the soft chairs opposite.

"First, I need to thank you, Rachel. We have a full confession from Dave Hughes. He said he attacked his uncle and you – although he didn't realise it was you – and it appears *we* were right about Dominic Venables. He was murdered – Dave's confessed to that murder too."

Waverley beamed from ear to ear while rubbing his hands together. Marjorie gasped and Rachel remained silent.

Waverley explained how Hughes had said he'd got angry with his father for ignoring him on board ship, they'd had a row. Venables was drunk, Hughes punched him and walked away. Later, he realised he must have punched him too hard and his father staggered and fell.

"Manslaughter rather than murder. He didn't realise he'd killed him."

"So why attack Gordon?" asked Marjorie.

"Revenge for humiliating him on the lido deck, he decided he'd get his own back. You're quiet, Rachel, I thought you'd be pleased – another case solved by PC Prince."

"Sorry, I find it hard to believe, particularly as he sounded pretty convinced that Gordon had murdered his father when I spoke to him this morning. He clearly stated he held Gordon responsible and threatened to kill him, or words to that effect, although I think it's all bravado. He may well have punched his father, but the coroner said Venables had been hit from behind before the neat drug scenario changed everyone's minds.

"In fact, I now don't think Dave attacked Gordon at all, or me. It hasn't sat right since I spoke to Dave this morning. He didn't have the facts and didn't give the impression someone else – namely me – had been attacked at the same time. He was terrified when Gordon attacked him by the lido pool – I can see why he wants people to think he's brave and vengeful, but he's just a big pussycat trying to be macho in front of his mates."

"You're the one who had us arrest him."

"Yes I did, but now I'm not so sure. It might play into our hands, though, so we can catch the real perpetrator. Did Dave volunteer that he'd attacked me or did you ask him?"

The other two stared in confusion at Rachel, Waverley groaning and brushing back the imaginary hair from his forehead.

"Now you mention it, I asked him. Why didn't you tell me this was a ruse?"

"To be honest, it wasn't, but the longer I spoke to Dave Hughes, the more I felt in my gut it wasn't him. He's just an insecure young man whose dream of being reunited with the father who abandoned him and his mother died a death. It's like he's now trying to be the bad man like his father."

"Great psychology, Rachel," said Waverley disparagingly. "Where's the evidence – apart from your gut, of course?"

"Now, Chief, sarcasm doesn't become you, and I for one am a great believer in Rachel's gut," said Marjorie, taking Rachel's hand protectively.

Waverley groaned again just as there was a knock on the door.

"COME IN!" he bellowed.

Jason entered the office accompanied by the groom-to-be from the stag group and Sarah.

"Sorry to interrupt, sir, but you should hear what this lad has to say. This is Aled Lewis, best friend of Dave Hughes."

Waverley glared but gathered his composure. "Come and sit down, Mr Lewis, we meet at last. Your party has caused us quite a few problems."

Rachel and Marjorie exchanged glances with Sarah who took a seat with them on the sofa. Aled sat on the other soft chair while Jason remained standing. The young man looked sheepish.

"Sorry about that, sir, the boys do get carried away when they've had a few." His Welsh lilt and smile were disarming. "I've just heard about Davey's confession so I came immediately. He couldn't have attacked that cruise director – he was in our room with me. He'd drunk too much, and while he was thrashing about in bed, he cut his head open again, you see. I called the medics and this nurse came and glued his head."

"Is this true, Sarah?" asked Waverley.

"Yes. I checked the records, and they called me at 5am. I left their room at around 6am after being summoned to attend to Gordon Venables and Rachel."

"I don't suppose you were around when Dave punched his father?" Waverley asked Aled.

"As a matter of fact, I was, but Davey doesn't know that. He kept ranting about how his dad left his mother, how he'd hero worshipped the man – famous singer and all that. He's always been impressionable. Anyway, he flew off the handle, miffed that the man had been ignoring him since he'd told him he was on board and determined to have it out with him. He stormed out of the room. I followed to make sure he didn't do anything stupid because he'd had a few, like. Anyway, I saw the confrontation they had. His dad was horrible to him and told him to grow up – he wasn't the daddy type – and to go back to his whore of a mother. Davey did lose it and punched him. The guy was so drunk he reeled back and Davey stormed off. I stayed to see if the bloke was alright."

"And was he?" Rachel found herself holding her breath.

"He was fine, laughing out loud. Called Davey a few names under his breath, then lit up a cigarette as if nothing had happened. He walked unevenly over to the ship's rail and started yelling at the world what a great man he was. I returned to our room to check on Davey, but I never told him what I'd seen – he would have been gutted to know anyone had witnessed how dismissive his great hero dad had been."

"You're a good friend to have," said Sarah.

"Thanks," said Aled blushing.

"Thank you, Mr Lewis, for telling us. I need you to keep this to yourself for now because we want the real murderer and attacker of our cruise director to imagine they are safe. Do you understand?"

"Yes, sir. Will you be letting Davey go?"

"We'll hang on to him for now. I don't want his anger to spill over into actually doing something silly, and it will add to the real attacker's belief that he is safe." Waverley nodded to Jason to take Aled outside and record what he'd just said.

After they'd left, Waverley looked at Rachel.

"Right again, Miss Prince."

"Sorry," she said.

"So," he sighed, "we're back to square one."

"Not really," said Rachel. "We've narrowed the field and we're getting closer to finding out which one of the band is involved. As you say, whoever it is will feel safe now, and for whatever reason, they want Gordon Venables out of the way. I assume you've got a tail on him?"

"How did you know?"

"My gut!" They all laughed, including Waverley. "I knew you would need a better reason for letting him go back to work than blind belief in his innocence."

"He's agreed to be bait as long as he keeps his job if proven innocent, which is quite brave of him under the circumstances. I almost called off the watch, but I'm glad I didn't. We will catch whoever it is trying to kill him."

"What if they don't try again?" asked Sarah. "And worse, what if they do and they succeed?"

"I agree," said Rachel. "We need to work out the motive for a double murder – if we do that, we find the killer. Marjorie and I are meeting the band and the manager this afternoon. I'm hoping we'll find out something. They all seem to have hated Dom, but I don't understand why any of them would want to kill Gordon."

"And you're sure it's one of them?" asked Waverley.

"Ninety-nine per cent certain that one of them killed Dom Venables, and for some reason, now wants to kill his brother."

"What if it's all of them?" asked Marjorie. "Remember I joked about *Murder on the Orient Express* – what if they hated him so much they planned this together?"

"That is a possibility." Waverley scratched his head. "Horrendous as it may seem."

"We will probably find out today," said Rachel.

"Do be careful, Rachel, and you, Marjorie."

"Don't worry, my dear," said Marjorie, "I won't let her out of my sight."

"I'm not sure that's very reassuring." Sarah laughed. "The pair of you are as bad as each other."

"We'll continue the watch on Gordon and I will have one of my men hanging around when you meet with the band. Do you want to wear a wire?"

"I'll record on the mobile if you can give it back to me."

"Yes, we've taken what we need." Waverley walked behind his desk and took the mobile from it.

Rachel took her phone back and quickly checked for messages in case of any word from Carlos. Disappointed she returned her gaze to Waverley. "They won't try anything this afternoon, but I'm hoping they'll talk enough to give something away. Marjorie's going to be very generous with the spirits during our meeting."

The two women exchanged conspiratorial glances as they rose to leave.

Chapter 29

The fishing expedition with the band had been totally unproductive in terms of discovering anything new. They happened to be their usual argumentative selves, but Jimmy seemed determined to stick to his objective of getting Marjorie to book them for Rachel's imaginary birthday party later in the year. Each time Marjorie or Rachel tried to steer the conversation towards the death of the late lead singer, Jimmy interrupted, preventing anyone from pursuing the subject any further. In the end, Marjorie provisionally booked them just to convince Jimmy that they were genuine. Then, feigning tiredness, she said she would finalise details after her port outing the next day.

"It's as if he did that deliberately," Rachel complained.

"If he did, he's onto us. We should proceed with caution."

"There's only one thing for it now – my Plan B, which Waverley would not agree to."

"What's that?"

"I need to go through their cabins while they're performing tonight. Waverley said there was no justification when I suggested it earlier – not enough evidence against them."

"Why didn't I think of that? What a good idea – we'll go together."

"Oh no, Marjorie, I can't ask you to go down there, it's too dangerous. The stairs are steep, metallic and difficult to negotiate, the rooms are tiny, and no offence, but you'd stick out like a sore thumb. Besides, I need you to keep an eye on the band and send me warning if any of them disappear during their break."

"You can't go alone. Take Sarah with you."

"No, I almost got her in trouble the last time I ventured down to the crew cabins. Besides, she's on call and I can't have her radio going off when I'm on a secret mission."

They discussed the plan back in Marjorie's suite before dinner. Rachel bought walkie-talkies from the on-board gift shop and showed Marjorie how to use hers if she needed to warn her about anything. Marjorie was thoroughly enjoying herself. Rachel apologised to the old lady for having to subject her to another evening of loud pop music, but even that didn't put her off.

"If anyone thinks it strange I'm there, I'll stick to the hiring them for a party story."

What they needed to do now was get hold of a universal swipe key and Rachel knew just where to find one. Waverley carried spares in the top right-hand drawer of his desk – she had seen them when he'd offered her a job in the past. Their problem consisted of how to get into his room without him realising.

Marjorie and Rachel decided to pay him an unannounced visit to explain that they had got nowhere with the band, sharing their frustration. He took it all in and sighed.

"An update on the new singer, by the way: it appears he and his wife did board earlier on the day in question. A computer update caused a temporary glitch that has now corrected itself. And now that security has less to do, I can't ask you to continue your involvement, so leave it to my team. Thank you for your assistance."

Rachel nodded before Marjorie could protest.

"Good idea. We're on holiday, aren't we, Marjorie?"

"Yes indeed. Have you spoken to that young man yet, Chief?"

"I was just about to go when you two ladies arrived, so if you'll excuse me." He stood up.

Perfect, thought Rachel as he walked them out. Just as they were leaving, Marjorie tripped, causing Waverley to rush forwards to support her.

"Are you alright, Lady Snellthorpe?"

"Yes, silly old thing that I am. I do lose my footing occasionally these days."

"Sit down for a moment, Marjorie. I'll get you a glass of water. Don't worry about us, Chief, you go ahead." Rachel smiled encouragingly.

"If you're sure? I would like to speak to Hughes, and then I've got to join the captain's table for some paying dinner guests."

"Quite sure," said Marjorie. "You go along, I am quite alright."

As soon as he was out of sight, Marjorie looked at Rachel.

"Did you manage it?"

"Like taking candy from a baby." After checking the coast was clear, Rachel crossed the corridor back to Waverley's office where she had inserted a piece of card to prevent the door locking while the distraction caused by Marjorie diverted his attention.

"Stay put, and if anyone comes along, pretend you're waiting for someone."

"Strictly speaking, I am." Marjorie laughed.

Rachel entered the office and prayed he hadn't locked his drawers. She crossed the room quickly and crouched down on hands and knees – because he'd left the blinds open, she couldn't risk being seen. Her heart was pounding and hands were trembling by the time she got to the other side of his desk. Reaching up, she pulled the drawer to find it was locked.

Drat and blast. All this for nothing. Lock picking wasn't her forté.

She sat on the floor, trying to work out what to do next. Risking raising her head up, she peeked at what was on top of the desk. Minimalistic order was his thing: the desk top consisted of a computer, the keyboard and a photo of a pretty girl about Rachel's age who in all likelihood was his daughter. The desk-tidy gave her a surge of hope, but on checking if he'd dropped his keys in there, she found nothing.

About to give up, she spotted a shelf of books to the right of the desk. A small silver tin sat at one end. Again risking being seen, she stood up, quickly checking the corridor for people. A couple walked past with their backs to her as she grabbed the tin and slunk back down to the floor.

The tin was embossed with faux ivory, something Waverley had probably picked up in Asia. As Rachel removed the lid, her eyes lit up with delight at the sight of a small set of keys.

With her heart beating ever faster, she tried each key in the lock. On the third attempt, the lock clicked. Her hands were shaking almost out of control as she pulled the drawer open, grabbed a lanyard with a universal swipe card on it, and closed and locked the drawer, panting.

Raising herself up off the floor, she felt dread return on seeing Waverley heading in her direction. Panic set in as she saw him stop to speak to Marjorie. Then he turned and walked in the opposite direction, giving her the opportunity to quickly replace the tin and race across the room and out the door.

Breathless, she sat down next to Marjorie.

"What kept you? I was so worried."

"The drawer was locked, I had to find a key. How did you get rid of Waverley?"

"I told him I was worried about you as you hadn't returned with my water and sent him off in the direction you never went in. I think we'd better leave."

They bumped into Waverley in the midships area. "I was concerned. Where were you?" he said to Rachel.

"Sorry, I got caught short, and then bumped into Mario, our butler, and we got chatting. All's good now." Deceit didn't come naturally and Rachel crossed her fingers behind her back. Waverley seemed satisfied and headed back to his office to collect whatever it was he'd forgotten.

"There's only one downside to this plan, you know," said Marjorie.

"What's that?" asked Rachel.

"You'll be on CCTV."

Rachel slapped her head. "You're right. Let's hope they don't have any reason to check it tonight. After that, I'll own up if need be and take the consequences. If not, I can easily put the key back."

"How?"

Rachel waved the lanyard. "I have a key!"

As they walked arm in arm towards the restaurant for dinner, no-one would have imagined what they had planned for the rest of the evening.

Chapter 30

Rachel joined Marjorie in the Culture Lounge. The surprised look on her elderly friend's face made her laugh.

There was little chance they could converse above the noise of the band, by now in full swing belting out *Bohemian Rhapsody*, the delighted passengers reliving their seventies' memories by throwing themselves around the dance floor, much to the chagrin of the younger members of their families. One man in particular appeared to be getting a little carried away.

"He'll do himself a mischief if he's not careful," shouted Marjorie.

"Or someone else, most likely. Come on, let's go somewhere quiet, I've got news for you."

They left the bass behind and made their way to the main atrium where a string quartet was playing a mixture of Vivaldi and Mozart.

"Now this is much more my cup of tea!" exclaimed Marjorie.

"That's what I love about cruising, there's so much variety, something for every taste."

"What happened? You were too quick to have been through all the rooms."

"I got lucky," Rachel said triumphantly. "I know what's going on."

After she had explained her findings to Marjorie and her suspicions, they agreed the time had come to involve Waverley and set a trap. Rachel asked guest services to call the chief of security as a matter of urgency and she and Marjorie waited for him to arrive.

He looked a little flushed as he made his way over to their table, conveniently situated behind a large pillar but in full view of the small dance floor and a stage where the quartet continued to produce aesthetic sounds. Rachel looked closely at the chief and wondered if he had been drinking, or whether the post prandial exercise had caused his face to burn brightly.

He sounded sober enough when he sat down. "Good evening again, ladies. I was informed you needed to see me urgently." His curtness told them they had obviously interrupted something important – a date?

Rachel smiled. "Sorry to disturb you, but yes, it is urgent." She explained her discovery, neatly omitting to mention how she'd acquired a key card. Thankfully, Waverley seemed more concerned with the gravity of the situation and the shock revelation than with her method. "I have a flytrap plan, but we will need Gordon's cooperation to carry it out," said Rachel finally.

Waverley listened intently, only asking pertinent questions, and immediately sprang into action.

"Follow me," he instructed while speaking into his radio, requesting Gordon to come to his office along with two security officers.

Gordon tentatively agreed to the plan and left them to set proceedings in motion. They needed to wait until eleven-thirty, but set themselves up fifteen minutes before, moving to the bow of the ship and hiding themselves in the theatre where Gordon would be arranging his meeting. Although Rachel would have preferred Marjorie to wait in Waverley's office, she insisted on attending.

"I don't want to miss the action now we've got this far," the older lady insisted.

In the dark, Rachel could hear Waverley's breathing and imagined him sweating. He had the most to lose if this trap turned horribly wrong – second to Gordon, that was.

After what seemed an age they heard footsteps walking on to the stage, followed by shuffling as someone hid themselves. Rachel's heart was pounding with anticipation and she prayed their plan would work.

Silence ensued for what seemed an eternity, but in reality could only have been around five minutes. No-one dared move for fear of alerting the person hiding on stage. At one point, a couple mistakenly entered the theatre from the back, giggled at finding themselves in the wrong place and left again.

The silence became deafening and Rachel could feel her muscles stiffening with tension from the hunched position in her hiding place. She hoped Marjorie would be alright – she had ensured the old lady was in a more comfortable hiding place than the one she'd found for herself. Just beginning to wonder if Gordon had changed his mind and chickened out, Rachel heard footsteps approaching and saw someone shining a torch.

A commotion occurred and the man dropped the torch and grunted as if someone had attacked him.

Waverley flicked on the lights and shouted, "That's enough – the game's up. Let him go."

The dastardly duo on the stage looked stunned at having been caught in the act. Gordon sat on the floor with his head in his hands.

"I suppose you were going to say your husband attacked you and you hit him in self-defence," said Rachel to Shirley Venables, now handcuffed and held by a security officer. Dalton Delacruz was also in cuffs.

"How did you find out?"

"When I took that photo of you and Sarah in Tallinn, I remembered catching a brief glimpse of a photo of you with a man. At first, I assumed it was Gordon, but it came to me earlier this evening that it could have been someone else, someone I recognised. Tonight while you were performing, I slipped into the changing rooms backstage and found your phone with your clothes. I was grateful you used a combination of your date of birth as a pass code – not wise, by the way. I checked the photo, and sure enough, you and Dalton were in a lover's embrace. What I didn't understand was why you had Dominic killed or why you didn't just leave Gordon and take up with Dalton. But it was all about money, wasn't it?"

Gordon looked at Rachel, clearly unable to look at his wife. "Who killed my brother?"

"Dalton, under instructions from your wife, I'm afraid. Dom had seen them together and threatened to tell you unless she came clean with you herself. He hadn't tried it on with her at all – he really was trying to mend his ways as far as you were concerned. Dalton knew they had been seen by a passenger – Dave Hughes, as it turned out – so he made up a story about Shirley and Dom to throw everyone off the scent. Even though he wouldn't be believed entirely, it muddied the waters enough to draw suspicion away from him. Shirley convinced Dalton she would run away with him, but didn't want to lose out on her inheritance with you still alive. I think she played Dalton to get at your money. He'd do the dirty work, she would be very rich, and later she'd dump him."

"Why did he pretend he had tried it on with Shirley when I confronted him?" asked Gordon, confused.

"Old habits die hard, I guess," answered Rachel.

"I suspected she was having an affair. I told her I was going to change my will, so I guess that's what brought on the urgency."

"I'm afraid so," said Rachel, putting a hand on Gordon's shoulder. "You were never the controlling one in the relationship, either. Jealous yes, but controlling, no. Your wife had everyone convinced you were a psychological abuser. It was the other way round."

Gordon, horrified, finally looked at his wife. "Why would you say that? They told me I had to stay away from you because you wanted to leave me."

Shirley glared at him. "You're pathetic, Gordon. Always in your brother's shadow. I only married you when I discovered you'd made a small fortune from developing a stupid app, but cautious Gordon would never spend any money. Saving it for a rainy day! I might as well have married a pauper."

"So the only way of getting your hands on the money was by killing your husband. What a callous woman you are." Marjorie's voice betrayed her disgust.

"Humph," said Shirley.

"Who sent the letter?" asked Waverley.

"She sent it to herself. Am I right?" asked Rachel.

"It seemed a good idea and kept the security team off the scent."

"What I don't understand," said Marjorie, "is why Mr Delacruz would agree to murder someone on your behalf so soon after you met?"

"I don't think they had just met," Rachel explained, looking at Shirley. "You were never really kept locked away in Wales, were you?"

"No, we met up with the band whenever they were in Cardiff. Dalton and I had a fling then."

"So my suspicions were right about you having affairs?" Gordon looked at his wife in astonishment.

Ignoring him, Shirley looked at Waverley. "I did wonder why you allowed my husband back to work."

"Mr Hughes withdrew his complaint and I didn't have your husband down as a killer," said Waverley. "You nearly got away with it as Hughes had punched his father after an argument and later thought he was responsible for Dominic's death – he even tried to take the rap for the attack on your husband."

Gordon looked astonished. "His father? What do you mean?"

"Yes, Gordon. Dom had a son who he abandoned at birth: Dave Hughes, the man you attacked. He really had seen a band member kissing your wife, but it was Dalton, not Dom." Rachel put a hand on his arm.

Gordon cried, "I'm so sorry, I don't know what came over me. I was in a jealous rage – a nephew? At least I have something left of Dom."

"See? You're pathetic!" spat Shirley scornfully.

"Take her away," commanded Waverley.

Dalton, who had been quiet until now, said, "She does love me, she told me."

"You were being used, man. Take him away too," ordered Waverley.

"So it was Dalton who tried to drown me?" asked Gordon.

"Yes, but he ran when I came along. It was Shirley who hit me – she was probably acting as a lookout, or perhaps she didn't trust Dalton to do the job properly."

"As I said," remarked Marjorie, "not the shiniest tool in the box."

Gordon looked a broken man as he walked away, shaking his head.

"He'll be alright," said Waverley. "We'll help him."

After the excitement had subsided and Waverley had left them, Rachel walked Marjorie to her room and kissed her on the cheek.

"Sleep tight, we've got a busy day touring tomorrow."

"You didn't get to use that security key below stairs then?"

"Not this time, but who knows? Maybe next time. Goodnight, Marjorie."

"Goodnight, Rachel."

Chapter 31

Two days later, a ringing in the distance penetrated Rachel's deep sleep. Coming round, she recognised the ringtone immediately and leapt out of bed, grabbing the phone in the sitting room and pressing the button.

"Carlos!"

"Hello, darling, did I wake you?"

Her eyes filled with tears of joy at the sound of his voice. "I can't think of a better way to be awoken." She clutched the phone tightly. "I was so worried. Are you back home?"

"Yes, another case solved by PI Jacobi. It was a lot more complicated than I'd thought – I'll tell you all about it when you get back. Lady was the star of the day, but I'm trying not to let her know that. She already has me wrapped around her paw."

"Oh Carlos, it's so good to hear your voice."

"Yours too, I've missed you. How is the cruise? I hope it has been relaxing."

"Erm, I think I'll tell you all about it when I get back."

"Oh?"

"Don't worry, it's all over now, but I'll give you all the details in London. We'll compare notes."

"I'll settle for that over dinner. Just tell me you and Marjorie are alright."

"We're fine. In fact, I'm pleased you woke me because we're getting an early train to Berlin today. It's our final stop."

"Enjoy that beautiful city. I'll join the chauffeur on Sunday to collect you; I'm taking a few days off myself after the events of the past ten days."

"That will be wonderful, I can't wait."

"Rachel," he sounded serious, "I should have said this a long time ago. I'm sorry if you don't want to hear it, but I love you."

She thought her heart would burst, knowing that he wouldn't say it unless he meant it. They had never said the words before, in spite of dating for almost two years.

"I love you too, Carlos."

"Then I'm the happiest man alive. See you on Sunday. *Ciao.*"

When she collected Marjorie, Rachel was glowing.

"I take it you've heard from your beau." The twinkle in Marjorie's eye told her she understood all about love.

"He's accompanying Johnson on Sunday to collect us. I hope you don't mind?"

"I couldn't be more pleased. He's a good man and he loves you, you know."

"I know that now."

They met up with Sarah in the main atrium before leaving the ship to take the train into Berlin. The three women had lots to tell each other as so much had happened, and Sarah had worked solidly the day after the arrests while Marjorie and Rachel were exploring Poland. Sarah told them Dave Hughes had been released and that he and his uncle were getting acquainted. Gordon was determined to forge a special bond with his nephew and make up for the lack of support his brother had provided.

"Oh, I am pleased," said Marjorie. "I do believe they will be good for each other and may be able to provide the solace needed for healing to take place."

"I think you're right there," agreed Sarah. "I liked Gordon until his darker side threatened to overwhelm him. I do hope he learns to rid himself of that temper."

"Let's hope he can get help to recover from the wounds his brother and his wife have inflicted on him," said Marjorie thoughtfully. "The fact his brother was on his side in the end might help him heal."

"On the subject of Shirley Venables, Waverley told me yesterday he'd had a report back from their previous ship. Shirley had a fling with a fellow dancer and had to have treatment for a sexually transmitted disease. The report had been marked confidential to prevent Gordon finding out. The doctor suggested she make up a story about problems with her contraceptive implant to prevent Gordon catching it while she was treated. He still doesn't know."

"My, my, she had me fooled," said Rachel.

"Not only you," said Marjorie kindly.

"On a lighter note, the other news on the *Coral* grapevine is that Waverley's got engaged! Bernard overheard Graham congratulating him this morning."

"I told you so," said Marjorie triumphantly.

"That is good news." Rachel was happy for him.

"Will you cruise again, Rachel, or has this put you off for life?" asked Sarah.

"On the contrary, I get more experience on this cruise ship than I do in the police force. I very much look forward to cruising again in the summer. I have been offered a rather large compensation sum once again following the attack on board your beloved ship."

Sarah's eyes lit up. "I'm so pleased, I love seeing you during my contracts. It reminds me of home."

"I enjoy the travel too, despite the criminals you get on your ships. I've seen places I would never have dreamed of visiting. The St Petersburg ballet is up there with one of my best experiences to date."

"You've got the cruise bug, dear," said Marjorie happily.

The trio joined hands over the table and toasted each other with a mug of tea.

"To more cruises in the future," said Rachel as they clinked mugs.

"Preferably with proper china teacups!" Marjorie added, to which the girls laughed loudly.

THE END

Author's Note

Thank you for taking the time to read this collection of Rachel Prince Mysteries, I do hope you enjoyed the novels and that you have grown to like Rachel and her friends. If you have enjoyed the books, please leave an honest review on Amazon and/or any other platform you may use. I love receiving feedback from readers and can assure you that I read every review.

Book 4 in the *Rachel Prince Mystery* series. *Dying to Cruise* is available on Amazon and through all good book stores. I am currently working on books 5 and 6 for release in the 2019-2020 season. Book 5 *A Christmas Cruise Caper* will be released in late 2019.

Please Keep in touch:

Signup for my no spam newsletter at:
www.dawnbrookespublishing.com

Follow me on Facebook:
https://www.facebook.com/dawnbrookespublishing/

Follow me on Twitter:
@dawnbrookes1

Follow me on Pinterest:
https://www.pinterest.co.uk/dawnbrookespublishing/

About the Author

Dawn Brookes is author of the *Rachel Prince Mystery* series, combining a unique blend of murder, cruising and medicine with a touch of romance.

Dawn has a 39-year nursing pedigree and takes regular cruise holidays, which she says are for research purposes! She brings these passions together with a Christian background and a love of clean crime to her writing.

The surname of her protagonist is in honour of her childhood dog, Prince, who used to put his head on her knee while she lost herself in books.

Bestselling author of *Hurry up Nurse: memoirs of nurse training in the 1970s* and *Hurry up Nurse 2: London calling*, Dawn worked as a hospital nurse, midwife, district nurse and community matron across her career. Before turning her hand to writing for a living, she had multiple articles published in professional journals and co-edited a nursing textbook.

She grew up in Leicester, later moved to London and Berkshire, but now lives in Derbyshire. Dawn holds a Bachelor's degree with Honours and a Master's degree in education. Writing across genres, she also writes for children. Dawn has a passion for nature and loves animals, especially dogs. Animals will continue to feature in her children's books as she believes caring for animals and nature helps children to become kinder human beings.

Acknowledgements

Thank you to my editor Alison Jack, as always, for her kind comments about each book and for suggestions, corrections and amendments that make them more polished reads.

Thanks to my beta readers for comments and suggestions, and for their time given to reading the early drafts.

Thanks to my immediate circle of friends who are so patient with me when I'm absorbed in my fictional world and for your continued support in all my endeavours.

I have to say thank you to my cruise loving friends for joining me on some of the most precious experiences of my life and to the cruise lines for making every holiday a special one.

Other Books by Dawn Brookes

Rachel Prince Mysteries

A Cruise to Murder
Deadly Cruise
Killer Cruise
Dying to Cruise

Memoirs
Hurry up Nurse: memoirs of nurse training in the 1970s
Hurry up Nurse 2: London calling

Coming Soon 2019
Book 5 in the *Rachel Prince Mystery* series
Christmas Cruise Caper
Book 3 in the *Hurry up Nurse* series
Hurry up Nurse 3: More adventures in the life of a student nurse

Look out for new series
Carlos Jacobi PI

Picture Books for Children

Ava & Oliver's Bonfire Night Adventure
Ava & Oliver's Christmas Nativity Adventure
Danny the Caterpillar
Gerry the One-Eared Cat

Made in United States
Orlando, FL
27 November 2021

10765689R00386